PRAISE FOR

LARRY McMURTRY

AND

MOVING ON

"A TEXAS-SIZED BOOK. . . . Mr. McMurtry is blessed with an absolutely solid sense of place. His backgrounds and scenic descriptions are inherent parts of his story, contributing as much to the novel as does the completely natural dialogue."

—*Saturday Review*

"A marvelous book, funny, tough, filled with sensual good nature and nerviness."

—Herbert Gold

"*MOVING ON* is filled with memorable cameos. . . . McMurtry writes with intellect, compassion, and considerable skill. . . ."

—*Library Journal*

"McMurtry can transform ordinary words into highly lyrical, poetic passages. . . . He presents human drama with a sympathy and compassion that make us care about his characters in a way that most novelists can't. . . ."

—*Los Angeles Times*

"LARRY McMURTRY IS AMONG THE MOST IMAGINATIVE WRITERS WORKING TODAY."

—*San Francisco Chronicle*

Books by Larry McMurtry

Anything for Billy
Cadillac Jack
The Desert Rose
Lonesome Dove
Moving On
Some Can Whistle
Somebody's Darling
Texasville

Published by POCKET BOOKS

LARRY McMURTRY

MOVING ON

POCKET BOOKS

New York   London   Toronto   Sydney   Tokyo   Singapore

The verse quoted on page vii is from "Old Showboat," by Marijohn Wilkin and Fred Burch, copyright © 1962 by Cedarwood Publishing Co., a division of Musiplex Group, Inc. Used with permission.

POCKET BOOKS, a division of Simon & Schuster
1230 Avenue of the Americas, New York, NY 10020

Copyright © 1970 by Larry McMurtry
Preface copyright © 1970 by Larry McMurtry
Cover art copyright © 1988 Roger Kastel

ISBN: 0-671-74408-9

First Pocket Books printing July 1988

14 13 12 11 10 9 8 7 6 5

POCKET and colophon are registered trademarks of Simon & Schuster.

Printed in the U.S.A.

For the woman with whom I found
the unemptiable Horn

Oh I rode into Dallas,
Feeling kinda low;
Thought I'd pick me up some change
at the ro-dee-o . . .

Preface

The knottiest aesthetic problem I fumbled with in *Moving On* is whether its heroine, Patsy Carpenter, cries too much.

I might say that I had not even the haziest consciousness of this problem while I was writing the book. Then it was published, and I immediately started finding myself locked into arguments with women, all of whom resented Patsy's tears.

Though the women I was arguing with were often on the verge of tears themselves, and occasionally brimmed over with them, they one and all contended that no woman worthy of respect would cry so much.

Some of these arguments flowed and ebbed for months and even years, in some cases swelling back to flood stage just when I thought they had finally ebbed for good. I gradually came to feel that the question was not so much aesthetic as political. I had inadvertently left a copiously tearful young woman exposed on a lonely beach, just as the tsunami of feminism was about to crash ashore.

The fact that most women didn't much like Patsy was a profound shock to me. I liked her a lot—enough to devote much of an eight-hundred-page novel to her—and I fully expected women to like her as much as I did.

The book was written in the late sixties, and set less than a decade earlier. As arguments over Patsy's tears persisted, I gradually came to regard it as essentially a historical novel, one which attempted to describe a way of life—mainly, the graduate school way of life—in a vanished era. The era had only vanished a few years earlier, but it was definitively gone.

In that simpler era—as I explained to many skeptics—virtually all women had cried virtually all the time. The ones I knew were rarely dry-eyed, so it seemed to me that I was only obeying the severe tenets of realism in having Patsy sob through chapter after chapter.

My editor, Michael Korda, was evidently one of the few people alive in the late sixties whose memory for social and domestic history was as precise as mine. He too remembered a time not so long ago when virtually all women cried virtually all the time. I believe he was as shocked as I was when half the human beings in the Western world treated the book with scorn. And it cannot have helped that the other half of the human beings—i.e., the males—ignored it completely.

In the seventeen years since its publication, it's fair to say that a few enclaves of enthusiasm have formed. A number of women from Arkansas have written to tell me how much they like the book, and none have complained about Patsy's tears. It may be that in Arkansas virtually all women still cry virtually all the time, as they did throughout America in the late fifties.

A rather puzzling thing to me, as I look through the book today, is that it contains so many rodeo scenes. Few novels, then or ever, have attempted to merge the radically incongruent worlds of graduate school and rodeo. I am now completely at a loss to explain why I wished to attempt this. Apparently I deceived myself for several years with the belief that I wanted to write something about rodeo. A publisher once went so far as to option a non-fiction book about rodeo which I proposed to write. The option provided me with an excuse to drive around the West for seven thousand miles, but I handily avoided all the rodeos along my route.

I grew up in the land of the rodeo, saw a great many as a youth, and cannot recall ever being particularly interested in them. Why I felt the need to graft a rodeo plot onto something I *was* interested in writing about—i.e., graduate school—is a mystery I don't expect to solve, though I do know why I wanted to write about graduate school. In the late fifties, with no war on, the romance of journalism tarnished, the romance of investment banking yet to flower, graduate school was where many of the liveliest people chose to tarry while deciding what to do next.

The same milieu caught the eye of Philip Roth, who probed its textures in *Letting Go*, another long novel with a participial title. No rodeo cowboys strayed into his book.

My strongest memory of *Moving On*—aside from how much I liked Patsy and her dowdy friend Emma Horton—involved the struggle to title it. In almost all cases I have started with a title, and then tried to find a book I can fit to it. The title helps prepare me for the book I'm going to write; ideally it should also help prepare the reader for the book he or she is about to read.

In this case the ideal did not prevail. I started with no more than an image of a young woman eating a Hershey bar, at evening in a car. At the time I was calling the book *The Water and the Blood*.

This title soon found its way into my entry in *Contemporary Authors*. A college president for whom I was making a speech misread the entry and introduced me to a comatose audience as the author of a forthcoming book called *The Water and the Bloop*.

No one rose to ask me what a bloop was, but I soon abandoned that title anyway.

Then I batted out four drafts of a book called *The Country of the Horn*. Patsy wept like the Sabine women, and there was all the rodeo anyone could want.

A year or so later I figured out that the book was really about marriage, rather than bull riding. The first four drafts were swept down a manhole and a long, titleless book began to evolve. Once I realized how long it was going to be I stopped trying to title it, in the belief that it would grow out from under whatever title I chose.

I finished it in November 1969, expecting that it would be published the following fall. I planned to spend several happy weeks with poetry anthologies, seeking a glowing phrase that would resonantly describe the book I had just written.

To my horror, Simon and Schuster informed me that they were jumping the novel to their spring list, which was weak that year in fiction dealing with graduate students who follow the rodeo circuit. Catalog copy was due in three days.

I immediately read several thousand lines of *Paradise Lost*. I found many glowing phrases, but they had already been used to title other books. Then I ransacked such likely sources as ballad collections and hymn books, adopting and discarding dozens of titles.

Eventually I grew numb, and suggested simply calling the book *Patsy Carpenter*, rattling off a few historical precedents in support of this approach. I think I mentioned *Emma*, *Jennie Gerhardt*, and *Geraldine Bradshaw* as fine examples of books named after their heroines. Simon and Schuster remained unimpressed.

Finally, my editor's then-wife suggested calling it *Moving On*. I was too numb either to love it or hate it, and in my numbness I conceded, foolishly, I now believe. Except for one reader in England who loved Patsy's husband Jim—a man who would now be called a wimp—Patsy Carpenter, sobbing tirelessly, was the character everyone noticed, whether they liked her or not. I thought then and think now that her name would have done fine as a title.

Larry McMurtry
August 1986

BOOK I

The Beginning
of the Evening

Patsy sat by herself at the beginning of the evening, eating a melted Hershey bar. She had been reading *Catch-22* but remembered the Hershey and fished it out of the glove compartment, where it had been all day. It was too melted to be neatly handleable, so she laid the paperback on the car seat and avidly swiped the chocolate off the candy paper with two fingers. When the candy was gone, she dropped the sticky wrappers out the window and licked what was left of the chocolate off her fingers before picking up the book again.

Sometimes she ate casually and read avidly—other times she read casually and ate avidly. Another melted Hershey would have left her content, but there wasn't another. The glove compartment held nothing but road maps and a bottle of hand lotion, and if she walked to a concession stand and bought another Hershey it wouldn't be melted, probably.

And it was dusk, almost too dark to read. She had been in the grandstand, but the lights around the arena had come on too early, spoiling some of the softness of the evening, so she had come back to the Ford. Evening had always been her favorite time of day, and in Texas, in the spring, it was especially so. Dawn was said to be just as lovely, but she had seen only a few dawns and had been only half awake at most of those. It was evening that made her feel keen and fresh and hopeful.

The Ford was parked far back from the arena in a jumble of pickups and horsetrailers, far enough away that the lights and noise of rodeo scarcely intruded on the dusk. Soon she put *Catch-22* on the seat again and sat watching the sky to the west. The sun had gone down and all the lower sky was yellow. While she watched, it became orange and then red and then a fainter red, and the color lingered on the rim of the plains until the whole sky was dark.

She wore a gray dress and was bare-armed. It had been a hot afternoon for May, and the coolness of dusk felt good on her arms. Behind her, at the near end of the bleachers, a high school band broke into the National Anthem—it meant that the Grand Entry was in progress. The arena was full of horses and riders: rodeo had come again to Merkel, Texas. There were riding clubs, kids piled on ponies, pivot men unfurling the flags of the nations, cowgirls in tight pink trousers, and nervous businessmen on palominos. The procession into the arena had been very noisy, but before the anthem ended, the sound of hoofs and the jingling of bits faded out and the grounds became so quiet that Patsy heard it when one of the young clarinetists squeaked his reed. Everyone but her was standing up and the knowledge made her fretful and a little ashamed of herself.

The sport of rodeo did not interest Patsy at all—it interested her husband Jim. She herself had lumped it in her mind with cows, and cows did not interest her at all—not, at least, unless they were properly cooked. The fact that no cows were at hand was merely a lucky happenstance; in that part of Texas cows might appear at any moment. The only animal immediately at hand was a fat sorrel horse. He was tied to the sideboards of a nearby trailer, close enough that Patsy could smell him. Aside from one fart, he had been very polite and had gained her sympathies. Several times cowboys had walked by and slapped him on the behind to make him move over, and he had refrained from kicking them. If similarly provoked, she felt sure she would have kicked them. Occasionally the horse swished his tail against the fender of the Ford.

In the west a few very bright stars were out, though it was still not completely dark. She felt a little restless and was considering what she might do, when another cowboy walked by, a can of beer in one hand. He slapped the horse on the rump and the horse moved over. The cowboy burped, pitched down his beer can, unbuttoned his pants, and immediately began to relieve himself against the fender of the Ford.

"Hey," Patsy said, very startled. "Go piss on your own car!"

She was too surprised to sound very outraged, but she was no more surprised than the cowboy. He whirled around toward the trailer, liberally watering the whole area, horse included.

"My god, I never knowed you was there," he said. "Why didn't you speak up sooner?"

"Shock prevented me," she said faintly, for she *was* shocked—the more so as the first surprise wore off. She could hear him pissing.

"Lady," he sighed, "I would stop. I just ain't got the brakes."

"Oh, hell," she said, flustered.

The cowboy was silent until he finished and had buttoned up. He stood with his back to her a moment, apparently in thought, and then confidently hitched up his pants and turned toward the car.

"Ed Boggs," he said. "I guess I ought to apologize."

"I'm Patsy Carpenter," Patsy said, assuming that an introduction was taking place. Ed Boggs was clearly charmed. He leaned his elbows on the car door and peered in at her happily. His face was paunchy and he smelled of beer and starch and hair oil.

"Never meant to mess up your fender," he said, not bothering to affect remorse. "I just kinda needed somethin' to lean on there for a minute. Been puttin' 'em down a little too fast this evenin'. What I really want to do is ask you for a date to the dance. You look to me like you've got a lot on the ball."

"Why, thanks," Patsy said, smiling. Her cheeks colored. She could never help smiling when complimented. "I'm married, though."

Mr. Boggs neither moved nor changed expression, and she assumed he had not understood.

"I can't go to the dance with you, I mean. I'm really married."

Ed Boggs was in no way discouraged. "Who ain't?" he said amiably. "My old lady's married too. How about me gettin' in and sittin' down with you a minute to catch my breath?"

Patsy wanted very much to scoot toward the opposite door. Sitting beneath Mr. Boggs's face was like sitting beneath a heavy, badly balanced wooden object. He reached for the door handle, as if he were sure she wouldn't mind his getting in, but Patsy had locked the door and he didn't quite have the nerve to unlock it.

"No, you can't get in," she said. "You're being a little rude. I was about to take a nap. Why don't you go off and fill your bladder again?"

Her admirer attempted to take the rebuff in stride, but it was clearly not the sort of thing he was used to hearing from the lips of a woman. His paunches slowly shifted position and became a frown.

"I ain't gonna hug-dance with you if you talk to me like that," he said, attempting to jest. "I ain't out to rape you. I just want to sit down and rest a minute, maybe talk, you know."

Patsy was silent, hoping he would simply go away, but his face remained squarely in the window.

"I'm probably gonna get bucked off a bull tonight," he said finally. "Here I am drunk as dawg shit, I'll probably get my stupid ass stomped. Least you could do is be friendly." At the thought of his own peril his tone grew slightly husky and his frown more melancholy.

Patsy didn't melt with sympathy, but what he said did make it seem funny again. She had been about to get scared.

"That's a pity," she said. "We all have problems. Now please listen—the point is that I don't want you to get in and sit down. Just please go on away. If you're planning to get stomped maybe you better not refill your bladder after all."

Ed Boggs drew back. He had reached his wits' end. "What's my goddam bladder got to do with it?" he asked loudly. "That's twice you done mentioned it. I just want to get in and sit down."

He paused. "You're a good-lookin' thing, you know," he said, remembering that a compliment had got him his only smile.

"No," Patsy said, suddenly scared. He was terribly big and loud and she didn't know how to get rid of him. "You leave me completely alone! Don't you know better than to urinate on people's cars? It's very rude. I'm married, I told you. You ought to sober up instead of standing there trying to think of some way to seduce me." She started crying and began to roll the car window up.

At that Ed Boggs stepped away from the car. "Well, good snoozin'," he said angrily. "I'm glad I ain't the one that's married to you. I got better sense than to screw a woman as wordy as you are, anyway."

Patsy stopped the window halfway up and they regarded each other for a moment through the deepening dusk. Then Mr. Boggs stalked off, his dignity secure, and Patsy rolled her window back down and sat crying. Tears ran off her cheeks, into the hollows of her throat, down her chest. She could never find a Kleenex when she was crying and could only wipe the tears away with her fingers. Soon enough she stopped and felt more calm. She cried easily—absurdly easily, she felt. Half the things she cried about were merely silly. Her cheeks stung a little from the tears, but that soon stopped too and they felt cool.

By the time she was through crying it had grown quite dark, so dark that she could barely see the sorrel horse. She wished Jim was there so she could tell him about Ed Boggs. To her left, across the parking lot, she could see the glow from the circle of lights above the open-air dance floor, and she tried for a moment to imagine what it would have been like to go to a dance with such a man. Crushing, she imagined, but then she felt a little annoyed at her own fastidiousness. He might have been a good dancer. The remark about her being too talkative to sleep with rankled, though. It had obviously been sour grapes.

Far to the northwest there were flickerings of lightning. The quietness was broken by a splashing near at hand, a steady splashing that carried with it an odor like wet hay. The patient sorrel horse was pissing too. Patsy looked and saw the arena lights faintly reflected in the spreading puddle. In an instant it lifted her spirits, and she wished again that her husband was there. It was just the kind of coincidence he loved—the kind that might happen in life but that could never be made to work in a novel. Jim had tried to write a novel the first year they were married and had made it over a hundred pages before he got diverted.

When the splashing stopped, Patsy felt even fonder of the

horse than she had originally. She decided to get out and pet him. He was good company, and he seemed to have a sense of the absurd. Just as she was opening the car door she thought she heard someone call her name. She saw no one and was puzzled, until she realized that her name had come over the public address system. The rodeo announcer had called her name.

"Will Mrs. James Carpenter please come to the judges' stand. Mrs. James Carpenter."

Scared, aflutter, she started off immediately and got two pickups away before she remembered her purse. She might need it. Jim was hurt, she knew. Her chest felt tight. She hurried back and got her purse, looked futilely for some Kleenex, and then turned and ran through the cars and trucks toward the arena. Perhaps he had tried to take a picture of a bull and been gored. She began to cry and a few strands of hair stuck to her wet cheek.

As she came dashing out of the parking area, a roper who was warming up his roping mare came within a foot of running her down. Patsy hardly saw the horse, but she felt the rush of its body past hers. She was out of breath and slowed to a walk. The roper whirled his mare and came back—he was unnerved and furious.

"Let's look where you're goin', lady," he said. "This ain't no damn track meet. I coulda broke your neck."

"I'm sorry," Patsy said, sniffing and trying to get her breath. "I'm afraid my husband's been gored. If you could show me the way to the judges' stand I'll try and stay out of your way."

The roper was a thin young man, no older than Patsy. When he saw how pretty she was, and how distressed, he cooled off at once and got down from his horse to help. He held a rope in one hand and had a contestant's number pinned to the back of his shirt.

"I'm Royce Jones," he said. "Sorry I blew off. You scared the daylights out of me. How'd he get gored, bulldoggin'?"

He spoke quite calmly, as if a goring were something that came to one occasionally, like a toothache, and his spurs jingled lightly as he walked beside her—a comforting masculine sound.

"He's probably just got raked alongside the ribs," he

added, to soothe her. "Always happens sooner or later, doggin'."

"Oh, no, no," Patsy said. "He's a photographer, sort of. I don't really know what's happened to him."

Royce Jones grinned at her in the tolerant way men of experience grin at the folly of women. Distressed as she was, it annoyed her a little.

"I doubt he's gored," he said. "Them steers wouldn't take after a photographer. He probably just wants you to bring him some flashbulbs. Ask the clown, he'll know. That's him there with the cop."

Patsy saw the clown and the cop and turned to thank Royce Jones, but he had mounted his mare and was already riding away. When he was halfway across the dusty road he stood up in his stirrups and turned and waved his rope at her, as if to acknowledge the thanks he hadn't waited to receive.

As Patsy turned back toward the arena she bumped smack into a little girl who had been racing along carrying a Sno-cone. The Sno-cone popped out of its cup and fell on Patsy's foot, and the little girl looked at her angrily and neglected to hold the cup upright, so the lump of ice was followed by a stream of strawberry-colored water, part of which splashed on Patsy's ankles.

"Oh, damn," she said. "Why can't anyone see me coming? Don't worry, I'll buy you another one. I've got some money right here."

"Okay," the little girl said smugly. She knew the world owed her a new Sno-cone. "My name's Fayette," she added in a chummier tone.

Part of the ice Patsy managed to kick off, but most of it slid into her pump and began to melt beneath her instep and trickle between her toes. She dug in her purse but could find nothing smaller than a dollar. It made her feel a little desperate. Jim was somewhere, probably hurt, and the world was coming to an end amid an absolutely ridiculous mess involving her. Something in her rebelled against giving the little girl the whole dollar. She had taken a dislike to the little girl, and she hated to be exploited by anyone she disliked. She felt that her nerves were beginning to split and curl like the ends of her hair sometimes did, and she was on

9

the point of raking things wildly out of her purse when she looked up and saw the clown approaching. He had on baggy overalls, a ridiculous derby hat, and red and white greasepaint.

"I bet you're Mrs. Carpenter," he said in a quiet, agreeable voice. It was in complete contrast to his garish appearance.

"I'm so rattled I'm not sure," Patsy said. "Do you have any change?"

But he had squatted down and was already holding out a dime to the little girl. "I seen your plight," he said, glancing up at Patsy.

Fayette was slightly awed by the clown, but not too awed to be practical. "They cost fifteen cents now," she said. "Do you still have your skunk?"

Patsy would have liked to kick her, but the clown stood up and pulled a quarter out of his pocket. "If you got a nickel you can buy one for your little sister too," he said.

"I only got brothers. Did your skunk die?"

"No, it got stolen in Tucumcari."

The quarter grew bigger in her mind and Fayette said a perfunctory thanks and rushed off to find her best girl friend and tell her about the skunk.

"Thank you so much," Patsy said. "I guess I'm scared—my legs are shaking. Could I lean on you for one second? I've got a Sno-cone in my shoe."

She handed him her purse, quickly emptied the water out of her pump, and, with one hand on his shoulder, slipped the shoe back on. "How did you know me?" she asked.

"Kind of an educated guess," he said. "You don't look like nobody else here. Your husband met with a little accident, not very serious. Let's go see if he's come to yet."

His voice was low and unworried and sure of itself, and it made her feel better. She snapped her purse shut and he took her firmly by the arm, his hand above her elbow, and they hurried into the bright dusty arena. Sand stuck to her wet shoe. A crowd of cowboys stood near the heavy wire fence, all of them looking healthy and very cheerful. They parted for the clown, and she saw Jim lying stretched out on the ground, his head on a pair of brown chaps. She had never seen him stretched so flat. His lower lip was split, and there was dirt in his blond hair and a raw skinned place on one temple.

"Was he run over, or what? What's wrong with him?" Patsy asked, tears starting in her eyes. It was terrifying to see her husband lying with his eyes closed amid a crowd of cowboys.

"Just knocked out," the clown said. "He was in a kind of fight, he's not hurt bad. We'll get him in an ambulance in a minute."

"But Jim never fights," she said, kneeling and brushing awkwardly at the dirt in his hair. He was very blond and she could see the dirt against his scalp. "We don't even know anybody here—who could he have wanted to fight?"

The clown squatted beside her and silently took off his bandanna and handed it to her. "He ain't hurt bad," he said calmly. "You don't need to have no hysterics. What happened was a couple of bronc riders beat him up. He snapped 'em at the wrong time, I guess."

When Patsy looked up, all she could see was the legs of cowboys, long legs in blue Levi's, and large hands with the thumbs hooked in the pockets of the Levi's.

"Where is the ambulance?" she asked. "I won't be hysterical, but can't it come on?"

"Oh, it's right out there," the clown said. "It's the driver we can't locate. He went off with some woman and took his keys with him.

"Pete's my name," he added.

"But that's awful," she said. "That's awful." Jim's face seemed waxen to her. She had an urge to feel his pulse but was afraid to for fear she wouldn't be able to find it. The clown's hair was sandy and curly at the back of his neck, and only the fact that he seemed genuinely unworried kept her from breaking down completely.

Then, to her relief, there was the sound of a motor, and a white ambulance spun into the arena, cut sharply their way, and skidded through the knot of cowboys, almost to Jim's feet. It scared Patsy terribly, but the cowboys jumped gracefully out of the way and seemed amused at the driver's recklessness. Suddenly several of them converged on Jim. Pete helped her up, and in a moment Jim was in the ambulance and Pete was helping her in after him. When she looked around to thank him all the cowboys were standing behind him, arranged like so many wooden-faced sculptures, all of them staring at her. It embarrassed her, and she blushed.

"Have you to town in no time, ma'am," the driver said. Patsy turned and saw that he too was watching her. He was a balding man, with such hair as he had slicked down. His shirt wasn't buttoned.

"Couldn't you come?" she said, turning back to Pete. "I don't know what to do."

"No, got to work," he said. "He'll come to in a minute." He nodded kindly as he shut the ambulance doors.

She realized then that she had his bandanna in her hand, but it was too late to give it back. The ambulance was already spinning around in the soft dirt, and a cloud of dust hid the clown and the cowboys. "We're off," the driver said cheerfully, as if it were a race. The ambulance came out of its curve and almost plowed into two black Shetland ponies that had wandered into the entranceway to the arena.

"Shit-toody," the driver said, braking hard. "Get them goddamn ponies out of the way," he yelled, leaning out of the window. "I got a hurt man in here." A cowboy ran up and yanked the little ponies unceremoniously aside and the ambulance shot through the entranceway, only to brake abruptly again when confronted with the milling crowd of children and horses and men. The starting and stopping seemed to wake Jim up. He blinked and made a restless movement.

"He ain't hurt, he's already movin'," the driver said, looking back again. They passed out of the rodeo grounds, accelerated down a short dirt road, and lurched onto a highway. The rodeo pens were three miles outside the town. "Nothin' to worry about," the driver said, speeding into a curve. He kept looking back at Patsy, with more interest than he seemed to be able to muster for the road. She could see the lights of the little town, bright in the darkness, but the ambulance was going so fast it seemed to her they might not be able to stop even if they got there safely.

Jim suddenly raised up on his elbow. "Got to vomit," he said.

"Get the pan, get the pan," the driver said, and Patsy got it just in time. The sharp smell of the vomit made her feel nauseated herself.

"I hope you got my cameras," Jim said when he was finished and lying back. "I feel bad."

"Oh, I didn't," Patsy said. She started to explain, but her voice broke on the first word and she began to cry again. Jim had wiped his mouth on the clown's bandanna and it seemed that for the hundredth time in an hour she had nothing to cry into but her bare hands. Jim was white around the mouth, whether from weakness or from anger about the cameras she couldn't tell. As they flashed into the little town she lifted her husband's arm and wiped her face on his blue shirt sleeve. He cupped his hand behind her neck a moment affectionately, and she felt relieved. A few street lights were on and some frazzled-looking rodeo flags were strung between the streetlight poles. The ambulance driver began to grow irritable, even baleful, as they neared the end of the run.

"Ain't hurt a goddamn bit," he muttered. "I knew it. Made a trip for nothin' and was interrupted besides."

"Oh, please be quiet," Patsy said. "He *is* hurt. We'll pay you for your trouble.

"I know your kind," she added melodramatically, because the driver glanced back at her again.

"I wish you'd got the cameras," Jim said.

They squealed to a stop behind a small dingy-looking brick hospital with a big television antenna on the roof and a swarm of moths and insects around the yellow light bulb that lit the back door. Jim gamely sat up, but he didn't look mobile. The driver honked impatiently and they all sat waiting for attendants to run out with stretchers. None came. The driver sighed and stretched his arm across the back of the seat. He seemed content to wait, since he was there, and turned on the radio. A hillbilly song came over the air, plaintive and nasal.

Oh, my baby's not in town tonight,
This ole town just don't seem right,
Even my old friends don't seem the same to me . . .

13

Well my baby's not in town tonight,
 These ole lights don't shine so bright,
 And I'm cryin' tears till I can't hard-ly see . . .

"Can you walk if I help you?" she asked Jim. "I don't think there's anybody in there, but maybe we can at least find you a bed."

"Oh, there's *somebody* in there, most likely," the driver said, waxing friendly. He looked back at her with robust admiration. "I'll help you drag him in, ma'am," he offered.

He got out and opened the ambulance doors and the two of them helped Jim ease to the ground. Once on his feet, he waved them off and wobbled unsteadily toward the hospital, leaving Patsy to pay the driver. He stood watching her, scratching his stomach happily.

"We're sorry we bothered you," she said acidly. "I hope you can pick up where you left off, approximately at least."

The driver, nothing abashed, took out an old billfold and stuffed the money in it. "Ain't too likely, ma'am," he said. "Somebody else probably done already has, if I know that gal. Besides, I'll have to be hauling in them stomped-up bull riders before long. Such is the times. Glad to help you out, ma'am."

His complacency and the way he kept calling her ma'am were almost too much. "Oh, I'd like to kick you," she said hotly.

The driver was amazed, and silenced for a moment. "You sure you ain't crazy?" he asked after a pause, unable to arrive at any other explanation.

"I don't like being called ma'am," she said and walked away. The driver continued to scratch his stomach, but a little less happily.

Jim was in the waiting room alone, sitting on a couch with his eyes shut. "No one's here," he said, but no sooner had he said it than a fat implacably jolly nurse walked in and stood with her hands on her hips looking at Jim. She was as rouged as any harlot, but no one could have looked less like a whore.

"I see the bloodshed's begun," she said. "Doctor'll be out in a minute. He's pumpin' out a kid who had himself some rat poison for supper. It's a wonder to me any of us survive."

She gave Patsy a card to fill out, and they sat alone in the

14

empty waiting room for twenty-five minutes waiting for the doctor to come. The bright overhead light was so piercing that Jim had to keep his eyes closed. Patsy hunted through his billfold and found their insurance card. The beige leatherette couch they sat on seemed to her the ugliest piece of furniture she had ever seen.

"I'm sure those cameras were right there somewhere," Jim said. He had a way of being single-minded, even when in pain. "That's nine hundred dollars gone if somebody steals them. Besides, they had pictures in them."

"I just didn't see them. I had pictures in me too—pictures of you dying and me being left at the mercy of about a thousand stupid cowboys. Maybe the clown took care of them. He was the only nice person there."

But she felt guilty, anyway, for not having more presence of mind.

Soon a frail-looking doctor with a black hearing aid came in and led Jim off to be X-rayed, and she sat alone in the waiting room, fidgeting uselessly about the cameras. Jim had only been working at photography three months and she had difficulty taking it seriously. His decision to photograph rodeos seemed quite nonsensical to her. She was always unable to take his work seriously enough at the time when he was most intense about it; by the time she became enthused about one of his lines of endeavor he would almost invariably be bored with it and ripe for a new pursuit.

To escape the brightness of the waiting room she walked out into the front yard of the hospital. The grass was dry and crackly already, though it was not yet summer. She walked around the side of the building to the back, away from the street lights, and felt better at once. The depth and sweep of the sky was a relief after the tiny room, and the sky was sown with uncountable stars. Her hair was mussed; she took a comb out of her purse and stood combing it, her legs spread and her head bent back over one shoulder. Her hair was black and she wore it middling length, just long enough that it touched her shoulders. She felt refreshed and combed vigorously, looking straight up into the Milky Way.

It seemed very odd to her that anyone, even a cowboy, would want to hit Jim. He was mild-tempered and agreeable, and to her knowledge no one had ever hit him before.

She walked back around the hospital, combing more leisurely, and saw a car filled with teenagers race down the empty street. It was an old two-tone Buick with no muffler. There were eight or ten kids in it, boys and girls all mashed together, yelling and laughing and waving their arms out the windows. As they passed the hospital a boy pitched an empty beer can high in the air. It rang when it hit the pavement, bounced into the center of the street, and spun around a few times before it stopped. The sound of the car gradually faded and the silence of the empty summer town was complete again.

When she went back inside, the fat red-cheeked nurse was sitting at the desk clicking her tongue over a coverless movie magazine that seemed to be several years old.

"Pore little Debbie," she said. "Can't tell a no-good when she sees one, can she, honey? We've about got your hubby patched up."

Patsy felt defenseless. The slovenly ambulance driver she might have kicked, but no person of character would kick a jolly nurse. It irked her to be called honey, and it irked her more to hear Jim referred to as her hubby. It was on the tip of her tongue to say something very complimentary about Elizabeth Taylor, but before she could think of anything she glanced up and saw that the fat nurse was looking at the pictures with affection brimming in her face. Her voice had dropped with sadness when she said, "pore little Debbie," and she was studying the pictures with as much fondness as she might have bestowed on a family scrapbook.

"I'm sure it was hard on her," she said, choked for a moment, with a desire to be kind to the nurse.

"'Course Liz ain't had no easy life either," the nurse went on. "She was as sweet a little thing as there ever was when she was young. Growed up too fast, I guess, and let all them bright lights and them night spots confuse her. I was out there once, went with my sister and her family. We went to Disneyland and had us quite a time. You-all got any little ones?"

"Not yet," Patsy said. It was a question she disliked being asked.

"Well, you ought to. Lord bless us, they're what's worth living for. 'Course I never married myself, but my sister has

16

six and I love every one of 'em. Liz has been a good mother, seems like, but adult'ry's adult'ry, don't matter who does it. When you carry on like that you've got to pay. Thank goodness I've got a clean conscience, even if I don't have much else."

"Did they X-ray my husband yet?" Patsy asked, suddenly remembering Jim.

"Oh, they X-rayed him all right," the nurse said. "I don't know what showed up. All them X-rays look alike to me."

She rattled on, and in a few minutes Jim came out looking somewhat steadier. He had a badly swollen lip and a bandage on his forehead. Patsy went over and put her arm around him a little awkwardly. She had never been able to be gracefully affectionate in public.

"The doctor's been telling me rodeo stories," Jim said. "I must be lucky. I don't even have a concussion."

"Sonny, you wouldn't know the half of it," the nurse said cheerfully. "I've been a night nurse twenty-four years and you wouldn't believe the sights I've seen, specially after these rodeos. They brought in a boy one time with a hatchet stuck in his skull—never lived the night. And nine times out of ten it's all to do with women."

It was not until they were out the door, standing on the front lawn of the hospital, that they realized they had no way back to the rodeo grounds.

"It's unreal," Patsy said. "How many more things can go wrong?"

"Actually, they're not so *wrong*," Jim said mildly. "Just inconvenient. Who would have thought those crazy bronc riders would hit me?"

"I would have thought it. I'll believe anything about cowboys. A bull rider tried to seduce me too. I didn't get a chance to tell you sooner. He peed on our car and then tried to seduce me."

Jim seemed scarcely to hear. He wandered aimlessly and a little woozily across the hospital lawn.

"They didn't even bawl me out or give me warning," he said. "I would have quit if they had. I took two pictures, and a big one got up and knocked me loop-legged. I'm still loop-legged, I guess."

"Oh, listen to my problems," Patsy said, relieved that he

could talk again. "If you have to indulge in pity, pity me. There I was, about to be raped and pillaged in a parking lot and left to my unpleasant end. If that had happened I'd be loop-legged too, believe me."

"I wonder if there's a taxi."

"Of course not. What would a taxi be doing out in the wilderness? We'll have to wait two days for a bus, or else walk. What about my gallant stand for chastity?"

"It sounds like you made it up," Jim said. "Why would anyone want to pee on our car?"

She thought he was going to say, "Why would anyone want to seduce you," and was relieved.

"I think he chose the car more or less at random," she said. "Why would anyone want to knock you loop-legged? These people are crazy, that's why. Isn't there anything besides rodeo you could take pictures of? I don't like you getting beat up and I don't want to sit around getting raped and pillaged just so you can become a famous photographer. Why not take pictures of gypsies? Then we can go to Europe and look for them."

Jim was silent, looking down the empty street. He didn't enjoy joking about his profession, whatever his profession was at the time, and Patsy knew it; but she kept thinking that if she could make the right sort of a joke, in the right tone, he might relax about it and then everything would be a lot more fun. But demons got in her and she never made the right sort of joke or found the right tone.

"The bull rider's name was Boggs," she said. "He breathed on me. If my fair white body is going to be sacrificed to your ambition the least you could do is take me to Europe. Why must I be sacrificed in Merkel, Texas?"

It didn't lift his spirits, so with a wriggle of her slim shoulders she dropped it and went over and hugged him, her face against his throat. He had his hands in his pockets and she shyly pulled one out and held it.

"Maybe we could hitchhike back out there," she said.

Then they heard the thin noise of a siren in the distance and saw, far down the straight highway, the red revolving light on top of the ambulance.

"Aha," Jim said. "Here comes us a ride."

18

"No," Patsy said firmly. "That's not our ride. I refuse to ride with that man."

"Why? He surely didn't try to seduce you, did he?"

"No."

"Then why not?"

"Well, because I threatened to kick him," she admitted. "I'm the kind of girl who sometimes threatens people."

"You never threatened to kick me," Jim said, frankly astonished.

"You're nicer than him. He just prompted me to threaten him, never mind why."

"I don't intend to pass up a ride just because you were rude," Jim said. "I'm about to collapse. You can apologize. I'm sure you had no business saying whatever you said."

The ambulance shrieked into town and skidded to a stop on the gravel driveway. Patsy didn't want to look. She had the horrid conviction that Ed Boggs had indeed been stomped by a bull. She would have to watch him carried into the hospital, his entrails spilling out. Instead, a young cowboy in black chaps emerged from the ambulance and limped inside, holding one of his shoulders. Jim walked over to the ambulance and she followed timidly.

"Sure, sure," the driver said, waving them in. "I got your cameras for you. Pete Tatum gathered 'em up. Just keep between me and your missus, is all I ask. She's a little on the violent side, ain't she?"

He was lighting the stub of a cigar and seemed not to expect an answer. Jim got in the middle and Patsy sat by the window. In a moment they were speeding back past the street lights, toward the dark country. Patsy had her arm on the car door. As they gained speed the rush of air cooled her armpit and blew through her dress, across her chest. The lightning to the northwest had grown heavier; when it flashed they saw the dark shape of a cloud. The driver seemed to be making an effort to be polite and Patsy softened toward him.

"I'm sorry I said what I did," she said. "I was a bit overwrought. Did you say the clown's name was Pete? He told me but I'd forgotten."

"Pete Tatum. Knowed him for years. Only reason Pete

19

bothers with this little show is because his brother's a big man in the rodeo association here. He works them big professional shows. Santa Rosa and shows like that."

"It was awfully nice of him to take care of the cameras," Jim said. "Thank him for us in case we miss him."

Ahead, off the road, they saw the glow of the arena lights and a lower glow from the dance floor. The driver turned onto the dirt road and they were soon back inside the rodeo grounds.

"This'll be fine," Jim said. "Our car's right here."

"Okay. Watch out for your missus now. Don't let her kick none of these pore cowboys. Most of them get kicked enough as it is."

"I'd advise you not to run that into the ground," Patsy said. "I might make good on it yet."

The driver grinned at her engagingly. "I was teasin'," he said. "Be a pleasure to be kicked by a pretty young wench like yourself. See you-all next time."

He tooted his horn lightly with the heel of his hand and moved the ambulance expertly through the mob of men and women and children who were leaving the stands.

"You see," Patsy said. "He keeps calling me things. Could I be accurately described as a wench?"

Jim was too tired to be interested in such issues. Patsy took his hand and they walked through the swirl of people toward the Ford. The horses and cars and departing pickups kept the sandy roadway stirred up, so that the dust rose to their waists and made it seem like they were walking through a sandy mist. Car lights shone red through the sand, and whenever a horse crossed the road in front of a car the lights threw huge wavering shadows against the dust.

"I hope you don't mind driving," Jim said. "I still feel dizzy."

The sorrel was no longer tied next to the Ford, and the trailer he had been tied to was gone. Jim went wearily around the car. Patsy stood for a moment by the door on the driver's side trying to locate her car keys by the little door light. Finally she jiggled her purse and located them by the jingle.

"Let's sit until the traffic thins out a little," she said. Jim was quite agreeable. He slumped silently against his door.

By the time Patsy got her key in the ignition his eyes were closed, and very soon he was asleep. It annoyed her and dropped her spirits a little, even though she knew his head must hurt. She wanted to talk, and having him so soon asleep made her feel lonely, as it often did. Jim could go to sleep quicker than anyone she had ever known. He claimed he had always been able to, but she sometimes felt it was an escape technique he had developed for occasions when he didn't want to talk to her. She would have liked to scoot over by him, but there was a clutter of photographic paraphernalia in the front seat and she had to content herself with putting a hand on his shoulder. Over the way, the dance she had been invited to was in progress. As the cars drove out and the grounds grew quiet she began to hear the sounds of the dancing, a yell now and then, the scraping of feet on concrete, and, over that, the sound of the hillbilly band. At first she only heard the ring of the steel guitars, but as the grounds emptied, mournful snatches of lyric filtered through:

Keep those cards 'n' letters comin' in-uh-in, honey,
Tell me that you love me time 'n' time ugin-uh-in, honey;
It's many a mile from Memphis to Berlin-uh-in, honey,
So keep those cards 'n' letters comin' innn. . . .

Patsy kept time with her fingertips. When the song ended she started the Ford and drove through the almost empty grounds, squashing several beer cans but no bottles that she noticed. There was a very small trailer parked to the left of the exit gate, with a donkey tied to the fence nearby. As she turned to go through the gate her headlights swept across the front of the trailer. A man with no shirt on sat on the tiny steps of the trailer wiping his face with a towel. He looked up when she passed and to her surprise called her name. She braked, puzzled, and he got up from the steps and came to the car, the towel slung over one shoulder.

"Thought that was you," he said, and she realized it was the clown. He bent and peered in at her solemnly and looked past her at Jim.

"He's just asleep," she said. "He's fine. I'm ashamed of myself for being so flustered." But she felt embarrassed and oddly flustered again and didn't know whether to look at him or not. He seemed lankier than he had seemed in his clowning apparel. He was balding too. The hair that was so curly on the sides of his head was almost gone on the top.

"We're very grateful about the cameras," she said. A girl had come to the door of the trailer house and stood just inside the screen, her body a dark shadow.

"Well, glad he wasn't hurt," Pete said. "Maybe sometime I'll get to meet him when he's awake. If he'll come and see me maybe I can tell him who not to take pictures of."

"Oh, we won't be coming back here," she said. "We were in Dallas and heard about this rodeo and drove out. We're going to lots more, though—my husband wants to do a book of pictures about them. I'm sure we'll see you again."

"Hope so," Pete said, stepping back. He was sawing the towel thoughtfully against the back of his neck. Patsy never quite knew how to get out of conversations; she gave a little nod, raced her motor a little, and let the clutch out too quickly. The Ford jerked forward and almost died. In a moment she regained control and was out the gate. A cowboy was leading three horses down the middle of the dirt road that led to the highway, but as she approached he obligingly moved them over and waved at her cheerfully, his hands full of bridle reins. When she turned onto the pavement the slight bump caused Jim to slide farther down in the seat, his head still against the car door. Straining, Patsy reached across him and locked it.

The lightning had come close enough that she could see it flickering in her rearview mirror, but it seemed a dry kind of lightning, appropriate to the country. Ahead on the straight highway were five or six sets of red taillights, cars going back to town. Patsy drove slowly, in no hurry. She followed the taillights into the town and stopped at both lights. The cars that had been ahead of her had all disappeared, absorbed by the town. Except for a deputy's car parked in the driveway of a filling station, hers was the only vehicle in sight. The deputy was sitting with his car door open. He had taken one boot off, and the sock too, and was contemplating his bare foot with an expression of gloom. He held a pocketknife in his hand, one blade open, as if perhaps he meant to perform an amputation. It was just the sort of moment she would have liked Jim to take a picture of, though no doubt the deputy would have resented it. Probably the man had ingrown toenails from wearing such sharp-toed boots.

When the light turned green she went on, past a block of darkened grocery stores and laundries, still driving slowly and enjoying the almost pristine emptiness of the little town. Except for herself, the deputy, and one lank brown dog, the emptiness was absolute. Soon she left the town behind and turned onto the Interstate. On the broad highway she could not help driving fast. There was no one on the road but herself and the trucks of the night, the huge trucks with squares of red taillights that lumber nightly over the country, from the South to Los Angeles and from Los Angeles to the South. The trucks blinked their eyes when she passed them, purring and snorting like great nocturnal animals. She held to the left until she had passed half a dozen and was ahead of all that were in sight, pushing the Ford almost to its top speed, which was eighty-five. The darkness, the speed, the straining pulse of the car, and the rush of cool air in the window were keenly satisfying to her, as satisfying as the taste of the Hershey bar had been, and as brief, for the motel where they were staying was in Abilene, less than a dozen miles away. She would have liked another fifty miles to drive—the road all to herself and the wind blowing her hair and cooling her arms. She swerved slightly from time to time to avoid the flattened corpse of some possum or coon or armadillo, and much too soon she was among the lights and filling stations of Abilene. It was irritating to have to slow down when she was avid for more driving; she stamped the brake with annoyance at the first light off the freeway.

Their motel was called The Old Homestead. Its office was done in imitation logs, with a squirrel rifle hung over the door to complete the effect. She circled the office, the swimming pool and kiddy playground, stopped and killed the motor at the door of their room, yawning and stretching her arms back over her head as far as she could. The moment she stopped she was glad she had no farther to go. She considered Jim with a mixture of affection and petulance, and gathered up her purse and *Catch-22* and his precious cameras, only to have to set them all down at the door of the room in order to find her key. She found it, took the stuff in and dumped it on the bed, got a glass of water, swished some around in her mouth when she was through drinking, and walked back out and across the bare courtyard to stand on the concrete edge of the swimming pool a minute, staring at the greenish shimmer of the water. She yawned and leaned backward, her hair dangling. The stars were so much brighter than any stars they ever saw in Houston, where they lived. Once again she yawned, and she reached inside the armpit of her dress to scratch what felt like a mosquito bite. Then she strolled back to the Ford to begin the awkward but familiar task of getting her husband awake enough to go to bed.

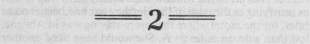

Sonny Shanks drew the last bull of the evening—a large white-eyed brindle bull. As soon as it humped out of the chute the crowd began to cheer. Usually by the last bull of the evening the crowd would have become blasé, bored with danger and tired of cheering. But Sonny Shanks was the king of the sport—the World's Champion Cowboy—and for him they cheered eagerly, even before they saw the ride. The brindle bull humped straight ahead, swinging strings of slobber left and right and kicking his hind legs high every second jump. He didn't twist or whirl, and Shanks rode him so confidently that to the crowd it seemed almost as if the ride were taking place in slow motion.

Pete had placed himself far back, by one of his barrels. He knew the brindle bull as well as Sonny did, and he wasn't worried. When the buzzer sounded he moved forward. Shanks stayed with the bull two more jumps and then left them. He went off his feet when he hit but was up in a second. The bull whirled back toward him dipping a horn, but at that moment Pete yelled and came into his line of vision waving his arms. Confused, the bull turned toward Pete, paused, made a short grunting dash at him, and when Pete sprinted aside, paused again, his head up and a string of clear slobber hanging from his lip. The crowd, knowing that the show was over, stood up and began to leave the stands.

Pete stood still a few seconds letting the bull look at him. He was a good-tempered bull, as rodeo stock went, a massive animal with the horns of a Brahma and a hide that showed every breed from Angus to Jersey. When he had studied Pete, he dipped his horn at him once more, snorted, and trotted heavily off toward the stockpens, the cowbell roped beneath his belly jangling at every step. As the bull passed, the rope came loose and Pete walked over and picked it up.

Shanks had not gone to the chutes but stood near the center of the arena probing in his mouth with one finger.

"Bite your tongue?" Pete asked in passing.

Shanks shook his head. "Feels like I jarred a fillin' out," he said.

"Well, you done fair," Pete said, handing him the bell rope. "You can afford a new filling."

Shanks's curly black hair fell over his forehead. He gave Pete a cool grin. "It beats clownin'," he said. "Reckon that rookie'll live?"

Pete walked on toward the chutes and didn't answer. He felt low enough about the rookie, and an argument with Sonny would not improve his mood. The rookie, a kid from Duncan, Oklahoma, had got a hand hung in his rope, and the bull had been a twister, almost impossible to get close to. When the kid had finally come free he compounded his mistake by moving at the wrong time, as Pete was trying to take the bull away. He had been kicked hard and was in the hospital with some broken ribs and a smashed collarbone. Compared to what might have happened, the injuries were minor, but knowledge of what might have happened was never any help to Pete. He took every such accident to bed with him, and had for years.

He found Boots sitting on the steps of the trailer waiting

for him. She had seen the accident and knew exactly what mood he would be in, and she was chewing her nails.

"That's where I like to find you," he said. Boots stood up and hugged him silently and then went to the rear of the trailer and talked to Hercules, the tiny donkey, while Pete went inside to clean up. A small dachshund named Jumbo had been sleeping under the trailer steps. He was jealous of the donkey and came over and nosed her ankle possessively.

"I wish nobody ever got hurt," she said, stroking the donkey's silky nostrils.

"How'd you do?" Pete called.

"Sixth," Boots said. She was a barrel racer. "That's not so bad—not at the Santa Rosa."

Pete came out of the trailer and stood on the steps looking down at her. He had washed his face and found a clean gray work shirt. He unbuttoned his britches to tuck his shirttail in, then turned his cuffs back almost to his elbows. He whistled when he was sad, and he was whistling.

"Let's go honky-tonk," he said. Boots had her back to him. All he could see was her white bleached-blond hair.

"Maybe sometime I'll win a first," she said. Barrel racing was her passion. Pete stepped down and embraced her and they kissed. Boots was eager and vigorous, yearning as she did every time they touched to prove with her young mouth, or her young self, that she was old enough to be his and his alone and his forever. Pete lacked a year being twice her age. Her mouth moved on his, fresh and uncertain, trying to kiss the kiss that would make him sure of her.

"You gonna drive or am I gonna drive?" he asked when they stopped kissing.

"Me," she said.

They got into her Thunderbird and cut at once into the stream of traffic that was feeding out of the grounds. No sooner were they on the highway than Boots passed three cars. "Don't worry about it so," she said. "The bull might have killed him if you hadn't been there."

"Sugar, hush," Pete said. "One thing you have got to learn is that you can't cheer me up by trying to cheer me up. Try not to plow into no trucks, if you don't mind. I'd like to survive to drink the matter off."

But no cautions reached Boots when the wheel was in her

hand. She drove like the road was hers. When she got into a clear stretch, ahead of the traffic, she put the Thunderbird up to ninety, her white hair whipping about her face. Pete watched the fence posts and the culverts and the road signs flash by, out of the darkness a second, into the darkness in another second. He almost never drove without pulling his horse trailer, and high speed worried him unless something else was worrying him so much that he was indifferent to speed. But fast driving made Boots feel bold; at the wheel she had absolute trust in herself. When the barrel racing was over she had changed from boots to sandals, and she wiggled her toes a little and kept the footfeed down.

"Hope there ain't no livestock wandering around loose tonight," Pete said wryly. "If you was to hit a cow, there wouldn't be a hamburger left of either us *or* her."

"I want to get there ahead of the crowd," Boots said. "Maybe if you get smashed enough you'll even dance with me. It's not your fault if people ride bulls. Think of all the people you've *kept* from getting hurt."

Her nose was round and a little too short and when she tried to cheer somebody up she tried hard. Pete reached a hand across the gap between the seats and began to rub her neck. Her swirling hair tickled his fingers. He rubbed high up, behind her ears.

"See, we're early," she said.

The honky-tonk was called The Hole in the Bucket and was located just across the line in a wet county. Twenty or thirty cars and a few pickups were parked in front when they got there. It was a long one-story frame building, set by the highway in a clearing in the brush, with a flashing neon sign to slow people down. In spite of Boots a lot of the rodeo crowd was already there, but they found a booth in the back and ordered beer. There were booths, a few tables, a sawdusty dance floor, and a bright squat jukebox. The barmaids wore Levi's and satin shirts.

Pete went over and fed a dollar into the jukebox and, in time, fed another and, in time, another, and Boots tapped her fingers on the beer bottles and matched him beer for beer, though she would much rather have danced. But Pete only danced when he was drunk, and that took time.

Long before Pete felt the beer, Boots was high on it and

talking loudly. She felt lightheaded and light-bodied and wanted all sorts of things from moment to moment: to dance, to have more beer, to kiss Pete and have him kiss her. The room was gray-blue with cigarette smoke and the neon of the jukebox; it was loud with shuffling feet and giggles, and curses, some happy, some angry. Pete dropped beneath his melancholy into a state of calm, now and then losing himself for a moment in one of Boots's hopeful beery kisses, now watching the shuffling dancers or the barmaids with their trays of beer bottles.

"There's old Sonny," Boots said. "The bastard. I guess he's a bastard. You hate him, don't you?"

"We ain't chums," Pete said.

"I don't like him, either," Boots declared loyally. "Even if you won't tell me why you hate him."

"I doubt he's in love with us, either," Pete said, amused.

"I know you had a fight on the bridge," Boots said. "Everybody knows that. It's the one thing I know."

It was the one thing that everyone in rodeo knew: that Pete and Sonny had had a fist fight on the bridge above the Rio Grande, in El Paso. It had been eight years since the fight. No one in rodeo had seen it, but no one in rodeo was without an opinion as to how it had started and who won.

Pete kissed her lightly. "Tell you one secret about it," he said. "Old Sonny gave me a present that night. Only thing he ever gave me. What it was was a dirty movie."

Boots could not have been more impressed. She stopped kissing to think about it.

"A real one?" she asked. "I didn't know you could buy them. What did you do with it?"

"Threw it into the Rio Grande," Pete said. "That was about when the fight started."

Boots could not get over it. None of the legends that had grown up around the fight included a dirty movie. "What did people do in it?" she asked.

"Oh, a little of this and a little of that."

The woman Shanks was dancing with was a tall brunette, fairly drunk. They were an easy couple to follow because the woman was wearing a white dress and almost all of the other women there wore cowgirl clothes. Shanks was dancing very

28

Western, with lots of bending and swooping; occasionally he bent the woman so far over backward that she shrieked and clasped his neck, but he always brought her up easily. When the number ended he spotted Boots and Pete and led the woman over to their booth.

"You children are up late," he said, grinning at Boots. "A young thing like you needs lots of sleep, honey."

"I'm not so young," Boots said, annoyed.

"Sit down, since you're here," Pete said. Shanks was willing but the woman pulled on his arm.

"Let's go on," she said. "We can take some beer with us. I want to get out of here before Monroe comes in."

"Piss on Monroe," Shanks said, still smiling at Boots. "I've survived a bronc and a bull tonight, why'd I worry about Monroe?"

"It's me that's worrying," the woman said. "I got to live with him, don't I?" She kept glancing around toward the door.

Sonny shrugged. "Looks like I got to choose between company an' adultery," he said. "See you boys and girls tomorrow."

The woman hurried toward the door and Shanks followed, picking his way lightly between the crowded tables. At one table he stopped and lifted a cowboy's hat, tried it on, and returned it to its owner's head. The cowboy didn't even notice. He was drunkenly trying to explain to his wife that he wasn't drunk.

"The hell you aren't," his wife said, crying. Her chin was propped on one hand and tears ran down her arm. "You're drunk as a bastard and all our kids right out there in the car asleep."

Shanks tilted the man's hat at a slightly jauntier angle than it had been and followed his date out the door.

"I thought his rich girl friend lived around here," Boots said. "Eleanor Guthrie. What's he doing fiddling around with people's wives?"

"You got me," Pete said.

She put her head against his neck, and he held her and before long she was asleep. When she slept she looked even younger than she was, sixteen rather than nineteen, and watching her sleep made Pete feel the more guilty about her, but also the more strongly drawn to her. He could not let her go, not after having taken her. He cradled her against his chest, motioned to the waitress, and listened to the jukebox through two more slow beers. When he finished and tried to ease Boots out of the booth she came half awake and with him guiding her stumbled out to the car. The wind had come up, with thunder behind it in the west. Some rain was on its way, close enough that Pete could smell it on the wind. In the dry country it smelled good.

After he folded Boots into the Thunderbird he discovered that she had the keys in her pocket and he had an awkward time digging them out of her tight Levi's. Boots thought he was wanting to make love and giggled a little and kept squeezing his hand against her in acquiescence, though she was limp and sleepy.

He got the keys finally and started back toward the town of Vernon. He had driven only two or three miles when he saw Shanks's hearse, dark inside and parked well out on the level shoulder.

For years Shanks had driven Cadillac hearses—they were an essential part of his legend. The hearses were white and he always had three sets of bulls' horns painted in gold on each one: a set on each door and one on the top, so people in airplanes would know it was him, he said. On occasions when he had to fly to make a rodeo he would hire a needy rookie to drive the hearse to him.

That's one place Monroe won't never think to look, Pete said to himself. As he passed the hearse he honked as loud as he could. Boots did not even stir. She slept with her head thrown back against the seat, her mouth open, her small light bosom barely stirring the satiny rodeo shirt as she breathed. Pete glanced at her now and then and settled it with himself definitely, no backing out, that the next day he would wake her early and ask her how soon she wanted to be married. Beyond Electra, on the straight highway leading to Vernon, he ran into the heavy early-summer rain, and he held his arm out the window until his hand and arm were wet. All tension had left him and he felt a little too tired. He wiped his face with his wet hand to clear his head. There wasn't much traffic on the road, but he had gone to sleep at the wheel a number of times in his life and was taking no chances. He took his time on the slick pavement and in twenty minutes swished into Vernon and put his sleeping sweetheart safely to bed.

=== **3** ===

Though he knew it was probably Pete who honked, Sonny sat up when he heard the horn. Pete was one of the few people who would risk disturbing him at his amours, but in this instance he hadn't been disturbed and was quite ready to sit up. The woman, whose name was May, lay asleep on the low bed, her mouth open, her legs open, everything open except her eyes. She had had more beer and more excitement than she was accustomed to, and had quickly spread out into slumber. Sonny had had no beer and only a most modest amount of excitement and wasn't sleepy at all. In The Hole in the Bucket, amid a crowd of cowgirls, May had looked better than she looked asleep, and he wished he had had the good sense to leave her strictly to Monroe.

"Hey, sweetheart," he said, shaking her foot. "Wake up and tell me where you live. Time you was getting home to your regular feller."

May mumbled something in a complimentary tone, but it wasn't her address, so Shanks pulled his Levi's up and climbed over in the driver's seat, leaving the mattress to her. It had begun to sprinkle. He turned the hearse around and drove slowly back to The Hole in the Bucket. A red Pontiac convertible was parked directly under the neon sign, and the top was down. Sonny parked the hearse beside the car and went around and opened the rear doors. His conquest was sleeping soundly, nothing on but her bra and a four-dollar bracelet. He reached in and eased her out, bare-assed and limp, and plopped her quickly in the back seat of the Pontiac. There was a bridle and a six-pack of Pearl beer on the seat but he managed to shove them onto the floorboards. He quickly crawled into the hearse and gathered up what he could find of May's clothes and took them back and piled them on top of her. She had begun to wake up and was mumbling vague complaints.

"What the hell—Monroe?" she said, looking at the Pontiac in sleepy astonishment. The neon sign flashed green and lit her body for a moment.

Sonny was tickled. "You need a shower, honey," he said. "Just stay there, one's comin'."

Before she had her eyes open good he was in the hearse and gone. In a few miles the rain met him, soft and slow at first and then a little heavier. He had taken a couple of pills after his ride and felt good. About halfway back to Vernon he saw a car stopped on the shoulder of the road. A young man and his girl were both out in the rain trying to change a tire. The girl was holding a flashlight and looked to be pretty—slim and black-headed and already soaked. Her boy was straining over his tire tool. Shanks swished on up the highway for half a mile, letting the hearse gradually lose momentum, and then he turned and went back. There was no point in not helping a man who had a pretty girl. He eased the hearse onto the slick shoulder and up behind their car, an old green Ford that looked as if it had been driven cross-country around the world. When he stopped the hearse he bent over the back seat and dug around in the litter in the back until he found an ivory-handled umbrella he had stolen from a TV producer in L.A.

The young man was having trouble getting his lugs unscrewed. He had three off and in the hubcap, which was rapidly filling with water, but the last two lugs weren't budging.

"Hi, boys and girls," Sonny said, sloshing up to them. He was barefooted. "Let's take shelter under here," he said, opening the umbrella.

"Thanks, but there's not much need now," Patsy said. Water dripped off her hair, her green dress was soaked, her bra sodden, and her bra straps clearly visible through the thin wet dress. She was annoyed and, since Sonny had appeared, embarrassed as well. Jim slipped in his effort to wrench loose a lug, and went down on one knee in the mud.

"Shit," he said. "You wouldn't have a good lug wrench, would you, mister? I can't get enough leverage with this miserable thing." It was a short lug wrench, of the sort that doubled as a jack handle. The footing was getting worse and worse and he could not keep the wrench on the lugs.

"It'd take a week to find mine," Sonny said. "Let me have a try. I'm fresh and you're done exasperated."

He grinned and handed the umbrella to Patsy. Jim gladly yielded the wrench. It had only been raining a few minutes and yet his pants and shirt were already smeared with mud. Shanks squatted by the tire bracing his elbow on his knees. He jammed the wrench onto the top lug, held it there with the heel of one hand, and put his arm and shoulder into the push. The lug gave, and the other one did likewise. He took them both off and dropped them with a splash into the brimming hubcap. "That'll get 'em," he said. The back of his red silk shirt was already as wet as Patsy's dress.

"Thanks," Jim said. "This isn't my day. I guess it's time I bought some new tires."

"Might buy a car to go with 'em," Sonny suggested. "This one looks like it's seen too many road signs."

He grinned at Patsy, but she didn't grin back. She was of precisely the same opinion where the Ford was concerned but managed to refrain from saying so. She sluiced the water off her hair with one hand and gave Sonny back his umbrella.

"You're Sonny Shanks," she said.

He nodded, looking at her more closely. He had a feeling he should know her, but he couldn't come up with a name. The two of them were not rodeo, obviously. The green dress was stylish, even if wet, and her husband's tone was a city tone.

"I'm Patsy Carpenter and this is my husband Jim," she said. "I recognized the hearse of course, but actually we met a few times years ago. I guess I was about twelve then. You used to know my Aunt Dixie."

"Dixie McCormack?" he asked, but it was a superfluous question. There was only one Dixie—or only one that counted.

"She's my aunt," Patsy said.

"My god," Sonny said. "I know her okay. The only thing that keeps us apart is that I ain't got the energy I once had. She cost me a world championship and I never went with her but three weeks. That woman's crazy. She could foul up a two-car funeral."

"She takes some keeping up with, okay," Patsy said. Jim let the tire slip as he was lifting it off the spokes and it splashed muddy water on their ankles and calves.

"I think a coincidence like this here calls for a drink," Sonny said. "I got a little bar in the hearse. Let's have a drink to Dixie while your husband finishes changing his tire. I been out of touch and ain't heard her recent exploits, anyhow."

He took Patsy by the arm, held the umbrella over her as jauntily as if they weren't both soaked, and led her along the edge of the wet pavement to the hearse.

"You look awfully smart to be a niece of Dixie's," he said. "Not that she's what you'd call dumb."

Patsy was annoyed with him for leading her away, and annoyed with herself for allowing him to, but he had done it so smoothly that she had not thought to stop him until it was too late.

"Nobody thinks of Aunt Dixie in terms of smart or dumb," she said. "Fast or slow, maybe."

"I'd like to see her sometime when she's slow," he said. "I've seen her other speed. Hop in."

He helped her in the back of the hearse and switched on a small light. A narrow mattress and box spring took up one side of the rear, and the other side was filled with an incredible litter: clothes, ropes, boxes of tapes and gauze, a case of whiskey, bridles, and chaps. A large saddle with what seemed to be a golden saddle horn was propped against the front seat. At the rear, near the door, was the tiny bar.

"It's kind of a mess," Sonny said ruefully. "My maid quit last week. What'll you drink?"

"A Coke if you've got one and if not, a little bourbon. About an inch."

Sonny stood at the rear, still in the rain, and reached inside to fix the drinks. He even had ice. "Make it bourbon," he said. "Soda water ain't good for a pretty girl's complexion."

There was a green high-heel shoe laying on the bed, and without thinking, Patsy picked it up and looked at it. It was cheaply made—the strip of inner sole was about to curl. Sonny handed her a glass. She put it to her lips politely and the odor of whiskey prickled her nose. She took a small sip and, when she put the glass down, became aware of another smell, which the smells of rain and mud and liquor had covered until then. It was faint but unmistakable and it came from the sheet on which she was sitting. When she realized what it was, anger and shock hit her almost at the same time. She pushed herself indignantly off the bed and one of her knees hit Sonny's hand. He had just finished fixing his own drink and the glass slipped out of his hand and fell into the mud. Patsy scrambled awkwardly out of the hearse, almost falling. She was embarrassed and very angry.

"*Damn* you," she said. "What do you mean, forcing me into your hearse when you've just . . . done something in it. You didn't even give her back her shoe."

She sloshed halfway to the Ford, crying, then remembered that she still had the green shoe and sloshed back and threw it angrily into the hearse. Sonny watched her. He was mildly disgruntled, but more at himself than at her. He had completely forgotten May.

"Well, kick me," he said. "I'm awful. I should have tidied things up. It ain't no reason for you to run off, though. It's messy everywhere tonight."

"Not like that it isn't," Patsy said. "This was a nice rain until you came along."

She turned and walked away, furious with her aunt for having had anything to do with such a person.

"Have a good swim," Sonny said, mostly to himself. He crawled into the hearse out of the rain, opened himself a beer, sniffed at the offensive sheets, and sat on the bed sipping his beer and watching Jim Carpenter wrestle the muddy tire into the back end of the Ford.

In a minute Jim came to the hearse.

"Thanks for the help," he said. "I guess we'll have to skip

the drink. The rodeo and the flat seem to have tired my wife a little."

"Don't matter. Where you headed?"

"A stepuncle of mine has a ranch not far from here. I imagine we'll see you again. I'm a photographer and I'm going to be traveling the rodeo circuit for a while."

"Oh, yeah," Sonny said. "You're the guy who got clobbered in Merkel."

"Right," Jim said. "However, I got through Santa Rosa without being beat up." He was a little awed to be talking to Sonny and would have liked to prolong the conversation, but, though Patsy hadn't said a word to him, he knew she was furious about something, and the longer he lingered the more difficult she was apt to become.

"Going to be in Phoenix?"

"Yes."

"Good," Sonny said. "If your car makes it, look me up. Your wife's a little peeved at me but she'll get over it by then. We'll have a party or something."

"Fine," Jim said, flattered. "I certainly will."

When he left, Sonny rolled one of the big windows down and sat with his back propped against the front seat, drinking beer. The rain was slowing down. The clouds had already broken to the north, and stars were visible. He bent over and got himself a handful of ice and sat crunching it. Now and then a car or a diesel swished by, but there was not much traffic. Noticing May's one green shoe, he picked it up and looked at it a minute before tossing it out the window. Then he took off his shirt and stretched out to sleep for a while. He had decided to go visit the love of his life, and she wouldn't be awake for several hours.

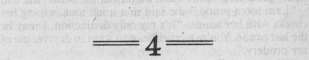

4

Patsy couldn't quite stop crying, and the reason she couldn't was because Jim refused to understand why she had started crying in the first place. He was annoyed with her and told her she was old enough to be able to control herself better. She was almost twenty-five, and it was quite true, but it didn't help. She was not crying freshets, but her eyes kept dripping and she felt wronged and her breastbone hurt from it. They had turned off the highway and were on a little dirt road that led to the ranch house of Jim's stepuncle, Roger Wagonner. As they drove west, the rain had slackened, but the shower had been heavy enough to make the dirt road a little slick.

"I didn't smell anything," Jim said for the second time.

"*You* weren't sitting on the mattress."

"All right!" he said. "I still don't see that it was so terrible. What different did it make, you're not a prude. You could have sat somewhere else. I wanted to talk to him."

"You're offending me," Patsy said grimly. "So I'm too delicate. I'm still not going to spend the evening in a puddle of sperm just so you can talk to some stupid bull rider about a lot of stupid bulls.

"It was very unsanitary," she added. "Much as I'd like to get pregnant, I don't want to do it by a mattress. Especially not his mattress."

Jim was silent. He was pretending to be very careful with his driving. Her abruptness annoyed him as much as her crying, and she knew it. His annoyance annoyed her. She would have liked him to be light and joshing—if he had been she might have become convinced that the whole thing was funny. But she had deprived him of a pleasure, and he wasn't immediately ready to let her forget it. They had been married over a year and a half and she had still not learned to control either her abruptness or her tears. He had just better get used to them—and the sooner the better, she felt.

"I am too a prude," she said in a small tone, wiping her cheeks with her hands. "It's my only distinction. I may be the last prude. You're a cruel beast to want to deprive me of my prudery."

"Oh, shut up," he said loudly, making her jump.

"I'm going to see him in Phoenix," he added, more quietly. "You don't have to come if you don't want to."

"I certainly don't," she said, perking up a little. She saw that he was ashamed of having yelled at her.

"If he was good enough for your aunt I don't see why you need be so snooty. After all, he's been World's Champion Cowboy three times. That saddle in the hearse was a championship saddle."

"That wasn't a saddle," she said. "It was an altar. I bet he deflowers a virgin on it every week."

They crossed a cattle guard and circled the dark ranch house. Jim parked by the back-yard gate and began to collect his cameras from the back seat. His annoyance would not subside. Patsy had a genius for fouling up evenings, but she did it in such a way that it was never clearly her fault, and he could never feel really justified in his annoyance.

"If he liked your aunt he couldn't have much taste for virgins," he said.

Patsy drew herself up. "Such remarks are not apropos," she said. "I love my Aunt Dixie and don't you be snippy about her. She just happens to have a weakness for organs, that's all."

It had rained more at the ranch house than it had on the road leading to it. They squished across the wet back yard, Patsy gradually getting her mood in hand. There was a towsack on the back porch for them to wipe their feet on. Jim wiped his, but Patsy merely slipped off her shoes.

The house was completely dark, and though it was the third night of their stay they were still unfamiliar with its layout. They bumped things and stepped on a great many squeaky boards. Patsy felt very tired. Jim offered her the bathroom first but she declined it and merely dried her wet hair on a towel from her suitcase. It was one of those times when she didn't feel like taking care of herself, and she undressed and got into her nightgown hastily and was in bed when Jim returned from the bathroom.

He came in shortly and turned on the overhead light—there was no other. The room was still a little dusty from long disuse, and there was nothing in it but a straight chair, a bed, and an old brown bureau. The wallpaper had once been green but was faded almost gray and was blotchy on the ceiling. The light shone right in Patsy's eyes and she hid under the sheet until Jim noticed and switched it off again.

"I guess people never read in this country," she said. "They haven't heard about bed lights."

Jim was standing by the open window. A light drizzle had started up again and he stood listening to it. "I ought to get those films ready to mail," he said. "I want to get them off first thing in the morning."

"Please do it in the morning. It's nice in here dark, and awful when you turn the light on."

Without answering, he came and stretched out on the bed, close against her, his body cool for a second. "Anyway, I bet you surprised him," he said. "He's probably not used to girls jumping out of his hearse."

"I'm not used to sitting in sluck, either," she said. "At least not in other people's."

Jim kissed her lightly on the shoulder. "Saint Patsy," he said. "Prude and martyr." He yawned and rubbed his forehead against her shoulder. "Maybe you aren't going to like being a photographer's wife."

She lay facing away from him, on her side, and he reached one hand across her as if to touch her loins but then rested the hand on her hip instead. In two or three minutes he was sleeping, and the drizzle and the sounds of Jim's breathing were the only sounds she heard. She fitted her back and legs against his body and soon felt warm and relaxed. She loved to listen to the rain. She drew Jim's arm across her and held it beneath her breasts. Often she felt closest to him just after he had gone to sleep, especially if he went to sleep at a time when she wanted quiet rather than talk. The rain made a lovely sound and a lovely smell, and as she became more content she became more wakeful. She would have liked to read, but there was no bed light.

After a time she slept, but not very long. When she woke it was still dark outside. She could never sleep long or deeply in strange beds. Jim had turned over, so that only the curves of their backs were touching. Patsy felt sure morning couldn't be far away, and she got up and put on her robe and tiptoed down the cool bare-floored hall to the bathroom. Her hair felt gritty from two nights of rodeo, and it seemed a good enough time to wash it.

The bathtub was old, narrow, and deep, with some of the enamel chipped off around the edges. The water pressure was very low, only a strong dribble, and she knew from the previous day's experience that it would take a good thirty minutes for the tub to fill to the level she liked. She left the water running and slipped back through the dust-scented hall to the bedroom and got herself a book and tiptoed down the cool stairs to the kitchen. In the darkness the kitchen smelled of oilcloth and linoleum and the strong gray soap that Uncle Roger used at the sink. She turned on the light, got a glass of water, and made herself a peanut butter sandwich. There had been no peanut butter on hand when they arrived, so she had bought some in Vernon for just such an emergency. The kitchen window was open; through it she could hear the squabblings of chickens. She was reading *Incidents of Travel in Yucatan,* a good book to read but annoying because the pages wouldn't stay open. She had been reading it at intervals for a month and was sixty pages into Volume II. She tried setting the peanut butter jar on the top margins, but that didn't work very well, so she gobbled her sandwich and then read, picking up crumbs with her fingertips and eating them. When she went back upstairs the bath was still not ready and she sat on the toilet and read until it was. She stuck the book in a closet on top of some towels, assembled her shampoo and several bath brushes, got in and soaked, scrubbed her knees and toes and back, soaked some more, washed her hair, and soaked still more, the wet ends of her hair dripping streams of water onto her chest and shoulders. Given half a chance she could bathe for an hour.

While she was drying herself she heard Roger Wagonner pass the door and go downstairs. The mirror over the lavatory was small and not very helpful, and she went back to the bedroom to attend to her hair.

Jim was sleeping soundly, his body curled toward the part of the bed where she had been. His shoulders were goose-pimpled by the morning coolness. Patsy pulled the sheet up over him and sat on the bed for a minute rubbing his shoulders until the goose bumps went away. He had not shaved the day before and in the gray early light she could see, when she bent over him, the line of light blond whiskers on his jaw, the same color as the light hairs on his chest. For some reason Jim took on authority when he slept; it was then that he seemed most like the man that she wanted him to be, and she felt respectful of him and pulled the sheet a little higher before she got up.

She went and sat by the window in the straight spindly brown chair, rubbing her hair with a towel. Outside, a cow was bawling at intervals, and in a few minutes Patsy saw her trailing slowly toward the barn. She was a small Jersey, and the calf that trotted after her was incongruously large and red. Uncle Roger had explained to her that the calf was adopted, and not the result of any irregular behavior on the cow's part. The country smelled cool and wet. The sky was quite clear, and a white moon, already fading slightly, hung high in the southwest.

Patsy concluded that they were right, those people who said dawn was as lovely as evening. She had never been awake so early, and the few times she had been up early at all she had been going someplace and had had to dash or drag around, hunting clothes and stockings and cosmetics, and it had not been pleasant. But she was there, and settled, and clean and wide awake, and had a book to read and a husband sleeping nearby and her hair to dry in its own time, and the morning seemed beautiful. The sun was up, she could tell, but the window where she sat was on the west side of the house and the sun was still low in the east. After a while its rays began to touch the green mesquite trees on the slope south of the house and to touch the wet grass. The damp ground had begun to give up a little mist. She used a

41

dryer when at home, but since she wasn't at home she rubbed her hair vigorously with the towel from time to time, examining the ends closely to see if they were splitting.

In a few minutes she heard Roger Wagonner slam the back door and saw him walk through the yard, his milk bucket over his arm. Their green Ford was parked by the back gate. He glanced at it with the curious unbelieving glance people always gave the Ford, as if he was pained and amazed that such a vehicle had been removed from the junkyard where it belonged and parked on his property. The Ford was six years old. Jim had had it four years before they were married. They could easily afford another car, but Jim was sentimental about the Ford and stubbornly refused to sell it. They had discovered each other in the car, and he had got it bound up with their love in some way. They spent their first full night together parked in the Ford on a hill near White Rock Lake, in Dallas, kissing and talking. Patsy was misty enough about the night herself, but not so misty about the Ford that she could ignore the fact that it was falling apart. Only the month before they had been stranded for six hours in a garage in Riley, Texas, with a broken timing gear. "Are we going to keep it all our lives?" she had asked then. She read three magazines and all of *Pnin* while the Ford sat in a blackened garage full of oilcans. Jim ignored her and talked to the mechanic. "Look, I married you for life," she said, trying again, once they were on their way back to Dallas. "If we're going to keep this car as our hearts' museum or something, we might as well have it bronzed."

"I fell in love with you in this car," he said, not impressed with her wit; and they continued to drive it.

The chickens came out to meet Roger, the hens scolding bitterly, and he clucked them out of the way and walked on to the barn through the milky shin-high mist. His pickup was parked between the chicken house and the barn, an ancient Chevrolet twice as old as the Ford, with sideboards that had not been painted in so long that they were gray.

He called to the milk cow and let her and the red calf into the barn. The sun was burning the mist away. When he emerged from the barn he had a full bucket of milk and set it carefully on a wheelbarrow near the lot. He filled a hayrack with yellow hay and got his milk bucket and carried it slowly to the house.

Patsy felt talkative. She laid her book and comb on the windowsill, belted her blue robe about her, and skipped quickly down the stairs to meet him.

"Hi," she said. "So this is what morning's like. Want me to help you with breakfast?"

Roger was a tall old man, with hair thin and quite white and so molded to his temples by years of being beneath the same hat that it stayed molded even when he took the hat off.

"Sure, start helping," he said. He set the heavy milk bucket on the smooth blanched wood of the drainboard. Patsy had watched him strain it through some cheesecloth into a strainer only the evening before, and she determined that straining the milk would be her first rural task. She began to open drawers at random, looking for the cheesecloth.

Roger became nervous as she rapidly progressed through the drawers. He got the cheesecloth, which hung on a towel rack over the sink. "You're an energetic creature, Patsy," he said. "Don't you have no shoes? You been here two days now and I ain't seen you with shoes on yet."

Patsy was busy reopening the drawers he had just closed, as she had in mind cooking bacon and wanted a fork to turn it with. She noticed that he was watching her as if he expected to have the entire contents of his cabinets dumped on the kitchen floor, and actually a good number of implements *were* scattered on the drainboard, but she intended to put them back as soon as she had a chance. The blue milk strainer, an antique almost, stood on the back porch. She held the cheesecloth between her teeth and used both hands to carry the milk bucket out there. How she was going to affix the cheesecloth and pour too she didn't know, and Roger Wagonner didn't know either. Whatever he envisioned her doing made him so nervous that he undiplomatically took the bucket and strained the milk himself while she went back and started the bacon frying.

"You don't trust me," she said. "You're perfectly right not to. I don't know why I think I'm a milkmaid, but it seems a

43

lovely thing to be on a morning like this. I guess I must have read about milkmaids. Thomas Hardy has them in numerous books and they're always at their best on mornings like this. If we're going to have biscuits you'll have to make them and I'll do the oven part. I've never made biscuits from scratch."

Watching her wandering about the kitchen in her blue robe, standing on one foot now and then to scratch her bare calf with a toe, Roger Wagonner shook his head and resigned himself with a smile to the chaos females bring to an orderly house. Patsy fried the bacon but then sat down at the table to peel an orange and eat it, dropping the peel and in time each seed on a white napkin spread on the checkered oilcloth. She talked all the while of the mist and the milk cow and this and that, and Roger fixed the biscuits and fried four eggs hard as stones and got the breakfast around her. It was not until he bent over stiffly and slowly to peer into the oven at the browning biscuits, and the hip pocket of his faded Levi's came into her vision, that Patsy remembered she had been going to cook.

"Oh, dear," she said, blushing and jumping up. She ran to the cabinet and looked desperately for something to do, but he had even put the plates on the table while she was chattering.

"I'm terrible," she said. "You have every right to be suspicious of me. I'm completely impractical."

"Now quit apologizin' and let's eat," he said, sitting down. He wore a clean brown khaki work shirt with the cuffs turned up. The hair on his wrists was as white as the hair on his head, but his wrists were strong-looking, old as he was. He cut through his eggs diagonally. They had been fried in bacon grease and the outsides were brown.

"I guess I'm a shade nervous," he said. "Haven't had to cope with a female in this kitchen in the morning for eleven years. That's how long it's been since Mary got killed."

He said the last merely as one states a fact, with no self-pity or nostalgia. Patsy could not understand how he could eat eggs fried so hard.

"How come you fry them that way?" she asked.

"Because it don't take no talent. You just leave 'em in the frying pan till they're hard enough to bounce."

The coffee stopped perking at just that time and Patsy noticed and jumped up before Roger could even scoot back his chair. She poured them cups. The cups were white and thick and had little thin cracks running down their sides. Roger immediately poured half of his coffee into a saucer. His food was already gone. He tilted his chair back, the saucer in one hand, and began to blow on the coffee gently and sip it as it steamed.

"Mary never went barefooted that I can remember," he said, still more thoughtful than nostalgic.

"Apparently ladies didn't in earlier days," Patsy said, contemplating the two brown eggs that seemed to be her responsibility. The peanut butter, the orange, and a sliver of bacon had filled her completely and she was nervous about the eggs. She had heard that in the country food was never wasted.

"Where you and Jim going next?"

"Phoenix."

"Going in that car?"

"Sure." She felt suddenly loyal to the Ford. She cut a little corner off one egg to see what the yolk of an egg looked like when it was fried that hard. "It's our only car. Your pickup is older than it is and you still drive it, don't you?"

"Well, naturally," Roger said. "No use buying nothin' new at my age. I don't go out tourin' the world in it, though. Besides, I'm pore. If old Jim's gonna haul you all over the country he oughta buy you a better automobile than that. He can afford it. You could probably even get a pair of shoes out of him if you sweet-talked him a little."

Patsy sighed and started to eat the bite of egg and then decided not to eat any egg. She felt too good to stuff herself with things she didn't want, duty or no duty. Perhaps there were pigs that the eggs could be fed to, though she had not noticed any.

"He doesn't like being able to afford so much, you see," she said gravely. Jim's wealth was one of their big problems. Her people were new rich, his not so new, and far richer. She did not think it would be polite to talk about the problem of having too much money to a person who had the problem of having too little.

"Just leave them eggs, honey," Roger said kindly. "I've

seen strong men who couldn't choke down my cooking. Why would anyone not like being able to afford things? I've wished I was able to afford things all my life."

"You're a nice man," she said smiling, but she felt almost tearful. Small gracious things, like about the eggs, sometimes flooded her with feelings of gratitude. A shadow came under her eyes and the old man saw it. "He doesn't really know how to do any one thing," she said. "But he can afford not to, of course. He just hates it. It's such a silly problem to have when there are so many people, you know, like the poor, who have real problems."

Uncle Roger looked at her and she saw in his lined, firm face and the twist of his smile that she had touched him, that even though they had only known each other three days he was fond of her, perhaps had just become fond of her as they sat at the breakfast table. Her throat closed and she was choked with feeling and began to scrape with her toenail at the white paint on the thin table legs.

"I'm so emotional," she said with a quaver.

He chuckled and reached across the napkin full of orange seeds and patted her hand. "Well, what you and him need to do is buy my ranch," he said. "Then pretty soon you'd be as broke as me and you wouldn't have no problems like that."

He stood up, neatly arranged his plate, knife, fork, cup, and saucer, and carried them to the sink. "Wish you'd clean up these dishes for me," he said. "I've got about three days' work to do today and I better get started."

He reached into the cabinet, got a toothpick out of a box, and stood looking at her thoughtfully while he picked his teeth.

"Only drawback to that is that you might not be no better at ranchin' than I am," he said. "I been at it fifty years and get worse at it every year. Least that's the way it looks in the bankbook."

Patsy looked up in disbelief. "Oh, come on," she said. "I can't imagine you not being good at things. You just look like you'd be good at things."

"Oh, well, that's just my noble bearing," he said, smiling and pleased. "You seen yourself how I cooked them eggs. One nice thing about a wife, she keeps a man reminded of how good for nothin' he is. Mary used to let me know her low opinion of me every morning and I worked like a dog all day hoping I could change it. Never did. She bawled me out the morning she went and had the car wreck."

He went out to the back porch and got his straw hat and then came back to the door of the kitchen. Patsy sat at the table, her feet drawn up to the top rung of her chair.

"I will wash the dishes," she said. "Don't worry."

"I won't. Hope you-all can find enough to eat to keep you from starving."

She was expecting some advice, some country platitude about life and its problems, but Roger just tipped his faded straw hat to her and turned and left.

When she heard the pickup start she got up and did the few dishes, leisurely, not liking the heavy soap but unable to find any detergent. She did like standing at the sink by the open window, smelling the cool morning and the trees and weeds of the north yard. It surprised her that such dry country could have so many nice smells when it was dampened a little.

Once finished, she put the dishes away where she hoped they belonged and, since Roger was not there to be nervous, poked around in the cabinet a bit to see what was there. The knives and forks and most of the utensils were old, so old that most of them had wooden handles, very smooth from many washings and with a faint woody smell of their own. She liked them, they seemed better to the touch than her own stainless and sterling, and it occurred to her that if she and Jim ever did do anything crazy like buy a ranch she would certainly have all sorts of wood in her kitchen— wooden spoons and wooden bowls and perhaps a huge wooden block for cutting meat on. With a bright woody good-smelling kitchen with a window that looked out on a slope and a deep sky, her cooking might even improve, though probably not. She would stand and look out too long.

She went slowly back up the stairs and got her hand lotion off the bureau and sat again in the chair by the window, rubbing lotion into her hands. Jim was sleeping on his back. She felt a little lonely and would have liked him awake, but probably he would wake up either sulky or sexy and at the moment she felt as cool and unpassionate as if she had become a virgin again. More likely still, he would wake up professional; there were four days worth of pictures to be mailed. The next day they were to go to Phoenix, and as Jim was a fanatic marathon driver it would probably be a very long day. She took off her robe, got *Incidents of Travel in Yucatan,* and lay on the bed on her stomach reading and occasionally tickling her husband's chest with the ends of her hair, until the warming day made her drowsy and she flopped the book open on the floor by the bed and went to sleep.

5

Eleanor breakfasted outside in the summertime, on the second-floor patio of her ranch house. She exercised early, on a yellow foam-rubber exercise pad on the patio, and then she showered and put on a slip and a white robe and went back outside, her heavy graying blond hair pulled back and held by an orange headband. The ranch house was a long two-story brown stucco that her mother had built in the twenties, when she was no longer able to abide the creaking three-story frame mansion that had been the Guthrie home for two generations. The patio was on the east side of the house, sunny in the mornings, shady in the afternoons, and was Eleanor's favorite place on the whole ranch.

She sat at a tiled table at the edge of the patio looking down on the long green lawn that stretched south almost to the barns and corrals. Lucy brought her a grapefruit and some French toast and coffee, and she leafed through a *New Yorker* as she ate, mostly looking at the ads and the cartoons.

Below her the Mexican gardeners were already at work, spading the flower beds and getting ready to water the hedges. To the south, in front of the barns, ten cowhands were saddling up, fiddling with their girths and rope and listening to the foreman outline the day's work. To the north were her wheatfields, stretching halfway to Red River, and, beyond the barns, to the south and west, the rolling broken country of the ranch spread in a great circle. The ranch house was almost on its rim.

She ate the French toast and would have liked more but didn't call Lucy. The sun was up, the air bright and still cool. Soon the air would be merely a shimmer of heat and she would be driven inside.

As she ate and turned pages and watched the cowboys mounting she saw a white elongating cloud of dust on the road that led from the highway to the ranch house. The highway was three miles away; the road that led to it ran between the wheatfields and the horse pasture. Long before the hearse swung into the circular driveway below her, Eleanor knew who was coming. Others drove as fast as Sonny, and raised as much dust, but seldom at that hour of the morning; and anyway, she always knew when Sonny was coming. In fifteen years she had learned to tell.

He parked the hearse just beneath her and got out but didn't look up. In a few minutes she heard the click of his bootheels as he crossed the bedroom floor. All the floors in the house were dark wood, kept bare except for a few Mexican rugs.

She looked up at him just as his hand gave her shoulder a quick hard squeeze. "Why, hello," she said.

Sonny bent and kissed her lightly and then went around the table. "I'm starved," he said. His chin was dark with stubble, his black hair tousled and uncombed, and his shirttail out. Though he smiled at her arrogantly, he looked a little bushed.

"Sit down and have breakfast with me," she said. "We can chat about old times."

"How you fixed for steaks?"

"I'm sure we have some. Steaks are our reason for existing. Ask Lucy to fix you one."

"I don't think I ate yesterday," he said. "Maybe I'll ask her to fix me two."

He did, and also fixed himself a drink, and came back and sat down across from her, swirling the ice in his glass.

"Beautiful as ever," he said. "You dye them streaks in?"

"I've never dyed my hair," she said. "As you well know." Her eyes were still on *The New Yorker*.

Sonny stood up, smiled, took the magazine from her, whistled sharply at one of the Mexican gardeners, and coolly sailed *The New Yorker* over the patio railing. Its pages fluttered as it fell to the ground. The gardener was fat and slow and didn't catch it, but he picked it up and without waiting for instructions took it into the house to Lucy, who understood all mysteries.

"You can be a bore," Eleanor said, a little irritated. "I like to read while I eat."

"If there was another woman like you around I'd marry her," Sonny said pleasantly. He squished some bourbon around in his mouth as if it were mouthwash. "If I was to get married, then you could sit around out here and read magazines for the rest of your goddamn life."

"I can, anyway," Eleanor said. "As a matter of fact that's what I've done most of my life. I love to sit out here and read magazines. I expect to do essentially that until I die."

Sonny sagged in his chair, one foot on the railing of the balcony. He looked very tired and said nothing more. Eleanor filed her nails. The exercise, the shower, and the breakfast had left her feeling good, but slightly lethargic; it was pleasant not to have to move. In a few minutes Lucy came in with Sonny's breakfast, two large covered trays. Under each cover was a platter with a rare steak on it. There was also a bowl of green onions, some hot bread and a plate of butter, his whiskey bottle and a bowl of cracked ice.

"You're worth your wages, Lucy," he said, pulling himself up to the table. Lucy was a heavy aging Negress who had done all her aging on the Guthrie ranch, most of it as Eleanor's personal maid. She had three gold teeth, a house in town, and enough sense to get herself out of the way when her mistress was in certain moods. "Thank you, Mr. Sonny," she said and left. In other moods, when Eleanor was gay, Lucy and Sonny enjoyed teasing each other. They were both expert at banter.

Sonny bent to his steaks and ate silently. Eleanor looked him over in quick glances. He had probably slept in the hearse, if he had slept. There were little flecks of lint in his black hair, and even a few stuck to the hairs at his wrists. He cut the steaks quickly and skillfully with a small steak knife and ate them without lifting his eyes from the plate, now and then crunching one of the garden onions in two bites, and now and then sopping a hunk of the hot French bread in the drippings from the steaks. The flash of his teeth as he bit into the green stem of an onion caused her to look away, back at her nails.

When he finished he poured some more bourbon into his glass, tilted back his chair, and put both boots on the railing. He grinned at her happily.

"Hardly anything beats a good meal," he said. His voice was fresh again. He often seemed able to shrug off fatigue, to freshen himself by some internal movement, some twist within himself.

"Well, I'm glad we could oblige you," she said, looking him in the eye. Sonny's gray-blue eyes were burglars, always looking for a crack, a lock left unlocked, a tear in one's screen. They had been lovers for fifteen years, but his look still made her feel stubborn. He crunched a piece of ice between his teeth and looked down idly at the three gardeners.

"I got to be gettin' to Phoenix," he said. "Thought you might want to ride along. We ain't been nowhere together lately."

For a second it was on the tip of her tongue to make a bitchy comeback, but she was suddenly touched with discouragement and instead straightened her legs beneath the table and looked down at her bare toes. She had tried to bitch him away on many occasions and had never succeeded, and anyway he was Sonny and she didn't feel bitchy. She smiled a little wearily and raised an eyebrow.

"Where did we ever go together except to bed, old buddy?" she said.

Sonny squinted at the sky, then got up suddenly and went

into the bedroom. He came back with a package of her cigarettes. He lit one and tossed the match onto his steak plate.

"I took you to some dances," he said. "And a bullfight down in May-hi-co. Them dances wasn't much, I admit. We must have gone somewhere, we been in the papers often enough."

"That's because I'm Eleanor Guthrie," she said. "If a man so much as holds my coat we're in the papers, at least in Texas. It's one of the small disadvantages of being an heiress. Of course it usually flatters the man who holds my coat. Sometimes it even flatters me."

"Yeah, that's the way it is being a world's champion cowboy too," Sonny said, grinning. "You pat some cutie on the butt and the next morning the papers have got you engaged. Ain't it awful what us heiresses and champions have to put up with? I guess that's why you and me always worked out so well. We got the same kind of problems."

"Okay, okay," she said. "Sorry."

He stood up and came around the table and bent to kiss her again but Eleanor jerked her head away. Sonny grinned. "Not feeling sweet?" he said.

"Not on your life, you arrogant bastard," she said. "I haven't seen you in two months. You haven't even called in two weeks. You can't just walk in here and con me into bed, not any more. Go away so I can read my magazines in peace."

"Well, you knew the rodeo was in town," Sonny said. He blew a puff of smoke her way disgruntled. "Got any pills? I ain't been watching and I'm about out."

"How careless of you," Eleanor said. "I hope somebody gets you pregnant. Look in the bathroom and help yourself."

Sonny did and then came back and stood restlessly on the patio tossing a little vial of pills in his hand. After a moment he stuffed it into the pocket of his Levi's and came around behind her chair, close enough that she could smell him— his breath always smelled faintly of whiskey and his skin faintly of sweat. She expected him to touch her, to run his hand down inside the robe and rub the furrow of her back. She knew exactly how his hand felt there. Her skin waited for it and the rest of her prepared to twist away angrily, but Sonny didn't touch her. He walked over to the bedroom door and stood looking at her thoughtfully.

"Thanks for them steaks," he said. "Tell Lucy she left 'em on a little too long. Still wish you'd come to Phoenix with me. Come on if you change your mind. I'll be at the Ramada. Nice seeing you even if you ain't feeling sweet."

"Oh, go on," Eleanor said. "Maybe I'll come, I don't know. If I do I'll fly. Why couldn't you have called me before you came out?"

Sonny shrugged again. "Just never thought to," he said. Then she heard his heels in the bedroom again and stood up, distressed. He often spoiled things, but when he did he always managed to leave her with the sense that she had only herself to blame. Her back had wanted him to rub it and the skin between her shoulder blades felt itchy and tight. She pulled the orange headband off her head and stood at the railing waiting for him to come out and get in the hearse.

He strode out and paused to kick at the left front tire of the hearse—it looked low. Before he got in he looked up at her.

"Hey, thanks for the pills too," he said. "I don't know what us celebrities would do without pills."

"You're welcome to them," she said. "Maybe I'll see you in Arizona."

He waved, and whirled the hearse around the driveway. She stood at the railing and watched him while he drove to the barn, where there were gas pumps and an air hose. He filled the hearse up and aired his tires. When he circled back near the house, the sun reflecting off the gold horns on the top of the hearse, things crowded into her head and chest and she stood crying, watching the cloud of white dust stretch back toward the highway. It was a wretched and indulgent thing, her sorrow—or so she felt, for who could be less worthy of pity than a lonely multimillionairess, one, moreover, who still had her looks. But there it was, and she could not help crying, the pride that had made her reject him all gone. The pride had not brought her solace in her whole life, yet she could never put it off. She went in and rinsed her face in cold water for several minutes, and she was dressing for a conference with her ranch manager when Lucy came in and looked at her fondly.

"Well, how's he?" she asked.

"Particular as ever," Eleanor said. "He reminded me to tell you that the steaks were overdone." She was standing in a walk-in cedar closet—she liked the smell of the wood. After a moment's consideration she took down a brown silk blouse.

Lucy chuckled, then sighed. "Mr. Sonny don't change," she said. "Particular ain't the word for him."

"It'll do," Eleanor said grimly. "I think he wants me to dye my hair."

She picked a tan skirt and stood musing. Her bra was too tight and she shrugged, trying to loosen it. "If Daddy had only let me date cowboys I might have been spared all this, don't you think?"

"Naw, Miss Eleanor," Lucy said and shook her head with such a ponderous assurance of her own wisdom that Eleanor could not help but be amused and a little cheered. She sat down at her dresser and picked up a bottle of coconut oil.

"Naw, honey," Lucy repeated without elaborating.

"Oh, scram, you fountain of sympathy," she said, considering the gray streaks. "I'm perfectly all right."

Lucy sighed heavily again and shuffled off and Eleanor sat at the dresser brushing her hair until the tightness between her shoulder blades had gone away.

MOVING ON

6

As Patsy had feared, Jim wanted to make Phoenix in one long drive. Their alarm went off at two-thirty A.M. It woke Jim, but Patsy, improvident as ever, had read late and was sleeping unusually soundly. The alarm didn't faze her. Jim dressed in the dark and made two tiptoe trips down the stairs loading the Ford. While he was peering into the back end trying to be sure he had everything, a light came on in the kitchen window. When he went back in, Roger was at the stove fixing breakfast.

"Sorry if I woke you," Jim said.

"Oh, it's might near mornin'," Roger said.

Jim really wanted to be off, but since breakfast was already half cooked he felt the only polite thing to do was eat.

"Patsy not going to eat?"

"I'll be lucky if I can get her awake enough to walk to the car."

"Well, I never cooked her no eggs, anyway. She don't care much for my fried eggs."

Jim ate hurriedly, restless and anxious to be off. He was always anxious at the start of trips, even routine trips, and the trip coming up was not routine. Roger sipped his coffee and watched him thoughtfully.

"Well, I hope you get some good photos," he said. "Seems to me like a long way to go just to take pictures of bronc riders, but then I'm ignorant as a bat about such things." He got up and stood by the stove a minute staring indecisively at the skillet of bacon grease, trying to calculate whether it was worth saving. Finally he set it in the oven.

"If I had to go to rodeos all summer I'd have to take a room in the loony bin by the fall," he said. "Never knowed a rodeo cowboy who had any sense. If you-all meet any, bring 'em by sometime."

Jim carried his plate to the sink and hurried up to wake Patsy. She slept lightly except on those few occasions when he needed her awake, and then she was all but unwakable. Jim pulled her upright and sat her on the edge of the bed, and she sat there sound asleep in a green nightgown, her head lolling over like a child's. When he finally got her half awake she stood up and stripped off the nightgown, dropped it on the floor, walked over to the bureau, and put her head on her arms and stood there nude, asleep.

"Come on, sweetie," Jim said. "We've got to go."

Patsy turned reluctantly and found her bra but had difficulty getting it on. She got her breasts in their cups and stood groggily in the middle of the floor, one snap fastened and her arms behind her back. She stood for almost a minute before Jim noticed her.

"Oh, damn," he said. "Hurry up. Please fasten your other snaps."

"Why are we leaving at midnight?" she asked. "I just finished reading."

"It's not midnight, it's almost three o'clock."

"Just as I thought, midnight," she said and collapsed in a warm sleepy heap on the bed, still clad only in her bra.

"Get up, Patsy," he said grumpily, his patience slipping.

"You're grumpy with me," she said, her face hidden under her hair. "Why are you grumpy? Come and make love to me for eight hours while I get some sleep. I don't want to go anywhere tonight."

Jim pulled her up a little roughly and pleaded with her, and she woke up, irritated. She shoved him away. "Get your grumpy hands off me," she said, going into a short frenzy of activity. She grabbed panties, blouse, and shorts and strode off to the bathroom to brush her teeth. In a minute she was back, dressed, and grabbed her book and purse and foam rubber pillow and stumbled down the stairs.

Roger and his old nondescript dog Bob were standing by the Ford in the faint moonlight. When Patsy saw them she pitched her stuff into the car and went over impulsively and hugged Roger. His brown shirt smelled of starch and tobacco.

"I like your house," she said. "I wish I were staying here. Thank you for being nice."

"Bye, honey," Roger said. "If this vehicle falls apart call me and I'll come and get you in the pickup. Old Jim can hitchhike back."

"I wish he'd hitchhike away." She got in the car, settled her pillow by the window, and went back to sleep. Roger peered in at her a little anxiously.

"I don't believe she's awake good," he said. "You sure she's all right?" Going off without breakfast was to him a shocking act.

"She's fine. Thanks for letting us stay. Maybe we'll get back by in the late summer when our travels are over."

"Hope so," Roger said. "Me and Bob will be here, if neither of us don't die. I guess I'll go in and drink some more coffee. It's too early to milk and too late to go back to bed."

When Jim circled toward the rattly cattle guard he saw Roger going in at the back door. A mile from the house, when he turned onto the highway leading to Vernon, he could still see the light in the kitchen window, as visible as a star in the darkened country. A coyote loped across the road in front of him, his eyes golden in the headlights. He ducked under a barbed-wire fence and vanished into the mesquite.

On the edge of Vernon, Jim pulled up at a cafe called The Big Rig. A thin short young man was leaning against the wall of the cafe, a small traveling bag at his feet and a pile of rigging beside it. He was a rookie bronc rider named Peewee Raskin.

"How y'all?" he said, coming over. "That's timing for you. I just waked up."

Peewee was friendly, informative, and broke. Jim had met him three days before and had taken a liking to him and promised him a ride to Phoenix—a promise he had not mentioned to Patsy. She was not very hot on the idea of going to Phoenix, or anywhere where there were rodeos, and he knew that presenting her with Peewee in the abstract would only lead to argument. Peewee in the flesh was harder to resist. They stowed his gear in the back end and Peewee managed to worm his way into the back seat through Jim's door. He eyed Patsy dubiously. "Snoozin', ain't she?" he said, settling himself between a pile of dresses and a cardboard box full of paperback books. He had spent the night in a horsetrailer behind the cafe and smelled of hay and horse manure. When they drove off, Jim left his window down, hoping the smell would blow away before Patsy woke up. As soon as the car started moving, Peewee leaned his head back against the seat and went to sleep, his black cowboy hat covering his face.

Jim angled southwest, driving a steady seventy-five. Though it was quite a bit farther, he wanted to go the southern route, through El Paso; the shorter route, through central New Mexico, held no attraction for him. He drove in darkness for more than an hour, then it was gray, then brightening. As he turned more and more westward the rising sun came up behind him and shone in his rearview mirror. The country was still and dewy, the fields freshly plowed, and the pastures white with mist. He passed a cluster of oil wells, with a little pumper's shack just down the road from them, the pumper sitting on his front steps with his socks in his hand, scratching his shins. Patsy was curled in the seat, her face hidden, goose bumps on her slim legs. The sun was well up before she awoke. She yawned, sat up, reached in her blouse to readjust a breast, and hooked a finger inside her shorts to scratch herself.

"Sleeping in cars makes my clothes feel too tight," she said, looking vacantly at the morning country. "If there are johns in towns in this part of the wasteland find me one with a john, would you?"

"Big Spring will have one."

Then Patsy caught a whiff of Peewee and turned and looked at him with astonishment. His only visible feature was his open mouth—the hat obscured the rest of his face. His belt buckle was also visible, a huge silver oval with a ruby-eyed steerhead for ornamentation.

"Hey," she said. "We've been invaded by a cowboy. What treachery is this?"

"He was broke," Jim said. "He barely has the money for his entry fees. I thought we'd give him a ride."

"Gee, he's small for a cowboy, isn't he?" she said, giving Peewee a friendly inspection. "Most of them are immense."

"He seems to know everything there is to know about rodeo," Jim said. "He'll make things a lot easier for me."

"It would make things a lot easier for me if you'd hurry up and get us to Big Spring, chum."

When they stopped she hurried off barefoot to the rest room, swinging her black purse by the straps. Jim got out to stretch his legs, had a Coke and went himself, signed the credit card slip, and sat in the driver's seat fidgeting for five minutes before Patsy emerged looking no different than she had when she went in. She got herself a Coke from a Coke machine, dropped a penny on the driveway and followed it leisurely until it stopped rolling, went and got herself a package of cheese crisps from a candy machine, chatted and laughed for two or three minutes with an attendant in a green shirt, and ambled happily back to the Ford, sipping her Coke and still swinging her purse.

"Got a nickel?" she asked cheerfully. "I want some gum and all I've got left is some pennies and a twenty."

"I've got some gum," Jim said. "Come on and get in. The rodeo starts tomorrow."

"What kind of gum?" she asked.

"Spearmint."

"Give me a nickel then, please," she said, reaching in her hand. "I want some Dentyne."

Jim only had a quarter in change, so he gave her that and she ambled back and leaned against the water cooler, looking at the sky and idly combing her hair while the attendant finished gassing up another car. Then she got some change, bought her gum, and skipped quickly back.

"Sorry," she said, biting open the cheese crisps and blowing the little tip of cellophane out the window. "Can't stand Spearmint."

Peewee had slept soundly through the stop, but the minute they started moving again he woke up and his hat fell over into the box of paperbacks. Patsy felt a little shy about him but she knew that Jim was annoyed at her for her laggardly qualities and she welcomed something to distract her from his annoyance.

"Hello," she said, turning around and smiling at Peewee.

She saw immediately, once his hat was off, that he was too young to be shy about. He had short reddish brown hair and a slightly crooked nose. He looked about sixteen.

Peewee smiled tentatively. He was blinking and trying to get the sleep out of his eyes, and it took him much aback to be spoken to at a critical juncture in his waking. And the girl who had spoken was so pretty that he just wanted to stare at her. Her eyes were merry and gray, and she had a straight nose that wrinkled a bit when she smiled, and her smile was merry too. She wore no makeup but she had a comb in her hand and now and then ran it through her black hair.

"I'm Patsy," she said. "Very pleased to meet you."

"Uh, yeah," Peewee said, feeling very, very shy. He wished he was tidier and tried to tidy himself a bit, but his canvas bag was in the trunk and there was not much he could do except try to tuck his shirttail in better. Patsy kept looking at him, her chin resting on her arm, which was across the back seat.

"Peewee Raskin," he said. "Nice to meet you."

"What do you do, Peewee?"

"Uh," Peewee said. For a moment he was honestly unable to remember what he did.

Patsy saw that he was struggling to collect his wits, and she politely looked at the road for a minute to give him a chance. Somehow he looked like a likable person, irresistibly hopeless. Jim was driving with iron concentration, determined to make up for the few minutes he had lost at the service station. He knew it was ridiculous, but despite himself he couldn't help making schedules and straining horribly to keep them. Patsy couldn't stand schedules and was glad Peewee had turned up in the back seat. They could make friends.

Peewee soon recovered himself and was glad when Patsy looked back at him again. He took up the question of what he did.

"Uh, I rodeo," he said. "Much as I can afford to, anyway. This here's actually my first year to be a pro. My folks thought I or-tent to a turned pro yet but I figure the younger the better, you know. So I done it.

"I ain't actually won no money yet," he added apologetically.

"Oh, well," Patsy said, stretching. "I bet you will any time. What do you ride?"

"Bareback horses," he said. "Try to, that is. I ain't actually stayed on one yet, either. These pro horses they're a different pot of beans from them amateur horses I was used to."

"My goodness, how complicated. I didn't know there were professional broncs."

"Aw, yeah," Peewee said seriously, warming to his subject. "You got to learn 'em, you see. Study 'em, I mean, so you know what to expect. Like the other night I drew this old red horse and the boys told me I ort to take a short rein so I done it an' the ol' son of a bitch, uh, the ol' so-an'-so stood on his head and yanked me off flat of my face."

Patsy giggled, delighted with him. He was not only hopelessly hopeless but hopelessly genuine too. "Those boys probably misled you on purpose," she said. "You shouldn't take advice from your competitors, should you?"

Peewee looked at her blankly, as if the idea that he would have competitors had never occurred to him. In truth, it had never occurred to him that anyone would regard him as competition.

"Aw, they wouldn't have needed to do that," he said. "I couldn't have rode the old son of a bitch anyway."

Patsy noticed that he was fidgeting—he had a look of discomfort on his face. He kept shifting the position of his legs.

"Are you too crowded back there?" she asked. "I'm sure we could cram some of that stuff into the luggage compartment."

"Uh, no, I'm just fine," Peewee said, still squirming.

He gazed out the window as if he had some inner pain, and Patsy felt perturbed. He was a very likable boy. One of his front teeth was chipped and his blue Levi shirt was at least a size too large. Watching him squirm, it occurred to her that in all likelihood his problem was the one she had had before they got to Big Spring: a full bladder, pure and simple. She was at once less perturbed, thinking he would mention it when they came to the next town; but in time they came to the next town, Midland, and passed through it, and Peewee didn't mention stopping. Jim had begun to chat

with him, quizzing him about rodeo and rodeo people, and
Peewee answered lengthily and fidgeted and looked stoically
out the window. Patsy grew worried, then annoyed. He was
plainly not going to do anything to interrupt Jim's ridiculous schedule, even if his bladder burst, and it probably
would if something weren't done, for there was no telling
how far Jim would drive before he stopped again. If they got
beyond Pecos without stopping, Peewee was doomed. The
longer she thought about it the more annoyed she became.
There she was again, involved in the workings of a cowboy's
bladder. It was ridiculous. But when she looked at Peewee
she found she could not be angry at him. He was obviously a
person who would never amount to anything, and who knew
it, and who had only his friendliness with which to face the
world. The way he tried not to look at her too much flattered
her and made her feel nervous and strangely powerful. He
was probably only keeping quiet about his bladder through
fear of offending her. She began to feel responsible for him.
He was a child in her keeping, virtually. Jim was the one
who was infuriating, for he should have anticipated the
problem, or asked Peewee, or simply stopped himself,
through common consideration. He was very insensitive.
He had no awareness whatever of other people's bladders. It
had been all she could do to get him to stop for her own.

She grew more and more fretful and squirmed a bit
herself. It had been a fine cool morning, and she had really
been very happy to be going on an endless drive, and the
cheese crisps and the Coke had been exactly what she
wanted for breakfast, and Peewee had been a nice surprise
—up until the time when he needed to pee. But it was all
getting spoiled. She grew angry at Peewee too. If he didn't
have gumption enough to speak up, he deserved to suffer.
Then they reached Odessa, passed the first stations, and he
was still silent. Patsy abruptly decided to act. She was tired
of suffering the thought of him suffering.

"Pull into that station, please," she said, pointing dictato-
rially.

"Why?" Jim asked, surprised. "We just stopped in Big
Spring."

Patsy had put on her shades, and she looked at him
imperiously from behind them. "True," she said. "We

stopped in Big Spring. Would you mind stopping again please? I have to do something."

Her tone left him no choice, so he braked hastily and swerved into the station. Patsy got out at once and strode to the rest room. The service station men looked at her hostilely when they saw they did not intend to buy gas. She waited in the rest room a minute, her bosom heaving with annoyance. Peewee's boots tapped by and in time there was the sound of a toilet flushing from the other rest room. Then the boots went back to the car. She waited another minute and went back too, her head down. Jim was drumming his fingers on the wheel. In the back seat Peewee looked content and comfortable and grateful, but she wanted none of his gratitude.

"Thank you very much," she said to Jim. "I hope this excessive stopping hasn't destroyed your career."

"Used to like outside Odessa," Peewee said. "Nice little town."

Patsy ignored his cheerfulness and Jim's silent, somewhat quizzical annoyance and turned and bent over the back seat to fish in the box of paperbacks. She fished out *A Charmed Life*, which she had bought only a few days before. Peewee was looking at the books curiously.

When she bent over to reach down into the box he had not been able to help looking down her blouse. All he had seen was the strap of her bra and the hollow of her shoulder, but it was the kind of glimpse that was infinitely tantalizing, and he quickly looked at the books in order to cover himself. There were a great many books, it seemed to him.

He picked one off the top and stared at it with surprise. It was called *The Decipherment of Linear-B*. He had never seen a book with such a title, and he stared at it silently. Patsy looked back at him again, still stern, but her sternness soon broke down. Peewee pushed his hat back on his head and stared at the book with innocent fascination, as if it were an unknown species of lizard. He looked so stunned and funny that she immediately remembered he was a child in her care and forgave him his modest reticence. She had also seen him glance down her blouse and felt slightly flushed.

"Read that?" she asked, grinning merrily again.

"Read it?" Peewee grinned too and grunted a little, pleased that she was friendly again. "No, ma'am," he said.

"Now look, call me Patsy. If you'll call me Patsy we can be friends and talk about literature."

"You read many Westerns?" Peewee asked, determined to do his best.

"Not many. I read *Destry Rides Again* when I was a little girl. Are there many good ones?"

"Uum," Peewee said. He was still looking askance at *The Decipherment of Linear-B* and glanced in the box of books as if he had suddenly discovered he was sitting next to an unknown mineral that might well give him radiation burns.

"I don't reckon there are many good ones," he said humbly. "I mean, they're mostly the kind of books *I* read. Westerns. If you read books like this here, whatever it is, then you probably wouldn't never think a Western was no good."

"I don't know. I like all kinds of books."

"Why would there need to be something like this here?" he asked, laying the book carefully back in the box. "It makes me glad I quit school when I did. I ain't got the brain power for such as that."

Patsy started trying to tell him what it was about, but she hadn't read it herself—it was a relic of Jim's flirtation with linguistics—and Peewee looked at her so raptly that it annoyed her a little. She soon broke off her lecture. It had grown hot and they all three gave themselves up to the boredom of a long desert drive. They lunched on hamburgers and shakes under the worn green awning of a drive-in in Pecos, and edged on west through the afternoon. Patsy read idly in *A Charmed Life,* stopping from time to time to look out the window at the bright empty country. It brought back the vacations of childhood. Every other year her parents would decide to go west and would bundle her and her sister Miri into a Cadillac and spend two or three weeks hurrying between scenic spots while the girls read comic books or Nancy Drew mysteries and waited irritably for the Grand Canyon or some other redeeming wonder to appear.

As the sun sank, it shone more hotly into the front seat, and Patsy slipped for a while into a sweaty doze. When she awoke she had a momentary sense of bewilderment and disorientation. It seemed strange that she should be in such barren gray country. If she had any sense, she reflected, she would be in a cool bed in Connecticut, having a tremendous love affair with someone sensitive—someone who would never be likely to have anything to do with Texas, New Mexico, or Arizona. But then Jim smiled at her fondly and she realized that such a fantasy was even more unreal than the locale—it was not her at all. She felt sweaty and tired and nothing seemed clearly the right thing to do.

"Couldn't we just stop in El Paso for the night?" she asked.

Jim looked slightly weary but shook his head. "Peewee needs to be there in the morning to get entered," he said.

She glanced around at Peewee and found that he had been exploring in the paperbacks again and had come up with *Sexus*—a fat red paperback and one of Jim's recent purchases. She hadn't read it and wasn't especially eager to, but it was obvious that Peewee had never read anything like it in his life. He was holding the book about four inches in front of his eyes and seemed to have stopped breathing.

"You're getting ahead of me," she said. "I haven't read that one. Is it pretty sexy?"

Peewee was stunned. When he opened the book he had forgotten everything. He had a terrific erection and when he saw Patsy looking at him he became horribly embarrassed, for he was sure his condition must be obvious. He dropped the book at once and tried to look out the window as if nothing had been happening, but his throat was dry and he had a hard time breathing.

"Uh, yes ma'am, it's kinda racy," he said.

"Patsy. Not ma'am."

"Oh," he said. "Patsy."

She felt cramped and sat with her back against her door, her legs on the seat, the soles of her feet pressed against Jim's leg. There was nothing to do but watch the distances, gray and wavery with heat, and so endless.

"God," she said. "I had forgotten this desert. Couldn't I just fly from El Paso and meet you gentlemen in Phoenix?"

"Sure," Jim said. "No problem about that. We can drop you at the airport as we go through. You'll have to change clothes, though. We'll find a station."

But when they arrived in El Paso three hours later and Jim asked her if she still wanted to fly, she shook her head. She did not like to do things alone, and it made her feel a little low to think that Jim was so obligingly going to let her fly. Another four hundred miles of desert with Jim and Peewee was a lot better than a pointless night alone in some motel in Phoenix.

"You would just put me on a plane, wouldn't you?" she said.

"Why not? You're grown. You have a right to fly to Phoenix if you'd rather. I know it's boring poking along in this car."

"You're just glad to get rid of me because my rest room habits aren't to your liking," she said sulkily, looking at the bare brown mountains behind the town. "Somehow I've been offended. Probably if I went on a plane you and Peewee would scoot right over to Juárez and carry on with women of the night. I know your types. Marriage vows mean nothing to you."

Peewee listened open-mouthed, amazed. She looked back at him sternly and he shut his mouth. He decided he had made some horrible mistake. He should not have let her see him reading that book. Clearly she had figured out that he had had a hard-on.

Jim was in traffic, an annoyance after the open desert, and he was not at all impressed with Patsy's shift of mood. "Oh, for shit's sake," he said. "You're ridiculous. You brought up the airplane. I wouldn't go to Juárez and you know it." But it had crossed his mind that if Patsy flew, he and Peewee might make Juárez for an hour, to rest themselves from the road.

Late afternoon depression fell on Patsy like a hot quilt and she felt ready to cry. "Don't say things like that to me," she said. "I'm sure they embarrass Peewee. You don't love me. All you do is yell excretory words at me. I was pretty once, until you robbed me of my youth." Tears ran out from under her sunglasses and she wiped them on her palms.

"If you don't go to Juárez it's because you're chicken," she said. "Any man in his right mind would dash right to Juárez the minute he got rid of me. You're both men of no spirit. Stop at that drugstore."

She grabbed her purse and went running into the drugstore crying, and Jim sat nervously at the wheel and tried to explain to Peewee that it was probably nothing serious, just one of Patsy's little fits of depression. Peewee was terribly worried and nervous and had already decided never to accept another blind ride involving a wife. He racked his brain for some excuse that would allow him to get out and hitchhike to Phoenix. Patsy was beautiful but altogether too scary.

"Don't look so worried," Jim said. "She does this sort of thing all the time. She'll calm down."

"What's gonna happen to us before she calms down?" Peewee said. "That's what's got me worried."

Patsy came striding back out of the drugstore carrying a number of boxes of Kleenex in her arms. She dumped them on top of the paperbacks, glowered briefly at Peewee, and sat down.

"Drive on, you wretch," she said. "I've decided to accompany you, even though I'm not wanted. Wither thou goest I might as well go. At least I've got some Kleenex now. I intend to cry a lot."

"You'll go, but you'll bitch about it," Jim said, driving on.

"I'll bitch if I feel like it, of course," she said. "Have you ever been married, Peewee?"

"Me?" Peewee asked. "Who would marry me?"

He said it so simply, with no trace of self-pity or melancholy, that it made Patsy stop feeling tense. There was always someone with a problem worse than hers. She wiped her eyes with a Kleenex and smiled back at him, and he looked at her with bewilderment and relief. They were curving west out of El Paso, with the thin winding Rio Grande visible in the valley to the south.

"Why, you look very eligible," she said. "You could use a shirt that fits but other than that there's no reason why you shouldn't get married and be as miserable as everyone else."

"All I can do to get a date oncet an' a while," he said, sure that he was being flattered.

"What do you do when you aren't riding professional broncs?"

"This an' that. Work in fillin' stations."

The sun was lowering, dropping more rapidly toward a

horizon far into New Mexico. The face of the great bare mountain to their right, El Capitan, was shining from the late sun, and the desert around them was cooler and more fragrant as the evening came.

"I never had a job," Patsy said. "I wonder what one would be like."

"You never?" he said. "You don't look like you have, now you mention it. They ain't so bad, most of 'em. The best one I ever had was in Houston."

"Goodness. That's where we live when we're home. What did you do there?"

"Drove a little train. It's over by the zoo, in Hermann Park. We lived in Houston a year. None of us ever liked the town much but I liked drivin' that train. It just goes around the park, you know."

"I know. How strange. I ride it all the time, or every time I go to the zoo. Maybe I rode it while you were driving it. Wouldn't that be odd?"

"Shore would," Peewee said, grinning at the thought. "We couldn't take that humid weather so we all moved back to the plains."

"Let's eat in Las Cruces," Jim said. Peewee's talk of jobs made him strangely envious. All his jobs had been arranged by his father and had been with oil companies owned by his father's friends. He had never felt that he could have gotten any of them if he had been applying strictly on his own merits.

They ate in the coffee shop of a large new motel, with red leatherette booths and fancy trays of syrups and jellies on each table. The place had a large plate-glass window; as they ate they watched the sun go down. Peewee had two cheeseburgers and Jim had a steak that was mostly gristle and Patsy had soup and a not-very-fresh salad and some rolls and butter; her legs were chilled from the air conditioning. When they left, the gray horizon had turned purple. As they drove away from Las Cruces, darkness came across the desert to meet them. The afterglow faded, there were taillights ahead and headlights coming and a swish from cars they met and a solid shock of air when they met one of the huge trucks. Before they reached Deming both Patsy and

Peewee had fallen asleep again, Patsy on her pillow, Peewee under his hat.

Jim felt fresh and drove easily. After a bad stretch of dippy road they entered Arizona and he could drive faster. He could not see the scattered mountains, but he knew they were there. Patsy shivered. He rolled his window up and lost himself in fantasies of himself as a photographer. For a time the road went through a valley, through little towns that were asleep and scarcely lit, and when he rolled his window down to freshen the air he smelled alfalfa fields. Once, just outside a little town, he saw some people walking on the shoulder, and he slowed and saw that they were Indian teenagers walking home from somewhere. The boys were fat and wore cowboy hats, and the girls wore sweaters and clumped together. Off the roads he saw lights, but very low to the ground, as if they came from tepees or little huts. The lights were scattered along a gentle slope. Except for the teenagers, it was a little like being in the Old West for a moment, the scout slipping past the Indian encampment. The strange low lights were eerily beautiful, in contrast to the teenagers, who were eating Popsicles and throwing the wrappers on the ground.

He had driven over six hundred miles and, except for an interval or two, had not felt tired, but not long after he passed the teenagers an unshakable fatigue hit him, and hit him very quickly. It tugged at his eyelids, slowed his feet on the pedals, made the roadway seem very familiar and his own speed quite natural and safe. He knew how such tiredness worked, and the second time he nodded and jerked awake he slowed and eased down a steep shoulder to park on a level place by a barbed-wire fence. He pulled a jacket and a cotton blanket out of the heap of clothes in the back seat, spread the blanket over Patsy, covered himself with the jacket, and went to sleep at once.

In a little more than an hour he awoke and got out of the car to piss. He was stiff and cold and felt like driving on. The moon had risen over the valley and the clear desert sky was pale. In the moonlight he could see the dark bulks of mountains across the valley to the north.

When he started the Ford and drove up the slope of

shoulder Patsy almost slid onto the floor, and the blanket slipped off her. She woke up and looked about in bewilderment. "Dumb fool," she said vaguely and then scooted over by him and cuddled against his shoulder. It was quite cold. She turned around and fished in the clothes until she found a red cashmere sweater of his that she liked to wear. She tugged it on and snuggled against him again, nuzzling her face beneath his arm, almost into his armpit.

"What's the appeal of my armpit?"

"Warmth," Patsy said. "My nose is cold." She covered her legs with the blanket and leaned her head against his shoulder, silent but friendly. When they curved up into the Superstition Mountains Jim slowed down and drove carefully, not fully trusting his reflexes. Patsy was still awake when they dropped into the flat desert east of Phoenix and saw the lights of the city brightening the sky.

"Please get a place with a swimming pool," she said meekly. "If I'm going to have to sit around all day by myself I want something to dip my toes into. It won't cost much."

"You deserve that much," he said. There were times when it was necessary for him to pretend he didn't have almost a million dollars of his own, and it was one such time.

He pulled into a station to gas up and get a city map. Patsy got out and stretched and took a quick walk around the block, although it was almost two A.M. The air was cold and the dark sky very liquid. The sweater felt good; her legs were cold. When she was coming back to the station he saw Peewee standing at the curb looking down the wide empty street. He had his rigging and his canvas traveling bag and had tucked his shirttail in neatly. When he saw her coming he began to kick his bootheel against the curb.

"Where in the world are you going?" she asked.

"Might as well hitchhike on out to the grounds," he said. "Ain't no use in you-all going out of your way. I sure am much obliged for the ride. Hope I get to see you agin while we're here."

"Of course you will," she said. "Don't be so humble. Will anyone give you a ride this time of night?"

"Somebody'll come along," he said. "Always have."

"He insisted," Jim said when she was back in the car. "You scared him back there in El Paso."

"How could I have scared him?" she said. "I didn't do anything unusual."

They drove down Broadway, the wide main street, rejecting block after block of palatial motels and settling finally on a modest stucco court with a small swimming pool. The manager had gone to bed, but cheerfully got up to register Jim. Patsy got out and walked across the gravel drive to stand by the water, which was bluish and lit by only two small lights. There was an old pool umbrella with five or six iron chairs grouped around it.

The room was modest and also poorly lit. The green bedspread depressed her and the green tile in the bathroom depressed her more. But whenever he was starting a new enterprise, Jim would have them poor for a time, and there was nothing to do but make the best of it. It was his one inflexible policy. Just as her spirits were sinking she caught an abrupt glimpse of herself in the bathroom mirror and pulled them up again. For a girl who had just traveled seven hundred and some miles, she looked okay, and she marched back out to the car to get her purse and her suitcase, determined that no cheap motel was going to control her spirits.

"Whee, we're starting a new life," she said cheerfully when she came back in. Jim was yawning, more tired than he would admit. He had brought only his cameras in. Without answering, he went back out to lock the car, and Patsy went in the bathroom to test the hot water. All the same, the life didn't feel so new. She made the shower drip and held her hand under the drip until the water got hot, wishing there was a bathtub. Behind her she heard the springs of the bed give as her tired husband sank upon it, and when she went in to get her gown he was asleep, the bed light right in his eyes. Some new life, she thought, but then he had driven all that way without any help and with her bitching at him, and she went over and took off his loafers and turned the bed light out before she went in to take her shower.

71

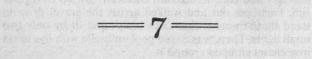

7

Patsy sat at the narrow little dressing table in the motel room, unhurriedly arranging her hair. The table had been designed to be a desk and a dresser both, and was not adequate to either purpose. It had a sheet of glass on top, under which was a map of a sort, showing all the spots of historical interest around Phoenix. The mirror was old and oval. Patsy lifted her hair, trying to imagine how she would look if it were long enough to be arranged in coils. Often she sat in front of mirrors for some time contemplating herself as she might be if she looked otherwise. She was far from indifferent to her looks, but on the whole she was content with them and felt no urgent need to make radical changes. She lingered at the dressing table because she found dressing tables nice places to meditate. When it came time to go someplace she could always be ready in six minutes. In the end she seldom did more than comb her hair and give a bit of attention to her eyes.

Jim was sitting impatiently on the bed watching her. He had his cameras and equipment bag ready and was merely waiting for it to be time to leave. Patsy had decided to skip the rodeo and go to a movie, and he was rather glad—if she had gone to the rodeo he would have felt responsible for her boredom. She had on her gray sleeveless dress and when she raised her arms to rearrange her hair the lift of her bosom made him feel sexy. He had slept most of the day while she had idled by the swimming pool reading and writing lengthy letters to her sister Miri and her friend Emma Horton. She was a happy idler—she loved to write long letters and sit by swimming pools, occasionally in the sun but more often in the shade. She never had been able to tan successfully—her shoulders and legs merely reddened.

As Jim watched her contentedly turning her head one way and another he became more and more horny, and with horniness came moodiness. He contemplated going over, kissing her, taking her to bed. She could usually be taken to bed, even if she had been planning on a movie; she cared more about impulse than she cared about plans. He cared about plans, though, and he had been planning to get some pictures taken. If they made love he probably wouldn't even get to the rodeo that night. Given any sort of chance, Patsy would loll in bed for hours and would want him to talk to her, and he would get lazy and not go. He knew his laziness problem and was determined to get on top of it.

The thing that complicated such decisions the most was his knowledge that if he did go sweeping over and make love to her it probably wouldn't be all too satisfying, anyway. Patsy liked for him to make love to her—at least she liked it okay, but she didn't like it as much as he would have liked her to. It just didn't seem to hit her terribly hard, or not very often, and though she was not critical of him particularly, he frequently felt that it was his fault that their transports were not more intense. If he made love to her and it worked out badly he would feel all the more that he ought to have gone to the rodeo and done his work. So, instead of going over and grabbing her he played out his desire in fantasy as he sat on the bed, and in fantasy it turned out a lot more gracefully and powerfully than it usually turned out in fact.

"I guess I'm ready," Patsy said, standing up and putting her comb in her purse. "I've got about thirty minutes to make the feature." Jim stood up too and managed to focus on the cool ready-to-go-out Patsy standing before him instead of the naked responsive Patsy in his mind.

She got a sweater, in case the theater should be too air-conditioned, and found her car keys. She was going to drop him at the rodeo and take the Ford. Jim kept a city map in his hand and gave her directions politely, but he was still horny and irritated with himself.

"I love these wide streets," she said. "The nice thing about the West is all the space."

"It wouldn't be so nice if you had to live in the middle of it."

Soon they saw the arena lights, with the sky behind them black and starless. There was a solid line of traffic. Patsy inched along irritably, tapping her fingernails on the wheel and compressing her lips with annoyance when a woman in a white station wagon stopped just in front of her and let two little boys out. Jim got out at the contestants' gate, got his cameras from the back seat, and leaned across the seat to kiss her. She was in the process of taking off her sunglasses, and the kiss got tangled in fingers and frames.

"Don't get yourself trampled," she said.

He hung the cameras around his neck and walked into the mob that filled the space behind the arena. A riding club was lined up. Women in tight pants that made their abdomens bulge grotesquely clutched their saddle horns nervously. They obviously never rode except on the first nights of rodeos and strove desperately to keep their spotless hats on and their horses in place. Some of them looked so incongruous that Jim wanted pictures of them, but he had not yet learned to take pictures unobtrusively and was nervous about taking any. Despite his Levi's and boots he himself felt incongruous—he no more belonged to the scene than the ladies on the horses. He felt almost as hopeless at photography as they were at horsemanship and wished for a moment that he had simply gone to the movie with Patsy.

He went up into the grandstand, but he stayed only a few minutes and took no pictures. The stands were a confusion of children, pillows, people in satin shirts, dropped programs, and Sno-cone vendors, and the aisles were already littered with popcorn sacks and paper cups. He went from the stands to the bucking chutes. The bareback riders paid him no mind at all. One tall man had his shirt off and was getting his shoulder bandaged. There was a smell of dust and horseshit, and the man who was being bandaged grunted almost as loudly as the broncs that were being cinched. He heard Sonny Shanks's name called and looked up to see Sonny sitting above chute three, bareheaded and in a bright yellow shirt. A heavy-set cowboy reached up and handed him some money without a word and Sonny grinned and folded it carefully before stuffing it in his pants pocket.

He wore black chaps and seemed without a care. When he saw Jim shooting pictures he nodded and gave a friendly wave.

Peewee appeared and was as glad to see Jim as Jim was to see him. "I would take you round but I got to help hustle the ridin' stock," he said. He wore the same clothes he had worn yesterday, but they were considerably dustier.

Jim found a place on the fence and watched the bareback riding. Shanks seemed to ride very well—at least two young cowboys standing nearby thought so. "I guess he's living proof that no amount of pussy can hurt a man," one said.

Instead of thinking of pictures, Jim found himself thinking of Patsy. He seldom photographed her—somehow it made them both self-conscious. He pictured her in his mind, sitting in the movie with a sweater over her shoulders. Her shoulders were lovely. Once before they were married they had gone in the evening to Fair Park, in Dallas, and sat on the grass by a little lake, eating fried chicken from a box. Patsy had worn a white dress with narrow straps, so that her arms and shoulders and neck were almost bare. She ate the hot chicken and wiped her fingers on the grass and talked about an Ingmar Bergman movie they had seen the night before, her voice soft and quick.

Jim sank easily and sometimes quite deliberately into reverie. As he was thinking of Patsy he was almost knocked off the fence by the two cowboys, who were scrambling up. He heard hoofs and snorting breath and looked down to see a yellow bronc charging straight up the fence line. The cowboys along the fence scattered upward before the bronc like grasshoppers before a mowing machine.

Jim got down and wandered to the stockpens to stare at the big lazy-looking bulls for a while. Three young would-be bull riders were looking at them too, one of them talking of how much he missed Idaho. When Jim got back to the arena the barrel racing had just begun. The first girl out was fat and a little scared. She let her horse go so wide on the second barrel that he almost touched the fence where Jim was standing. The second contestant was a woman in her thirties. She came out very fast on a well-trained gray horse, cut the barrels coolly and professionally, no more than a foot of space between the barrel and the horse's body, and quirted the gray out of the arena in a time of twenty-one seconds. The crowd seemed to think that very good. The third rider entered the arena at a dead run. She was bareheaded, her hair bleached white. She charged down on the first barrel so recklessly fast that the crowd shushed completely and then roared when her Appaloosa came out of the turn safely, almost on his knees. The second barrel was harder. The girl rode almost straight at it, keeping the horse at full speed until she was only a few yards away. Then she swung right to clear the barrel and sharply left to round it; but the horse had too much speed. The girl was up and forward in her stirrups, and when the horse tried to whip out of the turn his forefeet slipped and he went down, still straining forward. The girl was thrown clear and hit the ground several feet from the horse, right in front of Jim. He and three cowboys immediately jumped the fence, thinking she was hurt, but the girl got up and shook her head rapidly, flinging tears out of her eyes.

"My stupid fault," she said and began to cry bitterly. The clown came up and tried to put his arm around her, but she hit her fist against her thigh and stepped away. Still sobbing, she got her horse and began to lead him out of the arena.

"Well, bad luck," the clown said, shaking his head in discouragement. Then he looked at Jim and seemed to recognize him.

"Oh, hi," he said. "We met in Merkel, only you was knocked out at the time. I'm Pete Tatum."

"Sure," Jim said, shaking hands. "You saved my cameras."

They followed Boots and her horse down the fence line, and a girl in a pink suit dashed into the arena, overshot a barrel, and lost her hat. By the time they were out of the arena Boots's disappointment had subsided enough that she let Pete put his arm around her and soothe her and hug her a bit. Jim stood back awkwardly, not sure whether to leave or stay.

"I wish I would learn," she said.

"Aw, you will. Let's all go to the trailer and have a quick beer. I ain't busy till calf-scramble time."

On their way to the trailer they passed Shanks's hearse and saw him sitting on the back end of it, one leg out of his

Levi's, trying to wrap an elastic bandage around his knee.
He had a bandage on his hand too, and it gave him trouble
wrapping the knee. He had one end of the elastic in his
teeth. He glanced up and saw them passing and immediately
let that end go.

"Hey, Boots," he said. "Come wrap this thing for me. I
ain't got enough hands."

Pete went over to the hearse, took the wrap off, and
expertly rewound it on Sonny's knee. "Tighter," Sonny said.

"Not tighter unless you want gangrene. That ain't the first
knee I've ever wrapped."

Sonny nodded at Jim. "Your wife ever get in a better
mood?" he asked.

"She's fine."

Boots ignored Sonny entirely and walked on off, leading
her Appaloosa. When Pete was finished with the support,
Shanks slipped his leg back in his pants and began to tuck in
his shirttail.

"You-all come to the party tomorrow night," he said to
Jim. "My place, at the Ramada. You can come too, Peter, if
you bring your girl friend. You ain't much fun stag."

"I got to train my mule tomorrow night," Pete said,
walking off.

"See if you can train him to fuck," Sonny said, grinning at
Jim. "A fucking mule is what the circuit needs."

Jim promised to be at the party and followed Pete to the
trailer house. Boots was sitting on the steps and had a can of
beer for each of them between her legs. She sipped at hers,
and Pete stood with one hand on his hip, draining his. When
it was empty he threw the can under the trailer and reached
down to hold Boots's head against his leg for a minute.

"I got to be goin'," he said. "Come on, shake off that fall.
Everybody in rodeo falls sooner or later. See you, Jim."

He left. His attempt to cheer Boots up had not worked.
She still looked very disconsolate.

"We're going to get married next week," she said. "That's
why Pete acted embarrassed. He thinks he's too old for me."

Jim squatted down so he could see her better. Her nose
was a little too blunt but otherwise she was pretty, in an
open, energetic, unselfconscious way. Her straight white
hair framed her face nicely. He found her immediately

likable and was glad to be relieved of the necessity to be a photographer every minute.

"How long have you been married?" she asked.

"A year and a half."

"I wish we had," Boots said wistfully. "I'll be glad when Pete and I have been married ten years. Then we won't have any problems like this."

Jim was a little surprised. He thought she was sad about her fall, not about her marriage. He looked around for a place to put his empty beer can. Throwing things on the ground seemed sloppy to him, and he was always trying to break Patsy of the habit.

"Oh, just pitch it under the trailer," Boots said. "It gets messy around a rodeo whatever you do. That's one thing I like about it. I've always been messy."

It was really a one-man trailer, and so small that Jim could scarcely imagine how two people could even *get* in it, much less live in it; but its smallness and simplicity appealed to him. He loved the thought of being able to live on next to nothing—on the bare essentials. In his imagination he often stripped his life of all extras, all luxuries, everything wasteful. The difficulty was Patsy. He could not have persuaded her to live in the largest trailer ever made. In Houston they had the whole top floor of a large three-car garage, and she was not content even with that. She wanted a house and had threatened to buy one with her own money—she had just about enough. It was insane; she didn't particularly want to live in Houston, but she continually complained about not having a house, and he could never be quite sure she wouldn't just go out some morning and buy one. The value of keeping stripped down to essentials was lost on her, and his attempts to explain it did not impress her. When he quoted Thoreau she yawned. Boots was clearly more amenable to the simple life than Patsy would ever be.

"It's tiny, all right," she said, noticing that he was looking at the trailer. She giggled a little and looked happier. "Pete keeps talking about trading it in on a Volkswagen, so we'll have more room to screw. I guess we'll end up getting a station wagon."

"You ought to get a hearse, like Sonny has."

"He'd kill us. Us or anybody else who gets one. He's as proud of that hearse as he is of his dong. Want the rest of my beer? I feel like I may throw up. I get so excited running the barrels that I'm always throwing up."

Jim would have liked to talk longer, but she did look a little drawn. He stood up and said he had to go. Except for Peewee she was the only rodeo person he had met that he really liked to talk to. He was a little intrigued by girls who came right out with words like screw and dong. Patsy was more inhibited than he felt she ought to be where talk of sex was concerned.

"Bring your wife by tomorrow," Boots said. "I'd love to meet her." Jim said he would.

When he left, Boots went in and set her half-can of beer in the icebox and then went out and began to unsaddle the Appaloosa, whose name was Sprinkles. The dachshund had been run over the week before. She missed him, and now she laid her cheek against the horse's neck.

"It wasn't your fault, sweet thing," she said. "It was all my fault."

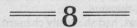

8

Patsy had gone to see *Lolita* and was delighted with it. For some reason she had missed the film when it first came out, though she had read the book three times and thought it beautiful. James Mason had been a perfect Humbert Humbert too. Still, the movie left her annoyed—vaguely annoyed.

The Ford was in a parking lot only a block from the theater, and as she walked down the wide sidewalk by the even wider street she tried to put her finger on what had bothered her. She passed a shop that seemed to sell nothing but sunglasses; there were hundreds in the window, with all sorts of strange frames, and as she loved sunglasses and liked to have numerous pairs in reserve, she stopped and peered in the window. A carload of boys passed in the street and let out a chorus of whistles. Alarmed for a second, she turned and looked. There were five of them in a new convertible, soldiers probably, all of them wearing the gaudy short-sleeved sports shirts that soldiers seemed to adopt for their nights on the town. When she looked at them they cheered and whistled and made it obvious they thought she was luscious, but they also seemed inoffensive and even a little shy, and they moved rapidly on down the street.

Normally, being whistled at embarrassed her, but this time it perked her a bit instead. As she walked on to the parking lot she reflected on the movie and decided that one reason she was annoyed by it was because she had been no nymphet herself, no Lolita, when she was that age. She had been thin and inhibited and had had no bosom at all and, as well as she could remember, no flair at all. She had had no trouble getting a respectable number of dates, but that was because she had always been pretty in the face, as the saying was in Texas. She would certainly not have attracted a Humbert Humbert, and except for one occasion when a boy had bumped his penis against her hand nothing memorably lascivious had happened on any of the dates. The movie left her all the more convinced that as a teenager she had been a complete stick-in-the-mud.

The question was, had she really changed? She had grown prettier, and had more bosom, and thought of herself as knowing the facts of life, but she was still not convinced that she was all a woman ought to be. She had always wanted to be beautiful and had always been slightly contemptuous of girls who just wanted to be sexy, but being sexy had begun to seem more important to her or, at least, important in a different way. Jim was not much help. It was a vague problem and he was vague himself half the time. He was often eager to make love to her, but that fact alone never seemed too convincing. His life, so far as she could tell, was one great interlocking structure of fantasies involving himself, and it was probably just necessary to the overall fantasy for him to think of her as sexy. In a way, being whistled at by a carful of boys was more convincing than Jim's attentions. At least the soldiers were something objective.

She started the Ford and drove slowly out Broadway, looking a little wistfully at the giant motels. Probably it was vulgar, a streak of Aunt Dixie in her, but she would much rather have been at a giant motel. She liked carpets and big bathtubs and good coffee shops and huge well-lit pools and television sets so there would be movies to watch at night. There would probably even be interesting people at a big motel. The only interesting person in theirs was a long-retired minor actor. He had a grenadier mustache, a chubby talkative wife, and a magnificent white Afghan so aristocratic that the whole motel seemed scarcely fit to be his kennel.

Around the pools of the big motels there were people sitting and drinking, some even swimming, though the night was cool. Patsy would have liked to be among them, and she felt a flash of annoyance at Jim. It was unfair, because if they had been at a big motel she would probably have been inside reading, but it was a strong annoyance, nonetheless. She had money and was glad of it and he had many times as much and his attitude toward it had been the cause of many fights, all of which she lost. From time to time he insisted on pretending they were poor, driven to earning their living from month to month, and when he set a budget at such times nothing could make him exceed it. Patsy pointed out in the wittiest possible terms that such budgets were ridiculous, but of all his fantasies the poverty fantasy was the one he was stubbornest about, and he never gave a foot of ground.

She pulled into the motel and locked the Ford. In contrast to the pools she had been passing, theirs seemed a small and uninviting fishpond. The old actor and his wife were just returning from walking the Afghan and said hello to her pleasantly. She felt depressed the minute she stepped into the room. The small room, the bare floor, the poor light, all seemed so confining in contrast to the wide streets and deep sky outside; and to make matters worse, Jim was already back. He sat on the floor with his shirt off, happily engaged in his favorite task, which was the rearranging of his files. She had seen it coming that afternoon when he had lugged the two small green cases of files in from the car. All of the hundreds of pictures he had managed to take were in piles on the floor, along with several stacks of folders, manila envelopes, pencils, felt pens, paper clips, and tabs of various kinds. He had even bought a bottle of bourbon—a pure affectation, it seemed to her—and had some, in a motel glass, sitting by his leg.

"Hi," he said, very cheerful. "Not much happening out there tonight so I thought I'd come home and straighten this stuff out. We're invited to a party tomorrow night."

"Ducky," she said, unreasonably annoyed. He had barely glanced up, and the sight of the absorbed, contented way he piddled with the neat piles of pictures and neat stacks of envelopes sent her spirits straight down. He was sitting there dreaming of being Walker Evans or Cartier-Bresson or Ansel Adams, whatever kind of photographer he wanted to be for the moment, and it made her furious and also, somehow, scared. She felt like kicking the bourbon glass, or kicking the piles of pictures into complete disorder, and could hardly stop herself from doing it. Three months as a photographer and he was already arranging his own retrospective in his mind.

Instead of kicking the pictures she tiptoed over them with exaggerated care, her lips compressed. If Jim had looked up he would have seen she was furious, but he was looking instead at a picture of the marquee of an abandoned drive-in theater they had passed in Texas. The local kids had visited it one night and done their best to spell out an obscenity with the letters still left on the marquee. The best they could do was HORS SHIT. It was one of his favorite pictures.

Patsy got her black bikini and a white terry-cloth robe and went to the bathroom and put on the bikini. Going back through the room, she took less care and one of her heels knocked a pile of pictures out of line.

"Where are you going?" Jim asked, surprised.

"I'm going to drown myself," she said hotly. "I'm feverish with envy because I don't have a noble profession to practice, like you do."

"What?" Jim said, puzzled. He had not really heard. The reverie he was enjoying had a strong hold on him, and he didn't want to be drawn out of it even if Patsy was miffed about something. She poised at the door, ready to argue if he wanted to argue, but when he looked down at the picture again she shut the door and strode angrily across the gravel driveway. The gravel hurt her bare feet, but not as much as she would have liked it to. She would have welcomed a flow of blood, either his or hers, but the only real pain was the pain at her breastbone, from the pressure of all her feelings. She sat down on the cold pool edge, let her feet into the water, and watched her own wavering reflection. The black of her suit and the white of her robe were plainer than her features or even her skin.

After a minute she began to cry helplessly. Jim was doing everything over. When he had wanted to be a novelist he spent two months arranging for it. He bought an electric typewriter—it only took the notion of a new career to drive all thought of economy out of his mind, then he used his money as lavishly and unconsciously as if it were air—all kinds of paper of different colors and grades, dozens of pencils, standard pens and esoteric pens, a new dictionary and a fine desk lamp, lots of manila envelopes, and good editions of the best novels by forty or fifty masters of the novel. He even bought biographies of novelists and criticism of the novel. He wrote letters to twenty agents (no replies), applied for three fellowships, wrote slightly more than one hundred pages of a book about growing up in Dallas, stopped one day to make notes, then instead of making notes began an elaborate chart of what was going to happen in the novel, improved on the chart and the notes for another month, and then began to spend his time in bars with fellow students while she read most of the novels he had bought.

After he had bought all the pens, pencils, papers, dictionaries, directories, and guidebooks he could possibly need he stopped even piddling with the actual pages of his novel, accidentally read a book on languages one day, and decided he would rather be a linguist than a novelist. It was more his sort of thing, he felt: more exact, more precise. It took experience to make a novelist, but anyone with a good brain could become a linguist. Patsy agreed and was glad he had decided to change careers. During his last days as a novelist he had been very gloomy and hard to live with, and besides she had read the hundred pages of novel and hadn't liked it much. Once the decision was made, she pitched in, helped him carry home books from the Rice library, applauded him when he tried to audit five language courses at once, and looked with interest into the grammars, dictionaries, journals, and books on linguistic theory that he ordered. The waiters at the local French restaurant smiled behind their menus when he tried to order in French, but Patsy didn't care. She got rather interested in Benjamin Lee Whorf herself and was happy at the thought of being a linguist's wife.

Then, after two months as a linguist, he bought a cheap camera to take snapshots with and within the next six weeks spent twelve hundred dollars on cameras and equipment and was thinking of setting himself up a darkroom. The way he meant to do it would combine writing and photography, he decided, and by the merest chance he got hot on cameras during the fortnight when the Houston rodeo was on. He went out to the stock barns, took a few pictures of the back ends of steers so pampered that their tails were kept in hairnets, and three days later decided they would spend the summer gathering pictures for a book on rodeo. It was only June, they were at their third rodeo, and Jim was already in the arranging phase and hadn't taken more than ten pictures that she thought were worth looking at. She felt scared and had no idea what she would do.

But almost as soon as she ceased crying, the depression left her. She wiped her face on the hem of the terry-cloth bathrobe and looked across the empty street, where there was a Pontiac agency with three gleaming cars spotlighted on the floor. She could be all wrong about it, she decided. Jim was smart and sensitive, perhaps he would become a good photographer. Perhaps he really needed to rearrange the files. Even if he didn't become a photographer he might hit on the field that suited him sooner or later. It was cowardly of her to become discouraged when he had had only three tries. It was all her own deficiency—she lacked faith in him. Even if he never found a field and just kept skipping from hobby to hobby, would that be so terrible? What would it mean for them? She didn't know, didn't know at all.

Sighing, she slipped off her robe. She hated the sense that she was becoming neurotic, slipping off into gloomy vapors; it was too silly and too self-pitying and she had nothing at all to pity herself for except that she wanted to have a baby and Jim didn't, and even that would probably work itself out soon. When she was in such moods she longed for something to lift her out of them, some purely physical sensation: heat or cold, to dance, to eat. Beneath her was a literal swimming pool, full of cold water. Bracing her hands on the edge of the pool, she began to lower herself into it slowly, watching the water as it came up her white legs to her knees, her thighs, her hips. When her hips went under, the sluice of water over the bikini bottom was very chilling, and goose bumps came out all over her upper body. The waterline was just below her navel, and she stopped it there for a second, enjoying the sensation of cold even though she wanted to turn loose and swim to warm herself. It made her shiver.

The bikini she had bought in Houston, on a whim. She had always been, if anything, an overly modest girl, given to one-piece suits all through high school and college; but when she had seen the suit in a window in Westbury she had a sudden immodest desire to wear such a suit and had taken it right home and tried it on. It was clearly the sort of suit that went best with a tan, but still she liked it; it made her feel loose and grown up in some way. Jim had been tremendously turned on by it and had tried to take her to bed while she was trying it on. It was a chink in the wall of her modesty, and he welcomed all chinks. Somehow the thought that it was the bikini that had prompted the seduction attempt had offended her slightly, and she put him off.

When the cold water had driven all the gloom out of her head she turned and with her hands still on the edge of the pool lowered herself until the water came over her breasts; then she shoved out into the pool and began to swim. For a few minutes she swam back and forth across the little pool in a vigorous but awkward crawl. She had had a good swimming teacher, and a good tennis coach as well, but she still swam awkwardly and played tennis so haphazardly that Jim had several times, in doubles matches, come close to pounding her with exasperation. She liked pools more than she liked swimming.

By the time she had swum four or five lengths she was warm and stopped beneath the diving board to rest, breathing hard. She was not meant for exercise, she decided. As she was resting, Jim came out in his swimming trunks, an old pair of gray trunks that he had swiped from a gym class years before. She considered them as much an affectation as the bourbon, but she was in a more tolerant mood and watched him tiptoe across the gravel, a little glad that he had come to keep her company. When he got to the pool he jumped in feet first, came up, treaded water for a moment, and swam over to her in an even crawl. When he looked up, streams of water ran out of his blond hair onto his chest and shoulders.

"I thought you were going to drown yourself," he said. He was in good spirits, and he was always sly at such times and infectious.

"My bosom wouldn't let me sink," she said. "Want to drive out into the desert and watch the sunrise? It's supposed to be great."

Jim ignored the question—it was his way of handling impulsive suggestions of hers that didn't appeal to him at all. Instead of answering he swam up to her, looked friendly, and began to kiss her. Kissing when their faces were both dripping wet was a bit of a novelty—it was slippery and his skin smelled differently and she compliantly kissed with him awhile, lightly and in fun, the water from her wet hair running off her eyelids and down her cheeks. She was holding on to the edge of the pool with her hands, her arms spread. Jim gradually began to kiss a little bit more than in fun. The bikini had done it again, she supposed. He put his hands on the pool side and wiggled between her legs, bumping at her suggestively while he treaded water.

"Quit," she said, not annoyed, but at the same time not wishing him to embark on any underwater gymnastics, none involving her, at any rate. She could tell from the bumps that he was feeling sexy and as usual that confused her a little, for while she was approving and a little glad she was also slightly reluctant. And anyway, cars were still passing on the street and the street was only yards away. And anyway, underwater sex was ridiculous even to think about, but Jim had read pornography and thought everything ought to be tried.

"Quit bumping me, please," she said, putting a hand on his shoulder. "I wouldn't be seduced in a swimming pool even if it were anatomically feasible, and I have a hard enough time keeping this suit on without you bumping me. Just desist for a bit."

"You have no pioneer spirit," Jim said. "I like to bump you."

Patsy put her legs around him and let him hold her up. She sank until only her head was out of the water, her eyes on a level with his chin. "You really don't want to see the desert sunrise?" she asked.

"Perhaps we can make a trade," he said, nudging her from below; but it was the sort of remark that didn't work with her and she ignored it as blithely as he had ignored the original suggestion.

"I saw the clown you like," he said. "Met his wife, too. She's a lot younger than him. They want us to come and see them tomorrow."

"Why not?" she said, not very enthusiastic. She had all but forgotten Pete Tatum. He had been very nice, but the circumstances had been unusual and she had the feeling that under ordinary circumstances they would have little use for each other. She remembered her embarrassment when he had come up to the car without his shirt on as she had been leaving to drive to Abilene. There was no reason why she should have been embarrassed, but the memory of it lessened her enthusiasm for a visit.

"His wife is a barrel racer. Boots is her name. She's very friendly. Even you might like her."

"So I might," Patsy said, still skeptical about Tatum. Names like Boots brought out the snob in her. Her chin was on the water and water got in her mouth. She tightened her legs around Jim to keep from slipping farther. Their loins were pressed together but in a position that was rather uncomfortable for both of them. Patsy unclasped her legs and ducked under his arm.

"Damn it, I forgot a towel, and you did too," she said. "I was angry with you when I came out here and you didn't even realize it." But Jim had started swimming across the pool and didn't hear her. It was not a remark that was worth repeating. She clung to the side, a little cold, contemplating a drippy dash to the bathroom.

"No towels?" Jim said when he swam back. "I'll get some." He left a little trail of wet tracks across the gravel and came back with a large green towel. "Damn it, I dripped on some pictures," he said.

Later, after she had dried and gone in and sat in the small warm bathroom awhile filing her nails, and was stretched on the bed in her green nightgown turning through an issue of *Vogue,* Jim left his pictures and came silently to the bed and began to rub her back. The ends of her hair were still damp. He folded her hair into two parts and tucked it around her throat, so her shoulders and the back of her neck were bare. "If you're through with your pictures turn off the overhead light, will you?" she said. He did and came back and massaged her shoulders and the base of her skull a bit. Tiring of that, he began a little timidly to move his hands under the loose straps of the gown, down her rib cage and around toward her breasts. Patsy knew she was being caressed but felt a slight catch of stubbornness in herself and kept reading the *Vogue* with concentration for a few minutes, until Jim's silent urging made her feel guilty. She turned on her side so he could reach a breast and then with a little excusing yawn dropped the *Vogue* off the bed and turned on her back acquiescently.

She liked the way he massaged her neck and shoulders and had begun to feel genuinely acquiescent, but Jim didn't know it. He was never quite sure when she wanted him to go on and when she didn't. As it was, he felt his desire to be something of an intrusion and became hasty about it. "Hey," Patsy said. She sat up, shrugged her gown off, and threw it on the floor with a quick gesture of resolve. The green gown billowed as it settled and Jim saw the line of Patsy's ribs as she stretched an arm to turn off the bed light. When she turned back to him in the sudden darkness he was not quite where she thought he was and their heads bumped. It took them a moment to realign their bodies.

"I'm sorry," Jim said, though it was just a slight bump. Patsy was silent. It seemed always just at that moment, at the beginning of lovemaking, that she was most silent, most mysterious to him. At that moment he had no sense that he knew what she really wanted, or really liked, and she gave no clues at all. He could not even hear her breathing, and he felt, as he always felt, that he must hurry or she would cease to be interested—perhaps already had. So he did hurry, feeling himself an imposer until he reached a point where his own pleasure became stronger than any thought of Patsy. With his face close to her throat and her hair against his mouth he could hear her breathe and knew that he was not imposing and moved at ease for a time. A faint light from the street came in through the window, enough so that when he raised up he could see Patsy's face, her eyes closed and her face tensed a little, pleasantly. It made him feel very close to her. Things were going to be lovely for them both, finally. She was idly, unconsciously stroking his back with one hand and without meaning to stroked too low. It touched Jim too keenly, he was suddenly past waiting. He wanted not to be, but he was, it was too sharp. And when he was done coming, the sense of closeness he had felt for a moment was replaced almost immediately by a sense of disappointment, a feeling that was brother to his earlier feeling of awkwardness.

It soon became kind of anger at Patsy, who was going on, moving very little but moving in her own deliberate way. He didn't want to communicate the sudden resentment that he felt, and he rested, his face in her hair, merely staying put. As he waited, some of his irritation passed away, he all but forgot Patsy and was thinking of pictures and picture books when her pace increased suddenly and he found it hard to stay put. She put her legs over his and flexed so rapidly that he was afraid he would slip out, but after a moment of straining high against him, she came, her legs loosened, and he felt her fast heartbeat beneath him. Filled with affection then, she began to rub her face against his throat. Her hair still smelled faintly of swimming-pool water. Jim remained where he was, but his irritation came back, and became anger. It was a cheat, somehow, and it seemed to him Patsy's fault; after two years of making love with him, she ought to have quickened. He wanted her passionate at the beginning, not silent and quiet; he wanted the affection and the nuzzling at the beginning, not long afterward when he felt detached and spent. He knew if he spoke of it he would speak angrily, so he merely lay as he was, sullen, resentful, and wanting to scratch.

Patsy knew he was not happy with her but tried not to know. Her pleasure had a short noon but a long evening if all went well; and though she felt selfish for wanting the evening to linger she was greedy and did want it very much, and she put her hands on Jim's hips to keep him where he was. She pressed him against her gently and appreciatively, but then for a moment felt briefly avid again and began to kiss his shoulders and rub her face against him. He didn't raise his face to her and her avidity quickly subsided. In a few minutes, without a word, Jim lifted himself off her and went through the dark to the bathroom.

Patsy lay with her arms and legs spread, feeling sleepy, but when the shaft of light from the bathroom cut into the darkness it also cut into her languor. She turned on her side and pulled the sheet up over her modestly. Jim turned off the light and came back, and she got up, fumbled on the floor for her gown, and went to the bathroom too. He hadn't spoken, and she felt lonely, as if she'd done something very wrong and was being punished for it; but she had begun to feel cold and stubborn too. In such a mood the bathroom light made life seem impossibly sloppy and dreary, and after flipping it on briefly she flipped it off again and made do in the dark.

When she returned to the bed, Jim was awake but silent as a stone and she got carefully into her part of the bed, silent too and determined not to cry. She had forgotten both noon and evening and felt low. It was a cheat and it was his fault, for if he could bring himself to say two or three kind words or even give her an affectionate pat she could melt and love him again and come close to him and go to sleep, and they would be like people were supposed to be after making love.

But Jim said nothing and they each kept carefully to their separate sides of the bed, and though there was the mutual pretense that they were going to sleep, they were both wide awake and tight as wires. The bed was none too wide, but they were careful not to touch. Patsy's urge to cry alternated with a terrible cold anger; despite herself some tears leaked out and the anger spilled with them.

"You haven't got a generous bone in your body," she said, choking. "You could say something. Even if you're mad at me you could say *something*. I'd rather you say you think I'm awful than for you just to lie there waiting for me to break down. It's just because you know I always break down, sooner or later. If you had any kindness you'd speak to me."

"I speak to you lots of times," Jim said, his voice quite firm and controlled. One of the things she disliked most about him was that he was always sure of himself at such times, sure he had a right to be angry, while she herself was never sure of anything.

"Not first," she said. "You never speak to me first. You know I'll cry when I'm wretched enough and you won't say a thing to help me. You like for me to cry."

"Okay, I'm sorry," he said, not sorry at all. "There's lots of favors you could do me too, if you wanted to."

"Oh, don't *sound* like that," Patsy said. "I hate you when you're smug. What have you got to be so smug about? Don't you ever touch me again."

"Okay," he said in the same firm tone. "I hope the next person I touch likes sex better than you do at least."

"Oh, Jim *quit!*" she sobbed, but then anger hit her again. She sat up in bed, distraught, her eyes very wide. In all their arguments about it he had never said that.

"If I don't it's because of you," she said, and though she felt many angry words crowding into her head only those words came out.

"Sure, sure, I know it's all my fault," he said, but his tone broke and his voice became ragged and hurt.

Patsy was glad—it released more of her anger. "I'm not a camera, you know," she said. "You can't just click a few things on me at the right time and get a nice picture of yourself in action, or me in action, or whichever one of us you're looking at."

"I don't click things," he said, guilt taking the place of his own anger. He sounded even more hurt.

"I love you," he said. "I'm no master of control—I can't

help it if it takes you six hours to come. It just makes me mad at you sometimes. I'm sorry."

"Oh, please don't exaggerate about it," she said.

"I didn't mean to say that," he said, truly abashed. "It was just accidental hyperbole. I'm sorry."

"Well, don't hyperbole about it," she said. "I can't help it. If you want me to be different you have to figure out how to make me your own self. Only don't let me see you clicking things, because then it doesn't work. And speak to me, anyway, please, just speak to me, whether it works or not. I can't stand not being spoken to."

And with that the last anger washed out of her on a new burst of tears and she lay down and without another word snuggled close to him and cried, and he put his arm around her and stroked her hair and wiped the tears off her cheeks and apologized and told her he loved her and asked her not to cry. "Just speak to me next time," she sobbed, and Jim said, "I will, I will."

After a while, lying against each other, they both relaxed. Jim quickly went to sleep, his arm across her, but Patsy lay awake for half an hour, feeling very dry and a little ashamed of herself. The quarrel wouldn't leave her mind. If such quarrels got worse, as they were said to, what would they do to each other when they were forty?

She slept for a few hours, but restlessly, not deeply, and awoke as the courtyard of the motel was turning gray. It occurred to her that there was no reason she couldn't go and see the sunrise by herself. She got up, found a dress and her shoes, and combed her hair. When she slipped outside, Phoenix was gray and quiet, and she didn't feel like starting the car and driving out into the desert. Walking would be better. She set out down the wide cool street. The quarrel came back to her mind. She felt it had been her fault, she was not a very good wife really and did not try hard enough to be like he wanted her to be sexually. She always meant to try, but when the time came she forgot to until it was too late, and it was easy to forget because she didn't know very clearly what it was he *did* want.

The filling stations were opening; attendants in green uniforms played streams of water over the oily driveways.

Patsy passed a drugstore and managed to extract a morning paper from a pile that had been tied with wire and left at the door. She had not brought her purse and had no way to pay for the paper, so she contented herself with scanning the headlines and looking at the movie ads. They would be there at least two more days and she was hoping the movies would have changed. But they hadn't. *Lolita* was still the only good movie in town. She put the paper back and went on with her walk. Far down the street she saw cars with their headlights on coming into Phoenix, and when they passed her she saw that in almost every car only the driver was awake. A face or two peered out at her, sleepy and vague from a night of driving across the desert. The sky to the east had become rosy. She passed the filling station where they had let Peewee out and she found herself wondering about him. She had smitten him, she was sure, but would they ever see each other again? She turned off the main street and walked a block or two to the east, curious to see what houses in Phoenix were like; she found that they were not interesting, not those near Broadway, at least. They were low houses, most of them, with sandy yards and a few dusty domesticated cacti on their porches. She soon lost interest and turned back to Broadway and, on her way along the street, saw the sun come up—not over the desert exactly, but over the filling stations, the little houses, and the quiet motels.

MOVING ON

=== 9 ===

Jim emerged late that morning and found Patsy sitting by the pool in her bikini and the white robe, writing a long letter to Emma Horton, her one true friend. She seemed very cheerful and friendly, and he felt cheerful and friendly himself. Their quarrels seldom had a kickback, not even quarrels involving sex. Jim got his cameras and left for the rodeo grounds and when he looked back to wave goodbye he saw that Patsy was chatting happily with the actor's fat wife, who was wearing a red bathing suit.

A score or so of contestants and a few sweaty spectators were idling around the rodeo grounds, most of them under the grandstand in the shade. A cowboy was shoeing horses, there was a card game in progress—in which a saddle blanket served as a table—and several young men were lounging around with their shirts off, drinking beer and flirting with some local cowgirls. Jim would have liked to photograph the card game, but one of the players gave him a surly look and he decided he had better find Peewee and get his opinion before doing anything rash.

As he was walking toward the empty bucking chutes Sonny Shanks waved at him. He was standing in the sun, bareheaded, talking to three women. He wore a blue short-sleeved sports shirt, Levi's, and a fancy pair of yellow boots. The women were all in their late thirties, bobby-pinned, bedraggled, and in pedal pushers.

"A hot place to talk," Jim said sincerely, after he had been introduced.

"Oh, we're talking about a hot subject," Sonny said. "Sex-u-al intercourse, to be exact." All the ladies abashedly

94

looked down at the ground, and Jim did too, surprised. They seemed like honest lower-middle-class wives and mothers, not the types to be in that sort of conversation with Sonny in the middle of the day.

"Least it ain't borin', though," Sonny said. "Boredom's the root of all wickedness, way I heard it."

"It's money that's the root of all evil," one of the women said, as if to remind him of an eternal law.

"Now let's get back to the point," Sonny said, grinning at Jim. "If none of you ladies ain't ever indulged with nobody except your husbands, how you know you're gettin' your dues? Looks to me like you'd need to make a comparison once in a while." He gave them his most engaging grin.

Two of the women giggled and looked at each other as if it were the most daring remark they had ever heard uttered. They appeared to give it some weight as argument too, but the third looked at Shanks belligerently. She was a tall rawboned, somewhat weathered brunette.

"I can't speak for everybody but I don't need no comparisons," she said. "You ain't never met Morris."

Shanks looked at her coolly. "The thing about me, I'm willing to learn from anybody," he said. "How does ol' Morris go about producing all them wonders?"

"You'll have to ask him about that," the woman said, not a bit flustered. "I sure ain't fixin' to tell you."

"You do look like you've got some mileage on you," Sonny said, winking at Jim. The women all looked astonished, as if some agreed-upon bound had just been overstepped. They moved away together, each secretly vowing to make the others promise never to mention the conversation to anyone, though each of them reported it in detail to her husband that very night.

"Take a ride with me," Sonny said. "I got to collect a wager."

Jim went, fascinated. He decided at once that if he knew anyone with charisma, it was Sonny. It was no wonder the women had all seemed bewitched. He had a way of making whatever he was doing seem interesting, and even his most casual gestures had a kind of authority. They went to a large motel nearby, but the cowboy Shanks was looking for wasn't in. His room was unlocked and his television set was on but the room was empty—just a saddle propped against the wall and a few clothes strewn about.

"He's probably two doors down the way," Sonny said, "puttin' it to somebody's old lady. Let's give him ten minutes."

He took a rope off the saddle, propped the saddle on a chair, and sat on the bed cross-legged roping the saddle horn. He demonstrated a number of throws for Jim's benefit. He never missed, and he never had to get off the bed to take the rope off. He flipped it off every time just before the loop closed.

"I thought you were just a rider," Jim said.

"Oh, I am," Sonny said. "Any nut can rope a saddle. I guess I could have learned to rope if I'd wanted to. Trouble with roping, it takes a horse, and then you've got to haul the goddamn horse everywhere in the world. I'd as soon have an anchor tied to me as a goddamn horse."

He stood up and quickly tied one end of the rope to the leg of the dresser and the other end to the bed and pulled the shades so the room was nearly dark.

"Let's go," he said. "If he's screwin' somebody, he's takin' too goddamn long. You can't tell, the bastard might be in Canada, he ain't got no sense. If he comes dragging in here drunk, maybe he'll trip over this and break his neck."

They sped back to the rodeo grounds, Sonny silent and angry. He ignored traffic lights when it suited him to, but by the time they pulled back into the grounds he had recovered his good humor and was whistling. "Well, that's rodeo life," he said. "I don't know what kind of woman would let that low-life son of a bitch screw her anyway."

He reminded Jim again of the party, and let him out with a nod. Pete Tatum was leading his donkey past the gate and Jim hailed him.

"Have you seen a guy named Peewee Raskin?" he asked. "I don't know if you know him."

"Hard to miss Peewee—but I ain't seen him this morning. You hungry by any chance?"

It turned out that Boots was off with a girl friend eating Mexican food, and Pete was afoot and hungry. Jim was enthusiastic about taking him to eat. He felt he was learning the rodeo world fast. Without his makeup Pete's face was rough, as if from many bumps and bruises, but confident and friendly. They went to a huge drive-in on the outskirts of Phoenix and ordered cheeseburgers and beer and ate rapidly. There was a south wind off the desert and paper napkins from the food trays kept blowing across the concrete of the drive-in. As soon as they blew off the concrete they stuck to one or another of the many small cacti and flapped in the wind. For fifty or sixty yards to the north of the drive-in almost every cactus had a few ragged napkins stuck to it. The sight annoyed Jim. A desert of napkins and hamburger wrappers was very unpleasant to look at. "How's picture takin'?" Pete asked in order to say something. Jim made him feel a little uncomfortable. Usually Pete made conversation easily with anyone, and yet he didn't know what to say to Jim. He was clearly a likable, pleasant young man—Pete liked him even without knowing him—but it was so obvious that Jim didn't know what he was doing that it made things a little awkward. He didn't even know how to pretend he knew what he was doing. He was young, so it was no crime. Pete had seen many young men who were more adrift than Jim. Normally he gave them a wide berth, even if he liked them—or especially if he liked them. Otherwise he made disciples and dependents that he didn't want.

"I'm none too expert yet," Jim said. "I get some good pictures but I sure haven't learned to be unobtrusive."

"Yeah, I remember you obtruded a little too far, back there in Merkel."

"I still can't figure out why they hit me. I would have stopped if they had asked me to."

"I wouldn't lose no sleep tryin' to figure it out," Pete said. "These boys ain't the gentlest folk in the world. I wish I had a dollar for every fight I've seen that there wasn't no reason for."

On their way back they stopped at the motel for Jim to get a lens he had forgotten. Patsy was still by the pool, still in her bikini. She had taken off the robe and had a blue towel draped over her shoulders.

"Want to come?" Jim asked, not really supposing she would. But he caught her at a gregarious moment.

"I guess so," she said. "I was having a try at tanning, but it won't work. Are you just going to take Pete back?"

"Yeah," Jim said, though he had really meant to take pictures.

Patsy felt shy at the sight of Pete and went in and put on a beach robe over her suit. Pete got out so she could slide in next to Jim and she found that she was glad to see him. He seemed relaxed and approachable.

"Hi," she said. "How many cowboys have you saved from horns and hoofs since I saw you?"

Pete smiled and said he hadn't kept count. Patsy discovered that she was sitting on a beer-can opener, part of which was wedged between the seats, part of which poked into her behind. She twisted around and fished it out and leaned forward to put it in the glove compartment. She was warm from the sun and smelled of suntan oil and the arm she stretched out was freckled a little above the wrist. Pete looked away from her, at the sun-whitened streets of Phoenix. Patsy's arm, or her odor, or her black hair, or her smile, something about her reminded him too vividly of his first wife, whose name was Marie. He had loved her very much, and lost her very painfully. She too had freckled in the sun.

When they pulled up at the trailer, Boots was sitting on the steps, barefooted and wearing Levi's and an old gray shirt of his. She had just washed her hair and was letting the hot sun dry it.

"Get out and have a beer with us," Pete said.

"I'm too nearly naked," Patsy said. "I'd like to meet your wife, though—I mean your wife-to-be. Maybe we could have the beer in the car." At first glance the trailer house seemed less roomy than the Ford, and she could not imagine the contortions that would be necessary for the four of them to crowd into it.

Boots came over and got introduced and Pete went in and got the beer. When he came back Boots was in the car chattering rapidly.

"You're our first guests," she said. "I don't count rodeo people. They're around so much it's like brothers and sisters."

Patsy felt drawn to her at once, partly because she was so completely unpretentious and partly because she and Pete were just getting married. She was more comfortable with people who had not been married very long. She didn't really want the beer but sipped it politely, and some foam stuck to her upper lip. Being in company, even the company of two people, suddenly made her feel that she had been a recluse of late. She began to feel very sociable.

"Look," she said, acting on impulse, "why must we sit in this car to drink. It's obvious that trailer house is too small for all of us. Why don't we go back to our motel? Nobody but us ever uses the pool. We can sit around the pool and you men can get potted if you want to."

"Great," Boots said. "I love swimming pools."

Pete looked slightly uncomfortable about the invitation, but Boots didn't notice. "I can't do much boozin' in the afternoon," he said. "We might come over and take a dip with you afterwhile."

Patsy felt a little cast down, for she felt sociable at that instant and hated for the company to dissolve, but Pete was too firm a man to argue with. He added that he needed to work with his donkey awhile. Patsy would have liked to watch and regretted she hadn't changed clothes. Sitting around a rodeo grounds in a bikini and a beach robe was out of the question.

"Well, we'll be there," Jim said. "Come on when you feel like it."

Boots waved her beer can at the Carpenters as they departed, and Pete pitched his under the trailer before following her inside. Once they were inside Boots turned to give him a light kiss and to her surprise found that he wanted her and wanted her at once. "My hair's wet, honey," she said, startled.

"Well, you have to take the good with the bad on a honeymoon," he said with a wry grin.

Her Levi's were old, and so tight that he simply turned them wrong side out as he peeled them off. Boots had never known him to be so sudden about it, or so resolute. Throughout their courtship she had made most of the first moves, feeling that he would be ashamed to make them because she was so much younger. But for once he made the moves, and without hesitation. All she had to do was answer, never a difficult task for her. It seemed, when she looked up, that the trailer was shaking—someone might notice. Maybe that was why they had never done it in the daytime before. But the fact that Pete suddenly wanted her so much excited her past the point of caring about the trailer, or anything except what they were doing. "Oh, Pete," she said, quickly caught. The hot afternoon sun came through the little window and made the sweat shine on their shoulders. She kept an arm crooked around Pete's neck and went to sleep, the sheet beneath them cool with sweat.

When he knew she was asleep, Pete moved and lay beside her and wiped his sweaty face on the end of the sheet. He felt swollen and moody. Instead of being rested, he felt restless, neither empty nor at peace. He loved Boots—he had only to glance at her sleeping face to know that—but he had come to her wanting someone else. Not Patsy—Marie, still Marie, whom Patsy had reminded him of. He had never had enough of Marie, never had his fill of her at all. In that regard, his only accomplishment in ten years was the acquired ability not to think about her often. He wanted to want Boots and Boots only. He was old enough to know that he was lucky in her, lucky to have a girl so easy, so open and so honest—lucky to have anyone who cared about him as unselfishly as she did. She wanted nothing better than to be in his keeping. And yet even Patsy had distracted him from her. Her chatter, her smell, the beer foam on her upper lip, her slim torso: no more than that and he had become, for a time, drawn away from Boots and had ruthlessly forced himself back.

He looked down at his bride-to-be sleeping contentedly despite the heat, the sun on her shoulders and her small relaxed breasts. It made him sad, he felt confused—but at least she didn't. She had been purely pleased. For a few minutes he grew more and more depressed, wishing almost that the whole business had never been invented; and then Boots woke up, her eyes shining when she looked at him, so cheerful and tender herself that he could not help but be glad after all that the whole business had been invented.

She sat up and rubbed his belly fondly then flushed a little and shyly got up and squeezed into the tiny bathroom. In a minute she came back and sat on the bed to brush her hair, her face quiet and relaxed.

"I guess we better start staying in motels," she said. "The trailer was shaking."

"I never thought," he said. "You really want to go swimming?"

"Sure. I like them." But she put down her brush and stretched out beside him. "You don't have a suit, do you?"

"I'll just cut the legs out of some old Levi's."

"I'll do it for you," she said, bouncing up again. "That's what a wife's for."

She couldn't find any scissors, and to Pete's amusement cut the Levi's with the shears he used to trim Hercules' mane and tail. She kept cutting, trying to get the legs even, and soon little snips of denim covered the bed. Pete grew easy and drowsy and watched her with his eyes half shut. She was right. It was time to sell the trailer.

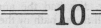

10

The Carpenters went back to the motel to await Boots and Pete, and as the afternoon lengthened and they didn't come Patsy grew terribly annoyed. She had wanted them to come right away, and when they didn't her sociable mood soured, her spirits dropped, and she soon reached a point where she didn't want them to come at all.

"He's no better than any other cowboy," she said, moping. "I hate cowboys, clowns, rodeo, and the whole business of cowboyism."

"What's cowboyism?" Jim asked lightly. He was sitting on the floor putting his pictures back in the file cases.

"I beg your pardon?"

"For shit's sake," he said, though still lightly. "You hardly know them. They may not be great minds but they're perfectly likable. Just because they didn't show up the minute you wanted them to, you make up some vague bitchy label that doesn't really mean anything, even to you. Maybe they wanted to make love or something. Maybe he really did have to train his donkey. You told them to come any time, so what difference does it make?"

He was sitting with his back to her as he spoke, and Patsy considered his back gravely, wondering how it would really be to plunge a knife into someone's back. But she knew that Jim was right: she was merely bored and being bitchy, and she didn't want a quarrel, at least not wholeheartedly.

"So I'm bitchy and smarty," she said. "You have no right to complain now. Besides, what I said about them was true—it was just fallibly put. I do like them. I'm no snob. You're the essence of vagueness yourself and you have no right to criticize my terminology."

"Boodly-boodly," Jim said. "I'll criticize all I want to."

Patsy felt it was surely not possible for life to be any vaguer and duller than it was at that moment. She lay on the bed with her chin on her wrists staring at the little brown dressing table. Through the open door of the bathroom she could see the white end of a motel towel that had been dropped in the shower. Jim had the annoying habit of drying himself while still in the bath or the shower, and he invariably got at least the ends of the towel wet, if not the whole towel. If he was going to go through life getting all their towels wet what was there to hope for?

"Feel like doing perversities?" she asked with no change of tone.

"What?" Jim asked, not looking around. "Want to do what?"

"Perversities," Patsy said. "Per as in persimmon, versities as in universities. You know, unconventional activities, like people do in pornography."

"Oh," Jim said, sliding pictures into envelopes. "I don't think you're serious."

Patsy didn't answer. How could she blame him for dismissing the invitation? They had only made love the night before and she had seldom been inclined again so soon. It embarrassed her a good deal even to have said what she said, because she had been more or less serious. While Jim was at the rodeo pens she had peeked into *Sexus* and it had affected her. If life was just going to be a matter of dullness and wet towels and waiting and reading, such things might be worth trying. She was in a mood to accept almost any diversion, and besides she was curious. For him to dismiss her so cursorily, without even glancing around, annoyed her. It was certainly not an invitation she intended to issue twice.

"Why are you so completely vanilla?" she asked.

"Because that's the way you want me," he said, not turning around.

"I did to begin with, but maybe I'm changing," she said. It was true that she had repulsed some experimental attempts on his part early on in their marriage, when she had been easily embarrassed, but it annoyed her that he thought her so static.

"I'm going to be new, dynamic, debased," she said gloomily.

"You might get a chance tonight. Shanks is giving a party."

"Oh, god." She reversed herself instantly. "We're not going, surely. At least I'm not."

"Be a great opportunity for the new you," Jim said.

"Oh, quit baiting me," she said with a little heat. "I know I'm duller even than you. I give up. I don't want to go. He's awful. He's cowboyism personified. I want to stay home and read."

"Suit yourself. I'm going. Maybe some cowgirl will seduce me. Then we'll have some guilt to work with. What our marriage needs is a little guilt."

"I said hush," she said. "Don't talk to me in that vein."

But they continued to talk in exactly that vein throughout the afternoon. They kept up a running low-grade argument of a sort they were expert at. They couldn't seem to drop it, but neither did it flare high. When Boots and Pete finally came, Patsy was relieved and quickly forgave them for their tardiness. Pete looked sort of comical in his snipped-off jeans. The late afternoon heat was terrific and the water felt good. Boots dove a lot, not gracefully, but with great energy. She wore a two-piece green suit, not quite so skimpy as Patsy's bikini.

After a while they all got out and sat on the cement letting themselves drip. It was obvious that Boots at least was very,

very happy to be getting married. She sat by Pete and hung on to his arm or his shoulder constantly. Once she kissed him shyly behind the ear. Patsy was amused and a little envious—she would never have kissed Jim behind the ear in public. Pete was relaxed and quiet. He scarcely looked at Patsy and took Boots's affection gracefully, now and then circling her waist with his arm. It turned out that both of them were from Fort Worth.

"Different sides of town, of course," Pete said. "Different sides of the track."

"We're both from Dallas," Jim said. "Same side of the track, worse luck." Patsy was irked by the remark but said nothing. Boots's father owned a big Dodge agency but spent most of his time racing horses in Colorado. Pete volunteered no information on himself.

They dried and changed and walked down the street to a diner and ate fried ham sandwiches and chocolate icebox pie. Boots thought Jim's occasional small witticisms were uproariously funny. She laughed so loudly at them that Patsy was at first annoyed and then a little touched. Pete looked at Boots fondly when she laughed and occasionally made some dry response of his own. Once he reached up with a napkin and wiped a bit of mayonnaise off her cheek. Boots was talking to Jim and scarcely noticed, but Patsy observed it and found herself liking Pete more and more. He seemed like a watchful, gentle, very trustworthy sort of man.

When they had eaten, Boots and Jim wandered up the street together, talking about Fort Worth, and Patsy waited for Pete. He had stepped back into the diner to get a toothpick and emerged smiling, the toothpick held between his teeth. To the west the sky was changing color. The two of them walked quietly along the sidewalk for almost a block, hearing Boots's light rapid voice ahead of them in the dusk.

"You have a nice bride," Patsy said, though it was not exactly what she had wanted to say. Walking beside him made her realize that he was several inches taller than she was. His appearance was a little contradictory: he was tall and at times seemed lanky, but he had a heavy belly.

"Nicer than I deserve," he said, glancing at her. Patsy was used to people who put themselves down as a matter of course, but Pete was not putting himself down at all, which made it a very nice thing to say about Boots, she thought. She felt slightly uneasy. Pete did not seem unusually bright and she was used to using brightness as a standard in judging men. There was something to him, even if he wasn't unusually bright. His walk was not like most men's. It appeared to be a slouch, but it had a springiness too, so that when he moved he seemed both slow and quick. Walking beside him, she could well understand Boots's habit of hanging on to him: he looked easier to touch than to talk to. If she could put her arm around his waist as they walked along, there would seem less need for talk.

It did disconcert her that she was so at a loss for small talk with him; it was for her a very rare thing. Since childhood everyone had always made much of her because she said interesting, slightly unusual things; and yet she couldn't think of a thing to say to Pete that he would be likely to find interesting. Casting about, she thought of Sonny Shanks's party.

"Will you and Boots be at the party tonight?"

"No. We don't party much. Who's having one?"

"Sonny Shanks."

"Yeah, I forgot. He invited us, sort of." He frowned and tilted the toothpick down. "Sonny and I can do without one another," he said.

They stepped off the curb at a corner and just as they did two high school boys in a red Mustang cut sharply around the corner, so close that they had to step back. The car squealed away into the dusk. In stepping back to avoid it, they touched, her arm against his arm. The brief contact startled Patsy and she forgot what she had been about to say. Then she remembered Sonny.

"I don't like him either," she said. "He seems to have made a better impression on my husband. Why don't you like him?"

She had not meant the question to be bold, or probing, but saw at once that it was a mistake. "Oh, it ain't worth talking about," he said. His tone was not unfriendly, but there was a strong note of reserve in it. Patsy felt she had accidentally put him off, and she didn't know how to remedy the matter.

"He used to go with my Aunt Dixie," she said.

"Dixie McCormack?" Pete asked, surprised. He looked at her with friendly astonishment, and Patsy immediately felt lighter.

"None other. You know her too? Everyone seems to know her."

"I worked for her husband for about six months one time. Never would have picked you for her niece."

"Sonny Shanks said exactly the same thing," she said.

The street lights came on as they were walking. Pete glanced at her and Patsy caught the glance and was a little unsettled. He did seem to like her, and she was glad, but she had no idea why he liked her, or what aspect of her he liked. It was confusing and not altogether pleasant, and she was glad when he and Boots were in the Thunderbird driving away.

After they were gone she stood on the driveway a little while making patterns in the gravel with her foot. Jim put his arms around her waist.

"You see, they're nice," he said. "You were just being unfair to them this afternoon."

"Of course I was," she said, stepping away from him. It irritated her for him to remind her of it. "I'm a very unfair person. If you haven't learned that about me yet, what have you learned?"

Jim went in without answering and she stood where she was, watching a white airliner slice gracefully down through the blue evening air.

===11===

"I wish I had the will power to stay here," Patsy said, twisting in front of the mirror so she could see the back of her dress. "I don't think this dress is right, but then I have no idea what *would* be right for a party Sonny Shanks is giving. If the place is swarming with cowgirls I'm going to look odd."

"That's never bothered you before," Jim said. He wore a red sports shirt and his gray sports coat and had been ready to go to the party for fifteen minutes. He was sitting in a chair leafing through an issue of *Playboy.*

"Hush. Whatever my faults, I seldom look odd." She had put on a green cotton dress. She liked it but decided it made her look a little too much like a college girl attending a lecture by a famous lecturer. That struck her as being the wrong look for the evening ahead and she shucked the dress off and selected a simple brown sleeveless blouse and a skirt. She had been experimenting with her hair again and as she was bent over taking her slip off one of the slip straps caught on a small hairclip. She struggled for a moment but could not get an arm free to loosen it.

"Help, please," she said, walking over to where Jim sat. He was actually looking at the Playmate of the Month, not with desire or even admiration, but when he looked up and saw Patsy peering at him trustingly from deep within her slip he felt a little guilty and at once closed the magazine and stood up to help her.

"Looking at cows again," she said. "No wonder you like rodeos if those are your ideal." She turned her back and stood waiting for him to free her.

"I was looking at that picture out of professional curiosity," he said. "Yours are my ideal." And when he had undone the slip so she could remove it he put his arms around her, his hands on her bosom, and held her against him for a minute. They swayed a little from side to side. It made her feel nicely wanted, nicely touched.

"You're nice," she said. "I'd really rather you photographed rodeo cows than *Playboy* cows, if you don't mind."

"I don't mind," Jim said.

Sonny's motel was a vast network of two-story structures made of sand-colored brick and arranged in what appeared to be a great square. "It's a walled city," Patsy said. She sat in the Ford while Jim went in to get the number and approximate location of Shanks's room. Three large fountains spurted colored water thirty feet in the air. The water was now orange, now yellow, now blue. When Jim came back he was puzzling over a large sheet of paper.

"His room is about two miles from here as the crow flies," he said.

It proved to be a corner suite on the upper story, not so hard to find as they had feared. When they rang, a tall expressionless middle-aged man opened the door for them. He was dressed in a conservative gray suit, set off by a neat pink tie; he nodded but didn't speak when they said hello. He simply left the door open and turned and went across the room to a white chair near the large picture window.

On a rack not far inside the room was the enormous ornate saddle they had glimpsed in the hearse. The saddle horn appeared to be gold-plated and the pommel was covered with silver inlays. The saddle clashed grotesquely with the rest of the suite, which was roomy, nicely lit, and nicely furnished. The picture window looked out on a central courtyard and a large curved pool. There was a double bed in the room, a very large one covered with a blue bedspread. Sonny sat on it cross-legged, a drink in his hand. He was barefooted and wore Levi's and a red satin shirt. A short, stolid young cowboy sat in a chair nearby and looked at them resentfully when they came in. Sonny uncurled himself from the bed and made Patsy a half-bow.

"The party's made," he said. "Never expected you to forgive me."

"I can't resist parties," she said somewhat stiffly.

"You'll have a Coke and Jim will have what?"

"I'll have a gin and tonic, if you don't mind. I can't stand being predicted."

"Well, just keep telling me what you can't stand and little by little I'll improve," Sonny said, grinning.

Though there was a liquor table with a Negro barman standing behind it, Sonny went over personally to fix their drinks. The two of them felt stranded. The gray-suited man stared out the window with an expression of quiet boredom. "Well, no cowgirls, at least," Patsy said. As she said it a lady they both instantly felt they ought to know emerged from the other bedroom in conversation with a short, slightly chubby, grizzled man in a Hawaiian sports shirt. As soon as the woman saw them she came over.

"I'm sorry," she said. "I didn't know anyone else had come. I'm Eleanor Guthrie. In a sense I'm the hostess."

"My goodness," Jim said. He had brightened the minute she walked over.

"Come now," Eleanor said, smiling at Patsy. "If you weren't from Texas you would never have heard of me. It's just my bad luck to be the last cattle queen."

They walked over with her to meet the man in the sports shirt. There was a phonograph in the far corner of the room, and a Beatles album was on, turned rather low. Patsy was a little surprised. The man in the sports shirt was quietly snapping his fingers and doing a slow dance step by himself. He stopped and shook hands firmly when they were introduced. He had a merry, slightly rakish look, for all his chubbiness, and a mustache and a good smile.

"This is Mr. Vaslav Percy," Eleanor said. "He's a novelist, a poet, and a screenwriter."

"Vaslav *Joe* Percy," he said, smiling cheerfully at Patsy.

"It's an awful nom de plume," he added. "Don't take it seriously. Joe will do. You got tagged with names like that in Hollywood in the thirties. I picked the Vaslav because I liked ballet and it was Nijinsky's first name. Dance with me, Eleanor?"

"Oh, I better pass," she said. "There will be people to greet." Sonny brought Jim and Patsy their drinks and immediately left to answer the door.

Joe Percy began to move again with the music. "You two in college?" he asked. "Young revolutionaries of some kind?"

"We're graduates," Patsy said. "We're both very inactive. What are the names of your books? Maybe I've read some of them."

"My books?" he said. "Be serious. Eleanor was flattering me. I'm a screenwriter. I wrote a couple of books long ago but kids nowadays don't know them, thank god. They read enough junk without reading me. Terrible books, as I remember them."

"Come on," Patsy said. "Tell me. I never met a published writer before, I don't think."

"Good god," he said. "Have you been living in an egg or something? I've met six thousand novelists in the last year alone. *You* dance with me—maybe we can put on something a little more raucous. I never reveal the names of my books to a woman unless I've fucked her, beaten her, or danced with her."

Patsy was quite shocked, but the shock didn't linger long. Mr. Percy had said the word too casually and in too merry a tone, with no evident intention of shocking anyone at all. She was used to hearing the word used at semi-bohemian student parties where everyone was exaggeratedly drunk or genuinely high, but she was not used to hearing it in the company of someone like Eleanor Guthrie. Fortunately Joe Percy was one of those men who could make the frankest speech sound innocent. His good nature was so obvious that it would have been almost impossible for him to sound obscene. Patsy decided that the essence of sophistication was the ability to absorb such shocks with a gay smile, so she accompanied Mr. Percy to the phonograph table and they looked through the records together.

"Actually, for you I'll make an exception," he said, for he was also perceptive and had noted the shock he had given her. "If you'll excuse my crudity I'll reveal the names of my books right now and we can dispose of the subject. You won't believe what they're called."

"I will too," she said. "I'm gullible."

"Okay," he said, lifting his drink in a kind of salute. "My novel was called *The Opalescent Parrot* and my book of poems was called *The Final Albatross*. The thirties were as unbelievable as my titles, at least where I was. Everybody had their bit and mine was bird imagery. All my screenwriting buddies were writing proletariat crap about the wretched of the earth, so to be different I wrote Firbankian crap about tubercular degenerates. If you happen on either of the books, love me a little and don't read it. I'd do as much for you if you wrote a book."

"I believe you," Patsy said. "I promise."

Most of the other records were hillbilly or pop vocalists and they ended up dancing to the Beatles after all. Patsy loved to dance, and it turned out that Mr. Joe Percy, despite his slight chubbiness, danced with flair. The room filled very suddenly, almost in one rush, as they were dancing. Patsy didn't notice the people closely until they stopped to rest, but when she did she felt lucky to have got Mr. Percy to dance with. He was a very appealing man and he admired her and let her know it, but without giving her any more starts. Most of the other people who poured into the room looked depressing and slightly shabby. They looked like night-club announcers, or disc jockeys, or young restaurateurs, and their wives were mostly thin and had dyed hair. They would have made her feel depressed and lost and wretchedly out of place, but Mr. Percy, by dancing with her and treating her generally as if she were the loveliest woman around, kept her feeling pleasant. Now and then she caught glimpses of Jim and Eleanor Guthrie. They were sitting on a couch and seemed to be talking rather gravely.

When Mr. Percy had had enough he stopped and led her to the window. "Boy," he said. "You almost inspired me to a coronary. Excuse me. I've got to find the place."

"Come back," she said. "I think you're the only one here I want to talk to."

As he was leaving, Sonny Shanks came over. "See you're having fun," he said. "You don't have to dance with that fat little writer all the time. I can do them dances too."

"All right," she said, not enthusiastic. The minute Joe Percy walked away she had begun to feel out of place. Jim was still talking to Eleanor, and it was hard to blame him. In looks and dress and manner Eleanor was all she might have been supposed to be—a very lovely woman, rather grave and not at all vulgar. She wore a white dress and her dark blond gray-streaked hair was pulled to one side. Now and then her face lit briefly as she made some remark to Jim. She wore a gold bracelet and a green pendant of some kind, set in gold. Watching her, Patsy felt like the merest schoolgirl, like a college freshman and a prim and proper freshman at that.

"I expected more cowboys," she said to Sonny. They had moved to a corner where there was room to dance.

"You got me down for a hick just because I rodeo," he said. "I ain't such a hick."

She really did not feel like dancing with him and was merely swaying with the music, moving her arms a little. Sonny followed suit, a yard away.

"This is just how I had it planned," he said. "Ol' Jim can keep Eleanor happy and I can dance with you. She likes to have someone young and smart and up on this 'n' that to talk to and I don't know many people who can fill the bill."

"She could talk to Mr. Percy. He's got a fine gift of gab."

"He ain't young an' en-tranced, though."

"No. He's *en*-tranced with me."

"Ain't we all?"

She kept her eyes off him, looking at the dancers. Most of the male guests might have been chosen expressly to make Sonny stand out—thin-chested, dull-looking men whose suits or sports coats didn't fit. Joe Percy was the only one among them who seemed to have any character, or even any energy. He was dancing again. A silver blonde in green Capris had snagged him when he emerged from the john.

Even without the red shirt and Levi's and bare feet Sonny would have stood out. In such a crowd his confidence of movement was striking enough. And he was not so imperceptive as she had supposed. He very quickly figured out that she didn't want to dance with him and stopped suddenly and dropped into a chair. He draped a leg over the chair arm and waved his bare foot in time to the music. From being gay he had become moody, and in her eyes the change improved him. His hostly gaiety was too superficial; it made his handsomeness seem brittle. When he frowned, as he was frowning at her, his face filled with hollows and shadows and became a more formidable face than it had been.

"So what's so good about you?" he said, looking her in the eye.

"I don't know," Patsy said, startled by the question. "I never said anything was."

"Eleanor's as good-lookin' as you," he said, as if arguing with himself, though he continued to look at her. "That redhead over by my saddle ain't bad, if you set her in the right light. What do you think you got on 'em, hunh?"

"Nothing," Patsy said, disturbed. "Nothing. What are you talking about? I don't have anything on anybody. My god, what a conversation."

"Nothing wrong with it," Sonny said reflectively, waving for the barman to bring him a drink.

"Well it's absurd," she said, impatient with him. "I didn't say anything to make you talk to me that way."

"Right," he said, smiling suddenly as if she had just reminded him of something. "It was just seeing you, you know. Milk right from the cow. You ain't even had time to cool. You're right as you can be. Who wants to talk to a nice pitcher of milk." And he grinned at her over the glass the barman handed him.

The comment offended Patsy to the quick. Not only was he presuming to size her up, but the result of it all was that he had sized her up precisely as she had sized herself up every time she looked at Eleanor Guthrie. She was a girl. It did not please her at all that he found her girlishness entrancing. She could not think of a comeback to his remark about her being a pitcher of milk—though later she thought of a hundred. She turned abruptly, went to the bedroom, and shut herself in the john, very depressed and wishing she had had the good sense to stay at the motel. But a look in the mirror improved her spirits. The dancing had given her color. She was not going to let a bastard like Sonny Shanks chase her home. What she needed was to find Mr. Percy and dance some more.

When she came out, Shanks was standing in the bedroom looking even moodier than he had been.

"Never meant to tick you off," he said. "I was just paying you a compliment."

She didn't like him being there waiting for her. He spoke quietly enough, but she didn't like his stance, or his eyes. There was a force in him very much stronger than any she had ever had to deal with, and it scared her.

"Oh, just leave me alone," she said, going past him. "Go bother my aunt, if you have to bother somebody."

Sonny pursed his lips quizzically. "Eleanor's gonna like you," he said in a very casual tone. It was as if he had suddenly decided to switch off the force.

Patsy went back to the party a little confused. Sonny was too shifty—one second hateful, the next almost likable. She went over and sat down on the floor by the couch near Jim's legs. Joe Percy was there, mopping his brow, and Jim looked slightly pinched around the mouth, as if he wished Joe Percy weren't there. When Patsy sat down Jim glanced at her fondly, but it was an absent, abstract fondness, as if his mind and not his eyes had registered her presence.

Joe Percy held a whiskey glass with a single ice cube in it. He twirled the glass in his fingers in such a way that the whiskey and the cube spun around and around together, the cube never touching the glass. "How do?" he said when Patsy sat down. "I never made it back. I was intercepted. Let me finish this drink and we'll dance some more." His eyes were friendly and intelligent, and he did not appear to be fooled by anyone, least of all himself.

"Yep, I've written every kind," he said, turning back to Eleanor. "Jungle movies, pirate movies, serials, spy movies, movies about the Mounties, everything. I've worked for more fourth-rate directors than any man alive, unless it's Randolph Scott. So now I guess I'll write a rodeo movie. From what I've seen of rodeo, it deserves me."

"A versatile man," Eleanor said.

"I should say, versatile," he said. "You wouldn't know the half of it." He winked at Patsy and gave her a sly, confidential, surprisingly tender smile, as if to neutralize in advance any vulgarity he might feel called to utter.

"There was once a famous actress, plagued like myself by

fourth-rate directors, who assured me I was the best lay in Hollywood.

"After Bob Mitchum, of course," he added with a broad grin. "Always excepting Bob Mitchum."

"I think you're a trifle vain," Patsy said, deciding she liked such conversations when they were with people like Mr. Percy. She was positive no actress had ever told him any such thing, he was merely being entertaining, probably for her benefit.

"Trifle!" Joe Percy said. "I should hope I'm vain. A writer without vanity would be like a woman without a cunt, if you'll pardon the usage. Drink, anyone?"

He got up and went to the bar. Jim was patting his foot nervously in time with the music. "I wonder what makes Californians so blunt," Eleanor said. Patsy had no idea. She felt a bit flat and noticed that Jim was getting drunk. She didn't have to look at him to notice it, she could tell by his voice. He had only been drunk four or five times since they had been married. She got up and went over to the picture window. The lights of Phoenix were brilliant in the darkness. Looking down, she saw that Sonny and the man in the gray suit and one of the girls in Capri pants were standing by the swimming pool. Sonny still had on the red shirt but had changed to swimming trunks. He stripped off the shirt, slid into the pool, and swam two lengths, cutting right down the center of the greenish water. Then he pulled himself smoothly back up on the side and shook the water off himself with a twist or two of his body, almost like a dog. The girl handed him his shirt and the three of them disappeared beneath the ledge of the motel.

Mr. Percy came over and suggested they dance some more, but Patsy shook her head. "I'm sorry," she said. "I've had enough of this party. I like you, though. I'm glad I met you."

"Mutual," he said and kissed her on the cheek. It pleased her.

"That's it," he said. "Smile. You've got a smile all your own."

When she told Jim she wanted to take a cab back to the motel he was surprised and confused and followed her shakily to the telephone.

115

"Aren't you having a good time?" he asked.

"I did for a while. I'm just worn out. You're getting looped, you know. I think that lady's gone to your head."

Jim looked guilty and fumbled through the yellow pages, trying to select a taxi service.

"Don't look abashed," she said. "Stay and have a good party. She ought to go to your head. If I were a man she'd probably go to mine. I'll expect you to tell me everything she says. Let me take the Ford. You're the one who will need a cab."

"Okay," he said. "I love you." He followed her out the door and insisted on kissing her, as if to prove it. She didn't need proof, and the kiss was interrupted by Sonny and the girl and the silent man.

"Leavin' us?" Sonny asked. "Shame. I'll walk you to your car."

As before, he gave her no choice, but he seemed to be feeling good and went ahead of her, doing a little dance step. She was embarrassed to have been seen kissing her husband.

"Who is that man who was with you?" she asked. "Doesn't he speak?"

"Not much. That's the pill man. He sells pills."

"Pills?"

"Yeah, all kinds. Good pills. Ever take any?"

"Only the pill with a capital P. And aspirin occasionally."

"Well, you ain't keepin' up with the times," he said.

"If you've got a pill that will get my husband home to me, give him one. I have a feeling he may pass out on you."

"I'll bring him home myself if he does." He gallantly opened the door for her and bowed her in.

"Is that Western courtliness?" she asked. "You're always bowing and dipping."

But Sonny had turned and was already trotting lightly across the motel parking lot, his shirttails flapping as he ran.

MOVING ON

=== 12 ===

Patsy was glad that Jim had elected to stay at the party. Though it disconcerted her a little to *see* him drunk, she had the notion that drunkenness was good for him. It seemed to her that if he was really going to try and be some kind of artist he probably ought to live a little more wildly than he did. Him getting drunk was fine, but she had no desire to stay around being the responsible wife of a drunken man. She couldn't imagine anything bad happening to him, or him doing anything bad, and was sure he would wander in in an hour or two, voluble, contrite, and secretly pleased with himself.

She discovered after it was too late that she would have liked to dance more, but the only man there she had wanted to dance with was Mr. Percy, and she was not sure how long he would have held up. She put on her green gown and got in bed to read. They had a bedraggled paperback copy of *The Sot-Weed Factor* that she had been whimsically picking her way through for weeks. She read a page or two and put it down and went to the book box to dig out Gibbon. They had an old three-volume Modern Library edition that one of Jim's teachers had given him in high school. Patsy had been reading it intermittently ever since they had married and was almost through Volume II. She dug it out, but after a page or two of it she concluded she was not in a reading mood and got a pen and some paper and began a letter to her friend Emma Horton. Frequently in their letters to each other she and Emma adopted the pretense that they were the heroines of epistolary novels. In their junior year they had both taken a course in the English novel and had read

Pamela together. Their letters were usually full of all sorts of sophomoric literary showing-off, and they both enjoyed them immensely. Emma was married to a graduate student in English. She was fat and rather slovenly but very bright and sweet and kind of heart, and she had two children already, both boys.

> *Dear Em,*
>
> *I'm too tired to write long sentences. I just got home from a wicked party. Why people sleep with the people they seem to sleep with is beyond me. Why anyone sleeps with anyone is sort of a puzzle, actually.*
>
> *The party was given by Mr. Sonny Shanks, World's Champion Cowboy. He's the one who sat me down on the bed where he had just done it, as you'll recall. I met his mistress—at least I assume she is. Eleanor Guthrie, who owns the big ranch. Very lovely—she could do much better than him. Jim was stunned and is still there getting smashed. She made me feel underweight. I was the second-most-ogled, though. I met a real screen writer who used real dirty words. It was a very worldly party. There was even a pusher there, very sinister. I think it was William Burroughs.*
>
> *We're going to Utah next—god knows how long that will take, or where I'll be stuck. I'll be glad when we get back to Houston. We can exchange secrets, if either of us have any by then.*

She paused, and was debating whether to go into a description of the Tatums, or the Tatums-to-be, when she heard a car drive up outside. After a moment there was a gentle knock at the door.

"Jim?"

"Me." It was Shanks's voice. "Just making a delivery."

"Oh, okay," she said. "One minute." She went to the closet and got her terry-cloth robe, a little surprised that Jim had passed out so soon. Usually when he drank he drank for hours, getting more and more voluble as the night progressed. She belted the robe around her so that as little of her nightgown showed as possible.

But when she opened the door there was no sign of Jim, just Sonny standing there smiling at her cheerfully. He was just as he had been at the beginning of the party, in the red shirt and Levi's and still barefooted. His heavy black hair was tousled and still a little wet from his swim. He strolled in and looked around the room with interest.

"This is how the pore half lives, ain't it?" he said. "You-all ain't poor, what are you doin' here? I wish I had a dollar for ever crappy little motel room I've stayed in."

Patsy's heart was pounding. He had walked in so quickly that she couldn't think. She merely stood where she was, her hand on the doorknob.

"Where's my husband?" She saw the hearse outside and felt a momentary relief. Jim was probably in it, somewhere.

"He's probably about ready to fall over in Eleanor's lap, if he ain't already. I come right on as soon as you left, but I had to run an errand or two on the way."

"Please get out," she said. "I thought you were bringing my husband. I didn't invite you here."

Sonny waved a hand at her as if what she said was only a joke between friends. He sat down on the bed, picked up the volume of Gibbon, and looked at it curiously.

"Wonder why I've taken to women who read in my old age," he said. "First forty or fifty I went with couldn't read the directions on a mousetrap."

"Would you get off my bed and get out," Patsy said, anger replacing her fear. She flung the door back so hard that the doorknob made a dent in the cheap plaster, and she stood clenching and unclenching her fists, waiting for him to be gone.

Sonny put the book down, peered for a moment at her letter, which was on the bed, and got up and moved toward the door. Just as she was ready to slam it behind him and start crying, Patsy realized he wasn't going out. His moves were always surprises—she was never quite up with him. He came right to her, before she realized that was where he was coming, and took her and scooped her off her feet. She stiffened, but his surprises had a kind of paralyzing effect; they all but stopped her heart. Sonny nudged the door shut with his heel and crossed the room and laid Patsy on the bed, taking some care not to mash her letter. The paralysis wore off when he put her down and she began to cry, very confused and expecting instant rape. But Sonny brought a box of Kleenex and kept handing them to her until her crying fit passed and she could see him again. She lay as stiffly as possible, trying to stop her mouth from quivering and her chest from heaving.

"Calm down," he said. "I ain't gonna hurt you."

"Then what are you doing?" she asked weakly. "Why are you here? Why aren't you at your own party?"

"Well, you seen what kind of a party it was. I mostly got it up hoping you'd come."

"What do you *mean?*" she said. "Hoping *I'd* come. Mrs. Guthrie was there. Why bother *me?*"

"Miss Guthrie," he said. "She's one of those folks that are so rich they don't change their names when they get married. One reason I ain't never married her. She don't want to be named Shanks and I sure ain't gonna change my name."

"Oh, anyway," Patsy said. "It doesn't affect what I meant. This is all absurd."

"It ain't," Sonny said. "You got looks all your own. I just wanted to get you by yourself a few minutes to see if you might not turn out to like me. If you do, we can sort of take it from there."

"To hell with that," Patsy said. "I could have started liking you at the party if I was going to. I'm not going to start liking you now, and I certainly don't like you barging in on me with some subterfuge and then refusing to leave when I asked you to. I'm married! Don't cowboys understand marriage at all?"

"Understand *what* about it?"

"Oh, please, just go away," she said. "I don't want to argue with you and it makes me very uncomfortable for you to be sitting on my bed. I'm married, that's all, and you and I are not going to take anything from anywhere. Just go away. You scare me in here."

Sonny regarded her with an air of friendly and tolerant amusement.

"Well, that's a start, anyway," he said.

"It's not a start! Don't twist my words favorably. I'm not going to suddenly stop being scared of you and throw myself in your arms. Just get out. *Please* get out!"

"How long you been married?" he asked.

"No," she said. "No conversation. I don't want to talk to you. If you want to know anything send me a questionnaire and I'll answer it in detail. I don't want to talk any more."

"Well, I just hope I ain't fallin' in love with you," he said with light sarcasm and put his hand on her calf. Patsy rolled off the bed and clenched her fists.

"I knew you'd try something," she said. "Go back to your party, you stupid slob. I'm going to call the police unless you leave right now."

But she was not accustomed to men who could really move, and as she turned to go to the phone Sonny caught her and scooped her up in his arms again. His face was a few inches from hers, and the genuinely amused look he had when he came in had been replaced by the hard varnished smile he had worn at the party.

"I hate to be called stupid," he said. "Specially by young bitches who don't know up from down. You could learn more from me than you'll learn from your goddamn books." The Gibbon had been knocked on the floor and with a single kick Sonny sent it flying across the room. He was holding her so tightly in his arms that she could feel his muscles, as hard and ungiving as wood. With no further ado he carried her to the door, lowered her a bit so he could open it and carried her out.

"I ain't kidnaping you," he said. "You ain't in no danger unless you yell and if you yell I'll break your goddamn jaw."

The set of his face and his wooden muscles convinced her that he meant it. She had never been close to real violence in her life and was scared almost breathless. He would certainly hit her if he felt moved to, and the thought was terrifying. He boosted her abruptly into the back end of the hearse and shoved her toward the bed where she had sat once before. Then he climbed in after her and pulled the doors shut.

"Let's go, Coon," he said. Patsy looked around and saw that the sullen young cowboy who had been at the party was in the driver's seat. He looked back at her, still sullen.

"Oh, please, I apologize," she said. "I'm sorry I called you stupid. Don't take me anywhere, just let me go back in."

Sonny seemed to have recovered some of his earlier good humor. He stretched out one leg and propped his foot on the mattress where she sat. "Nope," he said. "You got to take the consequences of being insulting. That's Coon Carter driving. Coon, Mrs. Carpenter."

"Mr. Shanks, please," Patsy said. "You know you didn't have any right to be in my room. I apologize again. Please let me go back."

But Sonny waved Coon on and the hearse pulled out of the courtyard. Patsy looked back sadly at the Ford and tried to straighten her hair. She felt too numb to cry.

"You didn't even shut the door to my room," she said. "Suppose people go in and steal us blind? I have things I don't want stolen. What kind of person are you?"

Sonny reached his bare foot in the direction of her calf, but she avoided it by scooting back on the mattress. She enveloped herself as totally as possible in her bathrobe.

"Where we goin'?" Coon asked. His voice was husky, like the voice of a child just awakened from sleep.

"Oh, the rodeo grounds, I guess. I didn't have nothing definite in mind. I just thought we ought to get Mrs. Carpenter away from her books for a while."

Patsy felt she disliked him more than any person she had ever known. He was arrogant and irritating when he was being pleasant, but when he was being unpleasant, even slightly, he was terrifying. She felt she had rather eat a fair amount of crow than risk making him angry again.

"Arizona ain't got many crooks," he said. "Nothin' much'll get stolen."

He seemed to derive a great deal of amusement from the way she huddled over her knees clutching her bathrobe. He drew his foot back and rubbed his other shin with it.

"Hurt my toe, kicking that book," he said.

"I'm glad. This strange farce is all your doing and I'm glad you aren't going to come out of it completely unscathed."

"Ain't the kind of scar I was hoping for," he said. They passed his motel, the colored waters still spurting high behind the ornamental palms. Soon they were approaching the darkened rodeo grounds.

"Everybody here's probably asleep," Sonny said. "Let's go out in the arena."

"I find this exceedingly bizarre," Patsy said.

The young man named Coon got out and opened a gate and got back in and drove them through the entranceway to the arena. He seemed to find it bizarre too, and a little nerve-racking. He cut off his lights and kept glancing at the bleachers. They proceeded slowly out into the arena, lit only by the desert moonlight. The bleachers were dark bulks. Patsy was feeling scared again; her legs were trembling and she hugged her knees to keep them still. Sonny was fumbling in the pile of junk, clothes, and equipment that littered one side of the hearse. When they reached the middle of the arena Coon stopped the hearse.

"Turn on the goddamn lights," Sonny said. "The inside lights. We ain't botherin' nobody but Patsy, and we got her too buffaloed to yell."

"You better be polite," she said. "I'm not too friendly with you just now and I may yell any second."

"When you start yelling, that's when we'll be leaving," Sonny said. "Knew I had a piggin' string here somewhere. This hearse is like Fibber McGee's closet. Let's get out and stretch our legs."

He opened the doors and got out, an old towel and a short piece of rope in his hand. "I don't want to get out," Patsy said, still hugging her knees. "This is not my idea of a good place to be this time of night."

"Aw, come on," he said. "I don't want to drag you out. It would just embarrass you and Coon both."

Patsy changed her mind. He sounded good-tempered, but it was clear he meant for her to get out, and he had handled her twice already, as easily as an experienced mother handles a child that doesn't want to be diapered. Her best bet was to keep him in a good humor, she decided.

"Okay," she said. "If you insist, Mr. Shanks."

She kept the bathrobe tucked about her, and he helped her down. "Just stay in the car, Coon," he said and walked a few steps away from the hearse and squatted down. "If you'll just have a seat this won't take a minute," he said.

"You're really out of your mind," Patsy said. "Have a seat where?"

"Right here on god's earth," Sonny said.

Patsy sighed and squatted down a little distance from him, but she was nervous and lost her balance and sat down. When she did Sonny grabbed her ankles, scaring her out of her wits again. She would have screamed if she hadn't remembered what he had said about breaking her jaw. But Sonny was talking soothingly, as he might to a frightened animal.

"Just take it easy now," he said. "Not what you think at all." He crossed her ankles and began to wrap the old towel around them. Patsy was shaking, but she didn't say anything. She felt quite speechless. When he had wrapped the towel around her ankles he wrapped the short rope around them too, over the towel, pulled it tight, and tied it.

"I brought the towel so you wouldn't get no rope burn," he explained.

"Thanks," Patsy said. She was becoming not quite so scared as it dawned on her that what he had in mind was not ravishment but something in the nature of a crude practical joke. Sitting in the sandy arena made her feel very undignified, but better indignity than a broken jaw.

"Now," Sonny said, squatting in front of her. "You know what this demonstrates, honey?"

"I'm afraid I don't," she said in a shaky voice.

"Quit shaking," he said. "I told you not to be scared. Ain't nothing more gonna happen. I'm just gonna drive off and leave you here. Probably be the last we'll see of one another for a while."

"I must say I hope so," Patsy said.

Sonny chuckled good-naturedly. "Yeah, I bet you do hope so," he said. "What it demonstrates is that you can't never tell what might happen. I bet when you was primping for the party you never thought you'd finish off the evenin' hogtied in the rodeo pens."

"No," Patsy said. "The possibility never occurred to me." Sonny leaned down and pulled at the knot again and she smelled bourbon on his breath.

"Never occurred to me, neither," he said. "I was really kinda countin' on making up to you, if you want to know the truth. We might have had a fling, if we'd gone about things right. But one of us screwed up, don't matter which one, and now we ain't never gonna have a fling, I don't guess."

"Pity," she said, tense, wishing he would just go.

"Sure is a pity," he said. "I could get killed any old year now and that'll be one beautiful memory won't neither of us ever have. I'm kinda sweet to girls, when I want to be. And I always figure the more you have, the more you have, you know."

"I thought you were going," Patsy said.

Sonny laughed a quick deep laugh. "I am," he said, and as he stepped past, ruffled her hair playfully.

"If you can't get that knot untied, just yell," he said. "Lots of folks sleeping around here. Somebody'll untie you and see you get home."

In a moment she heard the hearse's doors shut and a warm puff of exhaust blew over her, followed by a small cloud of dust as Coon shot the hearse forward too quickly in the loose dirt. It became very quiet, no sound but that of the departing car. Then she heard the clank of the aluminum gate as Coon shut it, and then the sound of the hearse accelerating as it left the grounds. Then no sound at all. If there were animals around they were apparently asleep. Patsy bent forward and discovered to her chagrin that she simply could not untie the rope from around her ankles. She couldn't see it, to begin with, and Shanks had pulled the knot so hard that the rope felt as hard and tight as iron. She tried to wiggle her feet out, but it didn't work and just got her gritty. There was nothing to do but yell—only what to yell? It was going to be humiliating to be found like she was. The arena was huge and dark, though the sky overhead was bright with moon. The thought of a sudden noise was frightening, even though she was going to be the one to make it. There might be bulls sleeping nearby, for all she knew. It was both vexing and scary.

"Help," she said, so hesitantly and quietly that she could barely hear it herself. No answer. "Oh, shit!" she said, feeling like crying. Then, struck with inspiration, she yelled —not "Oh, shit!" but "Oh, hell!" as loudly as she could bring herself to. It was not very loud, but it was adequate.

Almost immediately a flashlight began to bob around near the entrance to the arena.

"It's me," she yelled, encouraged. "Over here."

Soon the flashlight began a cautious approach. "Here, here," she said, to give its owner confidence. It approached to within several yards, flickered nervously over her, and quickly withdrew, to shine incongruously into the dirt several yards away.

"Who-all's there?" a man's voice asked.

"Just me," Patsy said. "Please don't be scared. I'm a very harmless maiden in distress. A sort of maniac brought me here and tied me up. It would be very Christian of you to untie me."

The flashlight zeroed in on her again and then came nearer, followed by the man who held it, a young bulldogger from Idaho. His name was Clint Brink and he was accompanied by his properly pajamaed sweetheart, also from Idaho. They had been spending the night in a sleeping bag in one of the bucking chutes.

"I know I'm a surprising sight," Patsy said, "but don't worry. I'm not a trap or anything."

"Goddamn," the boy said. "How come you to be out here?"

"I doubt I could make it very clear to you. Could you just untie me? Sonny Shanks tied me up more or less on a whim. I believe he's a well-known cowboy."

"Oh," the young man said, as if that made the phenomenon quite comprehensible.

"Hon, I'm scared," the girl friend said, peeking hostilely at Patsy from over his shoulder.

Clint Brink squatted down at her ankles, very conscious that Patsy's legs were bare and that his girl was with him. He pointed the flashlight irrelevantly out into the arena and peered through the darkness at the rope.

"Couldn't you just cut it?" Patsy asked, but as she asked she jerked expertly a time or two and the knot came loose.

"No use ruining a good piggin' string," he said, happy to be able to be practical in such a situation.

Patsy got up and straightened her gown and robe, brushing off as much sand as possible. It occurred to her that Pete and Boots must be somewhere around, and when she asked Clint Brink he seemed relieved that she knew them and said they would show her the way to the trailer. His girl hung on to his arm as they walked out of the arena. Patsy kept well back, walking on tiptoe most of the way, worried that she might step on broken glass.

At the chutes the young man courteously pointed her to the trailer and handed her the flashlight. "I'll get it from Pete," he said.

She thanked him profusely and he and his girl went back to their sleeping bag, speculating in whispers about it all.

When she got to the trailer it was quite dark and she tapped gently on the door. "Pete," she said. She had to rap very loudly before he answered.

"Yeah?"

"I'm afraid it's me. Patsy Carpenter."

In a minute the inside door opened and Pete appeared behind the screen, holding a sheet bunched in front of him.

"My lord," he said.

"I'm so sorry. I hate to wake people. I got into a strange predicament and thought maybe you could help me get home."

"Minute," he said. "I'll get dressed."

"Please don't wake Boots, if I haven't already. I'm very embarrassed to be such a bother."

"Boots ain't very wakable," he said and shut the door.

She sat down on the narrow aluminum steps, feeling very foolish and out of place. In a moment the door pressed against her back—it was Pete coming out. He stepped down and stretched, his shirt on but not buttoned.

"I know this is incredible," she said. "I really don't fit in the rodeo world."

"If I was to guess," he said, "I'd guess all this come about because you went to Sonny's party."

"Right. If you understand it or him I'd appreciate an explanation. I went to the party and he followed me home and sort of made a pass. I suppose that's reasonably clear, but then when I got mad at him he simply carried me off. He didn't really hurt me, but he tied my feet with some kind of rope and left me out there in the middle of the arena. A

127

young man named Brink untied me. Does that make sense to you?"

"Well, it sounds like Sonny. Hop in the Thunderbird. I'll run you home."

She was glad to be in the car, hidden from people. There was an empty beer can on the floorboard under her feet, and she nervously rolled it back and forth with one foot. The inside of the car smelled of beer and leather and dried horse sweat, from the bridles and halters Boots kept in the back. Pete had difficulty fitting himself under the wheel.

"It's like driving a sardine can," he said.

"I would get a taxi, if there were a place where I could call one."

"No, I'll run you home. Sonny might still be lurking around. Where's Jim?"

"I left him at the party. I guess that was my mistake.

"Eleanor Guthrie was there," she added. "That's why Jim was so eager to stay. What in god's name does she see in that man?"

Pete shrugged. He was driving slowly, his face still a little puffy from sleep. "Don't know the lady," he said. "I guess women see something in him."

There was a note of flat undisguised sadness in the way he said the last sentence, a sadness so noticeable that it made Patsy look at him more closely than she had. He wore a long-sleeved shirt and had not got one of the sleeves buttoned, so that the cuff hung awkwardly off his wrist. She wished he would button it and had an impulse to reach over and do it for him, but she didn't.

He glanced at her sharply, as if he had realized he had said too much. Patsy was huddled in the seat in her bathrobe, like a child that was up past her bedtime. Her look was so open that he relaxed a little.

"My first wife seen somethin' in him," he said. "That's the story of me and Sonny, but don't go spreadin' it around. She wasn't no more the type to take to him than you'd think Eleanor Guthrie would be. Even less. Women are hard to tell about."

He stopped talking, as though to close off a morass of memories that he had floundered in too many times. Patsy was disappointed but didn't show it. She had begun to feel secure and comfortable and a little lightheaded and would have liked to chatter about Sonny and probe his psychology, but it was clearly not the sort of thing that Pete would enjoy.

"I'm sandy," she said. "Another thing he did that infuriated me was that he drove off and left the door to our motel room open. I was afraid to blast him for it. He acted as if he might hit me.

"Do you think he would have?" she asked. "I don't know anything about such men."

"Sonny? Sure."

There was no hearse at the motel, and the door to their room was still open. "Please come in a minute, until I see if anything's gone," she said.

Pete got out and followed her into the room, but he was nervous. The sight of her made him nervous—the flash of her calves as she went through the door, and the way she tossed her hair back from her face. He didn't like being susceptible to anyone but Boots and knew that Patsy was someone he would do just as well to avoid.

"The bastard," she said, going over to pick up the Gibbon. "Now my book's all crumpled."

Pete stood awkwardly, just inside the door, watching her as she moved rapidly around the room. She peered vaguely at things, as if to try and remember what should be where.

"It was kind of black humor, you know," she said, looking with relief at Jim's pile of cameras. But then she looked at Pete and realized he didn't know. It was on her tongue to mention novelists' names, but he wouldn't know them either and her remark suddenly made her feel shallow and inconsiderate. He had got out of bed to bring her home, and what right had she to go talking over his head?

"I guess I'm still nervous," she said, peeping in the closet. "This sort of thing doesn't happen to me every night. In fact, nothing remotely like this has ever happened to me. You don't suppose he'll come back, do you?"

"No, he probably went on back to the party," Pete said. "Might have been someone else there he was interested in."

"No, just me," Patsy said and blushed immediately when she realized how vain it sounded.

Pete sighed and moved restlessly in the doorway, neither coming in nor going out. "I guess I could go by and beat hell out of him," he said.

"What?" Patsy said, very surprised. "What do you mean? There's no need to do that. He didn't really hurt me."

"No, but he's got it coming," Pete said. He was clearly on the horns of a dilemma, and his restlessness was beginning to make Patsy uncomfortable.

"Please don't," she said. "I don't like things like that. Fighting. There's no point in beating him up just because he's slightly crazy. It's like those people hitting Jim. Besides, it's nothing to do with you—"

She stopped, confused. She had been going to remind him that it was not his place, that Jim was the one who would be obliged to defend her honor, if it came to that. But Jim fighting Sonny was inconceivable. Not that he lacked courage—it was just inconceivable. Pete fighting him *was* conceivable. It was frightening to think of, but it was conceivable. What she knew for certain was that she didn't want to be involved in it in any way.

"No point tonight, I guess," he said. "I'm too sleepy and he's probably pilled up a mile high. I better get home."

She followed him out and thanked him again, and he turned and rested his elbows on the open door of the Thunderbird for a minute, rubbing his eyes with one hand.

"Poor man," she said. "You seem to be my guardian angel lately. I'm afraid I'm a very inconvenient person to guard."

Pete looked up at her. She was standing on the sidewalk, her hands in the pockets of the white bathrobe, with a foot of green nightgown showing underneath it. She looked a little moody, but she did not look like an inconvenient or difficult person to guard. She looked lovely. He told her to be careful, eased back under the wheel, and missed her a little as he drove home.

Patsy showered the grit off herself, feeling very keyed up and wide awake. She had begun to worry a little about Jim and contemplated calling the party, but that would merely announce that she was back again, easy prey. It was not really likely that Jim would come to harm, so she didn't call. She made sure the door was really locked and turned off the light and pulled the bedsheet up under her chin. It had been

130

an incredible evening. Grown men had looked at her, and that was very unusual. She was used to being ogled at student parties, but grown men were different. Mr. Percy, in his friendly way, had clearly admired her—so had Sonny, although it was strictly a disadvantage to be admired as he admired. And Pete Tatum had looked at her very strangely, particularly as he was about to leave, when he was leaning on the car door. She had no experience at reading looks, but his had made her uncertain. The evening had made her uncertain. She wanted to go away and be by herself. It was all she could do to cope with being wanted by Jim, her own husband. She looked out the window at the pale light on the street, wishing she were in Houston.

In Houston it was clear to everyone that she belonged to Jim. Rodeo people did not seem to see that clearly. Pete saw it, but she could not be sure that he really liked it. Sonny Shanks quite refused to recognize it, as had Ed Boggs. Civilized admiration, such as Mr. Percy had given her, was one thing—it was acceptable, it was even her due for being pretty. But uncivilized or ambiguous admiration was quite disturbing. Lying awake, wide-eyed, it occurred to her for the first time how terrible and complicated life would be if she didn't belong to Jim—if that simple truth weren't true, or weren't all-covering. What if Jim didn't absolutely and automatically belong to her? What if Eleanor Guthrie wanted *him*, as Sonny had seemed to want her?

Suddenly she wished very much that Jim were back with her, so she could hold him, touch him, get it all clear again. She felt like crying, from confusion. But she didn't cry and in time felt better. Perhaps it was only that she was getting older, or getting presence enough that grown men would naturally notice her.

Only the thought of Pete Tatum continued to trouble her. He seemed always vaguely troubled himself, and she could not help wanting to know why. He was really the only interesting person that rodeo had turned up and it was frustrating not to be able to really talk to him. She would have liked to know what made him look the way he did, at once confident and a little melancholy. She would have liked to know about his first wife, and why he had married Boots. But she didn't expect to. He did not seem like a man who talked much, and there was no reason why he should talk to her about such things.

Jim could talk to her, if he would only come home. They could have talked over the whole evening and gotten it all clear. But Jim didn't come. Patsy turned for a while, restless, neither unhappy nor content, and then switched on the bed light and got the volume of Gibbon. Its pages were badly wrinkled, but she straightened them as best she could and read until daylight.

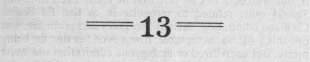

When Sonny left the party, the party began to drain out the door. Eleanor had seen it happen often. Though no one there particularly liked Sonny, they all immediately noticed it when he left and became nervous and restless. The tone of the party broke—the company seemed to become collectively insecure. Where was Sonny? Perhaps he had gone to a better party. Perhaps they were no longer where the action was. It bothered them, and after gulping a little more free liquor, they left.

A few came over and told Eleanor it had been nice, but not many did even that, and the few that did were diffident toward her, as if they were not sure they ought to say anything.

"Why is everyone scared of you?" Jim asked. He was tipsy and not scared of her.

"It's uncertainty," she said. "They don't quite know where I fit in. If they were really sure I was Sonny's mistress they'd be on solid ground."

"Mistresses," Jim said vaguely. He thought she was the

132

most attractive woman he had ever seen. He liked her smile, he liked the way she spoke, he even liked her chuckle. Eleanor, in her turn, found him a pleasant young man, very easy to talk to. If he had not been there she would have spent the evening exchanging sophisticated witticisms with Vaslav Joe Percy, who, besides themselves, was the only guest remaining. He was at the liquor table drinking his dozenth drink and telling the bartender jokes.

"Don't tell me you've had mistress problems," Eleanor said, smiling at Jim shrewdly.

"No. I haven't had any to have problems with, unless I count my wife just before we were married. I don't suppose a fiancée is the same as a mistress, even if you're sleeping with her."

"Not in the classical sense," Eleanor said.

Jim put his hand to his mouth suddenly, as if he had just received a bad signal from his stomach, but he quickly lowered it again and went on talking about Stanley Kubrick. Eleanor had never seen a Kubrick movie but listened politely, pretending that she had. Jim began to talk more rapidly, as if he knew he was going to topple over asleep at any minute and was desperately trying to keep himself awake. He was talking about *Dr. Strangelove.* Suddenly he stopped, set his whiskey glass carefully on the floor, and looked blank.

"Come on," Eleanor said. "I think it's time you slowed down. Stretch out here on the couch for a minute. I have to excuse myself for a little while, anyway."

Jim obeyed. Eleanor went to the bedroom and when she came back he was asleep. She turned the lamp at the head of the couch so it wouldn't shine in his eyes. Asleep, he was very good-looking, and very young. She went over to the picture window, where Joe Percy was standing. It was late, he was without an audience and looked tired.

"Drank him under, I see," he said. "Nice boy. He's probably got a crush on you already. I could probably get a crush on that wife of his if I let myself." He looked at her and smiled. "And on you as well," he said, raising his glass. "Isn't it awful?"

"What?" Eleanor said.

"The way people go around getting impossible, inappropriate crushes on one another."

"Awful," she said.

"Where did the cowboy go?"

"He didn't tell me."

"Pursuing that young lady?"

"Very probably," Eleanor said.

"Well, he's a dumb-ass," Joe said. "It would take her twenty years to catch up with you, if she ever does. Besides, he won't get anywhere with her."

"My feeling exactly," Eleanor said.

"Well, you don't seem very insulted," he said. "I doubt he has much luck with women of intelligence." But he realized instantly what he had said and gestured uncomfortably, as if to brush the remark out of the air. But Eleanor was amused.

"In all frankness—as we say in Hollywood—I've had none with them myself," he said. "Fortunately they're a rarity. I guess I better be going."

"I hope your script works out all right," she said as he was at the door.

"It will. Mine always do. I'm a screenwriter, if there's one left in the world."

Eleanor was taken with a sudden slight melancholy, brought on by the talk of Sonny's absence and probable whereabouts. Though it was a tranquil melancholy, and an element in her beauty, it showed, and Joe Percy looked at her kindly.

"Cheer up," he said. "It's all ridiculous, you know. If you ever happen to be in L.A. and bored, I wish you'd give me a call. Oddly enough, I'm listed."

"Oddly enough, I might," she said. "Who can say?"

She went back and looked at Jim, regretting that she hadn't made him take his sports coat off before he passed out. She went into her bedroom and found three empty glasses on her dressing table. It annoyed her and she carried them back to the other room. She was sitting on the bed pulling off her stockings when Sonny came in. He looked moody—half pleased with himself, half depressed.

"Where's your new beau?" he asked.

"Don't be smart," she said. "He's asleep on the couch and he's a very nice young man. Let him sleep."

"Seen some of the party going down the road," he said. "Hope you took care of everything."

"Not very well. You're an insulting bastard, I must say."

He grinned, sat down beside her, and ran his hand along her smooth calf. "Well, it never got me nowhere," he said.

Eleanor shifted her leg away. "Mr. Percy and I had already concluded that. He remarked that you probably had no luck with intelligent women."

Sonny snorted. "I never had no *luck* with any kind," he said. "Who's that dull little turd to talk?"

"He's not dull. He's a little chubby but his essential charm comes through. And he's certainly no fool."

"Spend a week with him sometime and see what you think then." He stood up and stretched. "I'm worn out," he said. He tossed the red shirt in a corner and slipped out of his jeans.

"You're really going to make a movie? Finally?"

"It won't be worth seeing. What I want is a TV series. That would be real money."

Eleanor went to the bathroom to undress and clean her face, and when she had finished went to the phone and called her pilot. "I want the plane in four hours," she said.

"Where for, ma'am?" he asked groggily.

"Dallas. But we'll stop by the ranch first. I need some things."

When she returned to the bedroom Sonny was stretched on his back, asleep. She got in bed and lay resting, looking across him, seeing the rise and fall of his chest. In a few minutes he groaned and turned toward her and groaned again. His bad leg was cramping—it often happened. He didn't wake up, but he kept groaning. His foot, calf, and thigh were drawn tight as iron. Eleanor tried to knead them, but as always it was like kneading a section of iron pipe. She persisted, but when the cramp finally loosened she didn't know whether the muscles had relaxed because of her efforts or merely of their own accord. His foot remained drawn, but she rubbed it and twisted it until the toes loosened. Sonny half awoke and raised on his elbows, but then lay down again. When his foot was normal she lay down too and he reached over sleepily and fondled her belly, just at the place where she was heaviest.

135

"I'm in better shape than you," he said.

"Well, you're a professional athlete. You ought to be."

But he had gone back to sleep, and she was glad. She awoke easily when it was time and dressed, feeling content and ready to leave. She felt at peace with Sonny. Jim was still on the couch. It was very dark when her cab came and only faintly gray in the east when she got to the hangar where the pilot was waiting. She saw the desert sunrise from the air as they were winging east, saw rose and gold spread upward from New Mexico. The pilot had a thermos of coffee which they shared. She dozed again over West Texas, tired, lulled by the smoothness of the flight and the brownness of the land below. When the plane dropped over the ranch house the gardeners were tending the flower beds and the cowboys had gone for the day.

She was there an hour. Lucy was furious. She hated Eleanor's spates of irrational traveling. In Dallas she told the pilot she would be back in four or five days and caught a plane for New York.

That evening, alone at the Carlyle, she found herself tired and depressed and regretted that she had not had the good sense to stay at the ranch. She had a theater date with a man who had hoped for eleven years that she would someday marry him. Her depression deepened and she called and broke the date. She put on a robe and sat at the window drinking brandy and watching the lights of the city come on. It had begun to drizzle and the window dripped and blurred, softening the lights. Eleanor felt grateful for the drizzle. It was a time when she preferred things blurred and misted to things dry and clear. In time she replenished her brandy. She became very glad she had broken the date and opened the window a little so she could smell the rain. A fall of rain on New York City smelled so different from a fall of rain on the country.

The next morning New York seemed a wonderful city, and she felt fresh and cheerful and had lunch with the banker who hoped to marry her. In the afternoon she shopped a little, dropped in at a couple of galleries, and strolled up Fifth Avenue. She went back to the hotel and pulled her shades, meaning to nap and go out in the evening.

But she couldn't nap. A familiar restlessness hit her, a desire to be somewhere else, somewhere she had never been. With it came a desire for something strange and harsh, something unfamiliar, inappropriate, something in contrast to the good bed, the quiet service—all the ease she was accustomed to. She regretted not staying in Phoenix longer, and she broke another date with the patient banker—not exactly to his surprise. It was Sonny's doings and had always been that way. If they could not be together for a week or more it was better not to go near him at all. It left her with an edge. She called Phoenix, but Sonny was gone and no one knew where. She looked out the window, but New York no longer seemed attractive—merely noisy, crowded, dirty.

On a reckless impulse she called Mr. Joe Percy in Los Angeles and reached him at a studio.

"Hiya, Joe," she said. "Isn't that what girls say in movies?"

"At one time it was. Is this Eleanor?"

"This is Eleanor. I thought I might come and see you tonight or tomorrow, depending on connections."

"Sure, delighted," Joe said. "Passing through?"

"No, coming especially," Eleanor said, feeling wild.

"Especially to see *me*? I'm flabbergasted. Why, for god's sake?"

"Because my father wouldn't let me date cowboys," she said. "It had a complicated effect on me."

"It sure must have," Joe said. "Well, now that you've explained it, come ahead."

"Do I detect a note of trepidation?" she asked.

"Oh, no," he said. "What have I got to fear? Neither of us has any reason not to do anything we want to do, that I can see."

She hung up and that evening they had a good late dinner in a restaurant off La Brea. Eleanor realized as they were eating that she liked Joe Percy very much, and all the sense of harshness and strangeness that she had felt on the flight west left her. She began to feel herself again, and very foolish, and Joe Percy realized it and did his gentlemanly best to make a graceful exit possible for her, but his tact only made Eleanor feel the more confused. He offered to get her a hotel room but she declined. "No," she said. "Maybe I better try to get a flight back to Dallas. I really don't know what I thought I was doing."

"You look a little worn," Joe said. "I've got a perfectly secure guest room you're welcome to. You can't get a flight this late."

Eleanor accepted gratefully. Joe Percy, modestly clad in green pajamas and a blue robe, came to his guest-room door to say good night and found her in bed crying. He came and sat down on the bed and patted her hand and then held it. "Come now," he said. "Cheer up. I'll survive the disappointment. I didn't let myself believe it, anyway."

"Oh," Eleanor said. "I'm just distraught. I don't know what I've been doing the last three days. This is the silliest thing I've done in years."

Joe smiled at her. He had good teeth and his mustache worked for him. He was clearly a man who had handled the tears of many women. Eleanor was trembling from her cry and held his hand tightly.

"Maybe you've been reading too much Iris Murdoch," he said. "Your coming out here like this reminds me a little of her stuff. People are always getting into bed with one another out of the blue."

"No I haven't," she said, beginning to feel a little less wretched. "I don't read very good books, really. I read a lot of magazines."

Joe chatted with her until she was feeling calm and pleasant. She told him about her ranch. He had seen most of the world but had never been on a really large ranch and she told him he would have to come sometime. He had been in Australia and told her about a couple of old Australian cattlemen he had known and the stories they told. As he was about to leave he bent to give her a light kiss, looked at her quizzically, smiled, and gave her a real kiss. Eleanor found she had been wanting him to. He drew back and gave her his little sly look, frank and merry and sexy, before he kissed her again.

The next morning she sat naked on the bed looking out at the smog-white Hollywood hills. The sheet was around her waist, and she felt heavy and good, uncombed and unkempt, but good. Joe Percy had just come to ask what she wanted for breakfast. He was wearing a pair of red briefs and a blue Hawaiian shirt.

"How'd I get here?" she said. "Did you hypnotize me in Phoenix. You need to lose some weight, you know."

"Nonsense," Joe said. "This potbelly is my secret. It was obviously my roly-polyness that got to you."

"You must have got to me with more than that," she said, yawning. "I feel downright despoiled."

"Well, I'd brag about you but nobody would believe me," Joe said. "They'd think you were a fantasy."

"Sonny would believe you," Eleanor said. "He knows my erratic nature. Besides, I told him you were attractive."

"You did? Somehow I've always felt attractive, despite my appearance. How did you contract that horse's ass? He must be worse than syphilis."

"No, talk nicely about him," she said quietly.

"I'm sorry," Joe said at once. "That was thoughtless."

Eleanor was silent, looking out the window. Joe looked at her and felt sad inside himself, for he would have liked to have seen her right where she was for many mornings, her hair uncombed and her breasts sagging just as they were—and he knew he would probably never see her there again.

"I must say you've got your nerve," she said, noticing his red shorts and grinning at him. "You certainly were greedy."

"Yep," Joe said, unabashed. "Get up and let's eat."

"I guess I'm glad you are," she said, pulling the sheet off the bed to hold around her. "Men have always rushed to give me things. Very few have ever dared to grab."

"Anyone who gets you in reach and doesn't grab is a fool," Joe said. "I can't figure you being single. All your looks, all your dough. How come?"

"Oh, I'm too sleepy to go into it," she said, yawning again. "Isn't it almost noon? You're better than sleeping pills.

"I really said most of it yesterday," she added, going to the window to look out at the hills. "Daddy wouldn't let a cowboy near me, or vice versa. There were only about five men in Texas rich enough to marry me when I came of age. The one I married was sixteen years my senior, and queer to boot, though he didn't know it at the time. I didn't know anything and Daddy paid no attention. He wouldn't have known it if he had paid attention. He had twelve thousand head of cattle to take care of. My husband and I lived together in honorable wretchedness for eight years and then he killed himself in a rest room of the Adolphus Hotel, in Dallas. It didn't get in the papers the way it was, I assure you. Three months after Daddy died I met Sonny. He took me off in one of his hearses to a secluded spot in Oak Cliff and I found out what a cowboy was. I found out a lot of things I hadn't known. I was twenty-nine. All that time I was married I did the conjugal act maybe twice a year. I didn't know enough to complain, and I had no one to complain to. For weeks after I met Sonny I wouldn't turn him loose. I couldn't believe it was me, but I liked it. That's why I can't help feeling protective of Sonny. He brought me into being. No one else had the nerve. You can't imagine how isolating wealth is unless you've lived in Texas. There are places where wealth makes people a little more companionable. In Texas it just guarantees you a comfortable loneliness."

"Have to look Texas over sometime," he said. "Sounds like a fine place for a novelist *manqué*. Lots of frustration. Hardly anybody screwing readily. There's too much ready screwing out here—it drains off the poetry of it all."

"You can have the poetry of it all," Eleanor said. "You're going to work, I take it."

"I have to," he said. "I'm an underling, comparatively. But I could take you to dinner at an even better restaurant, if you care to hang around."

"Nope," she said. He went back to his room and when she had put on a robe she went in. He was dressed in a conservative blue suit. On his dresser was a picture of a woman, a brunette in an off-shoulder dress. Her hair style belonged to the forties. She caught a glimpse of herself in Joe's mirror—she looked full, even a little overblown. She certainly looked her age.

"God," she said. "I can't imagine why anyone would want to go to bed with either of us. That's a nice suit."

Joe Percy turned from tying his tie and looked at her fondly. "Maybe not me, but certainly you," he said. "Of course, out here you might have problems. Out here you need to be sixteen and weigh about ninety-eight pounds to be considered prime."

"Your wife was lovely," she said.

Joe sighed. "Some old girl she was," he said. "A serial queen, if you can imagine it. She could swing through trees and fall over waterfalls with the best of them. I truly haven't been the same since she died."

"What happened?"

"Cancer," he said. "About ten years ago."

She looked out the window again. The hills were brown and the smog white as the white houses. It would be nice to arrive home, to fly through the clear plangent evening, with the whole of the Red River Valley spread out below her. She would exchange the neuter smell of Hollywood for the smell of alfalfa and mesquite and perhaps have a word with the cowboys if she got home in time.

"You really won't stay?" he asked. "I'll be so bereft without you that I'll have to get drunk."

"No," she said. "I have to go. Anyway, you failed me. I wanted to feel low and wicked. Now I just feel fat and carnal and a little goofy."

"So?" he said.

"Well, damn," she said. "You're too domestic, Joe. You make me feel like I might have made somebody a nice middle-class wife. I don't want to feel that way now."

"High romance just ain't my metier," Joe said. "I've written too many bad situation comedies." He looked in the mirror and could not help smiling a dapper smile. He turned his irresistible dapper smile on her.

"Quit," she said. "I don't want to get comfortable with you. I might marry you. That would throw my directors into a tizzy."

"You've got directors too?"

"Certainly. Daddy never figured I'd have enough sense to run the estate myself. I don't have much trouble, though. They're all scared of me."

They ate the breakfast Joe had fixed, chatting pleasantly. "You really will have to visit," Eleanor said. "I want you to meet Lucy, my maid. The two of you ought to be exposed to one another. She has a wit not unlike yours." After breakfast

Joe put on a driving cap and they kissed lightly at the door, as if they had been married ten years and had just remembered that they were fond of each other. He drove off in a Morgan with red seats, and Eleanor had more coffee and drank it while looking at his pictures and his books. She made the guest-room bed, called a cab, and when she got home that evening the bullbats were swooping over the long lake in the horse pasture, the cowboys were unsaddling at the barn, and her two dairymen were just turning the Jerseys into the oatfield for the night. She ate some cold shrimp while Lucy solemnly filled her in on the doings of the week. They prated awhile and Eleanor went to bed with the magazines that had accumulated in her absence. She didn't leave the ranch again for almost three months.

14

"You're getting sexier," Jim said, kissing her shoulder. Her shoulders were freckled from much sitting around swimming pools. Patsy glanced at him. She was in bed filing a nail. He had just showered and was suddenly there at her side, sexually aroused.

"I'm busy," she said pleasantly. "Take it away." But Jim went on kissing her shoulders—it was really more ticklish than sexy. "A minute," she said as he was turning her toward him to really kiss her. Just before he did, she managed to burp. She had been next door to a drive-in and had had a vanilla milkshake. Her burp tasted of milkshake and she could not really enjoy the kiss because she needed to burp again and was afraid she would. Still, matters went pleasantly enough. Jim had been off visiting a ranch for three days, rising early and working hard, and passed quickly from coming into sleep. Patsy made it belatedly and not very strongly—a short quiver of pleasure, quickly gone—but Jim was not awake to resent anything and she calmed quickly and didn't care.

She slipped from beneath him and lay with her chin on her arms and her arms on Jim's back, looking across him. Through the window she could see the green neon sign of their motel and the shallow end of a swimming pool. She was in no turmoil but felt vaguely bothered by the feeling that nothing in her life was ever going to be terribly intense. She would have liked sex better if it made her drowsy more often. She disliked being awake afterward, alone and think-ing. She had always supposed she would lead an intense life, one way or another, but it just wasn't working out that way. She wasn't starving, but neither was she feasting. Her sensations weren't very intense, her emotions weren't very intense, even her imaginings had ceased to be very intense. As usual at such times, her thoughts turned to babies. A baby would surely make for joy. She rubbed her hand fondly up and down her sleeping husband's back, for he had agreed two weeks before that they should have one. She might be pregnant already. And conditions for parenthood seemed very opportune. She was convinced that Jim was about through with photography—his enthusiasm was waning visibly. By the end of the summer he would be ready to try something more settled, and he was always at a peak of enthusiasm about life when he was starting something new. It would be a good time to be starting a baby. Besides, it had begun to seem to her that fatherhood might be what he was best at.

They were in Ogden, Utah, after almost a month of lonely circling through the West. The tying-up incident in Phoenix had scared them both. Jim had come in rumpled and guilty-looking from his night on Sonny's couch, and when Patsy told him about what Sonny had done he grew very depressed and they drew together and decided to split off from the pro rodeo circuit for a time. They started to Provo, Utah, where everyone else was going, but after several inconclusive arguments about whether or not Sonny was really dangerous they turned and went to Idaho instead. Jim was gloomy and troubled the whole trip. He liked Sonny and hated the complications of it all. They decided that the best thing to do was hunt out small amateur rodeos for a time and avoid the anxiety that having Sonny around would be sure to produce.

They went north through Idaho as far as Coeur d'Alene, then cut back through Montana to Missoula, went up to Great Falls, down to Billings, on down to Jackson, Wyoming, then up again to Miles City, to Bismarck, North Dakota, down again through South Dakota to Mobridge and Pierre, cut through a corner of Nebraska and slowed for a time in Colorado. Whenever they saw a rodeo poster they made a side trip if necessary. To her surprise Patsy found that she liked the country they were traveling through. Except for one childhood trip to Yellowstone she had never been in the high West, and she liked it. The towns they stayed in were another matter, for once they left the circuit, Jim developed almost an obsession for staying in the smallest towns he could find, towns even the chain motels had not heard of. They stayed in Grangeville, Mobridge, Killdeer, Swift Current, Cody, Belle Fourche, Pagosa Springs, St. Onge. Accommodations tended to be weird—it was Patsy's word. "Don't call this primitive," she said one night. They were in an old railroad hotel in Nebraska and a train had come through and had seemed to pass right underneath them. "Primitive life was never this noisy."

Some places had no movie theaters, and such theaters as there were seemed to belong so totally to the forties that it was a little incongruous to see sixties movies in them. Patsy took walks and got stared at. She read the box of paperbacks from top to bottom, got dangerously far into the third volume of Gibbon, and began to ration herself and subsist on what she could pick up at drugstores.

They decided to go to Calgary, mostly because Patsy wanted to see the Canadian Rockies, but the Ford picked that week to throw a rod and they spent two days in Lewiston, Montana, waiting for a part to come by bus from Great Falls. The country they drove through was cool and high, gray distance in the mornings, brown distance at noontime, blue distance in the evenings. Patsy came to love the distances and often sat for long periods watching the wavering horizon. Jim's picture-taking grew increasingly lackadaisical and they had little to do but talk, read, drive, and eat.

It was a month-long period of calm. The argument they had had in Phoenix left them both feeling chastened and a little ashamed. Each determined to be more considerate sexually and the next time they made love they were more considerate than enthusiastic. After that the driving seemed to sap them. They lived and slept together in placid, friendly chastity for three weeks, neither bothered, neither discontent. Jim had been very taken with Eleanor and had fantasies of her for a while, but he had only seen her the once and her memory soon began to fade.

The period of calm ended abruptly one night in a small town in northern Colorado. Jim went out to mail some postcards to their folks and completely forgot to bring back some cold cream Patsy had requested. He had also forgotten magazines—an essential of life. Patsy had suspected he would forget, since he often did, and had written him a little list, but he stuck the list in his shirt pocket and thought no more about it until he walked in the door of the motel room and saw her look up at him expectantly.

"Oh, no," he said. "I completely forgot what you wanted."

"I knew it," she said coldly. "Just give me the car keys. I'll get them myself."

Jim offered to go, but she left without another word as he was apologizing. It was a tiny town, just one drugstore and a couple of grocery stores and one or two other small-town enterprises. Patsy got her stuff and drove restlessly back and forth through the little town, fuming. Dogs ran out to bark at the car. The town was in a flat valley, with mountains to the west, just visible in the dusk. There was really no place to linger, and after ten minutes she gave up and went back to the motel, the only accommodation the town boasted and one that was not to her liking. The walls were peeling, the neck of the shower hung crookedly, so that she practically had to stand in the bedroom to get wet, and there was no air conditioning. The room was cool in the morning, but the sun shone on it all afternoon and in the evening it was hot.

Jim looked up guiltily when she came in and he tried again to apologize. "Oh, quit apologizing," she said. "I forgive you. I knew you had a bad memory when I married you. What I didn't know was that you'd take me to towns like this, with no warning."

"What do you mean, no warning? We've been staying in towns like this for weeks. You're getting soft."

The remark infuriated her. "Of course I'm soft," she said. "I was born soft. I'm not going to lead a crusade or anything. I'm just a woman."

"I didn't mean that," Jim said, annoyed by her tone. "I mean soft in the wrong way. You like luxuries too much."

"Hush, you hypocrite," she said, shucking off her dress. She flopped across the bed in her bra and panties, with *Cosmopolitan,* the only semi-readable magazine the drugstore had had. She felt more like arguing than reading.

"It's steaming in here," she said. "I'm sweating. You're heartless and a hypocrite. You like money more than I do. You love being able to spend hundreds on cameras and stuff any time you decide your lens is inadequate, but then you think you can make up for it by staying in sleazy motels and living on corn dogs. I'll never eat another corn dog as long as I live." She had just eaten a corn dog for supper.

"I didn't make you eat that corn dog," he said. "The drive-in had other things. You can eat what you damn please."

"Corn dogs are just my rallying point," she said. "It's the principle I'm attacking. I should never have married you." She flipped the pages of the magazine angrily.

"You're a puritan and a hypocrite and you wear your goddamn underwear three days in a row," she said. "I always thought I'd marry a man with the decency to change his underwear every day. Squalor is all I have to look forward to, squalor and neglect."

Jim felt guilty for having forgotten the things, and he let the accusations break over his head. She didn't sound seriously angry. Since he was directly behind her, sitting at a little lampstand that was all the room had in the way of a desk, her spleen was actually being directed at the head-board of the bed. He was writing in a journal that he had decided to keep. Sometimes he felt that he was more of a writer than a photographer, and the journal might come in handy. Besides, there was nothing else to do until bedtime.

Looking up, he caught an exciting hind view of Patsy as she lay on the sheets of the thin bed. Her legs were wide and she held one foot in the air, waving it erratically as she talked. A small tuft of dark hair showed beneath the edge of her panties. He ceased writing in the journal and began to doodle, and he looked at the rear view of Patsy again and got up and locked the door.

"I wish I had read Helen Gurley Brown sooner," Patsy said. "I'm sure she has some very practical ideas. Probably I should have been promiscuous when I was younger. I might have learned about men who don't change their underwear. According to this magazine, sex is everything."

"It would be everything if you lived in a town like this," Jim said. He sat down by her and ran his hand up her leg and underneath her.

"Quit," she said. "That was not a cue. I was merely remarking on a cultural phenomenon. I'm really glad I wasn't promiscuous and I don't feel sexy right now."

But Jim kept on rubbing her through her panties, intent on changing the way she felt. Patsy kept reading, feeling irritated, impolite, and stubborn. Finally she wrenched her bottom away from his hand.

"Stop," she said. "Go take pictures of small-town empti-ness, or something."

"You're getting sexier," he said.

"Well, you're not getting any more inventive. You've used that line for six months. Go away and suffer. You can't afford luxuries like sex. It would only weaken you as an artist. Sublimate. I'm reading and I don't feel sexy."

"I'm your husband," Jim said, annoyed.

"I'm your husband," she mimicked. "I'm sweaty and this bed is lousy and I have to read this and find out why sex is everything. I have the right to abstain if I want to and I choose to abstain."

"All you ever want to do is abstain," he said, trying to roll her panties down her hips. Patsy thwarted him by rolling off the bed. She went in the tiny bathroom, shut the door, and sat on the commode to read. When she came out fifteen minutes later, soaked with sweat, Jim was in bed looking aggrieved.

"You certainly don't seem to find me very attractive," he said. "I doubt you really love me any more."

"Don't lie there pitying yourself," she said. "It just makes me worse. I wish I had a milkshake. With all the cows around here you'd think there'd be milkshakes available."

But after a time she grew contrite and decided she was mean and bitchy and worked it so she got seduced. Jim was grateful and sweet, but also uncharacteristically slow. They were very sweaty and the bed was creaky and not at all firm. After a time, wondering what was wrong, Patsy turned her face toward him and saw from the rather strained look of pleasure on his face that he was considerately holding himself back, waiting for her.

"Oh, don't look like that," she said. "I'd rather you beat me than to look like that." She felt suddenly furious and hopeless.

Jim was startled, stopped moving, and then began again uncertainly. Patsy felt contrite at her outburst and gripped his shoulders, trying to get with him. But they had both become self-conscious and slipped further and further out of rhythm. Jim came and hardly felt it and Patsy simply gave up. She threw her arms wide on the bed and lay panting, shaken with a combination of frustration and hopelessness. Jim was silent and very depressed and Patsy cried a little and when he said nothing began to feel angry.

"Move," she said, just as he was about to. "I'm drowning in sweat. You can give me the silent treatment after I've showered, if you insist."

"I'm not giving you any kind of treatment," he said.

"Not the kind I thought I'd get when I married you," she said, going to the bathroom. The shower was cold and left her feeling edgy and more wrought-up than ever.

When she came out Jim was dressing, as if he meant to go somewhere, and it crossed her mind for a moment that he had stopped loving her—probably with justice—and was about to abandon her in a miserable little town in Colorado. He was looking for a sock that had been kicked under the bed. All he had on was a brown short-sleeved sports shirt and one brown sock.

"Why are you dressing?"

"I'm going out." He found the sock and sat on the edge of the bed to put it on.

"I hope you at least put some underwear on. Where are you going? Out where?"

"Just out. Away from your nagging tongue."

"There's nothing but prairie out there. You'll get snake-bitten."

"Snake-bit."

"Oh, hell. Bitten by a snake. Or else lost. Why do you want to embarrass me by getting lost? I'll probably have to hire a search party."

"Just shut up," he said. "I won't get lost. You're no one to talk to me about anything. You nag me and you don't like to sleep with me. I don't know what's wrong with you. You don't even like for me to see you naked."

Patsy had been holding a towel in front of her loins but she yanked it up and flung it at him. It draped over his shoulder but he shrugged it to the floor.

"There, I'm naked," she said. "Peer all you like, you're nothing but a goddamn voyeur anyway. An amateur voyeur. Take pictures of me if you want to. You think I'm frigid just because I don't come the minute you want me to. I can do it fine if you just let me do it like I like to and not bother with me so much. Get out and get lost—I want you to. I don't want you coming near me again."

"I don't know why I would want to. You always manage to make me feel I'm no good."

"Shut up," she said. "You're just feeling sorry for yourself. What do you think I am, some kind of applause meter? Look at me!" And she stuck one leg out and pointed to herself. "See. I'm just a woman. I'm not equipped with any gauge that registers how great you are."

"Let's quit," he said dejectedly. "I didn't mean it that way."

But Patsy felt wild and violent. She picked the *Cosmopoli-*

tan off the floor and flung it at the wall of the room. "To hell with sex," she said. "I wish I'd been a nun and never got involved with it at all."

"Hush," Jim said. He was putting on his underwear.

"I will not," she said. "I'd rather never do it than have to fight about it every time. Phooey on the penis—people were nuts ever to worship it. I think I'll write an article called 'Phooey on the Penis' and send it to that stupid magazine."

"My, you're witty," Jim said. His voice was so wretched that it broke Patsy's anger, though her bosom continued to heave.

She sighed and went over and put her head on his chest and hugged him. "You poor man," she said. "What an unlucky day for you when you married me. How could you suspect I'd turn out soft and frigid? I'm sorry I talked so mean."

Jim was relieved. Instead of going out he undressed again and they got back in bed and chatted and were friendly. "I wish we could forget about all this," Patsy said, her head on his arm. "Maybe if we forget about it for a while we can start over and everything will work."

"Maybe," Jim said, but he had little confidence that it would ever work.

Then, all unexpectedly, only two nights later, their sexual fortunes changed for the better. Late in the afternoon they crossed Berthoud Pass—crossed it at a speed of two miles an hour, in reverse. The Ford was not at its strongest and refused to take the pass in second or even in low, and Jim had to resort to backing over, while behind them a string of cars and trucks waited and watched, the drivers surprisingly patient, even amused. Patsy felt the center of all eyes. It was very ignominious to have to back over a mountain, and had she not been nervous and scared she would have been angry.

"Fool! Idiot!" she kept saying. "Why can't we get a new car?" She kept her dark glasses on and tried to look unconcerned and inscrutable. Jim tended grimly to his backing and ignored her. When they finally topped the pass he turned around and drove downward a few miles to a little mountain town, a sort of truckers' village. Both of them were edgy—Jim had been a little scared too.

"I want a new car," Patsy said. "I really insist. Our very life was in danger."

"Nonsense," Jim said. "You're too cowardly. Besides, that must have been the highest pass in the Rockies. We just won't come this way again."

"*I* sure won't, not in this heap of junk," she said. "I didn't see anyone else backing over. Most people have strong cars. You're insanely stubborn, Jim."

"You're insanely bitchy," he said, not yielding an inch.

They ate a silent supper, each determined not to weaken, but the little cafe where they ate was so unexpectedly jolly that they couldn't stay low-spirited. It was bright and noisy and paneled in pine. The kitchen threw out good smells, and the place was packed with a score or more of loggers and truck drivers, a boisterous and devil-may-care group of men. It was hard to be depressed around them. The stew they had was excellent, and that helped too. When they stepped outside it was dark and very cold and they walked up the highway for a mile or more, smelling the pine trees and the mountains. They were so high that even the height itself seemed to have a smell. They were both shivering, and Jim put his arm around her.

"Those were the first actual loggers I've ever seen," Patsy said. "They even wore plaid shirts, like loggers in books. I like this place, even if we did endanger our lives getting here."

She took his hand and they walked back to their motel. Besides the cafe, there was only the motel, one filling station, and a drugstore that doubled as a bus depot. As they passed it a Greyhound bus pulled away and the faces of the passengers looked down at them enviously.

They went to the cabin and read awhile. Then, unable to resist the cold and the good smells, they walked back across the highway to the cafe and had pie and coffee. The cafe was as full as ever, and the men still as boisterous and jolly. Patsy became infected with happiness suddenly, in the way she sometimes did. The loggers kept looking at her, which caused her to flush, and she became very animated. Her eyes shone. She and Jim sat at their table for almost an hour, talking of old friends, rehashing parties they had been to in college, and reminiscing about their honeymoon. It had been to Bermuda and had not been especially successful, but in retrospect it seemed charmingly silly and nice to remember.

The cabin was ice cold when they got back. The bed had real quilts on it, the sheets too were very cold, and the darkness cold around them. They snuggled together, shivery and goose-bumpy for a minute. Jim slipped his hand between her cold thighs and Patsy eagerly opened her legs and then closed them to squeeze his hand against her. He had put it there for warmth, but to his surprise she wanted to be touched. He had ceased to believe that she would ever want him to touch her, but he did and she was immediately responsive and soon twisted her gown up. No sooner had they begun to move than the quilts became a problem, their shoulders were cold and their feet uncovered. The quilts had bunched in the center of the bed, but they were, for once, so warmly into the act of love that they could ignore the quilts. Patsy came more strongly than she had in months, her legs hooked over Jim's, and they had both sunk almost into sleep when the cold brought them up from it. "We're freezing," he said. They hopped up by mutual consent and hurriedly straightened the quilts and tucked them in. Then they snuggled close again.

The next morning they woke early and huddled under the quilts for a long time, staring at the ceiling. It was very cold, and instead of smelling of air conditioning the cabin smelled of pine. Patsy, always a chatterer in the mornings, was unusually quiet and stroked Jim's shoulder from time to time.

"We should live here," she said softly. "Perhaps you could become a logger. I like the idea of your having something to do with logs. Cowboys are just about as wooden, and logs smell better."

"Nope," Jim said without elaboration.

Patsy looked out the window at the highway. Cars were going by. The sun had not yet risen above the peaks, and the mountains were gray, with white mist between the pines.

"I wasn't really meant to ramble," she said. "If we aren't going to live here I ought to go on back to Houston and wait there for you to finish your rodeo travels."

"But it's more fun with you along."

"Not really. I get too ugly. Everything gets disorderly when you're always moving. I lose control too easily."

"You were never terribly orderly at home," Jim pointed out. "You don't especially like Houston, do you?"

Patsy sat up and bent to raise the window so she could smell the morning. The cold raised goose-bumps on her warm arms and breasts. "No, but I'm changing," she said. "I'm ready to stop traveling."

Jim reached up and pulled her back under the covers until only her ears and nose and forehead showed. "I want you close at hand," he said. "It won't be too much longer. We're going back to the pro tour for a little while. I don't think Sonny Shanks will bother us now."

He cupped his hand over her groin and they lay quietly for another thirty minutes, watching cars and trucks go by and loggers in mackinaws going in and out of the cafe across the street. The mountains gradually took on definition. Patsy was not so sure about Sonny, not so sure about anything, but Jim's hand on her made her feel warm and she was willing to let it all rest. Perhaps they had reached a turning point of some kind.

Soon he got her up and hurried her through breakfast, determined to get to Ogden on schedule. All day, as they drove through the Rockies toward Utah, Patsy sat in her corner of the car, watching the curves of the road, the sky, the valleys and mountains, toying now and then with the ends of her hair and feeling unusually quiet and still.

15

"Stop that," Patsy said. "Stop pouring liquor into your glass like that. You act like you're Humphrey Bogart or some-body, getting drunk in a movie."

Jim continued to pour bourbon into the motel glass. He gave a good imitation of a hard-boiled actor getting drunk. "Alan Ladd, for your information," he said.

"Why are you getting drunk? *Now,* of all times?"

"I'm getting drunk because we fight all the time," he said. "If you want to bitch, fine—it's your privilege. I want to get drunk. My privilege."

Patsy was, indeed, in a flashing fury. She would have liked to stalk around the room, but there was so little space that her stalking made her feel ridiculous.

"If you weren't an insane fool we wouldn't be fighting," she said. "Now quit drinking. You're not a drinking type anyway. You don't even like liquor. My god. We're going to Laramie tomorrow. Your getting drunk is out of the question."

"I'll decide what's out of the question," he said. "You're scared to get drunk yourself. It might affect your dignity or something."

"Dignity!" Patsy yelled. "Dignity! When have I had any dignity to affect? Do you think it's dignified for us to be sitting around in some crummy motel in some crummy town in Utah, yelling at one another. They can probably hear us in the Mormon Tabernacle."

"You're yelling," he pointed out, sipping a bit more of his drink. "I'm just getting smashed."

Patsy sat on the bed and clutched her knees. She was wearing old jeans and a green blouse. "You're an abysmal person to bring me to this pass," she said.

"Well, you're abysmal too," he said.

"You're not taking that job, anyway."

"I'll take it if I want to."

"If you take it you're not getting near me again," she said grimly.

"Oh, shut up," he said. "I hardly ever get near you, anyway. Sonny Shanks does not have intentions in regard to you. If he asked me to work on his movie it's because he knows I'm inexperienced and need a start. It would be a start. I don't see why you're so set against it."

"Taking still pictures of some grade Z movie about rodeo is no start. I thought you had high ambitions. I will not have you working for that man. You should beat him up for what he did to me. Instead you make friends with him. He charms you a little and offers you a hokey little job taking pictures and you completely forget what he did to me."

"He apologized! I haven't forgotten. It was just a crazy joke. He was high, anyway. For god's sake."

"Don't blaspheme," she said. "It was no joke. If I hadn't had my bathrobe on I'd have been tied up out there in my gown. No, no, no!"

"You can go to Houston. You want to, anyway. Besides, it may be a year before they're ready to film. Why are we arguing about it now?"

"Sure, I can go to Houston," Patsy said bitterly. "By then I'll be aged. He'll bring his well-preserved mistress around for you to ogle. What a life."

"Isn't it about time for you to burst into tears," Jim said, snapping his fingers at her. "Argue argue argue, bitch bitch bitch, now it's time for you to cry. You always follow up with tears."

But when she did lie on the bed and cry for twenty minutes, he felt really bad and drank the glass of whiskey recklessly, and then two more, until half the bottle was gone. He hadn't meant to get drunk at all, but he felt like he had talked himself out of an alternative. Patsy's bare feet were toward him and it annoyed him that the soles were so dirty.

She was always padding around barefooted. Then he ceased to notice. She wouldn't speak to him, and the more he drank the less he cared.

The next morning he was deathly sick. It hurt him to open his eyes and he had to stop and vomit before he could get his socks on. Patsy felt that she had been cruel, though she still hated the idea of him working for Sonny Shanks. "You poor dope," she said and did the packing for him. He crawled into the back seat of the Ford and was soon asleep again.

Secretly, Patsy was glad he needed to sleep. She liked to drive, and he seldom let her. He felt she drove erratically. They had spent the night in Salt Lake City. The little pass to the east of the city had a gray cloud on top of it. She was a little worried, but when she drove into it, it was not so bad, much thinner than the fogs of Houston. East of the pass the country soon began to smooth out and she pushed the Ford along at seventy-five. She loved to drive on a flat road with mountains in sight. The sky behind the mountains was very blue.

When she had driven about eighty miles she heard a loud imperious honking behind her and looked and saw that Sonny Shanks and his hearse were right on her bumper. The young cowboy named Coon was in front of the hearse with him. It annoyed and frightened her, but she reflected that he could hardly do anything on a public road, with Jim in the car. She wouldn't let herself look in the rearview mirror. Then suddenly the hearse was right beside her; she was so startled she almost swerved into it. She was wearing her sunglasses but despite them gave Sonny what she hoped was a severe and discouraging frown. He waved pleasantly and gunned the hearse on by. Soon it was almost out of sight ahead, and she could enjoy the drive again. But then she passed the hearse as it was stopped at a small roadside station, and then a few miles later it passed her again. Coon was driving, and as they passed, Sonny leaned out of the window and made gestures to the effect that he was deeply sorry about the affair in Phoenix. Among the gestures were some indicating that if she would let him ride a little way with her he could explain. Patsy frowned again and did her best to ignore the hearse and him, although her heart was pounding. Finally Sonny gave up and the hearse pulled away for good.

A little later she glanced up and saw the Tatums' Thunderbird passing her, with Boots driving intently, her white hair blowing. She too had on sunglasses and didn't notice who she was passing. The Thunderbird left the Ford behind so rapidly that Patsy was a little irritated. She tried to get a little more speed out of the Ford and it inched up to eighty, but just as it did Jim raised up as if by magic and said, "Slow down or we'll throw another rod." She dropped back to seventy-five and he went back to sleep. It was a relief, a little later, to come upon Pete Tatum, his trailer hitched to a black pickup, chugging along placidly at fifty. The road ahead was clear, so she pulled up beside him and honked. She felt like a member of a caravan. He smiled when he recognized her and quickly made motions to the effect that they ought to stop and eat if the opportunity offered. Patsy nodded and moved on ahead.

The first decent-looking cafe she came to was in Green River, Wyoming, by which time she had gained several minutes on Pete. While she waited for him she studied herself in the rearview mirror, combed her hair, and fished a blue headband out of her bag. Jim remained sound asleep, and she felt hungry, impatient, and a little nervous. She glanced at Jim but had no intention of waking him. His stomach would barely be in shape for dinner, much less breakfast. Besides, she wanted to eat a meal alone with Pete Tatum. In company he gave her the impression that she bothered him slightly, and she felt it was possible that if they had breakfast together the feeling would go away. Finally he drove up. His donkey Hercules was in the back of the pickup.

Patsy got out a little awkwardly and Pete came over and peered in at Jim. "Every other time I look in this car Jim's lying there lookin' dead," he remarked. It was windier than it had seemed and the wind blew her hair across her eyes.

"He's hung over," she said as they went in. The cafe was log-cabin style on the outside but inside had the usual gum machines, truckers, and plastic booths. They took a booth, both of them feeling slightly awkward, and took refuge in the menus, which they pondered seriously. The drive and the altitude had whetted Patsy's appetite and she ordered two eggs with ham. She wore a clean white blouse and looked so fresh and so happy that Pete could hardly bear to look at her.

"Guess what that idiot Sonny Shanks did," she said. "He's offered Jim a job on a movie he's going to be in. I think it's insane, but Jim wants to take it."

"Too early in the mornin' to talk about bad things," Pete said. The sight of Patsy put him in good spirits. The waitress brought him coffee and her milk, and she drank and looked out the window, her chin on her palm and a strand of hair fallen across her cheek. From time to time she caught Pete looking at her, and then his gray eyes turned away and looked at the room or at his food. His look was always slightly wry, but she felt he did like her, after all, and it pleased her and embarrassed her. She ate with great concentration to cover her embarrassment. "Tell me about your job," she said. "Do you really *like* being a rodeo clown?"

Pete shrugged and blew on his coffee. The sun shone through the window on his curly sandy hair. He had often asked himself the same question. "It don't take much talent," he said, sliding past the question. "I just sort of stumbled into it. I was rodeoing and had a buddy who was a clown and one night he got hurt and I subbed for him for a few days. Turned out to be better at it than he was."

"Do you make all those scatological jokes, like other rodeo clowns?" she asked.

"What kind of jokes?"

"Oh, scatological. Scatology."

"What?" he said, grinning, and she realized she was in a dilemma, for he had no idea what she meant.

"Uh, bathroom stuff," she said, feeling hopelessly prim. Pete got the drift and seemed a little embarrassed himself, but their spirits were too high to be cramped for long. Pete told her a couple of his cleaner jokes. They were terribly corny but he told them with such confident charm that Patsy could not help giggling.

The meal went quickly and as they were going out Pete held the door open for her and offered her a stick of chewing gum. "You-all look us up when you get to Laramie," he said. "We'll go honky-tonkin', or something."

Patsy said they would but felt a little disquieted as she drove away. She didn't want to go honky-tonking with the Tatums, nor with anyone. He had suggested it as if it were the only form of mutual entertainment possible—in Laramie, Wyoming, it probably was. What disquieted her was that she liked Pete and was pleased that he seemed to like her, and yet there was some confusion in the pleasure. He made her feel both superior and inferior at the same time. She could not believe that he was very bright, and brightness had always been the first quality she looked for in men. Jim, for all his vapors, was very bright. It had always puzzled her that bright women could marry men who were plainly and glaringly dumb. And yet there was something impressive about Pete Tatum, and it had very little to do with brightness. She had never encountered his kind of impressiveness before and did not know quite how to value it. She glanced in the rearview mirror often until she had put a ridge between the Ford and his pickup and could no longer see it behind her.

A few minutes later, passing a filling station near Rock Springs, she saw a small cowboy standing by the road hitchhiking and, just in time, recognized him. It was Peewee, the ubiquitous.

"Lo and behold," she said as he came jogging to the car. He was absolutely covered with grayish dust and had to beat himself off as best he could before he got in. He still had his rigging and his small canvas bag.

"Ain't no country to hitchhike around in," he said. "I been standing there sucking dust for four hours."

"It's because you look like a sex fiend," Patsy said, grinning, and Peewee nodded in sober agreement.

"I got an evil face," he said.

Patsy broke up. "As a matter of fact you look angelic," she said. "You just happen to resemble that man in Lil' Abner who has all the bad luck. You know, the one with the small black cloud over his head. Joe something or other. Subconsciously people think a mountain will fall on them if they pick you up."

"I look like one done fell on me," Peewee said. "I even got dust in my pockets. You'd think this here was the Saraha. That big desert, you know."

"I know." She was delighted to have him to talk to, and Peewee was even more delighted. Not only did he have a ride all the way to Laramie, he had Patsy to look at as well. She was driving with her left foot on the gas pedal, which he had seldom, if ever, seen done. Occasionally she peered at him over the rim of her sunglasses.

"How goes your career?"

Peewee tried to remember something he had done that might impress her, but it was all but hopeless. "Well, I took a fourth in one go-round at Klamath Falls," he said. "Ain't had too much glory other than that. My big mistake was ever going to Salinas. Like to got killed on that Bayshore freeway and then on my way back to Arizona I got dropped off in Needles."

"What's Needles?"

"It's sort of a town. Hot place this time of the year. I squatted out there for four days an' wouldn't nobody pick me up. Had to go back to town and get a dishwashing job to keep from starving."

"You must be mad," she said. "All that so you can take a chance on getting killed by a horse."

"Well, you got to do *something* that's fun once in a while in your life," he said.

Soon afterward Jim awoke. He looked white and queasy. Patsy felt too good herself to be properly sympathetic.

"Welcome to the day," she said. "Here we are, citizens of the world, leading the life we've always sought."

"Don't bug me," Jim said weakly. "I'm entering a difficult period."

"If you need to upchuck, say so and I'll stop." She drove with her chin tilted up and looked very blithe. Jim managed not to throw up, but he had little strength for conversation. They had to stop for a few minutes while an old bearded sheepherder trailed his dusty flock across the road.

"I thought one only saw such things in Spain," Patsy said.

"You shouldn't have nagged me into drinking," Jim complained. "It would be nice to be back in Houston, wouldn't it?"

"Of course. I've been telling you that for months. Want to go? I can turn south at the next town."

Peewee was amazed—he had never imagined such whimsey. But Jim shook his head.

"I don't know what to think of you, Jim," Patsy said. "You aren't very consistent. If it would be nice to be in Houston, why don't we go?"

"I just thought of it because of the Orange Julius stand," he said. "They're good for hangovers."

"Well, next time keep in mind that you're not a drinker."

"I'm keeping it in mind right now. Please be friendly. I feel too bad for animosity."

"Quit fishing," she said. "I am totally without animosity."

"Could you open the glove compartment?" he asked Peewee. "There might be a candy bar left. I think a bite of something would be good for me."

Peewee did, but there was nothing there but maps, flashbulbs, and a box of Tampax. "You ate all my candy days ago," Patsy said.

Peewee felt scared. He was convinced that Patsy, for all her loveliness, was a dangerous and unpredictable person to ride with, and he was trying to decide what to do in case things went like they had gone in El Paso. Since he was in the front seat his position was all the more perilous. He looked at Jim for reassurance and Jim smiled and shrugged.

"Even though I love her she treats me ill," he said.

"Humph," Patsy said. "You wouldn't dare not love me, after all you've put me through."

"Oh," she added, "I saw Pete Tatum this morning. We stopped and had breakfast while you were crocked out."

"Glad you didn't wake me," he said. "Food would have undone me, and Pete and I don't have much to say to one another."

"That's because you're a snob," she said, looking at Peewee firmly, as if she expected his support for her opinion. Peewee tried desperately to remain expressionless, and Patsy smiled and let him off the hook. "I find Pete very bright," she said.

═══ 16 ═══

The Carpenters spent most of their first afternoon in Laramie at the rodeo grounds watching Pete train his donkey. The rodeo hadn't started, and no one was doing much. Patsy had developed motel claustrophobia and accompanied Jim to the grounds hoping some amusement would turn up. It was cooler than it had been in Utah—the wind blew constantly. Only Pete was uncomfortably hot. He had wrestled the donkey around so much that his blue shirt was soaked through. Boots sat on the rear end of the Thunderbird watching him struggle. She wore Levi's and a faded red blouse.

"It's the world's dumbest donkey," she said. "All it knows how to do is sit down, and then it won't get up."

Hercules was sitting down at the time and seemed quite content with himself.

"What is he supposed to do?" Patsy asked.

"Roll over," Pete said, wiping his face on his forearm. "What good's a donkey that can't roll over?"

Feeling curious, Patsy got Boots to show her the inside of the trailer house and immediately regretted it. Everything was in complete disorder, garments and bedclothes strewn together and three empty beer cans on the window ledge by the bed. For want of a better amusement the two of them sat cross-legged on the bed and played a game of double solitaire. Pete continued to wrestle with Hercules and Jim had wandered off with his camera poised.

Boots played cards like she drove—intently and rapidly. Seeing the inside of the trailer heightened Patsy's admiration of her. It was impossible not to admire anyone who could live with another human being in such close quarters, amid such complete disorder. Boots seemed not at all daunted. She noticed that Patsy was looking askance at the mess, but she was not offended.

"It's pretty horsy," she said. "It's very hard to rodeo and be ladylike. I never was ladylike, anyway, so I don't miss it."

Pete called for a beer. He had given up on Hercules and was sitting in a little folding chair. They got three beers and went outside, and Boots sat on her husband's lap while he drank. Patsy sat on the Thunderbird and sipped a beer and watched the high thin clouds blow over. A roper was loping his horse around in intricate patterns outside the arena. The horse was a beautiful slim sorrel whose neck was darkened by sweat. Patsy felt relaxed and loose. The Tatums themselves were so relaxed and loose that it was hard to be otherwise around them. Boots held Pete's hand and looked at him in a pleased way. The sight made Patsy feel a little lonely, for it seemed to her that the Tatums cared about each other in a way that she and Jim didn't, and she could not imagine what would become of her in the years ahead. Sugarpops, the Tatums' new dachshund, annoyed her slightly by licking her ankles every time she let her legs dangle.

The three of them chatted pleasantly until Jim returned, but as soon as they were on their way back to the motel Patsy's mood dropped. Jim noticed and asked her if she felt bad.

"No, just a vapor," she said. "I don't like Wyoming very much."

That evening the wind was very high and Patsy, who had been meaning to go to the rodeo, decided against it and went to a James Bond movie instead. They arrived back at the motel almost at the same time and were contemplating going out for hamburgers when there was a knock on the door. When Jim opened it Sonny Shanks stood there. He asked politely if he could come in.

They were taken by surprise. "Sure," Jim said. Sonny walked in, a drink in his hand, and went straight to the bathroom and ran some tap water in it.

"I was fixin' to run over to Cheyenne," he said. "I know a couple of crazy people there that you-all might like to meet. Why not come along?" He rattled the ice in his glass.

There were many reasons why they should not go along, but Sonny had put them both off balance, and he himself at the moment seemed the epitome of friendliness and balance. It was so obvious why they wouldn't want to go to Cheyenne with him that neither of them could speak, and he himself blithely ignored the obvious. His friendliness made everything that had happened in Phoenix seem remote and unreal. They couldn't articulate a protest and, without either of them actually making the decision, acquiesced to what neither of them would have thought possible five minutes before. Sonny had made the decision for them and somehow managed to enforce it. A few minutes later they were all sitting in the front seat of the hearse sipping Sonny's liquor as they sped through the night. It was very dark, with no moon and only a few stars. The country rolled and dipped and the road ahead was dotted with the red taillights of rodeo-goers returning to Cheyenne.

Patsy was in the center, next to Sonny, and could smell him. It was not a body odor exactly; he smelled of bourbon, horsehide, and himself. When he looked at her he smiled with perfect equanimity.

"Don't smile at me," she said, recovering her tongue. "Don't look so pleased. What are you planning for tonight? Going to tie us to a railroad track?"

"No, just feel like drivin'," he said. "Cheyenne makes a nice drive."

"I thought you decided never to see me again," she said. "I was perfectly happy with that decision."

Jim seemed rather cheerful, and it irritated her a little. He had let Sonny pull them into the evening without a word of protest, as if it were perfectly natural to drive off to Cheyenne, Wyoming, with a man who had scared and insulted her only a month before. If she had refused to go, he might have backed her up; but it seemed to her he ought to have refused himself, on principle. He had not even been wishy-washy—he had just left it to her, or to Sonny.

They drove to Cheyenne almost in silence and pulled up in front of a large two-story brick house. The driveway was empty and the house quite dark.

"They're probably just asleep," Sonny said, as if that were

of no import. It turned out, however, that they were not at home.

"I take it you didn't bother to call," Patsy said. They were standing on the lawn. While Sonny was ringing the doorbell she had informed Jim in a whisper that he was not under any circumstances to get drunk.

"Naw. I figured they'd be home. Nothing to worry about. I won't have no trouble breaking in."

And he coolly pried loose a screen on one of the side porches and went in through the window. "He's crazy," Patsy said. "Now do you believe me? He has absolutely no respect for civilization. He does just what he pleases."

"Don't be so hard on him," Jim said. "Maybe he's very good friends with these people." Despite everything, Sonny fascinated him, and he had a hard time hiding the fascination from Patsy.

Lights began to come on in the house, and in a minute Sonny opened the front door and beckoned to them.

"Who would have thought they'd be gone," he said.

"Maybe they heard you were around," Patsy said. "What are we going to do, wait for their unlikely return?"

"No, but we might as well have a drink on them. I got to make some phone calls."

The furniture and rugs were ordinary middle-class furniture and rugs. The only thing unusual about the house was the pictures, some thirty or forty of them, all oils, hung more or less at random on the walls. Almost all of them were nudes of the same woman, a massive redhead with orange pubic hair.

"This guy likes to paint his wife naked," Sonny said, as if that were sufficient evidence of their craziness.

"Maybe he can't get anyone else to pose for him," Jim said. "I can't even get my wife to pose for me."

"Don't talk about that," Patsy said.

Sonny left them to their own devices while he made a half-hour's worth of phone calls. The house was stuffy, so they wandered back out on the porch and sat on the stone balustrade drinking.

"When did I begin to drink?" Patsy said. "I was a milkshake and orange-juice girl until you debauched me. Now every time I turn around I'm drinking hard liquor."

Jim was two drinks ahead of her and just tight enough to feel slightly silly. "Think how far down that way Texas is," he said, remembering the lonely light in the window at Roger Wagonner's ranch house the morning they left for Phoenix.

"I'm thinking of how far away our motel is, and what perils beset us," Patsy said.

"If you'd just get drunk the way I get drunk you wouldn't worry so much," he said. "If we both passed out we'd never know what happened, if anything did."

Patsy was swinging her legs and didn't answer. The lights inside the house began to go out again, and Sonny crawled back through the window. He handed Patsy his drink and she held it while he replaced the screen.

"Locate your friends?"

"Nope. Wasn't trying to. I was talking to an ol' boy I know in Bossier City, Louisiana. Be a nice little surprise for those folks when that one shows up on the bill. Teach 'em to stay home."

Going back, Patsy rode in the rear of the hearse on the mattress. She thought she would be more comfortable there than she would be next to Sonny, but if anything, there was more of him in the back than in the front. Somehow he was always maneuvering her into his absurd seduction chamber, and it made her unreasonably annoyed with him, and with Jim. There was no reason she should even *know* Sonny Shanks, much less ride in his hearse and sit on his mattress. The range they were crossing was faintly starlit—it might have been lovely to watch if they had not been racing over it at one hundred miles an hour. Jim was silent, absorbed in his thoughts. Sonny too was silent, intent on his driving. She wished they would talk about the film job, so she could butt in and argue with them, but they didn't, and she had only her own irritation in which to be absorbed. That was not very satisfactory, because Sonny had not been directly offensive and there was really nothing to be irritated at except the fact of him, or his general arrogance, or something. The mattress had a rough spread on it and smelled dusty, but it was hard to keep from thinking about the things he must have done with women right where she was sitting. That was hateful. She could not imagine why any self-respecting woman would let herself be pushed into such an unlikely bed, by such an obnoxious man. That many did, that even such an intelligent woman as Eleanor Guthrie might have, made her feel she didn't really understand anything about men and women, and that made her feel scared. She looked at Jim, wishing he would look at her, smile at her, convince her that he would always take care of her and never leave her exposed to the things other women seemed to be exposed to. But Jim didn't look around, and the three of them rode to Laramie in silence.

Shanks let them out with a grin and a wave. "Sorry we never scared up no action," he said.

Patsy crawled out and went quickly into the motel, but Jim stood by the hearse a few minutes chatting with Sonny. Patsy was sure they were talking about the movie job and it angered her that they had not done their talking in front of her. She had an impulse to go back and tell them both off, but her desire to have Sonny gone was even stronger, and she didn't.

As soon as she heard the hearse pulling away she began to strip, wrenching her blouse off angrily. She threw it into a corner near the suitcases. Two drinks had left her just high enough that she felt careless about herself. She intended to shower. As she was unhooking her bra Jim came in the door looking sheepish. She let the bra fall where it fell. When Jim saw that she was undressing he quickly shut the door. Patsy flung her skirt in the corner where she had flung the blouse. She shoved her panties down and kicked them high in the air with one foot. They floated down near the bra.

"Nice kick," Jim said. He sat down in the one chair and idly picked up a copy of *Esquire*. Patsy strode in front of him, took off her watch and wedding band, and put them on the bedside table. She stood there a moment fidgeting and then sat down nude on the bed and stared at the wall, clasping her knees and pouting. Jim looked up curiously. "You look a little high," he said. "He sure drives fast, doesn't he?" Patsy lay back on the bed, her arms wide. She brought her legs up, one at a time, and held them as straight up as possible. She felt very odd. Jim glanced at her again and went back to his reading. It made her angry, and she chewed her lip in a way that she only chewed it when very unsettled. She felt sexy, and it seemed to her that it must be obvious, and that Jim had deliberately and callously rejected her just at the one time in their married life when she plainly wanted sexual attention. It seemed beyond belief that he could sit four feet away and not observe that she was in the mood to make love. But Jim was reading a piece about hallucinogenic mushrooms and noticed nothing of the sort. Patsy sometimes cavorted briefly and athletically in the nude, experimenting with exercises she soon grew tired of, and it failed to stir him. It was an interesting article on mushrooms and it simply never occurred to him that his wife was feeling sexy.

Patsy had never imagined that she would be, but she was, and being nude, eager, and ignored was very awkward. She had always responded or not responded to Jim's wanting her, never otherwise. She got up and stood in front of him scratching her hip, but he didn't look up. She went behind the chair and peered as if to see what he was reading, putting her hands on his shoulders.

"Your shower's running," he said, and it was. She had turned it on just before she began to undress so it would warm up.

"Oh, golly," she said and hurried off to the bathroom, which was full of steam. The water was scalding and she turned it off and went back to the bedroom uncertainly. She felt quite disoriented and got her gown and a hairbrush and began to brush her hair with quick furious strokes. Her mood made itself felt. Jim looked up and saw that she was agitated, but he was at a loss as to why and looked down again at his magazine.

"Oh, hell," Patsy said, sniffling and beginning to cry. She dropped gown and brush and went over and sat in her husband's lap, on top of the slick magazine. "Please quit reading," she said.

"Why?" he asked, surprised.

"Because I don't know how to seduce you," she said.

He was even more surprised but quickly kissed her, and Patsy was wet-cheeked and grateful. She was so eager that Jim was startled and a little discomfited, though for months he had hoped for precisely such eagerness. The passionate

Patsy he had fantasied so long had miraculously materialized right on his lap, and had only to be taken.

Yet, when he did take her, nothing was so dramatically different. He was deceived by her eagerness into thinking she was nearer the moment than she was, and yet when his was past she seemed, if anything, to be quieter and further away than she usually was. But he was not angry, not even later when she was ready and her movements became more dictatorial and he had to strain to stay with it. He was calm enough but puzzled and a little sad. If anything new had happened it had belonged to Patsy and not to the two of them, but better one of them than neither of them, he decided, and he was prepared to kiss her or make conversation or do anything she wanted in order to keep things pleasant. He lay quietly, a little bemused, until her heart stilled and her body ceased nipping at him. After a while she put her hand on his shoulder so that he would move off, and when she returned from the bathroom she put her hand on his hip and let one of her legs lie against his. She wanted that much touching but no more and moved her breast away when he reached out to hold it. It was quite hot, it seemed to her. "Well?" Jim said, as if there might be something to be discussed.

Patsy's stomach gurgled. She felt quiet and didn't want to discuss anything. "I'm glad we can sleep late in the morning," she said.

Later, when he was asleep, she felt gentle toward him and stroked his hip, regretting that she was not kinder or more congratulatory or something. Often since marrying him she had had the feeling that something very important was being ignored or misunderstood, but always before it had caused her to worry about herself, or to be scared for herself. The feeling came again, but it made her worried about Jim and a little scared for him. It occurred to her for the first time that of the two of them he might be the more insecure and the more exposed. When the wind cooled the cabin and her body dried she pulled the bedclothes out from under Jim and covered them and moved closer to him, as if her being close might remove the vague threat and make things right for him.

===== **17** =====

The next morning began as many did, with Patsy kneeling on the bed reading Gibbon while Jim slept. He slept on his back and she occasionally gave him a fond glance. One of the nice things about him, she decided, was the little line of blond hair that ran down the middle of his stomach toward his groin.

There was a knock on the door and she jumped up, frightened. She had a feeling it was Sonny Shanks returning to the attack. But it was Boots—and Boots looking uncharacteristically wifely, with a scarf around her head and the Thunderbird stuffed full of dirty Levi's and shirts. "Let's go wash," she said. Patsy was in the mood. She put on an orange shift and quickly gathered up their dirty clothes. Jim awoke and peered sleepily at Boots over the covers and she laughed. "He's cute when he's sleepy," she said.

They drove to a laundrymat with egg-yellow washing machines and chattered while the clothes whirled. The laundrymat was crowded. Patsy sipped a Fresca and peered through her sunglasses at the flabby wives in pedal pushers that seemed to predominate. Children were continually dropping gum from the penny gum machine and squalling when it rolled unretrievably beneath the washers. There was a pile of coverless magazines, *Redbook, The Saturday Evening Post, U.S. News and World Report,* but she was not in a reading mood. A cowboy with his shirttail out sat across from them and sharpened his pocketknife on the heel of his boot. He had a sad, lonely-looking face.

"You look so pretty in whatever you wear," Boots said. "I just look like me in whatever *I* wear."

Patsy was flattered. She felt happy and bright, but Boots seemed slightly sunken and kept twirling her Coke in her hand.

"Won't you and Pete have to settle down sometime?" she asked. "You can't just go on rodeoing forever, can you?"

"I don't know," Boots said. "Sometimes I don't think we lead a very normal life. Do you and Jim go to bed together very often?"

"Sure, every night," Patsy said, but when Boots's face fell she realized something else had been implied.

"Oh, no," she said. "Not that often. It varies. Sometimes two or three weeks get by us."

Boots looked a little less downcast. "I'll be glad when I'm in my twenties," she said. "Being so young makes me blue."

"No shirts?" she asked, incredulous, when she saw that Patsy's laundry was all underwear and towels. She was holding a sodden gray work shirt in her hand.

"We launder them. Where would I iron? I couldn't iron even if I had a place. What do you do?"

"Iron on the drainboard. Pete would never let me get his laundered. It would be a waste of money and we never waste money except on beer."

When the laundry was done they had a quiet cup of coffee in a noisy cafe and parted at the motel feeling that they were almost friends.

When Patsy left, Jim got up, shaved hurriedly, and went over to Sonny Shanks's motel. Boots's visit was a godsend. Sonny had asked him to come over and he had been wondering if he would lie to Patsy when she asked him where he was going. She almost never asked him where he had been, so he wouldn't need to lie. Sonny was lounging on the bed in his undershorts drinking a beer. He had asked Jim over because he liked an audience and Jim was an excellent audience. Before the morning was over he had regaled Jim with a great many of his exploits, some involving bulls and horses, some involving women, but all starring himself.

Jim, in return, showed Sonny his rodeo pictures. There were pictures of bulls, horses, cowboys, cowgirls, riders getting dumped, Pete training Hercules, ropers with pigging strings in their mouths, bulging matrons in riding pants, Sno-cone vendors, piles of rigging, one picture of a mound of bullshit, one of some dogging steers trying to screw each other, several of bleachers strewn with trash, one of a drunken Indian passed out under a pickup—pictures of everything that could be photographed around a rodeo. The one Shanks liked best was a picture of himself. Jim had caught him sitting on the rear end of the hearse, one leg cocked up, one leg stretched out, his shirt unbuttoned and a can of beer in one hand. He was talking to a cowgirl who had happened by.

"They oughta put that one on a billboard," Sonny said cheerfully. "Sell a lot of beer."

Jim left feeling good about himself and friendly toward Sonny, but he was slightly annoyed with Patsy. She never liked anyone he found really interesting.

That evening, tired of the motel and indifferent to such movies as could be seen in Laramie, Patsy went to the rodeo. Peewee ate supper with them and offered to sit with her while Jim attended to his picture taking. They sat high up in the grandstand, where she could enjoy the Wyoming sky and look down at the horses milling in the arena. Peewee had a hopeless crush on her but handled it very well, restricting himself to an occasional worshipful glance. She was wearing her favorite gray dress and had a green sweater to put on when the evening grew too chill.

"Okay," she said. "You have to explain it all to me. This going on right now is the Grand Entry, right? Why do they have it?"

Peewee was nonplussed. It had never occurred to him to question the importance of the Grand Entry.

"Well, you wouldn't want to just start off without it," he said.

He explained gallantly through three events and then had to leave to go ride his saddle bronc. It was a big gray horse and to Patsy's dismay dumped him flat on his back ten steps in front of the chutes.

"What went wrong?" she asked when he had made his way back to her.

172

"Everything. All I did right was land to the side. Half the time I land underneath 'em."

Patsy eventually grew bored and they left the stands and wandered along the arena fence. The barrel racing was about to begin, and to Patsy's delight Boots was announced as the first rider. She had Peewee help her up on the fence so she could see better. Boots came out very fast. The first barrel was close to where Patsy sat and she saw that the look on Boots's face was very like the look she had when driving the T-bird, only more intense. The horse whipped around the barrel and headed directly across the arena toward the second barrel. There, while running almost at top speed, it seemed to Patsy, he fell suddenly and rolled completely over. "She overrun it," Peewee said. "That's twice I seen her do it." Boots and the horse were both hidden by a swirl of dust, but when the dust thinned it looked as if she had come through unhurt. She clung to the side of the saddle as the horse got to its feet, and several of the cowboys who had begun to run toward her stopped, supposing that she meant to finish the ride. The horse, confused, looked around at her, and when he did Boots let go her hold and dropped to the ground.

"What happened?" Patsy said.

"No telling. He rolled over with her, though."

Patsy jumped down into the arena. By the time she got to Boots more than a dozen cowboys had gathered around her, and Pete had arrived. A doctor had been summoned, and while he was bending over Boots, Jim joined Patsy on the edge of the crowd. An ambulance, its red light swirling, entered the arena slowly and came toward the crowd. Pete glanced up from talking to the doctor, saw Jim and Patsy, and motioned for them to come. He looked very discouraged.

"Is it bad?" Patsy asked.

"Busted hip, at least," Pete said. "The doc says we oughta take her to Cheyenne. I was wondering if you-all could go and stay with her till I get there. I can't come until the bull ridin's over."

They quickly agreed. Boots was unconscious. As they were closing the ambulance doors Patsy caught a glimpse of

Pete, looking very dejected, taking the reins of Boots's horse from some cowboy. Then they were speeding out of Laramie on the dark road to Cheyenne. The trip was as fast as the one they had made the night before with Sonny, and they were just as silent. Boots moaned from time to time but did not really regain consciousness until they were wheeling her into a bright hospital corridor in Cheyenne. Her face was tear-streaked and her mouth quivering with pain. Patsy stayed with her in the emergency room, holding her hand until the interns came and wheeled her away.

Then there was nothing she and Jim could do but sit in the waiting room and wait. They held hands and sat almost in silence for more than an hour, now and then shifting their dry fingers in each other's hands. Then Pete came in. His face was streaked with greasepaint, though he had made a hasty attempt to wipe it off. He had already seen Boots's doctor.

"Smashed up her hip and leg, and she's got a little concussion," he said. "Didn't break no ribs, by a miracle."

He seemed tired and white, and they scooted over to make room for him on the bench where they sat. He handed Jim the keys to the Thunderbird. "You two just as well go on back," he said. "I'll stay around tonight and tomorrow. Maybe one of you could come back and stay tomorrow night while I'm working. Hate to ask. Course she may not need nobody by then."

"Why should you hate to ask?" Patsy said. "Of course she'll need somebody. We should just get a motel room here. I'd as soon be in Cheyenne as in Laramie."

They stood up but didn't leave immediately. Patsy hated to go away and leave Pete looking so forlorn. "Look, we can stay with you tonight, if you want us to," she said, trying to get him to look up at her. He did, but his gaze scarcely registered.

"No, no use everybody being miserable," he said. "Just come late tomorrow afternoon."

When they left he walked with them down the corridor to a pay phone, to put in a call to Boots's parents, in Fort Worth.

"Aren't you tired of all this?" Patsy said, as they were driving back. Jim was quiet. He looked almost cheerful, and

174

it disturbed her. She carried other people's pain with her for hours, and it always disconcerted her to see that Jim didn't. Once out of sight of suffering, his mind simply negated it and he could act as if it didn't exist.

"I'm not tired of anything," he said. "The only thing I'm really tired of is you waiting for me to get tired of something. I do get a little tired of you not believing in me."

"Oh, for god's sake," she said. "I wasn't not believing in you. I meant rodeo. Haven't we followed cowboys around long enough watching them get hurt? I want to go back to Texas and have a baby."

"I was thinking I might go to graduate school this fall," he said.

"Were you?" She was quite surprised.

"I haven't decided anything. I knew if I brought it up you'd accuse me of giving up on photography too soon."

"I wasn't meaning to accuse you of anything," Patsy said. "Please don't be so defensive." They fell silent again, and she felt very depressed.

The next morning she awoke before Jim and went down the street to a drab linoleum-floored cafe for breakfast. There was an item on the front page of the morning paper that chilled her so much that she couldn't eat. Two rodeo cowboys had beaten an elderly man almost to death, and all by mistake. One of them fancied his girl friend was sleeping around and he and a friend had gotten drunk and gone to the girl's house. Her father, whom they had never seen, answered the door, and the cowboys concluded he was the lover and hit him with their fists and a beer bottle and left him on his own living-room floor with a fractured skull. The cowboys' pictures were in the paper—she had the immediate irrational conviction that they were the same two men who had beaten Jim. She had ordered toast and coffee and a glass of milk, but except for a sip of milk she left the breakfast untouched and hurried back to the motel, very upset. She woke Jim and insisted that he look at the paper.

"Are those the men who beat you?" she asked.

At first Jim could make no sense of what she was saying, but when he did he shook his head. "Those aren't the guys," he said. "The ones that hit me were down in Texas."

"I know, I know," she said. "So were we then. That makes it even worse. It's not just two especially dangerous cowboys, it's some sort of insane violence this life seems to breed. I hate it. I won't stay around it any longer. We're going back to Houston."

She was sitting by him on the bed, looking so serious that he wanted to smile, though he knew there would be hell to pay if he did. Stories of violence seldom really touched him, and being awakened and given an ultimatum made him feel stubborn.

"We'll go in good time," he said.

"I knew you'd say that. I say we go now. It's insane to run the risk of some nut cracking our skulls with a beer bottle just because he feels like it. Shanks could do that sort of thing and you know it."

"You're paranoid about Sonny," he said, rubbing his eyes. "Just because he scared you once doesn't mean he's insane."

"Oh, Jim, why do you want to argue about something obvious?" she said.

"I don't. I was enjoying being asleep. I just don't like you waking me up and giving me blanket orders."

"I don't like being scared all the time for no good reason."

"You're not scared all the time. Besides, there are risks everywhere."

"Please don't generalize like that," she said, very annoyed. "I'm not general. I'm your own particular individual wife and I want to go home. That's not unreasonable."

"No, except we can't just go this instant, today."

"I could," Patsy said. She got off the bed and went to the dresser. "I could be ready in thirty minutes."

"You're always hasty." He peered at their traveling clock and lay back down.

"You're always inconsiderate," she replied. She was nervously twisting the ends of her hair. "I think I'll leave you. Then you can say the whole thing's been hasty. I seduced you hastily, I married you hastily, I was a very hasty wife generally and it would be perfectly in character if I left you hastily."

"*I* seduced *you*," Jim said with a yawn. "Don't try to make out that you were a bohemian. You were a prude."

"I wasn't all the time," she said. "I think I will leave you. I don't care which of us seduced the other, it hasn't worked out very well. We have nothing mutual any more except our ability to argue."

Jim decided to go back to sleep and ignore her until her mood changed, but he was a little too wide awake and he noticed after a while that she had changed into a dress and was combing her hair and actually making as if she might leave.

"Patsy," he said worriedly, sitting up.

She was tugging a comb through her hair, her teeth set. She didn't reply.

"Now calm down," he said. "I'm sorry. You can't leave." His tone was not entirely steady.

"Oh, go back to sleep," she said. "I know it. I'm too weak. I'm just going over to Cheyenne to see if there's anything I can do for Boots and Pete. I meant all that other, though. I really want to go back to Texas soon."

"We will," Jim said, relieved.

"You can have the Ford," she said, digging in the pocket of his pants for the keys to the Thunderbird. Jim held out his hand, hoping she would sit on the bed and be friendly a minute and kiss him, but she ignored it and went out the door holding a purse and her green sweater. She looked as if she would not be in a kissing mood for quite some time.

Patsy enjoyed driving the Thunderbird. When she was in high school she had begged her parents to let her get a Jag or a Porsche or even an MG for her first car, but they had refused, and while they were considering what sort of first car she should have, her Aunt Dixie had come to her rescue and given her a Corvette with white leather seats. The Thunderbird reminded her of the Corvette, and she sped across the brown sparsely grassed plains, remembering Dallas and high school and one or two of the boys who had been twice as eager to date her once she got the Corvette. One night while drunk her father borrowed the car and wrecked it completely while on his way to a U-Totem to buy some shaving cream. Neither he nor her mother had ever forgiven her Aunt Dixie for giving it to her in the first place.

She found Pete Tatum asleep on a couch in the waiting

room. He looked mussed, unshaven, and uncomfortable. She hated to wake him, but when she spoke he woke easily and seemed glad to see her.

"Pleasant surprise," he said. "Hope you brought a razor."

Patsy hadn't and was chagrined at her own complete impracticality. She offered to run out and get one but Pete wanted her to go with him to the ward to see Boots.

"Gosh, aren't wards awful?" she said. "Couldn't she have had a private room?"

Pete looked puzzled. "Best we could afford," he said. Patsy was embarrassed. She felt nervous and distressed, and in the light of morning the whole hospital seemed squalid. Boots had apparently had no nightgown and was dressed in a gray hospital gown. In the bed she looked smaller than she normally did, and younger. The contrast between her age and Pete's showed more. With no makeup, her lips pale, her hair short, she could have been in her early teens. The old lady in the next bed had on a bright pink bathrobe and looked at them inquisitively, as if she was trying to decide who was married to whom. She was too timid to ask, but her glances made Patsy uneasy, anyway.

"Pore darlin'," the old woman said. "She looks feverish. They just give her a shot." Pete felt Boots's forehead and smoothed back her hair, but she rolled her head from side to side, as if his touch made her hot. Patsy had no idea what to do, and when Pete looked at her again she realized he felt as helpless as she did.

"Let's go buy you a razor," she said. He asked the old woman to tell Boots they had gone to eat, if she awakened, and then quickly followed Patsy into the hall, as glad to get out of the ward as she was.

It was a cloudy day, with now and then a clear patch of pale blue sky showing through the clouds. The wind was blowing—Patsy's hair blew and blew and grew tangled. They drove to a drugstore and Pete bought a razor and some shaving cream. Patsy sat in the Thunderbird huddled over her knees while he went into the rest room of a Texaco filling station and shaved. When he came out his face looked clean and pleasant and healthy, in contrast to the dirty overalls and wrinkled shirt. He had nicked himself a little. They went to a restaurant on the highway and Pete ate what seemed to her an enormous unstomachable meal. Her own stomach had closed up nervously—she subsisted all day on Cokes.

"How can you eat?" she asked, watching him eat a breakfast steak. He had even put ketchup on it, which repelled her a little.

"One of the few things I can always do," he said, smiling at her comfortably.

A little later, back at the hospital, their hands brushed as they were going through a door and Patsy felt oddly embarrassed by the accidental touch. Boots was sleeping calmly, and as they had nothing to do but wait they decided to wait in the town rather than at the hospital. They drove to Frontier Park and sat at the curb in the car, talking and watching three mothers and their children. The park was brown and rather bare, and, as the day was so windy, Patsy didn't feel like getting out. She had the green sweater over her shoulders. She told Pete about the cowboys beating up the old man and he asked what their names were. She couldn't remember.

"Rummel?" he said. "Ed Rummel?"

"That's it. He was one of them."

"He told me she was two-timin' him," Pete said, looking at the women in the park. "I know her. She's a sorry little hussy."

Patsy was quite disturbed, first by the way in which he seemed to take the blame from the man and put it on the woman, but even more disturbed by his casualness in regard to the violence. It put a distance between them, gave her the feeling she had had about him before. They were not the same kind of people, and it was inappropriate, her being in the car with him.

"Oh, Pete," she said, "even so. You don't go beating old men with beer bottles, however bad she was. Even if he had been her boy friend that wouldn't be the thing to do. If his girl friend was so worthless he could have tried to get one who wasn't."

Pete saw that she was annoyed, but his mind was not really on what had happened in Laramie. "Well, that's true too," he said. "Ed Rummel just ain't that smart, or that nice, either. He's a mean bastard when he's drunk. I never

179

meant to take up for him. So far as I'm concerned he deserves whatever he gets."

A trash truck was moving slowly through the park, with an Indian in a red baseball cap standing on the back end. From time to time he hopped down and emptied one of the many trash barrels into the truck. Pete looked tired and solemn and Patsy ceased being annoyed with him. She could not stay annoyed with him for something that he had not done—it merely puzzled her that he would choose a life in which such things happened often. Probably they happened so often that he had become indifferent to them, and yet he didn't seem like a man who would be indifferent to such things. He looked worried and melancholy, probably because Boots was hurt. Patsy was not worried, exactly, but she felt lonely and very out of place. A park in Wyoming had nothing to do with her. She grew suddenly wistful for familiar places and familiar people, and regretted being ugly to Jim. He was familiar, and he had not been ugly to her at all. He had merely been sleepy.

She had her back against the car door and her arm across the top of her seat. Pete looked at her solemnly, and she expected him to say something else about the beating. Instead, he lifted one of his hands and put it on one of hers. The touch shocked her, and the shock did not stop with her hand but went through her. Her legs felt it, and her chest. "Oh, don't," she said. He smiled his quick wry smile but left his hand on hers. It was rough, much larger than Jim's hand, and very much larger than hers. Her protest had sounded thin and strange and she didn't repeat it. They looked at the windy playground and said nothing. For a minute the silence was very uncomfortable to Patsy, but then it ceased to be. The shock had diminished and it did not seem likely that the sky was going to fall. Because it was more comfortable she let her fingers entwine a little with his. He had not been offensive but had merely taken her hand, and it was restful enough to sit holding hands. The little ridge of sandy hair at the back of his neck was curly and led down into the rumpled collar of his blue denim work shirt. After the first agitation of the touch subsided a bit she saw that she had nothing to fear from Pete. He didn't want to kiss her, he didn't want to talk, he merely wanted to sit and hold her hand and watch the trash truck circle about the park. That was all right—it was even pleasant. Every time she had been with him she had tried talking and had ended up feeling shallow and frivolous. He had shocked her into silence, and once the shock diminished she felt more comfortable with him than she ever had when she had been trying to talk.

"Sure would have been a miserable day if you hadn't come over," he said, smiling tiredly, and Patsy felt even more at ease. He was really more worried and more worn down than he would have admitted, and it was flattering that such a strong man needed her, even if a crisis had produced the need.

She felt a sense of relief and with it a lightening of mood. The whole day had been strange, but she had suddenly begun once again to feel like her normal self. She felt quite friendly toward Pete, but at the same time she didn't want to sit by the curb holding hands with him all morning. She straightened up and disengaged her fingers.

"Let's go to a store," she said.

"What kind of store?"

"A ladies' store. I want to buy Boots a nightgown. She shouldn't have to wear those pajamas."

They went to one, and after some brooding Patsy bought a gown. She started to get a modest blue one, but decided Boots needed more cheer and finally bought a wilder yellow gown. Pete stood by uncomfortably, feeling badly dressed and awkward. They were in a large department store, and as they were passing the men's shirts Patsy stopped and asked him his shirt size. She picked out a nice red shirt.

"I'm buying you this," she said a little imperiously. "You'd look so nice in red."

He started to protest but she walked off to the counter and paid for her purchases, amazed at her own daring. She seldom bought shirts for Jim. When the package was ready she gave it to Pete to carry.

"Let's drive a little," he said when they were back in the car. He drove out the road toward Denver, and after eight or ten miles turned and drove back to Cheyenne. As they were coming into town he noticed a two-minute carwash and wheeled into it on impulse.

"Roll up your window," he said. "Boots ain't had this car

washed since we left Texas. We might as well freshen it up a little."

"I've never been in one of these," Patsy said, delighted. She had often meant to take the Ford through a two-minute carwash, just to see what it was like. They drove the car onto a kind of track, Pete put fifty cents into a coin slot, and they rolled up their windows as tightly as possible. After the breezy morning the car immediately seemed a little hot and close. Patsy took out a comb and began to comb her hair. Soon the washing mechanism started and moved them under a rectangular system of pipes. The pipes spurted very suddenly and a cascade of water broke over the car. The world vanished as suddenly as if they had driven under a waterfall. Water roared against the roof and sheet after wavering sheet streamed down the windows and the windshield.

"What a way to get a car washed," Patsy said. She glanced at Pete and caught him looking at her and was very startled, for there was no mistaking what was in the look. Hunger was in it. Outside, she might not have noticed it, or might have ignored it, but they were not outside. The pouring water hid them from the world, and hid the world from them, and it was very different from sitting by the windy park, with mothers following their children around a few yards away. The constant pulse of the water over the car was the only sound, and it made a disturbing background to the silence between them. It was not a pleasant silence—it was too charged with what Pete wanted, which could not have been more obvious if he had leaned over and kissed her or put his hand on her body. It had been only a minute since the track had carried them under the water, and in less than another minute they would be out again, into the air and the wind, but for Patsy it was a long and dreadfully complicated two minutes. She clutched her comb and tried not to look flustered, but the water kept pouring steadily over the car, and Pete was there, a foot away, and she *was* flustered. She looked at her hands. The silence was so uncomfortable and the tension between them so unexpected and so intense that it held her suspended, mute and uncertain. She almost wished he would lean forward and kiss her if he wanted to so much. At least it would be a movement that might break the tension. But Pete looked away from her face and soon the Thunderbird rolled off the track, the sound of the water died, and the world came into view again through the streaming windshield. The stream thinned to rivulets. Patsy put her hands on her temples for a moment and then began to comb her hair back. She was flushed and very agitated.

"Well, it's cleaner than it was," Pete said.

The fact that he drawled irritated her suddenly, and she was barely able to keep herself from saying something biting. Soon they were driving back through Cheyenne, the windows open, the wind cool. But Patsy felt very far from cool. Her emotions swirled: she felt foolish, she felt offended and angry, she felt bitchy, and yet she also felt apologetic and almost contrite. She didn't know what was wrong, but the more confused she felt the more determined she was to be casual. She chattered inconsequentially and even began to talk about Niagara Falls, where she had not been since she was eight years old. But her own talk rang thin in her ear and she was very glad when they got to the hospital.

Boots was awake, or half awake, and was pathetically glad to see them. She cried over the yellow nightgown and Patsy found herself crying too. Boots's gratitude made her feel guilty, and she avoided looking at Pete. The fact that they had held hands a few minutes seemed like a sordid secret, and she was glad when he left for Laramie. Boots drowsed and woke and drowsed and woke, and the afternoon passed as slowly as a season. When Boots talked it was generally of Pete, of how good he was to her and how much she wished her parents liked him better. Patsy scarcely listened. She felt a stranger to Boots, a stranger to Pete, and only wished she could leave the depressing hospital and the town and go back to her own motel and her own husband. She told herself again and again that practically nothing had passed between her and Pete, and that there was no reason for her to feel guilty and depressed about it. What little had happened had been the result of some accident of mood and meant nothing. But she continued to feel guilty and restless and depressed. About dusk, Boots went soundly to sleep and Patsy walked into the hall to get a Coke. She was wondering if she could risk a walk outside the hospital when Jim came into the corridor. He was fresh and cheerful and looked very glad to see her.

"Hi," he said. "I thought I'd come sit with you. I'm sorry I was so grouchy this morning. I don't think I was very wide awake."

He seemed all sane and familiar, and everything else seemed insane and unfamiliar, but nevertheless his sudden appearance only put her the more on edge. She felt taken by surprise. Jim was alert and saw at once that she was nervous about something, and he had the good sense not to push. "Would you like to go out and eat?" he asked.

"That's just what I'd like," she said. "I'm sick of this hospital."

In the Ford he said, "Something's settled."

"What?" She had not been paying him much attention, but when she looked she noticed that he seemed unusually cheerful.

"We can start back to Texas tomorrow," he said. "I'm really tired of all this too."

"Good," she said, not very surprised. "Let's go to a drive-in. I feel like a milkshake."

The clouds had finally cleared away and they watched the last of a long afterglow as they sat at the drive-in. "Should we stay a few more days to help Boots and Pete?" Jim asked.

Patsy's milkshake was so thick it clogged the straw. She ate it in globs, using the straw as a spoon. "Hum?" she asked. "Sorry. Hospitals make me so abstracted I can hardly listen. I'm really glad we're going." He repeated what he had said and she frowned. "I don't think we're needed," she said. "Her folks are coming."

Boots said the same thing when they told her they were going. She was glad to see Jim. He knew how to joke with her and they joked and chatted and again Patsy felt out of place. She was not bothered, but neither was she happy— she felt tired and out of reach of everyone. Pete came in, straight from work, smelling of animals and sweat. He thanked them for staying and walked with them to the Ford, chatting with Jim about routes.

Patsy avoided looking at him, as she had ever since they had left the carwash. He thanked her gratefully and gave her an awkward conventional pat on the shoulder as she was about to get in the car, but she looked away from him and responded just as conventionally to his thanks. It was only as Jim was backing the Ford out of the parking place that she looked at Pete. He was standing on the sidewalk slouching, his hands in his hip pockets, and he seemed very alone. His face was in shadow and she couldn't see it, but the way he was standing touched her. Something made her want to cry. She put her hand out the window to wave, and then on impulse put her fingers to her mouth and threw him a kiss. He turned away just as she did it and she never knew whether he noticed or not; but she felt much better for having acted on the impulse, even though Jim noticed and was disturbed.

"What in the world?" he said. "I never saw you throw anyone a kiss before."

"I'm different now," she said. "Perhaps I'll throw many people kisses."

"What will Pete think?"

"I don't know. He just looked so lonesome." She wiped her tears away covertly, with her knuckles.

Later that night Jim packed his photographic files. While he was in the bathroom Patsy poked among them and found a picture of Pete, one taken in Phoenix by the pool when he had been wearing the snipped-off Levi's for a bathing suit. She looked at it guiltily and thoughtfully and slipped it back in its envelope, wondering what might have become of her and of them all if the man in the picture had kissed her that afternoon when he had wanted to.

=== 18 ===

On impulse, they started south that night. Jim had slept most of the day and wasn't sleepy, and Patsy, though tired, felt so strangely wakeful that she could not imagine ever sleeping. She had looked forward to getting back to the motel, but once there she felt restless, and when Jim proposed that they start she agreed.

They had to go back through Cheyenne, which struck them both as a little absurd. For days, it seemed, they had done practically nothing but drive between Cheyenne and Laramie. They rode in silence. When they came in sight of Cheyenne Patsy began to fight an impulse to ask Jim to stop. She thought it would be nice to call Pete and say something, though she didn't know what. She was sure he would like for her to call.

But Jim had gassed the car in Laramie and had no reason to stop. He was humming hillbilly songs, a habit he had picked up. They passed quickly through Cheyenne, and Patsy felt sad. She tried to think of an excuse to stop, but even if she could have thought of one she would then have had to think of an excuse to call; and if she had called she would have had to think of something to say. But she really had nothing to say, to Pete Tatum or to Jim, and nothing to give, either, it seemed to her. She felt timid and ordinary and cowardly and contrary, and said nothing about stopping.

"Denver next," Jim said. The lights of Cheyenne were behind them. Soon they crossed a ridge and there was only darkness behind them.

"This is like in *On the Road,*" Patsy said. "All we've done is circle around. We are all a beat generation, I guess."

"I'm glad I married someone literary," Jim said.

"I'm glad I married someone who hums hillbilly music," she replied, stung a little by his tone. She regretted not calling Pete and woke up still regretting it several hours later in Pueblo, Colorado. Jim had covered her with a blanket and was not in the car. The Ford was parked in front of a diner with a neon campfire on top. Patsy was hungry but she also felt rumpled and strange and didn't want to go in. She lay with her head on her pillow, covered by a yellow blanket.

"What's the matter?" Jim asked when he came out. "You look sad."

"Nothing's the matter. I wish I'd called Pete when we came back through Cheyenne. It's miserable in that hospital."

"We could make Uncle Roger's by tonight. Want to stop there a day or two?"

"Sure," she said. "I like him."

By dawn they were almost below the Rockies. They stopped in Trinidad and Patsy had some milk and doughnuts and walked around a block while Jim was getting gas. It was cold and the tops of the mountains were still in cloud. When they went over Raton Pass Jim stopped and insisted they take a sky ride. The ride had just opened—the man who ran it could scarcely believe anyone really wanted to ride that early. It was so cold that Patsy had to rummage in her clothes for a pair of Levi's and a heavy sweater, but when she got out, the keen air picked her up and she ceased feeling melancholy. The sky ride took them hundreds of feet above a green canyon. Patsy became afraid and gripped Jim's hand tightly. When they got safely to the top she spent a half-hour looking through telescopes at snow-covered mountains, some of which were almost a hundred miles away. The telescope brought the mountains very close. They were snowy and golden with the morning sun and the sight of them thrilled Patsy to the core. She would have liked to stand in the keen air all morning looking at the beautifully colored mountains, but the telescopes worked on quarters and Jim refused to let her spend but a dollar and a half.

Riding back down, the cable car dipped over the face of a cliff, and she felt scared again. She could see, very far away and small and white-tipped, a peak that had been close and golden through the telescope. She watched the mountain until the cable car was low enough that she could look down at the trees beneath her without being afraid.

They descended the pass, went through Raton, and spent the day riding across the long rolling plain that extends from the foot of the Rockies almost to the Brazos River. Patsy finished Gibbon as they were going through Dalhart, Texas. She had been saving part of Volume III for just such a plain. Jim was very impressed. He had always meant to read long books himself, but except for *Middlemarch* he had never read any. He had been forced to read *Middlemarch* but had liked it well enough that he convinced himself he would have read it even without being forced.

"Well, that's that," Patsy said, yawning and looking out at Dalhart with quiet amazement. It amazed her to come upon towns in unlikely places. "Could we make a rest-room stop, please?"

"We just made one in Clayton."

"I know." She looked at the Gibbon affectionately and pitched it in the box of books. The box of books had long since overflowed onto the rear floorboards. "I think I'm getting a bladder infection."

"Obsession, I'd say."

"Anyway, I feel like peeing."

There was an old paintless grocery store across the street from the filling station where they stopped. It had a Nehi Orange sign on one wall and Jim went over and took a picture of it.

"Vanishing Americana," he said, returning to the car. "Have you?"

"Hum?" She settled against her pillow for a nap. Dust was blowing across the street, and the cars in the filling station were all dusty.

"Have you got a bladder infection?"

"Possibly. Drive on, please. I don't like to be stopped in dusty places."

"Remember that time you peed in the supermarket?"

"That was excusable. My doctor said all newlyweds do that."

"Newlyweds? We weren't even married."

"We were newly sinful. Can't you think of anything to talk about except my little urinary lapses?"

"What are you going to read now that you've finished Gibbon?"

"Magazines," she said.

"Read another long book."

"It would be strange, being Boots and Pete," she said apropos of nothing.

In Childress they had a flat. While it was being fixed Patsy walked around the town. There was an ancient railroad hotel where, as she imagined it, old-timey salesmen with garters on their sleeves sat and drank whiskey at night. It was long after dark when they got to the ranch. They had called Roger from Childress, and when he heard the car cross the cattle guard he came out with a flashlight. He was standing by the back gate when they stopped. Patsy was asleep. Jim shook her awake and she collected her pillow and purse and got out. She almost bumped into Roger, dropped her pillow trying to hug him, picked it up, and wove toward the house without a word.

"Ain't she woke up, all this time?" Roger asked. He shined his flashlight over the Ford, as if dubious that the vehicle they had left in could really have brought them back. The crickets were singing and the windmill creaked in the darkness above their heads. Jim could faintly see the white shapes of chickens roosting on the fence of the chicken yard.

A hailstorm had been prophesied, so Roger said, and at his suggestion Jim took the Ford and parked it in the hallway of the barn. The night was breezy. Roger was waiting for him in the kitchen, as brown, as thin, and as quiet as when they left.

Jim drank some milk and chatted with him for a few minutes. When he got upstairs he found that Patsy had flopped down on top of the bedclothes fully dressed. His calves were stiff and sore, but otherwise he felt almost fresh. Assuming that Patsy was sound asleep, he began to remove her clothes. He went about it deftly, but she was not really asleep. When he unzipped her shorts and yanked them down her legs she sat up.

"Are you a rapist?" she asked.

"No. Why?"

"I was going to ask you to turn me on my back if you were," she said, giggling a little. She felt lightheaded and strangely giggly. "I won't be had irregularly," she added. Jim scratched her leg with his fingernail getting the shorts off, and she kicked at him angrily.

"Sit up and take your blouse off," he said. "Where are the toothbrushes, since you're awake?"

"Don't ask ordinary questions," she said. "I prefer the fantasy that you're a rapist. You're such a timid one."

She sat up and took one arm out of her blouse, then leaned on the arm and smiled at Jim sleepily. Gusts of wind were rattling the windowpanes.

"What about the toothbrushes?"

"I may have been masturbating with them," she said, giggling. "It's very hard to remember." With a great effort she sat up, flung off her blouse and reached back to unhook her bra. Then she flopped on her stomach and went unwakably to sleep. Jim gargled a little salt water in lieu of brushing his teeth. He opened the window. The air smelled of rain. During the night the wind blew strands of Patsy's hair against his cheek.

Jim slept most of the next day and Patsy lay in bed with him, idling, reading through copies of a magazine called *The Cattleman*. Aside from the *Reader's Digest* it was the only magazine in the house. She washed her hair and filed her nails and discovered that she did have a mild bladder infection. It was a very hot day—the wind had the breath of August. It blew in their window from the south and the sheets of their bed grew as hot as if they had come from a dryer at a laundrymat. Jim lay in sweat. Patsy hunted up a little electric fan and set it near the bed. It didn't cool, but it made a kind of crosscurrent. Roger Wagonner was nowhere to be seen. When she tired of reading about ways in which brush could be combated and cattle made to gain more pounds per day she began *Love among the Cannibals*, which she had bought the evening before in a drugstore in Childress.

Later, well past the middle of the afternoon, Roger rattled up to the house in his old pickup, a brindle cow in the back end. He came into the house for a drink of water and Patsy went down to greet him, wearing a shift. His gray shirt was soaked with sweat.

He bent and kissed her on the cheek, his smell with him. Skin that was outdoors a lot seemed to smell different than skin that wasn't.

"Kind of orange, ain't it?" he said, meaning the shift. "I got a cow with a high fever. I thought you and Jim might want to ride in with me to take her to the vet."

"Jim might. He just got up. I've ridden all I want to for a while."

Jim did. He came down wearing Levi's and a blue shirt and made a peanut butter sandwich to take with him. Patsy noticed that the peanut butter was exactly at the same level she had left it weeks before.

She walked outside with them and leaned on the back fence looking at the cow. It was an old thin cow, with a black spot around one eye and two darkened twisted horns that looked like they might have grown into spirals if they had not been blunted. From time to time she bawled loudly and made awkward attempts to turn around in the narrow pickup. A string of slobber hung from her chin and her eyes rolled wildly, as if they saw another place. The bed of the pickup was already slick with green droppings.

"Poor thing," Patsy said. "What's wrong with her?"

"Not sure," Roger said. As he spoke the cow began to sway. Her front legs buckled and she sank forward onto her knees. Roger jumped to the cab, grabbed a long walking stick, and began to jab it roughly between the sides of the pickup, into the cow's ribs.

"Here," he said. "You can't lie down. Get up there! Get on back on your feet!"

And he continued to jab at the cow with the walking stick, poking her just behind the legs and poking her hard. Patsy was horrified. He had always seemed so gentle. The cow grunted every time the stick poked her, and then she began to bawl. It was an awful sound. Finally, desperate to escape the stick, she got her back feet under her and rose and whirled toward the cab of the pickup, hanging one horn on a sideboard as she turned. The horn came loose and the cow slipped in her own drippings but managed to stay on her feet, her flanks quivering.

"Poor *thing*," Patsy said, quivering herself. "Why do that to her?"

Roger removed his hat and wiped the sweat off his forehead. "A little rough," he said, noticing that Patsy was distressed, "but if I'd let her stay down she would have died. As long as she's up she's got a chance."

"But why can't she die, if she's dying?"

"Well, she's got a calf to raise, and she might be savable. If she wants to die bad enough, she'll die." He got a rope and after much soothing talk, much hanging over the sideboards, he managed to get the rope around the cow's horns. He tied her head as high as he could, so that her eyes were looking over the cab at the sky.

"Let's go," he said to Jim. "The sooner we get there the better."

When they left, Patsy wandered through the house for a while. Most of the upstairs light bulbs were burnt out and she could find none to replace them with, but she decided that the faded floral wallpaper looked better in dimness. About sundown she made herself a jelly sandwich with some plum preserves that seemed homemade—perhaps a present from some neighbor's wife—and had a glass of thin, slightly weedy milk. The milk seemed almost bluish. She went out and sat in an old glider on the front porch and swung herself gently and ate the sandwich as she watched the lovely late summer dusk descend. With the sun so low, the south breeze was more pleasant, though still warm as breath. Very soon after sundown a few clear stars appeared. The phone rang, a sound very different in the stillness than the sound of a city phone. Jim told her they would be late, perhaps another hour or so. She went back out and sat on the steps, and Bob, the old dog, lumpy and deferential, came and lay at her feet. He stared at her, his tongue hanging out from the heat. Occasionally he licked her hand.

The country was quiet in the early evening, so very quiet that Patsy found it scared her a little. It was like the too-quiet part of a Western movie, the part just before an ambush. As she watched the darkening range she managed to frighten herself with the absurd fantasy that she was a pioneer woman, her menfolks gone for some reason. She was absolutely alone in the vast still country, about to be leapt at by Indians bent on rape and pillage. She rubbed Bob's head and tried to dismiss the fantasy but could not help thinking how scary it must have been for real pioneer women. She turned up the collar of her thin blouse. Who could be sure there wasn't someone unfriendly around. Sonny Shanks, perhaps. It would be just like him to turn up at such a time. He might be lurking in the smokehouse, a little shack she had peeked in once. It was full of spiderwebs and empty boxes—nothing had been smoked there for a very long time. At her feet, Bob had fallen asleep, obviously no very trustworthy watchdog.

Thinking of Shanks reminded her of Boots and Pete. She ought to have bought Boots a decent robe to go with the yellow gown. If she was going to hold hands with her husband she owed her at least that much. But the store had not had any good robes. Pete's hand had been callused on the palm and had a rough scab on one finger. It seemed to her a pity he did not know how to talk, for if they could have talked, their vaguely sympathetic feeling for each other might have grown or shrunk or somehow taken shape. As it was, it had remained formless. It had been a kind of scent, and it seemed very unlikely she would ever smell that scent again. Her mind drifted and the breeze cooled as the upper sky darkened. Noises began: the whinnying of horses some distance away, a few crickets, the creak of the windmill.

She was relieved, when an hour had passed, to see car lights moving her way over the dirt road that ran to the house. It was the men, and her mood turned at once. It was so good to have men coming home. She hurried around the house, the dry short summer grass pricking at her bare feet. The windmill had been turning and water was sloshing out of the storage tank and dripping off the edges of the watershed with a cooling sound.

Patsy asked about the cow. "Lost cause," Roger said. "We took her to the hide-and-rendering plant. Let's eat something before we all starve."

He got out some thin steaks and fried them as hard as he had fried the eggs. He fried some potatoes too while Patsy made iced tea. Jim and Roger ate the steaks and Patsy drank some iced tea and nibbled at a French fry. Roger looked at her with concern.

"Stop that," she said. "I had a sandwich already. I'm supposed to be slim. Besides, this heat makes me sluggish as a reptile."

"I killed a reptile today that wasn't so sluggish," he said. "Nine rattles."

After the meal they went out and sat on the porch until almost ten enjoying the evening. Roger told them stories of his dead wife, Rosemary. He and Jim sat in rope-bottomed chairs tilted back against the wall of the house, and Patsy sat on the lower step.

Chuckling, he told them about the Bible argument that had been their nightly staple for thirty-five years.

"We never could get together on salvation," he said, "nor sin either. Six nights out of seven we'd get into it over one or the other. Thirty-five years that went on. After the first year or two I doubt we really listened to one another, but we got hot about it, listening or not. One night I got so mad I took off around the house and walked into a clothesline pole. Knocked myself flat. Mary thought it served me right." He paused a minute to light a cigarette.

"The first time I ever really gave Mary's side of the argument much thought was a night or two after her funeral. I was sitting out here all primed to argue and there wasn't nobody to argue with. Since then I've been kinda making up her part. In a way it's even better than having her here. I always win the argument and there ain't no way she can get revenge on me at the breakfast table.

"I got to admit the quality of the biscuits has declined, though," he added quietly.

He went on and told other stories, anecdotes about wounds and arguments, dances, frights, misunderstandings and exploding pressure cookers—selecting for them a kind of anthology of scenes from his decades of married life.

After a while it seemed to Patsy that he was delivering an elegy, probably the only one he ever spoke. His voice was calm and quite firm, as if its tone had long ago been purified by whatever disappointment, loneliness, or grief he had felt in that place, on that high-roofed old porch, alone with the night breeze and the dark pastures round.

Listening hurt Patsy more than the telling hurt Roger. A woman whose name was Rosemary had been alive and was dead—had sat where she sat and was gone. The old man sitting behind her had lived with the woman for almost forty years, had courted her, eaten her food, sat on that same porch with her thousands of nights, had fought with her, taken her places, made love to her. It was hard for her to imagine the people of older generations making love, but she knew they must have. And then one day without knowing it they did that act and each common act for the last time, rose from bed a last time, went to the morning's toilet, ate, spoke, rode the roads they had known, left their friends without being aware that they were leaving them, argued for the last time, touched for the last time, and, for the last time, were thrilled or hurt. Thinking about it, Patsy was wrenched with sadness, and she bent her head and put her face into the skirt of her dress and cried. She was very quiet about it and Roger went on talking and no one noticed that she was crying.

"Yeah, a lot happens in a lifetime," he said, as if he knew what she was thinking. "I roped an eagle once when I was a crazy young feller. I was batching out near Van Horn. Came riding out of a gully and there was an eagle eating a dead sheep. I had my rope off, sort of practicing, like a young feller will, and I shot the spurs to the old pony I was riding and caught the eagle when he was about four feet off the ground. You think that wasn't a may-lay. I finally threw my rope off and let him go, or me and the horse would have got clawed to death, I guess. It's a wonder he let us escape, anyway. Seen a lot of boys rope coyotes but I never heard of anybody else roping an eagle."

He stood up and yawned. "Speakin' of coyotes, you-all can stay up and listen to them if you want to. I'm going to bed."

He went in and they waited awhile and heard no coyotes

and Patsy stood up. "Let's go in," she said. It seemed to her that the porch belonged to other people. Jim was agreeable because he wanted to make love. The stories had left Patsy feeling tender and she wanted to too, but found out that she hurt. "Ooch," she said. Her breath sounded pained when Jim began to move.

"What?"

"I guess I do have a little infection."

But she wouldn't let him withdraw. She was only a little raw and they were not in disharmony. "Too bad for you," Jim said fondly, later. "You probably drink too many Cokes, or something."

After they were quiet they heard a long thin howl from far out in the pastures. "I think that's a coyote," Jim said. The howl came at intervals, like a call. Jim soon slept and Patsy got up and started a bath. She came back to the bedroom and sat by the window listening to the coyotes while it ran. She soaked herself and put on a gown, wishing she were in Houston and could see her gynecologist. Jim was extraordinarily nice to be with when he was asleep, she felt. He turned in the bed and made a sort of tropic shift toward her body. She reached down and straightened the tangled sheet and lay beside him on her stomach, wondering about Rosemary Wagonner.

The next morning, while Jim was loading the Ford and Roger attending to his cows and chickens, she sneaked into the other bedroom and looked at the picture of Rosemary that stood on the brown wooden bureau—an oval picture, apparently made in the twenties, of a young woman looking sideways, her hair drawn smoothly back. She wore a dark dress that seemed to match her hair. Her features were clean, her expression a little reserved, a little proud. The room she had lived in so long had a fireplace and a bed, a woodbox under the window, a closet, and a bureau with a small square mirror on top. There was no picture of Roger. On the wall was a calendar issued by a vaccine company. It showed a herd of steers watering at a river, with two cowboys on horses watching them.

Jim had not shaved, and while he was about it Patsy went out and sat on the stone storm cellar with Roger. A couple of speckled hens pecked in the bare dirt outside the yard gate.

"What's this about Jim goin' back to school?" Roger asked. "I thought he was done out."

"This would be graduate school. A simple B.A. isn't worth much any more."

Roger shook his head. "Folks in my day couldn't take school like you young folks can. You couldn't have got me to go back for love nor money, and I never even got out of grade school."

"I don't know how serious he is about it," Patsy said. "He's only been talking about it two weeks. It can't work out any worse than photography, as far as I'm concerned." The morning sun was already hot on the back of her neck and she could imagine how it was going to be when they got to Houston.

"Well, at least it would save wear and tear on tires," Roger said. "Might as well be optimistic."

Soon Jim came out and they all went to the car. "Do me a favor, please," Patsy said to Roger after kissing him on the cheek. "Come and see us sometime when you don't have ninety things to do. We've visited you twice—now it's your turn."

"Try to, first chance I get," he said. He took his hat off and ran his hand through his white hair and stood watching them as they drove away. Bob followed the Ford until it crossed the cattle guard and began to raise dust on the powdery road.

"I'll bet he never comes," Jim said. "He told me the other night that he hadn't been farther away than Fort Worth in fifteen years."

"But then he didn't have me to come and see," Patsy said. "I flirt with him and no one else does."

"How would you know?"

"A femme fatale always knows," she said archly. "You don't think I know how to flirt, do you?"

"Not if you pick my elderly uncle to flirt with."

"He's a lovely man," she said. "I like everything about him. Anyway, the beauty of my flirting is that it's whimsical. I flirted with Pete Tatum too."

"It doesn't seem to have driven him mad with desire," Jim said a little coldly. He had been troubled by the blown kiss. Also, he was in an intent driving mood and wished

Patsy would go to sleep so he could enjoy the country and the smooth almost trafficless road.

"I guess it didn't," Patsy said, wondering. She became solemn for a moment. "Though I don't know how you would know."

The road ran south, through a country of low hills. For a time the hills were grassy and lightly treed with mesquite, but then the mesquite gave way to stubby post oak. White thunderheads were blowing south too, small morning thunderheads as swift as birds almost. She looked with delight at the morning and wondered about Pete. He really *had* desired her, at least for a little while. It was strange that it should matter, but it had. He had seemed to notice something about her that no one else had noticed. She looked at Jim. He had been avoiding barbershops and his blond hair was the longest it had ever been. He was intent on driving and wasn't noticing her at all, and she had the feeling that he had never noticed whatever it was about her that Pete had noticed and wanted.

Then it slipped from her mind. It was pleasant to think about being in Houston. She could go for walks with Emma Horton, see real foreign movies again, read *Punch* in the Rice library, and have a baby and be settled. But when they had driven thirty miles in silence, Jim not once looking at her, she remembered Pete again. She was not annoyed with Jim exactly, but some feminine demon in her demanded its due. She smiled to herself and looked out the window.

"We even held hands once," she said, taking off her headband and letting her hair blow.

"With Pete?" Jim said, forgetting about the driving.

She nodded when he looked at her. She looked demure and clean and sweet, but her mouth was inscrutable and her eyes were hidden behind sunglasses.

"You're putting me on," he said.

"No. We held hands."

"Why, for god's sake? Did he make a pass at you or something?"

"No," she said sweetly. "I was just practicing flirting."

Jim felt very bothered, as much by Patsy's manner as by the fact that for some reason she had held hands with Pete Tatum. They had fought before and she had taunted him before, but never quite that way. She had always taunted him about his deficiencies, never about her possibilities. It made him feel awkward. He had a feeling he should just keep quiet, and he did keep quiet for a few miles. Patsy sat calmly, happy with the morning.

"When was this?" he asked finally.

"In Cheyenne, the day I was there."

"Oh," he said, relieved. He had been imagining some darker context. He looked at her again and remembered that, after all, she was not a femme fatale but just a lovely girl with a soft heart.

"Why do you say 'oh' in that superior way?" She lowered her sunglasses and looked at him severely over the rims.

"You were just being sympathetic," he said. "I know you. You want me to think you're a seductress or something. Actually you just enjoy comforting people."

"True. I do like to comfort people. There are all sorts of ways." She put her sunglasses back on and looked out at the low hills.

"I think I just did it to see how it felt," she added.

Jim let it rest, trying to imagine the scene. He was almost able to convince himself that her sympathetic nature accounted for it.

"I'm glad you picked him to practice on, if you had to practice," he said. "I can't think of anyone who's less your type."

Patsy didn't reply. The demon had had its due and she was not in a mood to needle her husband. She rolled her window partway up and fiddled contentedly with the ends of her hair. After a while she picked up *Love among the Cannibals*.

"I do like long books," she said. "With lots of short books strewn along the way. How many volumes is *The Golden Bough?*"

"A dozen or so."

"Let's get it," she said. "Could we? It might get me through my twenties."

Eleanor lay on her bed reading about Peru. The midsummer
sun turned the patio white and hot by seven in the morning,
and she normally spent her mornings in the long cool open
bedroom, reading and drinking iced tea with lots of lemon
in it. She had traveled a good deal in Central and South
America, but for some reason had never been to Peru. In
September she always traveled, September to November,
usually, and Peru seemed a possibility. For some reason she
liked the ranch best in the hard seasons, in July and August,
when the pastures shimmered and the cowboys were dark-
shirted with sweat at the end of the day. And she liked it too
in January and February, when everything was dry and bare
and gray-brown. Then northers sang around the barns and
thousands of geese fed in the wheatfields. In the spring and
in the fall she became restless, unable to be still, uninter-
ested in the ranch and the ranch work and money and Texas,
and she left. Lima had a lovely name.

The phone rang and she quietly picked up her receiver
and listened to Lucy, her private barricade.

"A mister who?"

"A Mr. Percy."

"Does Miss Guthrie know you?"

"What do you mean, know me? What kind of a question
is that? Of course she knows me. I'm her symbolic husband."

"Miss Guthrie ain't got no husbands, of no kind. What is
your business?"

"Never mind, Lucy," Eleanor said. "His business is foul,
but I'll talk to him."

There was an aggrieved silence from Lucy, and then she hung up.

"This is a surprise."

"I'm desperate," Joe Percy said. "I finally managed to weasel your phone number out of our cowboy friend. He's here with me, by the way."

"My phone number is no secret," she said. "Just call Texas, they'll put you right through. Why are you desperate? Where are you?"

"Ultima Thule," he said. "That's part of my desperation. I believe the name of the town is Boise. It's in Idaho."

"I've heard of it. How do you happen to be there?"

"I'm observing Sonny in his natural habitat. Last night he was apparently magnificent. Made an unheard-of score riding a bull. Very competent man. We're making a movie next summer after all and I've got to write it in the meantime."

"Why not this summer? There's plenty of it left."

"Not possible. Wheels don't turn that fast in L.A. these days."

"Is Boise fun?"

"For rabbits, maybe. If I could fuck rabbits it might be fun for me. I don't think there are five women in all Idaho."

"Must be nice for the five," Eleanor said. "Why did you call?"

"Partly because I miss you and mostly because I was coerced."

"I see. He wants to talk too, in other words."

"Precisely."

"He doesn't know about our symbolic marriage, I take it?"

"Nope. Wasn't listening. Want to come to Boise?"

"No. I was thinking of going to Lima soon. Know anybody there?"

"Not sure. Conceivably. You'll have to change planes in L.A., you know."

"Not if I go to Mexico first. I'm not at the stage of making plans. What does Sonny want?"

"He wants you to lease us a tiny corner of your ranch to make our film on. We're going to film in Texas. He doesn't think we'd be in the way much."

"He knows me better than that," Eleanor said. "That possibility is out, and that's final."

"Well, sorry," Joe said. "I didn't think it was such a good idea, anyway. I didn't mean to offend you."

"You didn't. You can get a location easily enough. All the small ranchers in the state are broke. Go to the Panhandle. You can lease all you want of it. But you can't come here."

"Would we corrupt the cowboys?"

"You certainly would. Is he awake?"

"It's hard to say. He's not in bed."

"I'd like to talk to him."

There was a pause as Joe Percy searched for words. "Okay," he said. "Nice speaking with you. Buzz me if you do pass through."

"You have a very appealing voice," she said. "I miss you."

Joe sighed. "I don't understand Texas women," he said.

"Sure you do."

"What do you do down there in your kingdom?"

"I read and I give orders."

"The opposite of me. I write and I take orders. We'd complement one another. I think Mr. Sonny Shanks, World's Champion Cowboy and soon to be the idol of millions of popcorn consumers, would like to talk to you."

"Okay. Call me when you don't have company. We can exchange tidbits of wisdom."

"I will."

There was a longer pause. "Mornin'," Sonny said. "How's the grassfire situation down in Texas?"

"Under control."

"Going to lease us some land?"

"Of course not."

"Joe's whistling. You must have been friendlier to him than you are to me."

"He's more polite than you are."

There was the sound of an ice cube being crunched. "Why not lease us some? Be good publicity. You could have your picture taken with me. We could get some rumors going again."

"No, thanks. My father would not have approved of his ranch being used as a movie set."

202

"The hell he wouldn't. He'd have taken the money and spent it on whiskey."

"I can afford all the whiskey I want."

Sonny was silent for several seconds. "Want to come to Denver next week?"

"Why?"

"Just to visit."

"I'm not in a traveling mood."

"Maybe I'll visit you. I always liked Texas in August. It's warm."

"You'd be welcome."

He chuckled. "I was wondering if you still love me," he said. "I've been wondering about that lately."

"Did I love you once?"

"You acted like it."

That was an understatement, Eleanor thought. "I'm not planning to leave before mid-September," she said. "Come any time. Are you winning much?"

"Yeah. Hurt my knee again in Laramie. My back hurts."

"I'll rub it for you," she said. "When do you think you might be coming?"

"Oh, maybe week after next."

"Drive carefully."

"Always do. Tell Lucy hi."

Eleanor hung up and lay on the bed on her stomach for a while, not thinking of Peru. After a time Lucy shuffled in frowning.

"Miss Eleanor, who was that man?"

"Sonny."

"No, ma'am. The one I talked to. What did he mean, your sym*bol*ic husband?"

"Nothing. He just meant we were good friends."

Lucy shuffled over to the patio and looked out at the white sky. "This weather's gonna melt me yet," she said. "They ain't got them cattle in. I thought they was gettin' some cattle in today."

"Maybe it melted the cattle," Eleanor said.

Lucy was still troubled. "A friend ain't no husband," she said. "No husband of no kind. You ain't gonna do nothing crazy, is you?" She had not forgotten the nightmare of Eleanor's marriage.

"Honey, you know me better than to ask that," Eleanor said. "Of course I'll do *something* crazy. I've always done crazy things. You're as much to blame as anyone. You raised me. But I'm not going to marry that particular man, if it will ease your mind."

"It sure does," Lucy said. "Eases my mind. He was jus' barely respectful."

"I think I'll swim a little. One of the most unpleasant men in Texas is coming this afternoon."

"Mr. Stob?"

"Mr. Stob."

"He ain't eatin' here, I hope."

"No. He's just buying cattle. We hope." She got up and dipped the lemon out of her iced-tea glass and sucked it. It was cold, and soft from the tea, but still tart.

"Sym*bol*ic husband," Lucy said. "I hope that man don't get in the habit of callin'. Me and him could have some fights, I see that."

"You'd love him," Eleanor said, slipping off her robe. "He thinks I'm beautiful and sweet and domestic. Men are easy to fool, aren't they?"

"You never fooled one yet," Lucy said, handing her the bathing suit. "Not while I was around, you ain't."

"Anyway, it will be nice to see Emma and Aunt Dixie," Patsy said. They had just passed through a town called Jacksboro, on the edge of which stood the abandoned drive-in movie theater where Jim had taken the picture of the marquee with HORS SHIT spelled on it. They had gotten a disgracefully late start, and it was close to noon.

Jim was silent and irritated, and Patsy had abandoned *Love among the Cannibals* and had decided to devote some attention to cheering him up.

"It may be nice for you," he said. "I think she's silly."

"I wonder who she'll have now?" Patsy said, calm and polite.

"Someone dumb. She's never had anybody who wasn't dumb."

"You don't know who she's had. Don't be needlessly rude to my aunt just because you're mad at me."

"Your aunt is a brainless woman," Jim said, feeling more annoyed the more he thought about Dixie.

"Oh, forget it," Patsy said. "I was just trying to make cheerful conversation."

They lapsed into a prickly silence for a few miles and then were startled out of it by the sight of a swarm of helicopters in the air. There seemed to be more than a hundred of them, buzzing over the fields, the pastures, and the low hills like swarms of giant dragonflies.

"What in god's name?" Jim said.

The closer they got to the swarm the more amazing and phenomenal it seemed. Helicopters were alighting and taking off mysteriously from both sides of the road. None of them were flying very high—some crossed the road over the car barely higher than the telephone poles. They had soldiers in them, soldiers wearing green fatigues. Some of the soldiers looked down at them curiously, some with embarrassment. All around, to the east and west, the swarm circled. To the south a long string of helicopters was visible coming north from some fixed but hidden point, like bees coming from a bee tree. Jim slowed down so they could watch the helicopters, and the soldiers in the lower copters pointedly ignored them, as if irritated by their watching. A little farther on they saw a sign that said DA NANG TRAINING CENTER.

"Weird?" Patsy said. "Are we in Vietnam?"

They stopped in the town of Mineral Wells and asked a filling station attendant, and he beamed and spoke proudly of the helicopters. "Ain't they something?" he said. "Biggest trainin' center going. They practice settin' 'em down out there in the brush. You want to see something spectacular

you ought to watch 'em going to the base some evening,
three or four hundred of 'em coming over those hills at one
time. It's awe-inspiring, what you might say. Somethin' to
see."

The sight made them forget that they were on bad terms,
and though the heat increased, their spirits picked up. "We
could go to Austin," Jim suggested.

"Why?"

"Oh, for the hell of it. We could see the Williamses. We
could eat Mexican food. We could sit in the beer garden and
drink beer. We could go to a party tonight—there's always a
party in Austin. We could smoke pot and argue about
literature. I miss all that. I don't know why I thought I
wanted to be a photographer. I'm really more of a literary
type."

"I don't want to do any of those things," Patsy said. "I
want to go to our apartment and not leave for years. I want
to go home and make a cream cheese sandwich." Elaborate
sandwiches were her culinary forte. She had not yet mastered cooking, though once in a while she made an ambitious effort, but she loved to concoct exotic sandwiches,
with cheese and vegetables and fish and meat.

"Just for one night?" Jim asked.

"No. I itch. I want to see my doctor tomorrow if possible.
We can do all those things you mentioned in Houston, you
know."

"I know," Jim said, "but Austin is so much more promiscuous. Now that you've become a flirt we have to consider
that. In Austin we could get laid, mutually, independently,
any old way. In Houston there's nobody to lay us but
ourselves."

He said it jokingly, but Patsy was not amused. "That's
very crude talk," she said. "I don't want anybody laying us
but ourselves. Stupid. We have enough trouble with sex as it
is. And I don't like the term 'get laid.' It has very repulsive
overtones to me. Just because I was teasing you a little you
needn't get salacious."

"Who's salacious? I was teasing you too."

And they continued to snipe quietly at each other as they
rode. When they passed through College Station the gray

buildings of Texas Agricultural and Mechanical University were blurred by the midafternoon heat.

"At least you're not an Aggie," Patsy said. "That would have been too much."

It had become very hot indeed. The back of her blouse was all sweat and likewise the back of Jim's shirt. She leaned forward and unstuck the wet blouse from her back, but it was almost as wet in front too. Even her chest and bosom were moist, as if water was oozing out of every pore.

In Navasota, a crumbling Southern hamlet, they stopped to get some ice. The sun was falling, but falling very slowly. Patsy sucked a cupful of ice, dipping her fingers in the cup and lifting the ice to her mouth. It was in chunks slightly too big to get in her mouth and she juggled them in her palms and sucked them. She slipped her cold wet fingers inside her blouse and let the cool water drip onto her chest, onto the tops of her breasts and inside her bra. They passed through Hempstead and turned east onto the coastal plain, only fifty miles from Houston. The highway cut straight through the flat pastures. The sun came into the car from behind and sweat shone on Jim's neck. When Patsy had eaten the last of the ice she wiped her face with her wet hands. Along the road, under almost every tree, was a Negro boy or an old Negro woman, with a small pile of watermelons or a basket or two of tomatoes to sell.

As they came near to Houston white clouds filled the horizons, but they were clouds that seemed to belong as much to the earth as to the sky. They were smeared and befogged with heat waves, huge indistinct clouds that were not at all like the clear fleecy clouds of the West, of Montana and Colorado and the Texas Panhandle. The clouds that hung over Houston seemed to drip and melt in the moisture-filled air, as if seen through the steam from a shower. About five-thirty they hit the outskirts of Houston and bogged in the evening traffic.

"God," Jim said. He was tired and soaked with sweat and itchy and irritated. "What an insane thing to be coming into Houston. We'll be an hour getting across town."

But Patsy, though as hot as he was, felt generally quiescent and good. She had ceased resenting the heat and the sweat, and felt almost cooled by it. She felt loose and tired and passive and a little somnolent, and looked at the unweeded foliage-clogged fields at the edge of town. She watched the fields turn into houses, into lots, into shopping centers, watched the cars, the red lights, heard the honking of irritated commuters, and was indifferent to it all, even to Jim, whose blond hair was darkened with sweat. In Houston she felt more located than she had in weeks, and the heat didn't matter. She was not even bothered when they got behind a wreck and had to edge along for ten minutes until they could brave their way into another lane and swing around it.

"Don't fret," she said to Jim. "We'll make it. There's nothing to hurry for, anyway."

Finally they got on a freeway. It too was clogged, but at least it was a freeway. They swung around the western edge of Houston on a loop that showed the downtown skyline with the heavy Gulf clouds as a background. In ten minutes they were on South Boulevard, where they lived. Their apartment was over the garage of one of the huge solid tree-hidden houses at the base of the Boulevard. The people who owned the house lived in Guadelajara much of the year, so they might almost have had the mansion. The owners were friends of Jim's father, and let them have the garage for eighty dollars a month. Their friends universally regarded it as a great apartment, though it wasn't air-conditioned. They had the whole upper story of an old frame garage, with great trees hanging over it.

Patsy jumped out ahead of Jim and ran up the stairs dragging her purse. She loved coming home, even though she knew the inside of the house would be an oven. She had meant to write Emma, who had been taking care of the mail and had a key, to come over and open the windows, but she had forgotten to write. It was very hot inside and the air was a little mildewy, as it was apt to be in Houston, but she dashed through the three rooms flinging the windows up. There was a huge pile of papers and magazines piled on their red couch, and although she would have read them already it was still lovely to have a pile of magazines to go through. Jim staggered in with his cameras and set them down and stripped off his sweaty tee shirt and went straight to the shower.

"Oh, goody," Patsy said, wandering into her kitchen to make sure all her plates were still in the cabinet. "Jim," she said. He was in the bathroom stripped. "I'm going to run out. I'll get some beer and stuff and some meat and cheese. We'll have great sandwiches for supper. You can unload the car when I get back."

"Okay," he said, bushed.

She went out and got bread and lox and cheese and chopped chicken livers and romaine lettuce and rye bread and beer and tea and some flowers from her favorite flower stand.

While Jim tripped in and out, cool in Bermuda shorts, unloading the stained untidy Ford she showered and put on a shift and set her table and put the flowers in vases and made sandwiches and stopped to call Emma.

"Emma!"

"Great, you're home!"

"Are you still my friend?"

"Uh, sure, I guess. What do you mean?" Emma was not easy to pin down, but her voice was the same.

"I was just checking. I'm making sandwiches. We're beat. I'll see you in the morning, okay?"

She finished setting the table and they ate and sat around after supper, Patsy unwrapping magazines and skimming through them, Jim gloomily watching television. Gloom had settled on him at the supper table. He had wasted two months and much money and had not done what he had meant to do and was nowhere again. *Casablanca* was on the late show and was one of his favorite movies, but before it was well begun, sleep crowded past depression and Patsy had to poke him to make him go to bed.

She sat up very late. It was hot even with the windows open and their one little fan on, but she wore only her gown and drank iced tea and read such *New Yorker*s as she had missed in the West and washed her plates and made a pile of laundry and wandered about the house straightening things. She got drawn into *Casablanca* about halfway through and cried helplessly at the end, remembering Joe Percy, who was

a great deal like Claude Rains except fatter. When she went
to bed she dispensed even with her gown and lay on her side
of the bed naked, listening. It was as though the heavy moist
heat had an audible quality, as though she could hear it,
something low but there, beneath the sounds of cars on the
freeway and the distant wheen of ambulances. After a time
she lay back, the heat her only cover, her upper lip, her
breasts and stomach and shoulders all slightly damp with
moisture; and when she could not sleep she turned on her
reading light and adjusted it very low, looking to see that it
did not shine in Jim's eyes. He was heavily, sweatily asleep.
She sighed, for she knew there would be trouble with him in
the next few weeks. He would be very dissatisfied with
himself. But being home again was a pleasure no prospect
could spoil. She got up and fixed herself another glass of tea
with ice in it and lay naked, reading *New Yorker*s until three
in the morning. Occasionally some warm gust of breath
from the Gulf came in the window and made the moisture
on her body feel cool. The breath stirred the edges of the
curtains and the pages of her magazines, and even the
moss-draped limbs on the great trees, so that they moved as
she read and brushed against the shoulders of the house.

BOOK **II**

Houston, Houston, Houston

1

Patsy sat perched on the very top of a jungle gym in Fleming Park, in Houston, watching Tommy and Teddy Horton. Tommy and Teddy were Emma's two sons. They were climbing a slide from the bottom up and clambering rapidly down the ladder on the other side. Both of them needed haircuts. Emma sat on a concrete bench by a concrete picnic table, below Patsy. She was trying vaguely to do something about her hair—keep it out of her eyes, at least—but she was not having much luck. Emma had wispy dull blond hair, neither long enough nor vivid enough to be spectacular and not short enough to be pert. Patsy could not look at it without wanting to beseech her to do something about it, but she could never quite decide what ought to be done. She had just broken some big news and felt happy but a little nervous. She held on to the top bar of the jungle gym with her hands and rocked back and forth on her behind.

"Well, it's nice you're so pleased about it," Emma said. "You look very pleased when you look pleased." She glanced at her sons and raised her voice. "Knock that off, boy! Ladders are to climb up, slides are to go down. Run it the other way around for a while."

Emma didn't really care. She had merely noticed that the boys made Patsy nervous, clambering so recklessly down the ladder. Patsy made *her* nervous, rocking so recklessly on the jungle gym; but she looked so happy that she couldn't be made to be careful, and Emma had a superstition against mentioning miscarriages or their possibility, so she held her tongue.

The boys each gave their mother a glance, saw that she didn't really care, and went right on with their game. "I think Patsy's the one that's going to fall," Tommy said. He was four and a half and extremely articulate for his age. At the very moment he said it Teddy lost his footing on the ladder and hung precariously by his arms for a moment. He slyly found his footing and continued down somewhat more cautiously, pretending it hadn't happened.

"I won't fall," Patsy said. "Maybe I won't know what to do with a child. Maybe I'll be scared to let him climb ladders." Tommy's remarks often put her off. She was aware that he was a child she didn't quite know how to handle.

"What do you mean, him?" Emma said, winding her hair into a loose knot. She wore a much-washed blue cotton dress. Patsy wore shorts and one of the old blue denim shirts that Jim had bought to disguise himself among the cowboys.

"I just think in terms of a him," Patsy said. "How long does it take to learn the essential things? I look to you for instruction, I guess."

"It takes until about the time the second one comes along," Emma said. Teddy had got sand in his eyes from climbing into the sole of Tommy's tennis shoe, and he came running to his mother weeping and rubbing his sandy eye with an even sandier fist. Emma cleaned his face with the hem of her skirt, and once the tears washed out the sand Teddy dashed away, back to the slide. Teddy was barely two. He tried to crowd in ahead of his brother and Tommy immediately kicked him off the slide. Teddy was barely two.

Patsy watched from her perch and said nothing, but she was secretly appalled at the savagery of Tommy and Ted. They fought all the time and were as violent as cowboys, only fortunately much smaller. Teddy got gamely up and Tommy kicked him off the slide again. Emma raised an eyebrow but kept out of it. Patsy watched with anticipatory smugness. Hers wouldn't be savage. Firm and resourceful, but not savage. Teddy seemed to accept the violence as his due. He was not offended by the kicks and merely waited until Tommy got well up the slide before climbing on again.

"So what's with Jim?" Emma asked. "I've been waiting for you to tell me, but my patience is wearing thin. I cry on your shoulder often enough, why don't you cry on mine? It makes me seem weaker than you. You're being inhumanly stoical about something."

"No I'm not," Patsy said, a little defensive. In musing about her baby she had been feeling so lifted and so cheerful that she had forgotten she had ever been depressed. She had been depressed all too frequently since their return to Houston, but a good mood always banished the memory of all bad moods, and she was a little miffed with Emma for bringing it up.

"Jim's just been withdrawn lately," she said, sighing.

Teddy, for some reason, chose that moment to make a dash for the street on the other side of the park. Being two, he was whimsical. Emma had to leave the conversation abruptly and dash after him. She was hefty and ran awkwardly, yelling, "Teddy, stop, Teddy, stop!"—words which had no effect whatever on Teddy. For a moment Patsy felt silly and looked across at Tommy. He was sitting on top of the slide watching the race with a slightly malevolent look on his face.

Teddy was making dead for the street and showed no sign of slacking off. His uncut brown hair bobbed on his head. Emma had to increase her pace. Her behind swayed, her elbows waved. It was a little funny and Patsy and Tommy watched with amused absorption. It was like a race between an ungainly giantess and a fleet midget, and it ended between the little strip of sidewalk and the street, with Teddy being grabbed just as he was breaking over the curb. It was as if Emma's instincts had set her in motion at the last practicable moment. An old lady passing in a Volkswagen had already swerved desperately for refuge, for once Teddy got his speed up he gave the impression of being a movable object more dangerous than in danger. Emma swept him up, both of them very red in the face and flushed from their run. The knot in her hair had come loose. She was embarrassed by the old lady, whose VW had died as if in terror at the streaking approach of Teddy. Emma was also angry, as Patsy and Tommy could see, but Teddy was a bundle of chortles at the effect of his dash, entirely merry, as if it had been a great joke on everyone, a marvelous little performance he had given the world out of the bounty of his young heart. Patsy, at the top of her perch, was won by his giggles even at a distance of thirty yards. Emma was too, rather quickly. She put him down and they trudged back together, the giantess and the midget, both content and looking remarkably alike. Emma kept her hand on Teddy's head, just in case. Tommy's expression turned to one of quiet contempt.

"When do you think Teddy will die?" he asked, looking at Patsy coolly. Patsy was shocked.

"Goodness," she said. "Why do you ask? Not for a very long time, I should hope."

"Well, I should hope not, either," Tommy said. "Because he's my brother."

Patsy looked at him, slightly aghast. She had had a similar thought about Jim, only the week before, and remembered it. There were moments when she felt a kind of dark rapport with Tommy Horton.

"He would probably like heaven very much," Tommy said, looking at her innocently. "Daddy says Teddy's the kind of kid who makes a hit anywhere."

Emma and Teddy returned within earshot and Tommy slid down the slide and regarded them a little sternly.

"You never spank that kid," he said.

Emma's neck was sweaty. "It's because I hate to bend over," she said. She swooped Tommy up as she had Teddy and tried to swing him into the giggles, but with no success. He merely gave a formal smile and when he was put down went over and tried to trip Teddy. Teddy walked around the trip and sat down in the sandpile. He had had his fun and was ready to ignore them all.

"The one advantage of kids is that they take your mind off husbands," Emma said, fanning herself ineffectively. It was only ten in the morning but the park was already hot.

"Do they take husbands' minds off you? If they do I'll have to take a lover or something, just to have someone to talk to."

"Well, you knew you were marrying a brooder," Emma said. "At least Jim isn't mean. He's just kind of boring sometimes. Frankly." And she glanced up at her friend.

Patsy was not offended. One of the things she loved about Emma was that she said the things other people were too polite to say.

"He's not really boring," she said weakly, not sure whether she meant it or not.

216

"You're not very borable," Emma said. "You're too lively to notice whether a man is boring or not. You could even live with Flap and not be bored."

Flap was Emma's husband; Patsy was caught somewhere between amusement and horror at the thought of living with him. "I'd rather hang myself than live with Flap," she said. "Frankly." Then she giggled.

Emma looked up and laughed. "Let's take these brats and get some ice cream," she said. "The heatstroke hours are approaching. There's no basis for friendship like a mutual dislike of one another's husbands, is there?"

Patsy climbed lightly down and went over to the sandpile to pick up Teddy. She seldom handled other people's children, but she thought she ought to start practicing and Teddy was easy to pick up. "Ready to go?" she asked.

"Um," he said and with a winning smile dribbled a handful of sand down the neck of her shirt.

"Oh, Teddy," she said. She had to set him down and try to shake the sand out of her bosom.

"But you do like Jim, don't you?" she asked, once they had the boys in the Ford. "I don't see how anybody could really dislike Jim." She was only faintly insecure.

"I like him better than you like Flap."

"Flap has his charms," Patsy said. "I like him a lot. I just think it's inconsiderate of him to go around trying to seduce me and other women at parties, with you right there."

"Not as inconsiderate as it would be if he did it with me *not* there," Emma said reflectively. "I don't take all that too seriously. I think he just likes to feel people up. It makes him feel deliciously guilty, or something."

Patsy dropped it. She knew from experience what a persistent feeler-upper Flap was, but, like Emma, she could never take it seriously enough to get really furious at him. Flap knew it. He was an appealing guy, in a baggy, disheveled way. He and Emma were alike in general rumpledness and seemed to get on fine.

They took the boys to a Baskin-Robbins ice cream parlor and stood looking at the hampers of ice cream. "I think I'll have something I haven't had," Tommy said. "Is coffee an adult flavor?"

"Very adult," Emma said. "Coffee pecan, how about?"

"Okay," Tommy said, hopping around the room. Teddy began to hop too, his hair bobbing.

"I'm going to have something major while I can," Patsy said and ordered a banana split. The boys were amazed. Teddy stopped hopping and looked at the split with solemn wonder while Patsy ate. The chocolate cone Emma gave him began to drip over his hand and onto his sneakers.

"Eat, Teddy, eat," Emma said. She herself was having chocolate chip.

Teddy turned and began to hop away, but kept his eyes on Patsy's split as long as possible. He ate and hopped, leaving a small trail of chocolate across the white floor. The attendant, also white, looked on with weary disgust.

"I suppose you have to get used to messes," Patsy said. Tommy was demonstrating the virtuosity of his own licking compared to the slovenliness of Teddy's. He sat at their feet licking skillfully and turning his face up to them for admiration.

"Not a drop on me yet," he said.

"You're a master licker, old boy," Emma said, reaching down to pat his head. "That brother of yours is a slob."

"No one likes slobs, Teddy," Tommy said when Teddy hopped by. But Teddy smiled a chocolaty smile at his mother, as if to say, Nonsense, mine is the kingdom of heaven, and the kingdom of earth too. Emma smiled back.

"You could use some messes," she said to Patsy. "When I first knew you, you were the most orderly person I knew. You even made your bed before breakfast—I remember that well. You're not nearly that bad any more. One good messy kid and you'll be human, with any luck."

"I did like order," Patsy said. "I wonder why I don't care so much, any more. I guess that trip we took convinced me order is hopeless, or something. I haven't been the same since we came back."

It was true—she was becoming what her mother would call shiftless. Once she had made beds promptly and done grocery shopping early and kept the apartment spic; but lately, since the trip, she had developed an inclination to do as little as possible. She liked to lie in bed in the morning eating oranges and listening to records, Bob Dylan or the Swingle Singers or the Supremes, while she read the morn-

218

ing paper. By the time Jim woke up, the sports section of the paper would be soaked with orange juice and there would be orange seeds in the bed.

"You could eat your damn oranges on the want ads," he said. "I like to read the sports pages."

Out of the window she could see the green back yard and the great branching trees and a back-yard glider and the brilliant flowers that a Negro gardener watered and cared for while the Whitneys were away in Mexico. She could feel the day's moist heat gathering, see the sun begin to filter through the trees and strike the screen, and she felt more and more a liking for just lounging in bed. She had magazines too and had got the first two volumes of Frazer out of the Rice library, and she liked just reading and eating oranges and listening to records, and if she felt active she could always walk the few blocks to Fleming Park and there would be Emma and the boys, most likely.

She had even developed an attack of immodesty, and since the nights were breezeless, heavy, and hot, she had taken to sleeping without her gown. She found that she had just as soon be nude as not, and a time or two in the mornings she had felt distinctly like making love, something in which Jim had apparently lost all interest. Once when she felt sexy she had rested on her elbows, watching him sleep for a while, and had picked a little lint out of his navel and then shyly slipped her hand down inside his underwear and held him for a while. He grew hard, and it was exciting to feel it happening. She wanted him to wake up, but it was still quite early and when he did wake up he merely raised on one elbow suddenly and looked at her as if she were a stranger and said, "Turn that loose, I'm sleepy," and went back to sleep. He had sat up most of the night reading Rosemond Tuve, on Flap's advice, preparing for his new career as an English scholar. Patsy took her hand away and sniffed and then cried, dripping tears onto the orange-juice-soaked ads, for he had always wanted her to be bold and sexually explorative and she had tried and been rebuffed and she didn't think she would ever feel like trying again. Later, when Jim awoke, he was conscience-stricken and chagrined with himself. He tried to apologize and explained that he had been dreaming, but explanations didn't help.

219

Nor did it help that night when he made love to her and took elaborate, overconsiderate pains about it. The little pip or response she finally had seemed not worth the sweat and effort, and Jim must have felt so too, for after that he let her alone. When the doctor told her she was pregnant she was grateful for whatever night it had been in Wyoming or Utah or Colorado. She had ceased to be sure she would get another chance.

Emma was happily munching her brown cone, and Tommy had licked his down to the rim and was licking inside the rim as far as his tongue could reach, and Teddy had grown tired of hopping and of his cone too and had abandoned it in a chair. He was walking in rapid circles around a penny gum machine, giggling at himself. Emma got up and found some napkins, gave one to Tommy, and caught Teddy by the suspenders of his overalls. She swabbed his face more or less clean as he spun his wheels and giggled and tried to continue circling the gum machine. Emma had heavy calves and rather heavy ankles and her old blue sneakers were very ragged. Her mop of hair came down again while she was wiping Teddy's face. Watching her handle the boys made Patsy feel strangely envious. She was twice as pretty as Emma, and at least as bright, but still she envied her friend her general know-how. Without meaning to, Emma made her feel that she was behind in some way—behind in life.

Once he was released Teddy trailed over to Patsy clucking his tongue. He stopped in front of her and held out his hand. "Um," he said, nodding brightly toward the banana split.

"Moocher," Patsy said. "Wait a minute." She was spooning up the sweet brown and pink syrup from the bottom of her split dish.

"Um," Teddy said again, peering approvingly at the syrup and opening his mouth.

"Moocher!" Patsy said again, giving him a spoonful.

"Of course you have to give me a taste now," Tommy said, popping up and smiling politely.

"Of course," Patsy said.

"I also get a penny if he gets a penny," Tommy reminded her. It was her custom to give them pennies when they saw a gum machine.

Patsy wiped her mouth and dug in her purse. She presented them with pennies and they raced to the gum machine, Tommy winning. "Yellow," he said with a satisfied air and popped his into his mouth.

Teddy's was black and rolled through his hand and bounced across the floor. He followed, set himself to pounce on it, missed, set himself again, missed again, and finally captured it when it rolled into one of the sticky puddles his dripping ice cream cone had made. "Um," he said, holding it up for inspection before he popped it into his mouth.

Emma had been watching the whole business studiously. "You boys are shameless," she said. "Let's be going."

They got in the Ford and Teddy crawled up behind the back seat to capture an old flashbulb that Jim had overlooked.

"Well, gee, I feel like crying," Emma said and actually sniffed. "You're pregnant and I'm not. You'll probably make a better mother than me too. I'm really a wretched mother. The other day I whopped Teddy twice as hard as I meant to because he wouldn't use the potty when I wanted him to. I was awful."

Patsy was amazed. She couldn't imagine Emma hitting Teddy too hard. "Maybe you were just overwrought," she said, not knowing what else to say.

"Of course I was overwrought," Emma said. "I'm always getting overwrought." She turned in the seat to see how the boys were taking the conversation. They weren't. Tommy was laboring to tie his sneaker and Teddy was gazing placidly out the window.

Patsy suddenly noticed that a driver in a blue Cadillac was zooming backward up the street in her direction. She swerved to the side and tried to honk, but she could never hit the horn when she wanted to. "Stupid woman," she said, not realizing until the Cadillac backed past her that the woman driving was her Aunt Dixie. "Hey," she said and tried to wave. But her aunt was apparently backing toward a restaurant, almost a block behind them, and did not notice Patsy. The cars coming down the street hung steady for a moment, as if incredulous, and then swerved to the left or the right. The Cadillac backed between them, never slowing down.

"That's my aunt that you've never met," Patsy said. "If we had had a wreck I could have introduced you."

Emma had turned to watch the Cadillac. "She's not even looking out the window," she said. "She's just using her mirror. That's very against the law."

Tommy and Teddy perked up. "Why does your aunt break the law?" Tommy asked.

"She doesn't know there are laws, I don't think."

"Does she break God's laws or people's laws?"

"Both," Patsy said, but Emma was exasperated by the question.

"People's laws, for god's sakes," she said. "You're too bright for your age, young man. Your daddy's been talking to you again."

"No he hasn't," Tommy said. "Gina talks to me. She says if you break people's laws the cops get you but if you break God's laws the devil gets you. The devil lives a few feet under the ground. There's such a thing as the devil's dodo too."

"Ick," Patsy said. "What will I ever tell mine about things like that? I used to have strict beliefs but something's happened to them. I don't know what I believe. My morals will probably be the next to go."

"Atheistic professors," Emma said. "The devil is not a few feet under the ground, Tommy."

"Uum," Teddy put in, very negatively, shaking his head. The concept of the devil was clearly not to his liking.

"How deep then?" Tommy asked.

"Who knows?"

"At least four thousand miles," Patsy said. "It's eight thousand miles through the earth and if he lives anywhere it's at the center of the earth, which would be four thousand miles. You boys are safe."

"Um," Teddy said affirmatively. He was glad to hear it.

"How can I be sure?" Tommy asked.

"Believe Patsy," Emma said. "She knows more about the devil than Gina does. She's read a great many books."

The Hortons lived in a large rather rickety unpainted garage apartment on West Main. When Patsy stopped in front Tommy tried to crawl out the back window, but the glass wasn't rolled down all the way and he had trouble. Emma yanked him out and he and Teddy ran up the driveway, past the family's old white Nash Rambler.

"Let's go somewhere without them," Emma said. "We never really get to talk. If I had any money we could go shopping."

"We could go looking," Patsy said. The Hortons' brokeness always discomfited her a little.

"The new graduate students have come in," Emma said. "If there are any lively ones Flap will bring them home. Maybe we can all go eat Mexican food or something. We might even get drunk. I need a party."

Patsy waved at Flap, who was standing in the garage in Levi's and a white tee shirt fixing his bicycle. "Okay," she said, willing but not enthusiastic. Emma trudged off after the boys, still trying to knot her hair, and Patsy drove away, relieved to be alone. An hour with the Horton boys always made her appreciate solitude. Jim was away when she got home. The apartment was cooler than the outdoors but still warm and humid. She took off her sweaty shirt and stood in the bathroom in her bra and shorts looking at herself in the shaving mirror and musing on how she would look when she was large. It was hard to imagine. That evening when it got cool she meant to walk to the library and bring home some books on it all.

================ **2** ================

"You could have been a little more polite," Patsy said, coming out of the bedroom. She was still in her bra and shorts.

"I was polite," Jim said. "What was I supposed to do, ask him in for a drink?"

"You could have asked him if he wanted a drink of water. He walked all the way up those stairs. Who's the package for?"

"For you, of course," Jim said, handing it to her. "It's from Miri. For a minute I had hopes it would be my *Cambridge Bib.*"

Miri was her younger sister, in school at Stanford. Patsy tore into the package and discovered that it contained a sort of psychedelic shift, very bright and long and rather fetching. She shook it to see if there was a note from Miri but there wasn't, and she put it on.

"It'll be great when I'm bigger," she said. "Hippie maternity clothes. I wonder if Miri's become a hippie?"

"Undoubtedly," Jim said. He was dressing to go to an indoctrination meeting for graduate students and felt generally sulky. Patsy's frivolity clashed with his mood. "I wish those books had come," he said, selecting a dark tie.

Patsy struck a few poses in the doorway, hoping he would tell her she looked nice in the shift, but he didn't. "I'm sorry I bitched at you," she said. "You weren't really rude to the postman."

But Jim's mind was on the books that hadn't come, and when she looked into the living room she felt a sinking of the heart. On the floor by the red couch were sixty dollars' worth of quality paperbacks, almost all of them criticism or scholarship. Jim had bought them the night before at a paperback store downtown. He had got in a conversation with several graduate students and a famous newly arrived professor and had bought every book that he could remember having heard mentioned. She had been with him and had wandered about the bookstore, feeling more and more frivolous and small-time, and had finally bought a copy of *Bonjour Tristesse*, which she had never read. When they were home she read it in half an hour, sitting on the bed in her nightgown while Jim sat at their desk carefully writing his name and the date in each of the new paperbacks. He read a few sentences from each one before putting it on a pile on the other side of the desk. She had felt a sinking of the heart then too, for it reminded her of the night in Phoenix when he had rearranged his photographic files, all of which were presently in a closet, forgotten. He had taken to ordering every book Flap Horton mentioned, it seemed to Patsy. Even Flap was taken aback when he found out that Jim had ordered a set of *The Cambridge Bibliography of English Literature*.

"My god," he whispered to Patsy. "A beginning graduate student with the *Cambridge Bib*. The professors here don't even own the *Cambridge Bib*."

"It's your fault," Patsy said fiercely, though it wasn't. "Just quit mentioning books to him. He even wants to order the OED and that costs three hundred dollars. If he asks you, tell him he won't need it. I don't want this apartment buried in unread books."

"The OED?" Flap said, staggered. "His first week in graduate school? He's either a genius or a fool."

"I don't care to vote," Patsy said.

When Jim had come to bed and noticed *Bonjour Tristesse* he asked her how it was, but he asked a little condescendingly, as if he already knew. The condescension irked her. She had just told him that afternoon about being pregnant and had hoped they could talk about it once they got to bed. She wanted to be made over. But Jim wanted to talk about William Duffin, a prize modernist that Rice had managed to hire away from Ohio State. All the graduate students were in a dither about him. Patsy was in a mood to think a baby more important than a modernist, even one who had written eight books, and she was glad when Jim went to sleep so she could at least think about the baby and be glad about it herself.

"Listen," she said, watching Jim knot his tie. "Emma needs to get away from those kids. Let's take them for Mexican food tonight. Maybe there'll be some interesting new graduate students to bring along."

"Maybe," Jim said, but he was too nervous about the meeting to really listen, and he kissed her as he departed without really looking at her. He would have been surprised to know that after he left she went out into the hot back yard and sat in a lawn chair crying for twenty minutes. Though it was early September, the heavy air and the moist earth seemed to hold all the fecundity of spring or early summer. Patsy remembered Emma and the boys going up to the garage where Flap was fixing his bicycle, and how glad he had looked to see them; in her breast she felt a bitter loneliness, as if she would be left to do everything she did alone. She had heard that pregnancy might make her draw apart from her husband, but instead she felt the reverse. She had wanted him to hold her and hug her before he left, and she felt very hurt that he had not noticed, or had not wanted to. When she had finished crying she went in to write her sister, thanking her for the lovely shift.

Jim need not have worried about the graduate meeting. It was pointless but not unpleasant and was in no way threatening. Outside the room where it was held he could see the formal hedges and bright green lawns of Rice University. Mexican gardeners worked at the hedges with long electric hedge clippers. The gardeners wore khakis and straw hats and looked very out of place in the quiet academic quadrangle. They looked as if they belonged on some remote hacienda shearing sheep.

Jim sat with Flap Horton and listened as Flap genially dissected the new batch of graduate students. Various more or less meaningless sheets of paper were passed out and studied with deep earnestness by all the budding scholars. Jim felt a little overdressed and mentioned as much to Flap, who wore a blue tee shirt and old slacks.

"No, rookies have to dress up," Flap said. "I have to hang loose myself—otherwise I feel like a suck-ass. Next year you can just wear slacks. Two years from now you'll probably wear Levi's. Three years from now you'll have to come naked, to show you've still got your self-respect. Four years from now you either won't be here or you'll be a member of the establishment and self-respect will be a moot question."

A very good-looking redheaded girl was sitting in the front row. She wore white net stockings. "She won't last," Flap said, "but it'll be fun while she does. The guy in Bermuda shorts, with the beard, he won't last either. His name's Kenny Cambridge. I kinda like him."

"Why won't he last?"

"He had never heard of Northrop Frye," Flap said. "Or Maynard Mack. Or F. R. Leavis. Or anybody I mentioned, come to think of it."

"Neither have I," Jim said, a little apprehensive.

"No, but you will," Flap said with a reassuring grin. "You're just illiterate. Kenny seems to be anti-literate, or at least anti-scholarly. You have to be really brilliant to get away with that."

Jim was depressed and remained so throughout the meeting. Nothing at all happened. A few polite questions were asked, and politely answered. William Duffin, the new modernist, came in for a few minutes but said nothing. He was a tall heavy man, very sure of himself, and there was a slightly devilish cast to his countenance. His black hair was a little longer than the professorial norm.

After the meeting Jim and Flap fell in with a new graduate student whose name was Hank Malory. Flap had met him already and liked him, and Jim found that he liked him too. He was almost as tall as William Duffin but was lank rather than heavy. His nose had a kind of dent in it, as if it had been broken, and his jaw was strong. In talking with him, Jim found out that his nose *had* been broken, and in Vietnam. He had survived a stint as a helicopter pilot and had broken his nose in a car wreck in Saigon the last week he was there. It turned out that he had trained at the training school near Mineral Wells, where Jim and Patsy had seen all the helicopters. His sports coat was old and a bit too short at the sleeves and he took his tie off and stuffed it in his coat pocket as soon as the meeting was over. He came from Portales, New Mexico. The three of them walked off the campus and up the tree-hung streets toward the nearest drugstore, talking of New Mexico, of the redheaded girl in the white net stockings, and of William Duffin. Flap had just checked out Duffin's latest book, which was on Samuel Beckett, and they passed it from hand to hand as they walked.

They stopped in at the drugstore on the corner of Bissonnet Street and to Jim's mild embarrassment there was Patsy, barefooted and still in her psychedelic shift, sitting at the soda fountain eating a thick chocolate malt with a spoon and idly reading an issue of *Seventeen*. She had come to the drugstore to mail her letter, and because she was feeling gloomy had gone in to have a malt. She knew most of the soda fountain habitués and could usually find someone to chatter with. If there was no one to chatter with she could at least read magazines free. When she looked around and saw the three men she brightened immediately.

"Gosh, you look great, Patsy," Flap said. His eyes began to shine. He could never restrain his enthusiasm for her, and Patsy could not help responding to it. She spun half around on the stool, her clean face coloring beautifully and her hair loose at her shoulders—so delighted with their presence that both Flap and Hank Malory were smitten by her and smiled without quite knowing what to say. Jim's reaction was the opposite. He could not quite look at her and could not help but be a little embarrassed by the fact that she was reading *Seventeen*. It clashed, somehow. The three of them had been talking about Duffin and Beckett and Northrop Frye, though only Flap had actually read the three men, and suddenly there sat Patsy, undetectably pregnant and looking like a schoolgirl on her way home from school, her lips stained a little by the chocolate malt she was eating. Jim was discomfited, but he quickly introduced her to Hank Malory.

"Hi," Patsy said and immediately began telling Flap about the conversation she had had with Tommy that morning regarding the devil.

"He's a Miltonist who can't read yet," Flap said, sitting down next to her. Jim sat on the other side of her and Hank

Malory took the stool just around the corner of the counter. Patsy knew Jim was displeased with her for some reason. He exuded waves of stiffness at such times. To avoid them she turned toward the other men, feeling for a moment disconcerted and slightly hectic. She was caught between the cold rays of annoyance coming from Jim, who was pretending to scan the Beckett book, and the somewhat breathy gusts of Flap's admiration. Hank Malory had already finished his Coke and was poking with his straw at the ice in his empty glass. He seemed quiet and relaxed and was easier to look at than either Jim or Flap, so Patsy focused on him.

"I bet you're from the West," she said. "You've got a Western jaw. Months of rodeos taught me to recognize them. You probably even smell from the West."

Her own remark embarrassed her—it was hardly an appropriate thing to say to a stranger—but he didn't seem to mind. "I probably do," he said, grinning as if there were something ironic about what she had said. She found she didn't like his sports coat, which was suede, and old, and far too hot for Houston.

"A year from now he'll smell like a bound volume of PMLA," Flap said. "So will Jim. Ever smell one?"

"I've smelled all sorts of books," Patsy said. She looked quickly at Jim and saw that he was ignoring her and gave the two men a confiding smile, helpless but happy, as if to let them know that even though her husband was ignoring her she was glad they had come. Flap spilled his coffee. He had ached for Patsy for years, and being with her when she was in a good mood made him fidgety with lust. He knew it was hopeless, but he ached, anyway. What he could do was yak with her, and yak they did, Patsy very animated and chattery and quick on the comeback. Hank Malory couldn't keep his eyes off her—he could not remember when he had seen anyone so lovely or so immediately delightful. They all left the drugstore together and walked down Bissonnet Street, Flap and Patsy ahead, still yakking. Patsy skipped quickly across the hot street and stood cooling her feet on the well-shaded sidewalk, leaving the three men to wait for the next break in the evening traffic. Jim gave Flap the Duffin book before he went to join her.

"Jim was born lucky," Flap said, noticing that Hank was watching them walk away.

"Must have been," Hank said. "There sure weren't any like her in Vietnam."

When they got home Patsy reminded Jim that they were taking the Hortons out for Mexican food, and evening found the four of them and Hank Malory and Kenny Cambridge, of the beard and Bermuda shorts, at a Mexican restaurant on Alameda Street. It was Jim's idea to ask Hank, and since Kenny had an apartment two doors from Hank's they asked him too. The restaurant had a patio with heavy tile-topped tables, excellent food, and huge cool pitchers of beer. The six of them drank lots of beer and enjoyed themselves enormously. As they were eating, it began to rain, softly and levelly, graying the summer evening, blurring the city and the green neon lights across the street. Flecks of rain touched them as they ate. Trucks rumbled by on the street beneath the patio, their tires swishing on the wet pavement. Alameda Street bordered the city's largest ghetto and lay on an ambulance route, so frequently all conversation had to cease as ambulances screamed by.

"Dead and dying from the bars," Flap said. "First thing to learn about being a graduate student here is which bars to stay out of."

"Which ones?" Kenny asked. His beard, like his hair, was reddish brown.

"All of them," Flap said. "They're all potential deathtraps. Even if you found one that was empty and went in for a beer someone would probably follow you in and shoot you."

"Flap's a little cowardly," Emma said. She had spruced up a bit and looked pink and pleased and very glad to be out of the house.

Patsy was pleased too. She was wearing her gray dress. Nothing was much pleasanter than company, particularly company that was part old and part new. Part of the fun would be talking over the two new men with Emma at the park next day, but even more of the fun was being there and being the object of two new pairs of admiring male eyes—as she definitely was. Both Hank and Kenny apparently regarded her as a woman worth looking at, for both of them looked at her frequently over their beer or their forks of Mexican food. Jim had forgiven her *Seventeen* and was happier than he had been in the afternoon, but he was still a little put off by the general insouciance and kept trying to steer the talk into literary channels. He wanted to talk about books and scholarship and graduate school. Flap kept trying to needle him out of it.

"For god's sake," he said, "you've got four or five years in which to sit around analyzing the graduate malaise, not to mention all the particular malaises of this department. Who cares about William Duffin, or his reputation? Screw him, for the moment."

"His favorite expression," Emma said, licking her lips.

"Screw you too," Flap said. "You're drinking more than me. I'm worried I'll have to cook breakfast. You shouldn't drink more than me. It's bad for our relationship."

Emma ignored him and poured herself more beer. Kenny Cambridge plucked at his beard and sighed, as if already the rigidities of the graduate life were weighing heavy on his soul.

"There must be safe bars," he said. "I can't stand this unless I can get potted regularly. That was a shitty meeting we had today."

"Sure, but we're counteracting it right now," Flap said.

"I'm thinking of quitting already," Kenny said. "It's no atmosphere for a writer."

He struck Patsy as funny and she laughed out loud. Jim looked embarrassed. Hank Malory had said very little. He seemed somewhat remote and a little melancholy, but when Patsy laughed he looked up and smiled. Kenny gulped his beer defensively. Had it been anyone but her he would have been offended, but as it was he was just nervous.

"What do you write?" Patsy asked, to make up for laughing.

"Poems," Kenny said shyly, looking hopeful. "Do you?"

"No. I just read." She felt pretty certain she was going to get a chance to read some of Kenny's poems before very long.

"I don't think it's such a bad life for a writer," Flap said. "You get lots of time to yourself. Of course, I spend all mine drinking coffee with my confreres, but if I didn't do that I could write. Maybe you'll have more strength of will than me."

"Flap used to be a writer too," Emma said, taking the last tortilla. "He wrote short stories. I was even a writer myself. I wrote short stories. But Flap sent his out. I never sent mine out. For all anybody knows, I'm better than him. If I'd sent mine out somebody might have bought them. Who knows?"

Patsy started to mention Jim's novel fragment but didn't. She didn't think he would want to be counted, somehow.

"Boy, do I like to eat here," Emma said.

"Houston smells like a crotch," Kenny said, sniffing the wet air quizzically.

"Male or female?" Flap asked.

It was a novel question. They all tested the smell of Houston against their memories of the smell of crotches. "Female, I think," Kenny said.

"How about you, Hank?" Patsy asked. "Are you a writer too?"

Hank shook his head, tilting his chair back. It annoyed Patsy a little that he didn't talk. She had been prepared to like him, and it was hard for her to like someone who didn't talk. Hank seemed quite content to listen.

"Hemingway wouldn't have gone to graduate school," Kenny said glumly. "Norman Mailer wouldn't either. Can you imagine Norman Mailer in graduate school?"

"Sure," Emma said. "He'd seduce us all. Us girls, I mean. Me and Patsy, I mean. That would be kicks, eh, Pat?"

"That would be kicks," Patsy said. She and Emma lifted their glasses to each other. Often they pretended they were Lady Brett. When slightly tight it was a charming thing to pretend. She smiled at Jim, hoping he would start liking the evening better. She wanted him to be in the mood everyone else was in; but he wasn't really in that mood and there was nothing she could do about it.

Emma patted Jim's shoulder. She wanted him to be happier too, for Patsy's sake. "This is fun," she said. "Let's go some place and continue it."

"Sure, come to our place," Jim said, trying to shake himself out of his feeling of withdrawal. He felt like being alone and reading, actually, but he saw that Patsy was flushed and happy and delighted with the company and he made an effort to change his mood.

"How come you like Norman Mailer?" he asked Kenny. "He's no poet."

"I don't like him so much," Kenny said. "It just occurred to me that he wouldn't go to graduate school. I don't much like prose, actually. It's all wasteful. I tried to write a paragraph of a novel once and it was all just ordinary words and sentences. It didn't have any specialness. No élan, no brio, no *joie,* no flair—" and he stopped, embarrassed. He had a habit of reeling off synonyms like a human thesaurus.

"Maybe they'll let you do a dissertation in couplets," Flap said.

"I guess I ought to write, if everybody else does," Patsy said, draining her beer. She had had three glasses of beer and felt light.

"Sure you should," Flap said. "It's something everybody starts doing at a certain age, like sex. If you're old enough to be pregnant you're old enough to write."

At the mention of Patsy's pregnancy Jim suddenly cheered up. He had been feeling very indefinite, very unestablished. But Patsy was pregnant, so he was not completely unestablished. And she looked very fresh and lovely. He put his hand on her shoulder to let her know he liked her. She noticed he was smiling at her and was glad. When they all got up to go to the car she walked with her arm around his waist.

Two hours later, at the Carpenters', the evening was running down. Kenny Cambridge was mumbling to himself over a bilingual edition of Lorca. He had smoked some pot and was pretending he was reading Spanish. Emma sat spraddle-legged on the floor, burping and wishing fervently that she hadn't eaten so much. Jim and Flap were looking at all the paperbacks Jim had bought, and Flap was going on about C. S. Lewis and trying to make clear to Jim the difference between drab poetry and golden poetry. They were drinking whiskey, as was Hank Malory. He was idly looking through their record collection. Patsy sat by Emma on the floor.

"I wish he would put something on and dance with me," Patsy said. "I feel like dancing before I get big."

"He's got a nice loose build," Emma said. "We're all going to like him. Kenny likes him because he doesn't write poetry. Flap likes him because he doesn't look academic. Jim likes him because he doesn't seem like competition."

"And you and I like him," Patsy said, giggling. "Why do you and I like him?"

Emma shrugged. "Because he's got a nice loose build," she said.

Patsy decided she must dance, though she was a little unsteady and wove slightly as she crossed the room. "Find anything we could dance to?" she asked.

Hank smiled and lifted his glass cavalierly. "One more little swig and I can dance to anythang," he said.

"Paul Newman really does that better than you," she said. "I saw *Hud* too."

He held up a Hank Williams record that Jim had bought on sale at a drugstore for a dollar ninety-eight. The cover picture showed Hank Williams in a white suit and white hat.

"Oh, not that," Patsy said. "Don't tell me you're one of those intellectuals who get sentimental about hillbilly music."

Hank was silent for a moment, as if he genuinely didn't know how to answer her question. "It's about the only kind of music I can dance to," he said.

"Okay," Patsy said. "Better that than nothing." They danced to "Jambalaya." Patsy soon discovered that she was a little too tight to dance enjoyably, though Hank danced well. Jim and Flap looked up at them with disbelief. Flap was talking about Yvor Winters. Their plane of discussion was so lofty that it was difficult for them to conceive of people dancing to Hank Williams.

"Maybe I shouldn't tell you, but I was named for Hank Williams," Hank said at some point while they were dancing. It took a while for it to soak in, but when Patsy realized what he had said she asked him if it were true and he said it was. "My daddy was a hillbilly musician," he said. "Not very famous, but he knew Hank Williams."

Emma had allowed herself to collapse sideways on the tiny little blue rug in front of the couch. Patsy noticed and was a little worried. But Emma was awake; she watched their feet as they danced. Patsy was barefooted, Hank in rather worn loafers. "I wish I were dancing," Emma said, but no one heard her. She could see Kenny Cambridge's knees pointed at her from across the room. He still sat crosslegged peering at the Lorca poems.

Patsy was sweating and suddenly became dizzy. Hank had to hold her up for a moment. The room was very still and hot and she felt nauseated. "This was not a good idea," she said, holding his shoulder. She stumbled to the bathroom, filled the basin with cold water, and splashed her face for several minutes. It made her feel better, although the bathroom itself was close and hot. She opened the door, her face and throat and temples still wet, and reached for a towel. When she looked out she saw Hank standing across the foyer, just inside the screen door that led out. His suede coat was slung over one shoulder.

"Hey," she said. "You're not leaving, are you? I'm okay. I was just woozy for a second."

"I just need air," he said.

Patsy patted her damp temples with the towel. "Let's go out," she said. There were drops of water in her eyelashes. They went out and sat on the steps for a while, neither of them very talkative. Patsy felt a little sleepy, but also very comfortable. Hank had his back against the screen and the light from the foyer shone on his rumpled brown hair. The air was muggy but cooler than it had been inside. "You don't seem very Rice-like," she said. "I hope you don't mind my saying so."

"Maybe I'm not," he said. "I can't tell yet. The only other place that offered me a fellowship was Indiana and I didn't feel like going there." She was sitting below him, and when she looked up, the light from the doorway struck her face. Once she straightened one leg and put her foot on the railing of the steps and Hank saw the white movement of her leg. Kenny Cambridge suddenly appeared behind the screen. He looked at them a moment and then disappeared into the bathroom.

"Do me a favor and take him with you when you go," she said. "Jim's no good at getting rid of people and I don't want to listen to Lorca all night."

They heard the occasional low rustle of tree limbs on the roof, the keen of an ambulance to the east, and the screech of the brakes of a city bus stopping a block away on Bissonnet. "Do you ever see stars down here?" he asked.

"Not very often," she said. She remembered the evening of the first rodeo, in Merkel, when she had sat watching the long sunset and had seen the first stars appear. She remembered the evening drives across Wyoming and the clear whinnying of the horses at dusk as she sat on Roger Wagonner's porch. The summer had had its loveliness, after all. She had stopped feeling high and tight—she felt very clear in the head and very relaxed and for a few moments was a little nostalgic for summer evenings in the West. She looked at Hank Malory, but his face was in shadow. All she could see well were his hands, which were crossed over his knees. They were large long-fingered hands, with prominent veins. She knew he was older than she was by three or four years, but somehow he gave the impression of not having attained his full growth physically. He had large bones that seemed to need more flesh than they carried. But he was a very comfortable person to sit with, even if his clothes didn't really fit him.

"How was Vietnam?" she asked.

He was silent for so long that she was afraid she might have offended him by asking. "Oh, very unpleasant," he said. Patsy didn't press him; she was sorry she had asked. For a moment she was afraid of finding out that they were on opposite sides where Vietnam was concerned. Kenny Cambridge came out of the bathroom and stood in the foyer pondering his alternatives.

"Ready to go?" Hank asked him, standing up. Kenny was, more or less. Patsy walked down the driveway with them to see them off. Kenny was still muttering.

"It boils down to Allen Ginsberg," he said by way of good night. He wandered into the street, bumped into a parked

Mercedes, and proceeded on fairly steadily. Hank and Patsy stood watching him.

Patsy lined her big toes up on the curb and hunched her shoulders. "Good luck with him," she said.

"Enjoyed it," Hank said and strolled off after Kenny, his suede coat over one shoulder.

Patsy felt a little dissatisfied. He could have stood and talked for a minute. Kenny didn't need that much watching. She didn't want to go back inside—it would have been pleasant to sit on the curb and talk. Hank Malory might have a nice loose build—did, in fact, though he handled it a little awkwardly—but he didn't have especially good manners. She had not even got enough out of him to know if he was bright. She almost regretted not walking along with them. There was no one to talk to inside. Emma would have passed out and Jim and Flap were either talking poetry or graduate-school politics. She didn't feel like sitting on the curb by herself, so she went back in.

Emma had her cheek propped on a palm and was listening sulkily to Flap, who was lecturing to Jim.

"Feeling bad?" Patsy asked.

"I'm thinking of the morning," Emma said. "Teddy is apt to get up at six and if he does, all this isn't going to seem worth it. Not in retrospect. You'll know what I mean someday."

But it seemed to Patsy that it would be a long time before she learned anything important, much less anything about babies. When the Hortons left, her mild discontent became a real depression and she wandered aimlessly about the apartment feeling almost sick. Jim was sitting on the bed cutting his toenails—he was also reading the first page of a book by Leslie Fiedler. Patsy went and sat by the open window in her favorite chair. It was a nice cane-backed rocker with a red cushion. She felt like crying and crying, and for no reason that she knew except that Jim was reading and seemed to be in another world from her. The snick of the toenail clippers was an irritating sound. There would probably be toenails in the bed unless she remembered to do something about them. It would have been more fun to sit on the curb talking to Hank Malory—assuming he could

237

have been made to talk. Even talking to Kenny Cambridge would have been better than listening to Jim cut his toenails. She put her hands to her face and caught her tears in her fingers, being very silent, for she knew that if Jim had to turn his attention from a serious paragraph to her vague vapors and glooms it would not help matters.

But Jim noticed anyway. He got up to drop his toenail clippings into the wastebasket and knew from the way Patsy's head was bent down that she was crying. Normally her tears made him feel pressured and annoyed, but just then he was feeling pressured from another direction, namely graduate school. There was a vast country of knowledge on whose rim he stood, and he didn't feel at all confident about entering it. Flap Horton and a good many of his fellow students had already explored it and seemed to know everything about it: the height of each mountain, where the desert areas lay, which guides to trust and follow. In comparison, Jim felt lost. Listening to Flap made him feel hopelessly behind, but being behind was better than being lost, and lost was how he felt when he wandered alone in the English stacks of the library pulling out books that looked interesting and putting them back in order to pull out others.

In comparison, Patsy and her tears seemed so familiar as to be almost comforting. When he had put his clippings in the wastebasket he went over and stood behind her rubbing her shoulders. He lifted her hair and rubbed the back of her neck. Patsy gulped back her tears and turned in the chair, trying to kiss his hand, but it was too awkward and she stood up and went into his arms, sniffing. She had felt so alone and worthless for a few minutes that it seemed the kindest and most thoughtful thing in the world that he would want to come and rub her neck.

"Party depress you?" he asked. "I guess Flap and I weren't too convivial. He's the only one I can talk to these days."

"It wasn't that," Patsy said, giving his throat and cheeks many grateful kisses. "I just got blue. I'm probably not very stable. There are times when I just get scared. I don't know what I'm supposed to do next in my life."

"Well, you're going to have us a baby next," Jim said, putting his nose behind her ear.

"Oh," she said. "Yes I am." She was irrationally happy that he had used the word "us," for he often went for long periods without seeming to consider them a unit of any kind. She kept her face pressed against his and they stood rocking a little on their feet in the middle of the room. Patsy's tears dried and the look of delight came back into her eyes. "I need a shower," she said when they broke apart. She went and showered and in the shower remembered that Hank Malory had said he was named for Hank Williams. She didn't know whether she should tell Jim or not. It might be something Hank didn't want everyone to know. But when Jim came in to brush his teeth she told him anyway.

"Oh, really?" he said. "He seems like a nice guy. Who will we name our child after?"

"I don't know," Patsy said, a little grave. Jim went out and she dried herself and brushed her teeth and then sat on the john for several minutes. They had a tiny bathroom bookshelf beneath the window, with a couple of Pogo books in it, Robert Graves's *The Greek Myths*, a paperback of *The Pocket Book of Modern Verse*, a Modern Library edition of Eudora Welty stories and a green *Ginger Man* which had come from Paris. Patsy pulled out the first volume of *The Greek Myths* and read a myth or two, rubbing herself with the towel. She shoved the book back in its place and contemplated *The Ginger Man* a moment but left it be. She had tried twice to read it and had been put off both times.

She went into the bedroom, still drying herself. It was not easy to get dry in a town as humid as Houston.

"Listen," she said, "we really have to get air conditioning before next summer." Emma had been telling her about the boys' bronchial troubles and it seemed more and more absurd to her not to have air conditioning. They would certainly need it with a baby. But Jim was already asleep, the light right in his face and the Fiedler book open on his chest.

Her mood, which had been rising, dipped again, though only a little. She turned off all the lights except her reading light and made sure the door was locked and sat on the bed with her legs pulled up and her chin on her knees, feeling balked and restive. Just as she had been feeling outward again she had been left alone, awake, and had no way to be but inward. She felt very peevish toward Jim. He had ceased to know his business as a husband, it seemed to her, for she was very much in the mood to be made, and had been three or four times since she had *been* made. She mused about it and became nostalgic for the time when Jim had been a suitor and had known his business better.

It was easy to be nostalgic for their courtship. It had been lovely to park at night and kiss a lot, with spring breezes blowing through the car. In a few weeks kissing and breezes and much talk had led them to the act of love—about which, it seemed to her, no nomenclature said anything accurate. It had seemed more an act of daring, or of curiosity, or of coming of age. Certainly it had not been, at first, so comfortable or convenient a way to express her feelings as kissing, in the days when she had really liked to kiss Jim. But kissing had got lost somewhere. She felt nothing to put into it any more except occasional gratitude for some small kindness or other, and it seldom made her feel warm in the way it once had. It was a pity, she felt, and it was almost as if sex had destroyed it, for the act called the act of love had led around to itself such a number of times that it had grown more major than kissing. At least it had gotten major enough that she was greedy for it; and for kissing she was only nostalgic. She touched herself for a moment and tightened her mouth angrily at Jim. If he had not been so dumb as to go to sleep, they could have had a good time. She got up and sulkily put on her nightgown and then reached over and got the Fiedler book, heavy, orange, its spine wrinkled and broken from the manglings of avid graduate students, and lay on her stomach, restively waving one heel and then the other in the air, and read, before she slept, one hundred and fifty pages on love and death in the American novel.

3

Dixie McCormack had a terror of parking lots, particularly large ones. They had fled into the store and were fleeing back to the car, Dixie well in the lead. She was carrying five packages in bright package bags. Patsy had only one package, a Jackson Pollock puzzle which she intended to send to her sister Miri. They were crossing a vast suburban parking lot and though it was late October it was still much too warm to be sprinting across large stretches of asphalt. Patsy slowed and walked at her usual pace and her aunt drew farther and farther ahead.

When they finally got to the blue Cadillac her aunt had dumped her five packages in the back seat, fastened her seat belt, turned down the sun visor, and was combing her dark well-dyed red hair. The minute Patsy was in the car Dixie pushed a button and Patsy's door locked.

"That's absurd," Patsy said. "We're perfectly safe."

"We are now," Dixie said. "Nobody's yanking me out of my own Cadillac."

"That rape was a month ago and she was just a high school girl," Patsy said. "Between us we could beat him off if he showed up. Just because it was in this parking lot is no reason to panic." Her window was remotely controlled, and she looked around to see it going up.

"We might inspire him," Dixie said. "Two sexy things like us." As soon as the windows were up she started the air conditioner and cold dry air blew against their legs.

"Between us we could scream loud enough to scare an army," Patsy said, arguing only for the sake of form.

"They use chloroform," Dixie said as the car shot backward. "You don't get time to scream. Let's go to Neiman's."

They whirled out of the parking lot onto the frontage road in front of a giant gravel truck, made a tire-screeching U-turn, and were soon on the freeway heading toward town at a clip so rapid it inspired Patsy to fasten her seat belt.

Dixie was driving with only the heel of one hand on the wheel, cutting smoothly from lane to lane and passing whole schools of cars. There was a look of delight on her face, which forty-five years of life had left plump and virtually unwrinkled. The skyline of downtown Houston appeared ahead of them, indistinct in the hot mists. The inside of the car had become chilly.

"Why must you pass everyone?" Patsy asked.

"The more you pass the more you're ahead of."

"I see why you liked Sonny Shanks. The two of you drive alike. On the other hand you hate rapists and I think he's probably a rapist. I told you what he did to me."

"He just has a crazy sense of humor," Dixie said. They curved off the freeway and stopped at a light in front of an antique shop. "I might like some rapists personally, if they weren't niggers or Nazis. It's the idea I hate. Sex is bad enough when you do it voluntarily."

Patsy was surprised by the remark, for her aunt's affairs were legend. She had been married only once, to a short, fat, goodhearted oilman named Squatty McCormack; they had divorced after three years but Dixie had lived lavishly ever since on the fruits of Squatty's undimmed devotion. He kept her in cars, clothes, and cash, and in return she kept his favorite bourbon in her liquor cabinet and let him come by and get drunk at her place once in a while, whenever he was up from South America.

"I thought you liked men," Patsy said a little timidly. "Most people think so, anyway. Momma used to hold it against Daddy, how much you liked men."

"Poor Garland," Dixie said, zooping past a blue pickup. "Married to her thirty years and she's more frigid than me. At least I'm a good cook. I do like men. I've had the greatest bunch of boy friends in the country. I even sort of like Squatty, especially when he's in South America. Now he's going to Alberta—did I tell you that? Big new field up there. The poor little bastard will probably freeze to death.

"The only bad thing about men is they're either queer or they want to screw you," Dixie went on. "The ones who want to screw you are the most fun to hang around with, so I keep having to do it. It's too bad it never much works, but I guess if it did I'd just go getting married all the time."

Patsy didn't know what to say and said nothing. Talk of sex made her shy, no matter who she was talking with. She looked at her aunt and her aunt looked quite merry and happy. She wore a bright orange dress and was as bright of eye as a girl of sixteen. Her energy and her good spirits were so attractive that it was easy to see why men took to her.

"Anyhow, men have always been the only people for me," Dixie said, looking at a man on the sidewalk, a Cajun type with long sideburns and a ducktail. "I did once know a trombone player it worked with. Boy would I have married him if I could have talked him into it. He wouldn't have me, though, and then he got shot dead accidentally in a bar in Lake Charles."

She was tapping her fingers irritably on the steering wheel and looking for gaps in the downtown traffic. "I wish Neiman's would get a suburban store," she said. "I hate coming downtown. My one objection to men is that I can't enjoy myself when somebody's grunting in my face. Maybe I started off wrong. I raped myself with a carrot when I was about twenty." She looked over and saw that her niece was blushing.

Patsy was sorry the subject had come up. The thought of her aunt poking herself with a vegetable was startling and unappealing.

"Jim a grunter?" Dixie asked. She had never much liked Jim, as Patsy well knew. She thought he was wishy-washy, and wishy-washy men put her off.

"No, of course not," Patsy said. "Don't say anything bad about him, please."

They whirled into a parking lot. The attendants knew Dixie and came on the run.

"Jim's darling," Dixie said, grabbing her purse and taking a final look at herself in the rearview mirror. "He just doesn't know the difference between living and existing. He should have hung around Sonny more. Sonny knows that much."

Patsy was angered, but her aunt was out and off and she didn't want to argue with her back. They crossed the street on a Don't Walk sign and were honked at, which flustered her. Going to Neiman's was not a good idea, anyway. Jim was on a poverty kick again and would not take it kindly if she bought anything, and he would take it even less kindly if she let Dixie buy something for her. She knew she would see something she wanted and be put in a quandary. More and more often, it seemed, she found herself in quandaries, some of them impossible to resolve. They were going to a party at the William Duffins' that evening—a great honor, apparently, for only a few of the most favored graduate students had been invited. For so serious an occasion she could conceivably get away with a new dress. She looked at several but bought none. Dixie's buying embarrassed her. It was completely random, but it seemed to delight the salespeople. Soon a string of them were following her like ants, each with his own bit of grain. Patsy found only one thing she could not resist, a lovely glass rose stem, heavy and beautifully simple. She paid for it and once again left with only one package. Dixie had seven.

"I'm hopeless," she said cheerfully, surveying the back seat full of shopping bags. "I don't know what I'd do if Squatty stopped giving me money. Most of the men who could afford me wouldn't be dumb enough to marry me. What did you buy?"

"Just something to put a rose in," Patsy said.

4

Lee Duffin was dressing but had gotten only as far as panties and a half-slip. She sat at her dressing table looking at herself in a triple mirror. Bill Duffin sat across the room in a cheap but comfortable green armchair reading a book catalogue and whistling happily from time to time.

"Happy, are you?" Lee said. Her hair was blond and cut very short. She was thinking of having it streaked.

"Damn right," Bill said.

"You're happy and I'm well preserved. I am, don't you think?"

"In the face. There was never much of the rest of you to preserve."

"Better thin than fat," she said.

"Books I picked up for four bits are now worth forty and fifty dollars," he said. "My prescience is making us rich."

"If books could only screw, it might even make us happy," Lee said, turning slightly. She was so small breasted that she seldom wore bras.

"What a trite complaint," Bill said. "I'm happy enough."

"Sure," Lee said. "I'm happy because I'm well preserved and you're happy because you've got six thousand books. Once every ten days or so we even have a pleasant conversation. I wish the girls were still at home. At least they talked to me."

"Find you a chum," Bill said. "There's bound to be a faculty wife or two who has similar problems."

"Nobody not married to you could have anything in common with me," Lee said. "When do the kids arrive?"

"Shortly. Want a drink? It might inspire you to finish dressing."

"Vodka and tonic," she said.

She finished while he fixed the drinks, and when the graduate students began to come nervously in, the Duffins were there to dazzle them. They had bought a house in Southampton, on Dunstan Street, an old high-ceilinged house with a long living room that had been shelved to hold four thousand of Bill's six thousand books. The Duffin library started with Henry James and came forward and included almost every modern writer of note, English, Irish, or American. Most of the books were fine bright copies and the collection shone brilliantly against the dark-stained bookcases. Among the nervous poorly dressed graduate students and their self-conscious wives the Duffins shone just as brilliantly—Bill tall and very confident and condescendingly amiable, ready with drinks and high-level academic gossip; Lee just as confident, quite impenetrable but poised and friendly and in a wild yellow dress. She moved from wife to wife inquiring about progeny and schools and the like. There was a Rolling Stones album on the phonograph, turned rather loud, a fact that unsettled many of the graduate students. The novelty of a professor who played the Stones was a little disquieting—almost frightening. In the past they had all done their level best to be conservative and unobtrusive at faculty gatherings, and it was unnerving to think that they might suddenly be expected to loosen up and be swingers. The Carpenters came in slightly late. Patsy was the only graduate wife with enough dresses to make brooding over what to wear a problem, and in any case she thought it ill-mannered to get to a party precisely on time. She had chosen a black and white dress with thin shoulder straps, so her arms were bare. Jim was as nervous as the other graduate students, and as soon as he got in the door and collected his drink he slipped over to the knot of males who were standing by the bookcases talking scholarship and admiring Duffin's books without quite daring to touch them.

Patsy was not at all nervous. Instead she was feeling happy and expectant and was just at that stage of her pregnancy when she seemed all bloom. She was looking splendid and knew it and was very in the mood for a party. The Duffins kept her a few minutes, exchanging pleasantries, and then she went over and stood chatting with Emma. Bill Duffin went to the bar and from that hostly vantage point stood watching her. He was impressed—a fact not lost on his wife.

"You look like a spider who's just come upon a fly," Lee said mildly. "Have another martini. It will blur your vision."

"Lovely girl," he said. "I saw her at the drugstore and never dreamed she was a graduate wife. I think I'll sit down and discuss profound issues with my students while I watch her."

"Try not to let your tongue hang out," Lee said.

Instead of sitting down, Bill took several of the students from his Eliot seminar over to the bookcases and showed them his Eliot collection, which numbered one hundred and thirty items. "It's not a bad author collection," he said modestly. "I was lucky and got my 'Prufrock' years ago, before it went out of reach. I wasn't so lucky with *The Waste Land*—I'll probably never own a first issue. Some of these magazine appearances are extremely hard to come by now."

He showed them some of the little magazines, English, American, or Continental, each magazine in a separate cellophane cover. The students scarcely knew what to say and handled the magazines fearfully, very afraid of damaging them. Only Jim was really at ease. He was fascinated. He had never seen such books or such curious magazines. A number of the books had Eliot's neat signature in them, and one or two of the late ones had short inscriptions to Duffin. Long after the other students had murmured their awe and gone back to their drinks Jim lingered by the bookshelves, Duffin with him. It had never occurred to Jim that books could be collected in that way or that they could look so attractive in a room. William Duffin, quick to respond to someone who responded to his taste, brought Jim another drink and continued to show him books. "My Pound collection is probably my best," he said. "I only know of one better in the world, and his bibliographer owns that. Did you know we're both from Idaho—Pound and I? I think that's what got me started on him. I even collect Vardis Fisher, another old Idaho boy."

Lee Duffin had come over and stood at her husband's elbow. She looked lovely and seemed in very good spirits. "I'm thinking of starting a collection of penises, myself," she said. "I'm planning to have them all in beautiful condition. I may even have a few rebound. I don't think I'll start with Idaho penises, though." She turned and left. Jim was very surprised, but Bill Duffin seemed not in the least ruffled.

"She doesn't suppress her resentments very well," he said. "It sometimes startles people. Let me show you my Faulkner."

They turned back to the books. Duffin noticed that Jim's clothes were better cut than the clothes of the other graduate students. "You collect?" he asked.

"No," Jim said. "I buy a lot of books but I never thought seriously of collecting them. Maybe I should."

"It takes money but it's very interesting," Bill said. "I better circulate. Look all you want to."

A little later, while Jim and one or two other graduate students were cautiously looking at the books, Patsy found that she wanted a drink of water and went to the kitchen to wash out her whiskey glass. Lee was talking to Emma, and Patsy was rather glad to get away from the wives for a minute. Her high spirits had flattened a little. For one thing, the Duffins both put her off. They were obviously sizing everyone up but doing it very slyly and, Patsy felt, not so much for political reasons as for their own exalted amusement. It was impossible to talk easily to the other graduate wives, largely because the Duffins kept the music a little too loud. The Stones or some other rock group were always hearable and were a difficult background to conversation. She had hoped that Hank Malory would be there and was disappointed that he wasn't. He was the only one of the new graduate students whom she found interesting. All in all it was not as good a party as it might have been, and she felt slightly wasted and a little bored.

When she turned around with the glass of water in her hand William Duffin stood in the kitchen doorway watching her. She felt embarrassed, as if perhaps she should not have entered the kitchen without asking. Duffin had loosened his tie and was clearly a little too warm, even though the house was centrally air-conditioned. He was a very tall man and looked more formidable alone than he had in the living room.

"Oh, hi," she said. "I needed a drink of water."

"You're awfully pretty," Bill said. "Let's go out in the back yard and neck."

Patsy was so surprised and shocked that for a moment she couldn't speak. She simply looked at him. He smiled good-naturedly.

"Don't look so surprised," he said. "Really. Why should I stand around dispensing social and professional banalities when what I really want to do is drag you out in the back yard and kiss you? I might as well be my licentious but attractive self." He had dropped his portentous lecturer's tone and spoke quietly and directly. For some reason the change in tone helped Patsy to recover her poise.

"Who says you have an attractive self?" she asked.

"Every woman I've ever slept with. Everyone except my wife, at least."

"Evidently your wife knows you best," Patsy said, setting her glass down. "I don't think you're so attractive. If you were two feet shorter and if your hair was curly instead of being too straight you'd look exactly like Eddie Fisher. Can you sing?"

Bill Duffin looked at her silently, as surprised by her remark as she had been by his proposition. She was looking at the Klee print that was thumbtacked over the stove.

"I guess I underestimated you," he said. "Sorry."

"Surely," she said, thinking perhaps he was drunker than he looked. She was in no mood to make a scene. The insult had actually pepped her up a little—it was a break in an otherwise boring evening. But Bill Duffin didn't move out of the door.

"Are you and your husband wealthy?" he asked. "That's a nice dress you're wearing."

"We're not starving," she said, standing up. "Excuse me, please."

"Sit a minute," he said. "I don't think you really considered my invitation on its merits."

"Oh, come on," she said. "Enough's enough. You know I'm married."

"He doesn't have much of an identity, does he?" Bill said, looking her in the eye. Patsy colored.

"If this is identity you're exhibiting I'm glad he lacks it," she said.

Bill was an excellent judge of how far was far enough, and he raised his glass to her. "Okay," he said. "I'll excuse you if you'll excuse me. I'm just impulsive and you looked kissable. My perceptions are probably dulled by drink."

Patsy went straight to Jim and told him she wasn't feeling well—could they go? Once they had paid their respects and were outside he asked her what was the matter.

"I just met the Sonny Shanks of the scholarly world," she said.

"Duffin? What do you mean?"

She told him as they walked. It was a clear pleasant night and their apartment was only a few blocks away. When she finished, Jim said nothing. Silence grew between them. It grew and grew until they were home. He sat on the couch, she sat in her chair.

"Probably drunk," Jim said finally.

"I knew you'd say that," she said. "He wasn't drunk, he was quite cold-blooded. No wonder she looks so uptight. Living with him she'd have to be."

Jim regarded her unhappily. "Do you think I'm cold-blooded?" he asked.

Patsy began to take off her hose. "No," she said. "You're nice. I wasn't comparing you to him, for god's sake."

"I'm just bothered," he said. "I was thinking of asking him to be my major professor. He seems to like me."

"Well don't," she said. "He likes me more."

Jim was silent, very depressed. Talking books with Duffin had excited him. He watched Patsy take off her hose, at a loss as to what to do. Marriage seemed to flatten his every expectation, but it had seldom flattened one so quickly. He looked at the shelf of quality paperbacks with dull dissatisfaction and went to get himself a glass of milk.

* * *

When the students were gone, Bill Duffin wrote out an order for two books, one by Lawrence Durrell and one by Oliver St. John Gogarty. He put an airmail stamp on the envelope and put the book catalogue in a neat stack he kept on the bottom of the bookcase near his desk. Lee came into the study in a white cotton nightgown and stood watching him.

"You look like Joan of Arc," he said. "It's your hair."

"I feel like her too. I know what it is to burn."

"Play with yourself," he said, smiling up at her. "I don't mind."

"What'll you be doing?"

"Reading 'Gerontion.'"

"My god," she said, yawning. "I'd think you'd be as bored with it as you are with me."

"'Gerontion' is ever fresh," he said. "Maybe I'll just listen to the record." He went to the living room and put on the record of Eliot reading and listened to "Gerontion." Lee went to bed and tried to read *The Hobbit*. Their oldest daughter, Melissa, was just then very big on it. She went to Mills College, in California, and they were practically certain that she had begun to smoke pot.

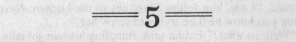

5

"I don't see anything so bad about them," Emma said, yawning. She was in her gown and an old flannel bathrobe and was watching the Johnny Carson show. Flap had just returned from taking the baby-sitter home. The party at the Duffins' had left him darkly depressed. Flap was normally cheerful, but when he got depressed he got very depressed, and it seemed to Emma that it was happening more often.

"You're the world's last optimist," he said, switching the TV to the late show, which was a Maria Montez movie called *Tangier*.

"They don't seem any worse than any other middle-aged couple," Emma said. "At least they're both smart. I thought you were glad Rice was finally getting someone like him. It was all you talked about for months."

"I didn't foresee him being a prick," Flap said. He went and got himself a beer and sat down on the couch by Emma, taking off his tie.

"Want to watch the movie or Johnny Carson?"

"Oh, the movie awhile, I guess. Let me have a sip of beer."

"I think Mrs. Duffin's getting worried she's too old, or something," Emma said. "She's a little tight under all that poise. I guess having a handsome husband who teaches young darlings all day would be worrisome when you got to her age. I'll probably be that way when you're a famous professor and I'm forty. Only she's thin and I'll be fat."

"He's not so handsome," Flap said.

"I thought he was."

"Anyway, he doesn't teach many girls. He mostly teaches hung-up graduate types like me and Jim."

"I thought you said he was good."

"He is good. I just don't trust him."

"You're paranoid. I like the movie better."

Flap got up and switched back and went and got another beer. His depression was lifting a little.

"He's the type who'll make trouble just for the hell of it," he said. "I saw him follow Patsy out to the kitchen. Next thing you know he'll be trying to screw her."

"Well, so what?" Emma said, rumpling his hair jovially. "Everybody tries to screw Patsy. I don't think you have any room to talk."

Flap grinned sheepishly. "Do you have to preface every remark you make with 'Well'?" he asked.

"No," Emma said. "That was the first remark I'd prefaced with 'well' all evening. Don't evade my accusation."

"I can't help it if I'm a flirt," Flap said.

Emma yawned again. "It's a good thing she doesn't take you seriously," she said. "She won't take William Duffin seriously, either. Let's have Hank over for dinner this weekend. Now there's a guy I could take seriously, if the chance arose."

"Okay," Flap said, yawning too. Emma was lying rather spraddled out on their old green couch. Flap glanced up her gown and saw the crotch of her white panties. Idly he lifted one of her legs across his lap and began to rub her with one hand. "Want to ask Jim and Patsy too?" he asked.

"I guess," Emma said, closing her eyes. She opened her legs even further, to facilitate being rubbed. On the screen Sabu was serenading Maria Montez, who was about to lose her heart to a hard-bitten newspaperman.

"Maybe Duffin won't bother me," Flap said. "I'm not in his century. Why would he bother a nineteenth-century man?"

"I admit the Rolling Stones were an affectation," Emma said.

"I've seen this movie. The villain gets killed in the elevator. He's a Nazi war criminal."

They heard a cough and both were silent. "Teddy," Emma said. "That sitter covers them up too much. She always has. It's a bad Southern habit, smothering kids." They listened, but he coughed only a couple of times and was silent. They relaxed again and Flap continued his stroking.

"Do that some more," Emma said, settling her hips a little. Flap did it for a while and then abruptly got aroused. "Hey, want the TV off?" he asked, standing up.

"It doesn't matter, I'm not watching it," Emma said, pulling up her robe and gown. When Flap got eager, he got very eager, and there was no such thing as getting it home too quickly. He took just time enough to drop his pants and switch off the light by the couch. The glow from the TV screen lit Emma's large hips and her loins, but Flap was not one to sit and look. He liked the way she smelled behind the ears, and the way her throat smelled. They soon grew very hot, for Flap still had his sports coat on and Emma her gown and robe. Her face was pink and sweating. Neither of them cared. When Flap came, Emma raised her legs and reached under him with one hand so she could hold his balls against her—it was a thing she really liked to do. Flap gave her a few soft little socks and, as always, was surprised, even worried, by the sound she made when she came. He knew it was only pleasure breaking through, but it was so like a sob that until her quietening grateful sighs followed it he was afraid to lift his face from her hair, fearful that he had goofed or hurt her somehow. They went almost to sleep, Flap comfortable between her ample thighs, and were brought back to themselves by a Dodge commercial. Besides being very rumpled, they were confronted with their usual problem: no Kleenex in reach and a fair amount of sperm ready to dribble out on the couch—an object which had already received an embarrassing number of dribblings.

"Well, hell," Flap said. "Here we are again. I can't reach my handkerchief without coming out."

"You don't have a handkerchief, anyway," Emma said, feeling around behind her head with one hand, hoping to find something useful on the radio table by the couch.

"Why don't we ever manage to get to bed?" she wondered, sighing.

"The fault of television. Find anything?"

"No. Go on. Who cares?" He went. "Eech," she said, covering herself with one hand. She went to the bathroom and Flap sat on the couch and took his shoes off. His left sock had a hole in the toe. Teddy began to cough again, and Emma came back in, in just her gown, with a washrag. She did what she could for the couch.

"Want some coffee?" she asked.

"No. I want another beer. My sock's got a hole in the toe."

"If you'd cut your toenails once in a while they wouldn't cut holes in your socks."

"You never remind me," he said.

Emma brought him a beer and made some coffee for herself. She got her sewing box and sewed up the hole in his sock. "I'll forget it and it will get too big if I don't do it right now," she said. They watched what was left of the late show and listened to Teddy's intermittent coughing. "If he's got fever in the morning we're canning that sitter," Emma said, yawning more broadly. "Let's go to bed."

"I want to see the elevator crash," Flap said. "Go on to

bed if you want to. I ought to read some eighteenth century, anyway."

Emma got out of the chair and came over and sat by him. She ruffled his hair again, yawning. Preston Foster was the Nazi. "I guess I'll wait for you," she said.

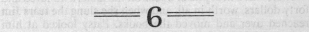

6

"I don't believe it," Patsy said. "You couldn't be that stupid." She was staring at Jim, injury in her face, and he sat at the kitchen table holding a book in his hands as if to protect it from her.

"There was nothing stupid about it. I asked Duffin and he said it was a good buy and a good book to start with."

"To start what with?"

"A collection of the Beats."

"Oh, shit," Patsy said and began to weep. She put her face on her fists and tears ran down her wrists and arms and off the crease of her elbows onto the blue tablecloth. Jim watched bitterly.

"What are you crying about?" he said. "So I bought some expensive books. Why not? I've got the money. Why shouldn't I spend it?"

"We haven't even paid the doctor for the baby," she said, sniffing. "We sweltered all fall without an air conditioner. You don't even want me to buy new dresses. We don't even go out and eat. We don't even go to the movies. And you spend forty dollars on a book we've already got, just to please William Duffin."

The book was a first edition of *Howl*, a copy that had belonged to a friend of Ginsberg's, for whom he had written in the words that had been censored out of the original text.

Jim had bought it from the catalogue of a book dealer in Florida and had patiently explained to Patsy what an important, unique copy it was; but the minute she had heard the price she became furious.

"I don't care what edition it is," she said. "Why should you squander forty dollars just to get the word f-u-c-k written a time or two in Allen Ginsberg's hand? I could have written it in our old copy for nothing."

"You won't even say it," Jim said. "Fat chance you'd write it."

"You shut up," she said, slinging tears off her face.

There was a neat pile of books on the table, a hundred and forty dollars' worth in all, and when she slung the tears Jim reached over and moved the books. Patsy looked at him contemptuously.

"Maybe I've forgotten what the word means," she said. "We haven't done it in months. Even if I am pregnant I don't think I'm that ugly. You just don't like to touch me any more."

Jim was a little jolted. "It hasn't been that long," he said. "You always exaggerate. I don't think it's been that long. Anyway, your being pregnant has nothing to do with it."

"Oh, I don't care how long it's been," she said. "It would just be nice if you wanted me once in a while. I don't know. It's that bastard Duffin."

"He's not a bastard and he has nothing to do with it."

Patsy snorted and went and got a dishtowel with which to dry her eyes. "It's him," she said bitterly. "You've got to be somebody's disciple, don't you? I wish I could understand why you invariably pick bastards."

Jim put the copy of *Howl* on the pile of books. Patsy was staring dully out the window. A couple of late tears had leaked out of her eyes and were caught beside her nose. It was Saturday afternoon, darkening and wintry.

"I don't want to argue about him," Jim said. "We've argued that a dozen times already. I don't know why he adopted me but he did and that's that. You're not realistic. He hasn't done anything but help me so far. You're more paranoid than Flap."

"Flap and I can tell a bastard when we see one," she said. "That's not paranoia, that's just good sense."

"It is *not* good sense," Jim insisted. "I'm going to be a scholar, right? Duffin is a famous scholar. If I work under him and do well he can help me get a good job. I've got to work under somebody—why not him? Anyway, I'd rather read moderns than anything else. You're just being irrational."

"I know it," she said, more quietly. He could always convince her she was being irrational if he tried.

"Maybe he's not so bad," she added. "I don't know. It doesn't strike me as particularly rational to spend forty dollars for a book you already have. A hundred and forty dollars for how many books? Nine? My god."

"Okay," Jim said. "Please hush."

They both hushed and sat silent, brooding. Patsy scratched her hair, which needed washing. Saturday afternoons depressed her, and they had nothing at all doing for the weekend. In a moment Jim came over and tried to make her stand up so he could hug her. She did, finally, but she was stiff in his arms.

"I'm not rational about money," he said. "I've admitted it before. I tell you what, I'll change. We'll spend all the money we want to. There's no point in pretending I don't have it when I do. We could even buy a house if you still want to."

Patsy kept silent, but she softened enough to rub her nose against his shirt. Her nose itched. It was a breakthrough, in a way. He had never offered to try and change before. Yet something in her was still disquieted and unappeased, and she didn't raise her face to him.

"What's the matter?" he said. "I'm sorry. I should have bought air conditioners. I just feel strange about being rich when the Hortons are so poor. Flap's my best friend."

"They could eat for two weeks on what that Ginsberg book cost," Patsy said, but not angrily. It was a problem she could understand, for she had often gone shopping with Emma and felt so guilty that she had not bought things she really wanted. Usually she snuck back and bought them later. It was particularly wrenching to watch Emma shop, because Emma loved things, objects, clothes, furniture, and had good taste and was always finding things she yearned for and couldn't buy. What made it even more wrenching was that Emma's mother had money and never gave Emma any.

"You're just afraid it will be like my dictionaries and my cameras," he said. "Just a new hobby. What if it is? It's nothing to get upset about. The books will get more valuable as time goes on. They're a kind of investment."

"You don't give a damn about investments," Patsy said. "You could buy municipal bonds if you wanted to invest. It's just a way of impressing William Duffin and showing him you want to be like him. I hate him. I don't want you to be like him. I like you because you're *not* like him."

"Okay, okay," Jim said. "I'm not going to argue about it."

"I wish you didn't have your money, anyway," Patsy said. "I wish the Hortons had half of it, or something. I would like for Emma to have new dresses. She doesn't fix herself up very well."

"Well, we can't do anything about the Hortons," Jim said. "What would you really like to do? We'll do it right now."

Patsy thought he meant make love, and she didn't want to, not just because her tears had made him contrite. But when she looked up at him she saw that he meant something else.

"I mean like go out or something," he said.

"Oh, yes, let's do. Maybe we could go to Galveston. We haven't been in months." She brightened at once, and the tense look left her face.

Half an hour later they were in the Ford, slipping onto the Gulf freeway. Patsy was curled against her door, wearing jeans, a sweater, and an old trench coat of Jim's. The warm car and the straight even highway calmed and almost mesmerized them both. As they sped out of Houston across the flat coastal plain, Patsy realized how much she had missed driving since the summer. In four months and more they had not been out of the city of Houston. All fall Jim had read at home at night or gone to the library, and she had read at home or gone to the library with him, the only break in the routine being an occasional hour or two of beer drinking with the other graduate students. She had even begun to avoid the beer drinkings, not because she didn't enjoy them but because she had discovered in herself a latent competitiveness in regard to Jim that was rather awful. The talk was always of books, and she had read many books and had a good memory for them, much better than Jim's. All too frequently she was unable to resist showing off how bright she was. It discomfited Jim, but the other graduate students appreciated her memory and her wit and she couldn't help responding to their appreciation. When the conversations got lively she became almost demonically inspired and could remember quotations and incidents in novels and bits of biographical minutiae that impressed the other graduate students mightily. Jim grew moody and told her from time to time that she ought to be getting the Ph.D., not him. Sometimes his moodiness merely made her worse. She became quite unable to shut up, and it was only later, remembering the conversations, that she found her aggressiveness distasteful. When she watched Jim study, saw him methodically reading scholarly books in order to get their theses clear, she would feel ashamed of herself and resolve to try and be a help rather than a discouragement, but the next time there was a literary conversation she invariably forgot her resolve. Flap Horton sometimes grew irritated with her, particularly when she came up with some oddment of information that spoiled his own theory on a given author or book. He told her she was a brilliant amateur, but essentially belle-lettristic, and she told him she considered that more of a compliment than a put-down.

The real trouble was that Jim was an amateur too, and a cautious one. He had been at work for three weeks on a paper on *The House of Fame* and was still far from satisfied with it.

It was a relief to be going somewhere where there were no graduate students. For once there would be no talk of books. There was nothing to see beside the flat road except an occasional filling station and, in the distance, the wavering orange flares from the giant oil refineries that lay along the ship channel. She looked at Jim, who was in a brood of his own. He had had his hair cut that afternoon, irritatingly short, she felt. It made him look too boyish. It seemed to her that the two of them had been living together almost all their lives, and that consequently it was time Jim stopped looking so much like a boy. She was growing heavier, her breasts were larger, she was changing, but when she looked for some development in him to match the development in her she could see none. The fact that they would soon have a baby left him unchanged, and almost unaffected. It worried her deeply. She wanted to feel that she could depend upon him taking care of her when the baby came, and she couldn't feel it. He had gone away, further away than he had ever gone before—into the library, into the coffee conversations of graduate school, into a world that didn't involve her at all, and she had no confidence in her ability to draw him back. His face was not happy—she had a feeling he would really rather be reading articles on *The House of Fame*. The drive to Galveston was just a duty, something he was doing to be courteous.

They crossed the high bridge over the coastal waterway and curved down onto Galveston island, drove up Broadway, passed the cemetery where the victims of the great flood were buried, and on past the few blocks of old turreted many-porched houses, virtually all that was left to suggest the Galveston of the past. Imperious dowager aunts should live in such houses, Patsy thought, though she had never been quite sure what made a dowager aunt. When they came to the ocean Jim turned right and they drove along the sea wall, passing the hotels, the arcades, the pier pavilion, and the seafood houses. They went on a mile or more south, past the old military embarkments, and parked and got out.

The gusty salty wind immediately blew Patsy's hair into her face. The tide was in and flecks of spray hit them. They looped arms and silently walked along the sea wall, the gusting wind causing them to weave a little. They walked far on, until they came to the last of the sea-wall lights. It was very foggy. They heard a ship's horn from the dark Gulf. The patterns of white foam and dark water repeated themselves and repeated themselves as they walked. They stood at the last light on the sea wall a minute or more, reluctant to go back; but the foggy darkness beyond the light seemed uninviting and they turned. "Hart Crane's washing around out there," Jim said. William Duffin had got him interested in Crane.

Going back, the wind was colder and stronger. Once it almost pushed them into the street. Between the wide-spaced lights were rows of parked cars, with lovers in them, mostly students and nurses from the nearby medical school. Every few feet or so there was a car, its windows rolled up, as private in the salty fog as if the lovers were on another planet. Patsy could not resist peeping a time or two, but even near the lights all she could see were vague shapes.

"Ah, young love," Jim said, and Patsy nodded, but as they passed more cars and remembered their own parking days—comparing them silently with the present—the thought of young love became more painful than pleasant. Jim regretted saying it. When they came to the Ford the door handles were sticky with salt spray.

"Do you envy those kids?" Patsy asked, once they were in the car. Jim took her cold hand and they tried to play with each other's fingers but didn't feel like it.

"I guess," Jim said. "Our folks still think of us as kids, you know."

They were silent, thinking about it, and then moved closer together and tried, out of mutual nostalgia, to be young lovers kissing. The attempt turned Jim hot and Patsy cold. When she put her hand behind his head she felt his newly barbered skull instead of the fine thick blond hair she liked to twist with her fingers. The kissing didn't warm her: she felt loose and indifferent and languid. Her hair was damp with the spray and the strands got between their mouths. Patsy sat carelessly, her eyes shut, while Jim patiently picked the strands away and smoothed them back. As he grew eager she grew more uncaring and idly looked past his head at the salt-smeared windshield as he kissed her. Whatever pleasure there had once been when their mouths touched was gone and she cared so little and at that moment remembered it so dimly that she did not even feel sad or like crying about it. She let him have her cold tongue, but it meant nothing. She just wished he would grow tired of kissing her. It was distasteful to be cold in a kiss and she wished he would realize from the slackness of it that she didn't want to kiss him any more.

But it was only when he began to kiss her that sex returned to Jim from its three-month leave. Somehow it had been absorbed by school, or killed by the worry about whether he would do well in school. There were always books and talk, one more chapter to read, one more authority to consider, one more text to scan. What was important was being bright, being alert, being informed. What he had done in three months was to become more adept at concealing his ignorance, and it had taken all his energy. Patsy had been a wife, which was enough; he had had no eye for her as a woman. But when he kissed her, sex came back, and he scarcely noticed that she was without tenderness or interest. He became too horny too quickly. His breath grew heavy and he worked a hand under her sweater. All he could reach was her heavy stomach, which had begun to curve with their child. He could not work his hand under her brassiere, nor under the waistband of her pedal pushers. She was slumped with her ankles crossed and her head back against the car seat, and he couldn't touch any of the places he wanted to touch. When she grew tired of being kissed she turned her head and her breath tickled his neck.

"Fine place you picked to come alive," she said. Her hair was a sticky tangle, she felt flat, and Jim's pressing eagerness made her feel removed and remote. The male was a curious creature, she decided. She had slept by his side in a thin nightgown for six or eight weeks and he had not so much as rubbed her belly.

"We could manage here, I think," he said, rubbing her just above the top button of her pedal pushers.

Patsy abruptly straightened up. "No, sir," she said. "Nobody's getting me in a car, not now. You might have managed it when we were younger, but you missed your chance." She turned and watched the ocean roll in.

"I don't want to drive home like this," he said, still stroking her under her sweater. "Let's go to a motel."

"There's a great suggestion," Patsy said, not meanly, but with a yawn. "Spend ten bucks to do what we could have been doing in our own bed all this time. You can make it home. If you've gone this long you can go another hour."

"Oh, quit," he said, stabbed by the indifference in her tone.

Patsy looked at him and saw that he was hurt and that he did want her, just as she had been wanting him to. She took his hand and tried to turn herself warm, but nothing in her

262

would turn. Holding his hand was the best she could do. She didn't feel hostile, just very uncaring.

"Sorry," she said. "I guess there isn't any point in my being penny-pinching about it. Suit yourself. I'd probably just as soon get screwed in a motel as anywhere else."

She had never used the word "screwed" before in reference to them, but she felt too generally uncaring even to use polite language. It startled Jim a little, but he saw that that was all the encouragement he was going to get, and he started the car. There was something coldly exciting about going to a motel solely for sex, and as they passed the sea lights he kept glancing at Patsy, hoping she would scoot over by him. Each light showed her face differently—one petulant, one a little frightened, one aged somehow, so that she looked older to him than she ever had. She did not scoot over, and she looked at the sea instead of him.

The first four motels he tried were full, and when he finally found one that wasn't, it was a dismal place with green and pink walls lit by green and pink neon. Patsy had been lulled again by the warm car and had all but fallen asleep against the door. When he stopped at the motel she looked at it once and then closed her eyes. The mood of emptiness was passing—she felt some emotion gathering in her, but it was a vague emotion. She was not sure what she felt, except that the motel looked dismal. Life seemed generally dismal too. When she saw Jim coming out with a key she kept her eyes closed and let her chin sink into her sweater, curious to see how far his own mood would take him. She was not sure he would actually wake her up and take her inside the drab place and make love to her. She felt willing to abide by his decision, but she refused to help him decide, and she didn't open her eyes when he got in the car.

He got in and sat looking at her. "Patsy," he said.

She yawned, knowing he wasn't fooled. "What?" she said. "Do you really want to come in?"

"I don't want to decide," she said, closing her eyes again.

"You're a cheat," he said and got out and went and pitched the room key to the desk clerk, who looked up in astonishment from the wrestling match he had been watching.

Patsy had no quarrel with the judgment he had passed on her, and even felt slightly more kindly toward him for saying it. He was sullen during most of the drive to Houston. It had started a drizzling rain and streams of mist spewed up from the tires of the cars they passed. They swirled into Houston on the wet freeway, the lights indistinct in the mist. Patsy sat up. She felt freshened and glad they had gone, and much friendlier toward Jim.

"You're right," she said. "I'm a cheat. I'm very spoiled. Hungry too. I'll fix us a nice sandwich when we get home. Guess what?"

"What?"

"I wish we'd gone in. I'd like to know what that place looked like on the inside. It must have been awful."

"Great," Jim said bitterly. "Maybe we ought to go back."

"Please don't be sour," she said. "I know you have a perfect right to be but I wish you wouldn't. Houston's lovely when it's drizzling."

At home she turned and lifted her arms to him, offering herself, but Jim ignored her and peed and got a book, and Patsy happily washed her hair and made them both pâté sandwiches with pickles and hard-boiled eggs. She took him a sandwich plate and some beer. Jim was still aggrieved, but he ate hungrily. Patsy stood by his chair a long time, all clean in her robe and gown, reading Lumiansky on Chaucer over his shoulder and wishing he would touch her and forgive her her bitchiness. But he ignored her until thirty minutes later, when she was kneeling on the bed, her behind in the air, reading and fingering the drying ends of her hair. He sat across from her and saw down the front of her gown. Her breasts were heavier. She was quietly reading *The Rights of Infants,* her face calm. She seemed to him very sexy. His annoyance seemed silly—she was the same old Patsy, only a little sexier. She was not at all the distant stranger she had seemed in the car. He left his book and quickly circled the apartment turning out lights. When all but the bed light were out she looked up at him, wondering, slightly surprised, a strand of hair curled round a finger. He sat beside her and put his hand inside her gown, on her warm breasts, and desire pushed at him immediately, as strongly as it had pushed at him on the beach. Patsy was quiet and cooperative, but they had been off pace with each other for hours, perhaps for days and weeks, and off pace they remained. Jim was in a great hurry and Patsy simply never turned on. She was not angry, though. "Don't worry about it, just don't skip so long next time," she said, patting his arm.

Later, when he had gone to sleep, she felt itchy and a little raw and was annoyed, though at herself rather than at Jim. In earlier months, when he had worried so much about pleasing her, she had longed for him just to forget her, to approach her in blind desire and take what he wanted without worrying about her. But that was in earlier months. He had just done precisely that and instead of being carried away by it, it had just made her itchy. He had learned to be impetuous just as she had reached a stage where she would have liked some leisurely attention. She sighed and went to the bathroom, wondering if they would ever be at the same stage at the same time. When she was back in bed she shyly got Jim's book on Chaucer off the bedside table, glad that he was asleep. He had grown defensive about her reading scholarship—he seemed to feel that it was something she would steal from him if she got the chance. She watched him a minute, to be sure he was really asleep, and then turned on her side and covertly read about the Marriage Group to satisfy her curiosity, peering over her shoulder at her husband from time to time to be sure he didn't catch her at it.

265

7

The first time Patsy saw Hank Malory's apartment she grew irritated and walked around with her arms folded, pouting a little with the desire to throw everything in it out. It was a small two-room second-story apartment in a chunky brick house on Albans Road. As an apartment, it was totally drab. The floors were bare; there were no curtains and curtains were badly needed, what passed for a kitchen table had an awful yellow plastic top and spindly legs that weren't even even; some of his books were piled on an ugly white bureau, others on an old brown card table in the living room-bed room, where there was a black portable typewriter and a wastebasket full of blue books and beer cans. The bed was made but it had an ugly green bedspread, and the couch was a sagging blue object with the center cushion faded white. Surprisingly, the place was quite clean, but the cleanness only emphasized the drabness, and Patsy was annoyed. Hank Malory ought not to acquiesce to drabness, even if he was poor. She had an urge to bring him some red curtains and a bright print or poster of some kind.

They had walked over one evening to see him, for he and Jim got on well. They were both new to graduate school, and while Hank was a good deal less nervous about it than Jim it was only because he was not the sort of person to be very nervous about anything. The first time Hank asked them over they found him sitting on a little stair landing in back of the apartment looking down on the tiny back yard. He was dressed in Levi's and a blue shirt and was barefooted. He had been reading his eighteenth-century assignment, which happened to be the *Essay of Dramatic Poesy.* It was still early fall—Patsy wore Bermudas and a white blouse. As she came up the steps her eyes came level with his feet and she noticed that he had corns on both his little toes.

"You don't take very good care of your feet," she said. "I bet you wear cowboy boots when nobody's looking."

Hank looked surprised and held one foot aloft to see what was the matter with it. "I never noticed," he said, which struck her as a limp remark. It annoyed her when people she was prepared to like let themselves be taken aback by her observations; but then Hank was not very taken aback—he was just not much on repartee. She noticed later that he did have an old crumpled pair of boots in his closet. He had only one suit and one sports coat and not very many shirts. Patsy was a tireless snoop and went in and snooped the apartment thoroughly while Jim and Hank sat on the back porch drinking beer and helping each other straighten out the dramatic preferences of the speakers in the *Essay.* When she came back outside Hank had put the eighteenth-century anthology down and she found his place and snooped in the essay a bit. Reading the places where people stopped in books was always sport. After a paragraph or two of Dryden she sniffed and closed the book.

When she sniffed, Hank grinned at her. "You prefer *McCall's* to Dryden," he said. "I saw what you were reading this afternoon."

Patsy blushed, taken aback herself. She read the women's magazines idly but regularly at the Bissonnet drugstore, and though she said she did it for the horror of it she had come to enjoy them and knew it; but the disconcerting thing was that Hank had seen her when she had not seen him and for a minute she could not remember how she had looked. She seldom went out looking dowdy, but occasionally, when the afternoon heat made the apartment like the inside of a clothes dryer, she wandered over to the drugstore for a Coke and a magazine, sometimes in an old shift, sometimes in jeans and a shirt.

"I read everything," she said and brightened, for she remembered that she had been quite nice that afternoon, in a red dress that Dixie had prodded her into buying on one of their excursions. She had worn her hair swept up on her head. She was not sure it had been becoming, but it certainly had been cool.

A day or two later she saw him and again she was dressed nicely and he rather shabbily. She went right over and sat down just around the corner from him and when he saw her he said, "Hi," and scooted over two seats so they could chat. Patsy ordered a cheese sandwich and showed off outrageously about *Tristram Shandy,* which he was having to read and didn't like and which she had read and loved.

"You have a good memory for novels," he said enviously. What he really noticed were the curling wisps of black hair at her temples, and the curve of her lips on the milkshake straw, and the way she kept looking down into her glass instead of at him. What Patsy kept noticing was that he was tall and a little awkward. She was five six and a half and he was only six two, yet he was always leaning down a little and smiling at her. It made her feel strangely diminutive and feminine and flustered her a little. When she had first come up the steps and seen him on the landing she had noticed how long his calves were.

She soon concluded that he was pleased with her and didn't care at all that she had a better memory for novels than either he or Jim. They only chatted for fifteen minutes, but somehow the chat disquieted her. She was not still inside herself for two hours when she went home. She tried to put her finger on what it was that she liked about him and couldn't. It certainly wasn't his manners, or his general appearance. The only really appealing thing about his face was the dent on the bridge of his nose, which for some reason she liked. He was normally so silent and noncommittal that she really had no clear notion of what it was he liked about her, other than her general appearance, and from then on when she went to the drugstore she took some pains with herself, in hopes that if she met him she could tell from his response what he liked about her. She dressed simply but nicely and read either *The New Yorker* or the *Atlantic* or *Vogue* or some paperback, quality usually, until she had met him several times and knew they were friends and that he really didn't care what she read. Then she went back to reading whatever was at hand. He usually read *Sports*

Illustrated and scarcely had grounds for feeling superior, in any case. Soon, without really thinking about it, she knew when his classes were, what days he had seminars and what days he didn't, and the times when he would most likely be at the drugstore. If she didn't bump into him there when she expected to she would go home feeling slightly put out, her day lessened. They both soon noticed that they would just as soon not see each other in other places, such as at graduate parties or beer busts. It invariably made them both edgy. It was frustrating in some way, whereas a chat at the drugstore was always pleasant and helped make a day.

Eddie Lou, the little middle-aged frizzle-haired short-order cook who could turn out hamburgers with her eyes shut, knew there was something illicit afoot months before Patsy would have allowed such a thought anywhere near the front of her mind. Eddie Lou was from East Texas and had been left by two husbands, both shiftless no-counts with roving eyes; and every time she saw Hank and Patsy looking happy and glancing at each other between sips of something and chatting about books she would never read or picture shows she would never see, the East Texas soul in her stiffened and she burned their hamburgers, if they were having them, or left the grilled cheeses on too long, or neglected to give them pickles, which she knew Patsy liked. It annoyed her all the more that they were usually so absorbed in each other that they ate the burned hamburgers as if they were delicious. What made matters even worse, in Eddie Lou's opinion, was that Patsy had the sweetest husband in the world as it was. Jim was her special pet. He joshed her a lot and had spent the summers of his boyhood in Gladewater, where Eddie Lou was from, so they had much to talk about. To Jim she was especially nice. She kept his milkshakes thick and gave him potato chips whether he had them coming or not. She was convinced calamity was not far off and she was determined to help him through it in whatever way she could.

Eddie Lou's forebodings, though justified, were quite premature. All through the fall no improper word passed between Patsy and Hank, and no improper tone was struck. So reticent was Hank, so little prone to reveal whatever emotion he might feel, that Patsy even became a little frustrated. Their chats were, if anything, too proper. She felt his regard for her to be a little too slight and too impersonal. Often after a chat, sweating under her dress from the humid fall heat, she felt that pregnancy must have already taken its toll of her looks; but then, when she thought about it carefully, she knew that wasn't true. Her looks clearly pleased him, but that they did was really small consolation. Probably her looks were the only thing about her that pleased him. He probably thought of her as no more than a pretty bagatelle, someone who would do to chat with, to ogle a bit, perhaps even to flirt with, but only in the lightest way.

He told her nothing of himself, nothing of his past; he was so quiet and his temperament was so level, apparently, that it was even hard for her to tell what sort of mood he was in. It was particularly hard for her to accept such reticence, since Jim had always been the opposite. Jim had told her his entire life story fifteen minutes after he met her for the first time. They had talked about their pasts for hundreds of hours, exploring every minute wrinkle in their relatively unwrinkled childhoods. There was something in Hank's face, in his walk, his accent, his name even, that bespoke a background very different from her own—some poverty, some vulgarity, something Pete Tatum would know about. He sometimes reminded her of Pete; like Pete, he had a kind of presence that had more to do with physical confidence than with intellect. He was fairly smart, but what she liked about him was not that he was fairly smart. She liked the way he was, and it frustrated her that he wouldn't share more of himself with her. She felt that if he accepted her at all it was merely as the pretty wife of a friend, someone who could brighten a seat at the drugstore counter.

It was not until almost Christmas that a different quality came into their relationship. There was a Christmas party at the Hortons'. The boys had been packed off to stay at Emma's mother's, and all the more likable graduate students had been invited. The Hortons loved to give parties and were only inhibited by their lack of funds; in this instance the Carpenters were co-hosts. The Hortons furnished the place and the dip, and the Carpenters furnished the liquor and a goodly supply of records. Flap was drunk before the party started and made a slight fool of himself by going around with mistletoe and kissing all the women smackingly. Everyone enjoyed him; without his joviality the party might never have got moving at all. He had got drunk early to right himself with his principles, for after much brooding he had done the diplomatic thing and invited not only the Duffins but the department head as well. He hoped neither would come, but as luck would have it the department head and his wife showed up almost immediately and the Duffins a bit later in the evening.

The department head was an aging Spenserian named Timothy Ivan—a man retired from active scholarship, as he frequently said with a sigh. The graduate students jocularly referred to him as Loving Mad Tim, because he loved them all but could only very occasionally remember any of their names. The high point of his scholarly career had been a collaboration on a prose version of *The Faerie Queene* for use in high schools, and his chief pleasure in life was his collection of arrowheads. His wife was a petite Philadelphian who had stoically endured thirty years in Houston. She came in wearing her fur coat, as all had feared she would. The temperature was in the sixties but Mrs. Ivan seldom got even that good a chance to wear the coat and seldom missed one when she did. She lived for the rare years when the MLA held its convention in Philadelphia—then she could go home for Christmas. Flap shuffled a bit and kissed her on the cheek and she was pleased and said good things about him to her husband when they left thirty minutes later.

"Whew," Flap said. "I thought they were going to stay."

"They're not so bad," Patsy said. "I kind of like them." She was sitting on the couch. Hank was there but was chatting with Emma by the dip bowl. Jim was in a very good mood. He had given a report that afternoon on *After Strange Gods,* and Duffin had praised it highly. Jim was dancing with Clara Clark, the good-looking redhead whom Flap had said wouldn't last. She was from Santa Barbara and was very good at dancing teenage dances. Elvis Presley, one of Flap's musical passions, was on the phonograph.

"There's a nice limber girl for you," Flap said, admiring Clara.

"Humph," Patsy said. "You should see me do that, if I wasn't pregnant."

Not being able to dance when her husband was dancing made her feel a little out of it, but after a while Hank and Emma and Kenny came over and they all got in a hot argument over Terry Southern and she felt in it again. It was an argument over the relative merits of *Candy* and *The Magic Christian;* Flap, in his usual fashion, dominated it by being the only one who had read both books. Kenny's beard had grown shaggier and he was staying high a lot to protect his creativity, as it were. "I don't like Terry Southern much," he kept saying.

"I liked his piece on the twirling convention," Patsy said. "I don't think he likes women, though." She was more and more inclined to judge novelists by whether or not she felt they liked women.

Kenny didn't answer. He was staring fixedly at Clara Clark's pelvis, which was twisting and gyrating only a few feet away. The conversation drifted on, but Kenny kept staring at Clara's pelvis, as if he hoped, by staring with sufficient concentration, to bring her clitoris into view.

While they were all yakking, the Duffins appeared at the door, surprising everyone. They had clearly dressed down for the occasion, Bill in an old corduroy coat with leather patches at the elbow, Lee in a blue sweater and skirt; but even so they managed to look like two jet-setters arriving at a hoedown. All the men stood up, the dancing stopped temporarily, and the conversation stopped too. Flap let his mistletoe lie and did not kiss Lee Duffin.

"Well, let the merriment resume," Bill said with a slight bow. It resumed, but with a different tone. It became a little more frenetic and took on a slightly forced quality, as if everyone in the room were performing for the tall smiling slightly sardonic man and the trim woman. In a few minutes it worked out that Jim was dancing with Mrs. Duffin and Bill Duffin was dancing with Clara Clark. Dancing with a famous professor threw Clara slightly off and made her look like she was trying too hard. Patsy began to feel depressed the minute the Duffins arrived, and watching Jim dance with Lee only made her feel the more depressed. Lee danced intently, moving around Jim with swoops and darts, like a thin desert bird of some kind. She was smiling, but it was a taut smile; she moved well, but her movements too were taut. She moved around Jim watchfully, as if he were a small snake that she might pounce on at her leisure.

Jim was obviously having a great time dancing with her and Patsy was suddenly filled with repugnance, not so much for him but for the whole gathering—the whole business. It reminded her a little of the party in Phoenix. Maybe Jim was just naturally attracted to older women. Lee fascinated him, just as Eleanor Guthrie had. So where did that leave her? She was too heavy to dance and no one was paying the slightest attention to her, not Kenny, not Hank, not even Flap. Clara and Lee were both prettier, probably, or sexier, or something. She felt very alone and wanted very much to be home by herself. Impulsively she rose and slipped past the dancers and went into the Hortons' bedroom. The bed was piled with sweaters and purses and she sat down on the floor by a bookcase, her back against the bed. Something inside her was sinking like a stone, sinking far down. She didn't understand anything, didn't love anyone, wasn't loved, really, never had been, never would be. The Hortons' bedside books were at her elbow: a paperback of *The White Nile*, Northrop Frye's *Fables of Identity*, *The Hero with a Thousand Faces*, Emma's high school copy of *Wuthering Heights*—her favorite book—a gray Modern Library Giant of Jane Austen's novels, a mixture of smaller Modern Library books with their titles faded off, and several paperbacks. Patsy pulled out a red paperback of the *Kama Sutra* and leafed through it, growing even more dispirited by the thought of people doing all those abstract and acrobatic things with one another's genitals. She was quite sure none of them would work with hers; the simplest things barely worked with hers and anyhow the whole thing was sickening, she felt like she would never want to touch a living soul again. Everything in life was disappointing and irritating and worked out to make her lonelier. She didn't even want to cry, she just wanted to be home.

Hank Malory walked past the bedroom on his way to the john and stopped and looked in at her. She had a green ribbon in her hair and it was slightly awry. When she raised her arms to straighten it she noticed him. She felt too lonely to be embarrassed, and looked up at him solemnly.

"Something wrong?" he asked.

273

Patsy shrugged. Her depression was too obvious to deny. "I'm just not in the mood for this party," she said. "I guess I've become anti-social. I don't know."

"I'll drive you home," he said a little awkwardly. For weeks he had been wanting to be alone with her and he was made nervous by his own desire. He was afraid too much of it would get into his voice.

But Patsy jumped at the chance. "Oh, I wish you would," she said, stuffing the *Kama Sutra* back in the bookcase. She had been dreading having to ask Jim; he was having a good time and would resent having to leave. When they went back into the living room Elvis Presley was still on and Jim was still dancing with Lee Duffin.

> *Well since my baby left me*
> *I've found a new place to dwell . . .*

Emma saw that Patsy had her sweater on and came over, looking worried. "Sick or bored?" she asked.

"Equivocal," Patsy said. At that moment she didn't feel close to anyone and was hoping Emma wouldn't ask her to stay. Emma didn't. While Hank was in the john Patsy stood in the doorway watching Jim and Lee dance. Bill Duffin came over, a drink in his hand.

"How are you?" he asked.

"In the process of departing."

"I hope you and Jim will come to dinner sometime soon," Bill said. "He's turning into a fine student. Between the two of us we might make a scholar of him yet."

"What do you mean, the two of us? I have very little to do with it."

"Sure you do," Bill said. "You have to become a complete bitch, like Lee. Bitches like Lee are the making of scholars like me. You've made a fine start—just don't mellow."

"Do you get a sexual thrill from being offensive to women?" Patsy asked. "I really don't understand you."

"I was just paying you back for saying I looked like Eddie Fisher," Bill said and walked away.

Patsy was shaking a little with annoyance and went over and made Jim stop dancing for a moment. "I'm feeling poorly," she said. "Hank's going to run me home. Have a good time, okay?"

"Okay," Jim said, a little surprised. He started to ask if she wanted him to come home with her. He would not really have minded leaving, but Patsy had turned away and Lee was waiting a little impatiently for him to resume their dance. He did, but he felt slightly out of kilter, as if he might have failed to do something he should have done.

Outside, walking down the driveway with Hank a few steps behind her, Patsy's eyes seeped a little. Duffin's insult had a delayed kick, and she felt frustrated. She resolved that there would be no dinners at the Duffins', no encounters with the Duffins; Jim would not have Duffin as his major professor if any effort of hers could prevent it. Hank's car was an old maroon Oldsmobile of about the same vintage as the Ford.

"You're smart," she said. "You didn't take Duffin's seminar, did you? I wish my husband hadn't.

"I've only seen the man twice and he's insulted me both times," she added.

Hank nodded sympathetically but didn't ask her about it. She thought ahead to the dark apartment and felt lonely again. She wished he were more talkative. She felt like talking to one person, not to a party of people. But he just wasn't very talkative, and they were almost to the apartment.

"Want to drive a little?" he asked unexpectedly. "Or have some coffee or something?"

"Sure," she said. "Whatever you'd rather."

They drove out a freeway to where it ended, on the southwestern edge of Houston, and circled underneath it and drove back in. It was a clear December night, not clear enough that stars could be seen but clear enough that the brightly lit buildings downtown were visible. Patsy wished they were going to Galveston—it would have been pleasant to walk on the beach on such a night. Instead, Hank took her to a place called Yum-Yum's Lounge, on Richmond Avenue, a bar much favored by graduate students. It was in a small dilapidated shopping center, next to a taxidermist's; it had deep booths and served sandwiches. Hank and Jim had been there frequently but Patsy had never been and was disconcerted at first because the jolly blond barmaid clearly regarded her as Hank's date, or did until he introduced her as Patsy Carpenter, Jim's wife. "Jim's wife!" the barmaid said. "He never told me he was married. And me all set to ask him for a date."

Seeing herself changed back into a wife in the woman's eyes had a settling effect. The booth was cozy and all the things that had depressed her at the party was easily forgotten. She brightened, found that she was hungry, and had a Swiss cheese sandwich. "God, I was about to get morbidly depressed," she said, eating the last bite of crust. "Why is it you never come to our house?"

"I study too hard," Hank said.

Patsy looked at him gravely, a little annoyed. He never really spoke straight to her. He either kidded her or spoke past her in some way.

"If you'd ever really talk to me we could be friends," she said.

"You're too pretty to be friends with," he said, and for once he didn't sound like he was kidding. He even looked at her, which was disconcerting. She had a sudden sense that her hair was wrong and took the ribbon off, so that her hair hung loose at her shoulders.

"I'm not too pretty to talk to," she said. "We could swap out. I'll tell you about my childhood and you tell me about yours."

Hank shook his head. "Mine's too literary," he said. "Some writer should have written it. What was that young guy's name who disappeared? The Texas writer?"

"Oh, Danny Deck," she said. "Don't tell me he should have written it. I didn't like his book very much. The Hortons knew him, did you know that? They were very good friends."

Suddenly the thought that Hank might really want her struck her. What he said about her being too pretty to befriend had sounded strange, unlike anything he had ever said to her. She didn't know what to do and began to chatter.

"My childhood was too unliterary," she said. "I had a nice straightforward right-wing Dallas upbringing. I didn't even have any traumas. My sister got to have all the traumas. Somehow I think that if I had got to live in Fort Worth I would have had traumas and been morbid about my childhood, like everybody else. Every second person I know seems to have come from Fort Worth and had a dark childhood."

"I lived there four years," he said. "Who else do you know from Fort Worth?"

"I did know this rodeo clown and his wife. His name was Pete Tatum. I don't know if we'll ever run into them again. His wife is named Boots."

"You know Pete Tatum?" he asked, looking genuinely surprised for the first time since she'd known him.

"Sure. Do you?"

"His first wife was my aunt," he said. "My Aunt Marie."

Patsy was amazed. It was the first time it had occurred to her that it really was a small world, in the sense in which the phrase was normally used.

"She lives in Dumas now," Hank said. "Her husband owns a grain elevator. I never got to see her much. She was my daddy's sister and I was raised by my mother's sisters. They didn't like Aunt Marie very well."

They were silent a minute. "Let's have a little music," he said. Patsy was agreeable and they went back to the jukebox together. He gallantly offered her first choice of songs and she chose "California Dreaming." He played "The Gates of Eden," and it became her turn again. She was about to play a Rolling Stones song when she noticed that there were a couple of Hank Williams songs on the jukebox. "Want to hear your namesake?" she asked. He shrugged, and she played, "Cold, Cold Heart" and "The Lovesick Blues," and they went back to the booth and watched the beer foam drying on their glasses while the songs played. They both felt slightly melancholy but comfortable together. When they went outside they discovered that a norther had just struck. The trees were rustling over the garage when he walked her up the steps to the apartment. Patsy was thinking how strange it was that Hank and Pete should have that connection, a woman named Marie whom neither of them had seen, probably, in many years. And what was stranger still was that she, who had never seen the woman, had found herself in a kind of harmony with two men who had known Marie so differently, one a nephew, one a husband.

"I think Pete mentioned your aunt," she said, trying to get the key in the lock. "It was about them breaking up, but I don't remember what he said."

Just as she got the key in the lock the phone began to ring. She rushed in to get it, missed the light switch, and answered it in the dark. It was Jim, sounding very worried.

"Gosh, have you been calling?" she asked. "Hank and I just had a beer at a place you and he go to. Yum-Yum's."

"I just called once," Jim said. "I was afraid you might have had car trouble."

"No. I'm sorry I left so abruptly. Your mentor insulted me again, I'm afraid. I do wish you'd find another mentor. You're sweet to call. How's the party?"

"Drunken. The Duffins just left. I'm looped enough that I might as well stay until it's over."

"Do," she said. "Apologize to Emma for me. I not only left, I took away Hank. Tell her I'll send him right back."

She didn't push about Duffin—Jim would just resent it. She turned on the bed light by the phone, feeling suddenly awkward. Her husband had disappeared from her mind for an hour—though it seemed like he had been gone for days and weeks—then he had reappeared, his pleasant self. He had sounded very concerned about her. She had been about to ask Hank in. She had an urge to make hot chocolate and wanted him to drink it with her. Perhaps he would really talk to her if she kept trying. Despite Jim's concern, she still felt lonely. But mightn't he be jealous if she didn't send Hank back to the party as she had promised? The idea of Jim jealous was so strange and new that she could hardly imagine it. Except for the one strange moment in Cheyenne when he had seen her throw Pete Tatum a kiss, he had never had the slightest reason to be jealous of her. She felt very uncertain and took a comb out of her purse and combed her hair quickly. It was an entirely new problem, and new problems made her frantic. She and Hank had just begun to get comfortable with each other, and she hated to rush him off. She went back to the door and switched on the porch light. He was sitting on the railing of the landing, his hands in his pockets. The new norther whistled around the corners of the garage.

"You didn't have to stand out there," she said. "You could have come in where it's warm."

They looked at each other through the screen but could not see each other clearly. It was only when he turned his head and looked away from the garage that the light shone on his angular face. "I don't call this cold," he said. "You ought to try a wind like this out where I come from." He got off the rail, as if to go, but paused a minute on the top step looking toward the country where he came from—the land of northers.

"Homesick?" Patsy asked. That was how he looked.

"I don't know what for," he said.

"I was going to ask you in for hot chocolate but I told Jim I'd send you back to the party," she said.

She had meant to ask him which he would rather do but found she couldn't. She stood inside the screen, silent and a little impatient. She was not sure he had even heard her, and she did not feel like repeating her remark. He kept looking out into the darkness and it annoyed her; she felt her impatience swelling, and yet when he turned suddenly to face the door she felt a tremor, almost a moment of fright. She looked at him with longing, but all she longed for was someone friendly who liked her, someone to drink hot chocolate with. He looked at her with desire—he knew it, even though she couldn't see him clearly. If he had stepped inside she would have had to make the hot chocolate and it would have all become scary.

"I'll run on back to the party," he said. "Enjoyed the beer, though." He waved and started down the steps, turning up the collar of his suede coat as he went. Instead of feeling relieved she was once again very impatient with him.

"I wish you'd get another coat," she said, putting her head out the screen. "I'm sure you could afford a better coat than that."

Hank turned and looked up at her, quite surprised. "What's wrong with this one?" he asked.

"Everything," she said hotly. She was as surprised at her

remark as he was. She had not been thinking of the coat until she saw him turn up the collar. Once she had given her views on it she had nothing else to say, and he had nothing to say in retort. There was a strange silence. They looked at each other across the landing, both of them irresolute.

Hank finally grinned and lifted his hands, at a loss for a solution. "You think I should burn it?" he asked.

"Yes, please burn it," she said, feeling ridiculous. He waved and went on and she went inside and sat on the john for a long time looking at *The Greek Myths* without reading a word. Once her feeling of ridiculousness diminshed she felt strangely good—warmer toward the world than she had in some time. When Jim came in at three she was still awake, reading Frazer. He wasn't too drunk but he was drunk enough to go immediately to sleep. She pulled his arm across her and held his hand against her swelling stomach, feeling quiet, protected, protective, and lucky. Somehow the few odd awkward moments with Hank made being in bed with Jim seem all the cozier. The norther grew stronger, strong enough to rattle the windows of the apartment, and the harder it blew the warmer and drowsier Patsy felt.

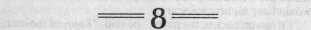

By the next evening the norther had blown itself out. The temperature, which had dropped only to the low forties, returned to the seventies, and the heavy December sultriness which sometimes occurred in Houston settled in.

Hank Malory had a date with Clara Clark that evening. They had been seeing each other for a six weeks. The only reason he hadn't taken her to the Hortons' party was because she had gone with a girl friend who had no date. Clara had initiated it all by asking him to take her surfing. She had no car. Hank had been glad to take her, though the surfing part didn't work out very well. She had lived on the coast of California all her life and was voluably contemptuous of the gray lukewarm Gulf.

"Mini-waves," she said, and they never went surfing again. Instead they ate—seafood, usually—saw several movies and a play or two, and finished the evening at Clara's, in bed. Her apartment was on Bissonnet, scarcely three blocks from his. She was a very attractive twenty-four-year-old redhead and she loved two things completely: herself and California. Except for a mild regret that she was not slightly taller and slightly slimmer, Clara was as nearly satisfied with herself as any human being Hank had ever known. She was quite convinced that she could handle anything that came along—emotional, sexual, or intellectual—and she could. There was no uncertainty in Clara, not in her movements, her speech, her reports and term papers, her orders in restaurants, or her plans for the future. She always knew what she wanted, and one of the things she wanted was a degree good enough to get a teaching job at some junior college in California. She did not particularly want to get married and she could not conceive of living any place but California.

She liked Hank at once. He was attractive and friendly, and didn't seem to be particularly hung up in any way. She would actually have preferred to sleep with Jim. He was the type of boy she was accustomed to, and he and she had more to say to each other, and she had always been attracted to blond men, for some reason; but she had also twice had things with married men and had found them very harassing. Graduate school was providing all the harassment she needed, so she kept it cool and friendly with Jim. He bought her lots of coffee and complimented her and they talked endlessly, but when it came time to get someone to sleep with she picked Hank. He didn't have much to say, but he was silent in a relaxing way and it was a relief to go with someone who wasn't eternally bitching about graduate school. Everyone else felt, or at least declared, that graduate school was really no place for them, that the life was unreal, the projects inane, the themes and theses worthless, the professors disagreeable, the social conventions artificial, the competitions silly. Nonetheless, most of them stayed hermetically sealed in the graduate life, wrote the papers, kowtowed to the professors, plodded through the texts, consumed lakes of coffee a cup at a time, griped, whined, exulted over triumphs so minor they would have been unnoticeable in any other context, competed with one another endlessly, and, by the time they had been at it a few months, would scarcely have known what to do in any other world. To go back into what they liked to refer to as "real life" they would have had to be reconditioned slowly, like divers coming up from the deep.

Hank and Clara both participated in the syndromes of apprentice scholarship, both did fairly well, neither felt particularly bored or particularly griped by the requirements, and neither was nostalgic for any other existence—though Clara did miss California very much. Hank didn't even have that problem. In comparison to Vietnam, graduate school was an idyll.

On the Saturday evening after the Horton party they saw *The Pumpkin Eater* and were both a little depressed by it. Hank was slightly uncomfortable all evening, wondering if Clara was going to mention his having left the party with Patsy. They were not going steady, officially, but he knew she must have noticed it. Also, Patsy kept occupying his thoughts, and it was strange to sit holding hands with one girl while thinking of another. Clara said nothing about Patsy. After the movie, at her apartment, he sat on her bed watching her strip, wondering what he ought to do. He had a sense, very new to him, that somehow he was not being fair to Clara. She was quite lovely, with rather small breasts but fine legs, and she stripped and hung her clothes in the closet as quickly and methodically as if she were about to put on a bathing suit and go surfing.

"Pooped?" she asked. "You don't look too spry."

"Just watching you," he said, taking off his socks.

She had recovered from her own mild depression and

talked brightly while he undressed. Movies seldom moved her—very little *did* move her, though she was not unfeeling. It was as if her needs were purely metabolic; she was too nearly complete, too fully possessed, to need very much emotionally. Food, sleep, a job, sex, pleasant company: those were her needs. She was not dramatic, not neurotic; ultimately, she was athletic. They had made love often and Hank knew what she liked. Part of what she liked was to be on top, the first time. She liked to do a lot of moving herself. That he didn't mind. He had never known a girl who really liked to be on top and the novelty was enjoyable, though since he was accustomed to being the surfer and not the wave he found it took a little catching on to. But Clara always worked things out to her satisfaction. Then she usually liked to be on the bottom, where she worked things out to her satisfaction a time or two more. Once favorable conditions were provided, she was a natural three-orgasm girl. She saw no reason to try for four—that would have been hubris, or childish, or too tiring—but neither did she feel inclined to stop at two when a third could be had. She was very quick, which was fortunate, since Hank was not normally multiple. He was often amazed at Clara's proficiency and wondered from time to time if it was simply a unique gift of nature or if perhaps it was something bred into young Californians. Clara seemed to assume the latter.

While they were resting she looked at him with a small good-natured frown. She was perceptive and had no trouble reading the handwriting on the wall. He had his eye on Patsy Carpenter and she saw no point in beating around the bush about it.

"Something tells me you're not too rabid about being my boy friend any more," she said. "Am I right?"

Her remark left him at a loss. He was no good at lying, and besides he had not really given the matter very much thought. He felt on the hook and Clara knew it and quickly took him off. She was not a mean girl.

"I just asked," she said. "Don't look so pained. It's no tragedy—don't look so blue."

"I'm not blue," he said. "I'm puzzled."

"I don't know why you should be," Clara said. "It's no big

mystery. You just want to fall in love, and it isn't happening with us. I saw you looking at Jim's wife. I'm sure she'd be great-looking if she wasn't pregnant, why shouldn't you fall in love with her? I'm just not much on love, really. Maybe I grew up too fast. I was heartbroken twice before I was sixteen, I mean I was *heartbroken*. I don't see how I could ever be that way again. It just means you get put down sooner or later. It seems kinda childish to me, but there's no point in knocking it. Too many people go for it."

"I've never been in love," Hank said truthfully. "I don't know if I'll go for it or not."

Clara sat up and straightened out her hair. "It leads to marriage, I've noticed," she said. After sex she seemed to become older; it was then that she talked with the greatest precision and clarity. She was sexually greedy without being particularly tender, but release brought out what gentleness there was in her, and her intelligence, normally rather programmatic, became more whimsical.

"Or else there's already a marriage and it leads to problems," she said. "I used to screw married guys—twice I got into that. They were from the Midwest, both of them. I pass on the Midwest. Both of them wanted to leave their wives and marry me. Why should they want to leave their wives just because they liked to screw me? Their wives were nice girls—I knew them both. I tried to persuade the guys to regard me as a little vacation, but they couldn't see it that way. It had to be the big show or nothing."

"Maybe I've got Midwestern blood in me," Hank said.

"You're not rabidly Midwestern," Clara said. She grinned at him critically. "You should have been a cowboy," she said. "You're great when you don't have to make conversation."

"I've never known anyone who talked," he said. "I'm just now learning. Don't rush me so."

But Clara was looking serious again. "You know, I think Dr. Duffin's getting a thing for me, maybe. He's taken me to coffee twice. What do you think I should do?"

"Run."

"Why?"

He shrugged, not sure.

"It's probably good advice," Clara said. "I trust your instincts, and I can tell you aren't jealous. If I thought you were jealous I wouldn't pay any attention to your advice."

There was a keen look of concentration on her face as she considered William Duffin. Hank had seen the same look on her face the day before when she was trying to decide whether to do her Chaucer paper on the "Knight's Tale" or the "Prioress's Tale." She reached out and held his genitals, still thinking. "You know me," she said. "So far as I'm concerned the horn is always greener on the other guy. He looks fine to me. But he's not just a guy, exactly. It's the repercussions you have to consider. If it didn't work out he might put the screws on me, you know, and he's in a position where he can put screws on people. What if he turned out to like to do that sort of thing? I basically don't understand men of an older generation."

"That's a small problem," Hank said. "I don't understand women of any generation. Think of all the trouble that's apt to get me into."

Clara shook her head. "You don't particularly need a woman you understand," she said. "I don't think you want one. That's our only problem. You're the romantic type and I'm not. You probably really crave guilt and mystery and all that sort of stuff. I'm too simple for you, I guess. You're not a type who just goes in for fucking. You do sort of want the big show. Well, maybe you'll get it with what's-her-name." And she smiled coyly. "I can never remember the names of wives of husbands I want to sleep with," she said.

"Jim seems very intellectual right now," she added, frowning. There were an awfully lot of nice men in the world. The complex of possibility was sometimes almost scary.

"You could get Flap," Hank said. "Since we're speculating."

"Naw, he digs his wife," Clara said. "Maybe I'll get Dr. Duffin, if I have the nerve."

She stepped in and took a quick shower while he was dressing. Hank sat in a chair and opened a book called *Paradise Lost As Myth*, which he was supposed to read as soon as she got through with it. Clara came out and stood by her dresser, sprinkling baby powder into her pubic hair. She took off her shower cap and held it over his head, so that a few drops of water dripped on him. Her hair was long, almost to her shoulder blades. "Bring me that Skeat tomorrow," she said. "I need to get started on my Chaucer paper before I go home for Christmas."

"Okay," Hank said. "Can I borrow this book overnight?"

"Sure. Hungry?"

"No."

"I am," she said, going to the kitchenette, her panties in her hand. "Don't forget the Skeat—I really need it."

"I won't," Hank said. He went in and gave her a light kiss and went to the door. She looked at him blithely and stepped into her panties gracefully, all balance, a surfer who had left her native surf. She was unscrewing the top of a peanut butter jar when he went out. A moment later, as she spread the peanut butter on a piece of bread, a frown crossed her face and she felt a touch of depression. Hank was nice. He didn't strike her as being the brightest boy she had ever known, but he was certainly a fine lay. She was not sure where she was going to find his equal. In California it would have been no problem, but then she wasn't in California. It depressed her for half an hour, but the sandwich and a Sprite helped her to shrug it off. Someone would turn up. Someone always had.

9

"Quit bitching about it," Jim said grimly. "It's over and it wasn't so bad. There are two things I really hate to do. I hate to drive on bad roads in holiday traffic and I hate to listen to you bitch while I'm driving on bad roads in holiday traffic. Please shut up so I can have a happy New Year."

They had been to Dallas for Christmas and were returning to Houston. As far ahead as they could see, the narrow two-lane highway was clogged with slow-moving cars and trucks. The day was gray and chilly and the heater on the Ford was broken. It had been so warm in Houston that Jim had neglected to get it fixed. Patsy was swathed almost to the neck in a twenty-year-old fur coat that her mother had passed down to her a few years before. It had been the first real present her father had bought her mother when it had become apparent that he was getting rich. That had been in the forties, and the coat was fairly shabby. Patsy called it her Creature. When she sank down into it, as she had, it was hard to tell where the coat stopped and she began.

"You're very gruff," she said. "I get to bitch if I want to. I certainly get to bitch about my own Christmas if I want to. My bitching about Christmas is a ritual, and if you expect to live with me successfully you had better get used to it."

"You better outgrow it by next year," Jim said. "I want our children to have merry Christmases."

"Children!" Patsy said vehemently. "That's a laugh. Where would we get children? I refuse to adopt one and it may be years before you get time to father another on me, even if you have the inclination. I'm not complaining, though. I recognize the claims of scholarship. Don't worry about me—write some more papers. Pretty soon I'll learn to efface myself completely." And she sank an inch lower into her coat.

"For god's sake," Jim said. "How can anyone be so insecure?"

"Me? Insecure?" Patsy said, coming up two inches. She peered at him over the collar of the Creature. Jim looked at her for a second and almost rammed the truck in front of them. The truck had a bulldozer on it.

"Okay, okay," Patsy said. "I'm insecure. Forget about me. I don't want our family wiped out just yet, wretched though we are."

"I enjoyed Christmas," Jim said. "I like your family. They're just like most people's families. At least they make an effort. Mine just run away."

His had gone to Yucatan—they always went south for Christmas. Patsy snuggled down into the Creature and looked out at the gray grass and scrubby trees, trying to imagine how it would be to spend Christmas on a white beach, where the water was very blue. She decided it wouldn't be any good unless she could wear her bikini, and she was considerably too pregnant for a bikini just then.

"I'm not just bitching," she said. "My parents depress me terribly, if I really think about them. The only way I can help being depressed about them is to avoid them. Such sad lives they lead. Why is it somehow worse when people won't admit that they're sad? We could never be that sad, could we, old pard?"

Moved by a sudden impulse to be close to him, she scooted across the seat and put her head against his shoulder. She slipped one hand inside his shirt and rubbed his chest. Jim was moved, glad. He had lost the ability to draw her close to him by his own efforts and was always delighted when she came close of her own accord. He took one hand off the wheel and stroked her cheek.

"They do lead pretty awful lives," he said. "It just doesn't do any good to analyze it that I can see. We can't change them now."

"At least yours like to travel," she said. She kissed his

palm and just as she did a car full of Negroes passed them and recklessly cut in ahead. Patsy shut her eyes.

"Mine travel without really liking it at all," she said. "I don't think they were always that way. When do we get to the freeway?"

"Thirty more minutes," Jim said.

Patsy kept her eyes closed, casting back in her memory for when her father and mother had been different. Her father's name was Garland White; his father had owned a country hardware store in Denison. Her mother's name was Jeanette; *her* father had repaired windmills and windchargers. Garland and Jeanette married in the mid-thirties and moved to Oak Cliff, then a rough suburb of Dallas. Patsy vaguely remembered the little one-story box of a house they lived in, for they were only normal broke oil people then. Garland worked in the East Texas oil camps. What Patsy remembered most clearly was how different her parents' clothes had been then: khakis, blue sweat-smelling work shirts, thin print dresses, cheap underthings. She had liked as a girl to sit in the laundry basket on the tiny back porch. One of the few things she remembered with nostalgia was the smell of the porch and the unlaundered clothes. The only other memory she had of Oak Cliff was of a row of washer holes in the bare dirt of the back yard, for Garland liked to pitch washers with the neighbors in the evening. Patsy remembered how the washers clinked as they dropped. There were domino games too, and she and her earliest friends chased lightning bugs while the men hurrahed and drank beer and the women sat on straw-bottomed chairs talking about their families.

Years later, in college, when her friends grew nostalgic about the past—about washer pitching or lightning bugs or old comic books or radio shows—Patsy felt puzzled and a little disquieted, for the memory of such things stirred no emotion in her. What moved her was the memory of how much friendlier her mother and father had been in the days when they did their own laundry, but she could never be really sure that the memory was not just a fantasy of her own.

Garland had a heart condition that should have killed

him but didn't. It made him florid, made Jeanette permanently anxious, but it had kept him out of the war. He went in with another man and bought a cheap oil rig and by the time the war was over was a small millionaire. Patsy started school in Highland Park, not Oak Cliff. Jeanette was a simple soul. In twenty years of practice she never mastered the game of bridge. Church was the only thing she felt good at. Garland gave up washer pitching for golf, joined two country clubs, bought a little ranch and a little airplane; he tried his level best to learn how to enjoy himself. He failed—but he kept trying. He worked harder at fun than he did at the oil business, but he had come to the oil business at just the right time and had just enough energy and enough judgment to keep himself in the money. It was small money, as oil money went, but it was enough to confuse him. He learned to drink, seldom got seriously drunk but got slightly drunk often enough that Jeanette began a ritual complaint—a complaint that Garland found stabilizing, on the whole. He would not have known what to do with a wife who didn't complain about her husband's drinking.

On Christmas Eve, two days before, Jeanette had had a long fit of weeping, all over Miri, who had inexplicably refused to come home for Christmas. She had called and been pleasant, but had simply refused to come home. The excuse she gave was term papers, but it didn't convince Garland or Jeanette or Patsy either, though Patsy didn't care. She was convinced she could have got the real reason out of Miri but, with her parents on the extensions, had no chance to. After supper Jeanette had broken up—it was the first Christmas the family had been separated. She wanted to fly out and find out what was the matter, but she was afraid to. Miri had a rebellious spirit and was very apt not to welcome a visit, and in any case Jeanette was afraid of what she might find.

"What if she's pregnant?" she wept. "What other reason could she have for not wanting to see us on Christmas?"

"She could just be bored with Christmas," Patsy said. "It's a possible human emotion. If you ever spent a Christmas away somewhere, without all this trapping, you might find you loved it. It doesn't mean she's forsaken us forever. Don't cry so."

"She may be living dishonorably," Jeanette said. "And be pregnant too."

"Probably not both," Patsy said. "Girls who live dishonorably usually do it sensibly these days."

"She might even be smoking marijuana," Jeanette said, looking to Garland for support. He was wandering around the room in a stiff new Christmas suit, drinking Scotch.

"Bad influences out there," he said. "It's my damn fault. I should have kept her at SMU." Miri had had an early and disastrous marriage, lasting three months, and since then neither Garland nor Jeanette had quite known what to do with her.

"You hush," Patsy said to her father. "She's probably not pregnant and she hasn't had time to get on heroin or anything. It's only been one semester. My god. If you'd kept her at SMU she'd be mentally paralyzed by now. She sounded just fine to me."

"But what'll we do with her presents?" Jeanette said. "She didn't get a single present from us. We expected her here."

"We could open them and divide them," Patsy suggested. "In my present state none of them will fit me."

"I guess you don't think there's anything wrong with smoking marijuana," Garland said. He and Patsy tended to get more and more at each other's throats as arguments progressed. Their fights invariably reduced Jeanette to a wash of tears.

"I don't know what's wrong with it and what isn't," Patsy said. "And neither do you."

"I know it's against the law."

"I believe it's against the *Reader's Digest* too."

It seldom took Garland more than five minutes to drive Patsy to extremes. Soon she was arguing passionately for Communism, free love, drugs, the banning of alcohol, and compulsory racial intermarriage. Finally Jim intervened and turned the conversation back to the Packers and the Cowboys, and all were grateful to him. Jim was adept at calming them down. Patsy and Jeanette went upstairs to look at snapshots, that being the only activity that soothed Jeanette when she reached certain depths of despair.

In the early fifties Garland had decided that travel was broadening, so the family, Miri only a tot at the time, had broadened themselves to the extent of five or six trips a year. There were boxes of color snapshots from every trip. They had gone to all the old places—Florida, California, Hawaii, Canada—and to all the new places as soon as they became known. Patsy and Jeanette sat on the floor of Patsy's bedroom, the boxes of pictures between them, and there they were, hundreds of color pictures of her and Jeanette and Miri the tot, with a background of the Grand Canyon or Lake Louise or the Royal Hawaiian, or a deep-sea fishing boat, sans deep-sea fish, the girls' grins always toothy and sun-blinded.

"I was all knees and teeth in those days," Patsy said. The only funny picture was one taken in Las Vegas. The family was grouped around a roulette wheel, with a thin croupier behind them looking obligingly evil.

"She was such a darling then," Jeanette said, holding up a picture of Miri, a tiny curly-haired bump on the back of a mule, about to descend to the bed of the Colorado.

"She's a darling now," Patsy said, but she could not stop her mother from worrying. Worrying had become her function. The one unworried moment she had had in years was when Jim, all handsome and proper, his family wealth three generations old, had landed Patsy, or been landed by her, whichever it had been. Jeanette assumed that with a little one coming nothing could be righter than Patsy and Jim, and when they left to go back to Houston it had taken Jim thirty minutes to load the baby stuff in the Ford. Garland followed him halfway down the driveway, pointing out the financial advantages of buying a house immediately. Real estate was always rising.

"I must call Miri tonight," Patsy said, peeking once again at the gray day and the line of traffic. "I sympathize with her not wanting any more Dallas Christmases, but I suppose there's a chance she might be in some kind of trouble."

"I wouldn't have wanted you loose in California at that age," Jim said. His neck was stiff from the strain of watching the traffic so closely. In fifty miles he had managed to pass one truck and three cars.

"That's a little condescending of you," she said. "I could have taken care of myself." But she didn't believe it, really, and rubbed his stomach some more. "I like you better in cars," she said. "Why is that? You're so tight at home. That's my basic impression of you, these days. You're very tight."

"It's just graduate school," he said. "That's not serious. I'll relax sooner or later. I'm not tighter than you are, anyway. You're very withdrawn, you know. You don't even want to talk about the baby, any more. We haven't even decided on a name."

It was true. At first she had had a great need to chat about the baby, to plan and consider and theorize, but as the months passed, that need passed with them, and as the event drew closer she ceased to want to talk about it at all. As soon as it became publicly evident, it became for Patsy very private. She thought about it often, calmly and at length, but she felt no urge to talk to anyone and often found herself even resenting her doctor's questions. Her life with Jim went badly or went well but it didn't seem to affect her feelings about the child inside her.

"There's time to decide on a name," Patsy said to close the subject. She sat close to him the rest of the way to Houston, but they scarcely spoke again. Jim was thinking of the finals he would have to prepare for, Patsy of her child and of her sister. Whatever they had been about to conclude about themselves and their parents got lost on the road, somewhere near Centerville, Texas.

That night, when she did call Miri, Patsy herself grew somewhat alarmed. In the first place, a boy answered the phone, and though she asked clearly for her sister another boy succeeded the first; she asked him for her sister and yet another boy came to the phone. They all sounded friendly, but rather vague and puzzled, and they all kept assuring her that Miri was right there. By the time Miri's voice finally came over the wire, Patsy was angry. She had spent five long-distance minutes and it was the sort of expenditure that brought out the Scotch in her.

"Who were those boobs?" she asked. She and Miri were always extremely blunt with each other. Their affection was built on bluntness.

"Boobs?" Miri asked. "Do you mean breasts, or what?" She did not sound blunt at all. She sounded fully as vague as the young men.

"Those boys," Patsy said crisply. "What's wrong with you? Come on, be incisive. I've paid for five minutes of heavy masculine breathing."

"Oh, those were just some guys."

"Momma thinks you're leading a dishonorable life," Patsy said. "She thinks you're pregnant and a dope addict and is thinking of coming out to check. In their world it's a pretty radical thing, not coming home for Christmas."

"I didn't want to," Miri said. "It's too much more fun. Out here is too much more fun, I mean."

She sounded unlike herself, quite foggy, as if she might simply wander away from the phone at any moment.

"What's wrong with you?" Patsy asked. "I hate to probe like this. I don't particularly care if you're living dishonorably. I'll even tell Momma you aren't, if you're okay and all. But what's up? You hardly sound like you're there."

"I'm just high," Miri said. "It's okay. I was gonna call you. We're having a party right now."

"It must be a slumber party," Patsy said. "I can't hear it. I thought California was noisy. I don't know if I like you being high if it's going to cut you off that way. On what are you high?"

"Just pot," Miri said. There was a silence. She was clearly having to strain to talk.

"Exactly as Momma feared. You better watch it now. I don't know which would be worse, the cops finding you like that or Momma finding you like that."

Miri didn't respond.

"Miri?" Patsy asked.

"Hey, you know I think somebody fell down the stairs," Miri said. "We have very bad stairs in this house."

"If it was one of those boys, don't worry about it damaging his brain," Patsy said. "You're too high to talk to. When do you expect to be down to earth again, like low enough to talk to your sister?"

"Oh, any time," Miri said. "I can talk any time."

Again Patsy got the feeling that Miri was not on the phone at all but was watching something that was happening in the room.

"What's happening!" she insisted. "I can't believe it's you. Are you in the midst of an orgy or something?" Miri

294

normally talked her ear off. She was, if anything, more verbal than Patsy.

"Oh, no," Miri said. "Don't tell Momma that. We never have orgies any more, anyway. Nobody's much interested now."

"What?"

"The guys had just rather get high, mostly. Hey, you're having a baby soon, aren't you?"

"Yes. Are you, by any chance?"

"Me? I'm not having a baby. I'm not even going with anyone special. I don't think my grades are going to be too good this year."

"I don't wonder. Between marijuana and orgies I don't know when you'd study. Have you really been in an orgy, Miri?"

"I guess so," Miri said. "At least there's been a lot of us around doing things a few times. But everybody's done that."

Patsy was silent, suddenly very shocked. It occurred to her for the first time that Miri might have become a person she didn't know.

"Hey, don't let Momma come," Miri said. "Why don't you come?"

"I'm having the baby, remember? Now you've depressed me. Why don't you call me sometime when you're low, okay? And watch out for the cops."

She hung up, put on her nightgown and robe, and sat on the couch weeping. Jim had gone to the library to get some books and when he came in her face was red from crying and the front of her gown was damp above her breasts.

"What now?" he asked wearily. He wanted to take a hot bath and read.

"Momma's worst fears are realized," Patsy said in a very broken voice. "Miri's smoking pot and having orgies. I never heard her sound so disconnected. It upset me. I guess I miss her."

Jim looked at the title page of a book on Swift and then looked at Patsy again. "Why should you cry?" he said. "She's always been pretty wild. It doesn't surprise me at all. Your father was a fool to let her go to California. Given her temperament, she was bound to do exactly that."

"Don't be so smug about her," Patsy said sadly. "She's my little sister. It isn't her being wild that made me cry. She just sounded so dumb tonight, and she's always been so bright. She's really brighter than me, and she sounded like a moron. The boys that answered the phone were as stupid as cows and I bet they're the ones she has orgies with. I don't mind any number of boys if they're bright boys, but it makes me sick to think of her having orgies with morons. If that's what pot leads to I'm against pot."

"She's very undisciplined," Jim said. It was unfortunate, but he could not help sounding stiff and moralistic when he spoke of Miri. Her behavior had always annoyed him, not because he cared so much about Miri but because he considered that Miri embodied in pure form all the bad qualities he disliked and feared in Patsy. Miri had had a marriage, a strange love affair with a bisexual gynecologist, and a nervous breakdown, all in eighteen years. Whenever Jim thought about it he grew uneasy about Patsy, for whatever had broken out in Miri might break out in Patsy any time, and he doubted his ability to control it.

"I think she needs a good psychiatrist," he said. "It wouldn't hurt if she were put in a good strict girl's school, either."

"Oh, go away and read scholarship," Patsy said. "Don't carp at my poor confused sister."

"Poor? She's had everything money can buy and she gets more pathetic and more neurotic by the year."

Patsy stood up in a fury and grabbed an ashtray. His cool assured tone at such times all but maddened her, and she just managed to stop herself from flinging the ashtray at him. "My sister is not pathetic!" she yelled and stood quivering. "Maybe she's sick but she's not pathetic! Don't you say that again. You're pathetic—you wish I would just vanish and not exist, so you could get on with your work. What are you going to do when I have the baby? You'll be twice as bad. You'll have to find some way to hide from both of us."

Jim felt like hitting her, but he turned quickly and went to the bathroom; he had visions of some horrible miscarriage occurring if he hit her, or if she didn't calm down. When he came back in she was in bed, her face turned away from him.

It took him twenty minutes of coaxing to get her to turn and look at him. Her back and neck stiffened when he tried to rub them and she covered her eyes with her hair. Though it had only lasted an instant, it had gone deeper in some way than any fight they had had. Patsy wouldn't cry—she just kept her face hidden from him.

"Okay," she said finally, turning toward him. Her face held no feeling at all. "I'm sorry. Miri and I both are just what you said, pathetic and neurotic. You're just lucky I'm the scaredy cat of the two. If I wasn't I'd probably be smoking pot and having orgies. Be thankful you got the inhibited one."

"Don't look so flat," he said. "I'm sorry I said it. I know I shouldn't get so priggish about Miri. She's just young and confused, like you say."

"So am I. I'm everything she is, only less honest."

"You're not. Remember how good we felt today when we were driving."

"I don't remember anything," Patsy said truthfully. "I don't know what I'm doing, bringing somebody into this world. I'll just be responsible for their unhappiness."

Her eyes, usually so quick and clear, were spiritless and hopeless. Jim couldn't stand it. "Don't look that way," he said. "It was just an argument. I was tired and I apologize. Put your hand on my stomach again, like you did today."

Patsy looked past his head. "Don't request things like that," she said, sitting up. "Please remember not to. I only do things like that when I feel like it."

She got out of bed and went to the kitchen. One of her remedies for low spells was to pour herself a glass of milk and then crumble five or six crackers in it and eat the soppy crackers with an ice-cream spoon. Then she would drink the milk. She brought her glass into the living room and sat on the couch eating the soft soaked crackers and looking at Jim thoughtfully. He was lying on the bed reading the acknowledgments page of the book on Swift. He looked up at Patsy and was relieved to see that she seemed to have reclaimed a little of her spirits.

"You're a cool one," she said. "Reading when I'm in despair."

"You aren't in despair any more. I wasn't reading when

you were. I guess I might as well have been, for all the good I did you."

"Why didn't you clobber me?" she asked. "I deserved it. I probably deserve it frequently."

Jim was at a loss. "You're too pregnant," he said.

Patsy sniffed. "That's a weak excuse. You'll never clobber me. Nothing tastes quite like milk that's had crackers soaked in it."

"It occurred to me to clobber you," Jim said. "Do you suppose it would have helped matters if I had?"

Patsy shrugged and managed to work a particle of soaked cracker out from between her teeth, pushing with her tongue. Her tongue was milky. She set the glass on top of a paperback of *The Armed Vision* and stood up.

"How would I know about getting clobbered?" she said. "I never get to have primordial experiences like that, living with you. I suppose I might leave you if you hit me, but more than likely I'd just cry." She stood on tiptoe, her belly large under the green nightgown.

"It was that Miri sounded so flat," she said. "I think I caught the mood from her. She's always sparkled so." She walked over and stood behind his chair and stroked the back of his head for a moment. Then she went to her dresser and rubbed hand lotion into her hands. "I'm too superficial to hate you for long," she said. "Let's go to bed." They did and, what was very rare, went to sleep almost at the same time. When Patsy awoke the next morning Jim looked so nice and handsome and undemanding that she felt she had been a bitch, if not a fool. She got up feeling very cheerful. He was there, and it was another day, a sunny winter day with bluer sky than was usually seen in Houston. She had wheat germ and sausages and when Jim awoke made him sausages and very good French toast and quartered him oranges and sat on the bed with him, reading the paper. When she was really merry it showed in her mouth, her eyes, and her every movement. "Your bosom gets better all the time," Jim said. She shook them for him a little, provocatively, and then, her behind in the air and her chin on her crossed forearms, went back to reading Dear Abby.

10

The following night a norther blew in, bringing clouds with it. The next day, which was the day before New Year's Eve, Patsy had two unexpected encounters, one in the morning one in the afternoon. Jim was doing a long term paper on *The Cloud of Unknowing;* he departed for the library early and returned from the library late, which left Patsy with a day to fill up by herself. She had ceased to feel like running about the city, and usually divided her days between the apartment and the drugstore. The apartment was cozy and the norther keen, but still she felt like getting out, and she didn't feel like the drugstore.

The afternoon before, a disturbing thing had happened there. She had gone in, hoping to see Hank Malory. He had not left town for Christmas and she was thinking it would be a good day to ask him over for hot chocolate, although it was sunny and not very cold. He was there, okay, but he was chatting with Clara Clark, and it disconcerted Patsy terribly. It was not unnatural that the two of them should chat, since Clara lived just down the street and was often in the drugstore. Patsy felt slightly inimical to Clara on principle, but she sat down with them and was at first not much bothered. What upset her was the discovery—it came out in the chatter—that Clara had just returned from California, and Hank had gone to the airport to meet her and give her a ride in. Again, that was only natural; it could have been no more than a friendly favor, but it all but spoiled Patsy's day. Clara seemed remarkably trim and happy and well dressed in a suit that was not wild but was certainly not frumpy either, whereas she herself was at a stage where it was not so easy to look good as it had been. She felt herself outclassed, or outsexed, or out-somethinged, and left before they did in order not to see them leave together.

Very moody, almost crying, she walked down to the Museum of Fine Arts and wandered moodily around for more than an hour, getting more and more tired, but no less reluctant to go home. Jim would not be there. No one would be there, and she would have nothing to do but sit and think about the likelihood that Hank was sleeping with Clara Clark. There was no reason why he shouldn't be, of course, but for some reason it had never occurred to her that he could be sleeping with anyone. Clara was obviously a good choice—sexy, single, and smart—though finally there was something too brisk about her, Patsy felt. She looked like a good tennis player. She herself was convinced that good tennis players were not very womanly—certainly not voluptuous. She couldn't play three licks of tennis herself and would have scorned being able to play any better. There was no explanation for her mood, and yet she felt betrayed. She had been convinced for a month or two that Hank liked her better than any woman he knew, and it seemed to her suddenly that it was all her own fantasy, completely unrealistic. He obviously just liked her as a person to chat with once in a while. Clara was certainly his mistress—it was too obvious even to question.

She went home low and weepy, and when Jim returned late in the evening he found her prickly and difficult. She made him go back into the traffic to buy pizza. Later, in bed, he found himself horny and made a sudden attempt on her from the rear. Patsy was reading and kicked him away without a moment's hesitation.

"Quit mauling me," she said. "Have you been sleeping with Clara Clark?" For it occurred to her in a flash that Clara, unattached and probably amoral, might have lured more than one man away from her. She sat up and whirled on Jim, who looked guilty and defensive. He had never touched Clara, though he had looked up her dress a time or two at boring points in the Chaucer seminar and had had a number of fantasies in which she was involved.

"Have you gone crazy?" he said. "I was trying to sleep with you. What brought Clara into it?"

"I don't know," she said, giving his erection an unwelcoming glare. "Just fold that back up. Or down. Something's stimulated you. I think it's very abnormal, this sudden desire you've developed to jump on me from behind. Who did you learn that from?"

Jim fell back on his pillow in an attitude of feigned despair, his erection falling with him. "I swear to god," he said. "You bitch at me if I don't make love to you and then you bitch at me if I do. Can't you be consistent. I wasn't doing anything abnormal."

"You might have if I hadn't stopped you," she said. "Of course I want you to make love to me, what's that got to do with it? I just don't want you going near Clara Clark."

"But I haven't touched her," Jim yelled. "You've gone out of your head."

Patsy's bosom heaved and in a moment she began to sob violently. He sat up and she collapsed against his chest.

"Honey, what's wrong?" Jim asked, alarmed. He supposed it to be a manifestation of pregnancy and patted her shoulder. "I scarcely even talk to her," he said. "Just at coffee breaks now and then. Hank dates her, you know."

Patsy sobbed harder, but in a few minutes her sobs stopped. Jim dried her face. She was quite calm but unmollified.

"I knew she was promiscuous," she said. "You stay away from her. It's bad enough that Hank's fallen into her snares." Jim put his arm over her comfortingly, but she flung it off. She didn't want to be touched. "From now on come around on this side, where I am, when you want me," she said.

"Okay, okay," he said.

In a minute Patsy felt guilty and took his hand, but his hand was all she wanted. She lay awake a long time, feeling burned by Hank's treachery. She decided that he had deliberately let her make a fool of herself, and she determined not to go to the drugstore any more. She would be very cool to him if she ran into him and very matronly— even though she was only potentially a matron.

So, to get out of the house without going near the drugstore, she bundled in her Creature and took a taxi to the zoo. It was a gray day, the seals in the seal pond were not to be seen, and she felt tired from a day and a night of emotion and decided to ride the zoo train around the zoo. She got a seat near the front, buried herself in her Creature, gave the driver her ticket without looking at him. She peered out dispiritedly from the depths of her coat, wishing she had not been a fool and a coward, and wishing also that she had gone to the drugstore. Hank sometimes had a ten o'clock breakfast there and she might be lucky enough to find him without Clara Clark. She had decided to ignore the fact that he had a mistress and remain warm friends with him, anyhow. She wished he had come to the zoo with her, for it was fairly dismal in the cold train almost alone.

The train started and swung to the right to go between two rows of bird houses, and the driver of the train, whose job it was to deliver thumbnail lectures on the various animals that they passed, began his recitation.

"And on your right yew have the South A-merican ma-*caw*," he said. "On your left you have the pere*grine* falcon, then the fascinating condor, largest of the vultures . . ."

The drivers always twanged their way through the animal kingdom, but there was something in that particular twang that struck Patsy as familiar and she looked at the driver, who was none other than Peewee Raskin, back on the job he loved best. He wore a faded Levi jacket and a red baseball cap.

"Peewee!" she yelled, popping upright.

Peewee turned in surprise, wondering why a pregnant brunette in an old fur coat was yelling at him, and discovered to his astonishment that it was Patsy. The train was still in motion; they were on the backswing, near the guanacos and llamas, and the sight of her threw him completely off his spiel. He waved and she waved and Peewee let the train run off the sidewalk. He tried to recover himself, but the thought that the girl who had read so many strange books was listening to him gave him an awful case of stage fright; he could scarcely remember the animals' names, much less the particulars of their origins and habits. His pronunciation grew increasingly unconfident, but fortunately none of the few freezing passengers particularly cared. When the train

302

stopped, Patsy ran up and kissed him on the cheek, to his deep embarrassment and the amazement of the few spectators—three Mexicans and a skinny mechanic and his wife and kids. Nice surprises, such as finding Peewee, filled Patsy with delight, and she hopped from one cold foot to the other beaming at him. Except for the baseball cap he seemed completely unchanged.

"My goodness, I never knew I'd be so glad to see you," she said. "How long have you been here? Why didn't you call us?"

Peewee shuffled about awkwardly, hardly knowing whether to look at her or not look at her. He had never imagined anyone would be so glad to see him—least of all Patsy.

"Never been here but a month," he said.

"Why are you limping?" she asked.

"Been gimpy. Got a broken ankle in Flagstaff."

"Well, I'm glad you've chosen a safer occupation. You've got to come to dinner tonight."

Peewee turned sideways and expertly blew his nose with his fingers, something that had always horrified her, but which he did as naturally and almost as neatly as if he had had a handkerchief. He had a moment of apprehension about the dinner, for he had no better clothes than what he had on, and had visions of being embarrassed in some splendid restaurant; but Patsy reassured him and soon he left with another huddled trainload of animal lovers, a happier man. Patsy went into the small-animal house and watched the delicate little fennec fox pace back and forth in its cage. Peewee had said he meant to go back to redoing when the rodeo arrived in Houston in two months, and it occurred to her how strange it would be if all the people they had known during the summer suddenly came back into their lives. She called a taxi and directed it to the drugstore, convinced that her luck had changed.

To her surprise, it had. Hank was there eating a bowl of chili. His brown suede sports coat seemed to be his only jacket.

"I saved you a seat," he said when she walked in. She had pretended not to see him. She was quite disconcerted. She felt alternately bold and shy and covered both feelings by launching into an account of her miraculous rediscovery of

Peewee, in the midst of which it struck her suddenly that it was presumptuous of her to mention that he had saved her a seat. She felt irritated with him and dropped Peewee.

"I doubt your girl friend wants you saving seats for other women," she said.

Hank looked surprised. "Nobody cares who I eat with," he said, ignoring Eddie Lou, who had just glared at them from the grill. The fact that Patsy had come to meet him in a fur coat seemed to her a clear indication of immorality. The few times she came in with her own husband she was usually in jeans and sneakers.

Patsy felt immediately rebuffed. She had had no right to say it, and after all, she had a husband and was on the verge of having a child. She was the one who was doing something inappropriate, and for a moment she felt hopeless, blocked in every direction. But Hank smiled a little apologetically, as if he understood what she was feeling, and it kept the depression from closing in around her. The warmth of the drugstore brought the color back to her cold face. They ate their lunch companionably, both silent and thoughtful.

"Walk to Rice with me," he suggested. "If a blizzard hits we can both take shelter in your coat."

"Okay," Patsy said at once, delighted. They went out into the cold wind and began to walk, as silent as they had been while eating. Both of them recognized that, in a way, they were flirting, and neither was quite confident about it. Patsy looked up at him from time to time. She liked the way his hair never stayed combed. The image of Clara Clark rose up and plagued her again, and she grew moody. He and Clara were scholarly colleagues, after all—they probably had all manner of things to talk about. He would scarcely talk to her at all, and it made her feel dumb and unserious, pretty but purposeless, only a bit of fluff.

"What time's your class?" she asked, but Hank had dropped a step behind her, and with the wind behind them too, he didn't hear. Patsy turned and he leaned down to get the question again—their faces bumped. He put his hand on her arm for a second, smiling, and she had a momentary giddy sensation that she was about to be stopped and kissed, right there on the corner of Ashby and Sunset, in full view of two filling stations. But Hank had no such intention, and when it didn't happen Patsy became flushed and disoriented and had to look up and down the street several times to keep in mind whether cars were coming. Then, after all, she started too late, when one was coming, and Hank had to grab her hand and pull her across the street at a trot. His hand was warm and hard.

"Do you think women ought to be scholarly, and thoroughly educated?" she asked, watching him closely.

"Only ugly ones," Hank said.

It was not an answer that pleased her. Suddenly she wanted to be away from him. "I'm going to the park," she said. "It's just a block. You don't have much time to make your class."

Hank was slightly irked. He had wanted her to walk all the way to the campus. "Okay," he said. "Maybe I can snatch a few minutes with my fellow scholar Miss Clark." He was instantly sorry he had said it, because it made Patsy blush and look away. She took several steps away from him and then turned back, a hurt look on her face.

"I'm sorry," he said. "I'll walk you to the park. I can still get to class."

"Out of the question," she said. "You go right on to Miss Clark—she talks your language. My stomach and I are too frivolous for you. We're going to the park. Maybe we'll see you sometime."

"Patsy," he said.

It was very nice that he used her name. Even though she was hurt and angry, it was nice. Jim had taken to calling her "you." He had called her "you" for years, it seemed to her.

"What?"

"Don't be mad."

"Why should I be? It's only natural that you would prefer the company of your intellectual peers. I'm just a girl who reads *McCall's*. I feel very inferior, and you did it to me."

"It was accidental," he said. "You're certainly not inferior to her."

"I'll thank you not to compare us," she said stiffly. "I'm sure you know her well enough to speak with authority about her, but you don't know me."

She turned and walked to the park and Hank walked with her, not asking her permission. She cried a little but the wind quickly dried her tears. When they got to the park she felt very strange, confused, and agitated but also absurdly warmed by the fact that he had followed. He seemed very depressed, as if he feared that he had spoiled their friendship.

"I apologize," she said. "You really are going to be late. I don't know what's the matter with me. I interrupted you in the midst of your bowl of chili and made you late for your seminar. Do go on."

"I'm sorry I teased you," he said. "You're all full of emotion."

Patsy didn't know what to say to that and stood watching his face, hoping he would tell her what he meant by it. He had said it in a tone of surprise, as if the fact that she was full of emotion made her unique in some way. He was looking at her face too. Both of them felt that there was something explanatory that ought to be said, but neither could think what. Patsy felt suspended, immovable, very at the mercy of the moment. All she could think of to do was stand and watch Hank watch her.

"Anyhow, I'm sorry," he said finally, as if he could not quite remember what he was apologizing for. He sighed and said he had to go and started off in a leisurely jog, so leisurely that she felt she could sit on the park bench and watch him jog through most of the afternoon. She looked and he was there, and looked and he was still there. The third time she looked he was gone. The whole park was quite empty. She wandered over to the swings. Falling leaves were blowing and a cloud had covered the sun. The park, in its wintry grayness, reminded her of the brown park in Cheyenne. "I'm always having adventures in parks," she said to herself. Increasingly since her pregnancy had advanced, she was prone to uttering statements into the air. She was sure that when her baby came she would say such things to it—one thing she felt sure of was that the baby would be a baby she could talk to.

She sat in a swing and swung, thinking of Hank, who was somewhere in the tree-hidden buildings of Rice. Nothing had really happened, and yet she felt as if something had. There was the bump that had almost turned into a kiss—she was sure he had wanted to kiss her. There was his hand pulling her across the street, then the silly argument, then the mean thing he had said. In the park he had looked so confused that she hadn't known whether to walk away from him or not. Images flickered through her head like frames from a movie, but a movie with no plot. She swung while they flickered, lifting her legs, happy that her ankles were still neat ankles, pregnancy or no. In the midst of swinging she decided that she had wanted to be kissed, and the thought didn't bother her. But how could he have wanted to kiss her—she was too pregnant. She thought about it some more and decided she really had no idea what he might have wanted. It would be nice if Emma happened by, but it was Teddy's nap time and there was little chance that she would.

She bent her head, arms locked around the chains of the swing, and watched the gentle movement of the ground beneath her. When she looked up she discovered that she was no longer alone. Lee Duffin stood on the sidewalk a few yards away looking at her. She had on sneakers, white socks, gray slacks, and a trench coat, all drab enough, but Lee had managed to turn all the drabness to good effect with a wonderful blue driving cap, sharply peaked and perfect with her short hair.

"Hello," she said. "You're Patsy, aren't you? Mind if I swing too? The truth is I'm bored to desperation."

She took the swing next to Patsy's and began to swing lightly, pointing her toes in the air but not trying to make the swing go very high. She wore no makeup, and her face was not as Patsy had remembered it; her character seemed not so definite as it had the night of the party. She looked both older and younger. Without the marvelous cap she would have looked quite ordinary, Patsy decided; but she was to learn that Lee Duffin always had a marvelous cap, or the equivalent of one. She never looked quite ordinary.

"I envy you that baby you're going to have," Lee said. "They're a great out. Even the ability to have them is a great out."

She dipped a toe into the sand and dragged it, slowing the swing. "I'm tied off," she said quietly. "Bill willed it that way. After three girls he decided the odds were against him

307

getting a son out of me and the thought of endless girls was not to his liking. I've been tied off ever since they learned how to tie you off."

"Where are the girls?"

"Schools. They all left last night, going back. Bill isn't home from the MLA yet. I guess that's why I'm so mopey. I always get blue when the girls go."

Patsy's sympathies were near the surface. She saw Lee Duffin in a new light and felt sorry for her. She was not the ultimate sophisticate she had seemed; she was just a lonely woman. Lee got up from the swing and turned restlessly, looking into the wind.

"Why don't you walk down to the house with me for a bit?" she said. "I'll make us some tea and show you some pictures of my girls."

"All right," Patsy said. She was a little tired and would rather have gone home, but Lee seemed nice and she was curious to see the Duffin house without the distractions of a party. They walked along silently and when they got there Lee went immediately to make the tea and Patsy had a very nice time wandering about the large living room and den looking at the pictures, the chairs, and the books. The living room had high windows and the afternoon light came through them and seemed warmer on the books, the fireplace, the couch, and the blue Mexican rug than it had seemed outside. "I love your rug," she said when Lee came in with a tea tray and some rye crackers.

"There were a couple of lucky years when we summered in Mexico," Lee said. "It came from San Miguel."

Lee moved her chair slightly so as to catch the occasional ray of sun and looked at Patsy through the smoke that rose from her teacup. Patsy was restful, slightly drowsy, quite relaxed. She fiddled idly with her hair and rested her feet on a stool Lee had provided.

"I'm glad we're going to Connecticut this summer," Lee said. "If we weren't you'd probably have some trouble with Bill."

Patsy was startled. She had forgotten for the moment that she had ever had trouble with Bill. Lee seemed neither hostile nor desperate—she was just quietly depressed.

"Does he proposition people just for a joke?" Patsy asked. "I can't quite figure him, frankly."

Lee was silent for a moment and Patsy became embarrassed. "I didn't mean to be too frank," she said.

"You couldn't be," Lee said. "Not with me. I'm at a point in my life where I don't care ever to beat around another goddamn bush. That's all I did for fifteen years, while Bill was on the rise. Now I couldn't care less who knows what I think." A throb of anger had come into her voice, and she was pressing a fingernail into the flesh of her thumb. "No, he doesn't proposition people for a joke. He's too well organized for simple flirtation. When he propositions somebody he usually means it."

Patsy didn't know what to say. She had never been in such a conversation. "I don't understand it very well," she said.

Lee set her teacup on the table and hugged her knees. "You said that," she said. "Lucky you. I understand it so goddamn well that practically the only thing left to do is cut my throat. If I weren't a coward I would cut my throat. It's awful to be trapped and a coward."

There was a quality in her voice that frightened Patsy terribly. She spoke of cutting her throat as matter-of-factly as she had spoken of the blue rug. Her face had become pinched and pained, as if she were having a waking nightmare.

"But this is so nice," Patsy said, meaning the lovely room.

"Yes," Lee said. "I love this room in the afternoon. But it isn't always the afternoon." She stood up, got herself a cigarette, and lit it.

"Bill and I have been married twenty-one years," she said. "The way it's worked out is that I still love him and he doesn't give a damn about me. I'm sure it works out that way for a lot of people who have been married that long, but I'm really only interested in how it's worked out for me. He likes to have me around to cook his breakfast and do the normal wifely stuff, but that's it. He doesn't need me as a woman. If he doesn't think I'm worth screwing I get to where I agree with him. It's got so about the only times he thinks I'm worth screwing is when somebody else is screwing me, or trying to. I used to be quite a piece, I guess. All his colleagues were hot for me and we worked it out pretty well, but here I am forty-four and those of his colleagues who go in for that sort of thing have got to the age of screwing graduate students, or undergraduates if they've got the guts. Lately none of his faculty pals have wanted to be bothered with an aging damosel like me—maybe they don't think I'm worth screwing, either. I can't tell. All I know is that nobody's made a pass at me since we moved here, including Bill. Once in a while I make a successful pass at him, but it gets to be humiliating, having to seduce your own husband. It's particularly humiliating with a bastard like Bill, who seduces hard. If I didn't love him it wouldn't be such a trap, but I seem to love him. I guess I'm a masochist. Usually when we get to this stage he starts bringing home queers. Nice ones, but it makes my predicament even worse, because I scare them to death. It really only leaves me graduate students. I took my first student lover in Michigan, four years ago, and it got Bill and I going again, for a little while. So here we are in Houston, which seems to be a wretched town for men, or anything else, as far as that goes. What am I going to do to survive here? I don't want to cut my throat, so I'll have to take another graduate lover, most likely. Maybe the lucky victim will be your husband—Bill's certainly grooming him for me. Sooner or later you two will get in a slump or something and I'll probably strike. He'll like me. I could make him awfully pleased with himself. I'm very good at that, and you probably aren't. Then Bill will get awfully pleased with me and we'll have some fine times and you'll get sad and confused and miserable because you won't have anyone and Jim will have quit screwing you, and one day when you're all sad and vulnerable my rapacious husband will leapfrog right from my bed to yours and screw you about nine times before you know what's hit you. He's a master at such leaps. He'll wait until just before we're ready to go away, and as soon as he's got the maximum mileage out of your confusion we'll be gone and you and Jim can muddle along for a year or two and get divorced and Bill and I will be off somewhere doing it all over again. I suppose it will work until I'm about fifty. I'm that well preserved."

And she sat down again, perfectly composed, as if delivering the prophecy had freed her in some way. She clasped her graceful hands on her graceful knees and looked at Patsy shrewdly and not unkindly.

"Do you think I'm crazy?" she asked.

Patsy had taken her feet off the stool. She was staring at Lee. She felt herself begin to tremble and couldn't stop it. No one had ever spoken so to her.

"I don't know what I think," she said. "I wouldn't be so scared if I did. You can't go around doing things like that."

"Why not? We *have* done things like that. Nothing is likely to stop us from doing them again. I don't want to, particularly. I'm not naturally predatory. I've really had to push myself to do what little preying I've done. Bill's the natural predator, I guess, and since I'm stuck with him I've got to survive somehow."

"But you can leave him," Patsy said. "If he's that kind of monster why don't you leave him?" She was trembling noticeably.

"Oh, stop shaking," Lee said, pouring her some more tea. "Maybe it won't happen. I've given you warning, maybe you can thwart our evil designs."

"But why don't you leave him?" Patsy insisted.

Lee sighed and gave her a long look. "You could be my oldest daughter," she said. "She knows a bit about her father and me and she asks the same thing. I was going to show you some pictures, wasn't I?" To Patsy's astonishment she went off to the bedroom and came back with some color snapshots of the three girls, all of whom were tall like their father and thin like Lee. All were pretty, with long dark hair.

Lee sat down and rubbed her eyelids with her forefingers, as if she were very tired.

"Do leave him," Patsy said. "It's your only hope."

Lee snorted. "Don't go presuming to tell me what my only hope is," she said. "For all you know, your husband might be my only hope."

"But why stay?"

"Because I'm scared to leave. Twenty-one years is a long time. I'd never really get free, and besides it's just scary, unless you have a bird in the bush. I don't know what kind of bird I could find at my age. We don't have any dough, either. We live well and Bill buys lots of books, but the girls cost a lot to educate and we never have any ready money. I'd have to go to work and I don't want to. I worked for years and I want leisure now, even if just to be bored.

"I don't have enough guts to leave," she added. "I only have guts enough to play around now and then, when I can find someone young and nice."

Patsy stood up. She had been about to get calm, but at the thought of Jim and Lee her agitation returned and she wanted very badly to be away. "You better leave us alone," she said. "I'd have to be put in a cage before I'd come in this house again." And to her great annoyance she began to cry. She wanted very badly to be strong and stony, but instead she cried.

Lee got her some Kleenex. "You're a little like Melissa," she said. "She's our oldest. It's too bad you couldn't have met them. You might like me better if you had. At least I'm a good mom, I think."

Patsy whirled around, very distressed. Everything was so confusing. The girls had looked intelligent and happy in their pictures, and the woman who had raised them stood before her talking of seducing Jim. She moved toward the door, still crying.

"I'm sorry," Lee said. "I really didn't set out to spoil your afternoon." Patsy turned to look at her, too confused to answer.

"Sometimes I hate this fucking life," Lee said sadly. Patsy stood with her back to the door, tears dripping off her cheeks. "Come on, honey. Wipe your face. It's not so bad."

"It is bad!" Patsy said, bursting out. "I'd run away to China before I'd get involved in anything like that."

Lee sighed. "It was a mistake for me to say those things to you," she said. "I know too much more than you know for us to be really able to talk."

"I don't like that!" Patsy said, feeling suddenly vengeful and hateful. "You didn't say anything so smart. All you did was point out what a crud your husband is. I started out feeling sorry for you but I don't feel sorry for you any more."

"I should hope you don't," Lee said hotly. "Never feel sorry for a woman—we bloody well get what we deserve. By the same token I won't need to feel sorry for you when your husband comes dawdling around."

"He never will!" Patsy said furiously. "He'll never sleep with you. Why would he?" And she drew herself up in anger.

The moment she found her dignity and hit back, all Lee's dignity left her. She stood looking at the floor, not answering Patsy's question. She compressed her lips very tightly for a second, as if to hold in all words, all emotions, all hurts, and then to Patsy's consternation she began to settle to the floor weeping. She didn't fall, but she let herself fold downward until she was sitting hunched over on the hard floor sobbing and squeezing her hands into fists. Patsy was stunned. She didn't know what to do. Lee kept bending over until her forehead almost touched the floor, sobbing loudly. Then suddenly she looked up, choking but trying to talk. "Go away, you bitch," she said. "Why did you want to hurt me this way? What am I that everybody wants to hurt me . . . always wants to hurt me."

"I didn't mean to," Patsy said, her anger gone. She could hardly believe that the woman who had been so proud and so possessed a few minutes before had suddenly become the abject woman on the floor. "Please get up," she said. "I didn't mean to hurt you."

"You didn't hurt me," Lee said, sniffing and calming a bit. "You couldn't hurt me. I hurt myself. You're not smart enough to hurt me. Just get out of here and stay away from my husband."

Suddenly she got up, strode past Patsy out the door, and stood on her front porch wiping her face with her hands and looking far up into a big elm tree that stood in the yard.

Patsy decided there was nothing to do but leave. She went timidly past Lee, down the steps.

"I'm sorry again," Lee said. "I'm the one to blame, but you needn't come back here any more. I don't know why you'd want to. I hope you manage to keep your principles polished. With a face like yours it's going to take a lot of polish."

"You either cry or you say awful things to me," Patsy said.

"No, I'm going to rake some leaves. I only have fits once or twice a year, and you're not enough of a threat to make me have a real fit."

She gave Patsy one flat glance and then turned and walked up her driveway. Patsy walked home and lay on her bed for three hours, waves of agitation sweeping through her. They didn't completely subside for two days. Lee had somehow had the last word. Dozens of comebacks occurred to her as she lay on her bed, and it irked her terribly that she would never get to make them.

The whole encounter left her feeling weak and it was a real task to drag herself to the store and get groceries for Peewee's dinner. She did it, and made spaghetti, but her mind was on the afternoon. Peewee arrived, shiningly clean in Levi's, every hair slicked down, terribly awed even to be coming into the garage apartment of such a big house.

Jim was delighted to see him, and Patsy let them do all the talking. She listened only with the shallow part of her mind—the deeper part was arguing fiercely with Lee Duffin. It was almost midnight—and Jim had gone to take Peewee home—before her mind began to leave the afternoon. She sat at her dressing table combing her hair for a long time. While she was combing it she remembered Hank, and the moment on the corner when she had thought he was going to kiss her. It was a better thing to think about than the argument with Lee. Lee was a sad, disappointed woman. The things she said had not really been important. The moment on the corner was a little frightening, but it had been important.

When Jim came back she was in bed reading Frazer, and instead of looking restless and irritable, as she had all evening, she looked subdued and glowing. Jim sat down and kissed her, and she allowed him a light kiss before she moved her head. "Stop, please," she said. "I'm reading. I can't be interrupted until the end of the chapter.

"Fourteen pages," she added, checking.

"You ought to see the dump Peewee lives in," Jim said. "He'll be lucky if he stays alive in that neighborhood."

"I wish I had been nicer. I wasn't myself this evening."

Jim went to the closet and dragged out the box his rodeo pictures were in. He sat down and went through it, pulling out a file here and a file there. Patsy let Frazer fall on her bosom. "I doubt he's ever known a nice girl," she said, thinking of Peewee and the life of squalor he must lead. She could not imagine Peewee having any girl, and it made her sad. Her nice bed, nice apartment, nice husband made her feel cozy suddenly. She felt she had been wrong to be contemptuous of Lee Duffin for being afraid to leave a nice house with a beautiful blue rug.

"These are pretty good," Jim said. "I might have got the book published if I'd kept on with it."

"You can blame that on me," Patsy said. "I couldn't take any more cowboys."

"Maybe I'll go take some more next summer and leave you here to bring up Junior."

"Wait till you see Junior. You might not want to leave us."

"Bill said I should write my thesis next summer."

"When did you start calling him Bill?"

"He keeps insisting."

"I had a chat with her this afternoon," she said. "You'll never guess what they have planned for us."

"Well, we're supposed to go to dinner with them some night next week."

"No," Patsy said. "What they really have in mind is her seducing you and him seducing me, in that order. Not that they have all that much interest in us, of course. It's just that their sex life withers and they need a gay young couple for fertilizer once in a while."

"Are you crazy?" he asked, looking around.

"No," Patsy said. "She told me that in so many words this afternoon."

"Oh, well, don't pay much attention to it," Jim said. "She's nice but she's not very stable. Bill told me she's had two nervous breakdowns. He's had a lot of trouble with her."

"That's lovely," Patsy said. She sat up, very annoyed. "Now he's telling you his marital troubles. Next you'll be telling him yours. His wife tells me hers and probably expects me to tell her mine. Pretty soon we'll know all about one another, and the cozy little switch can take place. Me-him, you-her, just like she said."

Jim shut the picture file and yawned. He didn't take any of it seriously. "Don't get carried away with your own rhetoric," he said. "Lee's obviously a little neurotic, that's all. We don't have any marital problems to tell them about, anyway. They'd get bored with us."

"Like fun they would. Maybe after a few months of swapsy-wapsy they'd get bored with us. It's very condescending of you to call someone you scarcely know neurotic. I think that's very sloppy."

"What would you call her?" He sat down on the bed and kicked off his loafers, a habit he knew annoyed her and yet couldn't break. He remembered that it annoyed her just as one of his shoes narrowly missed a vase full of ferns.

"There you go again," she said.

"Sorry." His good humor was undisturbed.

"Miserable is what I'd call Lee Duffin. Miserable and neglected, just like I'll probably be at her age."

Jim chuckled infuriatingly, all masculine poise. He was in no mood to take female irrationality very seriously.

"Don't chuckle like that," she said. "I'll hit you."

"He says she's very demanding," he said. His head disappeared for a moment as he took off his pullover.

"Sure. She probably has to demand like hell to get one drop of affection out of him."

"You've got a block where he's concerned."

"I sure have." She got out of bed and stamped angrily off to the bathroom. Her belly was large enough to eclipse the toilet bowl. When she came back Jim was straining his eyes to read a footnote in the back of Robinson's *Chaucer*. The light was completely wrong and he had not bothered to change it.

"For god's sake," she said, exasperated. "How did you ever expect to be a photographer if you don't have any sense of where the light is?"

He looked up, a little abstracted, then put the book down and reached for her. "Don't grab," she said, but he did anyway and after a short tussle got her turned on her back. "We don't have any marital problems, do we?" he asked.

"I don't like to wrestle when I'm pregnant," she said, staring up at him. She was friendly but grim in her determination not to yield points unnecessarily.

"We don't, do we?" he insisted.

"We will if you insist on attaching yourself to that guy's fetlocks," she said. "I don't like him."

"Okay," he said. "But do me a favor and go to this one dinner. I promised, and one dinner is no more than your wifely duty."

He tried to kiss her but she squirmed and looked cheerfully at the ceiling. "Okay, one dinner," she said. "Never let it be said that I'm slacking my wifely duties."

"I sort of wish he'd quit pestering me about the massage parlors," Jim said.

"What?" she asked, relaxing.

"The massage parlors. You know, the ones that are really whorehouses—there was a story about them in the paper. You go in for a massage and get a girl. Bill's always pestering me to take him to one. He think's it's a novel way to work a whorehouse."

"He's a monster," Patsy said. "He's married, and he goes to whorehouses?"

Jim sighed. "Where have you been?" he asked. "Millions of men who are married go to whorehouses, apparently. It's not like he was the only roving husband in the world."

"After twenty-one years, he treats her that way? I never heard of anything so awful."

"That's a long time to be married," he said quietly.

"So what? Momma and Daddy have been married over thirty years and Daddy doesn't go off to any massage parlors."

"No, he just drinks and wastes money and lets his youngest daughter screw herself up in California."

"How do you know she's screwed up? Besides, that's evading the question. How many years before you become eligible for that kind of relief?"

"Oh, nag, nag, nag," he said. "If you didn't talk so much you wouldn't get ideas like that."

"Don't evade the question." She watched him closely.

"I don't know," Jim said. "It seems to me I've been eternally faithful to you already and probably I'll go on through several more eternities. Just don't yap at me about it. How do I know what we'll be doing in twenty years. The one thing I'm sure of is that you'll still be yapping."

"If you were a man of principle, you'd know now," Patsy said. But she lost her heart for the argument, light as it was. Lee Duffin came back to mind, crouched on her living-room floor weeping and raising and lowering her torso hopelessly. When she tried to imagine the scenes that lay behind that weeping her mind was blank. The thought of Bill Duffin simply made her feel cold. She drew Jim close to her and held his hand long after he was asleep.

The next day's mail brought a letter on the stationery of the William Duffins:

Dear Mrs. Carpenter,
   I'm very sorry indeed for my performance today. It was entirely my fault. I'm so ashamed of it that it's all I can do to write you this note. My only excuse is that I'm in trouble. It would be painful for us to meet right now, of course, but I hope you'll forgive me and not find it necessary to shun me entirely. I shan't ever be that way again.

                                        Lee Duffin

Patsy wrote, in all, seven replies, some long, some short. One she put in an envelope—she even stamped it. Then she carried it past mailboxes for days and one evening threw it away.

11

The spaghetti, the mushrooms, the candlelight, Patsy, the nice well-lit apartment hung with strange pictures and posters of movie stars—all of it was a little too much for Peewee. When Jim let him out at his place of residence, a decaying motel on Telephone Road, he was so agitated that he scarcely knew what to do with himself. Walking across the muddy driveway, he stumbled over the tricycle of the cross-eyed tot who lived in the cabin next to his. It was an old tricycle, one wheel tireless, no handleguards, but Donna, the tot, wheeled it across the shaly drive with great expertise. Her mother was a fat slut named Doreen. She worked in a drive-in on Griggs Road, screwed a succession of Cajuns, and sometimes, on bad nights, used Donna for a punching bag.

Peewee's quarters did not particularly depress him, though there were times when he could have wished for less mud. When he got home he felt restless, too keyed up for sleep. He had nothing to read but a few issues of *Rodeo Sports News,* and he had those memorized. He did have a couple of cheap dirty books, one called *Passion Flayed* and the other called *Her Talented Tongue,* but he was in no mood for dirty books. He got his black cowboy hat out of the closet and set out for his favorite drinking establishment, a place called the Gulf-Air Lounge.

No one could remember whether the Gulf-Air had originally been a cafe and turned into a bar, or had originally been a bar with ambitions to be a cafe, or what. It remained an uneasy mixture, largely bar but with a small grill where hamburgers could be cooked and chili heated. The clientele consisted almost entirely of the wretched of Southeast Houston—a motley collection of aging bar bums of both sexes, with an admixture of young vagrants, day workers, Cajun cowboys, truckers, and Gulf Coast roustabouts, most of whom came in to horse around with the shuffleboard or the miniature pool table.

Peewee took most of his dinners at the Gulf-Air, it being the place closest to his motel. Also, he had just turned twenty-one, and the people at the Gulf-Air knew it and weren't always making him show his ID. He had got to know most of the people who frequented the bar at night, and he usually spent his evenings there sipping beer and eating Fritos and watching whatever was on the old blurry TV. He didn't like beer, preferring Coke or Dr. Pepper, but all of his acquaintances regarded beer as the manly beverage and he felt obliged to drink it. He found that if he ate a package of

Fritos per bottle it wasn't so bad, and having to walk to the john to piss every twenty minutes or so was a comfortable, manly thing to do. All the people in the Gulf-Air called him Squirt, whether because he was short or because he pissed so much he didn't know.

"Hey, Squirt, you're late tonight," the barmaid said when he climbed up on the barstool. Peewee began to chew a toothpick. The barmaid was a thin redhead from Lufkin —Nancy by name. Her three kids were growing up in Lufkin with her mother; she didn't think cities were good for kids. She herself had never quite managed to get divorced from her husband, who worked off shore, and she was well known to a couple of truckers who laid up in the area. She was too faded to be mean, and Peewee sometimes aspired to her in his fantasies. The only encouragement he ever got was that Nancy would sometimes lean across the bar and put her hand on his wrist while she told him her troubles. The owner of the bar was a fat shaky drunkard named Big Woody, who sat at one of the tables with his shirt unbuttoned, drinking malt liquor and playing Moon with two other oldsters, an unemployed liquor-store clerk named Roscoe and a tire salesman from the Lawndale area whose name was Skeets. The bar's two female habitués sat in a booth nearby smoking and sipping beer and trying to goad one of the old men into making a pass at them. They were both part-time waitresses who lived off the money they scrounged from their multiple ex-husbands. One was named June, the other Gloria. The only other patron of the bar was a young man named Terrible Tommy. He drove a truck for a sterile-water company and wore a cowboy hat when he was off work. He was playing a solitary game of pool when Peewee walked in.

"Pearl or Bud?" Nancy asked.

"Pearl," Peewee said touchily. He suddenly felt infinitely superior to the milieu he was in and sipped his beer a little haughtily.

The old man at the Moon game regarded Peewee as canaille and never let him forget it. Roscoe, the ex-clerk, was particularly foulmouthed and loved to tease Peewee about his job at the zoo.

"Well, we was wrong," he said, turning a domino down.

"We figured the lions ate you, sonny. Figured you'd be a nice smelly pile of lion shit by this time tomorrow."

"Shut your goddamn foul mouth, Roscoe," June said. "Peewee's a nice boy. A lot more of a gentleman than some people I know."

"Horse turds," Roscoe said. "You wouldn't know a gentleman if one was to piss in your ear."

"Where you been all night, sugar?" Nancy asked.

"Having dinner," Peewee said, using the phrase for the first time in his life. "I was almost over to River Oaks tonight."

"Doing what?" Roscoe asked, winking at Big Woody. "Stealin' hubcaps or fucking poodles?"

Peewee remained impassive. "Visiting some friends," he said proudly. "They go to Rice. One of them's going to be a Ph.D. That takes a lot of studying."

"I guess that would leave me out of contention," Skeets, the tire salesman, said. He had a dry voice and when he held two dominoes up to look at them the dominoes chattered like teeth his hands shook so.

"The only thing I was ever interested in studying was pussies," he said. "They don't give no diplomas for that."

"Naw, you learn about them in the school of hard knocks," Roscoe said. "I've knocked against many a hard one too."

"You old turds," Gloria said. "You don't deserve no women, the way you talk."

"Oh, goddamn, what am I going to do?" Nancy said, turning white. "Here comes Lee Harvey. That's his Chevy driving up."

"What's the matter with that?" Big Woody asked. "I thought he was your sweet thang these days."

"We busted up," Nancy said. "He's been off in Seattle. Richard's been staying at my place while he was gone."

"So what the shit?"

"Lee Harvey never agreed we busted up."

Everyone looked worried. Everyone *was* worried. Peewee regretted not staying home. The one thing he didn't like about life on Telephone Road was that everyone there went armed. He was used to the concept of Fist City, which meant fist fights, but he had not adjusted to the gun crowd.

321

"Everyone just act natural," Nancy said. Terrible Tommy was sighting studiously down his cue at the eight ball.

In a moment Lee Harvey slouched in, a stocky middle-sized guy with a greasy forelock dangling over his forehead and his cuffs turned up two rolls on his hairy wrists. He walked around behind the bar and dispensed with preliminaries.

"Where's that goddamn Richard?" he asked. "Gonna kill that son of a bitch's ass."

"Why, honey?" Nancy whimpered.

"Gonna stomp his guts out," Lee Harvey went on. "Where is he?"

"I don't *know*. What are you picking on me for? I don't keep up with Richard, if you want to know the truth."

"Oh?" Lee Harvey affected surprise and glanced around as if to share the joke with everyone. He wasted the glance, for the bar was paralyzed. The Moon players might have been sculpted, and Terrible Tommy, a crick in his back, was still taking aim at the eight ball.

"Then what was them goddamn rubbers doing there by the bed?" Lee Harvey roared suddenly. "Fine thing to find, coming in off the road."

Nancy had been squeezing out a rag to wipe the bar with. She started to retreat but before she could Lee Harvey slapped her with one meaty hand and knocked her on her behind. She scrambled up, back-pedaling, but he grabbed her by the collar of her cheap uniform. It tore, one of her slip straps broke, and she fell again and sat on the floor behind the bar sobbing and holding her torn dress together pitifully, the strap of her slip still dangling.

At that Lee Harvey seemed to lose interest in her; he walked out from behind the bar and studied the position of the balls on the pool table.

"What's the matter, your goddamn back broken?" he asked. "Hell, you got a straight in."

Terrible Tommy flinched and shot so hard that the cue ball hopped off the table, hit the cement floor with a crack, rolled between Roscoe's legs, and came to rest against the jukebox. Lee Harvey snorted and leaned over the bar to glare at Nancy. "You better get your cheatin' ass on home when you get off," he said. "I'm going to look for Richard."

Without another word he left the bar and roared off. Nancy got to her feet and hurried to the ladies' room, sniffling and wiping her eyes. The bar relaxed again.

"Well, a two-timing woman don't deserve no better," Roscoe said pontifically. June and Gloria glared at him.

"I guess you was always the loyal type," June said.

"Son of a bitch made me scratch," Terrible Tommy said. "Shoulda climbed his ass."

"Wouldn't have been nobody to get you down," Big Woody said.

Nancy came back in wiping her eyes with a paper towel. She had managed to make some repairs and seemed relieved and rather cheerful.

"Lord, that man's got a temper," she said.

"I'm just glad we all survived," Roscoe said. "Hate to get my ass shot off over somebody else's pussy."

"Shut up," Nancy said with spirit. "Lee Harvey don't need no cheap gun. He wouldn't beat you up, anyway, you're too scrawny to bother with."

"It's pretty over in that part of town where I was," Peewee said. "You have to be smart as hell to go to Rice."

"You have to be a goddamn Communist, the way I hear it," Roscoe said.

As Peewee was finishing his beer a stranger came into the bar, a little man with neatly combed hair, baggy green pants, a white tee shirt, and tattoos on his arms.

"Anybody here know where Satsuma Street is?" he asked. "I been looking for that mother for a fucking hour."

"Shit, yes," Skeets said. "It's right off Seventy-fifth. I could find it blindfolded."

"Good for you," the man said a little belligerently. "I'm from Spring Branch, myself. We still breathe air on that side of town. What's this shit you breathe over here? Reason I can't find Satsuma Street, I'm afraid to stick my head out the window, 'fraid I'll asphyxiate while I'm looking at the street signs."

"Oh, horse turds," Roscoe said. "This air ain't so bad. What it really smells like is Japanese pussy."

"Well, I wouldn't know about that," the man said, still surly. "You-all got any chili?"

"See if that chili's turned to concrete yet," Big Woody

323

said, and Nancy went to the pot of chili and stirred it vigorously.

"It's fine," she said, and just at that moment the phone rang and it turned out to be for her. Lee Harvey had decided he wanted details. While she was talking Big Woody heaved himself up and went to serve the customer. He filled a bowl with chili, put some crackers on the plate, and carried it over to where the little man sat.

"Whatcha drinking?"

"Pepsi Cola," the man said moodily.

"Ain't got it. Got Cokes."

"Okay."

Roscoe swiveled around in his chair, a fresh match held between his teeth. "Lemme get a good look at you," he said. "You must be a member of the goddamn Pepsi generation."

"Aw, shut your mouth," the stranger said. "If you don't you're gonna have to shit dominoes for the next couple of weeks."

"Tough guy," Roscoe said, and the old girls twittered.

"Don't yell at me!" Nancy said. "I ain't your wife or nothin'!"

"Well, I'll be goddamned," the stranger said, looking at the chili with disgust. "You call this chili? Where's the beans?"

Woody was on his way back to the Moon game, but he stopped and looked calmly at the man. "They're in there," he said. "Poke around a little. The light ain't too good in here."

The stranger poked. "Not a fucking bean," he said.

"You ain't looking good." Woody waddled back, took the spoon, probed awhile, and came up with not one but two beans.

"There you are. Beans."

"Two fucking beans," the man said. "I ain't gonna pay forty cents for two fucking beans."

"You never ordered beans, you ordered chili."

"When I order chili I expect beans," the man said. "See if there's some in the pot."

"See yourself," Big Woody said. "I'm the owner, not the waitress, and the waitress is on the phone. Satsuma Street will be there all night."

"What kind of service is that? A man has to fish his own beans out of a goddamn chili pot."

"Best kind. You get more for your money. Take all the beans you can find, we don't care."

"What do you want to do?" Roscoe asked. "Fart in your wife's face or something?"

At that, to the horror of all, the little man leaped to his feet dragging a very shiny pistol out of his pants pocket. "Kill your ass!" he said, blasting at Roscoe as Big Woody struggled heavily for the cover of the bar. The bullet passed to the right of the Moon game and hit the top of the jukebox with a loud splat. "Hello, Vietnam" was playing and continued to play. Terrible Tommy huddled under a barstool, poor cover, and Peewee accidentally sucked his toothpick into his mouth and had a horrible gagging moment trying to bring it out.

"Cheat a man out of his beans," the stranger roared, turning the gun on Woody. Woody whonked into the Coke box, almost rupturing himself, and the bullet intended for him the hit the jar of pickled pigs' feet just to the right of Peewee. Vinegar and pigs' feet splattered into his face and onto his immaculate hat. Nancy had departed for the ladies' room again, and just in time, for the final bullet hit the telephone dead center, puzzling Lee Harvey no end. He assumed the niggers were rioting and had caused a panic in the bar, with everyone rushing wildly for their guns. Peewee didn't dare move for fear of straying into the line of fire, but fortunately the man abruptly stopped shooting and ran out the door, gun in hand. The bar quickly gathered itself for retaliation. Roscoe pulled out his gun and Big Woody grabbed the .38 that was underneath the cash register. They both hurried toward the door, firing a fusillade as they ran. The old dames had both knocked over their beers and were crouched in the booth sobbing and trying to keep the beer from dripping onto their skirts.

Roscoe and Big Woody stopped at the door of the lounge and tried to take aim at their attacker, who got into his old station wagon and sat calmly trying to get the engine to turn over.

"I'll shoot the son of a bitch's tires," Roscoe said and promptly sent three bullets into the Gulf-Air's neon sign, which went out. The station wagon started away and Big Woody snapped a shot at it which ricocheted off the driveway. The stranger was holding a city map in front of his face as he drove away.

"Turdhound," Roscoe said, panting.

Big Woody felt on the verge of collapse; he barely made it back to his chair.

"At least the dumb motherfucker went off the wrong way," he said. "He'll never find Satsuma Street now."

The two old ladies were standing up swabbing at their soaked skirts with napkins.

"God damn you, Roscoe, why'd you shoot that sign?" Big Woody said. "You think there was a sniper up there or something?"

"The motherfucker could have had a rifle," Roscoe said. "The less light the worse targets we make."

"Want me to call the cops?" Nancy asked. She had emerged from the ladies' room and was matter-of-factly cleaning up.

"No," Big Woody said. "I got to cool down and calculate the damage. If I call them son of a bitches they'll just beat us all up." The old dames were hurrying off, anxious to get home before the killer returned.

"Wisht he hadn't splattered my hat," Peewee said, and as soon as he had choked down the last of his beer he hurried to the Alamo Courts to try and clean it.

=== 12 ===

"Well, did Melissa confess anything significant?" Bill Duffin asked. His plane had been two hours late and he should have been tired from three days of boozing in Chicago, but instead he was feeling buoyant and was sitting in bed wearing the psychedelic pajamas his oldest daughter had given him for Christmas. He was drinking a stinger for a nightcap and was idly reading through a couple of book catalogues that had come in while he was gone. Lee was in bed too, reading Flannery O'Connor's last book of stories.

"Nothing we hadn't suspected," she said. "She had some marijuana with her. The other girls and I all smoked some the night you left."

"What a scene," he said, chuckling. "Why did you wait till I left?"

."I guess she was afraid you'd take it away from her."

"Maybe I would have. Then we could have smoked it sometime when we needed a thrill. Or I could have taken it to the MLA—it might have helped. I got trapped with the Southern crowd one evening. Tenth-hand Faulkner stories for the tenth time don't do much for me. I did hear some good gossip about our friends in Virginia."

"The girls and I missed you," Lee said.

"Not a few of your old acquaintances missed you," Bill said. "I don't seem to be as popular up there when you stay home. All your usual beaus sent their love and sorrows."

"I'm glad I didn't go," Lee said. "I can't think of one person from our past that I ever want to see again. That's goddamn sad, because I can't think of one person from our present that I feel any different about."

"It's your New Year's melancholy," Bill said. "Have some of my drink. You've got friends galore from our past."

"Sure. I don't want them to know me like I am now, though."

"That's stupid. How was the pot?"

"It made Helen a little sick. Janie and I got pretty giggly. It didn't seem to faze Melissa at all. I'm sure she's a hardened pothead. It was fun, really. We all felt wicked and companionable."

"Hum," Bill said. "Our first born a pothead. If she stays out West it's probably just as well she's hardened to it. In fact it's probably better. She'll be that much less likely to get knocked up by some unsuitable young mystic. No LSD?"

"I didn't probe and she didn't say. I have a horror of being a prying mother.

"I don't worry about Melissa," she added. "She's got your ability to take care of herself. Helen and Janie are something else. They're more like me."

Bill put down a catalogue and picked up his drink. "Speaking of probing," he said, "I guess you'll be glad to know that my days as a conventioneering cocksman seem to be over. I never even got laid. This profession could sure use some attractive females. I never saw so many drab bags, old and young. It made me think better of my beloved wife. At least she knows how to walk."

Lee smiled. "Is that my New Year's compliment?" she asked. "Maybe I'll go next year after all."

"This is a great story," she said later. "The one about the girl trying to strangle the fat woman in the doctor's office." She stared solemnly at the ceiling.

The stinger had one swallow to go. Bill set it on the bedside table and turned to Lee, an open book catalogue in one hand. "I wonder if I should collect Robert Coates?" As he read the catalogue he put his other hand under the covers and under Lee's gown and began to stroke her. She had been lying with her ankles crossed. She looked at him to see what was what. His eyes were going down the page of the catalogue but his hand continued to move lightly over her abdomen. She was not sure what to do. Sometimes she thought he was a sadist, but it was just as possible that he was only a normal absentminded man who even after twenty-one years didn't really realize what her feelings were. She had grown afraid to respond to tentative, ambiguous caresses for fear that just as she became really aroused he would turn out to have merely been idling. Often that happened and he would stop touching her and yawn or read or go to the john. If she became insistent at such a time he was apt to be spiteful, and so insulting that she would not recover from the hurt for days. She opened her legs but lifted the book from her chest and pretended to read. Bill went on reading the catalogue. He was down to F. "I didn't know Forster was published in America as early as 1913," he said, quietly surprised. "Live and learn."

"We've only got forty dollars in the bank, if that's a consideration," Lee said. His caressing had become very direct and she shut her eyes and ceased pretending to read.

"Oh, I forgot to tell you," he said. "I'm lecturing at La Jolla in February. If I like it we may just go there next year."

Lee gripped the covers of her book. Her husband glanced at her with amusement, shifted onto his elbow a bit more comfortably, and went deeper with his caress. He still held the book catalogue. Lee half opened her eyes and saw that he was as cool as if he were reading Tennyson; she put an arm across her face. For a second she wanted to rip the catalogue out of his hand and scream at him, but she was already past the point of doing that. The scream would come days later, probably in the kitchen, when he pushed the wrong button verbally. She kept her arm over her eyes. Bill was down to James Purdy when she came. He had never liked Purdy, but he sometimes liked to own the scarcest book by a given author, and if he had had a hand free, and a pencil, he would have put a check by *'63 Dream Palace,* wrappers, mint, $17.50." Lee sighed very heavily, her arm still over her face. Then she turned a little and hid her face against his shoulder. "Don't quit now," he said. "I was ever an indefatigable fingerfucker."

She made no comment. After a while she drew herself away from his hand and went to the bathroom. When she came back Bill had finished the stinger and the catalogue was lying on his back.

"Turn out the light," he said. "These pajamas are so bright they distract me."

"They're really breakfast pajamas," she said. She marked her place in Flannery O'Connor and turned off the bed light.

"See anyone while I was gone?"

"Virtually no one. I ran into Patsy Carpenter today and brought her home for tea. It didn't work out too well."

"Why not?"

"We got emotional."

"By god. What about?"

"I told her to be wary of your attentions."

"You bitch," he said. "Do I do things like that to you?"

"Chase the one from California if you have to chase someone," Lee said. She felt very tired and low.

"No, I'd rather play tennis," Bill said. "Keep my legs in shape. If I decide to sin I'd rather have a Puritan like Patsy. Give me guilt and fear and remorse and darkness and shame. Takes it out of the category of exercise."

"I guess that's what's wrong with us," Lee said. "No darkness and no shame."

"Of course not," Bill said. "We're mature adults, capable of rational mature acts like fingerfucking. I'll save Californians for when we get to California."

"I'm warning you," Lee said. "Not Patsy."

"Well, it's in the hands of fortune," Bill said. "Ordinarily I'd pursue her but I must be getting less compulsive as I grow older."

"No. You're working. When you finish the Pound book your compulsion will rear its head again."

Bill chuckled. "I always wanted to live with a cynical woman." He reached over, patted her on the shoulder, and attempted to stroke her cheek. Lee turned her head away.

"Go wash your hands," she said.

=== 13 ===

For the first two weeks of the New Year Patsy kept a guilty
secret hidden in her closet. After the walk with Hank, she
did not see him for several days. Either he avoided the
drugstore or they simply missed each other. It preyed on
Patsy's mind. One moment she felt he must think her
disgustingly brazen, the next she felt he must think her
disgustingly shy, or frivolous, or shallow, or immoral, or
whatever bad thing she herself felt herself to be at the time.
Then she had a dream in which she decorated his drab
apartment with posters and prints and curtains, and she
awoke from the dream feeling extraordinarily cheerful. It
occurred to her that there was really no reason why she
couldn't brighten up his apartment a bit, as she had in her
dream, so she drove Jim to school, took the Ford, and went
out to a quaintsy-posh shopping center called Westbury
Square. Usually when she went to Westbury she took Emma,
but for once she felt like going alone. Driving out, she
envisioned everything she would buy, and once she got there
was rather disappointed not to find everything she had
envisioned. She ended up buying two posters, one a London
Transport poster and one a bright poster of a droll blue cow.
She also bought a lovely red bottle—it was just what she saw
the apartment as needing. As she was about to pay for it she
suddenly felt very guilty about Jim and bought him a
beautiful leather-covered journal with a little steel clasp and
a key. He loved the idea of notebooks and journals and
would be delighted. It was a very well made journal and cost
twelve-fifty, much more than the posters and the bottle. She

331

felt it squared matters, and she rushed right home, meaning to take Hank's posters and his bottle right over to him.

It was not one of his class days, and she assumed she would catch him home. She freshened herself a bit, put on a bright headband and a short jacket, put the posters and the bottle in a bag, and started out for Hank's as briskly as her stomach would allow.

It was a bright lovely day, and she felt happy with herself. He would undoubtedly like what she had brought. It was not until she passed the drugstore that she began to feel a little nervous. It was really a rather odd thing for a pregnant woman to do, and as she approached Albans Road her nervousness increased and she walked more slowly. Then, just as she was about to turn the corner she saw Kenny Cambridge coming up the street. She was suddenly breathless with shock and turned quickly to the right rather than the left. If she had met him he would undoubtedly have known where she was going. Kenny was a little conceited, but not conceited enough to think she was going to *his* apartment with a shopping bag full of presents. It was annoying, and also scary. Kenny turned toward the drugstore rather than toward school, which meant that he might return to his apartment any time and catch her leaving Hank's. It was a dreadful let-down.

She walked moodily to the park and sat on a bench, depressed. The whole social fabric, for a time invisible, had suddenly sprung into view, set up as if by demonic will and design to prevent her from doing the one small innocent thing she wanted to do, which was to give Hank Malory some posters and make his apartment nicer. She bit her nail and looked with vexation at a dirty-faced child in the sandbox. His birdy mother stood nearby, clearly hoping for conversation, but Patsy was in no mood to make any. She was irritated with the world and also with herself. If she had any gumption at all she would march right over to Albans Road and knock on the door and go in and tack the posters where she thought they ought to go, and accept a word of gratitude and walk out. If she met Kenny or Lee Duffin or Emma or Flap or Jim she should have the courage of her innocence and say, "All right, so there, so what?" He needed some posters and a bottle.

But she knew she wasn't going to do anything of the sort. She was not sure, once she thought about it, that she would have had the nerve to knock on the door and give him the posters even if she hadn't met Kenny. She had a slightly comic vision of herself knocking, saying, "Here's some posters," and fleeing at once. It was absurd. She hated the birdy mother and the dirty little boy; she hated Hank Malory for being too dumb or too tasteless to fix up his own apartment; most of all, she hated herself for being so cowardly and stupid and extravagant and contradictory.

Eventually she went home and hid the posters and the bottle in a closet, far back behind some blankets. They stayed there for two weeks, a constant source of annoyance and trepidation. She became passive and could not bring herself to attempt to deliver them again. She had daydreams of Hank dropping in someday when she was alone, so she could surprise him with them. They met again at the drugstore and the mere fact of having the presents made her feel awkward. She talked fast and furiously. Several times she got scared that Jim might find them, and on one occasion she almost panicked and put them on her kitchen walls. But she didn't want them on her walls—her walls were fine. So far as she could see they were likely to rot in the closet. She could not imagine putting them in a shopping bag and walking over to Albans Road again, and in time could not remember why she had been so bold as to buy them in the first place. They were a conundrum, always there. She bitterly regretted not having taken Emma on the shopping trip; she could then have innocently suggested getting Hank some posters to cheer him up. Emma would have thought it a great idea. They could have taken them by together, and that would have been that. Still, it wouldn't have been quite the same; she didn't want Emma in on it particularly. She wanted to take the posters in and put them up herself.

After two weeks of brooding she gave up on everything and supposed she would just be the permanent possessor of two rolled-up posters and a red bottle. It depressed her very much to have them in her closet. One morning Jim had to teach a class for a friend who taught a class, and he awoke grumpy and bawled her out for not fixing him toast the minute he wanted it. The postman came just at that moment, delivering sixty dollars' worth of rare books Jim had ordered. When Jim yelled at her about the toast she yelled at him about the books and to his horror kicked the package, which almost went into the open oven. The books were undamaged, but Patsy wasn't glad. She went raging into the bedroom and sobbed until he dressed and left; then, feeling terribly lonely and ugly, she climbed up in the closet, got the posters, and tore them to shreds. She stuffed the shreds in a wastebasket and sat on the couch crying and holding the red bottle. She had never felt so irrational—it was all she could do to keep from getting the beautiful leather-covered journal and tearing it to shreds too. Jim had only written in it once. But after she had cried awhile she put on an old green coat that she liked and went to Emma's.

Emma was sitting on her couch idly reading the want ads. She liked to go to garage sales. She was smoking and playing "Sergeant Pepper" on the phonograph and Teddy was sitting under a card table with a purple mouth from drinking grape Kool-Aid. Tommy was in nursery school. They had been trying to get Teddy to drink from cups, but he hated them and Emma had eventually put his Kool-Aid in a bottle. When Patsy came in, Teddy, who liked her, came over and said, "Um," and offered her such Kool-Aid as was still in the plastic cup he had rejected.

"Thanks, sugar," she said, politely taking a tiny sip. The Kool-Aid was awful—lukewarm and with an orange seed floating in it.

Teddy merrily held up his bottle, gave it an inimitable little flick with his wrist to assure himself that the level of the contents was still adequate, and went cheerfully off to try and fire Tommy's Johnny Eagle Crackfire rifle.

"You've been weeping," Emma said. "What's the matter with you?" Teddy, very curious about the emotions of adults, temporarily abandoned the rifle and came back to stare at Patsy, wondering if she was going to cry some more. He patted her on the knee sympathetically.

"I'm in despair," Patsy said. "I'll never rise again."

"Neither will I," Emma said. "Look at this room. The car pool was late and Tommy made play-dough dinosaurs to

334

while away the time. Look at that. If there's anything I don't need on Monday morning it's an acre of play dough to clean up. That's not a bad stegosaurus, though." She pointed at a blue lump. Teddy went over and plucked off what must have been the stegosaurus' head.

"You ought to smoke," Emma said. "Despair is easier to take if you smoke."

"My kind wouldn't be. Where's Flap?"

"Sleeping, the lazy bastard. Finals are approaching and he stays up and reads all night. Want to do the laundry?" Sometimes the two of them did their laundry together at a sort of lower-class laundrymat on Bissonnet. It was called the Sudsy-Dudsy.

"No," Patsy said. "I'd drown myself in the washing machine. Jim said I was frivolous and lazy."

"Well, so you are," Emma said. "I hope you are, at least. I am, and I don't want you being better than me. It would ruin our friendship. You should learn to cuss. When Flap insults me that way I tell him what a dumb prick he is and it sets him back on his heels long enough that he gets confused. Learn a few coarse insults and your marriage will go much better."

"Maybe," Patsy said, not enthusiastic. The clutter on the Hortons' living-room floor was truly appalling: play dough, sheets of newspaper, an orange, splotches of spilled Kool-Aid, plastic pants, tinkertoys. If that was what motherhood entailed, she wouldn't be able to stand it.

"I feel like agreeing with every bad thing Jim says," she said.

"Of course. That's where they put it to us. We naturally tend to agree with their low opinion of us. You have to train yourself to disagree." Emma wore an old housecoat, and her hair was as disarrayed as usual.

"You know what I did?" Patsy said. "I bought Hank Malory some posters because I think that apartment of his looks awful, and then I lost my nerve and didn't give them to him. This morning I tore them up. It's insane."

"I thought you had a small crush on him," Emma said kindly.

"I don't think I do," Patsy said, worried. "I just like to

talk to him. My god, look how pregnant I am. I can't go having crushes on people."

"I'm mother of two and I wish I could find someone to have a crush on," Emma said. "I'd be too cowardly to do anything about it too, but at least it would be good for daydreams."

There was a loud, realistic *pa-cheew* from the Johnny Eagle Crackfire rifle. Teddy had at last succeeded in firing his brother's gun. Patsy jumped.

"Sounds real, doesn't it?" Emma said.

There was a crash from the bedroom, and the sound of breaking glass. They looked at each other wonderingly. Silence followed the crash. In a minute Flap slopped in in gray pajama bottoms and a tee shirt and barefooted. His hair was tousled and he looked abashed.

"Hi, Patsy," he said. "How about that? I fell out of bed."

"What'd you break?" Emma asked.

"Just the bedside lamp," Flap said. "I think I was dreaming and that goddamn rifle went off and scared me. I must have been right on the edge."

Teddy ran over and his father hoisted him onto his hip. Teddy was jubilant and delivered a sentence of rapid *uums,* the gist of which was that he could shoot Tommy's gun.

Flap lay down on the couch and set Teddy on his stomach. Emma went to get her husband some coffee. Flap scratched his head. "Hate Mondays," he said. Teddy turned around on his father's stomach until he was facing his feet and began to fiddle with the tie string of Flap's pajamas. Flap had picked up the paper and was peering at the front page but without his glasses. "Our President," he said in a sleepily critical tone. He was a Johnson hater.

"Want coffee, Patsy?" Emma called.

"I don't think so," Patsy said. She was sitting in a deep armchair that still smelled slightly of a dog the Hortons had had months before. She felt like staying. There was something comforting and cozy about the Hortons, even when they were at their most disheveled and disorganized; but on the other hand she also felt slightly like an outsider, a disruption in the family's morning. There was a rather smashed-up library copy of Lionel Trilling's *Matthew*

Arnold lying on the floor by the chair and she picked it up and read a few pages without much interest.

"I could make toast if anybody wants any," Emma called, but neither Flap nor Patsy answered. In a minute Emma came in, a cup of coffee in each hand.

"Oh, god!" she yelled. "Teddy! Oh, shit!" She had sloshed hot coffee out of both cups onto her hands and had to set the cups hastily on a windowsill. Patsy was scared—she couldn't imagine what had happened. She sat up and saw that Teddy had untied Flap's pajama string, Flap having gone back to sleep. He was exposed, and Teddy had been blissfully trying to make a loop in one end of the pajama string, the meanwhile eyeing his father's apparatus and occasionally peeking into his diapers to check on his own. He knew that his mother's shriek meant real trouble and instantly rolled over between Flap and the back of the couch, seeking cover.

"Aaah," Emma said, wringing her stinging hands. She flung a section of newspaper over Flap, who awoke looking hopelessly perplexed. When he discovered the trouble he was mortified and turned red. Patsy tried to pretend she was reading Lionel Trilling, but it was no good. She rolled her head in horrified sympathy with Emma, feeling neither offended nor shocked. It was only the second penis she had seen in her life and she was secretly rather grateful to Teddy for making it possible. She felt like giggling, but didn't feel it was a good time to giggle.

"This ain't my day," Flap said, trying to retie the knot while looking innocently at the ceiling.

"Oh, none of your fucking understatements," Emma said. "Give me that kid so I can beat him."

Teddy had anticipated such an impulse and had managed to burrow under his father's arm. Emma ran over and grabbed his leg, but Flap decided he had better not surrender his son while Emma was so angry. He held on, grinning resignedly at Patsy.

"Let go of him," Emma said, giving Teddy an ineffective splat on the behind. She burst into tears.

"Oh, sit down and enjoy life," Flap said. "Patsy's reading Trilling." He grabbed Emma by the waist and tugged her

337

onto the couch, holding on grimly until she had exhausted her capacity for struggle and merely sat crying. Patsy sighed and after a time Emma sighed too. Flap continued to hold her, just in case. Patsy dropped the book and stood up.

"I'm going," she said.

"Who could blame you?" Emma said. "Take me with you. I'll go anywhere. Just get me away from these men."

"Come and see us more often, Pat," Flap said. He was all but buried under his wife, his son, his uncombed hair, and the morning newspapers. "You add a note of sanity to the morning."

"Don't flatter her," Emma said. "She's lucky enough as it is. Let's do laundry tomorrow, okay?"

"Okay," Patsy said. "Please be careful with one another. I don't know what I'd do without you."

And she walked down their driveway crying, for no reason or for too many reasons. The day had clouded over and rain was coming. Perhaps she should have numbers of boys and live amid clutter and never be lonely, only she didn't know if lots of kids would appeal to Jim. He had gotten very fond of order. There was really no knowing what might work with Jim.

By noon it had begun to drizzle and the apartment was lonely and she put on her nice lined raincoat and walked to Rice, meaning to find Jim and have lunch with him and the other graduate students. But she went to the library first, to a corner where she often found him, and missed him and sat in a big leather chair reading *Punch* and watching it rain until she had missed lunch. She realized it when she looked up and saw Jim go past the wet window with Clara Clark and Flap on their way to the Eliot seminar. It made her immediately blue. There was a whole afternoon ahead and it was raining and cold and she was tired of sitting and reading and she didn't want to go back to the apartment. Jim had looked very happy, walking along with Clara and Flap. It was only a glimpse but it convinced her that he was always happy when he was away from her; he was so nice-looking, so personable and confident when he was away from her. She had never realized it until then, but he had another life, a life in which he was merry and pleasant and open, instead of nervous and sulky and reserved as he was with her. It upset her. She didn't have any life at all, except him, and suddenly it seemed to her that she didn't even have the best of him. If he stuck with graduate school he would surely get better and better at it and would surely have less and less use for her, for she didn't know anything much and wasn't even very pretty or sexy any more. She remembered what Lee Duffin had said would happen, and it no longer seemed like malicious neurotic raving but like very sane clear-headed prophecy. Perhaps it had already happened, perhaps Lee had already seduced Jim, perhaps that was why he looked so cheerful. Lee Duffin probably knew all sorts of things about being a good lay, things she didn't know or was too inhibited to do, or something.

Feeling utterly miserable, already deserted and forlorn, she wandered down into the basement of the library, where the English graduate students had a large communal office. Jim had promised to bring her some Evelyn Waugh books and she wanted to see if he had checked them out. She might as well go home and be forsaken and read Evelyn Waugh.

The first person she saw when she got down the stairs was Hank Malory, asleep on one of the long green leather couches that were scattered through the basement, relics of a day when the basement had been a student center of sorts.

Patsy was startled. She had not expected to see him there, and she hastily and a little nervously tiptoed around the couch and went to the office, which, to her annoyance, turned out to be locked. What was even more annoying was that she could see a pile of Evelyn Waugh books on Jim's desk, four or five of them. She turned the doorknob a time or two and then turned and wandered irresolutely around the basement. She had never felt quite so anchorless, so adrift. She couldn't get in the places she wanted in, and didn't particularly feel like doing anything. Hank had a key to the office, of course, and if she just had the nerve to wake him up and ask him for it she could at least get the books she wanted.

She walked over and looked at him again, hopeful that he might be waking of his own accord. He wasn't, but looking at him made her feel better. Men asleep were different from

men awake. She had always thought Jim was at his best
asleep—sleeping, he looked strong and stable. Hank was
different. When he was awake he seemed so sure of himself
that she was kept a little on edge; she didn't know how to
move in relation to such confidence and kept fidgeting and
fluttering, seeking tiny clues that might reveal what he
wanted her to be like. Asleep, he looked less confident and
more vulnerable. He didn't look so unreachable. One of his
shoelaces had broken and was knotted in the second hole of
his shoe, and the corduroy trousers he wore were almost
worn through at the knees, like a little boy's trousers. He had
on a rather awful high school ring, and his suede coat had
begun to tear at one pocket. Obviously he was no good at
taking care of himself, and if he had female admirers they
were obviously too lightheaded to inform him that his
trousers were worn out and his coat not fit to wear. Asleep,
he didn't look at all formidable, and she was glad. It was a
time when almost everyone in the world seemed more
formidable than her. She leaned back against a pillar and
watched him contentedly, glad to be around with him; she
was thinking that it might be nice to be married to a man
like Hank—a man who had problems with his clothes,
things that even a simple girl like herself could remedy.

When Hank awoke she was standing by the pillar looking
at him solemnly, her abdomen bulging under her raincoat.
He blinked, embarrassed, and immediately tried to tuck his
shirttail in. Patsy giggled. The gesture had reminded her of
Peewee Raskin's attempt to tidy himself when he had
awakened to discover her staring at him on their trip to
Phoenix. Getting their shirttails tucked in was apparently
an instinct with Western men.

"Surprise," she said. Hank swung his legs off the couch
and rubbed his face.

"You were talking in your sleep," she said, grinning.
"Mumbling romantic endearments. Unfortunately I didn't
catch the name of the girl."

"It was the Wife of Bath," Hank said, yawning. "I was
carrying on with her till four A.M." He stood up, and his
shapeless clothes fell into place around his body. His face
kept a moody look, as if it troubled him that she had seen
him sleeping.

"I'm starved," he said. "Want to have breakfast with me?"

"Come to my place," she said without thinking. "I'll cook you some. I don't have anything else to do. It's a good day for hot chocolate."

The invitation seemed to make him slightly more melancholy, but he didn't protest. It was only after they left the library together that her heart began to pound at her own audacity. Their faces were wet by the cold rain. He was nice to walk with, and good at steering her around mud puddles. She began to think about what to cook and decided in advance that she would have to wash everything the minute he left. Jim would be outraged, and properly, if he came home and discovered that she had cooked a better meal for someone else than she had for him.

When she let Hank into the apartment she found that she had become too embarrassed to look at him. He seemed larger than she had thought him to be, taller and heavier. The whole apartment felt different with him in it. She kicked off her wet sneakers, skinned off her socks, and hastily waved him toward some magazines; then she went in and amazed herself in the kitchen. She was usually a rambling, digressive cook, prone to much singing and chattering as she cooked and not at all appalled by thirty-minute gaps between courses even if the courses were as simple as toast and bacon. But in a few minutes, beside combing out her damp hair, she put together a fine breakfast —orange juice, some apricots, toast, bacon and scrambled eggs, and some hot chocolate. She served it to him on bright blue plates.

"I ought to eat breakfast here every morning," Hank said when he sat down to it, but he still looked strangely sulky. He ate her food to the last bite while she sat across from him in a chair, rather silent, looking out the rain-streaked windows at the wet back yard. She held her cup of hot chocolate in her two hands and looked everywhere but at his face. Quiet as he was, and lonely as she had been, she was not really enjoying his company. Feeding him had been a pleasant, useful task, but he was almost done eating and she felt tight in her chest. She didn't want him to leave, but neither did she want him to stay. What she wanted to do had been accomplished and she wished that he could be instantaneously transported back to the couch in the library, with not another word said. She didn't have any words.

"I'll be glad when the semester's over," Hank said. It was as conventional a remark as could be imagined.

"Why?" she asked. "I won't. Another one will just start. Ever since I can remember, people have been saying they'll be glad when a semester ends, or glad when one starts, when they really don't particularly care one way or the other. The one nice thing about rodeo is that it doesn't operate on the semester system."

She suggested they go to the living room and they went. She sat in her favorite chair by the rainy window, and Hank sat on the couch and picked up a copy of *Esquire* but didn't look at it. He looked at her strangely, as if he were waiting for her to say something. But she felt silent and still; something oppressed her. Sitting down in the chair had been the last act she felt capable of. Having him in the room was too much. Something dreadful was going to happen; she could no more stop it than she could stop the rain. He was gradually filling the room; he had been there too long. There was no way either of them could get out of the room without it happening. It seemed so inescapable that her hands began to tremble a little, and she wanted it to begin so there would not be such tightness in her chest. When Hank frowned and got up and came to the chair, she was not surprised, though when he turned her face up and kissed her she was surprised to see the planes of his face so close to hers. She felt no whirl of emotion, only a deep blankness, close to unconsciousness it was so deep. At first his kisses were soft and tentative; after a time she opened her eyes and came out of the blankness into a kind of dizziness. His position on the arm of the chair was uncomfortable. "Sit on the couch," he said, his mouth so close to hers that she felt his words like breath.

She sighed very deeply. "My feet are freezing," she said. When she got up to get her big fuzzy-wuzzy slippers she found that her legs were so weak she could barely walk. She was glad to reach the couch; she sank and he caught her comfortably. She felt overwhelmingly grateful to him; mixed with a kind of fear was a deep relief, as if she had just been saved from a bad fall, or had just missed being in a car wreck. She shut her eyes and let herself be kissed some more, melting into a deep and delicious blankness, a state not possible unless her mouth was on his. Occasionally she opened her eyes and saw things and said things, but the blankness was accessible, easy to sink back into. He was very soft and gentle with her, as she had known he would be, and she quickly let herself trust him completely. It was a mistake, for while she was dazed with pleasure, wanting only to be kissed, he put his warm hand inside her shirt, on her breast. The shock was like a burn. She sat up and began to cry. Hank drew back but she continued to sob. He didn't go away, didn't even seem much bothered by her tears, which disconcerted her.

"You mustn't do that," she said, knowing it sounded silly. Hank made her let him rub her neck. She felt disconsolate but after a few minutes she felt better and gave a little yawn of pleasure. She saw that he looked unhappy and reached up and put her hand on his cheek—it was a wicked but delicious thing to do. He started kissing her again, not so gently. She couldn't immediately resist or make him quit, but when she finally did she felt miserable. He kept trying to put his hand on her, on her breast, on her body, anywhere. He had crowded her into a corner of the couch and when she looked at his face between kisses she felt lost and hurt. He had stopped seeing her, and only wanted her; his fumblings were impersonal and crude. But when he managed to catch her mouth she stopped caring. The kissing was what she wanted; she couldn't help it. But his hands were strong, and having to fight them away finally upset her and she began to cry again.

"Quit, it's all over," she said, sobbing.

"What's all over?"

"Us," she said. "Jim's seminar's out in an hour and we can't ever do this any more."

"Sure we can," Hank said. It irritated her; he really expected to see her again, touch her again. He looked smug, as if she had become his in some way. "I'm in love with you," he said, and Patsy flushed. She had not been prepared for him to say it. It undid her and she let him kiss her again. He had given up on desire, for the day, and went back to gentleness, and when it was just time for the seminar to be

343

out they were standing near the door, Patsy with her face against his chest, smelling his smell and the smell of the suede coat, which she detested, except that it did look sort of right on him. She felt grave. Another hour of kissing had borne in on her that he was not really going away forever; he was only going four blocks to an apartment where he would be that night, the next day, and probably for years. She didn't know what was going to happen and was glad of the kisses, which made her feel trusting rather than scared. Just as he was about to step out the door she remembered something. She went to the closet and meekly presented him the lovely red bottle.

"It's all I have left," she said. "I had some posters but you didn't make it possible for me to give them to you so I tore them up. I haven't had a chance to tell you but your apartment is awful."

When he actually left she felt like crying. She peeked out, and he stopped on the wet steps and looked up.

"You're getting wet," she said, unable to think of anything else to say.

When he was gone she went to the kitchen and piled the dishes in the dishpan and covered them with too many suds and stood at the sink letting the dishes soak, dabbing in the soapsuds with her hands and occasionally smiling to herself. It was scary, really, but with her hands in her own dishpan she could not be too scared. She decided to go back to Westbury and get some more posters. Before they parted forever she could at least see to it that his terrible apartment got fixed up.

14

Events seemed to come in clusters, like grapes. The next morning Jim left early, to go book scouting with Bill Duffin. He looked very pleased and it sliced through Patsy's mind that maybe the reason he looked so pleased was because he was really going to a rendezvous with Lee. It was a silly thought, she decided, putting on some knee socks. She hurriedly combed her hair and made the bed. She wanted to rush out to Westbury and buy some more posters, and she had promised Emma that they would launder that morning and so had no time to waste. In her haste she broke a fingernail and sat down at her dressing table, annoyed, and was filing it when there was a knock at the door. She looked at herself, her heart pounding violently; she was sure it was Hank. It agitated her very much.

But it was not Hank on the landing. It was Sonny Shanks. Patsy was too surprised even to feel let down. He wore a nice maroon sports coat, a dark blue shirt, and Western pants. He smiled at her and nodded pleasantly, as if he had arrived exactly on time for an appointment.

"Howdy," he said. "Come to see the baby. Looks like I'm a day or two early."

"A month, actually," Patsy said. "You surprised me. You're always surprising me. Do you mean to tie me up?"

"Not if I can help it."

"Come in, then," she said. "Maybe I'm even a little glad to see you, I don't know. You're the first cowboy I've seen in months, not counting Peewee. I'm going somewhere in ten minutes, though. You can pay me compliments while I file my nails."

345

He really didn't look violent, and she decided that flirtation was the best way to handle him. She felt much more competent at flirtation than she had previously.

"That's long enough for me to have a mornin' toddy," Sonny said. "Point me at the liquor, why don't you?"

Patsy did. "Are you a compulsive drinker, or something?" she asked. "Every time I see you, you're drinking. Maybe you just drink because you're shy. Maybe you're tormented by feelings of inadequacy."

Sonny broke out some ice cubes, a little surprised by her new manner but not disconcerted.

"Say something," she said. "If you intend to keep popping into my life every few months you have to get used to my sharp relentless tongue."

"Used to it already," he said. He took his drink and strolled into the living room. "Hey, this is the way I like to live," he said. "You got your living room and your bedroom right together. Don't go crashing into so much woodwork that way. Used to know an old boy who got so worked up over a girl he busted through a plate-glass wall and almost cut his dingus off. Wouldn't have happened if he'd had his bed in the living room." He tipped his glass at her cheerfully and took a swallow.

Patsy sat on the couch filing her nail. "Don't be crude, now," she said. "Nothing of that sort goes on here. We're all dedicated to humane letters around here. We subjugate the flesh."

"What?" he asked, amused.

"Subjugate," she said. "Don't you know the word?"

"I know it sounds worse than running through a plate-glass wall naked," he said, looking at a small Chagall print. "I've got a girl friend who's got pictures like that. Only she's got the real ones."

"If I had her money I'd have the real ones too."

"If I had her money I'd have her," Sonny said. He finished his drink.

"We all have our problems. I've got to go."

"Any place I'd like to see?"

"No place I intend to take you. We'll just have to talk about your problems some other time."

"Well, liquor beats Listerine," he said, putting down his

glass. "Only reason I drink in the morning. Where's old Jim? He's who I actually had the business with. I need to know if he still wants that job. We're making the movie this summer."

"I think he's going to be helping me baby-sit this summer. I suppose he'd like to talk to you, though. He'll be back this afternoon."

"I think I'll look up Dixie, since I'm here," Sonny said. "Why don't we all go have a feast, or something—maybe tonight? Your little dancing buddy from L.A.'s due in this afternoon."

"Mr. Percy? I'd like to see him. Unfortunately we have something planned for the evening." It was the evening the Duffins were going to take them out.

They went out the door together and Sonny looked at her appreciatively and laughed. His good spirits were infectious and she couldn't help smiling. She was in good spirits herself.

"If I was ever lucky enough to get in the sack with you I'd have to prop a dictionary on the pillow so I'd know what was happening," he said.

"The first cowboy who ever tried to seduce me told me I was too wordy," she said. "Boy, did I scare him off. It doesn't seem to work with you."

"No," he said. "I'd probably take the chance, even without no dictionary. Thanks for the drink. Might see you this afternoon."

His hearse was parked by the curb, looking strangely incongruous under the huge waving trees. Winter sunlight slipped through the branches. Patsy walked over to it and peered in. Seeing him had brought back much. She would have liked to ask about Boots and Pete, but knew he was the wrong person to ask. The rear end of the hearse was still littered with ropes and rodeo gear. Sonny stood on the curb kicking at it with a bootheel, and he too looked out of place and even seemed to know it. He needed his rightful milieu: the plains, the long empty highways, the bulls and horses and violent men, the space and the deep changing sky. All that belonged with him, while the large houses and well-kept lawns of South Boulevard seemed to conceal the real Sonny and make him look like a different man. She was tempted to

347

ask him to ride to Westbury with her, but once he was gone she was glad she hadn't. Sonny was still Sonny. They might have run out of pleasant banter—the old scary force might have come out again.

She got the posters and a small cute turn-of-the-century etiquette book that had just been reprinted. She rushed home, hid the posters, and bundled up her laundry before Emma came. They went to the Sudsy-Dudsy and washed and yakked. Emma was envious of Sonny's visit.

"The boys would go out of their minds if they could meet someone like that," she said. "You have all the luck. What did I ever get to do but come to this laundrymat? It's a big night for us if there's something good on television. You're going out with the Duffins and you know a famous cowboy and a screenwriter. Maybe I better reduce."

"I was never less reduced," Patsy said. "Don't go envying me the Duffins—they're no blessing. I think they're evil. Maybe not evil individually, but evil in combination."

"Everything you say makes it worse. I don't even know anyone evil. Everyone we know is nice, more or less. This is supposed to be a crazy confused age and here I don't even know anyone who's all that crazy. What's the matter with me? Why did I get left out of the age?"

"You may know somebody crazy if you keep knowing me," Patsy said. "I'm likely to crack at any time."

It was a small squalid laundrymat, poorly lit, with old top-loading washing machines that were always konking out. The reason they liked it was because scarcely anybody else ever came there. Emma's machine did konk out and Patsy watched her adjust it.

"It's getting so these machines won't take two diapers at a time," Emma said. "Remember the night the man tried to wash the rug?"

Patsy giggled at the memory. They had been roommates at the time. In those days the Sudsy-Dudsy had been more prosperous and a number of people were there. While she and Emma sat talking a little man came in and, unobserved by anyone, stuffed his living room rug into one of the machines. He couldn't even get the top closed on it, but he did get the machine started. The first intimation anyone had that something untoward was happening was when the lights in the building flashed blue and went off and the cheap metal chairs all began to rattle. Then the machines all began to shake and a horrible vibrating sound was heard. Everyone leapt up and ran out into the parking lot, expecting earthquakes, crumbling buildings, air raids, Russian paratroopers, and mushroom clouds. When they calmed down enough to look back into the Sudsy-Dudsy they saw the little man clinging as nonchalantly as possible to the washing machine, which was flinging him from side to side and attempting to wrench itself from its bolts. He tried to indicate by his expression that nothing unusual or dangerous was happening—he was just getting his living-room rug cleaned in the quickest way—but finally all the fuses blew and several of the ladies harangued him mercilessly while he dragged the sopping rug out of the machine.

"That was crazy," Patsy said. "You see, your life hasn't been totally devoid of incident."

"True. Something like that is good for a laugh once every five years, when you remember it. Still, it's hardly wild debauchery."

"Small loss. I doubt wild debauchery's all it's made out to be." She remembered that she had almost been debauched the day before and wondered.

"I've got to quit reading novels," Emma said. "They're full of crazed sensualists. It makes me feel cheated by life. I never even met a crazed sensualist."

"Are you kidding?" Patsy said. "You're married to one, if you ask me."

"That's around you. He's only intermittently crazed around me and then half the time he's in too big a hurry to take his shoes off. I seldom even get laid by anyone barefooted and that seems the very least one can ask of life."

"Oh, come on," Patsy said, trying to remember if Jim had ever made love to her with his shoes on. She could not remember him being in that big a hurry.

When she got home he was there, and in a high state of excitement; but his excitement was social, not sexual. He had just managed what he considered a brilliant piece of social maneuvering. He had seen Sonny, been offered a job

349

as a still photographer on the movie, and had invited Sonny and Joe Percy to dinner with them and the Duffins. The only fly in the ointment, so far as he was concerned, was that Sonny had already made plans with Dixie, which meant that she would be coming along.

"This ought to be an evening," he said proudly.

"Shit, damn, and hell," Patsy said. So far as she was concerned there were more flies than ointment. To make matters even worse, they were going to her aunt's club. It was high atop a bank and everyone there was so conservative they were practically paralyzed, the waiters included. "I can see you're looking forward to my poor aunt making a fool of herself in front of your patron intellectual," she said. Jim was too cheerful to be affected by her mood and tried to hug her. She shrugged him off. "I slave over washing machines while you think up schemes to humiliate my aunt," she said. "Sonny was by this morning. He must be mellowing; he didn't even try to rape me. I hope you told him you weren't taking his crummy job."

"No, I sort of think I might," Jim said. "It would just be for six weeks and it might make a good change from graduate school."

Patsy was infuriated. It had never occurred to her he would seriously consider taking the job. Jim anticipated her.

"Don't go blowing off," he said. "I didn't make him any promises, but I can't see why I shouldn't take the job. It would be fun. Don't you have any curiosity about how movies are made?"

"Not much. Where is this one going to be made, may I ask?"

"Amarillo. Or somewhere near there."

"Oh, great!" Patsy said, striding about the apartment. "I'm supposed to take our infant child and live in Amarillo? Monster! Infanticide! Amarillo! You're out of your mind."

"Is that all the epithets you can think of?" he asked, amused.

"Don't you be polite to me," Patsy said. "I'll make you rue the day you were ever polite to me. I will not live in Amarillo."

"Well, it's six months away," Jim said. "We don't need to

fight about it just yet. You look great today. We should make love, not war. Pretty soon we'll have a baby and won't be able to in the afternoons."

"Yeah, well too bad that didn't occur to you months ago," Patsy said. "I feel more like making war." And she went off in a huff to put the clean laundry away.

Later, as she was dressing, she began to feel that her life was dissolving, losing its natural shape. What had happened the day before with Hank did not seem very real. It was much more natural to be fussing and bitching at Jim. But the dinner to come also seemed unreal, and the people unnecessary forces pressing in on her. She wished the baby were born, so she would have an excuse to stay home. She dressed with unusual care, irritated that she had to be so large, slow, and bulky on such an occasion. She was sure to be outshone by both Lee and Dixie. Since she could not be slim she combed her hair out to see if she looked good that way. It didn't work. Nothing worked. She simply had no glow. In the morning she had had some glow, but the afternoon had dissipated it and she felt flat and sallow. She was tempted to fake a stomachache and stay home but decided that would be ignoble. She chose a black dress that she thought made her look mature and austere.

They went to pick up the Duffins and found them already a little in their cups. They were throwing verbal daggers at each other. Bill was wearing a white dress turtleneck and looked a little too high-colored, whether from drink or anger Patsy could not tell. Lee wore a blue dress with a very short skirt and was dancing by herself to the Mammas and the Papas.

"Come in, fellow sufferers," Bill said. "My wife's just been castrating me." He used his deepest oracular tone.

"Ignore him," Lee said. "He dresses like George Plimpton, pontificates like John Kenneth Galbraith, and cries like Johnny Ray, if anybody but me can remember Johnny Ray."

"Everybody remembers Johnny Ray," Bill said. "In our circle everybody remembers everybody. It's one of your persistent delusions that you are the only one who remembers people."

"I don't remember Johnny Ray," Patsy said.

"Stout girl," Lee said. "I'm teaching her the art of castration," she said to Jim, smiling. "Hope you don't mind.

"Let's get on to the cowboys," she said.

"There's only one," Jim said. "The other guy's a screenwriter."

"One cowboy will wreak enough havoc," Bill said. "Two would just overstimulate Lee. She once had a thing on a shot-putter, as I recall."

"He was a javelin thrower," Lee said. "Shows how observant you are. Makes me wonder how you ever find those cute little things in the texts of poems, on which your reputation is based."

"I like poems better than javelin throwers."

"Or me, for that matter," Lee said. She saw that the Carpenters were a little disconcerted by the acrimony and dropped it. "Sorry. Bill and I should never have seen *Virginia Woolf.* Let's go."

They found their party at a nearby hotel. Dixie was resplendent in an orange dress. Joe Percy had on a conservative gray suit but a bright pink tie, and Sonny had a white turtleneck to match Bill Duffin's. It looked good with his maroon coat. He also wore a black Western hat, and that too looked good. They were all three in good spirits, Dixie particularly.

"Hi, duck," she said, kissing Patsy. "I love these people. Mr. Percy's the nicest man I ever met in my life. Isn't Sonny something in the sweater. I see your friend has one too."

Lee smiled, but Jim was uneasy. Bill shook hands gravely with all three of them. His gravity made an instant impression on Dixie, who got her impressions in an instant, most of the time.

"You have to promise not to mind me," she said. "Otherwise I'll be afraid to open my mouth. You're probably the smartest man I ever met."

"What?" Joe Percy said. "You just conveyed that distinction on me, not five minutes ago. I thought sure I'd hold the title a little longer than five minutes."

"Too bad," Dixie said.

"Good to see you again, honey," Joe said to Patsy, taking

her hand for a second. "Surely you realize I'm the smartest man you ever met."

"Give me your keys, Dixie," Sonny said. "I'm the dumbass in the crowd, but at least I can drive."

"Don't be surprised when I say dumb things," Dixie said to Bill. "Do you like *The Carpetbaggers?*"

"I don't believe so," Bill said.

"We just won't talk about books then," Dixie said.

They got in Dixie's Cadillac and Sonny whirled them smoothly downtown. Dixie regaled them with an account of life in Puerto Vallarta, where she had just been.

"I even took Squatty," she said. "He speaks all kinds of Spanish, from working in South America so long."

"Squatty?" Lee asked.

"My little fat ex-husband."

They were soon seated atop of Houston, with a view of half the city. Lee sat between Sonny and Jim, Patsy between Bill Duffin and Joe Percy. Bill Duffin did the ordering and did it in his most solemn editorial tone. The presence of Dixie, perky in her orange dress, right at his elbow, seemed to have sunk Bill into a kind of reserve; he talked to her as he might have talked to a class of graduate students, only more politely. Lee, on the other hand, was very pepped. Sonny was paying her a lot of attention and she liked it. Once she turned and said something to Jim, even put her hand on his wrist, but in a maternal fashion, as a lady of presence might put her hand on the wrist of her son's roommate.

Though it irked Patsy to admit it, it was Sonny who dominated the table. A few passing guests glanced at Bill Duffin curiously, or at Dixie, whose dress was so bright it was almost impossible not to glance at her; but the person they really looked at was Sonny. The force that Bill Duffin was able to project at a graduate party or a gathering of his colleagues was not being projected. He looked old and seemed scarcely the man who had been saying acid things to Lee an hour earlier. To Patsy's surprise he said almost nothing to her. He passed her the pepper mill, he gracefully poured her wine, but otherwise he left her be.

Sonny stood out. If he had seemed diminished that morning standing under the great overlapping trees of South

Boulevard, he seemed diminished no longer. His white teeth and black hair and white shirt worked for him; and unlike everyone else at the table he was perfectly at ease. Everyone else was eating fish, but he was eating steak. He gave most of his attention to Lee, grinning at whatever she had to say and occasionally putting in some quiet sardonic comment of his own. Once in a while he glanced at Patsy. She was almost glad, since he was the only one who did glance at her; but she was not entirely glad. In the glances she saw the only Sonny, the man who had lifted her like a doll in Phoenix. Once he looked at her just as he was lifting a buttery piece of French bread to his mouth, and his lips curved and he bit slowly into the bread, as if he had slowed down his bite just because he knew she was watching. He inclined his head to hear something Lee was saying, but his eyes stayed on Patsy for a moment. Then he bit into the roll.

Patsy nibbled her trout and felt low and confused. She had tried to chat with Joe Percy, but his mood seemed to correspond closely to hers. He had become suddenly and undisguisedly melancholy, and though he responded politely and even wittily, his heart was clearly not in the conversation. She gave up on the evening and sat silently looking out at the lights of Houston; she felt unwanted, unnoticed, and unsure. Everyone there was stronger and surer than she was—Joe Percy in his melancholy, Bill Duffin in his reserve, even Dixie in her bright strong ignorance. They were all strong compared to Jim and herself; they were all grown up; they all knew what they were doing. She thought wistfully of Emma and Flap; they would have looked incredibly out of place in such a posh club, but their wry out-of-placeness would have been a comfort. She thought of Hank Malory and could not picture him in such a place at all. He had said he loved her. If he did she could not see how it could help but make both of them more unhappy. She could scarcely believe she had spent an afternoon kissing him. She didn't know what she felt and took what comfort she could from the lights of Houston.

The company wanted to go to the bar for brandy, but she didn't feel like moving and fortunately Joe Percy came out of melancholy sufficiently to second her. "Stay here with me and have some more coffee," he said. The company went and they stayed. Jim was puzzled; he could not see why anyone would prefer the company of Joe Percy to that of Sonny Shanks and William Duffin. But he said nothing.

"You seem as down in the dumps as I am," Patsy said. "You haven't even said anything crude."

Joe looked down disconsolately at the sprawl of lights. "This is wretched food," he said. "You'd think with the goddamned ocean forty miles away they could at least keep a fish fresh long enough to cook it. Mine was almost rotten."

"Does my aunt get you down, or what?"

"Oh, no," he said. "She's fun. Let's see if they'll bring us some brandy here. I just needed to get away from that mob we were with. Mobs like that make me wish I'd done something."

"Like what?"

He waved vaguely at the ground far below. "Oh, been a turnip farmer or something," he said. "Then I wouldn't have had to spend so many sophisticated evenings. Crowds like this one hurt my goddamn colon, to tell the truth."

"Was this sophisticated?" Patsy asked.

"After a fashion. Maybe I was a little depressed by your aunt. She's a peach but she seems intent on kidnaping me for the evening. I don't quite know how to get out of it. Is this guy Squatty really in South America? Things like this make me miss my dead wife."

"He's in Canada, making millions."

"Maybe the scholar will beguile her away from me," he said.

"Maybe Sonny will beguile his wife away from him," Patsy said. "What do you think?"

"I try to think about more appetizing things," he said. "This fish didn't help much."

"How do you stand to work for Sonny?"

"For money. For money alone I've worked with the worst in the business."

"You mean my aunt just asked you to spend the night with her?" It had just registered.

"More or less. She's a type I'd forgotten. There used to be women like her around L.A. in the thirties and forties, but I thought they'd passed out of existence. A lot of them came from Texas, come to think of it."

"You'll have to admit she's well preserved."

"Sure. Ladies like her are always well preserved, and it's fools like me that have preserved them. I bet Squatty is a fool like me. The poor bastard probably loves her. He's probably off in Canada with his ass in a mudhole, thinking of her right now."

"Do you suppose he does?" Patsy said. It had never occurred to her. All she remembered about Squatty was that he was badly freckled and had skin problems from years of exposing a fair complexion to the tropical sun.

"She'll be well preserved for fifteen more years," Joe said. "Why not? She keeps all she's got. You'll be a withered hag before she will."

"Me?"

"Sure," he said, looking at her with real affection. "You're the food of the world." He looked up and saw the company returning and didn't elaborate on the remark, but Patsy felt deeply, embarrassingly flattered by it; for years, whenever she remembered the way Joe Percy said it, she felt warmed.

The company looked very gay and attractive and was in boisterous good spirits. "Arise, arise," Bill said. "Sonny's promised to take us dancing. Shit kicking, I believe the term is in these parts."

"That's the term," Joe said. "Read all about it in *V*, if you haven't. I'll have to pass. My favorite dancing partner is incapacitated due to pregnancy and I'm not in the mood to kick shit with anybody else."

"I want to go home, anyway," Patsy said.

"You're going with me, anyway," Dixie said to Joe. "We can take Patsy home and Sonny can take them dancing."

Jim tried to persuade her to come with them to the honky-tonk, but he didn't try very hard and she declined. He and the Duffins and Sonny got out at the hotel. "Hope you know what you're doing, going off with a wild man from Hollywood," Sonny said to Dixie.

"I wouldn't know what I was doing if I knew what I was doing," she said simply.

"I just loved that scholar," she said, once they were moving. "I never met a scholar before. Are their wives always skinny?"

When they got to South Boulevard Joe Percy gallantly got out and walked Patsy to her door. He kissed her on the cheek and started back down the steps. "Good luck," she said. "Don't let her drive you crazy."

Inside, in bed, her feet tucked under her, she felt very cozy, read a little, and looked up from time to time to stare at the hairbrush or the chair or the books on the bedside table. Hank had come back to mind, and she was wondering when he would find her again.

=== 15 ===

Joe Percy hung to the handrest, checked his seat belts three times, and tried to remember the prescribed position for car wrecks, if there was one. Dixie was whirling him out a freeway in a light drizzle, the meanwhile filling him in on her life. They came off the freeway and, just as he had feared, she miscalculated the slipperiness of the streets and slid completely through a red light.

"Oh, hell," she said. "I'll stop twice as long at the next one. Don't you like my niece?"

"Sure. I don't know her very well but I hope I live to see her again."

"I can tell you all about her. I practically raised her. Her daddy doesn't have any sense, even if he is my brother. Squatty's made six times as much money as Garland, and Squatty's no genius himself. I don't think we have geniuses in Texas."

"They're probably all killed in car wrecks," Joe said, but his point was lost on Dixie.

"I don't like Jim very much," she said. "She just married

357

him because he was the first one who asked her. I was off in the Orient and didn't even know about it until it was too late to stop it."

She sped into a large high-rise apartment building. The garage men sprang into action instantly. Joe barely had time to get his seat belt unbuckled before the car was gone. Dixie's apartment was on the top floor. For a few minutes he thought it *was* the top floor, but after she had taken him out on a balcony and shown him around he concluded it was only about one quarter of the floor.

"That's River Oaks down there," she said. "It's noted for trees. All sorts of great people live there. I guess this place is dinky compared to the ones they have in Hollywood, huh?"

Joe felt sleepy and suppressed a yawn. "It's not dinky compared to the ones they have anywhere," he said. "You'd have to be Howard Hughes to need more room than this."

"I never met him," Dixie said. "I'll make some coffee."

She did, and it was very good. Joe had been wanting very much to be back at his hotel and had even built up a slight hostility to Dixie, but he couldn't maintain it. Her friendliness carried the day. She sat in a deep leather chair frowning—something she didn't do often enough to do convincingly. The worst she could look was quizzical.

"I'm not sure I like the scholar after all," she said. "I hate it when I can't tell if somebody likes me or not. I couldn't tell about him. Let's go to bed, okay? I really do like to get enough sleep."

Joe followed her irresolutely into the bedroom. What had seemed like possibly a good idea that afternoon over drinks had come to seem like folly. The bedroom, like almost every other room he had seen all day, had a fine view of southwest Houston. It would have been a comfort to have a room that didn't have a view of southwest Houston.

"Do you mind if I wear a nightgown?" Dixie asked, emerging from the bathroom. Without makeup she looked younger rather than older.

"No," he said. "I don't care if you wear overshoes and a parachute. I really ought to go back to my hotel, you know. I shouldn't molest you, I don't think. The thought of your poor husband haunts me."

"Squatty? I haven't been married to him in fifteen years."

"He sounds pretty husbandlike. I thought all Texas husbands were apt to come in and shoot men their wives were in bed with."

"Oh, yeah, it happens all the time," she said. "I've known plenty of cases. It's perfectly legal, you know."

Joe put his coffee cup on the windowsill and sat down on one edge of the large triple bed. He stared unhappily at southwest Houston. "Somehow the legality of it dampens my ardor," he said. "If I was to get blasted for screwing I'd want some bastard to pay for it. Maybe he's winging his way back from Alberta at this very moment to check up on you."

"Not Squatty." She emerged from the closet in a demure white gown and sat down on the floor and began to do exercises vigorously. She made a strange snorting noise through her nose. "That's yoga," she said, stopping to explain.

"I don't have any pajamas," Joe said, grinning despite himself.

"Get in bed while I'm not looking," she said. "I have to exercise a little more."

"Well, it's not as if I'm a virgin," he said, a little fed up with life. He got in his side of the huge bed and lay on his back. Now and then he caught a glimpse of Dixie's head as she exercised. Finally she turned out the light and got in the opposite side of the bed. The only light came from the city far below.

"Well, it's been a great evening," he said heartily. "See you at breakfast."

"I haven't seen Sonny in years," Dixie said. "That scholar liked him. I wouldn't have thought a scholar would like Sonny."

"Intellectuals are all fascinated with athletes," he said. "It doesn't work the other way around."

They were silent for a bit. Joe was hoping she would go to sleep.

"Sonny would have made a good match for Patsy," she said. "He's older. People the same age have the same kind of problems. How can you get along with someone if you have the same problems they have?"

"You're off your nut," Joe said mildly. "Nobody I can think of should marry Sonny."

"I should have married him," Dixie said. "When are you coming over here?"

"You're not really interested in me, are you?" he said.

"Well, you're a man and I'm a woman. That's what men always tell me when they want to screw me. Come on."

"There must be some real dimwits in this state if that's the kind of line they come up with," he said. "I was writing lines like that in 1935. I'm shy and depressed tonight. I think we ought to wait."

"I know you're depressed. I'm not dumb. If you screw me maybe you won't be depressed. I can't stand people who are depressed."

"You don't know what you're saying," he said. "I'm a mad romantic. I feel like plunging a dagger into my breast at this very moment. Once I taste the delights of your body you'll never get rid of me."

"Come on," she insisted. "It will cheer you up."

He looked at her across the several feet of bed that separated them. "This is a swell bed," he said. "You could put a small football team in it. If I'd been sober this afternoon this would never have happened. I'll meet you halfway but don't place any bets on the outcome."

They both scooted sideways until they were about a foot apart on the bed. They lay silently, flat on their backs. The pillows had not scooted with them.

"I'm getting depressed," Dixie said. "I told you if you didn't cheer up I'd get depressed. I catch things from people."

Joe raised up on one elbow. She had the sheets pulled up to her chin, and the frown was back.

"I'm sorry," he said. "I haven't been taking all this seriously. Forgive me. You know, I don't think you have any notion at all of what a human relationship should be. Do you?"

"No," Dixie said simply. She didn't look at him but the young-girl perkiness had left her voice and she sounded like a woman who was getting on. Joe was touched. Everything that her bouncy manner hid was suddenly exposed. Dixie was exposed.

"Well, you poor thing," he said.

360

They were silent again. He was sorry he had exposed her, for he had no way to cover her again. She lay as she was, holding on to the top of the sheets, the puzzled frown on her face.

"I just go around keeping cheerful," she said. "I've done it for years. When I'm cheerful it doesn't matter to me whether I know anything or not."

Joe couldn't stand to see her lying there silently, strained and puzzled. He took one of her hands.

"Look," he said. "You don't want to go bringing strangers like me home. You shouldn't go around asking people. It doesn't make good sense."

"Oh, I almost never ask," she said, brightening a little. "Usually they just do it and leave, or go to sleep. If I decide I don't like them I wake them up and make them leave."

"My lord," he said. "How have you survived? You don't feel sexy and you know it. Why do you think it would cheer me up? Jesus, it would drive me out of my skull."

"It would cheer you up if you weren't so shy," Dixie said. "I thought Californians went around screwing people all the time."

"They do, the damn fools," Joe said. "Better they became Buddhists. The point is, you don't really want me. And if you don't, what's the point?"

"I guess I do," she said. "You're from Hollywood, that's enough for me. I'm not very snobbish about it."

"Snobbish!" he said. "You're crazy, that's what you are. My penis doesn't have Beverly Hills stamped on it, or anything."

"I meant you were someone sweet from Hollywood," she said quickly.

"Am I sweet enough that you'd want me even if I wasn't from Hollywood?"

"Oh, sure. I told you I wasn't very snobbish."

Joe sighed. "You win," he said. "I'm glad I came—you've got to be unique. Can I ask you one question? What do *you* really *like?*"

"You mean about screwing?"

"About anything. Start with that if you like."

Her frown went away and she gave him a shy, almost

mischievous look. "Maybe I'll tell you, now that you're jolly again," she said. "It was awful when you were depressed. Maybe I'll show you—it might be fun for you."

"Maybe," he said dubiously. "Why don't you kinda sketch out what's involved before we launch into it. I'm not very acrobatic and I'm a real novice at yoga and stuff like that."

"Come on," she said. "Don't think about it. If you do you'll get depressed again. I'll help you." She thrust a hand into his shorts and helped him. Somewhat to his surprise, he became erect. "See?" she said. "Why'd you talk so much?"

"I can't remember," he said, thinking, What the hell. He took off his underpants but his erection went as quickly as it had come and by the time he was in position it was mostly gone. He tried a bit, embarrassed, and Dixie decided that a little conversation might help matters. Just as he thought he was about to return to potency she became very talkative.

"I've got this wild hairdresser," she said. "If you were going to be here longer you could meet her. Her husband takes dope."

"Too bad," Joe said, still faintly hopeful, though he had discovered Dixie to be as unaroused as he would have supposed. She seemed to think that by being brightly voluble she was making a hard task easier for him. When she asked if he knew Gregory Peck he lost his patience.

"Look," he said. "I can talk and there are times when I can screw but I'm pretty sure I'm not going to be able to manage both just now. If you don't shut up I'm going to get a cab and go home."

"Sorry," Dixie said. "I was just wondering. *Duel in the Sun* was my favorite movie."

Joe sighed and gave up. "I'm sorry," he said. "If your thing involves me it's just too bad."

"Poor you," she said. "You must be impotent or something."

"I'm something," he said wearily.

"You can get off," she said. "You just didn't want any tonight. I've been raping you."

Dixie got out of bed and headed for the hall. "You don't have to come," she said. "I do it in the bathroom." She was taking off her gown as she went through the door. She had a large behind but almost girlishly thin legs. Joe heard water running and waited apprehensively. It ran for several minutes and then stopped. When Dixie came in she had a gown in her hand and a towel around her. She stood by the bed in the dimness drying her legs.

"I love to run water on myself," she said. "In the tub, you know. I didn't want you to think I was some kind of dumbbell who didn't like sex. I'm sorry you're impotent. The only thing I don't like about you is that you make me feel old. Everybody else thinks I'm young." She sat down on the bed and her mouth curved downward. She looked like she might cry.

"Now, now," he said and patted her shoulder. "You are a little old, you know."

"I know," she said. "But I don't know what good it would do me to act my age."

Joe didn't know either. He rubbed her back.

"Do you know Gregory Peck?" she asked. "I've been meaning to ask you."

"Sure, I know Greg," he said. "I helped write *Duel in the Sun*, actually. I think about four lines in it were mine."

"I knew you were a celebrity," she said. "Will Sonny's movie be good?"

"It's a matter of taste."

"Good. I've got great taste."

"Have you always preferred bathtubs?" he asked. "I'm just curious." He found himself liking her more and more.

"No," she said. "Just for a long time. There was this guy I was in love with. A trombone player. He was the best man in the world, and a goddamn nigger shot him by accident. In Louisiana. He was nice to me. He liked to sit on the bed naked and play the trombone. He could play whatever I wanted—he knew all kinds of songs. I liked normal things with him. I was crazy about him. He loved to sit in bed with me and play the trombone. You think that wasn't a sight to see . . ." She began to cry and put her feet under the covers and pulled the sheet up to her neck, still crying, her face turned away from Joe.

He reached over and rubbed her back as well as he could. "I'll bet you're right, sweetheart," he said. "I'll bet that was a sight to see."

16

"Anyway, I look just awful now," Patsy said. "I've never looked this awful in my life. It ought to be some consolation, getting away from a person who looks like I do. But what's going to be a consolation for me?"

"Come and lie back down," Hank said.

She was standing in front of his dresser, crying, puffy-eyed, eight months pregnant, unable to stop crying long enough to fix her face so she could go home. It was cold out and she had her coat on, but with no more urging she went back to the bed, covered her face with her collar and her hair, and cried some more. Hank patiently uncovered her face and wiped away tears until she stopped crying. He didn't have anything to say, but then he never did. Patsy ceased to feel tearful; she felt a little tired and sleepy. She felt she could lie there for hours—for days, possibly. She had no wish to move. It was unbelievable, but he was going away that afternoon, back to Portales, New Mexico. Everything beyond the next few minutes was unimaginable. All she knew was that as long as she lay as she was, with him close enough that she could feel his breath on her face, then things were all right and she would not have to force her legs to carry her into the unimaginable afternoon.

"You're a cad to go away," she said, trying to be funny about it. She was afraid that if he went while she was downcast then she might always be downcast. But trying to be funny didn't work. She started crying again.

They had not become adulterers, merely lovers. The romance that she had assumed could only last one afternoon had stretched itself through two weeks of afternoons, physi-

cally unconsummated. It was the question of consummation
that was breaking them apart. Patsy wouldn't, and couldn't
understand why he was so blind and selfish about it. For the
first few afternoons she had come to him alternately pale
and flushed, terrified and delighted, guilt-shaken but ecstat-
ic. Being with him was quite enough. It made her feel
happier and more secure than she had ever felt. Being with
him was simpler and more satisfying than being with
anyone else. They didn't talk much; Hank was really not a
talker. They held hands, kissed, sat, and the hours passed. It
was so wonderful for her, having someone to be with, that
she couldn't understand why it wasn't enough for him.
Walking over to his apartment, she sometimes reminded
herself that they were bound to come to a tragic end, but she
felt neither tragic nor wicked. She felt light and gay and
comfortable, neither lonely nor at loose ends. Jim was off
having what *he* wanted, a day among books and the gay
literate company of his peers, and try as she might she could
not feel very guilty about him. He never kissed her any
more, anyway, and for weeks at a time scarcely seemed to
need her, except in the most mechanical ways. Hank kept
saying he loved her—some afternoons it was virtually all he
did say to her—but she did not tell him the same. She didn't
know if she loved him; she hadn't felt like saying it. She just
knew that she liked being there very much.

She liked being kissed too, and touched, and it was that
that made it scary and left her no time in which to know
what she felt. He was very aggressive, and blindly so. No
matter how gently he began, he always got hard to handle
sooner or later. Their first two meetings were at her house,
where he was not so hard to handle, but then she discovered
that it was absurdly easy to get in and out of his apartment
unobserved by way of an alley. She immediately fixed the
apartment up to her liking, but the fixings were not destined
to last very long, all because he wouldn't be held off. He was
determined to have her bare, and in the bed.

The apartment was his territory too and so like him that
just coming into it weakened her. It was not domestic, had
no curtains, no nicely selected furniture, no kitchen, no
neatly made bed, no vacuum cleaner, no pictures, no
dressing table, no television set. It was too masculine; going

there quickly began to make her feel fluttery. Each time she went she grew more fluttery, and each time it took her longer to relax, to acquiesce to being kissed or touched at all. If he had pursued her relentlessly from the moment she stepped in the door she might have grown too scared and quit coming; but he didn't. He sat and looked at her, quite relaxed himself, and eventually she came to him. Each time it happened her acquiescence got a little deeper, and her reluctance to leave became a little greater.

Once, when it was time to leave, she began to cry helplessly, to her surprise and his concern. She couldn't stay and didn't want to leave. She felt, for a few minutes, completely dependent upon being able to stay or, at least, upon being able to come back. If only he would let her stay without continually trying to undress her. Her belly was so large that when she opened her eyes she could not see her feet. It was a ridiculous state in which to be vulnerable to somebody's kisses, but she was. He lulled her into a happy sensate daze and then began thrusting his hand inside her clothes or trying to drag her out of them. It was natural, she knew, but it was also depressing. She couldn't be undressed, not just then. It was painful and confusing. She wanted him; it wasn't that. He knew it. She felt like a tease, and it was painful and confusing, but she couldn't help it. They could only have so much, that was that. They had had scarcely a week of the bliss of mutual discovery before there began to be fights.

"Damn you," she said one day when he had managed to slip his hand between her legs. "Can't you understand? Please don't. I was perfectly happy." She kept firm hold of his wrist.

"I'm not," he said intolerantly. All he felt was impatience and desire, things he had felt almost from the first time he had seen her. Her objections didn't register with him; he wanted her too much. He tried to kiss her again but she stiffened and drew back, frightened by the faceless quality of his desire. The minute he really began to want her he stopped seeing her—it had been that way even the first day. He ceased to be the man she was so fond of, so comfortable with, and just became a man, thrusting himself at her so strongly that it was scary.

"For Christ's sake!" she said. "Look at me, please. I'm eight months pregnant! I would be grotesque. I don't think I'm even supposed to sleep with my husband. Besides, I can't sleep with you, anyway. You should have understood that. I thought you did."

"Why?" he said. "Give me one reason."

"Oh, damn," she said. "Because I'm *married!*" And she began to cry, still holding his hand away from her.

When put off, Hank ceased to be the pleasant, relaxed, tolerant person she had caught such a fondness for. He was not used to being put off and didn't know what to do with himself, or with her.

"Turn loose," he said, freeing his hand. "I can't help it that you're pregnant and married. Maybe it's inconvenient but I still love you and I still want to sleep with you."

Her only recourse was to cry, which she did genuinely enough, from shame and perplexity. And fortunately, he did know how to handle her tears. Once his desire had cooled a bit he became very nice again and kissed her and stroked her face and was able to seem amused by it all. He seemed amused by her, in a fond way, and that was very comforting. It made him nice to be with again. When he was nice to her she felt so secure, so completely in his keeping, that she could not imagine anyone as good or as understanding. It made her want very much to let him make love to her, and she did let him talk about some pleasant future time when they could, though once she got home she could not believe that such a time would ever come.

But desire gave them no peace. His was raging, and things began to work in Patsy too. Sudden touches left her vulnerable—she couldn't predict it or help it. She appealed to him but appeals did no good; sooner or later she had to struggle up from her own pleasure and fight him again. In the second week it became very serious. She had to fight too hard and cry too much. She became afraid that Jim would notice.

"Please don't," she said one day. "Please don't scare me, please don't push me. I don't want to be scared to come here. Please understand. I just can't. Not now."

"Then I'm going away until you can," he said. "I can't stand it."

"Oh, don't say that," she said. It made her more miserable than she had ever been, and more embarrassed. It had begun so simply, and for a day or two had seemed free and harmless, and already it had become a bad thing. It hurt him. Whatever she had expected couldn't be, and she felt she might as well give up. It was exactly what she deserved for stepping outside the bounds in the first place. It seemed to her that she had been more dismal and dishonest and inconsiderate than if she had set out deliberately to commit adultery in the first place.

"I'm so worthless," she said. "I just wanted to be happy without it being a bother." She was ready to put the blackest possible interpretations on her own behavior, to get up and go home and settle down to sewing baby caps. Hank managed to shake himself out of desire and coax her back into a good humor, but once out of his presence her spirits drooped again and she was so silent and chastened all evening that Jim became worried about it. She had been looking unusually lovely, he thought, and was disturbed to see her so sunk and withdrawn. He decided it was all his fault, for having been withdrawn himself. Finals were in progress and he had done nothing but read for weeks. He put down his notes and devoted himself to Patsy for the evening; he tried being funny, tender, judicious, reassuring, so many things in fact that she was amused and touched by him and as a consequence felt all the worse. Once he had gone to sleep she cried, feeling wretchedly selfish. She was no good to either man, and she couldn't help it.

The next day she straggled back to Hank's, still pale and chastened, determined to tell him she was never going to see him again. That was clearly what was called for. Let him go away. She tried to tell him as much, but it didn't work well. He kissed her into a daze. It was because he had been in the army, she had decided. She was no match for anyone who had been in the army. He could always kiss her and it always worked. It was only when he began to undress her that her resistance awoke, and it awoke later every time. But in the struggle he accidentally hurt her breast and the moment of pain left her rational and cool again. She shook out her hair and ticked off a dozen reasons why it could never be.

Quite accidentally, in conversation, as they were getting

friendly again, Hank mentioned that he had had lunch with Clara Clark. Rumor had it that she was sleeping with William Duffin, he said. Patsy went from cool to hot in seconds; she had never gone through so many revolutions of feeling in so short a time. First she cried because his having lunch with Clara made her feel betrayed, then she stormed because he had had anything to do with such a slut, then she fell on the bed and cried again because she realized that her emotions were out of control. She couldn't sleep with him, but it made her burn with indignation that he would have anything to do with Clara Clark, and she quailed before the thought that Clara would probably be only too glad to sleep with him—might have done so, in fact. In an attempt to placate her Hank mentioned that he had dated Clara for a time during the fall and was obliged to be at least courteous to her. At that confirmation of her fears Patsy went blind with anger and turned and hit him in the face. It surprised them both. She strode around the small room shaking. She had never hit anyone before. In a minute she felt cold and forlorn and went to the couch and curled up beside him, as best anyone her size could curl.

"I must be mad," she said. "What am I doing? Did I hurt you?"

"Of course not," he said, amused and rather pleased.

"Don't laugh at my frenzies," she said. "I meant to hurt you. I'll hit you again. I enjoyed it." Then she sniffed and pressed her face against his arm.

He tried to touch her and she shoved his hand away.

"Look, be logical," he said. "Sooner or later we're going to sleep together."

"I don't happen to be especially logical," she said. "Don't preach logic to me. Besides, I've read Norman O. Brown. People don't have to do all that. We can just be polymorphously perverse. Nonorgasmic love is supposed to be pretty great."

"I'm not oriented to it," Hank said. Sometimes the fact that she read a lot made him very discontented with her.

"I'm not oriented to adultery, either."

There they stuck for three days, the complexities multiplying, the pressures at each meeting becoming more intense. A weekend came and Patsy's parents were in town.

She thought it would be a relief, not seeing Hank for two days, not having to struggle with the dilemma; but it turned out to be almost intolerable. All surroundings but his apartment had become a little bit unreal, and all concerns except the struggle toward or away from him had become irrelevant. It might be painful, being with him; blood might flow and ruin might follow, but at least something essential was happening, something better than the insubstantiality that attended her everywhere else. The dinner she and Jim had with her parents seemed one of the emptiest, most vapid occasions of her life. Her parents' familiar phrases and mannerisms irritated her so much that it took all her control merely to be polite.

Jim was exemplary during the weekend. He was solicitous and nice to her and adroit at handling her parents. Patsy decided that for some reason she had not noticed him in several months; she took note and found little lacking and attacked Hank fiercely on Monday for betraying a comrade-in-arms. The attack was vitiated somewhat by the fact that she was lying in *his* arms at the time, but for that very reason it was all the more violent.

"Your own colleague," she said.

To her intense annoyance he refused to defend himself or try to justify what he was doing. "A man in love will do anything," he said, trying to kiss her.

"Ethics," she said. "Principles. The Judeo-Christian tradition. Western civilization. The marriage oath. What about all that?"

"I wish you'd shut up," he said. "I can't help it. It's a fact, even if it's catastrophic for Western civilization."

"Oh, shit," she said. "I knew you were fallible. Too bad. I'll never be seduced by a man with an inadequate moral philosophy."

"Yes you will," he said.

A little later she almost was. A kiss turned into a bite. Everything got sharper—she was almost overwhelmed. But some deep stubbornness gripped her and held her despite her own response. The same thing happened the next day.

"Maybe if I wasn't pregnant," she said, crying. "But never like this."

"All right, I'm going away," Hank said. He was rumpled and very aroused.

It made her furious. "Are you issuing threats?" she said. "I hate threats. Go away if you want to." She felt as if she had been slapped; she hurt so much for a time that she couldn't cry.

"I can't see you and not sleep with you," he said. "I'll drop out for a semester. The school won't care. I can come back next summer."

"Why come back?" she said, still angry.

"You won't be pregnant."

"I'll be just as stubborn. All this will have gone away."

When he calmed down he looked very solemn. Patsy found she liked him, after all. She put her finger on the little dent on the bridge of his nose. "You won't go away," she said. "You won't abandon me."

"Yes I will," he said. "You've got to calm down and have your baby. I really better go."

She saw that he meant it—it was not a cruel joke or a trick to get her to come through. He looked very firm about it. She was not used to such firmness and it shocked her a little that a man could be so decisive about a matter of feeling. He had no right to be so positive about a matter that involved *her* feelings too. The rest of the afternoon she indulged in a glut of emotion or, rather, an assault by emotion. She tried everything: silence, coldness, tears, fury, name calling, joking, argument, logic, tenderness, wistfulness, helpless-ness, finally even wantonness, determined to break the decision. He would put her first—he would not go away. All it did was almost get her seduced. She broke free and had a final writhing crying fit; it ended with her in a state of shamed collapse, feeling cheap and scared. He didn't change his mind but she left him anything but calm. He had never faced quite so much emotion and it unnerved him without making him any less stubborn. Patsy left without apology and went home feeling broken, her self-esteem gone, her feelings uncertain. She spent an awful, tearful night, but Jim worked late at the library and didn't notice.

Hank stayed four more days. Once Patsy saw that he was really going she accepted it and made no more real fuss. She sniped and made small petulant fusses, and there were times when she hurt inside and felt betrayed, but she was scared of her own emotion and tried to contain it. Once or twice she challenged him, trying to get him to change his mind. But he was adamant.

"Portales or you," he said when she pressed him.

"Why are you so goddamn absolute?" she said. "Can't you realize that life isn't that way? You have to make concessions. Compromise is supposed to be the law of life. What will I do without you?"

"Sleep with me if you're so worried."

"No," she said furiously.

The last two meetings were quiet, except for Patsy's tears. She accepted, finally, that he had a fairly good reason for leaving. It was even a little noble, since he was interrupting his career for her sake. It made her feel valuable, if not exactly worthy. On the last morning she saw with a pang that his old Oldsmobile was loaded. The nice bedspread she had bought him was off the bed where they had wrestled and kissed to no conclusion. She felt as bare herself, though all morning she never took off her coat. They lingered for two hours. She could not remember later that anything was said. She spent the afternoon rocking silently, listening to Bob Dylan and Joan Baez. Jim was at the library until midnight, and Hank was driving toward New Mexico, over the darkened plains. In the days that followed she avoided Albans Road. Where she missed him most was the drugstore; a time or two, eating, she could not quite keep her tears back. Eddie Lou, recognizing a broken heart and no woman to hold a grudge, began to take some care with her cheese sandwiches again.

===== **17** =====

For Patsy the two weeks after Hank went away were not only bad but strange. She had never in her life missed anyone and she found it a wretched, weakening experience. She had never supposed that anyone she really wanted would go away from her, and for a time she could not get over feeling betrayed. She knew it was as much her fault as his that he was away, but it didn't keep her from hurting or feeling betrayed.

Never before in her life had she felt so completely at a loss. Suddenly there was nothing to do. When she went to the drugstore she found she wasn't really interested in any of the magazines; the world had suddenly become dull. The improvement in her sandwiches was quite lost on her. When she went to the library all the books seemed inessential. Even Emma was spoiled for her for a time. She tried going there a time or two in the afternoons, but the boys somehow irritated her with their bright questions and their fighting. Emma irritated her a little too, by not being prettier, or more ambitious, or less slovenly, for being so snug in her domesticity. They went out shopping and it still didn't work; she didn't feel like herself, and their chatter didn't mesh. Finally she decided it wasn't Emma's fault; it was just that she didn't want to spend that much time with a woman. It was more pleasant to spend time with a man. It seemed incredible to her that she could have become addicted to Hank so quickly. It was as if with him she had acquired a new self, only to be forced back to her old self just as she was ready to give it up forever. When she tried staying at the apartment she did literally nothing. She sat and stared and thought about him or about the baby. That was the one good thing left—there would soon be her baby. It was the only thing she felt happy and expectant about, the only thing that kept her from feeling completely empty. With the time so short and her breasts filling, it was impossible to feel completely empty. She only felt desolate. She decided that if she had only known how much she would miss him before he left she would have gone ahead and surrendered her virtue, for it had come to seem a paltry and sodden thing, anyway. She decided that she had only put him off because she was cowardly, or else too vain to want him to see her so heavily pregnant; in either case her withholding was hardly worthy of being called virtue. That was dreary enough to have to think upon, but it was made drearier still by the fact that she missed him physically. Three or four days after he left she felt more restless and irritable than she ever had before, and provoked a screaming fight with Jim. Later she decided it was all sexual; she was frustrated; she should have slept with him, pregnant or not; but it was too late. He was gone, and it was all uncertain. He might never be back.

Then one day she got a letter. The sight of it shocked her, but it was addressed to Mr. and Mrs. Carpenter, and was a quite innocuous note telling them that he had a job on a surveying crew and that they were to say hello to everybody for him. The only real purpose of it was to give her his address, she knew, and she was miffed when Jim assumed it was mostly to him and filed it away in a huge letter file of his own. She knew he wouldn't look at it again for years, if ever, so she immediately stole it out of the file and hid it in a drawer of her dresser.

A few days later Jim came home looking blue and introspective, as if he were feeling sorry for himself. Patsy felt slightly more in touch with the world that day and badgered Jim cheerfully through supper, trying to perk him up. She had written Hank a long letter in which she felt she had succeeded in being witty and noble and compassionate and several other good things, and had mailed it that afternoon. Mailing it made her feel better. Then, after some questioning, Jim told her that he had had coffee with Clara, who was gloomy. She had confided in him that the reason for her gloom was that Hank had been her lover during the fall; with him gone she didn't know where to turn.

"I sort of suspected it all along," Jim said sagely.

Patsy felt for a moment like she had been kicked. The kick caught her in a soft, vulnerable spot, and came just at the moment when she felt least deserving of a kick. She was standing at the sink in her fuzzy yellow slippers and a baggy brown dress, fixing to wash a dishpan full of dishes. Jim still sat at the table drinking coffee and looking at a publication called *The Book Collector*. He had subscribed to it on Duffin's say-so and his first copy had just come that day.

Patsy stood in shock, looking at him. Had he not been there, hurt might have come before anger, but when her emotion broke it broke as anger.

"Oh, goddamn," she said. "You goddamn men. Stupid, crazy . . ." And she choked for a moment on the violence of what she felt.

Jim looked up, very surprised at her words and even more surprised by her tone.

"Don't look at me like that!" Patsy said. "So that's why you're so gloomy. You wanted to be her lover and you got stuck with being her sympathetic confidant. You're envious of him!"

Jim was taken aback. It was uncanny the way her most irrational thrusts sometimes hit dead center. That had been what he was feeling. He had been secretly wanting Clara, not rabidly but steadily. He didn't feel stuck with being a confidant, though. From Clara's manner he felt it quite possible that he could become her lover, and his desire to do so added to a predicament of conscience that he had already acquired. All during the fall he had tried to keep himself in the notion of being eternally faithful to Patsy, but despite himself he kept wanting Clara. Patsy's raw voice stunned him for a moment.

"Shit!" she said. "Stupid, vile, promiscuous! I'm going to break something."

And to his surprise, crying bitterly, she lifted the dishpan full of dishes and heaved it awkwardly at the window. The heave was unsuccessful, the dishpan struck the windowsill and fell to the floor with a loud clatter. All the dishes spilled.

Only a saucer and two glasses broke but Patsy had dashed out of the kitchen. She was going to her dresser to tear the letter to shreds, but Jim caught her before she got the right drawer open. She was in a fury and wrestled and tugged until she broke loose.

"Get your goddamn hands off me," she said. "Go read your goddamn magazines in her house, maybe she'll let you screw her while you read. Then you'll have everything you want. Keep your hands off me. I hate you and I hate her."

"Stop it," Jim said. "You're nuts. I haven't slept with her."

"You will," she said, crying. Her hair was down in her eyes and her hands were still wet and soapy. "You'll sleep with her. Everybody will sleep with her. Why should I care? I won't stay in this house. Go on. Turn me loose."

"Patsy, you're mad," he said.

She was, virtually. She had been kicked and there was no way she could kick back, not as she would have liked to.

Jim dragged her by main strength to the couch, but before they got there her anger turned to hurt and she stopped fighting and sat crying.

"Don't touch me," she said.

"Do you need a doctor?" he asked. "You threw the dishpan. You can't do things like that. You're going to have the baby soon."

"Oh," she said, realizing how awful she had been. "I can't, I can't." And she hurried to the kitchen and knelt sobbing on the wet floor, among the soapy dishes, trying to sort out the broken pieces, still sobbing and talking.

"I'm sorry," she kept saying. "I'm so sorry, I didn't mean to." Jim came and helped her but she wasn't talking to him. She didn't know who she was talking to.

He had meant to go to the library that evening, but he felt uncertain that he should. He had never seen her so wild and scarcely knew what to do. If he left she might think he was going to Clara's. But once the mess was cleaned up Patsy washed her face and seemed to come back to herself.

"No, go on," she said. "I'm all right. I just have an irrational dislike of that woman. I'm very sorry I was so crazy just now."

"I don't understand why you dislike her so," he said.

"She's not married. There's no reason why she shouldn't have lovers."

Patsy felt awkward and frightened; she was afraid she had given herself away and was relieved when he left. She felt sure that once he thought about it he would figure out why she had been so upset. She dreaded his coming home, sure he would have figured it out by then. She cried all evening, miserably and intermittently, well aware that she was entirely in the wrong in feeling the way she did. Hank and Clara had had every right to sleep together in the fall; she had no claim on Hank, anyway. She realized that in any fair estimate of matters she would come out much worse than Clara Clark. Clara was single and perhaps thought Hank would marry her—*she* was married and pregnant. Clara had had every excuse for sleeping with him, including that he was attractive—*she* had none, for she already had someone attractive. And, worst of all, Clara had actually slept with him, while she had merely flirted and teased. Clara had behaved legitimately, perhaps generously, at least honestly; she had been dishonest, selfish, and cowardly. She didn't have the right even to want a right; and yet her lack of a right changed nothing. She felt just as lonely, just as wounded, just as sad—and just as angry. She hated him for leaving. That was his cowardice. He could have stayed and waited, or made her into something better if he had really tried. He had done a weak, incomplete job, and jealousy of Clara continued to gnaw at her.

But when she heard the Ford in the driveway she felt very small and scared. She hastily got in bed and feigned sleep, not knowing what to expect. Perhaps Jim would have figured it out; perhaps he would beat her. Instead, he took a bath and ignored her for an hour, reading. She got bored with feigning sleep and finally had to feign that he had awakened her. Jim was glad. He hugged her. He had not figured out anything.

"Thrown any more dishpans?" he asked, and in time he came to think of the incident rather proudly, as a sign that she was a woman of passionate temperament.

Next morning her relief turned to annoyance that he could so blithely miss what seemed to her so clear. She decided it could only be because he took her so for granted

that he assumed there could never be anything to figure out.
She didn't like that at all, and in a bitter mood, feeling that
men were basically only impediments to life, she sat down
and wrote Hank a note.

Dear Hank,

*I might have known. Jim told me about you and
her—Miss Clark. How dare you not tell me about your
sordid past? I feel vicious toward you now; I broke my
favorite glass because of you. If you ever come near me
again I'll hit you twice as hard as I did the first time. The
best thing you can do is stay away.*

Hostilely,
Patsy

*P.S. If you have anything to say for yourself write me c/o
the Whitneys, this address. They are gone until April
and I take care of their mail.*

Apparently, though, the note didn't represent her true
mood. By the next day she regretted mailing it. It seemed to
her that she had severed all connections, without really
needing to. She felt completely alone—only the baby was a
hopeful prospect. Jim loved her but didn't need her or
understand her; Hank had at least needed her, despite that
she was cowardly and pregnant. She still missed him as
much as she had before she heard about Clara.

In four days she got an answer and opened it nervously,
quailing at the thought of all the things he could say to her in
perfect justice.

Dear Patsy,

*My work crew has moved to Childress, and chill is the
word for it, all right. It was 12 degrees this morning, and
windy.*

*I know I should have told you about Clara. You could
have been upset at my place and wouldn't have broken
your glass. It was such an unemotional thing that it
didn't seem important to mention it. Maybe I was just
scared to. You were hard enough to get near, as it was.
My feelings were a big mess, that whole time, and still
are. About the clearest thing is that I love you and wish I*

378

*was back. I feel very unconnected, out here, and hope
you get over being hostile. There wasn't much to Clara
and me. If you do get over it write me. I'll be back in
Portales early next week.*

Love,
Hank

The letter left her slightly shaky, brief though it was. She
got her coat and walked to the park and sat swinging. The
wind was cold and made her think of him, far to the north,
where it was even colder. She could visualize him—his hair,
his eyes, his hands. She read the letter again and felt terribly
grateful to him for not taking the chance to say the obvious
mean things to her. She wrote three long replies, but didn't
mail them. They didn't convey what she felt. It was very
frustrating trying to write him. For the first time in her life
words really failed her. Language wouldn't receive her
feelings, somehow. One afternoon she realized she wanted
to touch him and had been trying to make her letter the
equivalent of a touch. She gave up and wrote a quick letter
and mailed it.

Dear Hank,

*I'm not very hostile any more. I miss you. I don't
understand why you love me—I'm not very good to you.*

*I did tell you not to go away. You have nobody but
yourself to blame for that. I've felt fairly sinful since you
left, but by the time you return, if you do, I'll be a matron
and will have risen above it all, I guess. I wish I could
have made it a little more glorious for you, but I
couldn't.*

*Couldn't you get a job in Portales, in a nice warm
library? I don't like the thought of you freezing on the
trackless plain.*

Write me any time before April.

Patsy

It happened that the rodeo was in town, and the next
afternoon, having nothing to do, she called Emma and
suggested they take the boys to the livestock show. She felt
they might enjoy looking at animals.

"Tommy's got tonsillitis," Emma said. "Fever a hundred and three. I'll gladly let you have Teddy, but he might be too much for you."

Patsy could hear screams in the background and felt in a quandary. Emma's company was really what she sought, but she decided that motherhood was imminent enough that she ought to have some practice, so she agreed to take Teddy.

He had had his hair cut the day before and no longer looked like a midget rock singer. The prospect of the stock show put him in a bright conversational mood, most of the conversation being about his haircut. Once Patsy had to stop abruptly at a light and sent him rolling onto the floorboards. It didn't hurt him but it dampened his mood a bit and shook his confidence in Patsy's driving. After that he sat sucking his thumb until they were parked.

They accidentally entered the show barn by the wrong door and found themselves amid the hogs and sheep. It was past the middle of the afternoon and the barns had had time to accumulate almost a day's worth of mess. The sheep and swine were crowded into rattly aluminum pens, and the whole area smelled of lamb's wool and sheepshit. Two huge Rambouillet rams were snorting at each other, only a few insubstantial fences between them. Teddy was abashed by it all and hid his face against her leg.

They went on to the pigs and he recovered some of his nerve. They saw a huge whory-looking sow with six irritable little piglets bumping around her ankles. The sow's udders dragged on the straw and the little pigs kept lunging underneath her, trying to keep her still long enough that they could feed. Both Patsy and Teddy were fascinated and stood watching for several minutes. Teddy bent down and looked through the lowest gap in the fence, facing the little pigs on their own level, but when one of them stuck his snout out at him he straightened up and held out his hand to Patsy. They made their way out of the sheep section as delicately as possible, skirting yellow puddles and lamb turds. The barns were full of adolescents in blue Future Farmers of America jackets, many with prize ribbons pinned to their lapels.

The cattle exhibits were cleaner and much airier. The aisles were wider and huge rotating fans kept the air circulating. They stopped and watched, again mutually fascinated, as a young Hereford steer was primped up for his contest. His tail had been in a hairnet, but it was taken out, combed into an amazing puff, and sprayed with hair spray. It looked, Patsy thought meanly, not unlike the bouffant hairdos of the cowgirls who kept passing. The steer was combed and oiled until he shone; he stood chewing his cud while four men bustled about him. One was parting the hair long the steer's neck. He had a rat-tailed comb and a bottle of Vitalis and Patsy couldn't help giggling. When she did, Teddy giggled loudly, in support of her, as it were. The four men stopped simultaneously and looked at them.

"I'm terribly sorry," she said. "I wasn't making fun. It's just that your steer reminds me of Louis the Fourteenth."

At that the men looked relieved, if still a little puzzled. "Uh, no, ma'am," one of them said. "This one here was sired by Larry Domino. One Sixty-one."

It was Patsy's turn to feel blank, but not so blank as to linger. They stopped again in front of a demonstration booth containing an automatic milking machine. Teddy was bored but Patsy was fascinated. There was a diagram of the whole milk-making process, beginning with a cow eating a bite of grass and ending with a dull-looking youngster sitting at a dull-looking supper table drinking a glass of milk. Patsy was wearing a bulky gray sweater and a dark skirt. Her hair was swept back loosely and held by a yellow headband. The attendant at the booth welcomed her heartily.

"They don't make a better milking machine than this," he said. "You-all got Jerseys or Holsteins?"

"We don't got," Patsy said, allowing Teddy to drag her to the bulls. Her impulsive reference to Louis the Fourteenth had not been so inept, either; the bulls were definitely treated like grand seigneurs. Each had his own spacious neatly ordered stall, filled thigh-high with fresh clean soft-looking hay—the sort of hay to be rolled in, if one were to be rolled in the hay. Some of the more important bulls even had individual body servants, in most cases a Negro boy who slept on a blanket in the stall and saw to the animal's every need. "Um," Teddy said in fascination, as one of the huge Santa Gertrudis began to shit. As soon as the droppings ceased falling an attendant with a pitchfork immediately scooped up hay and excrement and carried it to a disposal barrel. The Hereford and Angus bulls had a squat, debauched look about them; it was hard to imagine one raising himself onto a cow for carnal purposes, and even harder to imagine a cow that could bear the weight. The Brahmas she thought magnificent, sleek, and restive and not nearly so domestic in appearance as the other bulls.

Teddy demanded popcorn and she got him some. She was feeling tired and was thinking what a long way it was to the car. The parking lot of the Astrodome stretched on and on, like the West. As they were passing the horse stalls, Teddy munching his popcorn, Patsy saw a familiar blond girl holding an Appaloosa and reaching up to do something with its bridle. The horse was holding its head just high enough that she had to strain and she suddenly lost her temper and gave the reins a jerk.

"Sprinkles, damn you!" she said.

"My goodness," Patsy said. "You've recovered."

Boots was astonished. "Patsy!" she said. Teddy had been a few feet behind and at that point caught up. He offered Patsy a piece of wet popcorn that he had tried and found not to his taste. Boots looked unchanged: Levi's, old scuffed boots, and a man's shirt. "Is that yours?" she said, looking with amazement at Teddy.

"Um," Teddy said positively, catching Patsy's hand.

Boots quickly made friends with him—their approach to life was very similar. She lifted him up on the Appaloosa and let him ride the horse to its stall. Patsy followed nervously, hoping he wouldn't fall off and crack his skull on the concrete. That wouldn't sit well with Emma. Fortunately, he didn't. Pete was at the stall when they got there.

"How do?" he said, as if they had seen each other yesterday. He knelt down to shake hands with Teddy, but Teddy gave him an odd suspicious look and clutched his popcorn to his bosom. Patsy was for a moment at a loss for words, for Pete looked years older than she remembered him. His sandy hair had thinned still more, and he was fatter in the face and looked tired. When he went over to help Boots with her horse Patsy noticed he was limping.

"Don't tell me you broke your hip too?" she said.

"Naw. Little sprain. I been having to compete lately,

trying to get the hospital bills paid. I'm too old to be riding broncs, I guess. I never was much good at it."

"You're good enough," Boots said. "Let's go to the motel."

Patsy and Teddy followed them. Pete drove a secondhand station wagon, Boots still had the T-bird. The motel was a third-rate establishment called the Primrose Courts. Emma had sent a spare diaper along, assuming Teddy might need one, and Patsy took it in with her. Teddy looked at her a little sullenly when he saw it.

"Our home away from home," Pete said.

"It's crummy," Boots said. "We should have got a clean stall in the stock barns. If I ever break my hip again we might as well kill ourselves."

Pete scooped Teddy up and sat him on a saddle that had been rolled against one wall. Teddy started to cry but every one grinned at him and he decided not to and was soon playing merrily on the saddle. Patsy was as appalled by the motel room as she had been by the Tatums' trailer house. The walls were peeling, the bed was unmade, there was a pile of dirty clothes in one corner—Levi's, shirts, bras—somehow giving the room a bad tone, of sour-smelling lower-class intimacy. Pete got himself and Boots beers out of an ice chest near the bed. Besides the smell of beer and dirty clothes there was also the smell of medicine in the room—several bottles stood on the bedside table. "Dope for my aches and pains," Pete said.

"If he competes for six more weeks I can get a job somewhere giving rubdowns," Boots said. "Boy, am I getting good at it."

"I think it's insane," Patsy said. "There's got to be something safer than rodeo. Couldn't you buy a ranch or something?"

She regretted saying it, for it was obvious that no one who stayed in such a motel could buy a ranch. But the Tatums were not offended. Boots even laughed. "We can't even buy a steak, much less a ranch," she said.

Teddy noticed that Pete was drinking beer, a beverage for which he had a taste. He got off the saddle and came over. Pete held out the can and Teddy licked a little of the foam from around the opening. Patsy decided it was time to diaper him and swooped him up from behind and plopped him on the bed. Teddy looked at her hostilely but made no resistance while she took the sopping diaper off. Pete gave her a newspaper to put it on. "All this room needs is a few wet diapers," he said.

Patsy felt a little self-conscious folding the diaper. Teddy was docilely sucking his finger, but just as she got it folded and reached for his ankles to raise him up and slip it under him he adroitly rolled himself away and scooted to the head of the bed, where he sat looking at her with quiet poise, as if to say, "Your move."

Patsy knelt and gave him a sorrowing, appealing look, trying to coax him with her expression, but Teddy's heart had turned to stone. He held his ground until Patsy tried to grab him and then rolled off the bed and deposited himself in Boots's lap. She giggled and Teddy giggled too, but Boots proved a treacherous ally. She carried him to Patsy, who deposited him firmly on his back in the vicinity of the diaper. "No more nonsense," she said. Teddy lay quite still for a second and then flipped onto his stomach. When Patsy flipped him back he began to struggle in earnest. She kept hold of his ankles but made little progress with the diaper. Every time she got close he would arch his back or knock the diaper away with his behind.

"Oh, Teddy," she said. "Please be reasonable. Lie still."

Teddy was growing red in the face from his efforts to flip onto his stomach again. The look he gave her was far from reasonable. Patsy had not expected him to be so strong. She got one side of the diaper pinned but could not get the other. "What's got into you, damn it?" she said. "You used to be my friend."

Pete came to her aid. "If you don't quit that wiggling I'm going to sit on you," he said, pointing a finger at Teddy. Teddy took it to heart and stopped wiggling immediately. Once diapered, he recovered his affection for Patsy and sat on her lap.

They chatted for a bit, and Patsy found that she was growing depressed. It was the crampedness, uncertainty, and untidiness of the Tatums' life that depressed her. She liked them despite it. They had an openness with her that she liked, just as the Hortons did. It was an even better

384

openness than it had been, because before there had been that small thorn pricking them all, that sense that she and Pete were edging toward each other in some way. That was gone. Boots was bright and cheerful, despite the room and their financial troubles, and the two of them seemed married in a way that they hadn't the summer before. They had become each other's sustenance, and it would have been hard to imagine them apart.

Still, she felt awkward with them, and it was because she pitied them and was afraid they would notice it. And it was mostly pity for Pete; his life seemed so tiring, so cluttered, so full of worry. Some of the springiness he had had the summer before was gone. He didn't move like he had. For a few minutes they allowed the ebullient Teddy to dominate the scene and then Patsy got up to go, the newspaper with the soggy diaper in it in one hand. The Tatums followed her out to the car—it seemed she had only known them in the vicinity of cars. Someone was always leaving, or being left. They looked at the gray sky while Teddy gathered a handful of gravel; they looked at the white Astrodome, not far away.

"Please be careful with those broncs," she said to Pete. "I wish you could find some other way to make money."

"Daddy's offered him a used-car lot to run," Boots said. "I guess when we get tired of rodeoing we'll take him up."

"I couldn't sell money, much less cars," Pete said, opening Patsy's door for her.

She waved, they waved, and Teddy waved at length. They drove home in the thickening four-thirty traffic, Patsy a little sad. She liked the Tatums and knew they liked her, and yet it was odd that they should even know one another. For a few minutes, poking along in the traffic, she felt very isolated. She knew almost no one who was really her companion in experience. Perhaps no one but Jim. Even Emma, whom she loved, was different from her. Emma would understand Boots and Pete better than she did, understand staying in cheap motels and having no money and not very good clothes. Hank would understand it too. He was even related to Pete Tatum in some remote way. Even the Duffins had been poor once; Lee had told Jim about them living over a lumberyard in Indiana when they were first married. She felt herself still but a child compared to them all. She didn't have to ride broncs to pay hospital bills. She wouldn't have to feed her child hamburger three times a week, as Emma did. She had never been in a really tight corner of any kind. Neither had Jim. He was talking, finally, of selling the Ford and buying them two new cars, a sports car for himself and a sober station wagon for Patsy, the young matron-to-be. The Ford had been wheezing too much of late. Jim had completely abandoned his poverty pose. He was buying too many books to be able to maintain it successfully.

The real mystery was not just that people like the Tatums could tolerate her, but that they didn't even seem particularly envious of her. Emma envied her her clothes, but that was about all. She was sure that if the situations were reversed she would be madly envious of everyone who had more money than she did.

"Very puzzling," she said to Teddy, who was in a brood of his own. As soon as he was home he climbed in Emma's lap and began to recount his adventures. Tommy was sitting on the rug in his pajamas playing with some tinkertoys. He looked feverish and not especially glad to see either Patsy or his brother.

"Thanks for taking him," Emma said. "They fought all morning. I was about to strike bottom."

That night, sitting in her nice clean bed combing her hair and watching Jim tinker with a new television set they had bought, she thought of the Tatums again. When would she see them, through the years? They might vanish—she might never see them again. Or they might meet once a year, during the rodeo, in whatever town they were in, and sit and visit about the little they had to visit about in some bar or motel. Her memory of sitting with Pete under the carwash had grown very vague. She remembered that it had happened but not how it had felt.

"It ought to be clearer," Jim said. "It ought to be clearer."

"Maybe the trees are in the way," she said, indifferent. Jim had reached that point in his graduate career where it was a handicap not to know more about pro football than he did. Their little portable TV had been given them as a wedding present and had gone on the blink so many times they had both lost patience with it.

Two days later Jim went to see the Tatums and had a

pleasant afternoon of beer drinking. Patsy found an excuse not to go, and when Jim returned looking cheerful she could not be sure whether she was sorry that she hadn't, or glad. That night he was still fiddling with the new TV. "You take too dark a view of the Tatums' life," he said. "Rodeo isn't bad. I think it compares favorably with graduate school."

"Oh, it does not," she said. "Turn that stupid thing off and come to bed."

18

"Why did we wait?" Jim said. They were in the hospital; time was running out. Patsy had had a shot and the pains were getting noticeably more frequent. She was squeezing his hand hard and seemed giddy, though she was quiet. Her dark eyes had ceased focusing on him, at least for seconds at a time, and they still had not settled on a name. Patsy wore a blue gown and had so much color in her cheeks that it made her look feverish and a little wild.

"We weren't waiting," she said. "We've been considering. I say David and Margaret. David, Davey, Margaret, Maggie. I like those."

"They're okay. They just aren't very inspired. After all, there are a lot of available names."

"You're not naming my child anything inspired," she said. "It's ill-bred to go afflicting children with literary names. Look at the Wasatches." The Wasatches were a graduate family at whose house they had endured one awful meal. They had a little girl Ariel and a little boy named Dylan.

An elderly nurse came in and gave them a stern look; they both fell silent and felt guilty. "Give her a kiss and trot off," the nurse said.

"Okay," Jim said meekly. Patsy's lips felt dry and feverish.

"David and Margaret," Patsy said. "Remember, now."

He promised and went out. It was six in the morning and there was a warm gray mist on the streets of Houston. The Toddle House where he ate breakfast was very brightly lit. Back in the green waiting room of the huge hospital there was little to do but look down at the mist that hid the other hospitals. There were only two other men waiting. Jim had bought a paper—peace marchers were in the headlines. When he dropped the paper on the couch one of the men, a large florid man, asked if he could read it. He was very nervous, and his fingers seemed as red as his face.

"I better find out what those goddamn bearded beatniks are up to today," he said. "If there's anything that upsets my potty it's a goddamn bearded beatnik. You know what they are? Swindlers. They even swindled me." His expression was ferocious but his voice was surprisingly mild.

"How'd they manage?" Jim asked.

"I'll never tell you," the man said. "I'm enough ashamed of it as it is—getting swindled by a bearded beatnik. My name's Rawlins, since we're getting acquainted."

Jim was tired and would have preferred just to watch the fog, but Mr. Rawlins was eager to talk. He asked Jim what his business was and then launched into a prideful account of his own career.

"I'm in relics," he said. "You know, old stuff. Branding irons, wagon wheels, steer horns, spinning wheels, all that kind of thing. I'm the relic king—least that's what they call me. Got a factory up in East Texas where we make 'em."

"I thought you found them," Jim said.

Mr. Rawlins looked at him as if he were a child. "No," he said, "you can't find act-ual relics no more. At least you can't find enough of them, and what you do find's sky high. Lot more profitable to make them. You know there's six thousand antique stores in Texas alone, not to mention Arkansas and Louisiana? Where you gonna find that many kerosene lamps and wagon wheels? I tried to buy some rusty old branding irons from a man the other day and the son of a bitch wanted five dollars apiece for them. I can make 'em fer two and a half, already rusted. It's a scramble, I tell you."

From time to time a nurse would open the door long enough for a few screams and groans to come through. None of them sounded like Patsy, but apparently all of them sounded like Mr. Rawlins's wife.

"I swear this is the last one," he said. "Got seven. Don't know what I'd do if my wife was ever not to make it. Hell, I'm crazy about my kids, but I stay so busy up at the relic factory that I can barely keep their names straight. If my wife was ever to die I'd have to get the neighbors to introduce us. How many you got?

"How 'bout that," he said when Jim told him the one being delivered would be their first. Mr. Rawlins fished in his pocket, took a printed slip out of his billfold, and wrote something on it with a ball-point pen.

"Here you are," he said, presenting the slip to Jim. "Good for five antiquing lessons at any of the shops listed on it. You know, antiquing, sort of like relics—teaches you to make your furniture look old. You don't want to take 'em, probably your missus will. Women get quite a kick out of antiquing. Compliments of Charlie Rawlins."

Jim was trying unsuccessfully to read *The Philosophy of Literary Form* when the door opened and their doctor came in to congratulate him. He went into the hall. There was no sign of a baby but Patsy was being wheeled down the hall. Her hair was tangled, sweaty at her forehead, and she looked woozy but triumphant.

"Hey," she said. "It was a David . . . I think I'll get to see him later."

"Fine, fine," Mr. Rawlins said as Jim passed back through the waiting room. "Don't let him grow up to be no bearded beatnik. We got enough of them. If you're ever in Longview, stop by and see my factory. Might give you a discount on some of our nice relics."

"I'm afraid he has my capacity for fury," Patsy said. "Of course you can't tell it now. Look at him." Davey, two days old, was at the breast. Patsy had on a bright new robe that Dixie had brought her, and her hair was loose. Jim looked and saw a baby at the breast, a nice sight; but somehow only a slight current of parental emotion flowed in him. He had not yet so much as touched the child and had a certain feeling of anticlimax. He had not been particularly worried, and nothing at all had swept over him at the first sight of his son.

"I wish he'd open his eyes," Patsy said. "He's scarcely seen you. He's so much better than the way I imagined him."

She was cheerful, shining. Davey stopped nursing, moved his head indecisively for a bit, then went back to the wet nipple. Ten minutes later Patsy was bawling. Davey had been squalling when the nurse took him away and it brought on a deep melancholy, followed by a gush of tears. "It's awful," she sobbed. "I feel awful . . . He barely got to burp. I wish we could take him home now." She cried so streamingly that Jim could scarcely hand her Kleenex fast enough.

"Stop it," he said. "He's perfectly all right. I'm sure they know what they're doing. You're getting your gown wet."

The stream slowed to sniffles and eventually stopped; she looked out her window at the huge late-evening clouds that seemed to hang in perfect stillness over the city. In time her face became calm again, even serene. She smiled, a little weary. Her lips seemed fuller. Jim had thought of her as permanently fixed at the age and with the looks she had had when they married. It was only now and then that he noticed she was older than that and that her looks were changing.

"You must be lonesome, old buddy," she said. "I bet you'd like a good sandwich. If I were home I could make you one."

Jim said he would love one, though he had been rather enjoying being able to eat out randomly. Patsy stretched out her hand for him to hold, and she didn't want him to leave when it was time. "After having Davey I get twice as lonesome when everybody's gone," she said. She looked so lonely when he left that it disrupted his evening. Duffin's Eliot seminar of the fall had turned into a Pound seminar for the spring, and he had a report to make on the first five Cantos. He could make no headway with it. The Duffins had had him to dinner the evening before, by way of congratulations, and both of them had got drunker than he had. Lee had insisted on dancing with him while Bill sulked and complained of the choice of records. Then Lee too had

grown sulky and told him he ought to be more affectionate
to her, though to have been more affectionate he would have
had to kiss her in front of her husband. The evening left him
confused, and not having Patsy to go home to confused him
more. Irritating as she often was, it was disorienting not
having her at home.

Soon, though, Patsy was home—or rather, Patsy and
Davey were home. They were seldom seen apart. The baby
bed, which had been a neat, clean unused piece of furniture
sitting in the corner of the bedroom for two months,
suddenly became the hub of the house, the place where
everyone went when they came in, the object of all visits—
and there were many visits, some wanted, some unwanted.
Both sets of grandparents appeared within days, nervous,
laden with presents, eager not to be in the way, and,
invariably, to Patsy's mind at least, squarely in the way of
everything. Emma came, even Flap and the boys; Kenny
Cambridge threw Davey a cursory glance in passing; the
Duffins came and stayed eight minutes; and once Kenny and
Jim even brought Clara Clark in—they had been having
beer somewhere and she asked to see the baby. Patsy was
polite and cool. It was the first time since the birth that
Hank Malory had entered her mind, and he entered it
vaguely then. All she felt was a mild anger that Jim would
bring Clara to see her baby.

Her feelings about the visitors were very mixed. Getting
home was a great happiness to her and her spirits were high.
Davey seemed a marvel to her. She was filled with pride and
wanted people to come and admire him, but once they
came, once they had seen him, she was ready for them to
leave again, so she could have him to herself. Ordinary
drop-in visitors, such as the ladies who lived on the block,
those she welcomed; to them she unashamedly showed
Davey off. But with others, particularly with Emma and her
own mother, she was more ambivalent. She wanted very
much for them to recognize how splendid he was, but it was
when they were there that she felt the shyest and the most
awkward. She found she could not do things smoothly with
Davey when they were around. If he became fretful, she
could not always quiet him, as she almost always could if

they were alone. Their experience, the almost casual way they handled him and talked about him, bothered her; around them she felt like a novice and was worried that Davey too might sense that she was a novice and turn to one of them for comfort. She could not help being relieved when they went away and she was alone again with her baby. She talked to him constantly, whether he was asleep or awake, and one of the things she was frankest about was her own inexperience. No use fooling him. Besides, she had nothing to do but learn.

It was for her a lovely spring, though it was half gone before she really began to appreciate it as a season. The afternoons and sometimes much of the morning she frequently spent on their big bed reading, with Davey on his blanket right in the center of it, where he could sleep, or kick if he was awake. Between chapters of whatever she was reading, she idled, watching him, a box of Kleenex at his head to wipe up spit-ups. She felt very relaxed, untense, even languorous, and enjoyed the afternoons one by one as they passed. Sometimes Davey held her finger as she read; sometimes she smoothed his short faint black hair; sometimes he slobbered and complained and she rubbed his back softly. Alternating with her comfortable languor were moods of great keenness, when life seemed sharper, clearer, and more wonderful than it ever had. Sometimes the spring winds blew hard and the great trees in the Whitneys' back yard waved their branches. The edges of Davey's blanket blew in his face and made him sneeze, or did unless she curved her body between him and the window, to knock off the draft. He used prodigious numbers of diapers, it seemed to her, but she had a diaper service and would block him in with pillows and leave him kicking and naked while she went to rinse out the diaper; then she would come back and powder him and sit watching him kick for a bit, touched with a kind of life wonder that she would have thought corny but could not help feeling at the sight of such a wiggly little boy. She often wished that Jim were there at such times; she felt that Davey was at his absolute best in the afternoons, and that if Jim saw him so he might feel as she felt. But Jim had started doing all his work in the library. When he was home she was continually involving him with the baby, so she didn't really blame him for staying away to work; she only felt sorry that he was missing so much of his son. It was hard for her to understand why anyone would want to be away from him that long.

When he was home Jim was, if anything, overconscientious in helping her with Davey. He treated her as if she were much more fragile than she actually was. She was amused by it; she had not been really angry with him even once since Davey was born. It seemed to her that Jim had to be helped, that he didn't know what to feel or how to feel; she felt so much more confident and so much more at peace than she ever had that it was a little saddening to think that Jim was still struggling with his psyche, still somewhat unhappy, still confused. She chatted with Davey about it while reading *Vogue,* but it didn't really worry her. She was sure that Jim would soon awaken to his son. Certainly he would do so long before a father would be needed to teach him baseball and other masculine practices.

It crossed her mind, once or twice as she watched Davey and the trees, that it was really irksome of Hank Malory to have gone away. It was odd, but she had a stronger urge to show Davey to him than to almost anyone. She had a feeling that he would appreciate Davey as she wanted him to be appreciated, and she also felt that once he saw Davey he would understand why she had been the way she had—why she had not been free to give herself. It made her a little sorrowful to think of him laboring on some dry plain, amid sandstorms, when Houston was so beautiful and green, the lawns of Rice so good-smelling, the trees so lovely, the spring so well ordered, and herself looking so well and feeling so well. It had all been needless, his going away; another month and she would have ended their sweet but foolish and childish indulgence, and somehow done it smoothly, so that he would not have been hurt and could have stayed and gone on with his work. She felt, watching her son, that she had done too much ripping up of people's lives, partly through carelessness, partly through ignorance, perhaps even partly through meanness or selfishness. But that had been an old Patsy, a self she had left, like a girlhood—it was a manner she would never resume. She could not understand it when Emma on her visits spoke so bitterly of Tommy's cruelty to Teddy, so disparagingly of Flap's laziness and neglect of her. She could not understand how anyone, particularly Emma, could have retained such a capacity for resentment and bitterness. She felt—her son holding her finger all the while—that she had at last got beyond that sort of thing, to an age where she knew what she was doing and to a station where she could be content—not frightened and at a loss, not bitter and selfish, and, surely, not mean to anyone.

19

For Patsy, April and May were glorious months. It seemed to her for a time that Davey, separate and individual as he was, had somehow completed her just by being born and being hers. Small nervousnesses, fears that she might inadvertently injure him, afflicted her, but they were very small fears. She felt stable and capable, she felt useful and valuable, she felt at peace. It seemed to her that having a child obliged her to put her own childishness behind. It seemed to her that it obliged Jim to do the same, but she was prepared to be patient with him, as patient as she could be. Emma had told her not to worry about Jim's low-key response to Davey. "It's nothing unusual," she said. "It takes about six months for men to turn on to their kids. Jim will discover him one of these days."

Patsy waited, hopeful that Emma was right. If Jim would really begin to care about Davey, in the way that she cared about him, it would knit them all together, and that was what she wanted. Too many times, before Davey was born, she had had the sense that she and Jim were not knit at all, but were merely drifting through life in comfortable, conventional proximity to each other, with only the formal accident of marriage keeping them in the same house. That was why Hank had been so scary. Whatever she had felt about him, it hadn't been formal or casual. But that was over.

They had had the garage air-conditioned, and as the muggy, steamy Houston summer came on, Patsy's content began to diminish. By early June it had diminished to the point where it seemed to her it had been euphoria, not content. The change in her spirits was not the fault of Davey, nor did it relate to him. He continued to absorb her, to fascinate her, to delight her. Her days were still shaped by his needs—she still spent hours on the big bed, reading, tickling him, playing with his feet. He had learned to smile, and he gurgled constantly.

But Patsy was aware that a point had been passed. Davey could not be the whole of her life—certainly he didn't want to be. When he was done with the breast he went to sleep, and watching him sleep had ceased to be very absorbing. He slept through the night too. He woke early, kicking and squalling, but once he had eaten and kicked awhile and wet several diapers he went back to sleep. It was the same in the afternoon, the same in the evening.

She began soon to pay more attention to herself, and that was very enjoyable for a time. It was fun to be slim again, and the spring and summer clothes were a delight. It seemed to her that she had probably never looked better, and she went on shopping trips and bought herself all sorts of cool, bright new clothes. She began to have a yen for parties to wear her clothes to.

She felt great, she felt her looks were at their best, she felt motherly, wifely, optimistic, cheerful, and was prepared to have a splendid time on all fronts. Only gradually was she forced to recognize that there was one front on which she was having no time at all, and that front was Jim. She had been completely wrong in her expectation that Davey would knit them all together, make them all close. What he did was make her want them knitted close. She and Davey had become knitted together, but if Jim was knitted to anyone it certainly didn't show. She was a long time realizing that anything was wrong, for he had been very nice, very helpful whenever she needed help, and he had worked hard and done well in his three courses. Two things combined to make her realize that something was amiss with Jim—or amiss with them. He unlimbered his cameras one day and in the course of taking a great many pictures of her and Davey informed her quietly that he had definitely decided to take the job with Shanks and the movie company. He had joined a photographers' union and the filming was going to start on June eighteenth, in the Texas panhandle.

Patsy took the news as quietly as he gave it, for she was very happy that day. If Jim wanted to take pictures for a few weeks, there was no reason he shouldn't. If she and Davey got desperate for his company they could probably endure a week or two of Amarillo. They might even go and stay at the ranch with Roger Wagonner. Anything seemed possible.

A day or two later she left Davey with Juanita and walked to the drugstore. She set out for the park but decided it was too hot and reversed herself and went home. When she arrived Davey was squalling. For some reason she decided Juanita was at fault and was sharp with her. When Davey was quiet again Patsy found she was upset. She felt unusually tense. In the john she began to cry, almost the first time she had cried since leaving the hospital. It was senseless— nothing was wrong. She tried to recover her spirits, but didn't until that evening. Her period started and she decided that the afternoon's depression had merely been premenstrual blues. Then, at bedtime, she and Jim had a little argument. He had once again balked at selling the Ford. Patsy was annoyed. She had no real prejudice against the Ford, but she wanted something air-conditioned and he said it couldn't be.

"I won't even be able to take Davey to the park without him getting a heat rash," she said. "It isn't sensible."

"You can't step outside without getting him a heat rash in this town," he said. "Why not come to Amarillo? It's bound to be cooler."

"No. There's too much junk to take. I doubt there's even a diaper service there."

The argument soon trickled off without ever having become intense. Jim just went to sleep. Father and son were both asleep and she got up to check on the latter. She dug his pacifier out from under his neck, where it had fallen. Asleep, he resembled his father. She wondered if they were to have a little girl how she would look. Then, standing by the baby bed with the pacifier in her hand, idly watching the butterfly mobile suspended over the bed, contemplating a baby girl—that would surely necessitate getting a house—it occurred to her that their sex life had stopped. Jim had not made love to her since Davey was born, and Davey was three months old. It had occurred to her before, a time or two, but something had always come up to distract her and she had just not thought about sex very much.

Puzzled and a little disturbed, she put the pacifier back on the baby bed and went to the kitchen. She got herself an orange and sat at the table peeling and eating it. Of all things she had not expected to feel again, neglected was certainly one, and she tried to decide whether it was really neglect, or what. She had never supposed they were the most frequent couple in the world, but four months or however long it had been seemed an unnaturally long time for a man to do without. Before Davey was born it was quite understandable —besides being huge she had also been cold and negative and bitchy. But she was none of those things any more. Everyone told her she looked marvelous and with Davey turning out so splendidly she had never felt more in favor of life and love and bodily pleasure and all. They had had their bad times sexually in the past, but she didn't feel discouraged, not at all. Remote bad times were scarcely a reason to stop doing it completely.

But then, perhaps, there was no reason for her to become anxious either. There might be a natural explanation that she was ignorant of. Jim might be jealous of Davey, or inhibited by him, or something, though he had shown no sign that he was. It might be that he was tired. For a time he had gone to bed early, to get a head start on the feedings. But all that was past. He never awoke for the early feeding. She and Davey sat in the rocker and he slept. It couldn't really be fatigue. She could not understand why he had stopped wanting her just at a time when it seemed to her she was most wantable.

She brushed her teeth and went to bed but remained wakeful, unable to make sense out of it. He was going away in ten days. Things had been so nice—she didn't want any problems. She felt almost like waking him and seducing him, just so she would know there weren't really any problems. But he didn't like being awakened, and anyway, that was not the way things were supposed to be.

Two more days went by, and she brooded and became more and more conscious that Jim's politeness, considerateness, and general pleasantness contained an element of reserve—an element new to their relationship. They not only didn't make love, they didn't even fight. Such tiny arguing points as came up he toned down immediately. It was puzzling and frightening, the more so because on the second day she presented him, it seemed to her brazenly, a chance to make love to her and he politely ignored it.

They had gone out with the Hortons to celebrate the end of the semester. Jim hadn't been too enthusiastic, but Patsy had. She was eager for some night life. They went to a good cheap restaurant owned by a family of Argentinians, and as the evening went on one of the young men brought out a guitar and the Argentinians began to sing wild, wailing Argentine songs. They danced and yelled and the Hortons got tight. Patsy was high herself, not so much from liquor as from general gaiety. She was wearing a new red dress and could tell from the way the young Latins looked at her that it was a great success. Jim was quiet and withdrawn but did not seem to be unhappy. Not long before they left, one of the young men came over, made her a little bow, and asked very politely if she would care to dance. The Hortons urged her to, loudly, and Jim didn't care, so she danced. The men all bowed to her and the man with the guitar played another wild song. She didn't dance very well to it, but she looked very well and the family was all grins, white teeth, black hair, and politeness; the heavy-bosomed Latin women were dancing too and it was all fun.

She felt a little giddy; later, when they were home, she had a hard time toning down. Davey was sleeping. She felt like dancing some more and put on a record. Jim was making out bills. He had begun a systematic tying of loose ends in preparation for leaving. Patsy danced a little in her slip and then washed her face and went in the kitchen to see what was in the refrigerator. She loved late snacks. There was a bunch of green seedless grapes she had bought that day, the first green grapes of the summer. She broke off a sizable stem and got a couple of napkins and took the grapes to bed. She put on her gown and sat in bed eating the sweet grapes and putting the little stems on the yellow napkins. Jim had finished and was brushing his teeth. When he came in he glanced at her, stole a grape, and picked up *The White Nile*, which he was rereading. It was a close, still night, but not quite hot enough for the air conditioner, which sometimes made them too cold. She took her gown off. "You shouldn't eat that grape," she said. "You just brushed your teeth." She leaned over and gave him a quick kiss.

"These grapes are juicy," she said. "I love you—I don't know if I've told you recently. Things are so good now. Talk to me a little. Do you feel I neglect you? Maybe I've been so taken up with Davey I haven't been fun for you."

"Sure, you're fun," he said, stealing another grape.

"You worked pretty hard all year," she said. "You deserve a wife who's fun for you."

"You're fun, you're fun," he said. "Don't get frantic about it."

"I'm just bubbling," she said. "I think I read too much last winter. I've burned out on it. Now I feel like doing things. Especially things for you and Davey."

"I know, you're a regular horn of plenty," he said. "Give me a few more grapes." They sat and ate the grapes until the stems were bare. Patsy wiped her fingers on the napkin and looked down at herself.

"I have more pubic hair now than I did before Davey was born," she said.

"An amazing growth," Jim said, glancing at her briefly.

She felt too good to feel rejected; her spirits didn't sink. She got up to look at Davey. "The lot of women," she said. "We bear your children and you lose interest in us. I never thought I'd see the day when the region of the Nile was of more interest to you than the region of me." But Jim didn't hear. They both read awhile before going to sleep.

The next day, thinking back on it, her spirits did sink. He just didn't want to make love to her. At least the idea that he didn't had to be entertained. He had always wanted to make love to her. In earlier times the reluctance had always been hers. She was no longer wanted—or else she was being punished.

Once that thought struck her, it seemed the more probable theory. Somehow or other he had found out about Hank and instead of bringing the knowledge out into the open he was giving her the silent treatment. He was going to go away and leave her in silence for six weeks, to pay her back. Someone must have seen them and told him.

She felt guilty and blue all afternoon and cried. Her mood didn't mesh with Davey's—he was all smiles and gurgles. But in time her guilt gave way to irritation at Jim. What a way to treat it! He could have beaten her, yelled at her, left her; instead, he was punishing her with politeness. He could have been wildly angry, at the very least. His politeness merely showed his true colors, she decided; probably he didn't particularly want her any more and was only punishing her for having dealt a blow to his dignity.

She held her peace until bedtime, alternately furious and fearful. The thought of how guilty she was held her in check. She resolved to forget it, to say nothing, but then the sight of Jim—quiet, polite, self-satisfied, morally inviolable, preoccupied with his own work and his own virtue—the sight of him made her tremble with irritation. Even if she were sinful she deserved better treatment. Rage or forgiveness or something, not polite chill. When they were in bed, this time Jim with a napkin full of grapes and, once again, *The White Nile,* she sat nervously fiddling with the hem of her gown. Finally she decided to have it out.

"Look," she said. "You're going away next week, right?"

"Right," he said, not looking up.

"Look, talk to me," she said. "I want to know. Are you punishing me for some reason?"

"Why should I punish you?" he asked. "You've been wonderful lately."

The word was not exactly what she wanted to hear. "Just wonderful?" she asked.

"What's wrong with being wonderful?"

"Nothing. I'm sorry. It just sounded so mental."

"It isn't," he said. "You look great too." But a strained, defensive look came on his face, as if he knew what was coming and wanted to avoid it.

"Then why don't you ever make love to me any more?" she said, blushing and avoiding his eye. He was avoiding hers too. "I'm sorry. I hate talking about it. I just can't understand it. It's been months. I know I probably wasn't always the most responsive person in the world, but I still would like to sometimes. You know? I just feel like you don't want me."

Jim became very defensive. "What do you want?" he asked. "Do you want me, or do you just want me to want you?"

Patsy, though she hated herself for it, had begun to weep. She had not planned to but couldn't help it. "I wish we weren't talking about it," she said. "I always lose out in talks, there's no way I can win. I always cry. I don't know what I want? What are you driving at?"

"I don't know," he said. "I can't tell if you really feel sexy or if you're just vain."

"Oh, hell," she said, sobbing. "I don't know. You always turn things around so it's my fault. I wasn't feeling vain. I was just wondering why we never do it any more. Just forget I ever mentioned it. I don't ever want to talk about it again."

She got out of bed and sat in her rocking chair wiping her eyes on a diaper and rocking. She stopped crying and sat quietly, very downcast. She felt wretched—an incomplete sinner and a vain and unwanted wife. The only place she could win was with Davey. At least his needs were not so mysterious. She could at least be a decent mother.

She looked over at Jim, expecting him to be reading, impregnable in his self-control, but he wasn't. He was staring at the ceiling, the book on his chest and a look of pain on his face. A look of real pain. In all their married life she could not remember him looking so anguished, and it was a shock. For weeks he had looked so smiling and pleasant. He was not the sort of man pained looks improved. It frightened her and she tried to think what could have made him look so hurt.

"Jim, what's the matter?" she asked. "I'm sorry, I didn't mean to say anything that bad."

He sat up as if he were very tired—as if his limbs were stone. "You didn't do anything," he said. "I guess I just have to tell you something."

Three weeks before Davey was born he had done something quite inexplicable, and since doing it had lived as one cut off. That he should have felt cut off was also inexplicable, for what he had done was not so major, as human actions go. It was something he should have been able to confess, put in perspective, accept, and forget. But he had done none of those things.

He and Kenny Cambridge had been idling around the campus bookstore one afternoon, thumbing through paperbacks and trying to decide whether to go back to the stacks or out to drink beer. "Let's go to Richmond," Kenny suggested. "The town, I mean, not the street. I know a whorehouse there. It's only a three-girl whorehouse, but it's fun. I could use it."

"Come on," Jim said. "I'm about to become a father. I can't be going to whorehouses."

"You don't have to do anything. You can play the jukebox and yak with the other two girls while I'm busy. They're all nutty Mexican chicks. It's not a bad place to drink beer. You'd be furthering my research and I could acknowledge you in my acknowledgments."

Kenny told everyone he was going to do a thesis on The Madam as Philosopher in American Fiction 1945–1960. It was only a twenty-minute drive to Richmond, so Jim decided to go. "Anything for scholarship," he said. They crossed the wide muddy Brazos river and pulled into the little town. Kenny directed him to a street of shanties, most of them with Negro women sitting on the porches watching their children play in the dusty street.

"This is it," Kenny said, pointing to a small gray cafe with a long two-story wing extending behind it. The wing looked like it was about to cave in. A gray sign on the cafe said, Dock's.

"This is your high-grade or Mexican whorehouse," Kenny said. "Right next door is your low-grade or Negro whorehouse. I've never been there. It's only an M.A. thesis—who wants to get themselves killed for an M.A.? Besides, that one has no madam—it's every girl for herself. This one has a certain structure, a certain aesthetic, as you'll soon see."

"I can't believe this is a whorehouse," Jim said. "The main street of town is just a block away. Besides, it just looks like a cafe."

"You haven't researched it like I have," Kenny said.

The cafe was very tiny—two tables set against the wall and a counter with only four stools. A Mexican woman was peeling onions behind the counter and a large paunchy man was watching kiddy cartoons on a tiny portable TV that sat on a shelf above the counter. Hercules and Newton were rushing up a volcano.

"Afternoon," Kenny said politely. He skirted the counter and passed through a tiny kitchen into the back room. It held a pool table and led into a long dark room extending almost the whole length of the wing. At the very end was another small room where three girls sat. One was standing up putting her black hair in curlers before a small mirror. The walls were hung with Mexican calendars, all featuring an Aztec warrior in a stiff stylized embrace with a bare-bosomed Aztec maiden. There were also several Playmates of the Month thumbtacked to the walls.

"Give them a quarter for the jukebox," Kenny said. "It's part of the ritual."

Jim obliged and the girls took the quarters a little shyly. One went with him to the jukebox and they considered the selection of records, half Mexican, half hillbilly and rock. The girl was named Nina. "You crazy?" she asked. "Kenny's crazy."

"I'm not as crazy as him," Jim said.

Kenny was talking to the girl who was curling her hair, the youngest and jolliest of the three. "I think we'll go upstairs for a while," he said. "I can't resist those curlers."

"You wanta date, huh?" Nina asked. She was a thin girl

and her age was not easy to judge—late teens, early twenties, Jim thought. He felt uneasy. The other girl sat at a card table doing a crossword puzzle. Kenny and his date had disappeared up a flight of bare plank stairs, the kind that lead to the upper levels of a lumber yard.

"Come on," Nina said, putting her thin hot hand on his wrist. "Not much. Ten dollars. Screw lots of positions. You gonna hurt my feelings?"

Later, Jim could not understand why he had gone. It seemed an incredibly weak and foolish thing to have done. But Nina managed to make him feel sorry for her. "Where you from?" he asked, unable to think of anything else to say.

"San Antone," she said. "I like it but I had to leave. Too many relatives. Might have lived it up with one of my own cousins." She had a thin pretty face, but it was not her appeal that caught him. It was the situation, irrelevant, naked, disconnected; what it stirred in him was not exactly lust but a kind of dry excitement. A woman was there to be had. She didn't attract him and everything about the place depressed him, but its very depressingness caused in him some lapse of will. He followed Nina upstairs without a word. Even in February her tiny room was hot. It was afterward, as she was squatting over a small basin, washing herself, that he noticed that her breasts were the breasts of an older woman, with lines under them. There was a scar down her abdomen. He was back downstairs, very depressed, listening to Johnny Cash, when Kenny finally appeared. Kenny was in a good humor, as was his date.

Jim didn't bother to conceal how depressed he was. "Coming down here was the worst idea I've had in years," he said.

Kenny was embarrassed; he had not meant to lead Jim into infidelity. "I should have made you stay in the car," he said. "It's almost impossible to resist them on their own domain."

"I didn't see a madam," Jim said glumly.

"Cheer up. It's just an act. Any two animals are apt to do it. In three weeks you'll have forgotten it. In ten years you couldn't remember it if you tried."

Jim was not so sure. It was a week before he could get his

mind off it for any length of time. Even though she was pregnant, Patsy was lovely, and the sight of her in bed made him even more confused about what he had done. He had not felt frustrated or lecherous, and Patsy was much lovelier than Nina. Apparently he had slept with Nina only because she was there.

He gradually pulled out of the depression and the incident began to fade, but it left him with a problem in regard to Patsy. He was not sure he wasn't diseased. He looked up the books on venereal disease in the library and pored over the symptoms. Gonorrhea he ruled out, but syphilis was not so easy. Of course Kenny had been there often and seemed in fine health, but that was not definitive. The room had not even had running water. He resolved several times to see a doctor, but somehow never got around to it. Once the baby came he and Patsy got along so well that he simply let it slide. Several times he wanted her and he knew that sooner or later he would have to do something, but day after day went by and he didn't see a doctor or tell Patsy or anything. Things were pleasant and he was going to the Panhandle for six weeks. He could see a doctor there.

But when Patsy challenged him and he watched her sit in the rocking chair crying he felt so wretched and treacherous that he couldn't stand it. He told her with no elaboration, merely that he had taken Kenny to a whorehouse and without particularly meaning to or even wanting to had slept with a whore.

When he said it a silence fell between them. She didn't look at him, nor he at her. And as the silence lengthened they both grew worried, then frantic. If it wasn't broken soon it might never be broken. They might never speak to each other again. Patsy broke first.

"Okay, okay, okay," she said. "You slept with a whore. Okay. I'm not going to scream."

And she didn't feel like screaming, or even crying. What she felt when she looked at him was polite. Polite and a little cold, and sorry for him. He was clearly suffering. But it was not the sort of suffering that made her want to draw him to her. It was his—real, but the pity she felt only made her the more chill, the more stiff.

"I'm sorry," he said. "It was awful of me. I don't have any idea why I did it. I haven't known what to do ever since."

"Please don't apologize," Patsy said. Her eyes were wide when she looked at him. "I don't want any apology, really."

"But I owe you one."

"I don't know what you owe me—I don't care what you owe me. If you had come home that day and apologized maybe I would have wanted it. But it's been four months. Why apologize now?"

"Because it's now that we're talking about it."

"That's not my fault," she said. "I don't want an apology. I don't want a big argument, either."

"What do you want?" he asked.

She looked at him but her face and mind were blank. "I don't know," she said. "I guess I'll just eat some Cheerios and go to bed."

She went to the kitchen and ate the bowl of cereal slowly. She had only wanted to get out of sight of Jim's suffering look. Then she sat at the kitchen table for a long time staring blankly at the pages of Frazer. Perhaps if she sat long enough he would drop off to sleep and she would not have to confront him until morning. She tried to picture him going to bed with a whore, but no picture appeared. She didn't feel like crying. She just felt dry and tired and lonely. Four months ago—it had been just at the time when she had been in love with Hank. Or had thought herself in love with him, or had liked being with him, at least. What did she know about those things—about love? At least it had felt like it for a few days. Perhaps what Jim had done was her punishment, what she had to suffer for Hank's kisses. But that made no sense. The two things were hardly equivalent, and anyway, it was Jim who was suffering. She didn't feel guilty about Hank—not very. Whether she had loved him or not it had been good. She had at least loved what they did. In memory it seemed to her that they had been more intimate than they would have been if they had made love. At least it had been personal, and close. But poor Jim. His had been merely quick and sordid. No talk, no warmth, no kisses. A minute or two of jiggling on a bed and then weeks of guilt. If he were going to deceive her it was terrible that he had done it so pitifully, for such small gain. Better he had had afternoons with Clara Clark, learning wild California variations. Better Lee Duffin, who might have delighted him and made him pleased with himself. Better either than what he had had. Instead of pleasure and confidence he got no pleasure and came home with less confidence than he had ever had. He was even afraid to touch her. And just as Davey was about to be born—just as they might have drawn close, become really attuned to each other. Perhaps they would yet, since the secret was out. Perhaps it was not so bad, nothing tragic, just something silly and small. And yet her spirits were at zero. She sat at the table watching one last Cheerio float in an inch of milk, too empty of spirit even to walk to bed. Finally Jim appeared in the doorway looking no better than he had.

"Please come to bed," he said. "I can't sleep without you."

"Strange," she said. "I thought that was one thing you could always do." But she didn't want to argue; she took a look at Davey and got in bed. After a few minutes Jim hesitantly took her hand, and she let him hold it.

"What are we going to do?" he said. "I would never have believed I could do such a stupid thing. Live and learn, I guess."

"Who's learned what? I haven't learned anything.

"Please don't sound like a kicked dog," she said later. "I haven't kicked you. Don't go making it tragic. I'm sure all men sleep with women other than their wives, sooner or later."

"I wasn't making it into a tragedy."

"You would, given half a chance. Don't ask me what to do. You're the husband, you figure it out. I'll be around."

"Well, I'll go to a doctor first. I guess I've been sort of paralyzed, or I would have already."

But he could not get an appointment until two days before he was to fly to Amarillo, and the report giving him a clean bill of health did not come through until two days after he left. It was not a pleasant week for either of them, though no unpleasant words passed between them. The movie job suddenly seemed like a blessing to them both. They felt they needed some time apart in order to figure out how to get back together. Patsy's spirits kindled when Davey woke at five-thirty, and as long as he was awake she was lively and natural and she and Jim were at ease. But when Davey was asleep, when the night lay ahead and they were alone with each other, a deep constraint lay upon them. They spoke, chatted, went to movies, all without really looking at each other. When Patsy drove him to the airport to send him away they chatted brightly, lightly, all the way, but without looking at each other. When they kissed at the flight gate it was a brief, awkward kiss. They were standing too far apart and had to stretch to reach each other. Even then their eyes didn't meet. Only after Jim was outside, walking to the plane, and Patsy a level above him, watching through the glass, did they look at each other. Jim stopped a minute and waved. He looked very young, with his blond hair blowing and his camera bags hung over his shoulder. Patsy felt a stab of feeling at her breast and waved too; then she turned away crying. He had looked so boyish. She had shed no tears for a week. Through it all, until that moment, she had treated him as he had treated her in the months since Davey was born: with cool, extremely considerate, polite reserve. Going back, she almost had a wreck on the freeway from crying so hard—bitterly sorry that she had been such a cold unbending fool.

= 20 =

Three days after Jim left, a short letter came from Roger Wagonner:

> *Dear Jim and Patsy,*
> *Well, as usual things are drying up around here. I have been feeling poorly, maybe some Gulf breezes would do me good. Besides would like to see the little boy, have always liked to keep tabs on my kin. If no emergencies come up will be down Friday—will just take a room at a hotel. Can just stay one day, don't fix nothing.*
>
> *Your uncle,*
> *Roger*

Patsy was very pleased. She had not had time to get lonesome, indeed, had barely had time to loosen up and relax from the last tense week with Jim, but she could think of no one she would rather see for one day than Roger Wagonner. Friday at noon it rained for an hour and then the hot June sun broke through and turned the rain to steam. At three in the afternoon Patsy heard a knock on the door and Roger stood on the landing, literally soaking with sweat.

"My goodness," she said. "You're soaking wet. Come in here."

He took off his hat and kissed her on the cheek. "This sweat's from worrying," he said. "My eyes ain't the best and I couldn't see them freeway signs in time to do nothing about 'em. It's a wonder I ain't in Mexico right now."

She made him sit down and got him some icewater.

Despite his joking, he was trembling with exhaustion. Davey was asleep. Roger drank the water slowly, not saying much. Patsy felt that his color was not good, and his face had grown thinner. Once in a while he glanced out at the city with clear dislike.

"One of the few good things about being old is knowing you'll never need to go to a place like this again," he said.

"You're just not used to it."

"I don't ever intend to be." He got up a little stiffly and walked over to look at Davey. "Don't see how the little thing can sleep in all this racket," he said. "Cars going by all day. Healthy-looking boy, though. Got your black hair. How's it suit you, being a momma?"

"Oh, fine," she said. "It suits me better than anything else I've hit on."

"I sometimes think it was a good thing me and Mary never had no children," he said. "Our arguing would have probably drove a child crazy. And then sometimes I think the other way."

When Davey awoke she left him on his blanket on the bed, with Roger to watch him, and the old man and the baby looked at each other soberly and for the most part silently while she fixed dinner. She held Davey on her lap while they ate. Her chicken had turned out well, her potatoes fair. She had made an avocado salad that she was very proud of, but Roger regarded it with chilling suspicion and picked in it carefully, looking for edible bites.

"Really, that isn't poison," she said. "It's just avocado."

"Oh, is that all it is?" he said, taking a forkful with a pretense of reassurance. "I didn't know but what it was a gourd, and I never eat gourds."

After supper they went down and sat in the Whitneys' lawn glider. Roger was a little distressed that Jim would go off and leave his wife and child in such a dangerous city, but Patsy pooh-poohed its dangers and pointed out that she was an experienced city girl. When it grew dark she moved over to a lawn chair and let Davey nurse, and Roger began telling her how his various animals were, calling them by name and giving little details of their daily lives as if they were people. It was only when he got up to go to his hotel and they walked with him to the street that she realized he had actually come in the old wired-together Chevrolet pickup.

"Why, of course," he said. "Only automobile I own. Did you think I had a Cadillac parked in the barn?"

Patsy felt oddly touched. "Do you still have imaginary arguments with Rosemary?" she asked.

"Oh, yeah, I'm getting battier all the time," he said. His face brightened a little at the thought of his own craziness.

Early the next morning, so early that Davey had barely finished nursing, Roger came by again, on his way out. Patsy was astonished; she was in her gown and robe and made some coffee, to stall him. She could not believe he would drive so far for just one afternoon. He had been to breakfast, but he had some coffee, just to be polite.

"Surely you can stay today," she said. "We could go to the zoo." It was the only thing she could think of that might appeal to him.

"Aw, no, honey," he said. "I got to get on back. I've got too much to take care of."

Other than the wind and a few animals she couldn't think what, but she didn't argue. Carrying Davey, and still in her gown and robe, she followed him down the driveway to his pickup. At the sidewalk he put his arm around her and hugged her against him and she smelled the starch in his shirt and the tobacco in his shirt pocket. For some reason she was on the verge of tears.

"Maybe old Jim will get tired of all them movie stars and come down and see me some weekend," he said. "Hope so. Always enjoy talking to Jim."

He got in the pickup and sat for a minute, as if girding himself for the ordeal of the freeways.

"I'm so glad you came," Patsy said, blinking. Everything she said sounded inadequate, but not to Roger.

"Glad I did too, honey," he said. "Sorry I missed Jim, but anyway I got to see you and old Davey. I like to check up on my folks once in a while. If you don't hear from me I missed a sign and am off in Louisiana, in some bayou."

She leaned in and kissed his cheek and he squeezed her hand and smiled. "Take care of the boy," he said. "When he gets a little older bring him to see me and we'll go riding."

411

"He just four months now," she said.

"Six months is a good age to start 'em riding," he said, smiling again. Then he put the old pickup in gear and drove slowly, deliberately away, the old black pickup looking as incongruous and strange beneath the trees of South Boulevard as had Sonny's white hearse.

Patsy turned to go back to the apartment, but before she got ten steps up the driveway she broke into such a shower of crying that she stopped, stood still for a moment, and then sat down on the Whitneys' lawn. She put Davey on her lap, but the burst of tears surprised and shook her so that she put her hands to her face to catch them and Davey rolled off and to his surprise found himself on his stomach in the soft St. Augustine grass. He was puzzled for a moment and then delighted and fingered the grass while his mother sat crying. Things that Roger did, such as the visit, went to her heart. She had begun to think her heart functioned only for Davey, but it wasn't true, it had only seemed true. The emotion washed out of her in one hard burst of tears and then they were done and she sat wet-faced on the grass and picked up her son. She wiped a piece of grass out of his mouth and brushed off his belly.

"Don't eat grass," she said. "You've been fed today." She took him up the steps and they sat on the landing a little while. It was early and still quiet, not even the sounds of lawn mowers in a part of town where lawn mowing began early. She felt sad but relieved, and whenever she thought of Roger, nervous on the freeways, tears ran out of her eyes. It was not every old man who would drive a thousand miles in a rattly pickup to see such curious folks as she and Davey, she was sure of that. Davey pawed at the neck of her nightgown and occasionally put his fist in his mouth, totally unperturbed.

When the sun struck the landing she went in, put Davey in his crib, and showered. She heard something and came quickly into the bedroom, drying herself with a large green towel, but what she had heard was merely Davey bashing a rattle against the side of the crib. "You peach," she said and bent a moment so that the ends of her hair tickled his stomach. It was something he sometimes liked and sometimes didn't. At the moment he was more interested in bashing his rattle. Patsy went to the dressing table, dried her legs, and uncapped some hand lotion. She was not quite sure what had caused her to cry so, but whatever the reason, she felt much better. It felt good to sit at the dressing table, good to walk across the room. Feeling whatever she felt had had the effect of giving her back her own body. During the days of coldness with Jim she had lost all sense of her own flesh. She might have been made of straw. But the sense had come back, and she felt it was a pity Jim was gone. In such a mood as she was in, they might have worked it out. But he was gone, and the only man there to take advantage of her was Davey, who had gone to sleep, his face pressed against the bars of the baby bed. She felt a little restless. She suddenly found herself with a surplus of energy, a surplus of self, and as soon as Juanita came she walked over to Emma's and went with her to take the boys to their swimming lesson.

A few days later a letter came from Roger:

Dear Patsy,

I am no good at writing letters but have been meaning to write and thank you for all that chicken you fixed, not to mention that gourd, I have thought it over and am sure it was a gourd. Last week sold an oil-lease, my first oil-lease in six years. Hope they get a good well, my eating system is gradually wearing out, could buy a section of land with what I owe doctors now.

Well, I thought Davey was a fine boy, will tell old Jim so if I ever see him. I hope you will bring Davey to see me sometime, Jim too if you can catch him, next time you come I will take Davey for a horseback ride. I wouldn't be surprised if we got a shower tonight, cloudy back in the west, think I left the windows down in the pickup and had better go check, it wouldn't take much of a gully-washer to drown that old thing for good.

Your uncle,
Roger

That night, in her robe and gown, during the late news, she wrote him:

413

Dear Roger,

It was nice of you to write. We are very lonesome these days. I agree with you now that it was a bad idea, Jim's going up there. I don't blame him for wanting to get away from my shrewish tongue but Davey is another matter—I'm sure he needs a father almost daily. Besides, it's me that's lonesome. I was never alone before. I've taken to watching television and the horrible part is I cry if anything sad happens, no matter how corny.

We will come, sometime. I imagine it will be a while yet before Davey can sit a horse. I hope your oil well comes in, but if you would try not frying those eggs so hard your stomach would fare better. You might even try eating a gourd or two, of the sort I had. If you were ever around me for very long you'd have to endure some culinary reform, I'm afraid.

If I get much lonesomer I guess I'll have to break down and go to the Panhandle, after all, much as I'm opposed to it. I guess I just wasn't meant to take care of myself. Anyhow, do write if anything comes up I should know. In the meantime, I love you.

Patsy Carpenter

She sniffed a little when she put it in the envelope. It was true, how the nights left her longing for Jim. Any silly late show could break her up, if it was sentimental enough; but TV was better than no TV. At least it was a voice. Jim called every two or three nights. She had told him that she missed him and had tried to let him know with her tone that she was sorry she had been so unbending about the matter of the whore; he had been polite, even comforting on one or two occasions, but he had not asked them to come to Amarillo and she could not quite bring herself to offer.

Davey began to cry. He had become a wiggly sleeper and often got himself contorted in corners, or his legs stuck between the bars. He was in a corner, crying heartily, and Patsy picked him up and shushed him and walked him a bit, humming "King of the Road." After a time Davey hushed, his face against her shoulder. She became aware that he had shat his pants and switched on a little light she had arranged for such occasions. When put on his back he began to cry loudly again, but she deftly undiapered him, made a face at the consistency of the mess, and increased the volume of her own singing while she cleaned and powdered him. "*Trail*er for sale or rent, *rooms* to let, fifty cents . . ." she sang loudly and giggled. Davey, as if sensing some mockery, upped the ante with the loudest cry he was capable of, his face red with effort. "Oh, goodness," she said, peering at his bottom to be sure it was clean before reaching for a safety pin. "Hush, baby, I wasn't really trying to drown you out. Hush, Davey," and in a minute she had him diapered and walked him again, humming. Soon he slept. When she eased him down on his stomach he stiffened and woke for a second, rubbed his nose with his fist, and tried to turn over, but Patsy stood by the bed and put her hand on his back, talking to him softly until he relaxed again. Soon it was so quiet she heard his breath. Then she stood up and yawned, tried to think of something she really wanted to read and couldn't, scratched her hair and regretted not having washed it that day, and took the soiled diaper and rinsed it in the toilet. When she came back she sat in front of the TV set and hugged her knees. Rod Cameron was getting things thrown at him by Yvonne De Carlo, who seemed to be keeping a saloon. Nothing to cry about there. A Dodge commercial came on. Numerous local Dodge dealers appeared in white hats, giving away cars for thousands less than any other dealers in the world. Then there was a commercial of a girl who got a handshake one night, changed her mouthwash on the advice of a hip girl friend, and got a kiss the next. Such commercials sometimes brought on self-pity. Patsy was quite confident of her breath, and yet never got kissed any more, or anything else any more, either. But before self-pity could set in Rod Cameron was back, having chairs broken over his head. She turned to Johnny Carson, who was talking to a songstress with a hairdo that went up and up and up, almost out of camera. She turned back, hoping the movie might have improved. Rod Cameron was arguing with a sheriff. She heard Davey kick the crib with one foot, as if he were going to start scooting in his sleep. Then she heard him sigh, and he was still. She reached out one leg, punched the turn-off button with her big toe, and watched the light become a tiny bright point and disappear. Then she sat in the pitch dark room and thought a bit and hummed a bit and hugged her knees against her breasts.

BOOK III

Sleeping Around

═══ 1 ═══

Patsy had never thought of herself as a lonely person and
had never believed that loneliness would be a problem—not
for her. First there had been her family, and Miri, and then
there had been Emma and her other girl friends at college.
She had not made deep friendships easily, but she chatted
easily and got deeply involved in her chats, and it was
almost as good; at least she had never lacked for companion-
ship. And then there had been Jim—constantly Jim. She
had to concentrate hard to remember when she had not
been living with him. Of course they had not got on
perfectly, but he had always been there, and she could
usually get him to talk to her if she really wanted to talk. He
was there in the bed at night, quiet and male, and she had
always assumed he could be counted on to take care of her if
she really needed to be taken care of. She had read a lot
about loneliness and knew it was one of the great problems
of modern life, but it had never been very real to her.
Besides Jim, there was Davey. Who could be lonely with two
males in the house? Even the trouble over the whore had not
made her really lonely. It was a bad time, but there was no
reason to suppose they wouldn't get past it, sooner or later.

Then Jim went off to the Panhandle, and just as he did,
Juanita had to leave for a week. She had a daughter in
Matamoros who was in some kind of trouble. Patsy and
Davey were by themselves for the first time. The first week
went by all right—Roger's visit helped—but by the second
week she had begun to feel strange. It was nothing major,
certainly nothing desperate, just a kind of restlessness. The
days seemed hard to order. She either had too much to do at
a given moment or absolutely nothing. Davey either de-

manded her total attention, or he slept and needed no attention at all. With Juanita gone she could not go out when he slept, and she found that she had suddenly lost her capacity for doing things. She had always been active, but her activity tended to come in spurts. She would do things and then lie on her bed and read, or else lie on her bed and read and then get up and bustle about doing things. But by the time Jim had been gone a week, she discovered that she had lost her taste for reading and also her interest in doing things. Very often, when Davey slept, she did nothing. She lay on her bed and didn't read, or she sat in the rocking chair, rocking, contemplating the ends of her hair, gazing at the hot back yard, waiting for Davey to wake up and need her. At night she watched television and didn't like it, but kept watching it anyway, feeling it might get better at any minute; sometimes she watched it because it was too much trouble to get up and turn it off. She only came to life when Davey was awake, when he was nursing or needing a bath or something, and she discovered, somewhat to her dismay, that she was not always as in rapport with Davey as she had supposed she would be. Davey was not always interested in her and didn't always welcome her interest in him. He developed a dislike for her bed, where he had once napped so peacefully. When put on it, he fretted and kicked and squalled and turned over. Sometimes he would be nice, would gurgle at her, poke his finger in her mouth, smile, grasp her hair, and he was quite healthy and took quantities of her milk, but there were times when she found his fretfulness a bore and times when he simply acted as if she were bugging him. Often he would just as soon be let alone. If anyone was lonely, it wasn't Davey.

Sometimes she thought of Hank Malory, but she tried not to. It made her feel sorry for herself, and she didn't want to feel sorry for herself. Whatever guilt she had felt at the time had completely evaporated and she looked back on their two-week romance as something pleasant but not quite real. Actual life could not be that warm and that easy for very long. Had he not gone away just when he had, the bloom of their relationship would surely have withered and they would have become mean to each other, or else indifferent. She was glad he had gone when he had; she only wished there were some way to get him completely out of her mind. The trouble was that he was lovely to think about, except that thinking about him sometimes made her fell sexy; there was no advantage to that. Her idleness and the fact that it was summer just made such feelings worse.

Almost every afternoon she took Davey for a walk in his carriage—usually to the Hortons'—and often as not she came back feeling sexy. It annoyed her and she attributed it partly to her idle daydreams of Hank and partly to the heat, the still, heavy, moist heat of Houston. Everything grew so in the heat. If it rained in the afternoon the spiky St. Augustine grass was up three inches overnight, or so it seemed. The foliage in the Whitneys' back yard was always sprouting and spreading, green and shining with rain, the beautiful ferns growing so fast that the gardener could scarcely keep them properly thinned. Houston in June was almost too fertile, too fecund; the Horn of Plenty was spilling over and Patsy decided it must be affecting her subliminally. Something was. At night, when some embrace on the late show reminded her that in the real world, as on the TV screen, humans did actually kiss and hold each other and make love she felt humiliated and small, for she was a woman, she had had a baby, she was ready to give such plenty as she had, and yet no man was there to touch her. She thought of the movie stars and what she had read of them and it puzzled her that it should be so easy for them to move from love to love and bed to bed and yet remain handsome and lovely and gay. It made her feel all the smaller. Not only could she not move from man to man, she could not really hold or please the man she had, and she had not been generous enough to accommodate the only other man who had really wanted her. The day before her period she felt swollen and irritable and gave Davey a slap because he wouldn't lie still while being diapered. She got tired to death of Frazer that same afternoon and flipped crossly through a paperback by Peg Bracken, wishing someone would call, or that Juanita would come back, or that something would happen to make either the spirit or the flesh work out better for her.

Lacking either consolation, she turned as usual to her friends the Hortons. Almost every evening, when it was cool enough to go out, she sprayed her arms and calves and ankles with mosquito spray and put Davey in his carriage and pushed him up Mandell Street to the Hortons' garage on West Main. The area beyond the freeway had once been a solid middle-class neighborhood full of two-story brick houses; but lacking the protection of even minimal zoning, it had gradually become pocked with apartment houses, most of them peopled by the young and the divorced. As Patsy walked along she was ogled by shirtless young men drinking beer on their balconies.

The Hortons were having a grim summer, in their way. They were too broke to leave town, and Flap was studying himself red-eyed for his preliminary exams, which came in the early fall. The boys were big enough to bash each other and have it really hurt, and they frequently did. They only had two air conditioners for four rooms, which kept them huddled together more than they liked to be. The kitchen wasn't air-conditioned, so Emma didn't cook except when absolutely forced to. She spent most of her time mediating elaborate arguments between the boys, or else protecting one or another boy from Flap, who had grown intolerant of being interrupted while studying. The boys invariably did interrupt him and he sometimes swatted them more heavy-handedly than Emma thought good, so they themselves were frequently in fights.

"Fire or ice," Patsy said, comparing their overcrowdedness with her loneliness, and they all sat around and drank beer for an hour or so every evening, talking about how in despair they were and in the meanwhile laughing uproariously at their own wit or the antics of their children. Teddy and Tommy were both reasonably respectful of Davey's fragility, and Tommy, who considered himself infinitely more responsible than his brother, was good at planting himself in front of the baby carriage to be stared at by Davey, who loved to stare at human beings closer to his own size. Teddy thought Davey a bore and once threw a ball up in the air in such a way that it came down—by sheer accident, he claimed—in the baby carriage. It was only a rubber ball, but Emma scolded him fiercely. Davey had not been hit and Patsy kept calm. Teddy took his reprimand casually, humming to himself while it was in progress.

One evening ten days after Jim had left, the Hortons walked over to her place. The Whitneys were gone and they all sat out in the big back yard while it grew dark. The boys had orange Popsicles, provided by Patsy. Davey lay on a blanket between his mother and Emma, wiggling on his stomach. "A few months and he'll be mobile," Emma said.

Patsy wore jeans and an old blue blouse. She had washed her hair that afternoon and felt clean and in good spirits. Flap lay on his back on the grass with a copy of *Ramparts* spread over his face. Occasionally Teddy sat on his chest for a few minutes while he picked particles of grass off his Popsicle. Flap pretended to be asleep but he was actually putting into effect a plan he had to see Patsy's breasts, or at least one of them. If she thought he was asleep she might decide to nurse Davey and he could peer out from under the *Ramparts* and watch. He had always wanted to see Patsy's breasts, and that was the only plan he could devise that offered any hope of success.

Unfortunately, it didn't work. It was not feeding time and in any case Patsy was not about to uncover herself around such a transparent lecher as Flap. When it grew dark they all went inside.

Patsy left Davey on his blanket and went to the kitchen to make lemonade. When she carried in the drinks, Emma had gone to the john, Flap was lying on his stomach on the floor reading an old book catalogue, and Tommy and Teddy were sitting politely on the couch awaiting their lemonade. Flap reached up for his beer and the boys took their glasses carefully and sipped sly sips. It wasn't until she was lowering herself to the floor that Patsy noticed a drastic change in the company. Davey wasn't on his blanket.

"Where's Davey?" she asked, her heart pounding. She looked around the open floor but didn't see him. In the moment of quiet they all heard the toilet flush. Patsy hurried to the baby bed, thinking she had absent-mindedly put him back in it, or that perhaps Emma had, but he was not there either. Her legs felt shaky. "Did Emma take him?" she asked.

"To the john?" Flap asked. He looked up, puzzled, just as Emma walked in.

"Davey's gone," Patsy said. "Where could he have gone? I was only out of the room for a minute."

"He couldn't be gone," Emma said. Then she and Flap both looked at their sons. Teddy was sipping lemonade, a picture of angelic innocence, but Tommy was red in the face from the effort it took to repress his laughter.

"Aha," Flap said.

"He's under the baby bed," Tommy said. "Teddy rolled him while you were reading." He began to giggle. Teddy pretended not to hear, but a sly grin touched his lips. Patsy rushed to the bed and sure enough Davey was there, on his back, and quite pleased about it. He was trying to reach the bedsprings. He only began to fret when Patsy swooped him out and held him. Her arms and legs were trembling from the scare she'd had, and she was afraid to look at Teddy for fear she'd go yank him off the couch and spank him. But Emma did just that, and in a minute he was properly spanked and was crying loudly, almost in tune with Davey, who started crying as soon as Teddy did. The Hortons quickly gathered themselves up and left, Tommy pleading to be allowed to finish his lemonade. Patsy cried a bit from relief and tension and tried to get them to stay. She felt silly for getting upset over nothing, but they were all embarrassed and glad to be out of one another's company for a time. Patsy made an awkward attempt to make friends again with Teddy, but he would have none of it.

"She's really uptight," Flap said as they walked home. Teddy was riding on his hip, totally exhausted.

"You can't blame her," Emma said. "Jim was a fool to go off and leave her with that baby, I don't care how temporary the job is. If one of mine had disappeared I'd have acted the same way. Fortunately you were always around trying to screw me when things like that happened and I never had a chance to get nervous."

"You think if I went back and tried to screw her it would help?" Flap asked, trying to be jocular. It came out wrong and he instantly regretted having said it. Emma was huffy the rest of the evening.

Patsy kept crying and wiping her eyes long after they were gone, although she knew it was silly. Davey was already blissfully asleep, not a bit the worse for having been rolled. But the sense of panic she had felt when she couldn't locate him wouldn't quite leave her. Several times she went over and looked, to be sure he was in the baby bed. It was absurd, but she was terrified. She checked all the windows and doors to be sure no one could creep in and steal him. A bath failed to calm her and she was in bed trying to go to sleep when the phone rang.

"My goodness, you're in bed early," Jim said.

"Oh, Jim," she said. "Please come home. I'm no good alone."

She told him about the incident and tried to explain why he had to come home and help her, but everything she said sounded silly and Jim was not at all sympathetic.

"But that's so minor," he said. "It's bound to happen to every mother. You wouldn't have been any less scared if I had been there."

"Yes, I would," she said and began to cry. It embarrassed her and annoyed him. He was silent until she stopped.

"That's about three bucks' worth of tears," he said.

"I can't help it," she said. "I can't. I'm lonely. I never said I was the independent type. I just don't know what to do with myself."

"Come on, now," he said. "That's silly. Take a painting class or something. It's absurd for me to come home and do nothing when I'm making seven hundred dollars a week. Juanita will be there. It doesn't make sense for me to quit. We can't just act from whimsey."

Patsy felt choked. She didn't know what to say. He was absolutely right—it was all minor. But everything he said felt wrong.

"Don't you love me?" she asked, hating herself for fishing.

"Sure," he said. "Of course I do. But that has nothing to do with it." And he went on to tell her about his work. It was fun and he sounded in fine fettle. Boots and Pete were coming in a week. Pete was going to be in a clown sequence.

Patsy calmed down a little, listening. She was hoping he would ask her to come up. She waited, trying to chatter naturally, but Jim hung up without inviting her, or even hinting at it. When she hung up her receiver she felt dry of tears, so flat with loneliness and disappointment that she didn't know what to do. She lay blankly until sleep came. And when she awoke she felt just as blank and flat. It was one of the few mornings in her life that seemed utterly not worth getting up for, though it was bright and sunny in the room. She started to call Jim and ask if they could come, but she looked at the phone awhile and didn't. He would be on the set, anyway. She looked straight up at the ceiling and listened to Davey wail for her for a full ten minutes before she found the spirit to get up and change him and take him to the rocking chair to give him the breast.

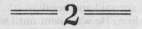

2

Her state of spiritlessness lasted all that day. She didn't go out until the evening, and then instead of wheeling Davey to the Hortons', she wheeled him to Rice. In the empty quadrangle there was a rabbit nibbling at one of the hedges. Patsy tried to point him out to Davey but had no luck. Except for a graduate student or two strolling along with their girls, the campus was empty. The twilight and the heavy silent buildings soothed her a little.

Jim didn't call that night and the next morning she awoke feeling agitated. She toyed with the idea of calling him, but Juanita came in while she was brooding and her spirits shot up. She flung off her robe and got dressed, thinking it would be a great day for random shopping. She called Emma, but Emma had just burned her hand on some grease and didn't want to go.

She went downtown alone and spent sixty dollars on two dresses for herself and some baby clothes for Davey. She watched half of *Youngblood Hawke* because she happened to be passing the theater and felt like seeing a movie. When she came out of the chill darkness the heat off the baking pavement was so great it almost made her faint. She made it to the Ford and drove to her drugstore for a milkshake and a grilled cheese sandwich before going home. Reading seemed feasible again, so she idled at the paperback rack while her sandwich was grilling. A fat historical romance called *Angelique,* with a stunning blonde on the cover, tempted her—a silly romance might get her through the evening. Then she noticed an unobtrusive paperback called *The Marriage Art* and on impulse took it to the counter with her. It proved to be mostly about sex and she turned through it as she ate, slightly repelled and yet slightly fascinated. There was a chapter on what the author considered more or less advanced variations; the one at which she paused the longest was a technique which required the female to place an icebag at the base of her partner's scrotum a moment or two prior to orgasm. It was, the author advised, not for amateurs. Patsy sipped her milkshake thoughtfully, trying to imagine herself lying down to make love equipped with an icebag. It did not seem likely she would ever be that advanced about it all.

As she was brooding about *The Marriage Art* an arm brushed her shoulder and she looked up into the face of William Duffin. He had quietly taken the seat beside her and was smiling and reading about the icebag variation, across her bosom almost.

"Hi," he said. "Just browsing, or do you go in for that sort of thing?"

Patsy blushed and closed the book. She was very embarrassed. Later it occurred to her that at that moment she felt very much the way Peewee must have felt when she caught him reading *Sexus.*

"Why did you have to sit down there?" she said irritably. She wanted to move over two or three seats but didn't.

"You're blushing," he said. "My goodness. It looks like a fascinating book. Loan it to me when you finish it. A double cheeseburger please, and coffee." He was in tennis clothes and his long angular face was sweaty.

Patsy nibbled at her sandwich. She could not go on reading the book and she didn't particularly want to make conversation, but she was determined not to let him rattle her. All the same, she felt very stiff.

"Want a job?" he asked.

427

"From you?"

"Sure. My Pound book is done and I need somebody to help me with the index. I have a flunky but I'm not sure he knows the alphabet. Anyway you're much lovelier than he is."

Patsy looked at him a moment to see if there was anything at all in his face that she liked. He was opening a bag of potato chips. He had very long fingers and deep curved lines around his mouth. He looked sweaty and melancholy and a little more human than he ordinarily seemed. She didn't feel sympathetic toward him, but neither did she feel actively antagonistic.

"Your wife is very nice," she said. "Let her help you."

"Lee *is* nice," he said. "Maybe I should buy her an icebag."

"Now really," Patsy said. "Quit talking like that. Act your age. I'm trying my best to like you."

"You haven't been my age," he said. "I am acting it. I'm a fifty-two-year-old snob and you're a delicious-looking young woman in her twenties. It's only natural I should scheme about you."

Patsy was disconcerted, but not by what he said. Eddie Lou had just scowled fiercely at her from the grill. To Eddie Lou she was clearly the Madame Bovary of South Boulevard, and Eddie Lou scared her worse than Bill Duffin. She had a feeling she could hold him at bay with her wit.

"Okay," she said, "so you have desires. By the age of fifty-two you ought to have acquired perspective, right? After all, you have a reputation, a wife and daughters, and all that."

Bill laughed. "Don't be so pompous," he said. "Do you say things like that in bed? No wonder Jim left. Perspective has nothing to do with it. Life isn't a critical essay, you know. As it happens, I lead a fairly dull life—more or less true to my wife, more or less good to my daughters. What it lacks is variety, and the older I get the more I realize what a truly marvelous thing variety is. There are all sorts of people and all sorts of experiences to be had with them. What did I have to lose by asking you outside that night at our party? Nothing. Only the bold deserve the fair. You might have been drunk enough to take me on. Don't you ever have the impulse to take some big chance with a stranger, just to see if something interesting might happen?"

"No," Patsy said. "Is that your philosophy of seduction?"

"I guess," Bill said. "I don't suppose you play tennis, either?"

"No," Patsy said, getting up. She had begun to feel nervous again.

"Too bad. Say hello to Jim next time you hear from him. I'd be glad to pay for your milkshake."

"No, thanks." She stood nervously, *The Marriage Art* concealed by her purse, waiting for Eddie Lou to come and take her money. Finally Eddie Lou did, and she bought some cold cream and went to the park. She sat at a picnic table, in a grump, grimly reading *The Marriage Art*. Bill Duffin seemed so clear about his motives and his principles that in contrast she felt doubly confused. He had also managed to make her cowardly and inhibited and various other things she didn't like to feel. She read on, determined to read about everything that could be done with the human genitals, even if she never wanted to do any of the things herself. It was hot in the park and ants kept crawling on her ankles.

Jim called that night just as she was about to bathe. She found that she was very annoyed with him for being so far away and sounding so blithe and cheerful about it, but she was determined to be as cheerful as he was and not put herself in the humiliating position of having to admit how much she needed him.

"I saw your mentor today," she said. "Apparently he plays tennis. He still wants to ravish me."

"That's silly," Jim said. "You're always imagining yourself getting ravished. Probably due to growing up in the South."

"I grew up in Dallas. So did you. Do you never imagine getting ravished?"

"No."

"You don't have much imagination. I read a sex book today. Like me to hold an icebag against your scrotum sometime? It's supposed to be quite a thrill."

"Don't be ridiculous," he said. "You'd never do that. How's Davey?"

Just before he hung up he told her that he loved her; he said it a little stiffly, as if he had been waiting for a place to slip the statement in. She told him good night and marched in to bathe, determined not to grow low-spirited. Later, after her bath, she sat at her dressing table. Her bosom was okay but it seemed to her that her thighs were growing flabby. After all, she was getting older. It was twenty minutes until midnight. She turned on the *Tonight* show but nobody good was on and she went back to the dressing table and began to brush her hair. She felt petulant. Having Davey hadn't affected her figure much, but still, with age coming on, it might be a good idea if she prodded Emma into exercising with her, or something. It was depressing to think of drifting into her thirties, unappreciated, alone, and with flabby thighs. Lee Duffin probably played tennis—she gave no indication of flab. Trimness wasn't happiness, but it might be some consolation. She stood up. It seemed to her that her hips were too broad. She might spread. Still, Duffin had obviously thought she looked okay; delicious had been his word. If so, it was a little sad, for nobody was getting much of a taste of her except her son, who was asleep. She went over and stood smoothing the fine hairs on his head with one finger as he slept. Then she yawned and went to her bed and picked up the phone. She dialed Jim at his motel in Amarillo. He answered in a very sleepy voice.

"It's me," she said. "I'm lonesome and I don't understand. I was a spritely girl once and now I'm a matron and I'm going to get dowdier year by year. I know I am. Why aren't you here enjoying me while I still have my looks? You're not supposed to go off like that until I'm in my forties and faded and fat."

"For god's sake," he said. "You're the vainest person I know."

"I am not," she said categorically.

"I'd like to know who is, then. Waking me up just because you've decided your looks are fading. I'll be home in a month. Will you fade in a month?"

"Probably. They go quick once they start going."

"I'm going back to sleep. I wish you weren't so vain."

"You want us to come and see you?"

"No." There was a silence. "Not while you're in your present mood. I'm working very hard and I don't have time to cater to your vanity."

Patsy took it coolly. She felt she was getting what she deserved. "Okay," she said. "It was nice to argue with you again. The only time I feel married any more is when we argue."

But after she hung up she found that her last sentence hadn't been true. They had argued and Jim had been entirely in the right, but she didn't feel married and she didn't feel chastened, either. She felt clear, dry, undepressed, restless, and a little hungry; and she went to the icebox and got a stem of grapes and some icewater and dug around in a pile of library books until she found William Duffin's book on Beckett. She found that she was curious about the Duffins—how they had got as they were—and it occurred to her that Bill's scholarship might provide a clue. The book was dedicated to Lee, with love. She wondered what, in their life, that word meant. It had certainly not come to mean anything very definite in her own. Bill's prose was confident and heavy and a little portentous, like his voice. She hadn't read much Beckett and hadn't much liked what she had read, and the faces of Lee and Bill kept clouding the page. To Lee, with love—it was disquieting. Was it possible that despite the malice and bitterness of their conversations they still did care for each other? Did they sometimes have tender moments, still? She would have liked to see through the pages into their lives for an hour. It might tell her what to hope for. But the book didn't tell her what she wanted to know, and she grew annoyed with it and with herself. Jim was right: she was vain, weak, without character, full of vapors and gloomy speculations. She snooped in the book for thirty minutes as she might snoop in a drawer, hoping that somewhere, at the end of a chapter or the top of a page, she might find some clue to Bill and Lee, some small leakage of personality that would help her understand how very intelligent middle-aged people really *were* in their married lives. But all she found were insights about *Endgame,* and she yawned and switched off her bed light. She was sleepy and it was a comfort—small, but genuine—to know that she had six whole hours to sleep before Davey would wake up and want his mother.

The Duffins at that moment were sitting with both bed lights on. The bed was rumpled and they were drinking coffee that Lee had just made. Lee had been crying but was dry-eyed again. She gathered up several sodden Kleenex and pitched them in a wastebasket. They had just had a harrowing telephone fight with their oldest daughter, Melissa, who was in California. She had dropped out of Mills and was thinking of going off to Big Sur to live with a young man who was a nudist. He had been in a public wade-in, apparently. Lee had not particularly liked that, but Bill had not at all liked the idea of her dropping out.

"You're going to stay in college if I have to chain you to a desk," he said. "If you don't like Mills you can go to Stanford next year. Or anywhere, almost."

"It's college I don't like," Melissa said. "It just doesn't interest me. Why spend a lot of money on something that doesn't interest me?"

They tried to be patient, but nothing they said seemed to have any effect on Melissa, and finally they both lost their patience and began to yell at her and she lost hers and yelled back. "You two don't know anything about me," she said. "Quit trying to force your life style on me. I don't like alcohol and books and dull people."

"What have you got that's better?" Bill said. "Pot and dull films and moronic nudists?"

"He's *not* moronic! You haven't even met him! He's smart. He's just very essential!"

"I hope he's not too essential to let you take pills. I don't want you off at Big Sur having a daisy child, or whatever they call babies in the love generation."

"They call them babies."

"Babies, then. Where's your intelligence gone?"

"It's *not* gone! You and your mother just emphasize all the wrong things."

"Shut up," Bill said. "If you quit school then you can pay your bills with your own superior emphasis from now on. I won't pay them."

Melissa hung up, crying, and Lee cried and Bill sulked. "One gone, two to go, I guess," he said. "What are you crying about?"

"I don't know," Lee said. "I don't think she thinks we're good parents. Even if we weren't I thought we had our children fooled. I just hate to see her quit school. She's so bright."

"At least she *was* bright," he said. "Education apparently isn't where it is any more. It's probably a handicap. If one is going to live with an essential nudist I can see where it would be. What happened to the anthropology professor she was going with?"

"I guess he lost out. I think he may have been married, anyway."

"Hard for anyone articulate to compete with essential nakedness," Bill said. "The nudist probably screws better."

Lee put her coffee cup on the floor and lay down on her stomach. "I don't want to get ten years older," she said. "I'd be no sort of grandmother. I don't want to go on getting older day by day until I look like a prune. All my daughters will think me an absolute anachronism in another five years. I won't have a chance."

"What do you mean, chance?" He looked at her with curiosity.

"As a woman. What will I do? You won't want me twice a year, probably. The girls will be off with their men. I won't be able to do any of the things that make me happy."

"Well, who will?" he said.

"You will. You'll have your reputation and your students and your books."

"Robert Frost has a poem about what you're talking about," he said. "It's called 'Provide, Provide.'"

"I read it. I waited too late to provide."

He reached over and stroked her back, but she didn't change expression. "So what's your solution?" he asked.

"No solution. I'm going to sleep."

"Patsy Carpenter really hates my guts," he said. "I was at the drugstore today and caught her reading a marriage manual."

"I'm glad she doesn't like you."

433

Bill switched off his light and lay in the darkness. "Melissa has a nudist and you have five or six years," he said. "My, my."

"What do you have?"

"Fantasies. Want to help me index the Pound book? We haven't done an index together in years."

"I guess," Lee said. "Ask me in the morning."

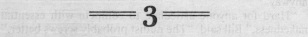

Joe Percy was griping about how bad the movie was going to be, and Jim was listening to him without much interest. They were making the evening ride from the movie set to Amarillo, across the shimmering summer plains. Jim ordinarily rode in with Sonny Shanks and Catherine Dunne, a lithe blond starlet from Fargo, North Dakota, the home town of Casey Tibbs. In the film she was Sonny's principal conquest, but whether he had managed to conquer her in real life was a matter for speculation. Almost everyone connected with the production speculated about it constantly. Catherine had left on Thursday to spend a weekend with her boy friend, but neither Jim nor Sonny was depressed about it. Eleanor Guthrie was flying in that evening and they were dining with her at the home of a wealthy lawyer. Jim was looking forward to the weekend—the thought of seeing Eleanor again excited him. Joe Percy had nothing to look forward to but a weekend of drinking in Amarillo and was depressed.

"We should have settled for a straight grade-C movie called *The Sonny Shanks Story,*" he said. "Everybody was willing except the producer. 'I want something more resonant,' he said. 'Something a little more Conradian. It needs more moral ambiguity.' He's an idiot but he has a Harvard education and doesn't want anybody to think he's wasting it. I told him horseshit didn't have resonance. Fragrance we might could have managed, but not resonance."

"Maybe it won't be as bad as you think," Jim said. "I hate movies about the lives of athletes."

"They're okay if they're clearly labeled," Joe said. "What we've *got* is a movie about the life of an athlete. Only a dumb-ass like our producer could mistake it for *The Heart of Darkness.*"

Their car was at the head of a squadron of rental cars. Every morning at dawn the squadron sped out of Amarillo toward the location on the plains, and every afternoon the same squadron sped back to the huge motel in Amarillo and emptied its dusty cargo of actors and technicians into the greenish water of a large swimming pool. Jim jumped out as soon as the car stopped, hoping to get a quick swim before the mob filled the pool. A fat matron in a bright blue bathing suit was trying to teach her terrified son to float on his back. Hank Malory, his skin darkened by three months in the weathers of the plains, sat in a pool chair nearby. His surveying crew was working about sixty miles away and he had driven up to have a beer with Jim.

Instead, they had gin and tonics in Jim's room. Jim made his light. He remembered that he had passed out the first time he had been in Eleanor's company, and he didn't intend for it to happen again. He showered and came out to find Hank leafing through a *Playboy*.

"I thought you had principles," Hank said. "I knew I'd sink to this level once I was out of school, but I wouldn't have thought it of you. Why aren't you reading René Wellek and people like that?"

"It takes too much energy," Jim said. "By the end of the day all I want to do is lie around and look at breasts."

"How's Patsy?"

"Fair," Jim said, frowning. "I think the baby makes her a little claustrophobic." His own memory of Davey had grown so vague that he felt guilty about it. "When are you going back?"

"Oh, pretty soon."

"Good, go by and see her. Take her out to dinner or

something. She must be bored out of her mind, with nothing to do but change diapers."

They chatted amiably for a while, reminiscing about the graduate life, but Jim's side of the chatter soon grew a little forced. It was not that he didn't like Hank—he had been glad to see him—but he couldn't quite get his mind off Eleanor Guthrie. He had spent the day thinking about the evening, and Hank's presence broke into his visioning a little unpleasantly. Besides, it was almost time to go; when they finished their drinks they went out and stood by the pool a few minutes watching a pink blond getting the make put on her by an intense young cameraman.

"You might like to meet Joe Percy," Jim said. "He's a wacky old screenwriter. Patsy's fonder of him than I am, but he does tell good Hollywood stories. I'll feel I've failed in my duty if I can't introduce you to somebody."

Joe was in the coffee shop, at a table by the plate-glass window, eating a honeydew melon. He rose politely and shook Hank's hand. Just as he did, Sonny strode into the room; he had had a swim and his black hair was not quite dry. He wore a red shirt and a white sports coat and was in high spirits. When he heard Hank's name he turned and studied him a minute.

"Used to know some Malorys," he said. "Any kin to Marie?"

"She's my aunt."

"Thought so. You got the same build, all things considered. Wish I had time to sit and visit. Ain't heard from Marie in years. We better go, though, Jimbo. Eleanor's at the airfield."

Jim apologized for having to run off, and they left hurriedly. Hank felt a little awkward. "Nice to have met you," he said to Joe. "I didn't mean to intrude on your supper."

"Not at all," Joe said. "You're welcome to sit a spell, as they say in the South. Who are you?"

"Just a friend of the Carpenters," Hank said. "I went to school in Houston for a while."

"Oh, yes, the town where they rot fish. Compared to this place it's delightful. Amarillo is the skin-cancer capital of the world, I find. Judging from your complexion you must live around here. What was that about Sonny and your aunt?"

"I've never known. They may have had a romance."

Joe took a box of medicinal toothpicks out of his pocket and thoughtfully picked his teeth while Hank ordered and received a steak sandwich. They looked out the window at the skyline of Amarillo, the few tall buildings as blocklike as if they had been set there by a child. Behind the buildings was the wide beautifully colored evening sky.

"You're not a young writer, I take it?" Joe asked.

"No."

"Good. It's nice to meet a young man who's not a writer. Know any good places to drink around here?"

"Just a few honky-tonks," Hank said. "They're pretty ordinary."

Joe stood up and reached in his pocket for some change. "If you've got nothing better to do let's go to an ordinary honky-tonk," he said. "I'll tell you my philosophy of history or something while we drink. If I can find the Tatums we'll take them along. He's a rodeo clown. They know the Carpenters too.

"He likes to drink and his wife likes to dance," he added. "So she and I dance while he drinks. A sociable arrangement."

"Small world," Hank said. Jim had made him feel a little out of place and he had been sorry he came, but he stopped feeling sorry. "Did you know Pete Tatum was once married to the aunt of mine who knew Sonny Shanks? It's amazing they both know the Carpenters."

"That's not so amazing," Joe said. "I'm always meeting people who've met or been in love with or married or screwed or divorced someone I've met or been in love with or gone to bed with or something. It's bound to happen, even in a place as big as Texas."

Outside, the huge pool was empty. All the movie people had gone off to their dinners. The evening shadows covered the pool, making the green water dark. The Tatums proved easy to find and easy to entice. They were sitting in their messy motel room watching television. Boots was glad to see them, and happy to be going out. Joe's love of dancing had been a great boon to her, for she had had nothing to do for two weeks except sit around the motel. Pete was tired and would just as soon have watched television, but he got up and put on a clean shirt and came along, quiet but willing. They went to a nearby dance hall called Elmer's Lounge, a very dark place. The only strong light came from the jukebox.

"The waitresses here must learn to count their steps," Joe said, but soon he and Boots were on the sawdusty square of dance floor, laughing and dancing, while two or three melancholy roughnecks peered at Boots through the gloom.

Hank had diplomatically waited until Boots was out of hearing to mention that he was Marie Malory's nephew. Pete looked up from his beer in surprise. "My god," he said. "You're Monroe's boy?"

"I'm Monroe's boy."

Pete was silent for a minute. "I never met your dad but once," he said. "That was just after the war. I think we meant to get him to fiddle at our wedding, but then we run off and got married and did without the fiddling."

Then, instead of talking, they both fell silent, Hank thinking of his father, Pete of his first wife—of Monroe and Marie, people from another time. The jukebox was turned up loud and one song followed another as quickly as the record arm could shift. Joe Percy barely had time to wipe the sweat from his forehead before the music started again. From the booth, Hank could see Boots's white blond hair moving in the gloom. The music that filled the bar was so familiar to Hank and to Pete and to Boots that they scarcely heard it consciously. It was merely one of the sounds behind their lives. Someone played a war song about a veteran whose balls had been blown away in Vietnam—"that old crazy Asian war," as the song put it. The soldier's wife was named Ruby and the song was a raw plea that Ruby not leave him, despite his sad condition:

Oh Ruuuuuby, Ruuuby,
Don't take your love to town . . .

It offended Joe Percy; he tried not to listen. Pete and Hank were drinking beer. Pete had danced to such songs with Marie, in the days when he danced more. Then it had been

"Dear John"; it had been "Fräulein." A decade earlier Monroe Malory had danced to such songs with Hank's mother—to "The Soldier's Last Letter" and the war songs of World War II. They had danced in the same darkness, on the same sawdust dance floors, with the same onlookers looking on—roughnecks and truck drivers, cowhands and mechanics—all of them sitting in their booths musing of women. George Jones or Johnny Cash, Hank Williams or Ernest Tubb, Roy Acuff or Kitty Wells—only the shape of the beer bottle had changed over the years. When Pete spoke, idly spinning a fifty-cent piece between his fingers, it was not of Marie at all.

"Seen Patsy since she had her baby?" he asked.

Hank said no. Joe and Boots came over, sweaty and out of breath. Joe drank whiskey from a bottle he had brought along, and the rest of them drank beer. Eventually it was midnight. Boots had been asleep for an hour, her head against Pete's shoulder.

"We got to quit drinking with you, Joe," Pete said. "You wear her out and then I have to carry her all the way to bed. Wake up, honey, we better go."

"I'm awake," Boots said sleepily.

Back at the motel the Tatums said good night and staggered in to bed, Boots with both arms around her husband's waist. Hank had had eight beers and felt a little fuzzy himself. His motel was in Clarendon, sixty miles away, and he was wondering if he could make it without getting sleepy. Joe seemed fresh and clear-headed. He stood by the swimming pool looking up at the high, clear Panhandle moon.

"Do you know Dixie, by any chance?" he asked. "Patsy's aunt."

"No."

"Your mentioning that it was a small world made me think of her. She's one of Sonny's old girls. One of my old girls too, I guess. So in theory at least, both your aunt and Patsy's aunt have been had by Sonny. Dixie's supposed to come up here one of these days. If she were to elope with Pete—god forbid—that would really close the circle."

He sat on the diving board and smoked a small cigar, enjoying the quietness of the night, and Hank drove sixty miles across the still, moonlit plains to his motel. When he got there he tried to write Patsy a letter telling her he was coming back to Houston, but he found that he was too fuzzy. He wrote it the next morning as soon as he awoke.

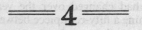

Hank's letter was short—only a note, really—but it took Patsy's breath. It came on one of those mornings when she had not felt like dressing; she felt cheerfully sloppy and lazy and on the whole calm, and when she heard the postman's steps going down the driveway she left Davey undiapered for a moment and stepped out on the landing, where the mailbox was, hoping some magazines had come. She was in her gown and a blue summer robe. The boards of the landing were hot against her bare feet and the noon sun warm on her face and her calves.

There were no magazines, just some bills, a letter from her mother, who was in Colorado Springs, and the envelope with Hank's name on it. When she saw his name she had a moment of shock and immediately tore it open and read it, standing in the hot sun:

Dear Patsy,

Rice has renewed my scholarship, so I will be back soon. I have enough money to last until school starts. I saw Jim last night, but he had a dinner engagement and we didn't get to talk much. I don't know exactly when I'll get to Houston but I want to see you very badly. I thought I ought to warn you. I'll come by when I get in.

Hank

Davey had begun to yell for her, but she scarcely heard him. All the terrible strange feelings that had possessed her when Hank was there came back for a moment, and it was hard to get her breath. She stepped inside, into the shade. Everything was complicated again. With him gone, life had simplicity—a drab simplicity, perhaps, but at least it wasn't complicated or scary. The flush of feeling that passed through her became a kind of anger. Who was he, to write her such a letter? What was he presuming? So they had felt romantic, months before. So they had kissed. That was all past; he had no right even to write her a letter, much less assume that he was still a factor in her life. It was very rude of him. Miffed, she dropped the note into the bathroom wastebasket. She shook her hair free on her neck and straightened her robe over her breast and looked in the mirror to see if she looked like the kind of woman he apparently thought she was. Her image reassured her. She looked formidably domestic—a mother. Actually she had never looked better, and she knew it; the way she looked would be fitting torment for him if he came by. She felt completely inaccessible and hurried in to Davey, who was crying lustily, lying on his back undiapered. The minute Patsy went to the bed he stopped crying, looked up at her through his tears, and began to pee, wetting his stomach and the new diaper she had laid out. "Oh, you're always doing that," she said, swabbing him efficiently. She abandoned her matriarchal expression long enough to nuzzle his stomach. Davey grinned in response. When he was diapered she carried him over and plopped him on her unmade bed amid the morning paper.

Then she went and got the letter out of the wastebasket and came back to the bed to reread it. Davey had managed to bite off a piece of the newspaper and she dug it out of his mouth with one finger and patted his back until he stopped yelling. He caught a strand of her hair in his fist and mouthed it; he could tug hard enough to hurt her scalp. She read the letter and folded it again and pressed the thin edge of the paper against her lips. There was a sag inside her, a kind of softening. She remembered how pleasant it had been to come into the drugstore and find him there eating. It had made her feel better all day. She disentangled Davey's fist from her hair and took him in her arms and jiggled him a little, hoping he would lift her mood. He was in a merry mood himself, but she began to cry. "I'll stop," she said, feeling silly. She said it again, as if Davey might be worried about her, but he wasn't. When she got tense and stiff he sometimes got stiff too, but she was the opposite of stiff, she felt as if she had suddenly gone all soft and muscleless. She got up and with Davey on her shoulder went to the kitchen and fixed herself some iced tea; she sat at the table by the kitchen window letting him play with the buttons on her robe. Her cheeks dried and she found herself smiling. She put her forehead against Davey's, something that always amazed him. Then her hair fell between them and tickled his nose and he rubbed it with his fist. It was funny; her lips curved happily. Things were not so bad, after all. She suddenly felt like getting out and popped Davey into his bed and dressed. As soon as Juanita came she went out and spent a happy afternoon poking in antique stores. She never bought real antiques, but she liked to poke in antique stores. She spent a pleasant hour going through a huge stack of old sheet music, reading the songs. All she bought was a tortoise-shell comb and a shabby book by Ouida that cost a quarter.

That night in bed she was trying unsuccessfully to read the book when Jim called. He sounded even more cheerful than usual.

"I was just reading Ouida," she said. "I'm thinking of going to graduate school and doing a dissertation on her. Are you really as happy as you sound? You never sound that happy when you're around me."

There was a pause. "Please quit that," he said. "You're always on the attack."

"I just asked a question. Is a question an attack?"

"Some questions are."

"I'm sorry," she said. "I didn't mean anything."

"It always sounds like you mean something," he said angrily. "You have a great memory for everything except the fact that I love you. You act as if I'm deserting you, just because I want to make decent money for once in our marriage."

"Okay, okay," she said, chastened. "Please don't go on about it. I really didn't mean to pick at you. I don't want to have an argument with you. I always just cry after you hang up."

"I knew you'd say something like that," he said. "Every time I criticize you, you tell me to stop or you'll cry. Aren't you tired of being a crybaby?"

"I'm tired of it, I'm tired of it," she said, dispirited. "Couldn't we forget I ever said anything wrong and start the whole conversation over. I really didn't mean to sound bitchy."

"I don't know what we can do," Jim said. "How's Davey?"

They managed, by talking of Davey, to be pleasant and chatty for the remainder of the call. Patsy was hoping he would say something nice, something gentler, before he hung up, so she could go to sleep feeling in rapport with him. Jim was hoping she would do the same. Both of them concentrated on not saying anything wrong; neither said anything very positive, or loving, or even spontaneous, and the rapport was not achieved. Jim felt guilty for having flared up, but it was a slight feeling of guilt that had made him flare up. He had yet to tell Patsy that Eleanor was in Amarillo, but she was there and he was infatuated with her and what Patsy had said about him sounding unusually happy was no more than true. It had been so true that he had had to attack it, but he felt even guiltier after he hung up.

Patsy continued reading. She was very discontent but hoped to read the discontent away. She hated to lie in bed awake, feeling cold and cut off, unwanted and untouched; but when she finally turned off the light, that was how she felt. She thought of Hank, but the thought only made her feel the more hopeless. She felt completely closed off, to him and everyone. If he tried to seduce her it would only make her feel the colder, or else make her angry, and she would drive him away forever and be truly alone. The nicest possibility she could think of was that he might be considerate and stay at the drugstore eating sandwiches a lot, so that she could go in and talk to him when she was lonesome. If he would only do that she might at least have a friend, and she could wheel Davey in from time to time and show him off. Somehow the thought of the three of them at the drugstore was very pleasing to her, and she lay awake awhile, considering which dress it would be best to be wearing when she saw him the first time.

The next two nights there were no calls from Jim, and Hank did not appear at the drugstore. She found that in the idle intervals of her day she could not help thinking about him or stop trying to imagine how their meeting would be. She decided it would be better if she could somehow manage to meet him first in company—at the drugstore or the library or with the Hortons, perhaps. In company she might be able to indicate nicely that he could not simply return and pick up where he had left off, if that was what he was planning on doing. In company she might convey to him by her manner, and with some delicacy, that their romance—such as it was—had ended when he left. The thought that he might think that he could come marching in after months in the wilds and simply grab her again brought back the feelings of hostility that she had had when she first read the letter. At times the feelings of hostility were very strong.

But Hank did not play fair. He chose to arrive at an extremely unlikely time, when Patsy had neither hostility nor thought: five-thirty in the morning. The bedroom was gray, barely light, when she realized someone was knocking on the door. She sat up, startled. No thought of Hank was in her mind at all. For a second she thought Jim must be returning, but Jim had a key. It must be Miri. Her mother had told her that Miri was wandering about the country with some friends in a Volkswagen bus. It would be just like Miri to arrive at five-thirty in the morning, totally unannounced and with several shaggy friends. But it would be good to see Miri, anyhow. She got up, yawning, and pulled on her robe. She went to see if Davey was all right. He was asleep on his stomach, with one foot poked through the railings of the baby bed. Then she hurried to the door and opened it, expecting her little sister to fall into her arms.

Instead, to her shock, Hank stood on the landing. He wore jeans and some kind of work shirt; he looked brown and his hair was tousled. Patsy had not belted her robe, but she held it together over her breasts, too stunned to do more than look at him. She was still half asleep, and despite herself, yawned again, not thinking.

Hank seemed to find that amusing. He smiled and, without asking, stepped inside the screen and put his arms around her and his cheek against her warm cheek. His face was browner. When he turned to kiss her, her hair got between their mouths and he stopped to brush it aside. Patsy couldn't think. In the kiss she became dizzy, almost lulled again into sleep and warmth, and too surprised to do anything but surrender. Hank moved his foot to steady them and stepped on her bare toes.

"Oh, damn it," she said. "Why'd you come so early?"

"I drove all night," he said, yawning.

They guided each other to the couch. Patsy found that her legs were shaky. "I was sleeping," she said, suddenly feeling awkward. When she sat down she tried to keep her gown and robe decently down over her thighs. Hank had never seen her look so desirable and pulled her to him, a bundle of woman still warm from the bed. Patsy felt dazed, confused; her face was so hot, so prickled with feeling that she felt it would singe if he didn't put his cool cheek against it again. In the midst of kissing, his hand worked its way inside her robe and began to stroke her bare shoulder; then it covered a breast and the feeling that went through her was so strong that she could only grasp his wrist and hold his hand where it was. She began to shake her head, to bump her face against his in soft protest, but it did no good; he had lost sight of her, the way he had so many times before. Soon the hand that had been on her breast got free and was under the robe and she began to twist, to move her loins back from his hand. Finally, almost desperately, she turned her hips and sat up, straining for breath. "No, what do you mean?" she said. "My son's in here."

Hank had not even noticed the baby bed behind its screen in the corner. He looked at it curiously; he clearly didn't think it was very important. She felt hurt that he should be so insensitive. Davey turned over and they heard the sound of his foot hitting the baby bed. Hank ceased being so aggressive and as soon as he did, Patsy began to feel comfortable and meek and quiet. "You've got to see him," she said. She stood up, belted her robe, and led him by the hand to the baby bed; she went and got her hairbrush and stood with her shoulder against his chest, watching Davey. He was rubbing his fist against his eyes as if he were about to awaken. "I wish you'd known him when he was younger," she said. "He's very changed now from how he was."

Hank yawned, not very interested in Davey. Patsy smiled. "See his toes, they're like mine," she said.

"So they are," he agreed, unable to think of anything to say about her son.

She grimaced and stepped to her dressing table to put down the brush. It suddenly felt odd, having him in her bedroom. "I don't know why men don't like babies," she said. "Don't you have a better shirt than that? The collar's fraying."

He frowned, as if he found it a little insulting that she should notice such things at such a time. He had to go to the john; she followed him partway to the bathroom and stood with her forehead pressed against a wooden doorjamb, waiting, feeling awkward, suspended, and a little dreamy. When Hank came out he kissed her again and touched her a little roughly; they were out of sight of the baby bed. Patsy was not offended, but she broke away. "Stop doing that," she said. "I can't breathe. Leave me so I can breathe—otherwise I can't cook. You're probably starved from driving all night to sneak up on me. You'd never have got in if I hadn't been asleep."

"Sure I would," he said, a little too positively. Her robe had come unbelted; she could not keep his hands off her.

"Damn it," she said. "Please go get the paper. I want to cook breakfast before Davey wakes up."

When he came in with the paper and his shaving kit Patsy was at the stove scrambling eggs, and there was a grapefruit on the table ready to be eaten. When the eggs were done she let him hold her a bit and stroke her back; she wanted to feel his hands on her shoulders, and by shrugging this way and that got the urge across. He slipped his hands under the robe and held her shoulders. Patsy smiled at her own wiles and broke free and piled up a huge breakfast—cereal, eggs, bacon, toast, and grapefruit. She left him to it and went to see about Davey, whose morning gurglings they had been hearing for several minutes.

She brought Davey in while Hank was eating and showed Hank to Davey and Davey to Hank, so pleased and unlonely suddenly that her face and eyes shone. Davey was hungry too and she turned her chair aside and fed him while Hank politely read the paper. Instead of feeling shy she felt content and comfortable and full. When Davey was full she strolled around the kitchen with him until he burped and then handed him to Hank, who was finished. She was hungry herself and ate an orange and some toast and strawberry jam. Hank was slightly awkward with Davey, but Davey was quite content to be held by him. He stared at Hank curiously while Patsy read the paper.

"It's almost worth getting ravished to be able to read Dear Abby without him slobbering on it," she said. Then Hank jiggled him too roughly and there was a rush of spit-up. "Should have warned you," she said, wiping the spit-up off his pants with a dishtowel. When she bent, her robe opened and she saw Hank glance at her breasts. "Sex fiend," she said, closing the robe. "He's peeing on you now, in case you hadn't noticed. Bring him in the bedroom."

Later, when Davey had been diapered and was grabbing happily at his butterflies, they sat on the couch again. Patsy stopped feeling cheerful and began to feel oppressed. She cried a little. Things suddenly seemed too much. She didn't know what was going to happen. Then the flurry passed and she calmed down; Hank kissed her wet cheekbones and wiped the last tears from the hollows beneath her eyes.

"I hope you like salty things," she said. "I'm always crying."

"Why don't you ever talk?" she said irritably a few minutes later. It was the most annoying thing about him; unless she talked they just sat silently. Instead of answering he began to kiss her again. Her conversation intimidated him a bit, and his kissing shocked her and left her more and more helpless. Davey was growing bored and was making squalls. They ignored him, and his squalls grew more insistent. Patsy felt very wanton, and Davey's voice in the background made her feel guilty and sexy at the same time.

She wanted to stay where she was but she finally got up and brought Davey to the couch, her lips curving merrily.

It was certainly a very odd morning. She saw that Hank looked tired; she felt unusually tender and sat stroking his hand, with Davey on the couch between them. Fifteen minutes before Juanita was due she made Hank go away. He had to find an apartment and she gave him precise instructions on what kind to get. His shirttail had come out, and she put her hand under it at the back—both hands, finally— and slid one up and down the trough of his back while they stood at the door. Her robe had come open and he kept drawing her hair tightly around her face. He went out on the landing but then stopped and looked back, smiling. Patsy realized that one breast was exposed. She pulled the robe tight and then stretched, tilting her head to one side so that her hair hung free. "Suffer, sucker," she said. "You'll never see that sight again."

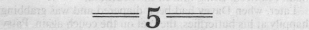

5

Eleanor did not stay at the motel. She didn't like motels and would not have stayed there even if there had not been the gossip factor to consider. The hotel she chose had a top-floor suite that she had stayed in before when it was necessary for her to be in Amarillo. It had a balcony, and she was very addicted to balconies. At night she and Sonny and Jim sat on the balcony, drinking and watching the white clouds move over the city and over the plains beyond the city. Then, when Jim was gone and Sonny asleep, she sometimes put on a robe and sat on the balcony alone, enjoying the breezes that crossed the plains at night. Rising at dawn and working all day was not what Sonny was used to, and he went to bed earlier than usual, sometimes by ten o'clock. Often, after he was asleep, Eleanor would see the ten-thirty plane from Dallas passing over the city, its red wing lights winking. Sometimes Sonny woke before midnight, to use the bathroom or ease a cramp in his leg, and he would usually grouch at her because she was not in bed.

"But I don't have to get up at dawn," she said. "I want to sit awhile."

Usually, though, she did as he asked. He always slept on his back and he liked her close to him, liked to draw one of her legs across his and hold it as he slept. He made love to her the night she arrived, but since then had seemed more interested in sleep than in sex.

"Who's been wearing you out?" she asked.

"That director. This was a big mistake, this movie. I didn't know making it would be so fucking dull. One day of standing around watching them move the goddamn cameras and I don't feel like doing anything."

She was there several days before she found a convenient time to call Joe Percy. Sonny was putting in a guest appearance at a rodeo fifty miles away.

"How are you?" she asked when Joe answered the phone. "I thought I'd wait to call until we could talk."

"Where's your steady fellow?" he asked.

"Borger. I think he wishes he could get back to the life he knows."

"I wish he could too," Joe said. "With all my heart I do. Then I could get back to the life I know."

"Did you bring that little car you had in Hollywood? I wouldn't mind being taken for a drive. I wanted to at the time but you didn't suggest it."

"Oh, the Morgan. No, I left it home. I could call the studio and have them air mail it. When am I going to be blessed with your company?"

"I'm not sure. I'd just as soon Sonny didn't get the idea that we were old flames. At times he's pretty possessive."

"Can't blame him," Joe said. "This is no place for intrigue. Trying to have an affair in this town would be nerve-racking as hell, no matter who you are or who it's with. Monogamy must have been invented for dumps like Amarillo."

"I'm curious about the starlet I read about," Eleanor said. She had been curious about the starlet ever since she came to Amarillo.

"Catherine? Do you really care?"

"Yes, I care," Eleanor said.

"That's depressing. What's the good of millions of dollars if they can't keep you from being jealous of Sonny's conquests?"

"So she's his conquest. Is that for sure, or is that just your opinion?"

Joe hesitated. His opinion was that Sonny screwed Catherine Dunne in her dressing room, in her motel room, in his motel room, and in the hearse, pretty much as the spirit moved him. But he didn't want to give his full opinion.

"They may have done it just to be able to put one another on their scorecards," he said. "It's unlikely either of them gives a damn about the other."

Eleanor was silent. "You seem to have made a kind of conquest yourself," he said. "Jim Carpenter can do nothing but sing your praises."

"He's young and easily dazzled," Eleanor said. "I like him a good deal. He's very bright when he's encouraged to be. He seems to like being in the movies. I think he feels a little guilty for going off and leaving his wife and baby."

"He ought to feel guilty. His wife's a delight. So far as I can see, you and her are the two best things Texas has produced. I wish one of you were President."

"Me and her," Eleanor said. "I'm not sure I like the sound of that. How would you rate us?"

"Cut it out," he said. "If you're not going to come and see me you don't get to be jealous. Besides, I don't really know her. We've had two slightly moony conversations in which I waxed profound about life and love. She soaked it up as if I knew what I was talking about."

"I guess I'm just still peeved because Sonny chased her home that night in Phoenix."

"Well, like it or not, he does get around on you, honey," Joe said. "I doubt it was Patsy's fault."

"That's no consolation," Eleanor said. "I wish I knew why talking to you makes me feel so domestic."

"That is a mystery. What do you want to do, come over and wash my socks?"

"I wouldn't know how," she said. "I never washed a sock."

They chatted a few minutes more, inconsequentially, of this and that, and when she hung up Eleanor went out on her balcony and looked down on the lights of the city. She felt very melancholy, but it was a familiar late-night melancholy, one that she had known for years. She did not expect to be alone long enough for it to get serious. Somewhere on a road to the north the hearse with the horns painted on it was already speeding back toward Amarillo. Sonny would be different for having been to the rodeo. She had never known a rodeo not to leave some residue of excitement in him, and whatever it left always got through to her. They seldom approached each other casually after he had been to a rodeo. Always he had that recklessness about him that made him so beloved of the crowds—it showed in his walk, his manner, his way of smiling. Frequently she hated him at such times, for he was never more arrogant or less affectionate. Sometimes they fought, sometimes they made love, sometimes they did both—whatever they did was apt to be violent. Sonny made the terms at such times; if she didn't like them it was too bad. Frequently she didn't like them and fought with him and left, but almost always when she left she regretted it bitterly later. Then, after quiet months at the ranch, or travels that were too smooth, to places she had been, there would be moments, hours, sometimes days, when she was forced to wonder if she had ever been really alive, really in the mainstream, or the maelstrom, or whatever it was. Only the memory of those nights with Sonny after rodeos, when they were both at their wildest, convinced her that she had. The fights were terrible, for she fought to have him all, or to be done with him completely, and neither thing was possible. And the lovemakings generally began as fights, with her cornered near some bed. Her anger did not give way to gentleness, but it gave way to something rawer, something more compelling; then her greed sometimes grew faster than it could be fed. Sonny hated her at such times. She outlasted him, exhausted him; in such a state he could not scare her, could not intimidate her. She held the power and it disturbed him. Sometimes he left, sometimes he fell asleep. Sometimes, though, he was too much; he beat her at her own game. Sometimes the greater energy was his, and he weakened her so with pleasure that she became frightened. It left her hopelessly at his mercy; it was hard to fight him when her body was not with her. Her body was with him, and only some part of her intelligence, some woman in her skull, fought desperately for existence while the rest of her cleaved to Sonny. Sometimes she fought free and left. She would have to keep fighting as she dressed and often would get caught again and pulled back to the bed. It was at just such times, when he could have let her go, that she might abruptly turn the tables on him. When her fright turned back to hunger it was usually Sonny who left. He could sometimes stop her when she tried to leave, but she could never stop him. When he started out, he went. If she managed to get away, she could not relax for days; her body kept wanting him and expecting him; but if he left her she knew it was over for a while, perhaps for a long time, and she lost all fear and nervousness, soaked in a hot bath, and slept in deep relaxation. But whether she left or he left, the memory of such times was a comfort in empty seasons. She need never doubt that she had had the real thing. The real thing sometimes got too real, while it was happening, but she would not have wanted to be without it.

In coming to Amarillo she had known there would be a problem, but she had supposed it would be Joe Percy. Instead, it was Jim Carpenter. She had all but forgotten him and was surprised the night of her arrival to see him approaching with Sonny. She remembered then how attractive he had been to her in Phoenix, and it was evident before the night was over that her attraction had not dimmed. He put himself out conversationally, and it was obviously for her benefit. He immediately made something of a fool of himself by attacking the Vietnam war in a company that was conservative in the extreme. Jim apparently assumed that she shared his liberalism, which she didn't, but she liked him for the way he defended it. His boyish attempts to dazzle her had their charm and their appeal, all the more so because he was young and romantic and idealistic in a company that might almost have personified cynicism. The company consisted of half a dozen Panhandle aristocrats, cattle and oil barons and their fattening wives, people who were just polished enough to have remained naïve about the ruthlessness of their own motives, but who took for granted the ruthlessness of everyone else's. They all, men and women alike, admired Sonny—he was most of the things the men would rather have been than what they were, and one of the people the women would rather have had than who they had—so it was a great evening for him. Nothing made his ego shine like the admiration of people who were wealthier than him. At first it puzzled her that he had brought Jim along, but then she saw that Jim was as awed by him as everyone else, and that explained it. Sonny loved to awe.

Later, the party over, they chatted casually about Jim. Eleanor was undressing and Sonny was sitting on the bed in his briefs wiggling his ankle and frowning.

"I think your young friend is going to turn up with a crush on me," she said.

"Jimbo? He's had a crush on you ever since Phoenix. One of the reasons I hired him. I thought if I kept him around to admire you, you might stay and visit awhile."

"I don't think I'm quite that vain," she said. "Why don't you do your own admiring?"

He looked at her shrewdly and lifted an eyebrow, and Eleanor felt annoyed, for she was in very good shape. She had been strict with herself for months, had exercised and ridden and dieted and had just spent a week in a very expensive beauty spa. She was feeling splendid and felt she was looking splendid and she wanted him to say so.

"You are right shapely," he said, but with mock gallantry. "All these Hollywooders will be trying to zap you the minute they see you. That's what they call it now. About all we do all day is sit around and bullshit about zapping

"You brought enough clothes," he remarked, watching her hang up her dress. "You didn't use to carry around so many clothes."

"I didn't use to be forty-four, either," she said. "I find they do more for me all the time."

Sonny snorted with amusement and she looked around at him, but she didn't explain. He had been thinking precisely what she just said—she had reached the age where he liked her better with her clothes on. That evening at dinner she had been just the way he wanted her. Every man at the table had felt a little more male because she was there, and had envied him for being the one to bring her. The way her presence worked on the men had been a real pleasure to him. But watching her cross the room in her slip didn't make him feel anything, and when she took the slip off she didn't seem quite such a prize. Her calves were a little thin, her thighs a little slack, her behind slightly too broad, and with her hair undone and her makeup off, it all told.

"Zap sounds like something you do with a ray gun," she said.

"Naw, that ain't what they use," he said. He didn't mention that on several occasions he had zapped Catherine Dunne, whose twenty-three-year-old thighs, breasts, midriff, bottom, and face were perfect and twenty-one years fresher than Eleanor's. Nor did he tell her that his steady zapping for the past month had been with a girl named Angie Miracle, who had a very small part in the film. Angie lacked Catherine Dunne's perfect face, but she was only twenty-one and her body was the color of a nicely turned French fry. He had never zapped anyone with such a perfect tan, and it was consistent right down into her pubic hair. She had spent five years on the beaches of Southern California and could surf and could dance and was, so far as he could remember, the limberest girl he had ever zapped. Angie had been annoyed when she heard Eleanor was coming, and had moodily arranged to get herself zapped by a young camera-man.

Eleanor's tan did not compare and her legs did not compare, and it irked him, watching her prepare for bed, that she could not hold what she had had at the dinner party. She came to bed more eager for him than he was for her. Her body had ceased to interest him, whether tempo-rarily or for good he didn't know.

Often, in the days that followed, he felt like kicking hell out of the young cameraman. Angie Miracle knew how such things should be handled, and she never said a word about Eleanor or went out of her way to talk to Sonny. She passed him on the set as indifferently as if he were a statue. One day in a flash of anger he attempted to trip her, so she would have to acknowledge him, but she avoided his foot as gracefully as if she were doing a dance step and went on her way without speaking. Sonny was not used to being walked past, nor was he used to any of the things he was doing. For the first time in many years he was in a situation that inhibited him at every turn. Every day he grew tighter, more irritable, and more exhausted. When he had decided to do the movie he had merely assumed that acting would suit him, particularly simple acting. Numerous people in Hollywood told him there was nothing to it. When the shooting began and he discovered it wasn't so simple as he had supposed, he was not immediately worried. He would catch on to it quickly, he assumed. Everyone on the set was patient with him; no one treated him like the fool he felt himself to be, and he kept his presence off camera even when he lost it on.

But he had never been a foolishly conceited man. He was a shrewd judge of ability, his own and other people's, and he knew quite well that he knew less about what he was doing than anyone in the cast. He could feel his own stiffness, his own awkwardness, and it infuriated him. His confidence was so natural that he had long since ceased to be conscious of it, but he was conscious that it deserted him the minute he went under the cameras. He was at a loss as to what to do, and his frustration carried over into his leisure hours. Ordinarily he would have given Angie Miracle a good shaking and gone right on zapping her when he felt like it. And ordinarily he would have insulted Eleanor and got rid of her. She was proud and brooked very little insulting, and would have gone home on ten minutes' notice if he had rubbed her wrong. But he kept her there and didn't make love to her, and he put up with Angie's snubs and didn't approach her. He became a little more short-tempered with the menials of the crew, and he kept Jim Carpenter in his company more and more, bringing him to the hotel almost every evening to eat with him and Eleanor.

At first, none of it registered on Eleanor. All spring she had been in a mood to make crucial decisions, but in the end she had made no decisions at all. She felt herself at a crossroads. She had to decide whether to marry, but she couldn't; it was too abstract a decision. She knew no one she wanted to marry, and yet she felt the urge to be married. She felt she was at an age when she must marry if she was ever going to. If she didn't, her life from then on until she died would be the ranch and traveling, and traveling and the ranch. That she could marry well, find someone attractive, someone likable, someone she might even love, she didn't doubt. It would only be a matter of putting herself out a little, letting herself be found. She would only have to stay for a time in places where there were good potential husbands. But she didn't go to any such place, nor ever came close to going.

From time to time she heard from Sonny. Sometimes she saw him, often she thought about him. It seemed to her that it was time she made a decision about him. It had been a long time since he had taken her away in his hearse to Oak Cliff and brought her into womanhood. She had few regrets, but one regret she did have was that both of them had fought so long against the notion of marriage. She had been almost forty before she got around to admitting to herself that he was, for better or worse, the only man in her life, and by then they had buffeted each other so long and so strangely that neither of them thought a marriage possible. They had something strong—no doubt of that—something essential, but it brought her no peace and she had begun to want something more like peace. She thought of giving him up, shutting him out, but she never got around to it, and when he asked her to come to Amarillo she was nearer a decision about him than she had ever been. The ranch was settling into its summer lethargy and she had idly considered and put off a trip to Scandinavia. When he called her the fourth time to demand that she come to Amarillo she acquiesced in five minutes. Peace was not so all-important after all, and crucial decisions could be made in the fall, or during another spring.

She was a little surprised, after a few days, to discover him so listless. Listlessness was something she had never seen in Sonny. Usually they came together at times when they were both whetted for each other, but Sonny was not whetted at all. He was not even eating much. He had always taken meals as he had taken her, sometimes leisurely, sometimes quickly, but always with a relish that communicated itself at once. Yet in Amarillo he seemed to have lost both appetites, and it worried her.

Jim Carpenter didn't worry her, not even when it became obvious that the crush he had on her was going to be a serious crush. His infatuation was as obvious to Sonny as it was to her. Sonny took it so for granted that it irked her a little. It was if he had deliberately procured Jim to pay her courtesies and gallantries and small attentions so that he himself would not have to bother with her at all. Jim's pleasure in her company was quite genuine, of course, but the fact didn't lessen her irritation with Sonny.

When Sonny came in from Borger, not long after midnight, he was, as she had expected, more like his old self than he had been since her arrival. Rodeo was his world, and he was the biggest name in it. In Borger he had only to ride a horse into the arena to get a standing ovation; that and a couple of hours standing around the chutes talking to cowgirls and absorbing the adulation of young contestants had restored him. His official function had been to crown the rodeo queen, something he did with aplomb. The kiss he gave her was one of the high points of the young woman's adolescence. He left the arena feeling good and whirled the hearse back over the plains, the wind whipping his shirt sleeves. When he came into the hotel suite, Eleanor was still sitting on the balcony watching the clouds. He emptied his bladder and pulled a chair up beside her. He crossed his feet on the stone railing and put his hand on the back of her neck.

"You'd have a balcony if you was to live in China," he said.

"Lots of balconies in China," she said. "I've been there. Did you crown the queen?"

"Yep. Tried to get old Jim a date with her but he wouldn't have one. At least he got to see the sights of Borger." He put his hand under her robe and rubbed her leg, squeezing occasionally so that she felt the full strength of his fingers. "I think the only reason he went was because he thought you might go. He was talking about how depressed he was that he had to go in and call his wife. Can't blame him. I wouldn't want to talk to her, either. Sharp-talking little bitch. If he had slapped her down three or four times when they was first married she might have cut that out."

"Slapping's your method, is it?" she said. "Do you think my tongue is properly dulled?"

"Duller than Patsy Carpenter's," he said.

Eleanor moved her leg away from his hand. "Pawing's your method too. That was a stupid thing you just said. Go back to your rodeo queen."

He reached for her leg again but she scooted her chair out of reach.

"What I meant was that you ain't ordinarily as mad at me as she is, day in and day out. I know you're both smart as hell. You both got tongues like razor blades."

"I don't like to be compared to her," she said. "Why is she mad at you, day in and day out? I didn't know you saw her that often."

"Ain't seen her since February." He scooted over so that he could put his hand on her neck again. She tried to pull away but he tightened his fingers and she couldn't. She relaxed and he began to rub her gently behind the ears. It was enjoyable, but she was still irritated.

"What did you do to make her mad when you saw her in February?" she asked.

"Well, I never screwed her," he said, "so why don't you shut up about it. I came out here to enjoy the breeze, not to argue about her."

"Fine," she said, getting up suddenly. "You enjoy it. I'm going to bed. I obviously don't interest you, anyway. Who *have* you been screwing, if not her?"

He looked away without answering, his expression a little sullen, and she went angrily into the bedroom and yanked the spread down on the bed. The thought of Patsy filled her with fury. She tried to imagine what could have taken place in February—a tussle of some kind, she imagined. She heard him get up from his chair and come into the room behind her, but she didn't turn around.

"What's the matter with you?" he asked, catching her shoulder. She shrugged loose and turned on him.

"You're what's the matter with me," she said. "I just realized it. Who do you think I am?"

"A goddamn silly woman," he said, growing angry but still trying to treat it lightly.

"Don't call me silly," she said. "I don't know what I'm doing in the same county with you, much less the same bedroom. I didn't come up here to sit on a balcony for a week while you cavort around with starlets and rodeo queens. You've hardly even looked at me since I've been here. I'm going home. I'm sick of you."

"Shut up," he said. "I didn't come out here to start any fight. You're too old to be acting this way."

Eleanor's arms were shaking. "I'm forty-four," she said. "Forty-four. And I've wasted fifteen good years letting you push me around, just because you got to me at the right time, in the right way. Well, so long, buster, you've had me. Maybe it's time I started on young men, since you're so good with young women—starlets and bitchy young wives and the like. Maybe I'll find me someone young."

"Maybe you'll get your goddamn teeth knocked out first," he said, no longer trying to hide his anger.

"Cheap talk," she said. "Go try and scare somebody else. You don't have any guts, all you've got are big muscles and a big ego and a big mouth. Your heart's the size of a knuckle and I don't even think you have a brain. Well? My teeth are still clicking and my razor-sharp tongue is still slicing. I don't see you doing anything about it."

They stood quivering, two yards apart, neither moving. Both were filled with such uncertain rage that they couldn't act. Eleanor was not sure whether to slap him or to run—for all her talk, he frightened her. Every time his arm moved she expected to be hit. For seconds they simply stood.

"I wouldn't talk to a dog the way you talk to me," Sonny said. "You call me gutless again and I'll break your goddamn neck. Wasn't for me, you never would have been screwed. None of them fairies you was brought up with had the guts to kiss you, much less do nothin' else."

"Thanks very much," she said. "Thanks for fifteen years of your splendid charity. Now why don't you get out and go help some other poor creature with her womanly troubles? I can get by on my own from now on, thank you."

"Go on, then," he said, turning away as if he meant to drop it. "Go back to your ranch and let Lucy get you fat. I guess you've worn everything out but your goddamn tongue, anyway."

"You *bastard!*" she said, tears suddenly streaking her face. A purse of hers lay in a chair nearby. It had a long shoulder strap and as he turned away she grabbed the strap and swung the purse at his head as hard as she could. He had taken his eyes off her for a second and the purse caught him on the neck, but his reflexes were very quick and before she could swing it again he grabbed the strap and yanked her toward him. She tried to cling to the purse but Sonny easily twisted it out of her hands. He whirled and threw it out the door and off the balcony. She tried to slap him but before she could swing her hand, he punched her on one shoulder so hard that she was knocked backwards and fell against the endboard of the bed. After the minutes of quivering, unsupported tension the shock of the hard bedboard against her back was almost a relief. Sonny reached down and caught her by the shoulder, meaning to pull her up, but she writhed and kicked at him and managed to scoot away. "Get out, you bastard," she said. "I wish I'd broken your neck." And she did. The *whop* of the purse against his head had been very satisfying. Undignified as it was to be crouched on the floor glaring at him, her shoulder slightly numb and her side aching, still she felt good, felt she had won. He had said the unforgivable, finally, and she had struck back as hard as she could, and she was sure, for a moment, that that did it, finished it, made it over. After that remark he would never be able to reach her again. She looked him in the face, not at all scared, indeed triumphant, proud that finally she had outdone him, berated him into a mistake that he could not undo. Her lips curled. For a second in the battle she was enjoying herself.

But the enjoyment was brief, because Sonny did not understand her, or did not care to. He dropped to his knees and shook her violently so that her head whiplashed. "You don't kick me out," he said. "You started this, and for no goddamn reason in the world."

As she was being shaken the sense of triumph dissolved and the words he had said earlier began to burn. "I . . . had my reasons," she said. "You . . . never give me any hope, you don't know how I . . . hope for things."

"Hope for things," he said, his hands still on her shoulders. One of her shoulders hurt and she twisted, trying to make him ease his grip. "What do you need to hope for? You've got half the money in the world."

"Oh, hell," she said. "You goddamn child. Quit squeezing."

"You fucking well better shut up," he said flatly. She looked back at him, still furious.

"What will you do, throw me off the balcony?" she said. "That purse had a thousand dollars or more in it. What's in me that you want?"

"Nothing," he said. "You can't make me, any more than you can take care of me . . . or give me what I hope for. You treat me like a teenager."

"You act like one."

"No," she said. "I'm acting like a woman scorned. And I scorn you back, you callous son of a bitch. Turn me loose so I can leave. I never want you to touch me again."

In desperation Sonny tried to kiss her. He wanted her to shut up and he had to kiss her or slug her. She strained back and butted his face with hers, then twisted her face aside. Eleanor's hair was tangled in her face, they were both panting, and their breaths crossed.

"No," she said. "I don't want you to."

He finally caught her head in the crook of his arm and kissed her, but she killed it by being passive. "I want to go," she said when he took his mouth away.

"You're not going nowhere," he said.

"I am. We've done all this. Maybe I liked it when I was young. Maybe I thought it was the way women ought to be wooed. Maybe I was melodramatic." She could not stop talking and he kissed her again. She met it passively, but it was not so easy. She wanted to do as she had always done—let go, meet him. But part of her refused. "I meant it," she said. "I've changed. I don't want you."

Sonny had passed through violent anger into a state of complete exasperation. He tried to put his hand on her and she fought it, and he could not make her stop talking. They had passed the point where their anger usually turned to passion, and she was still talking. He lifted her and pitched her unceremoniously on the bed. Then, before she could move, he went to the lamp and the light switch and turned them off. The room was dark.

"Shut up, Eleanor," he said. "You're not going nowhere. I'm coming to bed."

Eleanor sighed. She stayed where she was. In a moment he was in bed beside her. They were both out of breath.

"Turning off those lights was a smart move," she said in a minute. "I can't stand the sight of you right now."

"That's the way I feel about you too," he said. He reached for her leg and began to stroke it, but it was not really a caress, it was something he did automatically to calm himself. She scarcely felt it and he scarcely felt her. The tension and fury began to drain out of Eleanor and she lay quietly, feeling beaten but not so bitterly beaten, after all. She had just worn down, she was too tired to go anywhere, and anyway, she had stopped feeling such hatred of him. It might have been her fault—she had cut him terribly. She put her hand on his wrist to slow the stroking.

"Come on, relax," she said. "I won't dig at you any more tonight."

But it was not to be quite that simple. Sonny's anger was gone, but a tension and a restlessness remained. He was too keyed up to go to sleep. He was not finished with it—or with her. He too lay quietly, but angry statements welled up in him. He never said them, but they turned in his mind. He wanted to say something that would hurt her so badly she would have no strength to fight, no will to attack him again. But he knew her well enough to know that, with her, there was no certain kill. Worn down, beaten, half asleep, and she was still dangerous. So he held his words and when his restlessness did not subside, ceased stroking her leg automatically and began to caress her in earnest. The minute he did he felt fine, for he knew that in desire he was more stubborn than she was, particularly when she was tired. In that state she could be dealt with. When what he was doing reached her she tried to stop him. "No, please don't," she said. She felt too spent already, too tired in spirit, to either join him or fight him. And she was tired in body too. For a minute it seemed as if he might revive her, but he didn't; in her protest she had been right, she was too spent. Sonny was the opposite; the fight had lifted him out of his boredom. He was a long time with her, and Eleanor became sad, tears streaking each of her cheeks, for she loved that strength and if she had not spent so much of hers in fighting they could have had much more from the night. She had wasted herself. When he did grow tired, when he had had enough, she felt tender toward him. She was wakeful in her fatigue and saw by his face in the dimness that so far as he was concerned all was well again. His face closed in some way when he was done. He became his own man again, without the need of anyone, and she smiled at him. "Am I really worth the trouble?" she asked, and did not expect a flattering answer. He was getting out of bed to go to the bathroom.

"Yeah, once in a coon's age," he said without turning. "Before you go to sleep call the desk and tell them to look for that goddamn purse."

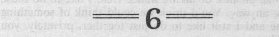

"Don't say those things, Emma," Patsy said. "Please don't sound so hopeless."

But Emma looked hopeless. She seldom cried, but she had just cried for twenty minutes. The crying had left her clear-headed, and she was not feeling particularly sorry for herself any longer. She was feeling realistic, and it was the things she said after she calmed down that had Patsy on the verge of tears. Crying was one thing, but dispassionate hopelessness was much worse. In her concern for Emma she didn't even notice that Davey, on the floor at her feet, had found a Tinkertoy and was about to pop it into his mouth. Emma reached down and took it away from him and he began to fret. She got up and found him a toy truck in compensation. He gummed it and began to slobber.

"He's teething," Emma said. Patsy scarcely noticed.

"But I know he loves you," she said, meaning Flap. "He's bound to."

"Oh, probably," Emma said in a tone that wrung Patsy's heart. "It doesn't really seem to matter. Sometimes he's good to me, but then there are times like this summer. I think I would be less upset if I thought he didn't love me.

We've loved one another for ten years now and it ought to have changed things more fundamentally, don't you think?

"Damn it," she added flatly and was silent awhile. "And it's nothing, really. It's just some deficiency in me, I guess. He's working himself blind studying for those exams—why should he be bothered to cater to my whims?"

"What whims?" Patsy asked, looking down at her son, who was chewing the truck.

"Well, not whims exactly. I just have to have about fifteen minutes' masculine attention a day or I get blue. If I'm not flattered every day I get sour, and Flap just doesn't want to bother with flattering me any more, or fucking me any more, or doing anything with me any more. The only things we really enjoy together any more are things we do with the kids, like picnics, or taking walks. Hell, I like to do those things, anyway. You'd think we could think of something that he and I still like to do just together, privately, you know?"

"I bet it's just the exams," Patsy said. "They must be a terrible strain. Flap's so good-natured I can't believe he'd mistreat you if it wasn't for some reason like that. After all, the exams sort of decide your life."

Emma sighed. She stuck her foot out and waved her toes in front of Davey. He grabbed her big toe and tried to get it in his mouth, but she grinned at him a little wanly and wiggled it so he couldn't. He grinned too and held on to the toe. Patsy felt sad. From being messy but still content and still glowing, Emma had grown wan, and her sloppiness did not complement her wanness as it had complemented her glow. Her hair was dull; when her face was alive and changing it didn't matter, it went with her. But her face had fallen. It didn't dimple or change, and the only things alive in it were her sorrowful eyes.

"It isn't just exams," she said. "It's always irked him that I need him. It doesn't bother him that he needs me to cook for him and take care of the boys and get him clothes and be here when he wants me, but it strikes him as utterly irrational and weak that I should want to be flattered ten minutes a day."

"Can't you just tell him what you need?"

"I tell him all the time. 'Quit pestering me, you know I

464

think you're great,' he says. Sometimes he doesn't even look up from whatever he's reading."

"Sounds like Jim," Patsy said and grew confused. It was the first time Jim had crossed her mind in days. It reminded her that she too had a marriage that was far from ideal. Hank had been back three weeks and she had almost ceased to think about Jim or worry about her marriage. Jim was apparently not worrying about it either, for he had taken to calling only once or twice a week.

"If you and Flap aren't happy I guess nobody is," she said.

"Oh, don't look so blue," Emma said, smiling, for it was obvious to her that despite a temporary melancholy her friend was happy. When she had come in that morning, in sneakers and shorts, with Davey in his carriage, she looked as lovely, as blooming, and as full of happiness as Emma had ever known her to look.

"You don't look so bad," Emma said.

Patsy felt even more confused. Emma did not know that for more than two weeks she had been an adulteress. Several times she had wanted to speak of it, but the words never came to her lips. The Hortons knew Hank was back, and whenever his name came up Patsy felt deeply uncomfortable. She knew within herself that she was not going to speak, that she had not the courage to expose what she was doing, even to Emma, and yet she could not master her confusion. She reached down and swooped Davey up in her lap to cover what she was feeling.

"Who knows?" Emma said, yawning. "I don't care any more. I can't think of any way to change anything. I'm not going to change and he's not going to change. I want what I want, by god, and I don't think it's fair that I should have to want any less. I can't help my deficiencies. I get as twitchy as a teenager when I'm ignored for days. We just have temperamental differences, that's all—nothing's going to make them go away. I just don't know what to do that would be worth doing. I can't leave him—I don't even want to. What would the boys do without him? *I* couldn't even do without him."

Patsy tried to imagine Emma and Flap living apart and couldn't. Emma had always had Flap. They had been engaged when she and Patsy met. Emma too tried to imagine separation—as she had several times—and couldn't. The best she could do was to imagine herself in a posh job, or the sort she would be very unlikely to get.

"Maybe I'll just have to train myself not to want what I want," she said. "He never trains himself. All he does is study. God help us if he fails those exams."

"He won't fail them. Jim always said he was the sharpest graduate student here."

"He better be. I'm not going to put up with any failures from him. If he failed the exams and tried to use me for an excuse I think I'd kill him."

"I'm glad I'm not in school," Patsy said. "I hate artificial pressures like that. Essential pressures are bad enough."

"Flap used to be so enthusiastic," Emma said wistfully. "That was what I loved about him first. Now he isn't enthusiastic about anything and lack of enthusiasm about life just kills me. I have to have someone who's enthusiastic or I can't operate."

Just then there was a howl from the driveway, where the boys were playing. They both listened, hoping the howl would diminish, but instead it rose higher and higher. The cry was from the throat of Teddy, and in a minute the door slammed below and they heard the boys on the stairs. Teddy burst in, howling and weeping, and flung himself into Emma's lap. Tommy came in behind him, trying to appear calm but betraying a certain nervousness.

"Oh, baby," Emma said, hugging Teddy. "What's the matter?"

"It's nothing really serious," Tommy said. "I just ran over his toe with my tractor."

At that Teddy made an effort to choke off his sobs, and he fought clear of Emma's lap. He plopped himself down on the floor and held up one foot mournfully. One of his toes was bleeding slightly and another was a little skinned.

"Oh, poor toes," Emma said. "That's not so bad, though. You can have a Band-Aid."

But Teddy's temper was up. He shook his head and pushed out his lower lip. He contemplated his injured toes unhappily, and clearly felt he deserved more sympathy than he was getting.

"Was this an accident, Tommy?" Emma asked. "Did you tell Teddy you were sorry?"

"Oh, sure," Tommy said. "I told him I was sorry."

But Teddy shook his head in vigorous denial and gave Tommy a dark look. Davey was staring at the boys with his usual solemn amazement.

"He says you didn't tell him you were sorry. Who am I going to believe?"

Tommy came over, keeping a judicious distance from Teddy, whose sorrow seemed about to turn to violent rage. "I didn't really tell him I was sorry at the time," he said. "I wasn't really sorry at the time. But later I told him I was sorry."

"You mean after he began to howl," Emma said. "Maybe he didn't hear you. Couldn't you tell him again? It might help matters."

There was a silence. Tommy pondered; Teddy waited.

"Well?" Emma said.

"I asked him to move," Tommy said. "He was standing in my beanfield and I needed to plow. I asked him *several times* to move."

"Couldn't you have plowed around him?"

"It was my field," Tommy said, frowning. "Teddy could have stood somewhere else. I was going to grow a beanstalk and he was standing right where the stalk was going to come up. I needed to plow right there so it could come up."

"They're big on farming just now," Emma said. She tried to smooth her hair back from her face. "I gave them some seeds, but it's not working out very well. If he asked you to move, why didn't you move a little, Teddy?"

Teddy's vocabulary was filling out. "No," he said, looking sullenly at his bloody toe.

"Look," Emma said, reaching down and shaking his foot. "You do not need to be stubborn. When Tommy asks you nicely to move off his beanstalk, move off it. Then your toes won't get tractored."

"No," Teddy repeated, giving her a dark look.

"So it wasn't my fault, was it?" Tommy asked. "I had to plow, so the beanstalk could grow. Teddy even said he was going to pull it up when it did grow."

"Me beanstalk," Teddy said, getting up. He gave Emma an all-right-for-you look and meandered over to Patsy. "Me toe," he said mournfully. Tommy had begun to edge toward

467

the door, with a view in mind of going down to plow, but Teddy saw him. "Me beanstalk," he yelled, red in the face with fury.

"It's my beanstalk!" Tommy yelled back, even louder.

"All right, hold it a minute, Tommy," Emma said. "I think farming's out for now." She suggested they play jungle; the suggestion diverted them and they pattered back down the stairs.

"I've got to take this one home," Patsy said, standing up and lifting Davey to her hip.

"I'm ashamed of all that crying," Emma said. "Flap's not as bad as I make him sound. Maybe I need a girl. All these males get me feeling outnumbered."

"What would a little girl be like?" They were silent—neither knew.

"I'd just have another boy," Emma said, and she laughed like her old self and followed Patsy down the stairs.

Davey was inserted into his carriage with some effort.

"Come back to see us," Emma said, yawning. She looked sleepy and relaxed and no longer nearly so blue. "Next time you need to cry about the miseries of marriage let me know and I'll listen."

"Okay, perk up now," Patsy said, but she wished Emma had not made the last remark. She didn't think she would be crying about the miseries of marriage with Emma any more, because Emma, unhappy or not, was still a good wife. Come good or bad, Emma was true to Flap. She herself, with much less reason to stray, had strayed anyway, and whatever miseries came her way as a result she would have to cry about alone. She couldn't tell Emma.

As they were walking home they met Flap pedaling home for lunch. He waved and said, "Howdy, y'all," but his look was almost hostile, as if he suspected Patsy of having just listened sympathetically to lies about him. He looked despondent and paranoid, his hair needed cutting, and he didn't stop, as he normally would have, to stall her in the broiling sun for ten minutes while he chattered and admired her legs or her looks in general. He didn't even glance at her legs, though she wore shorts. He kept pedaling. It made her almost angry with him, for he had established a kind of lecherous ritual with her, involving unserious flirtatious remarks, and it seemed rude that he should pass her so curtly. But that too was bad for her, for it was Emma who needed Flap's flirtatious remarks and his attentions. She felt it was sad that Emma had got herself in such a hole with a fickle, inattentive man—Emma of all people, practically the one person she knew who was steadfast in her affections.

The carriage was unshaded and Davey was hot. By the time she got him home Davey was yelling as loudly as he could yell. Juanita heard them and came down the stairs and gathered him up, and Patsy, still sad, followed them up to the apartment, bringing the baby gear.

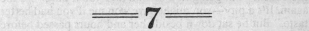

7

The sadness was still with her that afternoon when she made her way through the sullen, sticky heat to Hank's apartment. To her intense annoyance he had chosen an apartment only two doors from his old apartment, on the same dead-end street. Except for a slightly less faded couch and a noisy old air conditioner it was exactly like his first apartment. The sight of it made her angry, and had continued to make her angry every time she stepped into it.

"I knew you weren't perfect," she said the first time she went there. "You have an utter lack of exploratory zeal. You can survey the whole goddamn Panhandle but when it comes to finding a decent apartment you won't even drive around the block. Did it ever occur to you that there are apartments in Houston that aren't on Albans Road?"

"I was tired from driving all night," Hank said. "I didn't feel like looking very hard."

"Oh, sure," she said, flinging open the closet and sniffing as if she expected to smell a dead animal. "You could have

stopped at a motel and slept and then arrived at a normal
hour. You drove all night so you could sneak in on me when
my defenses were down. Then you're too tired to drive
around five minutes until you passed a pleasant apartment.
I can't stand lazy men. I'm going home to my son."

"I don't think this one is so bad," he said. He didn't think
it was bad at all, but he watched her closely to see if she
really planned to go. Evidently she didn't. She was striding
around the room, growing more and more furious.

"It's awful," she said. "Stark, dusty, and awful."

"I didn't know it mattered. I'm not especially attached to
it. I can get another one next month."

"Where, next door? No, thank you. I *told* you it mattered,
five minutes before you left to go look. You just stay right
here and find a girl who likes ugly furniture and dust."

"Maybe it can be fixed up," he said.

"Never, it's hopeless," she said moodily, sitting down on
the couch. "I'm going in a second and you'll never see me
again. It's a pity—you might have won me if you had better
taste." But he sat down beside her and hours passed before
she left.

When she came up the back stairs and into the room,
Emma on her mind, Hank saw at once that she was
unhappy. She didn't frown at the apartment, or look in the
icebox, or come to him to be kissed; she walked into the
bedroom, took off her clothes, and got in bed without
speaking a word. She pulled the sheet up to her chin and lay
looking at the ceiling, her mouth curved down sadly.
"What's wrong?" he asked, sitting on the bed.

Patsy shook her head. "I'm just low," she said. "Emma's
not happy. I think we're all done for—I really do."

He tried to kiss her but she wouldn't let him, so he stood
up and began to take off his clothes. "I don't feel done for,"
he said.

"You aren't married," she said and looked at him hostilely when he slipped into bed beside her. "If I were married to
you I'd do for you soon enough."

Hank had already learned that he could not talk to her
moods. The few times he had tried he had only made
matters worse and got sliced to ribbons in the process. He

didn't like to talk to her unless she was in extremely good spirits; otherwise he kept silent and relied on his one constant asset: his physical presence. He lay beside her and held her as closely as she would let him, and Patsy's spirits began to rise, almost imperceptibly. She was not as sad as she had been when she undressed. It was pleasant to lie with her cheek against his shoulder, his arm across her breasts. After a time she turned her head and bit his shoulder, thoughtfully but hard. "I ought to be whipping myself with nettles," she said. "Poor Emma. She's miserable all the time now because she's good. I'm not good and I'm too shallow even to stay sad two hours out of sympathy."

Hank had no interest in Emma or her troubles; what he wanted was to make love. But the intensity of Patsy's moods had already taught him caution, and he waited until her spirits had risen to a safe level before he turned to her and asserted himself. It was very successful. They dozed, and Patsy awoke first, feeling calm and happy. She was quiet and very tender to the touch, and she lingered past the time when Juanita was expecting her home. When she finally got up and put on her panties and bra Hank was still on the bed and she could not resist going back to lie down for a few more minutes, to rub her cheek against his shoulder. It was only in the alley, as she was making her way home in the heat, that she thought of Emma again and felt guilty. Somehow the thought of Emma made her feel guiltier than the thought of Jim. The horns of the five o'clock traffic sounded on Bissonnet, as virtuous wives and husbands made their way home to their equally virtuous mates. She had just been reading *Anna Karenina*, and for a moment saw herself as the Anna Karenina of Albans Road. Perhaps someday, instead of the railroad track, she would fling herself under the five o'clock traffic and be laid out dead in the driveway of the filling station. A crowd from the Seven-Eleven would gather to view her remains, grocery sacks and beer cans in their hands.

But by the time she got across the street she had stopped feeling guilty, and when she got home to Davey she was quiet and cheerful and very calm. The feeling that suffused her was something new—it had not come immediately. Her beginning, with Hank, had been so nervous and weak that she had almost given the whole thing up at the outset. Nothing had been wholehearted. Clothed, they seemed close, but naked they were strangers—awkward strangers. Patsy was terribly disappointed. She could hardly believe she had fallen from virtue for so little pleasure. Months she had been without sex, and yet at first she had to strain very hard for even a small tweak of orgasm, and that left her so flat that she could not even cry wholeheartedly. It had been lovely discovering him, and even lovelier letting him discover her. Love was the only word she knew to use for the feeling it gave her. And then the seduction reduced it, made it all small. Hank too was low. Patsy went home, the first time, and showered and fed Davey and found herself even without remorse. She could not feel remorseful for having done something she hadn't enjoyed. For a few hours she felt a kind of dull relief. To have found adultery so piddling and unattractive made her feel clearheaded about marriage. She had got less pleasure than she had had with Jim, and she considered it a lesson well learned. It was trivial, really trivial. She had learned the hard way and need have no more foolish hopes.

That evening when Hank came over, she let him in without nervousness, thinking there was no longer any reason to be nervous; surely he would not want her again after she had been so depressed and so depressing. She fell deep into self-pity, waiting for him to arrive; it seemed she was not meant to have a very sexy life. But when he came in both of them ceased feeling depressed. They forgot the dismal afternoon and lounged around together, watching a hilarious Peter Sellers movie on TV. The warmth came back and they felt cheerful again, and to her surprise, sexy again as well.

She went back to him the next day and the next and soon knew that she was not going to stop going, even if she wasn't finding it as wildly sexy as she had thought it would be. If she wasn't, Hank at least was; no one had ever wanted her so badly, and his desire drew her back. He made her feel so wanted that she couldn't stay away; her own feelings seemed almost irrelevant. He was so greedy that it left her shaken. He was not especially considerate about it, either. He was so keen for her at first that he rushed over her own feelings and gave her little chance to catch up with him. Nothing went quite right for her at first. Their bodies did not behave in classic fashion, as bodies were supposed to. Graceful beginnings gave way to amazing awkwardnesses; they found themselves snarled in tangles of garments and bedclothes from which passion alone could not extricate them. Sober cooperation was often necessary. Such things deflected her, sometimes completely, but nothing seemed to deflect Hank for long. She came back day by day to the place where she was wanted, and gradually the fact that she was off pace in the lovemaking ceased to disturb her. Apparently it didn't disturb Hank at all; he had not even mentioned it, and she was grateful. His silence on the subject made her feel the more prized. She stopped feeling self-conscious. His own desire was blind—it was for her, but it took little account of her, except as a body, and once she got over being shaken by it she found she liked it that way. It was also mute, his desire. There was no talking to it, and she found she liked that too. Once she relaxed and accepted the new terms on which she was desired, she began to respond, and soon responded more strongly than she ever had. In the hot afternoons, in the dim apartment, questions of heart got blurred; they seemed secondary. For all she knew of them Hank's emotions were in his penis, or his hands. She realized she scarcely knew him, but she didn't care. The focus of her curiosity shifted suddenly and became physical. She was more curious about how it felt to touch him or be touched by him than she was about what he was thinking or what his emotions might be. She concentrated on his body and hers, and for whole afternoons was almost as silent as he had always been.

Then one day, snooping, she opened the tiny little broom closet and discovered that there was an old guitar in it. It had not been there the week before, when she had looked in the broom closet. She was naked; they had made love and Hank was dozing. She felt cheerful, loose, and hungry. She had gone to the kitchen to make herself a peanut butter and honey sandwich. As she was looking at the guitar some of the honey dripped out of the sandwich onto her hip. She wiped it off with a finger, ate the sandwich, drank some milk, and went back to bed. She lay on her stomach, looking at Hank for a while. Her hair covered her shoulders.

"Whose guitar?" she asked when he awoke. "And where have you been hiding it?"

"Oh. It was Daddy's," he said. "It was in the back end of the car."

"Why hide it?" she asked. All he had ever said about his father was that he was a small-time hillbilly musician.

He didn't answer her question. Instead, he put his hand on her and began to play with her gently, but as he did he looked past her, over her shoulder, avoiding her eye. It bothered her badly. She wanted him to look at her, not over her shoulder, when he touched her. For the first time in days she felt alone. Though they didn't talk much, she felt completely open to him, and the look chilled her, for it made him seem very closed somehow.

"Well, are you ashamed of him, or what?" she asked. "If you have some kind of father hang-up I'd like to know it. Don't look away from me."

Instead of telling her what she asked, Hank told her his life story. It was an unpleasant life story and unpleasant to listen to because he didn't look at her while he was telling it. His face had a sulking look, as if she had insulted him by asking him a question. In the days ahead she was to discover that he hated to be questioned and always sulked if she persisted in pursuing some point about his character or his feelings or his past. All she was to remember about his life story was that his father and mother had been killed when he was six; their station wagon collided head-on with a truck full of oil-field equipment on a bridge over Red River while they were on their way to a dance at an army base in Oklahoma; that he had been raised by a mean aunt in a trailer house in North Fort Worth; that she had once whipped him with a clothes hanger because she caught him masturbating over a picture of Esther Williams; and that once he and a gang of boys had found a dead Mexican baby in a warehouse they broke into on Christmas morning. From time to time, when he wanted sympathy, he told her more about his past—sad, wretched details from his loveless adolescence, usually—but only the first recital really touched her and even then she didn't like the tone in which he spoke. She took him in her arms afterward and petted him and kissed him, and her sympathy was genuine. She was moved that he had at last spoken to her about himself. But the self-pity with which he spoke bothered her, even the first time. She didn't like it. She had no doubt that she would pity herself if she had lived such a life, but that didn't matter. She didn't like self-pity in him. She was sorry, going home, that she had found the guitar and asked about it, for she didn't feel as secure or as happy as she had been before she asked.

Still, she was happy. That he occasionally pitied himself was, at the time, a very small erosion. They had three lovely weeks of mutual discovery, the weeks stretching themselves as weeks never had for Patsy. Time stretched as she stretched on his bed, and she seemed always to be stretching, turning lazily, stretching as she dressed, as she turned to check the time or turned to check him. The act in the bed took on an importance it had never had and that she had never expected it to have. For a time only Davey held his place with it. Everything else moved to the perimeter of her life. The Hortons scarcely saw her; Juanita got little out of her. Jim had almost ceased to figure, since he had almost ceased to call. There was Davey in the morning and the late afternoons, and Hank in the morning, or the afternoon, or at night, whenever it could be managed. The days had suddenly become complete—there was nothing more to want, nothing missing at all. She was too happy in body even to lament the loss of her virtue. Occasionally, late at night, combing her hair before her mirror, she would remember that she was adulterous and would brood for a time, but she could not feel really remorseful. Her body made it impossible; she simply felt too keen to be able to feel bad. Everything she did, with Davey or with Hank, was really pleasing. Her future, her position, what would happen when Jim returned—those were things she seldom thought about. Her days were a constant motion, and she could not disengage from the motion long enough to do much thinking. She awoke when Davey insisted she awake. He was charming in the morning, once she had taken him out of his bed. She fed him and dawdled with him a bit and then fed herself, rather amply usually, French toast and Canadian bacon and orange juice, reading the paper from the headlines to the auction notices while Davey sprawled on the clean kitchen floor at her feet, amid balls and plastic blocks, sometimes grasping her toes or the hem of her nightgown. She had decided that estate auctions might be fun to go to, but she somehow never got around to going to one. Her son and her lover left her no time. After breakfast she bathed Davey and they lounged on the bed, talking to each other in their different languages until Patsy began to feel energetic. Then she would dress and pop him into his car seat and off they would go. Davey would be admired by her grocer, her druggist, or whoever happened to be in the park. She had found a nice garage man who had given the Ford a good going over, and it got them wherever they were going. Juanita came at noon and Patsy gathered a few notebooks for cover and strolled off to pursue her studies, generally stopping at the Seven-Eleven to buy whatever sandwich makings appealed to her. Then she went to Hank's apartment. Sometimes he would be at the library, pursuing real studies, which was okay with her. She snooped, made herself a sandwich if she was ready for one, listened to his records, most of which she disapproved of, or lay on the couch reading *Middlemarch,* her long book of the month. Hank had a somewhat soiled Riverside edition that he had read as an undergraduate in a course in the novel. It had his annotations in the margins, most of which Patsy thought extremely dull. Occasionally she wrote in counter-annotations.

His books were mostly paperbacks and mostly shabby, which she found pleasing after watching Jim pile up impeccable copies. Some of Hank's marginalia were so solemn that she penciled in expressions of despair beneath them. He had so little to say to her, about literature or anything else, that she could not really imagine him teaching, but she did not particularly care what he did or planned to do. She was quite content to seize the day.

Sometimes she undressed and got in bed and slept until he came. He liked to tiptoe in and awaken her by putting a cold bottle of Fresca between her breasts; when he did Patsy generally sat up and drank half of it, and the small ring of moisture the bottle had made would dissolve and trickle down her stomach. She felt a kind of bodily luxuriousness she had not known before. Everything she did seemed simpler. Her former self, in so far as she could remember it, seemed frantic in comparison with her new self. She was silent more and could sleep almost any time she found herself on a bed. Nakedness no longer made her feel awkward or scared. There was no knowing what the horn of carnality might yield on a given day—anything from a cool touch to a rough, sweaty excitement. All she knew when she went to his apartment was that it would be hours before she left. Finally, after the luxuries of the afternoon, she would dress and stroll home and take Davey for a walk down South Boulevard, under the great arched trees. When he was put to bed she made sandwiches and Hank came and they ate and drank beer or iced tea. She read magazines; he might read Jim's books; they watched television and sometimes made love again, on the floor, safely out of view of the baby bed. Patsy found she liked it on the floor, and Hank liked it anywhere. When he left she was so sleepy she had only to crawl in bed to be asleep, but Davey had no trouble waking her in the morning. Morning was welcome. Davey had never been better, and the greens of Houston had never seemed lovelier. She had developed a fondness for Bob Dylan and often cooked breakfast to wild harmonica.

Their first real fight was over something very minor. Hank had gotten into a long conversation with Kenny Cambridge and was very late in getting to the apartment. Patsy was petulant. When she found out it was Kenny he had been talking to she became furious. He never talked to her at all; what could he have had to say to Kenny that was so important. Hank couldn't remember—it had merely been a conversation. She became furious. In her furies she was always silent, for a time. Hank, like Jim, was very unnerved by her cold silences. He tried to kiss her—the only tactic he knew—and she became volubly angry and tried to leave. Hank wouldn't let her go. He blocked the door and dragged her back to the couch. Patsy succumbed, coldly, and when she got a chance tried for the door again. He dragged her all the way to the bed. It was as hard a contest of wills as she had ever fought. She would have jumped from the second-story window if she could have; she stood up in bed to see if it was feasible, but Hank dragged her down again. She fought until she simply wore out. She was very rumpled, her chest heaved, she was out of breath and bedraggled and felt herself ruined and wretched and messy, a disgrace and ugly.

Hank was as ruffled as she was rumpled; when she finally stopped fighting he almost wished he had let her go. The look in her eye was anything but friendly and he didn't know what to do or say. He tried stroking her cheek and she allowed it, but then she took his hand and after holding it a minute bit his palm as hard as she could bite, annoyed with his pretense of patience. He pretended the bite didn't hurt but she coolly inspected the teeth marks and knew it had. That pleased her, but angered him. He fell on her, trapped her head, and began to kiss her.

She was too tired to fight but she didn't want to be kissed. "No, no," she said. "Please let me go. I'll give you fifty dollars. I'll give you a hundred dollars. I want to go." She meant it, but somehow the idea of offering him money to let her leave struck them both as amusing. They ceased to fight in earnest and began to haggle in fun. While they were haggling Hank got his hand on her, and the negotiations became confused. "Good god," she said, sitting up to struggle awkwardly out of her dress and underclothes, "I can't believe it. If you'd taken either of my offers I'd have given you up forever."

There was a long calm, afterwards, and Patsy felt very clear in it. Hank was sleepy. "It's a good thing you're potent," she said. "If you ever become impotent I'm quitting you on the spot. I'm not going to be ruined for nothing. If I'm getting ruined I want lots and lots." While he slept she showered, and she came out feeling very energetic. She decided to go empty all of Jim's bookcases and spray them for bugs, something she had promised often but not done. She came into the bedroom, beads of water still on her body, rubbing herself with a towel. His bureau had an inadequate square mirror on it that had always annoyed her. "Do I look wasted?" she asked. "Isn't one supposed to get wasted from a lot of sex? I can't tell from this wretched mirror of yours." She bent forward, still nude, and began to comb her hair, and then flashed him a quick merry smile to see if he really thought her wasted. But he was still asleep and had not even heard the question. She flung the towel down, finished combing her hair, and began the search for her panties. Somehow, nine times out of ten, they managed to get themselves flung far afield, under things or into out-of-the-way corners.

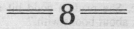

"Oh?" Patsy said. "When did *she* arrive?" Jim was on the phone and Davey was beside her on the bed, all bathed and powdered. She had been tickling the soles of his feet when the phone rang.

"You sound like you've got something in your mouth," Jim said.

"A grape. Concord grapes." A pile of them lay on a napkin by her elbow. Davey watched the phone. It was an instrument that interested him and he would have liked to be able to reach it.

"You didn't answer my question," Patsy said. "When did Eleanor Guthrie arrive?"

"Oh, she's been here a couple of weeks," Jim said. "I forgot to mention it.

"I haven't seen much of her," he added, but he shouldn't have. His voice didn't carry the statement well.

"Then why do you sound so defensive?"

"I'm not defensive," he said defensively.

"Have her looks faded yet?" Patsy asked. She felt a touch of anxiety and a touch of jealousy at the mention of Eleanor's name, and when it soaked in that Eleanor had been there two weeks and Jim had not reported it, both emotions increased.

"No," Jim said. "For god's sakes. She looks fine."

"You scrutinize her, I take it?"

"Look," he said, "be nice. We got rained out and I thought I'd call. Let's don't fight."

"Aren't you ever curious about your son?" she asked. "He's right here with me."

"Sure I'm curious," Jim said, but once again it didn't sound convincing. He could barely remember Davey.

"I suppose Eleanor and her paramour are staying nearby?"

"She stays at a hotel. Sonny stays here."

"How lovely. You and she are friends now, I suppose?"

"Well, sure," Jim said. "Sort of. I have dinner with them once in a while. She reads a good bit and likes to have someone to talk about books with."

"Great," Patsy said. Suddenly she felt vicious. "I stay around here cleaning the bugshit out of your goddamn bookcases while you hold profound literary discussions with an aging heiress who's screwing a bull rider. What a sucker I am.

"Or maybe your relationship's changed," she went on. "Maybe it's deepened. Maybe now that she's aging she sees there's more to life than bull riders. Probably she knows how to value a man with sound literary opinions. Maybe she's cast Sonny out and made you her Pekingese, or something."

"Oh, shut up," he said. "You're such a bitch."

Patsy ate a grape and kissed Davey's stomach. "She has a sweet disposition too, huh?" she said. "Millions, a good mind, and a sweet disposition. If her looks weren't fading she'd be perfect, wouldn't she?"

"You sound like you don't think yours can compete," Jim said.

"My looks can compete," she said. "You'll just have to lump my disposition, I guess. Are you in love with her?" She looked into the phone intently, as if by doing so she could see his face.

"Of course not," he said.

"Don't sound so positive," she said. "You could be, you know. Vague as you are you might not have realized it yet."

"Do you love me?" he asked.

"I guess," Patsy said, getting another grape. "I did the last time I saw you. I don't like the thought of you and her sitting around being literary critics. Deduce what you want to from that."

"Pleasant dinners are hard to find out here," he said. "Why should I deny myself a normal social life?"

"Joe Percy reads books. Let him eat with her. Actually I don't care. I'm just feeling bitchy."

"I wish you weren't. You sound so small when you're this way."

"I am small," she said, making a face at Davey. "I've just noticed that literary chitchat between men and women is apt to lead to fucking."

Jim was silent, very surprised. "Did I hear you right?" he asked. "When did you start using that word?"

"Just then, I guess. I might as well use the words everybody else uses."

"What about Davey?" he asked and realized it was a silly question.

"We speak very frankly. Are you insinuating that I'm a bad mother? I was meaning to ask you when you had in mind picking up fatherhood again?"

"That's one reason I called," he said. "I was thinking you and Davey might come up this weekend. We're almost done here. We'll probably be going to L.A. the last of next week."

"What? We? You too?" She was genuinely startled.

"Yes, the whole crew. I didn't know they'd want me, but they do. It will only be for about three weeks. I'm not sure I can get through Houston on my way. That's why I thought the two of you might come here."

"Great," Patsy said, angry and hurt, and surprised at herself for being so. In theory, she should have been glad he was going, for his return would complicate things immensely. But instead of being glad she felt like crying.

"Is Eleanor going to L.A.?"

"I doubt it. I haven't asked her."

But he knew she wasn't going, and one of the reasons he had asked Patsy up for the weekend was to clear his conscience on the score of Eleanor. There was a week's moving break and she had asked him to stop by her ranch for a day or two. He was looking forward to it very much, but he could not decide whether to tell Patsy or not. He knew she would be jealous.

"I *bet* you haven't asked her," Patsy said. "I bet you know her schedule for the next six months. You probably even know when her periods are due."

"Quit being so goddamn bitter and suspicious," he said.

"Why? You never come home. You hardly ever call. Davey will be in school before you see him again. How can you stand just to wander away from us like that? Now you're getting friendly with a beautiful millionairess. Why shouldn't I be insecure? Are we married or not?"

"You act like I've been gone for a decade," he said.

"It seems like it. Davey thinks the world is composed entirely of people with breasts."

"So come up and see me. That's what I called to ask."

She was balky and anything but enthusiastic, but in the end she agreed. She and Davey were to fly up on Friday and back on Sunday afternoon. As soon as they hung up she put Davey in his carriage and wheeled him down the Boulevard for a morning walk, very perturbed. Life was shifting—nothing could be kept in focus. She could not understand why the bile had flowed so when she found out that Jim liked Eleanor, or why it had bothered her that he was going to L.A. She was not lonely and would not be lonely. Certainly she had no ground for sniping at him about Eleanor. She was the adulteress, and anyway the two of them probably did only talk about books. The thought made her a little contemptuous of them both. She found that she had no desire at all to go to Amarillo. The very idea of bundling up a lot of baby paraphernalia and taking it up there was ridiculous. And what she and Jim would do with each other she could not imagine. Perhaps she would no longer be able to get in bed with him, even to sleep. Or she might discover that nothing he did, to her or anyone, mattered to her in the slightest any more. What then? She could not think of a worse place in which to have to cope with such imponderables than Amarillo, Texas.

When they got back to the apartment, both of them hot and a little prickly and irritable, she found another imponderable sitting on her steps. It was Flap Horton. His bicycle was propped nearby. He was sweating, one lens of his cheap sunglasses was cracked, and he took them off and squinted at her as she wheeled Davey up the driveway.

"Hi," she said. "To what do we owe this pleasure? You look hot."

"I'm exactly as I appear," Flap said. He stood up and lifted Davey out of the carriage for her, which was a help. Davey was getting heavy. Flap, the seasoned father, treated Davey with authority, and Davey responded to it and behaved. Flap's mustache interested him.

"I'll lug your infant up for you," Flap said. "I came by to borrow a couple of books. Someone seems to have absconded with most of the seventeeth-century scholarship."

"Sure," Patsy said. "Have a beer and cool off. How's Emma?"

"In the doldrums," he said. "Tommy's got an ear infection from too much snorkeling. Teddy's got a pseudo ear infection, in imitation. I've got prelim-itis and Emma sits around and cries most of the time. We're our usual happy selves."

"That's awful," Patsy said. "I think I'll give you a lecture, but maybe you should have a beer first."

"I better have two beers," Flap said, grinning. "Lectures are largely wasted on me when I'm sober. Where do you want Davey?"

"In his bed. Why don't you change him while you're at it? He's a sop. It's not often I get a man over here who knows how to work a safety pin. You want a sandwich while I'm at it? It's the least I can do if I'm going to blast you."

"Sure," Flap said. "Any largesse will be appreciated.

"Got any goose liver?" he asked. "I'm the only one in my family who likes it, which means I never get to eat it."

"I don't think so," she said. She stood in front of the air conditioner for a minute, lifting her hair to cool the back of her neck. Flap put Davey on the bed and began to mumble to him in a fatherly way while he removed his diaper, and she kicked off her shoes and went to the kitchen. She made a fine sandwich and put some pickles on a plate and opened the beers and brought them in on a little tray. Davey, snugly diapered, was kicking on the baby bed, and Flap was reading one of Jim's books.

"Odd-looking cheese," he said when he saw the sandwich.

"Looks great. Will Jim care if I borrow this? He's sure neat about his books."

"It's sickening," she said. "Don't judge that cheese until you've tasted it. I mean his neatness is sickening. Borrow what you want. I don't care. He's going to L.A. and won't be back for another month. By the time he gets back he may have forgotten he's a book collector. I suppose Bill Duffin, the great scholar, will remind him of it."

"Don't mention that name," Flap said. "It gives me a hunted feeling."

"Me too. Except I guess he's quit hunting me now. Why is he hunting you?"

"I don't think he wants me to pass my prelims. Emma says I'm paranoid, but Emma doesn't know him."

"You are paranoid," Patsy said. "Quit worrying. Graduate school isn't the whole world."

She was swinging her legs a little as the rocker rocked, and Flap looked at them and grinned his old rakish grin. Patsy noted it and frowned at him, but in a friendly way. It was hard to be angry with Flap when his eyes lit up.

"I'm glad to see you've recovered your interest in life," she said. "Still, you might as well quit letching."

"That's my only interest in life," he said.

"Then letch Emma," she said. "Why aren't you good to her any more, by the way? That's what I was meaning to blast you about. I used to think you were the best husband around because you kept Emma so happy. Why aren't you doing it any more?"

"I guess I just forget to," Flap said simply. "Could I have another beer?"

Patsy went and got it for him. "Well, try to remember to," she said kindly, for he looked a little sunken. He glanced over his shoulder at the scholarly volumes on Jim's shelves as if they were the Eumenides.

"It's making me sick," he said. "What if I fail those damn exams? I don't even dare mention the possibility around Emma. She either becomes hysterically angry or hysterically hysterical. I'd probably have to kill myself if I failed them."

"Nonsense," Patsy said. "You know worlds of stuff. Why should you fail?"

"I shouldn't," he said. "I should pass. It's the element of whim that scares me. Besides, I have theories and opinions. What if I put in the wrong ones?"

"Don't. All you have to do is be precise."

Flap looked at her caustically, as if he had never received less helpful advice in his life. "Thanks," he said. "You're as helpful as Emma. All she says is 'You're gonna pass.'"

"You worry too much. Drink more and eat more. Look at girls' legs if it really helps. I would hate to think a set of exams could daunt *you.*"

"I ain't daunted, just skeered," he said, standing up. "How many books can I get away with borrowing? For some reason Jim's books look more readable than library books."

"Not to me. Take as many as you want. He can only kill me." Flap carefully picked out four books and put them in his blue bookbag.

"I thought bookbags were supposed to be green."

"Only if you're from Harvard. Thanks for the meal. You sure have pretty legs. I wish you'd decide to have a fling with me."

"Get on with your studies. I'm your wife's best friend."

"So what? She makes friends easily."

"Is Tommy really sick?"

"He had two bad nights. It's hard for a kid to sleep with his ear hurting."

"We'll bring him a little present."

Flap stepped out into the white noon and put on his cracked sunglasses. He slung the bookbag over his shoulder. "Bring Teddy a little something too, if you do," he said. "He's feeling underloved just now."

She went back and got Davey and sat with him on the couch. She liked the way the books tilted over where Flap had removed volumes. It was tempting to rearrange the books completely. She decided to do it but then sat and kissed Davey on the top of his head and wondered. Flap, for all his faults, was a comfortable man, and it seemed to her that when all was said and done, her sloppy friend Emma had made an excellent choice, and probably had more basic good sense than she herself would ever have.

9

Flap had scarcely left when Juanita arrived, and none too soon to suit Patsy. The thought of the weekend ahead made her restless; she slipped her shoes on and was at the door, ready to go to Hank's when the phone rang. It was her mother, calling from Dallas, and the moment she spoke Patsy knew something was wrong.

"What is it?" she asked. "What's wrong?"

There was silence on the wire.

"Is it Daddy? Is anybody dead?"

"No, no," her mother said, almost wistfully, as if simple death would have been preferable. "It's something that . . . upset me. I was wanting to come down and see you today. You and Davey. I could stay at a hotel."

"You can stay right here," Patsy said. "Don't be silly. What is it? Please don't cry." For she could hear the beginning of her mother's tears on the phone, and her mother's tears, once started, were apt to flow for days.

"I'd rather not talk over the phone," her mother said. "All these extensions—anyone could pick one up. I'm so distressed about Miri—it's her."

Silence again. "Well, what has she done?" Patsy asked. "Has she been arrested or anything?"

"No. Has she written you?"

"We never write. What's she done?"

"I don't know," Jeanette said. "I'm just so frightened, though. I'm afraid she may be involved with a colored man."

"Oh, goddamn," Patsy said, both relieved and annoyed.

"You didn't have to scare me so. I thought somebody was dead."

"I know, but I was too upset. I called and one answered the phone."

"For god's sakes," Patsy said. "Isn't that jumping to conclusions? Maybe she's hired a butler or something. What did he say?"

"I hung up."

Patsy was twisting with impatience. She wanted to be at Hank's. "Listen," she said. "Get a plane and come on. I'll call Miri. It probably isn't half as disastrous as you think."

She hung up and went to Hank's, so agitated that she forgot to buy anything to make sandwiches with. Hank was not there. The apartment was dark and cool, but not chill in the way most Houston apartments were. The air conditioner was too old. It gave the air a musty smell that she had come to like. It seemed to her, in moments of fantasy, that real people, who hadn't money, probably lived their lives amid such smells, in such apartments, and she loved to lie on the couch and imagine herself an underprivileged housewife, one with a struggling young husband—the kind of wife who never wore stockings except to faculty teas. When Hank came in she was still on the couch, an empty milk glass on the floor beside her. Her thoughts were swirling—now to Miri and a possible Negro lover, now to her mother and the night of tears that lay ahead, now to Jim and a weekend that she could not imagine.

"I hope you've eaten," she said. "I forgot to get anything."

His appetite was of a different nature. Patsy was dizzy with willingness. It was bliss to be presented with a desire that blew away all that had been swirling in her head. Miri, Jeanette, Jim, all blew away and were replaced by the feel and smell of skin. They made love immediately on the couch. Afterwards they found themselves unduly sweaty and garment-plagued and got up and undressed and went to bed, to rest. Patsy rubbed her cheek against his shoulder. She told him about her problems but got little response. He never thought her problems were serious. He was reading *Tristram Shandy* but with reluctance. She dozed, and when she awoke the air conditioner seemed to have played out

completely and she was sweating. Hank was fiddling with it.
Everything beyond the bed seemed tinged with unreality. It
seemed to her she had at last found a way to manipulate
time. She felt like she had been on the bed for weeks. If she
could just stay there, more weeks might pass with nothing
bad happening.

When he sat down she stroked the smooth skin over his
arm muscle. He hadn't tried to stop her from going to
Amarillo, and she was a little annoyed. "I guess you can
finish *Tristram Shandy* while I'm gone," she said. "It would
hurt my conscience if I interfered with your studies." But
she was fishing. It wouldn't have hurt her conscience at all.
She was beginning to wonder what would. She wanted him
to ask her not to go. If he had, she would have found an
excuse to back out. But her hints never reached him, and
finally, feeling distinctly petulant, she showered and left him
to *Tristram Shandy*.

Miri simply could not be reached. Patsy tried four times
before her mother arrived on the doorstep, fighting tears.
Patsy popped Davey into her arms, hoping to plug the dike,
but it didn't work. She had to snatch him away again and
divert him as best she could from the spectacle of her
mother crying herself out. It was not hard to divert him, for
her mother cried quietly, like a gentlewoman.

"But you really don't know that anything's wrong," Patsy
said. "You really don't know a thing."

"I know," Jeanette sobbed. "If I knew maybe I wouldn't
act this way. When I see Davey I can't help crying."

"What's he got to do with it?" Then she realized that
Jeanette was envisioning him with a black cousin. Finally it
was Juanita who calmed Jeanette down. She took her into
the kitchen, made her some tea, and told her in her own
hesitant English about the various horrors that had befallen
her own daughters, in Old Mexico and South Texas. It left
Jeanette feeling that her lot was only the lot of all mothers.
"You have such a nice maid," she said, after Juanita left to
catch her bus. "I wonder how those people survive. Of
course Daddy and I were poor once, but we didn't have
these problems then."

"What problems did you have then?" Patsy asked, curious.

"You know, I don't really remember. Garland was very anxious about money. I guess he was afraid he wouldn't be able to provide for me. I wasn't anxious much, I don't think. You and Miri were both such dears as children that we never had to worry about you at all. You were both so sweet and pretty."

"But then we grew up," Patsy said. "What a change that's wrought." She was silent, trying to imagine Davey grown up to be a man. Was it possible that the day would come when she would be sitting, tear-streaked and poorly made-up and fifty-five, making one of her daughters nervous because another of them, or Davey, had grown up and was making what to her were hideous mistakes? She jiggled her son on her lap and could imagine it, for there might be thousands of girls, of all colors, whom she would not want him to marry. She sighed and Jeanette sighed and they turned the talk to Davey, who was cheerful. He helped the afternoon pass.

Late in the afternoon she took Davey and Jeanette next door to visit the matronly widow who lived there. While they were making a fuss over Davey she sneaked back home and managed to get Miri on the phone.

"You okay?" she asked.

"Sure," Miri said.

"I can't talk very long. Momma's here, going out of her mind with worry about you. Have you got a Negro boy friend, by any chance?"

There was a pause. "That isn't any of her business," Miri said hostilely.

"*I'm* the one that's asking. I don't care—I just want to know. I'm having to fight battles for you on this end. It's pretty tacky of you not to come home all summer. No wonder they're worried. You can have an Eskimo boy friend, for all I care."

"You're not really very different from her, though," Miri said.

"I *am* very different from her, and you know it."

"Well, there are lots of boys around. I don't classify them by colors. Are you still living with Jim?"

489

"I'm *married* to Jim," she said. "Why wouldn't I be living with him? He's in Amarillo making a movie right now."

"That's what I thought. I think you probably need some boys around."

Patsy was startled. "Listen," she said, "don't bitch at me. You're not all that worldly, just because you smoke marjuana. If you've got such good boys around why do you sound so bitchy?"

"I'm too much for them," Miri said. "You don't really know me any more. You're back there. It's different out here. Out here it's great."

"It's too bad there are no men there who can handle you, if it's so great," Patsy said. "I'm going to tell Momma you don't have a Negro boy friend, if you don't mind."

"It's a lie."

"I know it's a lie, but it will make her sleep better. It doesn't hurt to consider *her* a little, you know. She loves you, even if you don't like her."

"Okay," Miri said, sounding a little chastened. "I don't want her to worry. We were going to come to Texas but our Volks broke down."

"You sound like you've had a wild freshman year. Have you been taking LSD?"

"Sure. Have you?"

"No. I'm too old. I guess I missed it."

"Out here you don't have to miss anything."

"Okay, dear," Patsy said. "Try to miss getting pregnant or busted, if you don't mind."

The story she fabricated for Jeanette was so successful that she almost regretted it. All she said was that Miri was dating a law student from Stanford, but it cheered Jeanette up immediately and left her so grateful that Patsy scarcely knew what to do with her. She had meant to fly back to Dallas the next morning, but she decided to stay another day and enjoy her grandson. The morning turned out to be more trying for Patsy than the tearful afternoon had been. Once cheered, Jeanette became everything that was irritating to Patsy. She cooed too much over Davey, overpraised Patsy at every turn, and was enthusiastic at depressing length over Jim's new career. She went on about how glad she was Patsy had made such an ideal marriage, how much Garland liked Jim, how reassuring it was to them that they were so normal and well married, how they could hardly wait for another grandchild. Patsy gritted her teeth. In desperation she took her to Emma's, where Jeanette outdid herself in complimenting Emma on a rather dowdy dress and her generally shabby furniture. The only dark cloud on Jeanette's day was the Ford, which struck her as unnecessarily old and low class; she remarked four or five times how all the car dealers in Dallas were friends of Garland's. They would, she was sure, bend over backward to give them a good deal on a new car. "No, thanks, we like this one," Patsy said grimly.

But the Ford was a small cross to bear. Once back home, Jeanette began to overflow with compliments—on the books that looked so interesting, the pictures that were so novel, Patsy's new clothes, the matronly widow next door, the Whitneys' well-kept back yard, the sandwich she was given for lunch, Patsy's infinite skill in handling Miri, Juanita's neatness, and the spotless state of the floors and the silverware; even the iced-tea glasses were worthy of compliment. Patsy became grim, very grim, and was extremely glad when Juanita came to draw off some of the compliments. She felt on the verge of blurting out that Miri was taking LSD and sleeping around interracially, in order to turn the compliments back to tears. In sorrow her mother seemed human, forgivable, lovable even; but when happy she seemed like someone who had been created entirely by a second-rate advertising firm, someone whose chief function was to keep repeating testimonials to all products, no matter how dreary, and all approvable ideas, no matter how banal and empty. Even from the bedroom, as she was rocking Davey, she heard the drone of her mother's compliments from the kitchen, the inflections rising and falling in a Southern rhythm, interrupted now and then by Juanita's slow English.

Jeanette, after a little subtle prodding, had decided to leave that evening on a six o'clock plane. It seemed to Patsy that six more hours of compliments would be unendurable, particularly since Davey would be asleep for three of them. She rocked him, her cheek against his, wishing she could rock him all afternoon, but when she put him in bed and confronted her mother again she felt dry and nervous. Jeanette wanted to talk about Miri; she felt optimistic and wanted Patsy to tell her what to do to win back Miri's confidence. She was dutifully prepared to try anything Patsy could suggest. Her optimism depressed Patsy so deeply that she could hardly think. It seemed to her that Miri was absolutely justified in everything she did, and that she ought to go on, pushing her rebellion with integrity, taking each new drug as it came out, and sleeping with black militants or perhaps Chinese if China loving became fashionable among the young.

The prospect of listening to Jeanette, much less advising her, suddenly became unendurable; she seized upon the flimsy excuse that she had forgotten to return a reserve book to the library and in five minutes was out the door. She knew if she didn't move fast it would occur to Jeanette that she wanted to see Rice, and the thought of offering her mother a whole campus about which to be complimentary was too much. Once out into the hot one o'clock heat, with no voice in her ear and no grateful face across the table from her, she discovered that she felt fine. Hank was lying on his couch, reading a magazine. She came in briskly, kissed him, and saw that the magazine was *Sports Illustrated*.

"Why aren't you reading the *Journal of Aesthetics and Art Criticism?*" she said. "My husband reads it."

"Are you sure?" He reached for her but missed. She got herself a drink of water and went briskly into the bedroom, swinging her purse.

"He read one issue of it," she said. "Come on. I haven't got time for the amenities today. I had to lie to get out at all."

He came, but her approach took him aback slightly. He was not very sure of himself. It didn't matter to Patsy, who had grown quite sure of herself.

"What made you like that?" he asked as she was dressing. She felt fine, but he spoke in his sulking tone, as if he were offended that she had been aggressive. He did not realize that his statement was ambiguous.

"You think the romance is wearing off, huh?" she asked, fastening her bra.

"I wasn't talking about romance," he said.

492

"You don't talk at all," she said. "Occasionally you venture a cryptic observation, usually inaccurate. I'm not in such an odd mood, I'm just in a hurry. I came here to be had and I was had. Thank you. I've stopped being a nice person and become a competent person, but there's nothing strange about my mood particularly."

He tried to get her back in bed—he wanted the control back—but she was cool to him; all she would do was sit for a minute. With one finger she traced the little line of hair that ran upward from his groin.

"You've got a blue spot on your leg," Hank said, pointing it out.

Patsy sighed. It occurred to her that his conversation was as dull as any she had ever listened to. It was odd she should be sleeping with him. "Advancing age," she said. "You're not the sort who'll love me when I'm old and flabby, are you? You'll find someone young and nubile and leave me to spend my declining years in a snowdrift or somewhere."

She got up and looked in the mirror to see if she looked chaste and scholarly, as befitted a girl returning from a library. "Damn it," she said. "I look like I've been doing exactly what I've been doing. Maybe I better wear lipstick. Momma's idea of a bohemian is someone who doesn't. Actually I suppose if I were being had before her eyes she'd pretend it was a first-aid demonstration or something."

She went home and was sweet and kind and talkative, reassuring about Miri, concerned about her father's drinking, confiding about Jim's plans. She got Jeanette a cab, allowed Davey to be showered with last minute kisses, and stood at the curb with him, waving one of his chubby fists until the cab was out of sight. Davey thought it was absurd and so did she. Then she got his carriage and took him for a long happy walk, feeling calm and thoughtful. The world had resumed its normal course.

10

The next day the problem of Amarillo—complicated
enough to begin with—became more complicated still. In
the middle of the morning, as Patsy was meandering about
in her gown, enjoying not having her mother there and
looking for a section of the newspaper that she had managed
to mislay, there was a knock at the door and in breezed
Dixie, resplendent in a red and green outfit that hit her
halfway up her nice plump thighs. She looked as fresh and
firm as the apple Patsy had just washed for herself, and she
had brought Davey a huge red, yellow, green, blue, and
white truck, made out of plastic blocks that came apart. It
was several months too old for him, but they put him on his
blanket on a sunny spot on the rug and let him look at it.
Dixie's dress was even brighter than the blocks, so that
Davey had trouble deciding where to look.

"You look great," Patsy said. "Where'd you get that
miniskirt?"

"Oh, a crazy shop. There were hippies around. There
must be something wrong with me, you know. I kinda like
hippies. I always was one for men with lots of hair. It's too
bad they're all communists—we'll probably have to put
them in camps sooner or later. Jeanette called yesterday and
told me how worried she was about Miri."

"I might have known she'd call you," Patsy said.

"Sure, you know how polite she is," Dixie said. "It would
never do for her not to call her husband's sister, even if she
can't stand me. I didn't care. I always liked Jeanette,
anyway. Anybody who has to live with Garland deserves
some sympathy."

Patsy giggled but felt slightly on the hook nonetheless. She knew that Dixie was not as easily fooled as her mother.

"What's Miri really been doing? Taking dope?"

"Yes," Patsy said, thinking she had better yield that point. Dixie was not rational on the subject of race.

"You can't expect a kid not to take dope these days," Dixie said. "It would be like expecting me not to dance when I was that age. I just wouldn't want her to marry a communist or anything. If she starts to do something like that maybe you and I can go out and stop her, okay?"

"Maybe," Patsy said, not enthralled by the prospect.

"Just don't let Garland and Jeanette get wind of it. If they were to try and stop her she'd marry old Khrushchev himself."

The thought of Miri and Nikita Khrushchev made Patsy smile.

"Say, we can go to Amarillo together," Dixie said. "Jeanette said you were going tomorrow and I'd been meaning to go, so I called Joe and I called Sonny and made them both invite me. I called them in the middle of the night, when they were too sleepy to think of any excuse for not inviting me. You'll need some help with all that baby stuff, anyway."

Patsy felt an immediate sinking feeling. She didn't want to go to Amarillo; she wanted to stay where she was and do exactly what she was doing. She had been planning to call that morning and tell Jim that Davey had a minor illness and that they wouldn't be coming. But she had been too sleepy and had neglected to call. Dixie's words made her feel trapped. Dixie would certainly go, and there was Davey at her feet, healthy as a baby could be. She would have had no excuse except the truth, and she was not about to tell Dixie the truth. She couldn't keep a confidence any longer than she could keep a hundred-dollar bill.

Dixie noticed that her niece looked unhappy, but attributed it to a natural reluctance to see her husband. "Perk up," she said. "You're looking great these days. Maybe there'll be some fun movie stars around. I'll call and make us reservations."

Patsy's hopes rose for a moment. It was possible all the planes would be full. But the reverse was true—they were all empty. Crowds were not flocking to Amarillo. Dixie breezed out as cheerfully as she had breezed in, leaving Patsy very down. A promising day had been spoiled, not to mention a promising weekend.

Her spirits spiraled slowly downward, and by the time she reached Hank's that afternoon she felt hopeless. Her marriage was probably ruined, and no doubt her romance soon would be. It was exactly what she deserved, but, deserving of ruin as she felt, she could not help wishing it hadn't come so soon.

She might have stayed hopeless all afternoon had not Hank made her angry. "Well, it's not such a tragedy," he said when she told him why she was low.

He began to caress her even as he said it, and Patsy flared up and shoved his hand away.

"Get your hand off me," she said. "Of course it's no tragedy. I know that. You don't really care, anyway. You could have kept me here if you'd tried."

He looked surprised, as if it would never have occurred to him to keep her from going to see her husband, and Patsy smacked him. She had never resented a look so much. It had never occurred to him to stop her from going. She was bitterly disappointed and burst into tears. She felt very alone and confused, and while she was sobbing in confusion Hank managed to seduce her. The sport was all his, she was far away, but she didn't resent it. Why shouldn't he? She lay with her eyes half shut, listening to the rattle of the air conditioner and looking at the edges of brightness around the drawn shades. When she looked at Hank she saw, with no feeling of surprise, that he was scared of what she might do next. She surprised *him* by being very mild, both that evening and that night. Despite everything, she wanted to see him again. It was only just beginning, she didn't know what it might become, and she was not going to have it cut off because of one unfortunate weekend.

Dixie came by for her in the morning and *was* a big help with the baby stuff. Davey was agog and it was all sorts of fun. She hadn't gone anywhere in a long time, and Dixie's spirits bubbled so that hers began to bubble too. She didn't miss Hank until the plane was up, until it banked so that all

Houston lay out the window to her left. She could see the
trees of Southampton, where he was sleeping on the bed in
the shadowed room, with the musty air conditioner creaking. Then something dropped straight down inside her and
her aunt seemed a gauche stranger, the stewardess some
kind of cardboard woman, the well-dressed passengers all
foreigners, unreal. Even Davey, who was soon asleep in her
lap, seemed a blur. A longing for the other place seized her, a
longing for shadows and hands. All the way to Dallas it was
all she could do not to cry, and during the hour and a half
spent in Dallas waiting for a flight to Amarillo she had to
chatter and chatter, from the very lightest level of herself, to
keep the longing from welling up too high, to a point where
she would have to yield to it and somehow get herself back
to Albans Road.

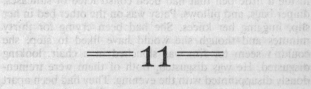

The motel had no baby beds, or rather, none that were
workable. It had not occurred to Jim that one would be
needed and he had neglected to put in a request. The
management seemed amazed that Patsy would want to
bring a baby into a motel full of movie people. The manager
scratched his head and the elderly blue-haired dotty lady
who seemed to be alternately cashier, room clerk, and
telephone operator called Patsy honey in the worst twang
she had ever endured, and took on over Davey in the same
twang. He was irritable, and Patsy wanted to brain the old
lady with a potted cactus. Finally a baby bed was located
and a sweaty Mexican was taken off grounds duty and
ordered to set it up, a task to which he proved unequal,

though he tried for dear might for more than thirty minutes. Jim stood by trying to help, Patsy stood by feeling frantic, and Davey wailed and wanted to be fed.

"Thees bed is not going up right," the poor man said repeatedly, trying it another way. The trouble was the springs, which obviously belonged to another baby bed. They could only be made to stay in if they were slanted. When they tried cramming the mattress down on them and put Davey on it he immediately slid into the railings.

"The hell of it is thees springs and thees bed," the man said. For a time the springs would not come out either, but finally, with a desperate wrench, he freed them. "They are not going together," he said, flashing the wailing Davey a look of exasperation.

Finally, to Jim's annoyance, Patsy tipped the man two dollars and sent him away, and they got a room with two giant double beds; and on those beds, at eleven that evening, the reunited family was concluding one of its grimmer days. Only Davey was at ease. He was sleeping on one of the beds, inside a little pen that had been constructed of suitcases, diaper bags, and pillows. Patsy was on the other bed in her slip, hugging her knees. She had been crying for thirty minutes and though she would have liked to stop, she couldn't seem to. Jim was slouched in a chair, looking disgusted. He was disgusted. Both of them were tremendously disappointed with the evening. They had been apart six weeks and had supposed they would at least have a friendly reunion, and it had turned out that nothing was any better between them, or even any different. It always boiled down to her crying and his looking disgusted, as if they had been cast by fate in those roles when they were together.

"I don't see why you asked us here," Patsy said. "Was it just so you could humiliate me in front of your Hollywood friends?"

"It was nothing of the sort, and you know it. Besides, I didn't humiliate you in front of my Hollywood friends. I didn't humiliate you in front of anybody."

"You did it in your usual strange way," she said. "No blame can possibly fall on you, don't worry. You're too smart to do anything I could feel good about blaming you for. You aren't that generous. You humiliated me by not doing anything with me at all in front of your friends. Am I such a leper that you don't want to be seen with me suddenly? You acted like you'd rather no one knew I was your wife—that's what's making me cry."

"Your vanity is making you cry," he said. "I guess you wanted me to arrange an occasion for you, so you could show off for the director and the producer and other big shots."

"I did not," she said. "You didn't even want to introduce me to those people in the swimming pool when we were coming back. They didn't look like big shots."

"I didn't know any of those people very well," he said, growing more disgusted. "They don't really care to meet anybody I know, or if they do it's just so they can try and screw you. They're a very hang-loose bunch."

"Even so, that doesn't make me a leper," Patsy said, reaching for the towel that she had been using to wipe her eyes. "You're looking at me as if I was a leper right now."

"I didn't know you'd been saving up tears for six weeks," he said. "If I'd known that, maybe I wouldn't have asked you."

Patsy lay down on the bed and put her face in the crook of her arm and said no more. It had been a dismal evening from the outset and it had become obvious that nothing was going to improve it. Dixie and Joe Percy and Sonny and Eleanor had all gone to dinner together, and Patsy had at first assumed that she and Jim would go along. She had a really fetching, wild summer dress that she intended to wear; but to her surprise Jim insisted that they eat alone. It was very unusual, for they usually got along better in crowds than they did alone. Still, it didn't bother her unduly. It struck her that perhaps she had misjudged him; perhaps he had really missed her and wanted her all to himself. That was a pleasant thought. She wore the dress, anyway.

The first unpleasantness had to do with the baby-sitter, who was fat, fortyish, had an enormous stiff bouffant hairdo, talked strangely, and handed them a pamphlet on Rosicrucianism only minutes after she had come in the door. "I tell you, it will open your eyes," she said. Davey was wailing. He knew he was in a strange place and had a notion his mother was about to leave him with a stranger, and he didn't like it. No more did his mother. The few times she had left him at night she had had Juanita; she had never gone off and left him wailing with a stranger who seemed to be a Rosicrucian. The sound of his wails affected her. They didn't sound like normal wails but like appeals for help, and her legs were trembling as she walked down the motel sidewalk. She had to fight down the urge to ask Jim to abandon the whole idea of dining out; but it was against her self-evolved principles of child raising to coddle her son or let herself become a slave to the sound of his voice, so she set her teeth and tried to keep from trembling and went on and got in the huge rental car Jim had. Jim himself was not overly affected by Davey's crying and had merely been amused by the baby-sitter. Patsy didn't like it one bit. If she could have had her wish at that moment she would have run the day backward like a home movie—would have gone back up the sidewalk, put things back in suitcases, gone back to the airport, back into the sky, back to Houston and South Boulevard. Then she could have put Davey into his own bed, where he was peaceful and happy.

But since that was impossible, she tried to make the best of things, for Jim's sake. Amarillo was an obstacle in itself, stark, sandy, and untreed. She felt exposed, and they were both nervous, though on the surface Jim seemed in a pleasant mood. They went to a steak house, which he said was the best he had found, and it was awful. Patsy had no appetite anyway. Davey's wails kept reverberating through her mind, and her stomach felt closed. Even so, it was a miserable restaurant. The bite or two of meat she forced down tasted like wood, the salad tasted like plastic, and even the bread was bad. Jim told anecdotes about the filming and the doings of the movie people, but somehow nothing he said got through to her. It was the sort of talk he would make with his parents if they visited; it didn't seem personally intended. She began to feel a groundless, unjustifiable irritation with him. It seemed to her that he had probably only chosen the steak house because it wasn't the one where Eleanor and Sonny and Dixie and Joe were eating—*that* was probably the good one. It seemed too that he had not insisted on dining alone because he had any desire to be

alone with her but because he didn't want his friends to see
him with her. It was an eerie feeling, one she had never had
before with Jim, but it persisted. He glanced around from
time to time, almost as if he were afraid someone would see
them.

When they got back to the motel, ten or twelve young
couples were sitting by the swimming pool drinking and
cutting up. All the girls were in bikinis. One young man
yelled at Jim, and Patsy's spirits lifted a little. She had a
bikini, and she had not been to a party in a long time. It
would be fun to sit around talking to Hollywooders. The
young men seemed loose and attractive and she was all for
running up and donning her suit. It was the kind of scene
she had imagined more than a year before, in Phoenix, after
she had seen *Lolita*. But to her surprise Jim seemed discomfited when the young man asked them to join the fun. He
introduced Patsy around, but a little perfunctorily, and
before she could really strike up a conversation with anybody he made the surprising remark that they needed to get
back to Davey, and led her away. She felt again that
somehow he was embarrassed by her, though certainly no
one in the group had seemed to find her odd. She looked
back at them wistfully across the sidewalk. The wavering
pool light made the scene all the more attractive. Inside,
they found Davey asleep and the baby-sitter reading one of
her pamphlets. Patsy suggested they keep the sitter and go
swim, but Jim said he was tired and had the sitter out the
door before Patsy could argue. It was only ten o'clock and
Davey was down for the night, and they had absolutely
nothing to do except sit and stare at each other. When Jim
switched on the big television set and began to watch the
news Patsy went to the bathroom to take off her pretty dress
and a feeling of lonely wretchedness came over her. She
wanted to be in Houston, watching television with Hank.
She began to cry, the tears burning her cheeks.

Jim tried to affect surprise when she came out of the
bathroom crying, but he was not surprised, and he didn't
blame her. He knew it had not been the sort of evening she
had been expecting. For some reason he had not wanted it to
be the sort of evening she had been expecting. He had not

known until she arrived how nervous he was about her, or how threatened she made him feel. What she said about him not wanting her to meet his friends was quite true, and it had been as big a surprise to him as it was to her. Normally, he wouldn't have cared, but the moment she arrived at the motel, looking beautiful and radiant and fresh, something stiffened in him. The little world of the movie set was the first world he had ever found on his own, the first place where he had felt like a professional among professionals. It was very different from graduate school, which was only an extension of worlds he had known. Despite himself, when Patsy arrived that day he felt she had come to rob him of what he had found. He simply didn't want to usher her into the company that had been his—she would immediately make it hers. Eleanor and Sonny and Joe were as surprised as Patsy that she was not coming to dinner with them; they had all, in their various ways, been looking forward to seeing her. Only Dixie was not surprised, and when somebody mentioned it she dismissed it as obvious. "I don't blame him," she said. "I'd hide her too if I was him. She always shows him up."

When the company had called them to the swimming pool Jim had felt the same awkward desire—to get Patsy away. Everyone would like her and she would like everyone, and the whole future he had been arranging might be altered. She might decide to stay for days; might even decide to come to California with him. He could not control his uneasiness, but he did feel ashamed later, once he recognized his own motives. When she had cried herself out and lay face down on the bed he felt even more ashamed. Her bare feet were sticking off the bed. He looked at her feet, at her ankles and legs, and the knot of anxiety inside him began to loosen. With her head hidden and only her calves and feet showing, she seemed very different—helpless, touching, hurt. He began to regret the whole evening. He had been a fool. She had been very beautiful in her wild black and white dress, and if only he had not been silly it could have been a wonderful evening. Patsy would not really have been likely to disturb anything. She was, after all, his wife. He did love her.

The future he had been arranging was unreal, anyway, and a little scary. The thought of visiting Eleanor on her ranch was a little scary. He had no idea what would happen or what Sonny might think. Los Angeles was a vague, strange prospect. Patsy was familiar and dear. Her legs were very nice, and they were there, not in the nebulous future. He remembered the trouble about the whore—he had not made love in months. He got up and went to the bed. "Turn over," he said. "I'm sorry and you're right about everything. I guess I was just competing with you again, or didn't want you competing with me, or something. I was awful. I'm very sorry. Tomorrow night we'll have the night we should have had tonight."

He put his hand on the back of her neck and she stiffened slightly. His hand did not feel like it belonged there, and what he had said made her feel no less hopeless, no less distant and cut off, and no less bruised. "It's okay," she said. "I didn't mean to seem so demanding." But she only said it hoping he would stop talking. His apologies just made it worse. They made her feel slightly contemptuous of him.

"I guess I should have admitted long ago that I felt in competition with you," he said. "I kept not admitting it to myself. Maybe I've just begun to grow up this summer."

"I hate conversations like this," Patsy said. "Please don't apologize any more."

Jim was a little annoyed but kept rubbing her neck. He felt genuinely sorry and genuinely loving toward her and it seemed to him that she never gave him credit for his genuine feelings. She was always ready to blame him when his good feelings got covered over, but she was almost never ready to love him when he felt loving toward her.

"I was just trying to tell you I was sorry I treated you that way," he said.

Patsy sighed, wishing he would take her advice for once. "All evening I felt like you didn't like me," she said. "I felt like I was offensive to you. You used to make me feel like you were proud of me but tonight you just made me feel like you were sort of ashamed to be seen with me. I'm sure I was wrong to feel that way but there's no point in your trying to explain it away. It doesn't make me unfeel it."

"But I was silly. I love you. I love you very much."

She sighed again, wishing she could simply go to sleep and be unconscious of all that was happening. "Maybe I'd rather you just liked me," she said. "Maybe I'm too simple-minded to appreciate love if it's so changeable and inconsistent. If you just liked me we might have a little more harmony. Ow!" A hair had caught in the stem of his wrist watch.

"I've never seen you more beautiful," he said.

Patsy felt too discouraged even to sigh. "I'm not sure you like Davey, either," she said. "You haven't held him much."

"We're just new to one another," he said, impatient with the subject of Davey. His relationship with Davey would take care of itself. "He'd rather you held him, anyway."

Patsy turned on her side to try and explain. "Sure he would. I've held him all his life. I'm familiar to him. If you'd hold him more he'd begin to like you." The thought of Davey and Jim really liking each other touched her. "I know you do love us," she said in a different, softer voice. "Please don't let yourself become unfamiliar to us."

But Jim had made his apologies and was only thinking of sex. Patsy saw it from his face and the moment of warmth she felt for him got mixed with guilt and dread. Though part of her wanted to be accommodating, she had never found it so hard. She had never felt so awkward in bed or found it more difficult to make a simple move. "You mean you haven't been sleeping with starlets all this time?" she said, trying to be light, as he was undressing.

"No, nobody," he said. And it only sank her spirits the more. She knew it was true and it made her feel the more guilty, the more obligated, and the more wretched. Her limbs didn't want to move. Her panties hung on one heel and it seemed to take an hour to get them off. She felt strange with him and didn't want him to touch her breasts, but Jim was so starved and impatient that he noticed nothing. It was fortunate. When he was asleep Patsy was surprised to find that she had recovered a bit of warmth for him. She had expected to feel like dying, but she didn't at all. She felt dutiful, and that was something. Jim was only Jim. It was not impossible. And sex was only sex. It hadn't counted, hadn't meant anything, but it was still only sex and it was a relief to find it didn't involve some kind of instant destruction. She had feared it might, and she got up and sat on the john awhile, depressed, but in such a light, clear-headed way that it was almost pleasant. It meant, she supposed, that she had become worldly at last, and she went in and went to sleep without thinking about it any more.

Perhaps because he was in unfamiliar surroundings, Davey woke early. It was only a little while after dawn. Patsy had not slept very deeply and woke as soon as he did. She fed him and decided to take him for a walk, even though it would mean carrying him. Jim was sound asleep and would be for hours and she didn't like sitting in closed rooms. She put on some jeans and a sweatshirt—brought in case she decided to make a quick trip to visit Roger—and sat Davey on her hip and went out. The red sun had barely risen above the plain when they left the motel. It was a clear ball, hanging in the gray sky to the east. The streets were quiet and it was cool and Davey was pleased to be out and moving. Cars passed them, cars on Route Sixty-six. Davey looked at them, and the weary occupants of the cars looked back curiously at the young woman in sneakers and jeans, walking her baby at dawn. "You're getting heavy, old chum," she said, switching him to her other hip. Davey spat up on her sweatshirt and kept his eyes on the road. There was dew on the grass by the sidewalk.

When they had walked a few blocks they turned and came back, and by the time they reached the motel Davey had grown very heavy. The sun was higher and had turned from red to orange. A truck full of horses passed; one of the horses whinnied and for a second there was the smell of horse manure. Patsy tried to show Davey the truck, but he missed it. When they turned through the portico and went up the sidewalk of the motel she looked a little sadly at the pool. She could see the remains of the party: glasses, a few beer cans, a pair of sandals. She walked over, thinking Davey would enjoy seeing the water, and discovered to her surprise that an old acquaintance was in the pool—namely Sonny. He had been resting at the edge of the pool, almost under the diving board.

"Well, hello," she said. "Fancy meeting you here. What a good time for a swim."

"Best possible time," he said, as nonchalant as if he had been expecting her. "Go get your suit on."

"What would I do with him?" she asked, tempted by the invitation.

Sonny swam lazily over to the edge where they were. Davey stared at him, amazed to see a man in the water. "You could dump him in bed with his pa," he said. "Be good experience for Jim, wouldn't it?" He was a little baggy under the eyes, as if he hadn't slept, but he seemed relaxed.

"It would if his pa were awake," she said. "Maybe we'll just sit and watch you."

"Naw, come on in," Sonny said. "I can tell you're dying to swim. I'm about swum out. Worst comes to worst I could baby-sit for you."

"Okay," she said. "We'll be right back."

She got into her suit, got a robe, a towel, a rattle and a clown doll and several other toys, bundled Davey and his paraphernalia in a blanket, and went back to the pool. The motel yard was still empty. She spread the blanket a safe distance from the pool and put Davey on it, his toys in a semicircle around him. Sonny got out and stood looking at them. He seemed to have no towel.

"Well, he can't be no harder to handle than his mother," he said. "I'll try and keep him from getting kidnaped."

Patsy took her robe off and he grinned at her. "Watch my child, not me," she said. The top of the water was icy cold and made her gasp when it covered her breasts. She waved at Davey, to reassure him, and began to swim to warm up. Davey looked very solemn, as if he could not quite believe what was happening. By the time she had done two lengths she had lost her chill and the cool water felt good. From time to time she swam over and talked to Davey. He had decided it was some kind of sport, and he grinned. Soon he ceased to pay her any mind and began to mouth his toys. After a while she got out and wrapped herself in a huge towel. The air made her cold. Davey and Sonny seemed to have established a solemn relationship. Now and then Sonny would push a toy Davey's way with his foot and Davey would look at him solemnly and take it and, after a moment, solemnly put it down again. Sonny was leaning back in a pool chair, apparently lost in thought. He was not really paying very close attention to Davey, who had found the ring of a pull-open beer can and was about to put it in his mouth when Patsy stopped him.

"I'm sorry my husband insisted on isolating us last night," she said. "I was looking forward to seeing Eleanor again. Maybe we'll all eat together tonight."

"Nope, you just missed her," he said. "There she goes now." He pointed into the sky. Far away, beyond downtown Amarillo, a small white plane was flying toward the southeast.

"Oh, I don't believe it," Patsy said.

"That's her. Going back to her ranch. Decided I was a lost cause, I guess."

"I'm sure you are," Patsy said, a little awed. It would be nice to have a neat little plane at one's command.

Sonny shoved Davey a rattle with his foot. Davey regarded the foot with more interest than the rattle.

"I guess I am a lost cause," Sonny said.

"I thought you were at the height of your fame."

"That's the trouble," he said. "I'm at the height of my fame." There was a strange bitterness in the way he said it. She glanced at him and he looked up just as she did and looked her squarely in the eye. The look hit home, frightening her a little. He was the same unpredictable, scary man.

"Well," she said, discomfited. She realized what it was Eleanor saw in him. "Don't look at me that way."

Sonny ran his fingers through his wet black hair and a drop of water hit Davey, startling him.

"What I meant was, I'd just as soon be a year or two back from the height."

"Maybe you are. Maybe you haven't really peaked yet—isn't that the term. You seem in pretty good shape."

"You never knowed me when I was in really good shape," he said. "Wisht you had. I peaked five or six years ago, where rodeo's concerned. I just been winning on finesse the last year or two. You can't finesse forever. Now you done

507

broke my heart, and it don't look like I'm going to turn out to be no movie star, like I thought I might. What do you reckon that leaves?"

"I didn't break your heart; I don't think you have one. I just turned you down. Don't get maudlin about it."

He regarded her silently for almost a minute, and it made her uneasy. She kept herself wrapped in the towel. He made her feel very unworldly and demure. The ends of her hair were dripping still. Life was constantly difficult, she decided.

"Someday you'll wish you hadn't turned me down," Sonny said quietly.

She didn't know what to say. She picked Davey up and held him in her lap. "Haven't you ever had an urge for one of these? I thought all men wanted children."

Sonny gave Davey a quick glance and shook his head. "I got a nephew in Big Spring," he said. "That's descendants enough for me."

"Not me," she said. "I wish I had two or three more just like this one."

"How long you had your boy friend?" he asked lightly.

Patsy was taken aback. She pretended shock. "Me?" she said. "How could I think of boy friends after rejecting you? You were my peak possibility."

Sonny grinned. "You ain't gonna be able to squeeze three more kids out of Jim," he said. "He's too busy winding film."

"That's an insulting thing to say," she said, but Sonny grinned his most charming grin.

"If you do finagle two or three more kids, that's when you're gonna wish you hadn't turned me down," he said. "Once you get all flabby and bedraggled it's kinda nice to have a little romance to remember. You could tell your girl friends how the king of the cowboys used to screw you in his hearse. I'll be dead and gone by then, probably—it'd make it all that much nicer to remember."

"You conceited bastard," she said. "What a vision of my old age that is—or my middle age. Does it make you feel good to envision this procession of girl friends putting flowers on your grave forever? I don't intend to be bedraggled, and I certainly doubt I'll sit around wishing I'd let you ravish me in that seedy hearse of yours."

"Want some breakfast? The water made me hungry."

"I don't particularly want to eat with you. I'll go dress and get my own breakfast."

"Wait," he said. "Joe's been pining for you. I'll get him up to sit between us and hold your hand."

He trotted around the pool and began to pound on one of the doors. In a minute it opened and Joe Percy stood in it in his underwear, looking so bleary and outraged that Patsy laughed. Joe was looking her way, but vaguely.

"Hi, Joe," she said. "I'm over here in a towel." She picked Davey up and went around the pool to introduce them. Joe was blinking unhappily, for the sun had risen higher and the courtyard was very bright. He went back into his room and emerged in his sunglasses, looking much more cheerful. They agreed on breakfast and Patsy hurried back to the room to dress. Jim was still asleep. She plopped Davey on the big bed and was dressed in five minutes. She changed Davey and put him on the bed with Jim.

"Wake up," she said. "I'm leaving Davey with you for a while."

Jim sat up, but still looked asleep. "Where are you going?" he asked. "Where can I get you?"

"Just down to have breakfast with a couple of old beaus."

"You better give me some instructions," he said. "He and I are practically strangers."

"I know. It's high time you got acquainted. All he needs at the moment is to be amused."

She was out the door before either he or Davey could protest. Sonny and Joe were both there when she walked in, Sonny in the midst of a platter of ham and eggs, Joe with a cup of coffee and a plate of untouched toast. Sonny had on one of his bright red shirts, which went well with his dark hair and his good mood. Even Joe was in a good mood, though clearly hung over. Patsy had ham and eggs and a cantaloupe and some tomato juice, and they had a pleasant chatty breakfast. Patsy fenced cheerfully with Sonny, who treated her to some of his lightest and least threatening charm. Joe was extremely obscene on the subject of Amarillo society. Patsy loved it. The two of them made her feel innocent and worldly at the same time.

They lingered, and when Patsy finally got back to the room Davey was red in the face and screaming his lungs out. He was on one of the big beds. Jim sat on the edge of it looking worried. Patsy picked Davey up and clucked him a bit and his screams subsided. He choked and heaved and grew quiet.

"You should have walked him a bit," she said.

"I tried," Jim said. "He just got stiff. I offered him everything in the room but he wouldn't have anything. What's the matter with him?"

"Nothing. He's just disoriented." She put her cheek against her son's. He was still a little stiff. It seemed too bad that Jim was unable to make either of them anything but stiff, but she didn't mention it. She felt too friendly and relaxed. Jim went and breakfasted and by the time he got back with a paper both his wife and his son were napping.

12

Saturday turned out to be fun. Patsy had envisioned boredom and arguments and was pleasantly surprised when neither materialized. She and Davey napped until noon and then went down and found the Tatums, who were leaving that evening for Laramie. They were very cheerful and it seemed like great luck, her arriving in time to see them and show them Davey. Boots thought he was the most delightful little creature she had ever seen and virtually took him over for the day. Patsy was glad to let her. In the afternoon, when it was time for his nap, they put him on Joe Percy's bed, with the door left open a crack so they could hear him, and sat around the pool playing canasta, Patsy and Pete against Boots and Joe. Pete played surprisingly well. He was wearing the same cut-off Levi's he had worn in Phoenix. His face seemed a little puffier than it had, but his eyes were lively again and he was loose and almost boisterous and kept up an amusing, self-deprecating chatter about his part in the film. It kept Boots in stitches, and as she played slap-dash canasta, anyway, Patsy and Pete won easily.

"How come you two are so cheerful?" Patsy asked.

"Hard to be blue when you're winning at cards," Pete said. "Actually we're just solvent again. This movie job got us out of the hole."

"Don't buy any yachts," Joe said. "This money is printed on a special paper—it vanishes two days after you get it. Come on, Boots, concentrate. Think who you're playing with. I used to be the best canasta player in Hollywood."

"How about Robert Mitchum?" Patsy asked, winking at him.

Joe looked blank for a minute and then grinned. "Don't think he's had time to learn the game," he said.

"Laramie is where you got hurt, wasn't it?" Patsy asked Boots. "I can't believe that was just a year ago."

It was, indeed, very hard to believe, and from time to time, through the afternoon, she dropped into reverie, thinking about it. Though Pete and Boots and Joe and Sonny and even Jim looked at her and treated her as if she were the Patsy she had been the year before, she knew that to varying degrees they were merely mistaking her for someone she no longer was. When she tried to remember herself in those days, she could not. She could not remember how she had felt, driving through the West with Jim; could not at all remember how she had felt the day she held hands with Pete in Cheyenne. She only remembered that those things had happened a year ago. It was hot by the pool, even though they had an umbrella. They were all sweating, all consuming quantities of beer, Coke, gin-and-tonic, according to their preference, as they played. Heat she could remember: the heat of the desert, and the heat of Houston. But not moods, not feelings, not sensations. In a year she had become a mother and an adulteress. Several times she had felt a moment of emptiness, from being so far from Hank, and had wanted to sneak away and call him, but for some reason he was stubborn about not having a phone and wouldn't get one.

"Who's that girl Sonny's after?" she asked at one point. Every once in a while she saw Sonny casually rub the girl's leg with his foot.

"Her name is Angie Miracle," Joe said.

"Great tan." In comparison, she felt distinctly pallid.

"Apparently even her clitoris is tan," Joe said. "Eye-witnesses have told me as much. I think I hear your son."

He did, and the card game was interrupted. Davey was brought out and allowed to gnaw on a joker, and the afternoon passed pleasantly. Patsy took him in the water for a bit and struck up a conversation with a nice long-haired young man from Redondo Beach. He had triplets and was lonesome for them. "They're thirteen months old now," he said. "They're just great. You ought to have some."

"That would finish my family at a stroke," Patsy said, momentarily enthralled with the young man, and the idea of triplets.

"Not ours," he said. "We want to try and have another set. The odds are really against us but what's it hurt to try? They're very individual, really. I don't know where people get the idea they're not. Come and see them if you're ever in L.A.

"You remind me of my wife," he added and splashed a handful of water on her shoulder wistfully. When he got out of the pool he went in and wrote his address on a card and stuck it in Patsy's pool bag. "My wife's name is Rhoda," he said, "in case I'm at work when you call." He waved and seemed to assume he would be seeing her shortly.

"Good luck with your second set," Patsy said.

The Tatums were packed to leave but consented to stay until after dinner. There was almost a scene with Dixie, who wanted Patsy and Jim to go to dinner with her and the director. She was amazed that they would think of going to dinner with the Tatums, who were clearly hired help, in preference to dining with a director. She had apparently decided that even Joe was a little déclassé. Patsy grew irritated and Jim was smug: it always gratified him when Dixie's *nouveau* streak showed itself.

Dinner with the Tatums was pleasant. They ate Mexican food and drank beer. It was Davey's first trip to a restaurant and he displayed an amazing ability for grabbing spoons and forks, and a preference for grabbing spoons and forks with food in them. Patsy's dress suffered so badly that the company began to wince every time Davey moved, but she herself remained unruffled. She had had three glasses of beer and felt a little high.

Soon after dinner they bade the Tatums goodbye. The sky behind Amarillo was deep violet, and the first stars had appeared. A breeze had blown up. Davey was asleep on Patsy's shoulder; she walked him back and forth on the sidewalk while Pete stuffed a few last items into the station wagon. Joe Percy, to everyone's surprise, gave Boots a big box of candy as a going-away present. She hugged him and burst into tears. Patsy too was strangely touched. Pete finished his packing, spat in the gutter, and regarded the scene with the little smile that Patsy remembered, the smile he had had the first night she met him. "Joe, you might have got *me* something," he said. "After all, I carried her to bed after all that dancing. Better get in, honey. I got so much food in me I'll be lucky to stay awake as far as Dumas."

Boots managed to kiss Davey without awakening him. Patsy hugged her, and Boots waved at Jim and got in. "Come see us," Patsy said to Pete.

He bent over to inspect a loose reflector and the street light lit his face and his curling thinning hair. When he stood up his eyes caught hers for a second and he smiled again. "We'll get by sometime," he said. "Take care of yourself."

"Well, there they go," Joe Percy said.

The dark sky over the plains was very deep, a vast sky, good to stand under and yet not a quietening or a comforting sky. Patsy was troubled. Something about Pete Tatum touched her still. It would be nice to know what the little smile meant, why it came when it did, went when it did. And yet she was glad they had left. It was fitting they should leave in the evening and drive across the breezy plains all night, higher and higher, upward to Colorado, upward to Wyoming. Vicariously, in the hour that followed, she went along on such a drive, though in fact she went with Jim to their room, put Davey down, and read magazines while Jim read magazines. But her mind drifted away from news and fashions, back to the car and the plains at night, and the lights of service stations, so bright after one had been asleep, and the smell of the coarse dewy grass in the early morning —all things she had known but a year before.

"Do you ever wish we'd kept on with it?" she asked Jim.

"What?"

"Traveling. Going to rodeos."

"No," Jim said. "Why?"

"I guess I just feel like a drive," Patsy said. "I mean a long drive."

"You sure didn't like it much at the time."

"Didn't I? I guess I didn't. I remember some of the mornings as being nice."

"Remember the first summer we were married?" Jim asked, apropos of nothing.

Patsy tried to, but couldn't very well. The first months they were married had no reality for her, not even in memory. When she stared at the present, at the room and at the man and the baby who scarcely knew each other, she felt only apprehension, and time after time her mind left the magazine and went back to the time when she and Jim had been alone together on the long roads in the Ford.

Not much later her apprehensions were justified. The present forced itself upon her—Jim was horny. A day of watching her wander around in a bathing suit had whetted his appetite. The night before he had been hasty; but he became the opposite. It seemed to Patsy that after years of haste he had picked that night to settle down to a leisurely and rather studious consideration of her body. She could not have been less in the mood to be played with. It made her sick. The worldliness she had credited herself with suddenly deserted her; she felt ashamed in so many ways that she could not even feel hostility. She didn't want to be naked, didn't want to be touched, and was afraid Davey would wake up. The shame she felt disarmed her. She didn't want Jim to know he was making her sick, though he certainly knew she was not responsive. "We've got out of touch," he said lightly, afterward. He said it nicely. They had got out of touch, but it was something he was sure could be remedied in a few days.

He slept but Patsy could not. She was too low. After a while she began to feel very strange. She didn't want to stay in the bed with him. She went to the bathroom but didn't turn on the light. She felt hurt, but she also felt sorry for Jim. It was all her own fault. But when she stood in front of the darkened mirror, in which she could only see flickers of her image, her mind began to spin. Confusion and hopelessness almost overcame her; she felt herself spiraling helplessly, felt that her marriage was over. She must take Davey and leave. She went to the door and looked out across the empty courtyard of the motel to see where she might go, or if anyone was there to help her or hold her back. No one was there. The moon swam in the empty pool. She went back into the room, still swirling in her mind. If she were dressed and packed she might leave, but she couldn't turn on lights and dress and pack. Toys and baby clothes were strewn everywhere. She couldn't go, but neither could she get back in bed. She felt terribly tight, as if she needed to cry, but her eyes were tearless and even the inside of her head felt dry.

She bent over Davey's bed and made sure his pen was secure, and then slipped on her robe and tiptoed down the concrete steps to the courtyard. She pulled a pool chair back into the shadows and sat on it, her feet tucked under her. She wanted to cry but couldn't. She chewed nervously on a fingernail, something she never did. Nothing was at an end; that was the awful thing. She didn't know how to bring anything to an end. She remembered what Jim had said: They were out of touch. What could put them back? So many things would have to change before they could be put back; she didn't know how to change them, nor did Jim. He didn't even know what the things were, neither did she, not very clearly. Perhaps they had never been in touch—she didn't want to think about it. She was grateful when a couple walked along the sidewalk. She could listen to their voices for a minute. It was Sonny and the girl with the marvelous tan. They didn't see her. The girl had her arm around Sonny's waist. They went into a room and Patsy was alone again. She felt such a dread of the future that it made her queasy.

Then she thought of Joe. It was not very late. She went to his door and his light was still on so she knocked. "Who goes?" he asked.

"Me." It surprised her that her voice sounded normal and not like the voice of a madwoman.

Joe had been lying on his bed smoking, reading *Herzog,* and intermittently watching a Lana Turner movie. Patsy's face startled him. She had been happy, chatty, and serene-looking during the afternoon. But her face was pale and she looked sick.

"What is it, honey?" he asked.

"Oh," she said and shrugged hopelessly. "What were you reading?"

He seemed unable to remember, the sight of her face had thrown him off so. "Ah, Bellow," he said. "More or less for professional reasons. We're trying to decide if a movie can be made of this. Do you want a drink?"

"I don't think so." The brightness of the room depressed her. She felt it was a mistake to have come. "You were watching a movie," she said.

Joe saw that the room depressed her. "I've seen it before," he said. "You have a caged look. Let's sit outside for a while."

"I feel caged," she said. "It's no one's fault, don't sympathize with me. I made the cage myself and it's not fair for me to have sympathy."

"Let's go outside, anyway."

"I don't want you to let me cry on your shoulder," she said, but she followed him out. "You probably have problems of your own, and they're probably worse than mine. You probably don't deserve yours."

"Don't be so hard on yourself, sweetheart," he said in a voice so kind and concerned that it turned the dust in her head and bosom to water, to such a flood that she could not see where she was going. She stubbed her toe painfully on the leg of an iron table. Joe could not quite reach her and she almost stumbled into the pool, blind with tears. But she found a chair and sat in it crying, and he pulled one near and sat smoking and watching the pool. After a while he fumbled in his pocket but found no handkerchief.

"That's me," he said. "I was never a ladies' man, as you can see. Always poorly equipped, never have a handkerchief, always on the wrong side of whoever I'm with when there's a door to be opened."

Patsy wanted to chide him but her throat was not in operation. She kept crying.

"It's a good thing you didn't fall in the pool," he said. "I would have leapt in after you and we might both have drowned. I always see black humor in these situations."

"Do you mind if I talk while you cry?" he asked a little later.

"No, but I'm stopping." She was, but her voice remained unsteady.

"It would be nice if it were an ocean instead of a swimming pool," Joe said. "Primordial emotions sort of go with the ocean."

"It wasn't so primordial," Patsy said. "I don't know what it was. I'm going to look awful in the morning.

"I broke my toenail," she added unhappily. "You sounded so sympathetic you started me crying."

"Well, I'm naturally on your side, even if I don't know who the battle's with. Cheer up a little."

"Please get me a Coke. My stomach's unsettled and I think my toenail's bleeding."

She sipped the Coke while he went to his room and got a drink and came back. He was reticent—almost too reticent. Patsy found herself hoping he would ask questions. If he would, she might find answers to them. She thought of telling him that she had a lover, but, as with Emma, she couldn't form the sentence that would expose her. "I guess something's gone terribly wrong in my life," she said finally, but even that sounded pretentious. She had ceased feeling so bad. Thin white clouds were passing overhead, rapid, lovely in the dark sky. The sense of constriction left her.

"You were happily married," she said. "You told me so. How did it happen? Or maybe you don't want me asking."

"I wouldn't mind telling you if I knew," he said bemusedly. "As near as I can remember it was mostly luck. I tend to be simplistic about these things. We met by accident and happened to get on beautifully."

"You're not much help," she said. "Except as a shoulder to cry in the vicinity of. Tell me the secret of it all, so I can be happy."

"You know me," he said. "Besides being simple-minded I'm a lecher. Maybe lechery is the secret."

"No, no, no," Patsy said. "Don't say that. You'll drive me to despair. Sex is not supposed to be overemphasized in marriage any more. What about stability and sharing duties and all that?"

"I've never known two people to keep one another happy by taking turns dishwashing," he said, as if that were the end of that.

Patsy felt very discouraged. Her legs felt heavy as stone. Joe noticed and did his best.

"Don't be so sad," he said. "If it doesn't work out with Jim it will work out with somebody else. You're in splendid shape. Lots of good fellows around. For god's sake, don't mope. You're too pretty to mope."

She stood up. It occurred to her that Davey could have rolled out of his pen. "You don't make me feel very dutiful," she said, "but thanks for being on my side."

"It's no accomplishment. Leaving tomorrow?"

"So far as I know." When she reached the second level he was still standing by the pool, and she waved.

Jim was awake when she stepped into the room. His bed light was on. He looked at her hostilely and she felt discovered—seen through.

"Oh, hi," she said.

"Been to see your friendly marriage counselor?" he asked.

"I was just talking to Joe awhile. Don't pick a fight now, please. Please don't."

"Why were you talking to him at this hour?"

"I felt wretched. It isn't so late."

"It isn't my fault you felt wretched," Jim said. "You didn't have to. I didn't do anything wrong."

"I didn't accuse you. I can feel wretched on my own hook, can't I? I know it was my fault."

"You think it's my fault, though."

"No, I don't," she said. "Please don't be angry with me now, Jim."

"Technically I didn't do anything wrong but I still lack some sort of generosity of spirit or something so that you become wretched when I touch you, right?"

"Well, you're lacking it right now," she said with a flicker of vehemence. "I asked you not to pick a fight. I'd like to try and go to sleep."

"I'm not keeping you awake," he said, flicking off the light. "Where I wish you'd go is to a psychiatrist. Maybe we could find out what's wrong with you sexually."

Patsy had been about to get in bed, but she stopped. "Listen," she said. "Shut up. I know I wasn't any barrel of fun tonight but there's nothing wrong with me sexually. I can not be in the mood. You were out of the mood for six goddamn months, until you happened to be in that whorehouse in Richmond. So maybe I got cut off, I don't know. You just be careful what you say to me."

"Big deal," Jim said. "What will you do, run back down and cry in Joe's arms? I know we were cut off. I was trying my best to turn us back on."

"You just tried on the wrong night," she said. "If you'll forget it and shut up, it will be okay. I didn't do anything so bad, either. I just got blue and went and sat by the pool awhile.

"I do not need a psychiatrist," she added flatly.

"Well, okay," he said. "Maybe you need a gynecologist, I don't know. I just know we need something."

"I was turned *off!*" she said. "I didn't want sex! Shut up before you ruin us forever. Can't you understand? Just shut up. Talking makes it worse."

She took a pillow and pulled the bedspread off the bed.

"What are you doing?"

"I can't sleep in this bed tonight," she said. "You go to sleep and let me alone. I'll sleep all right."

"That's childish," he said. "Come on."

"No. You think I need nine thousand doctors. I won't sleep with you."

"I'm sorry," he said. "I was just talking."

"I told you not to talk," she said.

"Shit," he said. "Come on, you can have the bed."

"Keep it. Go to sleep. I'm all right."

"Okay," he said. "Be stubborn."

"I will." She stayed on the floor, wrapped in the bedspread. She awoke so often that she could not tell if she had really been sleeping. There was a kind of vibrating silence in the room, as if Jim too were awake.

When morning finally came and Davey was awake things improved. They all had breakfast together and were as polite and friendly as if the night had never happened. Both knew that it had, but they ignored the knowledge. Patsy called Roger Wagonner and he insisted that they visit; she decided it might be a good idea. She did not want to rush right back to Houston, to Hank. If she went back in the wake of such discouragement anything might happen. Her marriage ties might snap, and she didn't want that, at least not on the basis of one bad night. They sat by the pool most of the morning in the bright sunlight. A few cheerful Californians sat around with them drinking Sprites and Frescas and joking about their hangovers. Jim took Davey in the water for a while and Davey loved it. Jim looked very blond and handsome and cheerful, and it seemed so right and so natural that the two of them were playing together that Patsy felt even less like returning to Houston. She knew she ought to think of some way to keep them together more. Soon they would not be able to help loving each other. But Jim was planning to go to California and leave them alone again. It irked her every time she thought about it. It was so inconsistent. He wanted them to love him but he wouldn't stay around so they could try. Davey gurgled and yelled and after a while Joe Percy emerged, looking truly hung over. He was blinking and holding his sunglasses out before him like a shield.

"Why don't you put them on?" she asked.

"I like to hold them out like this," he said. "It gives me satisfaction."

"Put them on. I can't bear to look at you when you're in pain."

He put them on. "You look lovely again," he said. "What became of your ravaged countenance?"

"My toenail still hurts," she said. "We're going to a ranch this afternoon, Davey and I."

"A little thoughtless of you, to go off and leave us all at the mercy of Dixie."

"Where is she?"

"With the director, but it's nothing that'll go two nights, if I know them. She's a kind of Norman Vincent Peale of the boudoir, you know. She believes in everyone she likes absolutely, for a night or two. Then she disbelieves in them absolutely."

They chatted the morning away, and then Patsy went up and fed Davey and packed. She stopped at Joe's door and said goodbye to him, and he kissed her on the cheek. A little later, at the airport, Jim kissed her lightly on the mouth as she held Davey. On the way to the airport and while waiting they had been polite; they had left things very vague, for fear of becoming heated. They talked of Davey and of the fall, skipping entirely the ambiguous weeks ahead. He was surprised that she had not seen more of the Duffins, told her to say hello to the Hortons, and didn't mention Hank at all. On the plane she and Davey took a seat by the window. Jim was still standing by the flight gate, the wind of the plains blowing his hair and making him look happy and rakish. She tried to make Davey wave, but Jim had not spotted them. Davey was gurgling; he liked planes. Patsy tried to smile in response to the stewardesses' appreciatory remarks, but she felt strange inside. There was her husband—they were going away from each other again. Then Jim turned and went back into the terminal, to do what, to go where, she really didn't know. She was alone with Davey and didn't really know where *she* was going, either, or what she was going to do. It was very lonely to be departing after such a short visit, with so little done and so little clear. They ought to be going somewhere together, though she didn't know where; she could not much blame him for wanting to go without her after the way she had behaved. Then the plane went up. Davey grew very still, his head leaned back against her breastbone, between her breasts. His head was warm and he gripped one of her fingers. A little of the strange

feeling went away. She talked to him and held him up so that
he could see the small white clouds below them. Then she
settled him back in her lap, his head where it had been, and
looked out fairly calmly at the brown land and the clouds.

===== **13** =====

The ranch house too was without a baby bed. There were
only two beds in the whole house. Roger gallantly offered
her the use of his marriage bed, but Patsy declined and put
Davey down for a nap on the bed in the guest room. He was
very tired, and so was she. Once she had made him a kind of
pen she took off her dress and lay across the bed in her slip,
meaning to wait until she was sure he was asleep before she
changed clothes. Though the heat outside was fearsome, the
old high-ceilinged room was fairly cool and she too was soon
asleep. Davey woke before her, knocked one side of his pen
awry, and she in the process of falling off the bed when she
awakened. She had been sleeping deeply and could not get
herself in motion in time to catch him. His heels disappeared and she heard a loud bump, as of a small boy's head
hitting a floor. It terrified her and she grabbed him up and
began trying to comfort him even before he began crying.
He cried loudly for a bit, surprised and outraged. Patsy felt
terribly guilty and strange and cried too, stroking Davey's
head with her fingers. The shock, the scare, the adrenaline
mixed strangely in her with grogginess and a desire to go
back to sleep. Her arms trembled.

Fortunately Davey quieted down rather quickly. He
looked for a time as if he felt the world had done him a bad
turn for no good reason, but then he began to look cheerful
again and Patsy felt enormously relieved. She had been

imagining permanent brain damage but could not even find a bump, only a small red spot on his forehead. She looked out the window and saw Roger go into the barn. She changed Davey and put on her jeans and a shirt and retrieved Davey from the edge of the fireplace, where he had scooted himself. "Let's go see some animals," she said.

They paused for a time in the chicken yard. Davey stared in wonderment at the hens, who walked around pecking at things and chattering. Patsy clucked at them inexpertly and they regarded her with scorn. They were white hens, a few of them fat matriarchs but most of them young and skinny. Davey eventually grew annoyed because none would come in reach; he grabbed a handful of chicken droppings, which he happened to notice before Patsy did. "Oh, shit," she said, holding his smelly hand away from her. She carried him down to a large water trough and washed the hand under a faucet.

Roger was standing near the lots doing something to the front foot of a large gray horse. He was sweating profusely. When he saw them coming he set the horse's foot back on the ground and wiped his forehead with his shirt sleeves.

"Up from your snooze?" he said. "How's he taking to ranch life?"

"He just grabbed a handful of fecal matter," Patsy said. "It was from a chicken. I would have expected a son of mine to be more discriminating."

"I ain't very pleased with this horse, either," Roger said. "The big idiot just stepped on my toe. Think he weighs a ton. After I worked myself down trimmin' his toenails too."

"I stubbed one of mine on a chair last night," she said. It seemed remarkable that the events of the night before, which had seemed so terrible and so final, already seemed distant and only rather ordinarily sad.

Bob, the big dog, came over and licked her hand. She let Davey pet him and after a while set him on Bob's back, an experiment that both he and Bob regarded with mixed feelings.

"About time he had a horseback ride," Roger said. "It's cooling off. We'll ride over to the mountain."

The mountain he meant, apparently, was a long flat-topped hill a mile or so away, to the southwest of the barn.

Patsy would have liked a ride, but she felt distinctly apprehensive about the combination of herself, Davey, and a horse.

"I don't think I ride well enough to carry him," she said. "Not even that far."

"No, but I do. Me and him will ride double and you can poke along behind us on this old gray idiot here."

"But Davey might not ride with you."

"Course he will. Why wouldn't he?"

He went in the barn and got a bridle and then went into the lots to catch his own horse, a trim red sorrel. Patsy sat Davey on the edge of the water trough and let him dangle his toes in the water. Their reflections wavered when he made the water ripple. She watched Roger saddling the horses and imagined catastrophe, runaways, horror, screams. It seemed a tremendously perilous undertaking, but she could not get up the will to put her foot down against it. When Roger got the gray saddled he got a sack and carefully wiped the saddle free of dust.

"Mary's saddle," he said. "Ain't been rode since she died. Hop up so I can see if the stirrups need changing."

He held Davey while she mounted, then handed him up to her while he checked the stirrups. Davey was amazed. Roger fixed the stirrups with dispatch and mounted the sorrel. He rode up beside her, took Davey, and set him firmly between himself and the saddle horn. "Hang on, young feller," he said and rode off. The gray followed, trotting heavily, and Patsy's sense of catastrophe deepened. She bounced ungracefully. She could see nothing at all of Davey, only Roger's back and his brown shirt. She was bouncing so badly she was not sure she would notice a catastrophe if one happened.

Soon, though, they slowed to a walk, and the horses picked their way off the low ridge on which the barn stood. At the foot of the ridge Roger reined in so she could come up beside him. She brushed back her hair and saw that Davey was quite all right. She had expected him to be frantic to come to her, but instead he glanced at her almost with disinterest when she came alongside. Davey's hands were on Roger's wrists.

"My goodness, he's taken up with you," she said. "What an independent brat."

"Hum?" Roger said. "Well, you can't keep him tied to your apron strings all his life. A boy's got to get out with the men sooner or later." Davey was trying to hold the saddle horn, but it was broader than his hands.

"That old thing will pace if you make him," he said. "Whop him with the reins a time or two."

He set the sorrel in a light, easy trot, and after some more heavy bouncing Patsy took his advice and lashed at the gray awkwardly. It took effect; he slipped suddenly into a comfortable pacing gait that didn't bounce her at all. The sense of catastrophe left her and the ride became very pleasant. They were crossing an old grown-over field, the two horses side by side, the weeds and taller grasses struck with late sunlight. The wide high sky was very clear and plangent and the evening clouds turned golden in the southwest. Gray mourning doves rose from their feeding in twos and threes and flew south. The air and the grass had one smell. The bridle bits jingled lightly in unison and Patsy found herself watching the sorrel's delicate strong legs pick their way through the grass, with dusty sunlight filtering under and through them. Davey suddenly made a pleased, emphatic sound, waving one hand.

"He's giving us his opinion on all this," Patsy said.

"Oh, is that what he's doing?" Roger said. "I thought he was calling for more speed."

When they left the field she fell behind again, sad for a little inside her pleasure. When would he be out with the men again, her son? And with what men? They rode through a short strip of thin mesquite, all dead—sprayed, Roger said—and the doves that had left the field and flown to the trees lifted themselves and flew back to the field, whistling over their heads in passage. As they started up the slope of the hill Patsy shook the little sadness out of her breast and forgot the future. It was so much fun to ride. She had ceased to be nervous about the gray horse, and she liked the sound of horses' feet and the leathery dusty smell of the saddle. Roger waited for her at the top of the hill and they rode slowly around the edge, Patsy smiling, enjoying the breeze and a sense of great well-being. To the south there seemed to be more ridges, more flat-topped hills, with pastures of mesquite in between. The farthest distances were already blue with evening but the sun was not yet down.

"I always forget how much land there is," she said. "It goes on and on."

"Wish I owned more of it," Roger said, studying the pastures below.

"Goodness, why?" Patsy asked. "Don't you have enough? It seems to me that this hill and that field and the place where the barn is would be enough." They could see the field, see the house and the gray barn, see the old pickup sitting at the back-yard gate.

"I never understood this urge you ranchers have to own the whole earth."

"Well, it would eliminate the fencing problem," Roger said dryly.

"Actually," he said a little later, "I wouldn't want the whole earth. I wouldn't want nothing east of the Mississippi or north of Albuquerque, and I ain't got much use for Old Mexico."

Mention of Albuquerque reminded her of Hank—it seemed to be his favorite town.

"There the hussy is," Roger said, pointing toward a patch of mesquite to the north of the hill. "You and old Davey get down and sit here a minute while I do a little chore."

She got down and he handed Davey to her, then dismounted and tied the gray to a small mesquite.

"She's calving," he said. "She's probably got the calf down there somewhere. I'll jog down and take a look."

Patsy assumed he was talking about a cow, though she had not seen any. "What do I do if a snake comes along?" she asked as he was mounting.

"Just kinda make conversation, and give him room," he said. "I won't be gone long."

She sat down at the edge of the hill, the short grass pricking her bare calves. Davey kept looking around for the horse and shook his head irritably when his mother tried to nuzzle him. Finally she saw the cow. She was standing in the edge of the mesquite, to the north. Roger was talking to her as he approached; sounds floated back. He was trotting slowly toward the cow, standing up in his stirrups. The sorrel's coat was red with sunlight. Suddenly the cow lifted her head and made a short clear bellow. She left the trees in an awkward, heavy run, her full udders swinging. She seemed bent on getting across the long clearing and around the edge of the hill, and because the man and the horse were caught slightly off balance it seemed she might be going to make it. The sorrel whirled and leaped a bush and ran in a straight perfect angle for the spot where the cow would turn the corner of the hill. Patsy was amazed, rapt, involved to the pit of herself, for the race took place just below her, in the clearest evening sunlight, vivid and splendid as some great race in a movie, only, for her, more urgent, for she was straining and did not know whether she strained for the horse or the cow or the old man, whose hat had blown off. He was still up in his stirrups, his eyes on the cow but his body urging the horse. Red cow and red horse converged toward each other, the red horse racing like a horse in myth, one red flowing line from neck to tail. When he left the grass and struck the hard bare earth at the base of the hill his hoofs left small clear identical puffs of dust. And for all the heavy awkwardness of the cow and the grace and beautiful speed of the horse, their two intensities were almost perfectly matched and the cow almost won; would have won had not the horse turned out of his angle slightly, toward the lift of the hill. At the moment of whirling Patsy cried out. The horse and the cow spun head to head, but the horse between the cow and the point of the hill. Davey jumped, frightened by his mother; he began to cry. Patsy tried vainly to soothe him, her eyes on the scene below.

The cow had been headed but she had not been stopped. Immediately she tried to cut behind the horse, and they were so close that again she almost made it. But the sorrel whirled backward and sideways and blocked her again, and with a fling of her tail she left the hill and ran north, still going away from the spot where she had been. There was another race, almost as intense as the first, but the sorrel had the long clearing north to the field to work in, and he caught the cow before she was halfway across it. Then, in the open, he had her, and the cow's angry, sullen stubbornness was gallant but almost annoying. She turned, stopped, darted one way, was stopped, darted another.

Roger and the horse were no longer really challenged. They stayed far enough from the cow that they could anticipate her, the sorrel pivoting gracefully, sidestepping, neck curved or neck straight, but always between the cow and where she wanted to go. Finally she stopped, head up, and horse and man stopped; all became as still as statues. They looked at each other and looked at each other. Then the cow turned disgustedly and began to move back toward the mesquite. From time to time she would attempt to turn to the right or the left, but Roger and the sorrel kept far off her flank and turned her easily. When she was back amid the trees Roger drew rein, turned away from her completely and rode over to retrieve his hat. The cow had stopped and was watching him. He got off to get his hat and stayed on the ground a minute, talking to his horse. When he mounted again the cow had gone to her calf.

Patsy saw it get up and stumble to its mother, trying to nurse. Roger and the sorrel approached in a slow walk; he looked at the calf a moment and turned back toward the hill. Davey suddenly began to choke. While she had been looking off he had put three small rocks in his mouth. She was frightened for a second but managed to get them out. Roger rode up and reached down for him. "Better go," he said. The sorrel's withers were dark with sweat but neither he nor Roger seemed tired or excited. Patsy felt limp.

She mounted the gray and they edged off the hill and jingled back across the weedy field and up the ridge to the barn. The sun had gone down, but the sky still held its light. Once they were unsaddled, the sorrel and the gray stood drinking at the water trough. Patsy and Davey stood watching. Their drinking made a thin sucking sound and when they lifted their heads water dripped off their noses. The gray romped heavily away, down the ridge, bucking and twisting, and the sorrel trotted lightly after him.

The jar of peanut butter she had bought the summer before was still there, and Patsy made supper on it. The bed problem they solved by having Davey sleep on a pallet of quilts on the bedroom floor. "Half the grownups in this part of the country slept on pallets when they was kids," Roger said, surprised that she considered the arrangement esoteric.

"That's not necessarily a recommendation," she said. Roger fried himself a steak for supper, overcooking it by about twenty minutes, to her mind.

"You've fried it so hard it looks wooden," she said. "It's not necessary to burn your meat, you know. I'm sometimes tempted to move in on you for a month to see if I couldn't coax some real food down your throat. I honestly don't see how you survive."

"You're as big a puzzle to me as I am to you," he said. "I never seen you eat nothing but peanut butter. I'd as soon live off burned meat as peanut butter."

"But peanut butter is extremely nutritious."

"Burned meat's so much tastier, though."

Once the plates were cleared away they went out and sat on the porch listening to the ringing crickets. The subject of land came up again. Patsy sat on the lowest step, where she could enjoy the stars. She stretched one leg out along the step against the cool concrete.

"What would you do if you was to inherit a ranch?" Roger asked. He was whittling, his chair propped against the wall. Once in a while, when he turned the knife blade over, she saw it flash in the light that came through the screen door.

"No possibility is more remote," she said. "Neither of my folks have any land left. Daddy has a place in East Texas where he takes his friends to play poker, but I doubt it would keep a milk cow. Won't you cut yourself, whittling in the dark?"

"Oh, this ain't whittling," he said. "I'm just smoothing a stick. Reason I asked, I was kinda considering leaving this old place of mine to you and Jim. I was gonna leave it to my sister's boy, but he got killed in Korea. My sister's older than me, so there ain't no point in leaving it to her. I'd kinda like to leave it in the family somewhere. If I don't my sister would just sell it, and pretty soon the money would be gone and the land too."

"Goodness. I don't think you ought to leave it to us," Patsy said, confused. The suggestion filled her with dismay.

"I know that must sound awful," she said a minute later.

"I don't know—the idea just surprised me. You don't really know us very well. If you did I'm not sure you'd think we were the sort of people to be trusted with your land."

Roger went on smoothing the stick, unperturbed. "I never expected you to jump at it," he said. "Still, you might talk it over with Jim. It ain't a bad little ranch. It's well watered, and the taxes ain't too high."

"Please don't misunderstand," Patsy said. "I love you for wanting to give it to us—I think it's wonderful of you. There are just such problems. I wouldn't know what to do with land."

"It would need you, don't you see?" she said later, growing even more confused.

Roger chuckled. "Aw, the country could get along without me, I guess," he said. "Besides, it ain't really *that* ugly. You might get to liking it, in ten or fifteen years. Be good for old Davey too. And Jim."

"I guess that's what really upset me," Patsy said. "Jim. He and I haven't been very happy lately. I'm not even sure we'll be together always."

"What's the matter, don't he want to stay home?" he asked.

"I don't know. Things don't seem to be a great deal better when he's home."

"Sorry to hear that," he said, and they fell silent. Stars were thick in the sky—there were almost too many. After a while the mood of confusion passed and she felt better.

"Well, aren't you going to give me advice?" she said. "I suppose it's time I went around collecting advice."

"Wouldn't think of it," Roger said. "I ain't no expert on the subject. Only reason I never got left in the lurch myself is because it's so far to the bus station out here."

"Come on," she said. "That woman would never have left you. I can tell from her picture."

"No, I guess not," he said.

"Did you ever love anyone but her?"

"Not that I remember," he said. "Flirted around a little when I was young. Thought I wanted to marry a schoolteacher, once. Pretty close shave. She's an alcoholic now."

"But she might not have been if you had married her," Patsy said. "Don't make her ruin sound so inevitable. I guess what I meant was were you ever in danger of loving anyone else after you married Aunt Mary?"

"Lord, no," he said. "Wouldn't never have dared. Mary was downright murderous at times, even without no provocation.

"Course this country don't exactly teem with women," he said thoughtfully a little later. "There ain't a whole lot of temptation between here and Fort Worth."

"Well, there's temptation where I live," she said. "I guess I'm in danger of loving someone besides Jim."

"Is he a scoundrel?" he asked, so kindly and seriously that she almost cried.

"Not really. Why do you think of people in terms like that?"

"Way I was raised, I guess," he said mildly.

After a while he went to bed and Patsy bathed and sat in the dark bedroom rocking by the open window, looking out at the moonlit ridge. The mesquite trees in the yard were very dark against the pale grass.

Roger persuaded her to stay a day, and she spent it cleaning. His cabinets had not been cleaned in years, and all the floors needed mopping. She mopped the downstairs but lost her impetus and left the upstairs for another visit. Davey rolled about on the dusty floor until he looked like he had been the mop.

When it grew late and cool they went riding again, back to the same hill. She had no apprehension and the ride was pure pleasure. They loped through the field, a gait that was pleasanter for her than for Davey. It caused him to spit up profusely on the saddle. They slowed to a walk and a flight of crows flew over. The cow and calf were nowhere to be seen. There was no wild chase. They sat on the horses on the edge of the hill, watching the evening land. The late sunlight made everything clear, perfectly defined. The fields and pastures were very bright, the brown burned summer mesquite leaves golden. Strings of doves flew in and out of the field, high as the hill they sat on and so distinct that each bird could be counted. Roger took off his hat and set it on Davey's head, tilting it back so it wouldn't blind him. Davey was not sure what to think but managed a lopsided grin. The sun struck the old man's brown shirt and brightened the rowels of his spurs. She took off her headband and hung it on her saddle horn. When the sun was just above the horizon the colors began to soften. The golds turned to grays and blues.

"The weeds have just about taken this old field," Roger said as they rode home. The weeds had a thin dry smell. That night they had the same suppers they had had the night before, and afterward sat on the porch talking of light matters. Roger lectured her at length on cows and their ways. She slept well, and the next morning at the airport told Roger she would speak to Jim about the ranch. She stood at the flight gate blinking in the bright sun and clutching Davey and her purse and a diaper bag. She had left her sunglasses at the ranch and had been too embarrassed to ask Roger to go back for them.

"Bring old Davey back to see me before he gets too old to ride double," he said, kissing her. He smelled dry, of the sun.

"I will, I promise," she said, half blinded. "Please take care of yourself and learn to do something besides fry. I'm going to send you a cookbook."

"Send her on," he said. "Be nice to have something new to read."

14

When Eleanor told Lucy there would be a guest for the week, Lucy was immediately apprehensive. Only very occasionally were there guests, and the few who came were usually there on business of one kind or another. Eleanor had never liked bringing her friends to the ranch; there was nothing for them to do there. The three or four women she liked, and the three or four men, she preferred seeing in cities, preferably in the East, where they could shop together and where there were theaters and galleries and shows.

She had learned while in college that it didn't work, bringing people to the ranch. They were fascinated by it and awed by its scale, and they expected to be given tours and treated as if they were on a dude ranch. They wanted to be taken riding, and to be allowed to watch the work. It made both Eleanor and her cowboys uneasy. Work on the Guthrie ranch had always been work—it was never sport. They had no show cattle, no race horses, no polo field. A few old family friends—doctors and lawyers mostly—were allowed to come and hunt, dove in the fall, quail and geese and duck in their seasons; but other hunters were warned away. The grand medieval hunts which the owners of the great South Texas ranches held seasonally for their hundreds of acquaintances did not appeal to Eleanor. She did not want to be mistress of a hunt. Her ranch was a great ranch, and that was enough.

For years Sonny had been the only regular guest, and he was too restless to stay anywhere for more than a week. Besides, he could join in the work if he chose. He seldom did, but he and the cowboys got on with one another and he was never a problem. When he came he came essentially to rest and eat and see her, and no one was made uncomfortable.

But Jim was a new name, and until she saw him Lucy was apprehensive. He might be a threat—some young man from Hollywood who would do Miss Eleanor harm. Lucy was a worrier, and it did no good to tell her that Jim was just a young man she was fond of. Fond was the word she used in speaking of him, and if it did not convince Lucy it was no wonder. It did not convince Eleanor, either. Lucy held a simple view of young men—they were out to get what they could, and get it free if possible. A young man, finding Eleanor miraculously without a husband, would be out to marry her. If he succeeded there would be no way he could lose. He would either get money or love or both. But the ways Miss Eleanor could lose were various. Lucy was the mother of seven boys—all tacitly assumed to be by her first and only husband, though he had not been seen in the vicinity of the ranch since World War II. She was a woman of position herself, and the wiles of the young were familiar to her.

For Eleanor the reverse was true. She had never known the young. The men she had known as a girl were invariably a decade older than herself, established men, of the sort her father thought might be good for her. She had had only two college romances, both short, for she had been very uncertain of herself and very puritanical—painfully so. Then there had been her marriage, and then Sonny. There were a few men, such as the broker in New York, who served as a contrast to Sonny. She liked them, but Sonny had no serious rival. She had no son and had observed only distantly and without much interest the sons of her few friends. She could see that some of them had a certain charm, but it was not a charm that drew her to them.

Thus, when she met Jim in Phoenix she thought him nice but no more. His image didn't linger in her mind. When he appeared again in Amarillo she thought the same. He was appealing, and, in his fondness for her, rather touching. When Sonny needled her about Jim's crush, she shrugged, not much interested. The first thing out of the ordinary that she noticed about Jim was that he never ceased noticing her. He could not be with her without looking at her. She had often been the object of admiring glances, but after a while Jim's admiration began to take on her in a way that was new. He looked at her constantly, and yet, she began to realize, he was blind to her. His vision of her was not her at all. It didn't include her age—to him she was without age. It didn't include Sonny, with whom she slept. To Jim she was a womanly ideal—beautiful and intelligent, rich in the flesh and rich in the spirit. When he left, on evenings when the three of them dined together, his eyes returned to her from the door, as if he were looking so as to be able to take her image with him and keep it for the night.

At first it irked her a little, his idealization. It made him seem childish and made her nervous. She found herself wanting to shake him loose from the image he had, or else shake the image until it became *her*. A time or two she dressed sloppily. Once or twice she said things which were coarse. But the vision refused to be dimmed. He made her sloppiness or her coarseness part of the womanly ideal. He wouldn't see or hear anything that he didn't want to see or hear. Eleanor began to understand why he had trouble with his wife. Adoration disconcerted her.

But by the time two weeks had passed it began to disconcert her less. She began to feel a little tender toward Jim, for thinking she was so much better and more beautiful than she actually was. And he made no demands, no unseemly displays of affection. It seemed to her admirable and quite touching that he could like her so much and want her so much and yet behave with restraint, so as not to risk making trouble with Sonny. She began, after a while, to be very sympathetic to him, sympathetic because of his loneliness and his marital troubles. For a few days, when his attention had made her nervous, she was sympathetic to Patsy, but that changed. He was obviously a very nice, very considerate, very loving young man. A woman who would not recognize that and make much of it was obviously either a fool or a bitch or both.

Gradually she began to wish she were the woman Jim thought she was. At times, combing her hair, she wished it. At times, with Sonny, she wished it. Sonny did not think her ideal; he knew she was proud and gluttonous. He had no interest in changing her, or in marrying her. He would never make her better, nor she him. They could only get worse, more violent, more emotional, more sordid. There would be less and less tenderness, less and less grace, less and less consideration; a great deal of lessening awaited her with Sonny. He had been a continent, her continent, Sonny had. What she feared was that she had come to the end of him. What was left of it, that country where she had been alive? Phone calls, a few visits, some sex, many fights. The plains, the forests, and the valleys, those were behind her. There was just the coast, with a nice wave now and then to watch for, and the beach littered with beer cans and chewing gum wrappers.

Jim could not be a continent, but he was at least a clean beach, and perhaps the best she would find. It would be nice to entertain him, to let him discover her. And when he did perhaps she would not be the lonely mistress of a great ranch or the shrieking bitch she became with Sonny; perhaps she would be the woman Jim saw, someone gentle, someone with grace, someone to give him a kind of comfort his nervous young wife was never going to give him. She began to feel considerate of him and a little responsible for him. It was a pleasing thing, to be suddenly guardian of the confidence of a young man. She began to feel an urge to teach him, to lecture him, to show him things.

Even so, as much as she had begun to like Jim, it would not normally have occurred to her to ask him to the ranch. Instead she had asked Sonny. There was to be a free week, while the production shifted to L.A., and she had supposed Sonny would spend most of it with her. Except for a fight or two they had gotten on well while she was in Amarillo. Sonny had more or less agreed to drive her home and spend three or four days. It was agreed upon for a week, and then, for no reason but restlessness, Sonny changed his mind. There was a rodeo in Flagstaff, and Highway Sixty-six ran right from Amarillo to Flagstaff to L.A. Eleanor was not overly surprised when he told her he was going to the rodeo, but she was furious anyway.

"Why go, damn it?" she asked. "You can't ride until the movie is finished. You've been to thousands of rodeos. What's so important about this one?"

"It ain't especially important," he said. "I just feel like going."

"Thanks," she said, crying a few angry tears. "It's always nice to be reminded how little I mean to you. It restores my perspective, for what that's worth."

"What are you bitchin' about? You been here three weeks." He was lying on her bed reading a rodeo newspaper.

"Oh, boy, keep on," she said. "You're in rare form. Three weeks. That's how long it takes you to get enough of me, is it? A year or two more and it'll drop to two weeks, or one week, or just long enough to screw."

In a fit of fury she snatched the newspaper out of his hand and flung it at the wastebasket. Sonny was mildly amused.

"Hard to resist the highway when I get an itch to go," he said.

"Fine. Don't resist it. Go on. I too can have itches that are hard to resist." She sat down at the dressing table, put on her shoes, and began to comb her hair.

"Going somewhere to scratch one?" he asked, grinning at her arrogantly. He knew she wasn't.

"No, I'm going to see Joe Percy. I've neglected him this whole visit. Maybe you can find a rodeo to go to tonight. Make it in North Dakota, if possible."

But her visit to Joe was brief. Eleanor was on edge, fearful that he might make a pass. Joe realized it and did nothing of the sort, but the edge remained. He fixed her a drink and they chatted and she looked about restlessly, so much so that he finally suggested they take a walk. The suggestion was so ludicrous that it restored her calm.

"A walk. Where?"

"I've discovered a back street," he said. "It runs behind the motel. It's possible to walk on it without getting run over. When do you suppose they're going to introduce sidewalks to Texas?"

So they actually went for a walk on the graveled street behind the motel. Dogs barked at them from yards, and the sky was pale with starlight. Eleanor began to feel comfortable again.

"I have no intention of letting that one-night stand spoil our friendship," Joe said. "In case you were worrying."

"Forgive me," she said. "I used you to get over a very bad mood. Why do you put up with me?"

He shrugged. "We could get snakebit on this road," he said.

He seemed to sink briefly into a bad mood of his own, but as they were standing on the motel sidewalk, waiting for her taxi, he cheered up again. For a minute she considered asking him to the ranch but decided against it. Los Angeles was the place to see him—his house was there. When she got back to the hotel Sonny was on the bed where she had left him, watching a Joel McCrea movie on TV.

The next day Jim announced that his wife was coming for the weekend, and Eleanor's mood dipped badly. It was an irrational dip, for Jim seemed nothing but depressed at the thought of the visit. Sonny was not depressed though, and his attitude depressed her. She found she still resented

Patsy. It was at such times that she hated the play and counterplay of desire, and would have agreed with Lucy that it was better to be done with it all, to be safe, serene, only interested in magazines and in the ranch. Unfortunately she was not serene. The weekend would be a tangle of emotion, most of it bad. She did not want to compete with a young wife for her husband's attention, nor did she want a young wife competing with her for Sonny's. When it occurred to her that she did not have to stay, it was a great relief. Immediately she remembered the ranch, and missed it, and was eager to be out of the hotel and out of Amarillo, back to her own balcony. If Sonny wanted a drive to Flagstaff, let him have it.

When she told Jim she was going he was very obviously disappointed.

"Gee, I'll miss you," he said wistfully. "There's no telling when I'll see you again."

His tone touched her. She was not accustomed to being missed. Sonny never seemed to miss her, or at least never admitted it if he did. Jim sounded as if he really would not know what to do without her.

"You'll hardly have time. You have to go to California next week."

"Sometime next week. I don't know exactly when."

It would be nice to sit on her patio with him and talk. He was looking very droopy and he looked much better when he was cheerful; then he was boyish and attractive. And she always felt awful after leaving Sonny, as if for a day or two her blood had stopped moving. She could do nothing and enjoy nothing and was nervous and irritable. She swung the sash of her dress thoughtfully. Jim was not the sort of person to put the cowhands off. He was too quiet. Effusive women and loud-mouthed men put the cowhands off.

"You might visit me for a day or two, if you're at loose ends," she said. "I'd like you to see my house."

He was no good at hiding delight, and it was pleasant to see his face change. "Gosh, I'd love to," he said. Then he looked confused for a moment, as if he were afraid she would ask him to bring his wife and baby; but when he realized she had no such intention he became very happy and animated, livelier than she had ever seen him. He even persuaded her to come to the motel and swim. She liked the water, but she waited until evening, when most of the crew was gone.

Later that evening she had second thoughts about the invitation. Sonny had been at the motel, and had brought her home after the swim. They were arguing about whether to eat out or eat in, while her hair dried. Somehow, seeing Jim out in the open, and not at dinner or with Sonny, had put the whole business in a different light. In that light he looked more of a boy, and his admiration had embarrassed her a little. She had been glad when Sonny had strolled up and taken charge of her. She had more or less forgiven him his decision to go to Flagstaff and they were arguing on good terms, so she told him about inviting Jim to the ranch and told him she had second thoughts about it.

"Uninvite him," he said. "It's your ranch."

"Yes, but it would crush him. I suppose there's really no problem. Maybe Lucy will like him. What's a day or two."

"A long time to be bored," he said. "Pore Jim. Nobody wants him."

Hearing him dismissed piqued her a little. "Don't run him down," she said, opening a jar of hand cream. "He's quite wantable. I don't know what bothers me about him."

Sonny came up behind her, bent over, and enveloped her in his arms, nuzzling and swaying her from side to side. She got hand cream on his forearms when she grabbed them They looked at themselves in the mirror, both amused.

"Probably too young for you," he said. "Ain't much sport to be had with kids."

"I'm glad to hear you say that. I thought young women were second only to bulls in your affections."

She had meant to leave before Patsy came, but in the end decided to stay another day. She felt too good to do any of the things that leaving involved and instead of packing spent the morning in bed reading. When Jim spirited Patsy away, she was just as glad. Sonny deposited her at her airplane at dawn the next morning. She felt better about him and about herself than she had in a long while.

"I'll see you when I get done in Hollywood," he said. "Maybe we'll go to May-hi-co this fall."

"Okay," she said. "Have fun in Flagstaff."

She stood by the plane trying to chat with her pilot but in reality watching the white hearse streak back down the highway toward Amarillo. It was soon lost in the morning grayness. She saw the sunrise light the whole Texas plain, but the sight didn't touch her. That night she called Sonny and he was not in, and what had seemed simple in Amarillo became a confusion in her breast. It had always been that way, as soon as they lost sight of each other. She remembered him well enough, but memory never brought her contentment.

Jim came on Monday, and it seemed to Eleanor that his mere arrival caused a demon to seize her. All weekend she had fretted about Sonny; she had come a dozen times to the old conclusions that she had been coming to for years: that they were bad for each other, that she would never have him like she wanted him, that he would trifle with her forever. If she were wise she would break it off. If she were even reasonably sensible she would break it off. Or, if she could not be either wise or sensible, she ought to move in the other direction, take a wild gamble and marry him. He would marry her, if only for the hell of it, or to be able to say he had. Or for the sense of triumph it would give him, or for the ranch, or because she really did have more that he liked than any other woman. She had always known that: Their peak was not an age, but each other. If that were not the case some other woman would have risen from among his anonymous seductions and made herself visible; and in many years none had. So she fretted, and missed him, and wondered if she ought to go back, ought to make some gesture. All she did was call, and he was never in.

The demon that infused her when Jim came took the form of a fever. She had expected to be bored and on edge for two days, doing her best to keep him from making a pass. She wanted to behave from the moment he arrived so that he would have no false hopes and Lucy no reason to be upset.

It should have been easy, for Jim was not a difficult person. From the moment he stepped into the house Lucy was for him. He was so quiet, diffident, nice, polite—Lucy all but adopted him. He was just the kind of boy she liked, for despite his diffidence he was in high good spirits and was anything but solemn. Everyone smiled when they saw him—even the gardeners.

She herself was the only one disturbed by Jim's presence, and before the first evening was over she was very disturbed. Things didn't go as she had supposed they would. She had imagined that she would have to make the conversation, and keep making it as an obstacle to him becoming romantic. But when they sat down alone to dine on the patio, she felt no desire to talk. Jim carried the conversation and it was she who was silent. She felt more than silent; she felt heavy and a little sullen. He still wanted her; obviously he did. The glances he sent her way held a clear longing, but he was as respectful and careful as he had been in Amarillo. It irked her. He looked so young and so fresh, in a short-sleeved blue shirt and white pants and loafers, his blond hair worn longish in imitation of the Californians. She had lost completely all the good emotions she felt for him in Amarillo. She didn't feel that she could be good for him, gentle with him, loving or tender or wise, the mistress-mother-confidante that she had once vaguely envisioned herself. She no longer wanted to restore his confidence in himself and send him back to his young wife experienced and secure. She felt something much coarser and didn't like it at all. It was a shock, but it was there. The formality and respect and conversation merely irked her. When she looked at his young face, his clean hair and tanned skin, she didn't feel loving or considerate, she felt an awful rapacious emotion that she had never felt before for a man so young. She could not put the sensation down, and his talk began to annoy her terribly. If he would only stop talking about French movies and make the pass he had been wanting to make for weeks he could have her. She could touch his fine skin. She had never felt such a desire to use a person physically as she began to feel for Jim. He was too nice. She had an urge to despoil him in some way. He continued to talk and didn't make the pass, and finally, appalled at his timidity and her own desire, she excused herself on the feeble grounds of a headache and he went downstairs to the library to read.

Alone, she felt very strange. How could she want such a child, so hotly and so incongruously, when she had never been so attuned to Sonny? She sat on her bed feeling dull and sad, wishing very much that Sonny would call and bring her back to herself. It was nonsense; she had never before in her life had the slightest desire to seduce a young man. They had flirted in Amarillo, and she had embroidered the flirtation a bit, but no such fever ought to have followed from it.

She didn't sleep well, and the next day all the people of the ranch walked small around her. She was quiet, but her quietness had passion beneath it, and anger, and the people who knew her kept their distance. Lucy talked little, and of the merest nothings. The foreman was careful too; he had just discovered that six yearlings had been poisoned by oil waste but he decided to hold the news until the weather was better at the big house.

Jim was the only one who didn't know anything was wrong. He breakfasted with Eleanor on the patio, and to him she looked great. There were shadows under her eyes, but they merely made her face seem lovelier, her beauty richer. At breakfast Eleanor tried to starve the fever. She starved it by looking at the land and not at Jim, by chatting about a John Cheever story, by eating more than she usually did. It was ridiculous; she was not going to enter on a sluttish middle age. If she loved him, then of course; but any glance told her that she didn't love him. Nothing could induce her to keep him two weeks, and probably not two days. What she wanted of him wouldn't take more than an hour, if he would only start it.

Jim did notice that Eleanor looked at him differently than she had in Amarillo. She seemed moody and withdrawn, but he did not suspect the reason. Yet he wanted her very much and was very excited by the fact that she had invited him to the ranch. He hoped a moment might come when they would be close enough that he could touch her. He had imagined the moment many times. Eleanor was so much kinder to him than Patsy, so much gentler, and so much more considerate. She really seemed to see him, whereas Patsy only seemed to need him—or else hate him. But he was a little surprised by the change in Eleanor. In Amarillo she had been relaxed and warm and talkative. At the ranch she was silent, and there was something a little threatening about her silence. She was much more reserved than she had been; he was puzzled and didn't know how to break through the reserve.

In the afternoon of his second day at the ranch Eleanor fell into an annoyed boredom. It was a hot still afternoon, with not a breath of breeze. White thunderheads hung motionless above the browning land. There was nothing to do but talk, and she was sick of that. With Sonny there, she would have shut Lucy out of the bedroom and lounged on the bed all afternoon, she reading and drinking iced tea, Sonny napping or drinking beer. But she could not shut Lucy out of the bedroom for Jim, even if Jim had done anything to make it necessary, which he hadn't. Annoyed, she put on some duck trousers and field boots and a khaki shirt and told Lucy to fix a thermos of icewater and one of iced coffee. She asked Jim if he would like to see the ranch. He said he would and changed into Levi's. She got a .22 and some shells and the two thermoses and they got in the old high-axled station wagon she used for ranch trips. The station wagon itself was like an oven, but Eleanor didn't mind. There were times when she liked the breezeless August heat. Soon they were both sweating. Her temples and upper lip were beaded, and a line of sweat dripped out of Jim's sideburns, bisecting his cheek.

"I thought we might drive across the ranch," she said. "This feed road goes straight through it. It's about eighteen miles."

But the drive worked no better than anything else had worked since he came to the ranch. They drove west, off the level plain where the headquarters stood, into rolling mes-quite country, cut by gulleys and crisscrossed with low ridges. In contrast to the white clouds the sky seemed almost yellowish with heat. The road dust and the mesquite and even the car seats smelled hot. Eleanor didn't care—the heat at least was positive. The sun came straight through the window and shone on them, making their clothes hot. She kept the thermos open and drank iced coffee as she drove. Jim irked her terribly. He sweated and listened attentively to her offhand remarks about one pasture and another, as if he were a child being taken through a museum.

Six or eight miles into the ranch she abandoned the idea

of driving across it. It would be too tiresome a drive back, and the ranch got rougher the farther west she went. She grew tired of easing the station wagon across creek beds. There was a large lake up a side road to the north and she turned and drove to that. The bank had tall cottonwood trees shading it and a good covering of green Bermuda grass. The water was as still as a sheet of brown glass, its surface broken only when a dragonfly or a wasp dipped into it. They got out, taking the thermos and the gun, and walked up the bank, both glad of the shade. Eleanor thought he might use his imagination, or if not his, some novelists', and suggest they go swimming, sans suits, but if such an idea entered his head he didn't voice it. Instead they did some shooting. They found cow chips and sticks and a few beer cans some fisherman-cowhand had left behind, and threw them in the water; they ran two boxes of shells through the .22 shooting at them. Jim was a better shot than she was, to her surprise. A hawk alit in the flat behind the tank while they were shooting, and she shot at it and missed it clean. Jim's shot hit the branch the hawk sat on; the hawk slowly took flight and alit again, out of range.

When they had used up all their shells and were amusing themselves by plinking the shell cases into the brown water Eleanor felt some pressure ease. She told Jim he shot well, and he looked pleased. She grew ashamed of herself for being irked with him—he was very nice. He clearly knew very little about women and had not suspected or understood her fever. Her own expectations had gone awry; perhaps he loved his wife more than she had supposed. She lay back on the Bermuda grass, her eyelids pressed down by the heat; she dozed a bit and when she awoke Jim passed his hand across her damp forehead and stroked her hair. She smiled and closed her eyes again, waiting, but he did little more, only stroked her hair and once her arm. She did not become angry. He was young. Perhaps he could not imagine making love to someone in the grass, by a tank. It was not the young who were reckless in that way. She was expecting the wrong thing of him again. Probably it would seem too Lady Chatterley to him; he was shy and conventional, and screwing an older woman in midafternoon on a bed of Bermuda grass was not conventional. It would require a different kind of ardor entirely from the sort he had. She had never been the older woman before and decided it required patience and kindness and a willingness to lead. She had never been inclined to lead, but she could not feel angry at Jim. Perhaps his feelings were as confused as hers. If he were merely confused there was no point in her being cruel.

The heat and the nap had relaxed her. She sat up yawning, and Jim wanted to hold her hand. She let him, and they sat by the tank until the sun was falling, chatting pleasantly. He told her she was beautiful and she smiled and said nothing; they chatted of things unrelated to their confusion. Eleanor had no thoughts. Sometimes she came to the tank with Lucy, who loved to fish. She sat under the cottonwoods reading, or merely thinking, while Lucy kept an intense watch on three or four poles. Finally she got up and led Jim to the station wagon. They drove back to the ranch with the sun behind them. The sky turned blue again as the air cooled.

Eleanor drove slowly, looking at the pastures and the clouds. She would have liked her own feelings to cool and clear like the sky, but they didn't. The time on the tank dam had been a respite. The fever came back, stronger and more hateful than it had been the day before. It was an awful urge. When they got to the ranch house she left the station wagon in the circular driveway and strode inside. "Come on up," she said to Jim and he followed her upstairs. The patio was in shade, but Eleanor did not go out. She stopped at the desk in her bedroom and turned to watch him, gripping the edge of the desk with her hands.

"I'm glad we didn't go the other ten miles," he said, waiting for her to come to the patio. "What now?"

"Oh, I don't know," Eleanor said, tossing her hair free of the high-collared shirt. "I feel kind of wild." He looked at her in surprise and she tried to smile, but a smile did not go with her emotions. She felt wrong, too bold, too exposed. If only he would move toward her—any sort of touch would begin it—and cover her again.

But Jim was not sure, and for a moment he was afraid to gamble. It had sounded like an invitation, but he wasn't sure. Her look was wild and a little frightening. She kept pulling one hand through her heavy blond hair. He didn't know. A canyon lay between them, deep with ambiguities. He was not sure what her look meant, and he didn't leap. The moment stretched as slowly as a shadow.

"I guess I should shower," he said uncertainly.

"Yes, so should I," Eleanor said and looked down at her feet, her face at once changed, as if she had felt a rain of cold water on it. Then Jim started to her; something in the change of her face convinced him, but she had stopped looking at him. She moved slowly toward the patio, as if she had suddenly grown tired. When he took her arm she looked at him with contempt, but he held her, anyway, and she let him kiss her. But she had gone flat, and the kiss was flat. She had wanted him to kiss her all day, but she had suddenly stopped wanting it. Jim was the opposite. He wanted desperately to make up for having moved too late. Eleanor felt like herself again but heavy and cold. Finally she shook free, crying a little, and went to the patio and sat down in a chair. He followed but she wouldn't let him kiss her again.

"Don't, now," she said. "Please go and take your shower."

"No," he said, kneeling awkwardly by the chair. She let him have her hand. He was so upset that she tried to smile, but she could not really smile.

"You don't know much about women," she said quietly, looking off the balcony. Eight cowboys were coming into the barn, riding abreast across the dairy pasture.

"I guess I don't," Jim said. "I've fallen in love with you and I don't know what to do about it."

Eleanor smiled sadly and shook her head. "Please go shower," she said. "Then we'll eat some supper."

When he left, reluctant and abashed, she felt a moment of keen relief. At least it was finished, it was clear, it was done, whatever it had been. She felt quite without fever. No one was dead and she had not been allowed to be the slut she had wanted to be. In her relief she called in Lucy and briskly ordered supper, and by the time Jim returned, clean but gloomy, she had showered and put on a white dress and felt immeasurably better. It was a fine feeling, having got through something without a real catastrophe. For an hour she felt grateful and at peace.

Jim's gloom at supper was even endearing. She felt warm toward him, forgiving, and kept Lucy with them, so he could have no chance to launch into protestations of love. She wanted him to believe that missing whatever they had missed was really for the best—missing it had saved their friendship. But Jim was no longer interested in their friendship. He didn't want it and it didn't please him that she had become gracious and friendly again. He did not accept his mistake in the bedroom as being definitive. He knew she had wanted him, and he did not believe she had stopped completely just because he had hesitated at the wrong time.

Eleanor knew that he was in the throes of an intense disappointment. She blamed herself and was as nice as she could be. She knew he was going to make another effort and made no attempt to avoid it. They went back upstairs after supper, and when he came near her on the patio and told her again that he loved her she thought she was prepared to be kind and tolerant.

"You don't, really," she said. "You've just never known anyone like me."

"I do, though," he said. "I do love you."

He was sincere. Eleanor sighed. He kissed her, trying as hard as he could. The fine clarity that had come to her in her relief began to slip away. Her feelings were a jumble, and in the jumble somewhere were all the bad feelings she thought she had thrown out. It seemed for a moment that she herself had been scattered, thrown away. She was somewhere there, if he could salvage her and put her parts together again.

Jim tried, but he couldn't find all of her. When she ceased to feel clear and tolerant and kind she dropped into a stupor of discouragement and merely felt dull. In the dullness she let him close to her again—she had no shame in the dullness—and took his kisses leaning back against the patio wall, where anyone walking across the courtyard might have seen her. She let him kiss her as long as he wanted to, let him stroke her hair and her throat, let him move his body against hers. Once he stopped kissing her, discouraged by her discouragement.

"What's the matter?" he asked.

"It's hopeless."

"No it isn't."

547

Eleanor smiled a little. He tried to show her it wasn't hopeless, but she felt as heavy and sluggish as mud, and when he did something that caused her to tremble it was not the trembling of passion but the kind of motion mud makes when it is shaken. She let him move her to the bed in her bedroom, hoping he would find her. She would have welcomed the fever, but it didn't come. Her skin might have been dead, her nerves disconnected. Every touch was flat. Sometime, somehow, she had set her brakes. Perhaps Jim could release them. She wanted him to, and he tried. He brought all his eagerness to the task, but eagerness was not sufficient. Her brakes stayed on. Whether they talked or whether they embraced the brakes were on. She would not undress. They twisted on the bed, rumpled, exhausted, separately frantic, not knowing what to do. Eleanor kept hoping for the fever long after she had ceased to expect it. Finally she despaired of it and slid off the bed to the floor. She sat with her back against the bed. Dim moonlight filled the open doors of the patio.

Jim was silent, and very depressed, she knew. Once her dress and her hair were straightened, she felt better. A little clarity came back. Once they stopped touching some of the deadness went away. She looked around at him and stretched out a hand for him to hold. He held it and looked at it in a way that amused her a little.

"You're looking at my hand as if it held the answer to all mysteries."

"I wish it did."

"It's just a woman's hand."

"Do you want me to go away? I mean leave the ranch?"

"No," she said, lying. "Don't be silly."

But the question piqued her. "For a smart young man you ask awfully stupid questions," she said. "It's not really necessary to talk to women, you know. Sometimes it's pleasant and other times it's very stupid."

She checked her anger with difficulty. She wanted to tell him he could have had her practically any time in the last two days. No one should be so stupid—particularly no one who had been married for almost three years.

"Maybe you ought to go back to your wife," she said finally. "I imagine she needs you. I don't, really."

548

"I don't know what she needs," he said stiffly, as if offended that she would mention Patsy at such a time.

"No, and you won't find out while you're pursuing me," she said. "This is my fault and I feel badly about it. This kind of fluttering around doesn't become either one of us. The longer we wallow in it the sorrier we'll feel for ourselves and the less we'll like one another. I hate the whole business."

Jim released her hand. He got off the bed and began to tuck in his shirttails. "I guess it was too much to hope for," he said.

"That's exactly why it didn't happen," Eleanor said. "You were convinced in advance it was too much to hope for. Well, it wasn't at all. You were mistaken. I'm just as vulnerable as anyone. You shouldn't have built me up into someone unattainable. If you hadn't we'd have attained plenty."

"I know," he said. "But I know better now. Why is it too late?"

"I don't know why. How should I know why? Please go to bed."

He kissed her before he left, and she allowed it. When he was gone she got up, undressed, and listlessly put on her dressing gown. She turned the bed down and sat on it for a time, discouraged and dispirited, jiggling a couple of sleeping pills in her palm. It was all such a mess, and it was not finished, either. She had been stupid not to tell him to leave when he had asked if she wanted him to. He would keep at her for another day and she would reach a point of not caring and let him. It would just make things worse, but it would probably happen. She was not a terribly hard person to wear down. Just having him gone was the nicest thing she could imagine, and yet she knew she was not simply going to walk downstairs and tell him she had changed her mind, he would have to leave. Instead, she would take the sleeping pills—in a minute she would.

As she was sitting on the bed she heard a car approaching the house. It came into the circular driveway, stopped, a door slammed. Curious, she walked out on the patio and looked down. The pale moonlight shone on the long white hearse. It seemed such luck, such a miracle, that she could scarcely believe it; her legs shook a little at the thought of what would have happened if he had come an hour earlier. When she went back to the bedroom, Sonny was there. The smell of the room had changed. He sat on the bed and began to pull off his boots.

"Hi," he said. "Never got to Flagstaff. Complications come up. How you?"

"I'm glad to see you," she said, sitting down by him. He gave her a light kiss.

"You sound as tired as I am," he said, peeling off his shirt. "What you been doing?"

"Oh, showing Jim the ranch."

"Oh, yeah, Jim's here," he said. "Forgot. Maybe he'll ride to L.A. with me."

He lay down and stretched out an arm, and Eleanor lay down beside him. "Don't wake me for breakfast," he said.

"Don't worry," she said. After he was asleep she got up and put the two pills back in their bottle and closed the doors to the patio and pulled the shades so the morning sun would not wake them. Lucy would see the hearse and take care of the telephone and Jim and anyone else that needed taking care of. They could sleep.

15

"What are you doing? Why are you telling me this?" Patsy said, so agitated that she wanted to fling the phone down. She looked around in distraction. Davey was in his highchair making a great spectacular mess with his carrot goop. She had almost finished feeding him and was making herself a salad involving cottage cheese and black cherries when the phone rang. Jim began a confession and the evening was spoiled. She wanted to fling the phone down.

"Do you enjoy hurting me?" she asked. "Why would you tell me that, otherwise? It's terrible of you."

Jim was surprised. He had not expected her to be upset; he had expected her to be glad to hear what he was saying. In a way, Sonny's arrival had been a relief to him as well as to Eleanor, though it had eliminated a tantalizing possibility. But his conscience began to hurt him and he felt an urge to call Patsy. He went into the little town near the ranch and called from a phone booth near a truck stop, so his voice was occasionally drowned out by the sound of trucks pulling away. Down the highway from him the sun was setting, but the phone booth was still hot.

"I just thought I ought to be honest," he said. "Nothing happened. I didn't sleep with her. I'm really sorry about it all. I guess I did have a crush on her, but it didn't come to anything. It didn't hurt anything."

"What do you mean, it didn't hurt anything?" she said. "You leave me all summer to go have a crush on another woman and then you don't even sleep with her and you call me up when I was perfectly happy to tell me all this! It hurts everything! Now I don't know what to do. I want to rip this phone out!"

"Don't do that," he said. "Why?"

"So you can't call me and hurt me any more," she said, beginning to cry.

"Wait," she said. "Davey's got carrot in his ears." She went over and swabbed him briefly and sat him on the floor. She was crying, very agitated, her chest heaving. The receiver of the wall phone dangled. She didn't want to pick it up. Davey eyed it hopefully, but Patsy finally picked it up.

"I don't know why you're so upset," Jim said. "I couldn't help having the crush. What you should be glad about is that it didn't amount to anything. I didn't sleep with her."

"Well, thanks, only don't do me that kind of favors," she said. "I can't stand self-pity and you're dripping with it."

"I am not," he said. "I just called thinking you might be lonesome. I thought you might be unhappy. Is it so bad to call?"

"I don't know. I just hate you. It's too bad you didn't get

to screw your aging millionairess. What are you going to do now?"

"Tonight I'm going to an amateur rodeo with Sonny. Tomorrow we're driving to L.A."

"Sure you are," Patsy said. "Can I depend on that, or will you figure out some way to get left behind, so you can have another try? Better try quick, before another of her low-class boy friends comes in and beats you out."

"Shut up," he said, stung. "She doesn't have low-class boy friends."

"Ha," Patsy said. "How do you know who she screws, you've only been there two days. She may screw her gardeners for all you know."

"Shut up," he said loudly. "I don't like you using that kind of language anyway."

"And you especially don't like me using it about your fading violet," Patsy said, the venom rising in her so rapidly that she could hardly pour it out fast enough. "I can use any word I want to. How close did you get to this prize, may I ask?"

"I'd like to brain you," he said. "I called to be nice. I never wanted this fight."

"I never wanted your confession, either," she said. "I was having a pleasant supper. I didn't need to know you had gone off to try and screw an aging heiress. If that's the kind of husband I've got I'd just as soon not be reminded of it."

"I called to tell you I love you," Jim said. "Don't you understand anything? I do love you. That was the whole point of the call."

"Oh, fuck your noble motives," she said bitterly. "Fat consolation they are. Tallulah or whoever she is wouldn't let you screw her so you love me again. That's music to my ears."

"I ought to come home and beat the hell out of you," he said, not very convincingly. Her anger shook him a little.

"Oh, no, I think you ought to stay there," she said. "You might get another chance at Tallulah. Maybe you could find a cowgirl or something while she's busy with Sonny."

"Come on, Patsy," he said helplessly.

Patsy was clenching and unclenching her fists, trying to calm down. Her venom surprised her too. "Don't Patsy me," she said, but a little wearily. "You've ruined things now. I don't know what to do."

"I haven't done anything," he repeated. "I was just intrigued with her. I didn't sleep with her."

"That just makes it worse," she said, all spirit running out of her. She remembered what she had been doing all afternoon.

"Why?"

"I don't know," she said. "Maybe it doesn't make it worse. I'm going to hang up. Go on to your rodeo."

"No, don't hang up," he said, frightened at the thought of the uncertainty he would be in if she hung up at such a time, in such a tone.

"Why shouldn't I?" she asked listlessly, no longer particularly caring whether she did or didn't.

"Because it's not that bad," he said. "I know it was foolish, but I do love *you.*"

She was silent. He repeated it. It sounded true. "Surely it isn't so unforgivable," he said.

"Oh, Jim," she said. "Why did you go away just when we had Davey and could have been happy? We didn't have so many problems then."

"I didn't know going off would make problems," he said. "I really wanted the job."

"Couldn't you get out of going to California? We just get farther and farther apart this way."

Jim didn't know what to say. With her voice in his ear he missed her and would have liked to be in Houston; but at the same time he wanted to go to California in the morning, with Sonny in the hearse.

"No, it's too late to get out of it," he said. "I won't be there long, and I won't make any more mistakes of this kind. It'll work out. You'll see."

"You don't know that," she said, her discouragement growing heavier. "You're just saying what any man would say. You don't really want to come home and do anything about us, or you would. You don't know what to do about me, or you would. You don't even like to think about what to do about me. Go on and have your vacation. Enjoy Disneyland. Maybe you can find an aging actress to admire."

"Please don't start that again."

"A young actress then," Patsy said. "I don't care. Listen, I've got to get Davey. I'm going to hang up."

"I'm sorry," he said. "Don't sound that way. I'll call you in the morning. Maybe it won't seem so drastic then."

"Don't count on it not seeming drastic. Go on to your rodeo and stay away from that woman."

Davey had scooted into the hall and was staring at a small gray cat that had appeared at the top of the landing. "Goodness, see the kitty," she said, sniffing. She opened the door and with her foot and the little cat walked in, past a startled Davey. It rubbed itself against her ankle. She picked it up and they stared eye to eye for a moment. Then she took it to the kitchen and gave it some milk. "I oughtn't to feed you," she said. The cat ignored her. She let it drink and took Davey to the bed. He was not happy about leaving the cat but she put him on his back and tickled him until he forgot it; he grinned and kicked happily. While he was playing with a toy giraffe Patsy began to cry again. The cat came in and jumped up on the bed. It licked its paws and watched her cry. Davey mouthed the giraffe and watched the cat, who ignored him.

Patsy did not cry hard or long—she felt too listless and unenergetic. Her throat and chest felt stuffed, as if she were an unemptied vacuum cleaner. Such a mess and such a cheap mess, common and hopeless and yet puzzling. She could remember vaguely that she had been unhappy at times, a year before, two years before, but in retrospect it seemed such a mild, guiltless, unessential unhappiness that it scarcely deserved the name. It was the kind of unhappiness two aspirin should have cured. Then her dissatisfactions had been normal and natural ones, at least, and not so confusing.

That kind of unhappiness was all past, all past for good, she felt, looking at the young child and the young cat. The cat reached out a paw and tapped one of her hands. She scratched it between the ears and it closed its eyes. Davey was delighted and made sounds. The kitten stretched out on its side and the blue spread, yawned, got ready to go to sleep. Davey would have liked to touch it but didn't quite dare. Once when he advanced a hand the cat raised its head and looked at him sternly. "Un-uh," Patsy said. "Let the kitty-cat sleep."

Evening was closing down. The room was almost dark. Patsy picked up the phone and called Juanita, asked her to get a taxi and please come, she needed to go out. There was to be a graduate students' party that evening to celebrate the decline of summer and the impending resumption of graduate miseries. She had not meant to go, mostly because she didn't want to see Hank publicly. She was afraid something might show. She had gone to Amarillo with some slight hope that she and Jim might bind themselves together again, in a way that would exclude Hank, but it hadn't happened. Her marriage was simply out of control. Jim was spinning off into some new orbit, far from her, and there was no way she could check him. She had come back to Houston with the sense that it was simply all beyond her, finally. She couldn't reach Jim, and he couldn't reach her. But Hank could reach her, in at least one way. He wanted her more than ever and the night of her return she was very vulnerable to being wanted. His desire carried her with it; when he touched her she felt all the things she had always hoped to feel. Most of the four days she had been back had been spent in his bed. Life became so physical that she had no time to think, no way to think; the bed was their country and thought only a kind of evening shadow that sometimes stretched across them when they were tired, their skins still smelling of the sun.

But Jim's phone call made the new country seem unreal. She was back with herself, her marriage, her guilt and loneliness, her child and a cat. Where had she been? What had she been doing? Details of the day's passion rose to mind, sickening her. Poor Jim had done nothing. He loved her. Why had she berated him so? She was the one who was guilty. She knew she didn't want to sit there all evening thinking about it, the cat asleep, Davey soon to be asleep. Better to go to the party. Better, perhaps, to see Hank in public while the country seemed so flat and barren to her. Perhaps she would give him up, make Jim come home, try again. Anyway the Hortons would be there. She could get drunk and not have to think about it all night. She had not been drunk in a long time. She put on a green summer dress and was ready to go when Juanita arrived. Even in her gloom it was nice to think how surprised everyone would be to see her, especially Hank. She herself did not ever expect to be pleasantly surprised again. Jim's little confession might have been her last surprise.

Six hours later everyone was drunk or, at the very least, tipsy and danced-out and sweaty and feeling happy and doomed. All the windows in Kenny's hot bare-floored second-story apartment had been flung as high as they would go, giving the neighbors an unwelcome earful of rock music. Only the host and his girl—a stocky junior from Harlingen—were left on their feet. Everyone else was sitting on the floor, drinking and watching them dance. Patsy sat between Hank and Emma, and they were all slightly high. She had not really paid Hank much attention and was sure that no one had noticed anything. There was so little to notice that it almost upset her, for it seemed to her that he was much less interesting and much less forceful in a group than he was alone. In a group Hank faded out of sight; Flap had more to say, and even Kenny Cambridge was livelier.

But Patsy was not really bothered; like everyone else she was mostly interested in watching Lee Duffin. Bill was out of town and she had come to the party with her acknowledged boy friend; there had been gossip about them all spring but actually seeing them together was something else. He was a slim young graduate student named Peter, a nice boy with a neat soft blond beard. He danced awkwardly and clearly felt awkward; coming had apparently been Lee's idea. Lee looked splendid, Patsy thought. She wore a white summer dress and was neither nervous nor abashed. She took good care of Peter, danced with him, kept him drinking until he relaxed, and treated him very tenderly. "He's so slight," Patsy said to Emma. It was strangely cheering to have another adulteress in the room.

"I like him, though," Emma said. "I admit it seems a little too Henry James. But they look nice together. I kind of envy her. Nobody's ever going to make me into a Madame de Vionnet. Peter's certainly nicer than her husband."

"Who wouldn't be?" Patsy said, drinking some more

vodka punch. It had a nice limey taste. Lee looked pensively into her glass and then smiled at Peter. It occurred to Patsy that she was playing the role with Peter that Eleanor Guthrie had played with her husband; she might be playing it with him at that moment, at some distant rodeo, while Sonny rode a bull. The world seemed very confusing. It bothered her that Hank was not impressive in a crowd. He never had anything to say. He was good-looking in his way, but she didn't care about that. She wanted him not to be so dull. Then he slyly hooked one of his fingers through one of hers and she forgot that she was worried. Lightness filled her head and she felt happy. The touch reminded her of other touches. Kenny was fondling his sloppy girl friend, who seemed neither pleased nor annoyed. They suddenly sat down in the middle of the dance floor. "Hey, your beard needs trimming," the girl said.

"Let's talk about literature," Kenny said, ignoring her.

Flap was lying full length on the floor, his arms over his eyes. He had drunk twice as much as anyone else—everyone observed it—yet he held it well. Patsy had danced with him for an hour while he was getting drunk. "Bringing It All Back Home" was on the phonograph.

"I hate literature," Flap said. "Don't we all?"

"Not me," Emma said. "I hate mornings. I also hate cereal. It's so goddamn unpleasant to look at, once it soaks up. Some cereals particularly."

"Don't hate literature," Kenny said gloomily. He had been smoking pot, as had his stocky girl. "Hate the English department if you want to. Fuck the English department, in fact."

"Fuck Post cereals," Emma said. "I don't like them."

Patsy drank more punch. She felt lighter still, and happier. Hank was stroking the inside of her hand with one finger. Lee Duffin looked quiet and thoughtful. Peter lay stretched out on the floor with his head in her lap. Lee stroked his forehead. Patsy suddenly found herself liking Lee enormously, for her poise, for her courage, for her kindness to Peter. She found herself liking everyone enormously: Emma, who went on morning after morning feeding her boys cereal; Flap, who went on day after day studying for prelims, and who drank well at parties; Kenny, for having the party; even the stocky girl friend, for being so tolerant of Kenny. She had not been to a party in a long time and had forgotten the feelings that swept over her; she had a strong sense of being involved along with everyone else in the ruin of something. What was being ruined scarcely mattered: a civilization, a generation, or only the summer, or only an evening, or perhaps only themselves. What seemed important was that they were all in it together. No one seemed unhappy, and yet no one was likely to be spared. She drank some more and peeled her wet blouse loose from her chest. "The humidity is getting worse," she said.

Kenny Cambridge took offense at her remark. "It ticks me off," he said. "Here we are, the smartest people around, and nobody wants to talk about literature."

"Why should we talk about literature?" Flap asked. No one had an answer.

"I'd rather have an orgy," the stocky girl said, startling everyone.

"I vote against it," Lee said mildly.

"Me too," Patsy said. "There's nothing I'd rather not see than all of you naked."

To everyone's dismay, Peter asked Kenny to read some of his poems aloud. Everyone else had been grimly determined never to ask Kenny to read. Kenny went to an old scratched-up desk and opened a drawer, and a huge cockroach ran out and across the desk.

"Shit," Kenny said. "A cockroach was in my poems."

"Maybe it was Kafka," Emma said. She looked like she was getting sleepy.

Kenny hastily read a poem. There was silence. "You're all too drunk to appreciate me," he said.

"Let's talk about Norman Mailer," Flap said.

"Kenny made me read *The American Dream*," the stocky girl said. "I didn't see anything so good about it.

"I hear he acts crazy," she added, yawning and scratching her stomach.

"Don't put him down," Kenny said angrily.

"I wasn't."

"I didn't like that story that happened in the loft," Emma said. Her eyelids were falling.

"Why are we talking about him?" Patsy asked. She was

annoyed at Hank because he didn't say anything. She wanted very badly for him to say something brilliant. She felt she might stop loving him if he didn't. But he said nothing; he didn't even seem to be listening intelligently. It worried her. She could not help wondering if he was smart, and she didn't want to wonder such a thing.

"We could talk about Mary McCarthy," she said.

"What's there to say about her?" Flap asked.

"She was one of Edmund Wilson's wives," Lee said. She was amused by it all.

"Well, what's so good about Edmund Wilson?" Kenny said. "It's always Edmund Wilson this, Edmund Wilson that. Who told him he could be the boss of literature?"

"Don't be impertinent," Flap said. "Edmund Wilson isn't even on a faculty. How could he be the boss of literature? Northrop Frye's the boss of literature at the moment. There are some regional bosses. F. R. Leavis is the boss at Cambridge. Lionel Trilling is the boss at Columbia. Yvor Winters is the boss on the West Coast."

"I don't believe in anal intercourse, anyway," Emma said drowsily.

"Quit mumbling," Flap said. "Nobody was talking about it. We're talking about the administration of literature."

"Sorry," Emma said. "Let Patsy talk. She never gets to express herself."

"This department is a collection of turds," Kenny said sincerely.

"They're just a bit Galsworthian," Flap said mildly. "I don't mind. Why should you mind?"

"That's very condescending," Emma said. "I like most of them very much."

"Fuck you," Flap said. "Go on to sleep."

A sullen young couple nobody liked were arguing in the corner, as they had been all evening, passing marijuana back and forth to each other. "We would be just like them if we were married," Patsy said to Hank. Her sense of doom was deepening.

"Why don't you stop drinking and take Emma home," Patsy said to Flap. "She has to get up in the morning."

"Emma is old enough to solve her own problems," he said. He looked oddly haggard and was drinking again.

Lee and Peter left, and Hank and Patsy followed them. Lee and Peter were holding hands. "So it's really true," Patsy said. "I saw Bill two days ago. I guess he knows and doesn't care. Everyone sleeping with everyone and some caring and some not. I'm getting sick. I don't like being drunk."

On the corner of Dunlavy and South Boulevard she was sick. Hank made her sit on the curb to rest a minute. "It's awful," she said. "Now Jim has a girl friend. Only he doesn't sleep with her." She was sick again. "We're not even equals in sin," she said, beginning to sob.

At home she washed her face and felt much better. All evening at the party she had wanted Hank to touch her. Her skin had wanted that, even when she was annoyed with him. She turned the lights out and went to the couch where he was, only to find that she no longer wanted it. She still wanted to want it, but she had gone cold; the heat and the need had gone. She didn't want it to have gone; she became desperate for the heat to come back. She was sure that if they made love it would, for she had never made such love as they had made in the last four days. She was sure it would come back, but it didn't. It did for Hank, but not for her. The harder she tried the less good it did to try, and afterward she was almost sick again, not nauseated but disappointed and confused. "It's ruined," she said. "Even that's ruined now."

"It was just the liquor," Hank insisted. The look in her eyes scared him. It was the first time in weeks he had not been able to reach her. "Don't go yet," she said. She did not want to be left cold and dreary and a mess. He held her and she grew very sleepy and went to sleep, her face against his arm.

Then Hank was shaking her in the dark. It was very hard to understand. She just wanted to sleep. There was a very distant ringing. "Wake up," he said. "Your phone's ringing."

That was the ringing. It was an awful feeling. She could not move. Hank turned on a small lamp. Their clothes were strewn about the couch. Her legs were shaky. Finally she reached the phone, blinking in the light. "It will be Jim," she said fearfully, as if he would be able to see through the phone, into the room.

But it wasn't Jim. It was Sonny Shanks.

"I was about to give up," he said. "Sorry to get you up."

It seemed a miracle that it wasn't Jim. "That's all right," she said. "I was very sound asleep."

"Got bad news," he said. "Jim had an accident. It ain't gonna be fatal or nothing like that, but he's kinda busted up."

"God," she said, shock breaking through her drowsiness. "What? A car wreck?"

"Sort of," Sonny said. "We was at a rodeo and he borrowed a horse from an old boy I know. He just wanted to ride around a little. The horse wasn't very well broke. Something spooked him and he kinda had a runaway. Ran into a car and threw Jim into another car. Nobody hurt but Jim. Awful bad luck."

Patsy was waving one hand, pointing at the closet door where her bathrobe hung. Hank went and got it for her.

"Where is he? How bad is he?"

"Wichita Falls, General Hospital. Eleanor and I are both here but I got to leave early in the morning, probably before you get here. He's got a broken hip, one leg broken in two places, broken collarbone. Don't get in too big an uproar. I've seen a lot worse accidents than this one."

"I'm not you, Sonny," she said. She felt blank and cold and hopeless.

"Tell him I'll come as soon as I can get a plane."

"Eleanor'll stay till you get here," he said. "Sorry I didn't have better news."

He hung up, and she hung up. Then she realized that she had already forgotten the name of the hospital. Still, there couldn't be many in Wichita Falls. Hank had put on his pants. He sat by her on the bed. When he tried to put his arm around her she shoved him away, sickened. He tried again and she let herself rest against him, not up to fighting anything. If only the call were some sort of dreadful dream, the sort you realize is a dream as you wake from it. But she was not dreaming. Her green dress and panties and bra were on the floor.

"It's all over," she said. "Jim's badly hurt. A horse threw him into a car. I've been being a fine wife while he was getting hurt." she looked with disgust at her scattered garments.

"Accidental," Hank said.

"Sure. Everything's accidental. It doesn't make me feel different. Why don't you just go away now and leave me to my mess? I deserve it and there's nothing more you can do, ever."

He picked up her clothes and made some coffee before he left. Patsy lay on the bed crying. When he was gone she dressed and sat up the rest of the night. There were few thoughts in her mind. When it was light she called Emma and asked her to see about Davey and Juanita from time to time. Emma sounded sick at the beginning of the call and solid at the end of it.

"We'll take care of them," she said. "Give our love to Jim."

She called her mother, and Jeanette insisted she bring Davey and Juanita to Dallas. It meant taking a later plane, but it was obviously a good idea. Three hours later she handed Davey's diaper bag to her father in a yellow waiting room at Love Field. Juanita was nervous, and Davey was crying. Patsy couldn't make him stop. He was still crying anxiously when she had to go to her plane. It was fifty long minutes before the plane left the ground. She sat with her hands clenched, worrying about Davey, wondering how Jim would look, what she would do, what she could say to Eleanor Guthrie, what she would do . . . what she would do.

=== 16 ===

When the doctors told her, the afternoon she arrived, that it would be at least three weeks before he could be moved to Houston, Patsy had thought nothing of it. He was alive, that was enough to ask. His face was a shock. His cheeks were sunken, and it took an effort for him to turn his eyes. He had a concussion that Sonny had forgot to mention. His face had so little life in it the first two days that she could think of nothing to say to him. Silence enveloped her. The nurses chattered, the doctor spoke with authority, Jim asked for Coke; she answered with the thinnest and most convenient conventionalities. She remembered a dream she had had of Jim dying in a plane crash, and herself a widow, and the memory only made her feel lower. It had been almost a pleasant dream, and the reality of the hospital room was anything but pleasant. The room was air-conditioned to an almost intolerable degree of chill. Patsy's hands were always cold; she had not brought a sweater and had to buy one. Jim's hip was in traction and at first he was very dopey. There was nothing to do or say, and at first she could not read. With his face looking so thin he seemed pitiful. She could not even have a genuine warm fit of crying. When he was clearheaded she could think of nothing to say. It was all she could do to call him dear. There were indignities: enemas, and the constant urine samples which she was left to coax out of him. He had blood in his urine at first and the doctors were worried about kidney damage. The room was never quite dark and she couldn't sleep; the nurses were always coming in; shafts of light fell across her face.

Sometimes she held Jim's hand, but neither her hand or Jim's had any grip. The only places to walk were the hot treeless streets, baking hot until seven in the evening.

There had been no scene with Eleanor; the sight of Jim left Patsy feeling numb, and Eleanor left within twenty minutes of her arrival. She was neither overfriendly nor oversolicitous. Patsy watched her through the blinds as she walked down the hospital sidewalk. She got in a blue Lincoln and drove away. That afternoon some flowers came with Eleanor's name on the card. After that there was nothing.

As soon as Patsy knew that Jim was not going to die or be seriously crippled, an overwhelming boredom set in. By the evening of the first afternoon she was bored. By the third morning she could hardly believe she was herself. It seemed impossible that she could sit in a hospital room with her own husband and him badly injured and have so little feeling, for him or anyone. The Hortons sent a spray of mums; through no fault of theirs, the florist put them in a horrible brown football-shaped vase. Patsy was too bored to be annoyed. She called Dallas twice a day to see how Davey was, but once she was assured he was okay she was too bored to do more than make small progress reports on Jim. She really didn't want to talk about anything with anyone. The chill room immobilized her and seemed to slow her blood. She sat for two and three hours at a stretch, not reading, not thinking, just sitting. The entrance of the nurses annoyed her. Jim was too dopey to talk. Hank had told her he was having a phone put in, so on the fourth day she called to see if he had. He had, but she didn't want to talk to him, either. Nothing he said reached her. Still, out of boredom, she called him back that night. On the fifth day she moved out of the hospital into a downtown hotel, so she could sleep whole nights, and she began to talk to Hank more often. He suggested that he come to Wichita Falls to keep her company. The thought sickened her. "I don't think I've sunk that low," she said and didn't call him back for a week.

It occurred to her to call Roger, whose ranch was not far away. He would come and stay as long as she needed him, but she didn't call. She had worked out an existence, at the hospital and the hotel, the first existence she had ever had that involved an absence of feeling. She didn't cry, she didn't complain, she didn't pity herself; she did what little there was to do, and then she sat. She didn't want Roger to come. A real person might break through the feelinglessness, and she wouldn't be able to handle it. Her mother wanted to come, but Patsy wouldn't let her. She wanted nobody—nobody.

Before a week had passed, however, someone appeared: her husband Jim. At first he seemed not Jim but an object made of plaster and white skin, a bad sculpture with one leg permanently extended in the air. He said almost nothing and slept a great deal. She did not think about him much, because there seemed no one there to think about. She thought about her own heartlessness, in not feeling more, but couldn't help it. Holding his hand was a little unpleasant, as was the whole business of urine samples. Little of Jim seemed to be there. She could hardly remember a time when he had been all there, when they had handled each other with love, or at least with heat. There was no heat in the room anymore, not in the air, not in Jim, not in her.

Then, gradually, he began to come back to himself. For three days he was very restless, tormented by the casts and his own immobility. He began to want liquids, and to need attentions, and Patsy ceased to be able to be immobile. He began to look at her through Jim's eyes, not through the dull eyes of a doped person. She would see him looking at her and be reminded of herself. She had all but forgotten her appearance. She saw a dull face in the mirror in the mornings, sometimes a dull body in the same mirror as she was drying after a shower; but she didn't really see herself until Jim began to see her again. He itched, he was hot, he was thirsty, he had to pee, he wanted a magazine, or he wanted to be read to. He began to want to eat.

She herself became hungry one day and walked several blocks in the blinding noonday sun until she found a drugstore where she could get a milkshake and a grilled cheese sandwich. She could not remember a bite of the food she ate the first five days in the hospital. She drank many Cokes; the taste of them was always in her mouth. Gradually she began to leave the room more often, when Jim was napping or reading. There was a brown little park a few blocks away, very hot during the daytime but not so bad in the cool of the evening. She sometimes walked there and sat in a swing, amid children. They made her miss Davey. It was a high park, with a long sweep of sky to the north, toward Oklahoma; once she saw an airman and his girl holding hands in a car and was reminded of the park in Cheyenne. By rights Pete Tatum should come and hold her hand, as she had held his when *his* spouse had a broken hip. It might be cheering, but it wouldn't happen.

Jim decided he wanted a TV in his room and they rented one and sat watching it for hours, dully, arguing a little, seldom seeing anything they liked but somehow lulled by it. At least it was something they could discuss with the nurses, whose absent chattiness was driving them both mad. Inasmuch as it was awkward to shave, Jim had begun to grow a beard, and that too was something to talk about with the nurses. Patsy felt noncommittal toward the beard project. Watching it grow was almost as dull as watching TV, but she couldn't think of any reason why he shouldn't have a beard if he wanted one.

As soon as Jim became really clearheaded they both began to feel like talking to each other, something it seemed they hadn't done in months. The only difficulty was that neither wanted to talk about what the other one wanted to talk about. Patsy didn't pick at him about Eleanor, not at all. Eleanor's cool attitude had convinced her that the whole thing was one of Jim's fantasies. She had a feeling his crush had got no further than a few double entendres slipped into literary conversations. Eleanor did not seem like the kind of woman who would be won by Jim, somehow. She mentioned Eleanor once, and Jim became annoyed and defensive, as if talk would tarnish the gold of his memory of it all, so Patsy dropped it. He was even less in the mood to talk about his disastrous horseback ride. All he knew was that the horse had bolted and he had been unable to stop it. What he was most eager to talk about was what everyone in Houston had been doing all summer. It was an awkward subject, since Patsy had paid scant attention all summer, and it was made even more awkward by the fact that Jim seemed mostly interested in Hank. His curiosity was entirely innocent, but it was still awkward to handle. She was forced into direct lies, for one thing, and at the same time was annoyed with Jim because he had managed, entirely through the workings of his own fantasy, to turn Hank into one of his best friends. A year before if he had wanted Hank for a friend she would have been glad. As it was, it seemed to her impossible, an indecent irony life had thrust upon them.

"We'll have to have him over a lot this fall," Jim said cheerfully.

The remark frightened her, as did all talk of the fall. Jim loved to talk about the future, but all his talks echoed earlier talks; they held tones that she could remember too well, and were filled with prognostications of things he would never do. Even Davey became a sore spot. She had begun to miss him severely; she would wake up in the night wondering if he were crying, unhappy without her, or what. When she called her mother and heard him babble in the background she could hardly keep herself from going to Dallas, though she knew that a hurried visit would only disorient him. He seemed to be fine. Jim loved to talk about him; he loved to listen to her tell about him. In a way it was natural that he would want to hear about his son, but in another way it annoyed her. It was as if he liked to think about Davey more than he liked to be with him. She enjoyed talking about him too, but it was no consolation for not having him in her lap. It worried her, and she tried to frame some careful sentence that would make Jim see that it was precisely that attitude of his that was at the center of what was wrong with them. She understood it so clearly, or thought she did, but she could never frame the sentence. She was afraid he would take it as a sign of her dissatisfaction with him and withdraw further into plans and fantasies.

Much of the time, though, they didn't argue. They were quite amicable. Patsy went downtown to a bookshop and bought lots of paperbacks, scholarly ones for Jim, more frivolous ones for herself, and they read and got on well through the second week and into the third. There were little problems, one being that Jim kept wanting to kiss her. She didn't want to be kissed. Once his pain subsided, boredom produced a kind of low omnipresent sexuality; he spoke happily of all the love they would make when he was well. He was always catching her hand, telling her how sexy she looked, trying to get her to sit on the bed. When Patsy did kiss him she felt afraid, afraid that he would discover how really turned off she was, where he was concerned. She pleaded the grotesqueness of the casts and the constant parade of nurses, and kept her distance. But what she wished most of all was that he would quit talking about it—stop talking about the future at all. The more he talked about sex the less she wanted it. Despite herself, she began to long for Hank, who didn't talk about it. She tried to keep the talk in the present, on the books they were reading, the ball game, or the soap opera on TV, but Jim's mind kept leaping ahead, and the more it did the more she felt her body dragging behind and setting its feet.

One morning a few days before they were to leave Jim spoke of the leaving in a tone of light regret. "I almost hate to go," he said. "It's so nice, just the two of us. It's been a long time since you've given me so much attention."

"Yep, you're a pampered invalid," she said. She had been out shopping and had brought him a Greta Garbo button and some new pajamas.

But that night, in her hotel, sitting by the window watching the neon sign of an insurance agency flash from across the street, the remark came back to haunt her. She saw it as altogether true. For the first time in a long time Jim had her just as he wanted her. His role and hers were clear. He was free to idealize her, to make much of her sexiness, of her wit, of her attentiveness. She was his wife again, in the purest and most handleable sense. His scholarly interests, his parental interests, his sexual interests, all were revived. He talked about his thesis, about Davey, about lovemaking. He seemed to have forgotten his summer crush, and of the mystery of her summer he had no inkling. To Jim their future was clear; to her it was even more obscure than their past.

She called Hank occasionally, but did not talk much. She refused to commit herself to anything, refused to say what she would do when she returned to Houston. She could not say because she didn't know, and she did not want to speculate, either in her mind or over the phone. She squelched all speculation, Hank's directly, Jim's with wit rather than conviction. She was not convinced of anything and did not particularly want to be. When Jim wanted to kiss her she felt as if the chill of the room had transferred into a central cooling unit, so that heart and body alike were kept stable at a very low but very even temperature.

And then, the second day they were back in Houston, with Jim comfortably settled in his bed, books on every hand, with Davey re-established in his kingdom, and Juanita there to see after them, and the Hortons expected in the evening, she concocted a mythical errand for herself and, ashamed and terrified and lonely, went straight to Hank's. It was a very hot day. Hank was lying on his couch with no shirt on, reading *Sports Illustrated*. His breath on her face knocked out the cooling unit in her breast; his hands turned her warm again. The apartment's old rattly air conditioner had been broken down for two weeks and he had been too dilatory to get it fixed, so, hurriedly, wet by the heat of August, they stripped and went to bed.

17

"Of the two of us my lot is definitely the darker," Emma said. They were in the park, late in a day in September, watching their three children and discussing their marital plights. Emma had nothing to do but watch; Patsy's role was more active. Davey had grown big enough for the park swings, those that had a bar across them to hold infants in.

They came to the park almost every evening and Davey's enjoyment of swinging had become an addiction. Patsy leaned against one of the iron swing supports, shoving him forward every time the swing returned to her. A promising little norther had blown in that day, very slight, no more than a breath of coolness, and instead of lifting their spirits it only sunk them further, for they knew the temperature would be back to ninety the next day. Patsy was blue, Emma was blue. A boy and a girl were laughing and throwing a frisbee on the north side of the park and the sight of such lightness, such happy frivolity, made them both feel middle-aged. It was hard for either of them to remember when boys had taken them to the park to play. It was the sort of gaiety that belonged to youth. Teddy and Tommy were playing in the sandbox and exhibiting what, for them, was unusual rapport. Emma sat in one of the swings smoking. She had taken to smoking more and had lost weight. She was shaped for plumpness and the loss of only a few pounds made her face look gaunt.

"But think," Patsy said. "The exams will be over in two weeks and then Flap will be a big success and get a job at some glamorous school. Jim won't even get his casts off for nearly a month."

"Psychic wounds never heal," Emma said. "Flap has psychic wounds."

"No he doesn't. It's just exam anxiety."

"Well, I do then. I keep wishing I were a book, so he'd look at me. He's even quit swatting the boys. Even their noise doesn't penetrate to him now."

"We have opposite problems," Patsy said. "Maybe we could swap houses for a few days. I'd love to be around a man who didn't notice me."

Davey squalled, looking at her indignantly. The swing was stopping. His hair was dark like hers and had grown longish; people were not sure whether he was a boy or a girl. It irked her—he seemed to her unmistakably masculine. She swung him high and his blissful expression returned.

"I didn't expect to feel middle-aged so early in life," Emma said.

"I don't feel middle-aged. I just feel unyoung."

As they were talking, the Duffins walked by and waved at them. They had just come from Rice. Bill had his black leather briefcase; Lee carried a couple of books. She was dressed like a college girl, in a brown sweater and skirt, and had let her hair grow a little longer. Bill wore a green corduroy sports coat. They were laughing and seemed in the best of spirits.

"I don't know where they get off, being happy," Patsy said. She was bored with swinging and lifted Davey out and put him in his carriage. He protested, but she ignored him. Emma gave her boys a come-on wave, but they ignored her and went on building a sand fort.

"Okay, boys," Emma said.

"Just two more minutes, please," Tommy said, patting the sand. He was secure in the knowledge that he could not be denied as long as he asked politely.

"They're probably happy because their kids are gone," Emma said. "Why shouldn't Lee be happy? Peter's really nice, and he's crazy about her. It must be nice having somebody crazy about you. Maybe Duffin is pleasant too, if you don't have to depend on him."

"I don't know why, but I'm annoyed with her," Patsy said. "She makes me feel more conservative than I really am."

"I think it's just that you really are conservative," Emma said, motioning sternly to the boys. "You're like me. I'd be scared to death if somebody was crazy about me."

The sandy boys kicked in their fort and they all walked home together, Patsy in a silent brood. She *had* somebody crazy about her, two somebodies, for that matter, and had just begun to realize that she wasn't really crazy about either of them, neither husband nor lover. It was a new problem. Davey sucked his pacifier and hung to the sides of the carriage when she wrestled it off curbs. Emma gave her boys a desultory lecture on what was fair and what wasn't.

"You could have another baby," Tommy said. "Then if it was a boy I'd have two brothers and if they tried to beat me up and I won, it would be okay because they would be two against one and that's no fair."

"You'd be bigger than both of them put together," Emma said. "That would make it unfair. I've got all the boys I need as it is."

Teddy was trudging along silently, a little morose, well aware that if anyone got beaten up in the near future it would be him. He was interested in pill bugs and when he saw one crawling along stopped and turned it into a pill. Once he did it suddenly and Patsy almost ran him down with the baby carriage.

"Oh, sorry," she said.

Teddy looked at Davey as if he were ripe for slaughter. Davey looked at him adoringly.

"I don't think Jim's the beard type," Emma said.

"Nope," Patsy said. "He just started it in the hospital to have something to do. He'll get tired of it pretty soon."

That evening before her mirror she concluded again that she didn't look well. She looked either feverish or anemic, either flushed and hot or pale and drawn. She did not look lightly happy, as Lee Duffin had looked that afternoon. She looked, it seemed to her, like a woman whose life had gone wrong and was apt to go yet more wrong. Both her husband and her lover told her she looked great, but she had taken to discounting both their opinions; she was not sure either knew her well, and she looked in her own face to try and discover what was wrong inside her.

And yet, what was wrong was not just inside her, it was outside her as well. Something had started that she couldn't stop, and something had stopped that she couldn't start again; that which had started, except in one particular, was really no better than that which had stopped, but whether it was better or worse scarcely seemed to matter. It was started, and the one particular was a strong particular, and there was nothing she could do about it. She knew the fault must be in her, for there was nothing drastically wrong with either of the men involved. Only that evening Jim had courteously yielded a point she had been pressing for days: he had agreed that they ought to buy a house. He had only resisted, so he said, because owning a house would set them above all the other graduate students. They had to have one, though; Davey needed a room of his own. Jim had given in, and had given in with grace. She could start looking the next day.

She should have been happy with her victory, but as she combed her hair she felt low. He was watching her as she sat at her dressing table. He loved to watch her, and his looks were expectant. And he had every right to be expectant; not of sex, necessarily, for he could still barely move, but of affection at least, a bit of lightness and niceness on her part. Instead, all she wanted was for the lights to be off. She had been sleeping on the couch because of his casts. It was an easy couch to sleep on, and until she was on it and the lights out she felt slightly pressured at night, pressured to give some wifely affection that she had ceased to feel.

What made it worse was that Jim had ceased to demand anything. For a time after he got home he had been very grabby and was always wanting her in bed, but he had apparently decided that his casts made him unpleasant for her and had started leaving her alone, except with his eyes and his voice. He was always paying her compliments. There were times when she read in the john, just to be alone, and she lingered in the kitchen as long as possible. She did not tell him that her reluctance had nothing to do with his casts. She did not tell him anything. She would have been hard pressed to recall five words she had said to him since their return, so inconsequential was her conversation. The house had been the only serious issue they had to talk about, and that was settled. It was awful to feel no gratitude, but she felt none, nor any particular delight at the thought of house hunting or decorating. A year before, even a few months before, the prospect would have filled her with happiness, with rapture and ideas and energy. Now it merely seemed like a necessary chore. Davey had to have a room that was not their bedroom. What she and Jim would do in the rest of the house she could not imagine.

"Need anything?" she asked, turning out the lamp on her dresser. She yawned and it was not a faked yawn either; she was always tired at night, glad of the time when she could leave it all alone and go to sleep.

Jim was reading, alternating between *The Rise of the*

Novel and a fat Eric Ambler omnibus that she had found him secondhand. "What's the late movie?" he asked. "I'm tired of reading. Want to watch TV awhile?"

"Not desperately," she said, but she went to the TV and wheeled it over where he could see it better. The guide was lost—it was always lost. She went to the kitchen and found the day's paper and looked up the late movie.

"It's something called *Vera Cruz*," she said. "Burt Lancaster, Gary Cooper, Denise Darcel, and others."

"Let's watch a little. Come and sit with me awhile."

She turned the TV on and went to the bed, but instead of sitting with him she lay on her stomach, her face on her arms. There was the sound of gunfire from behind her. "Burt Lancaster seems to be the bad guy," Jim said, stroking her hair. "It's about Maximilian."

He slipped a hand inside her gown and rubbed her back between her shoulder blades. "I really don't know what I'd do without you," he said, not in an urgent tone but merely conversationally. It was his new bit: needing her. One of the discoveries of his convalescence was that for years he had been needing her without acknowledging that he needed her. He attributed such troubles as they had had to his own pride, his need to appear independent. The admission of his need made him feel enormously hopeful. In the future they would function together, each needing the other.

For a few days Patsy liked it. It was a long overdue recognition, so far as she was concerned. She liked him trying to be honest about himself. She liked him playing with Davey—that too was long overdue. But he soon overworked the need bit. It led to problems. She could scarcely put mustard on his hot dog without him praising her considerateness, and she began to wonder if he would ever again put mustard on his own hot dogs. He had certainly adapted beautifully to invalidism. She had the feeling that he could be getting mobile again more quickly than he was, that he was boondoggling on his broken bones. She had the nagging feeling that he liked staying in bed, in casts, amid books, his need shining pure, more or less. It made her a little edgy. Being needed was nice up to a point, but as things stood she could not help feeling that his need had peaked at a bad time. A little of that need and appreciation earlier might have welded them together. As it was, she felt slightly uneasy, not sure she wanted him needing her all that much, and even less sure that she still needed him. She had been forced to be independent for two months and the result was that she felt independent. She didn't want anyone putting mustard on *her* hot dog. When, occasionally, she took a poll within herself to determine what she did need Jim for, the results were not encouraging. She was glad to have him her husband in the eyes of her friends, and she wanted him to be a father to Davey, but for herself, woman to man, she was not sure she needed anything from him.

When he said he didn't know what he would do without her she turned her face toward him and he stroked her cheek. "You'd make out," she said and kissed his hand a little guiltily. His sincerity sometimes unnerved her and made her ashamed of herself. He might be foolish but he was almost always sincere and she could not remember if she had ever been sincere with him. She kissed his fingers and wished she felt more. He had been hurt—his bones were really broken. He deserved an affectionate wife.

She sat up and let him hold her hand; they watched the movie awhile. She wished the feeling of dullness would leave her. Jim was too cheerful even to notice that she was dull. "Gary Cooper looks kind of sick," he said. "How long was this before he died?"

"Don't ask me," she said, idly picking up the Eric Ambler book and looking into it. Jim put his hand under her gown again, stroking the tops of her breasts. "Why do people like to read about spies?" she asked, hoping he would quit. She had come, automatically, to try and counter his touch with conversation.

"Why not? They're kind of interesting. There must be thousands of them sneaking about. It's a wonder we don't know any."

"I don't want to know any. I know too many people as it is." She shut her eyes, though it was not a bad movie. Burt Lancaster was bad with a flair. He had a great smile. Jim was touching her nipples, one and then the other, lightly. She wanted him to quit but she didn't move. "You have a nice bosom," he said.

"Thanks."

"Slow coming but worth waiting for."

"I'd rather it wasn't discussed in those terms." She grew drowsy and went to sleep. When the movie was over he awakened her. She was dazed with sleep and a little troubled to find herself asleep in bed with her own husband. She got up to turn the TV off.

"Sleep here," Jim said. "I won't crush you."

Patsy went to look at Davey and came back scratching her head.

"Maybe I'll change back tomorrow night," she said. "The couch is already made up." She gave him a sleepy kiss and went to the couch and turned out her reading light. Jim still had his light on. He was watching her.

"You're a funny girl," he said. "You don't act the way you used to."

"Well, I'm a mother now," Patsy said, taking off her robe. It was all she could think of to say. She looked at him. He seemed to be in a kind of reverie.

"Can I ask something?" she said.

"Sure."

"Did you really make a pass at Eleanor Guthrie?"

"Oh, sure," he said, surprised.

"You did?"

"Sure. I told you so over the phone."

"You just said you hadn't gone to bed with her. You could have not gone to bed with her and never so much as winked. I just wondered."

"I said I had a crush on her but didn't go to bed with her," he said. "I kissed her."

Patsy was startled. Somehow she had convinced herself that nothing physical had taken place. There was a long uneasy silence. She had asked the question unemotionally. It had occurred to her to ask him that several times. She had been certain he hadn't made a pass, but he had. It bred not only more questions, but a strange stirring of emotion. She felt puzzled and offended. Her body had been ready for sleep, but her emotions crossed it up.

"What did you think happened?"

"I don't know," Patsy said, wishing she had gone to sleep and not asked.

Jim sighed. It was a misdemeanor that belonged to the remote past. But he was much more relaxed than she was in regard to it.

"There isn't any mystery," he said. "I guess she loves Sonny. Maybe she sort of got interested in me too for a few days. I didn't realize it in time. It doesn't matter now. She loves him and I love you. I guess she gets pretty lonely there on the ranch."

"Poor thing," Patsy said. "I wish you wouldn't compare us."

"I wasn't. How did I compare you?"

"Oh, I don't know," Patsy said angrily. "Maybe you didn't."

"Then why sound so hostile? Nothing happened. She wasn't hostile about you."

"A kiss isn't nothing," she said.

"Well, it's not much, either. It wasn't so earth shaking."

Patsy wiped tears of anger on the pillowcase. She was aware that she was utterly in the wrong to be angry, and hated the illogic of her own emotions. An hour ago she would not have supposed she would care if Jim had taken Eleanor Guthrie and gone to Majorca with her. Yet she was hurt that he had kissed her. It was stupid and humiliating. Everything she did or felt was absurd, it seemed to her— everything except what she did with Davey. Only taking care of him made sense.

"I don't see why you're upset," he said. "It was just one pass and it seems like years ago. Besides, I like to kiss you better."

"I don't know how you'd know. We haven't done it in years."

"That's not my fault," he said.

"I don't want to talk about it," she said, feeling sullen and stubborn. Every word she said put her more clearly in the wrong, but the fact that she was in the wrong didn't seem to affect what she felt.

"I don't either, especially," Jim said, opening the Eric

Ambler book. "I do like to kiss you, though. I'd like to right now."

"No. I don't feel like being compared to an aging heiress."

"Screw you," Jim said angrily. "Will you quit making up cute little categories? She's not that old and the fact that she has money has nothing to do with it."

"From where I sit it does," Patsy said.

"Then come and sit over here. You seem to want to keep yourself twenty yards from me these days."

"I'm sleepy and I'm going to sleep."

"You're full of excuses. Have you stopped loving me or something?" His voice sounded worried, for the first time all evening.

Patsy was ashamed of herself. "No," she said, more meekly. "It's just a difficult time. Please let me go to sleep."

It was confusing to realize that he still wanted her to love him. Half the time she believed it didn't matter to him; the discovery that she was wrong always subdued her for a while, but it didn't really make anything simpler. Jim soon turned off his light. She stayed on the couch, sleepless, silent, and so stiff with nervousness and guilt that it felt as if her joints had hardened. She didn't cry. More and more, it seemed, she only cried in anger. Sorrow and confusion left her dry.

$$=== 18 ===$$

"Of course we know them," Lee said. "Jim's one of your father's best students. He just had a bad accident—a horse threw him. We're going to visit them tomorrow. Is her sister nice?"

Bill had been reading, but he stopped to listen. Lee was talking to Melissa again. He could have listened on an extension but he hated three-way phone calls. And he and Melissa were always getting angry with each other on the phone. She had as much temper as he had.

"I don't like anything I've heard about that drug," Lee said. "And I don't think mixed couples really further the cause of civil rights. Besides, they don't usually work out. Is she seeing a psychiatrist?"

"Ask her about her sisters," Bill said. "Tell her to ask them to write, if it isn't against their principles, or if they haven't forgotten how."

"Hush," Lee said. "I don't have a very good connection."

"Is who seeing a psychiatrist?" he asked when she hung up.

"Patsy Carpenter's sister. She's living in the same house with Melissa."

"Small world."

"Kids drift around too much out there. Melissa has a boy friend who sets up light shows. She says he's very good and he makes money."

"That's a novelty," Bill said. "A hippie capitalist. What's wrong with Patsy's sister?"

"Lots of LSD and a Negro boy friend who's mean to her. So Melissa says."

She sat down at her dressing table and began to clean her face. "Melissa and her boy friend are peace-marching tomorrow," she said.

"Did we ever march in anything?"

"We were in the Fourth of July parade, the year we were in Milwaukee."

"I've suppressed that year. I'm glad I was born without a social conscience. It leaves more time for basics like reading and fucking."

"Especially reading," she said with a small smile. "I can remember years when you've had almost unlimited time to read."

"Ah, but those years are past. You've taken bloom again. It's been years since you've looked so lovely."

"I wasn't aware that I had faded so," Lee said, but she was

aware that she was looking especially good. Her hair shone, her face was untroubled. She had taken to playing tennis twice a week at the River Oaks Country Club. They didn't belong, but she had a friend who did. The pro admired her; she played good tennis for a woman her age. And she had Peter, an affectionate and adoring young man, not very strong but that was all the better. He was just the sugar she had been needing. He had never dreamed he could seduce anyone as lovely as herself. They drove to Galveston often and took long walks along the beach. He had a neat apartment on Dunlavy, as clean and uncluttered as his psyche. He could not believe that he was actually getting away with a love affair, and with her, a professor's wife. She was gay and protective and reassuring, but he lived, nonetheless, in constant terror of Bill. It was an understandable terror, for Bill was formidable. But Peter was wholly and hopelessly in love with her, and the terrors which, for him, attended their meetings gave his ardors a kind of trembling eagerness which she found delicious.

"You certainly aren't faded now," Bill said. "Look, I've laid aside my book, and it's the best book on Joyce since year before last. What more in the way of passion could you ask?"

She took up her brush. "Would you even lay aside Joyce himself?"

"Don't be coquettish," he said, turning off his bed light. "No modernist worth his salt would lay aside James Joyce just for a woman, least of all his wife. Lesser men, yes. In your present state of bloom I'd lay aside Ford Madox Ford for you without a moment's hesitation."

"There have been those who thought me worth more than a minor novelist," Lee said. "Friends of yours, I might add. John Groton would have laid aside not only his specialty but his job and Mary and the kids if I had offered to let him unstring my bodice."

Bill chuckled. "That's a pretty phrase," he said. "It wasn't your bodice that won John, it was more likely your derrière. Your bodice has never required stringing."

"Oh, all right. The point still pertains."

"Sure, but it can take some amplification. For one thing,

his specialty is Wilkie Collins, and Mary Groton is dull of body and dull of brain. In comparison to her you're Greta Garbo."

Lee gave him an austere smile, went in the living room and found the novel she had been reading, and came to bed.

The next afternoon they visited the Carpenters. Jim had improved to the point of being able to get around on crutches, which fascinated Davey. Jim and Bill talked book buying while Lee and Patsy sat by, both feeling slightly left out and slightly bored. They chatted unoriginally about babies and then about houses.

"You ought to buy ours," Lee said. "It's the darkest of secrets yet, but the odds are we'll be moving next year. We've never even touched the third floor. It would be perfect for your son."

"I wish we could buy it," Patsy said, "but I don't think we can survive here until next summer." She did like the Duffins' house. It was large and solid and rather understated, and had good floors and a large fenced back yard.

Bill had perked up his ears. "The problem of timing might not be insurmountable," he said. "Lee and I could take an apartment for the spring semester." And he and Lee began to discuss various possible arrangements. Jim and Patsy listened, both skeptical, neither terribly eager, but neither willing to close the possibility completely. In the end, as the Duffins were leaving, Patsy promised to come by and look at the house more closely in a day or two.

Lee and Bill walked home feeling buoyant. "What a relief that would be," he said. "I'd rather sell a semester early than two semesters late, like the Indiana house."

"Patsy's the one to sell to," Lee said. "She'll do the deciding."

"I think we better clinch the deal before they fall apart," he said. "They look like losers to me."

"You're always so knowledgeable. It's too bad marriages can't be edited like texts. Think how good you'd be at spotting influences and borrowings. She didn't look so bad."

"A little sage counsel and a few good bangs wouldn't hurt her."

They stopped at the drugstore for Cokes and tried to remember how much the painting had cost them, and the landscaping and the upstairs plumbing, and by the time they got home had settled on $28,000 as the figure at which they would quote their house to Patsy when she came.

══ 19 ══

"Uh-oh," Emma said. "Of all times."

"Oh, no!" Tommy yelled. "Oh, no!" Then, from the living room where the boys were, came the sound of something being beaten.

"Don't do that, Tommy!" Emma yelled. She and Flap were at the supper table having coffee.

"But it's *Flipper*," Tommy said. "I've got to make it come back on."

"Don't beat the TV," Flap said. "We've told you about that."

But the beating continued. "What's he beating it with?" Flap asked.

"His stick horse, I think. I'll go fiddle with it. It is *Flipper*, after all."

"So what?" Flap said. "Stop that!" he yelled at Tommy. The beating had not stopped.

The Hortons, Emma and Flap, glanced at each other over the remains of supper, which had been spaghetti, as was more or less customary on Saturday night. Normally Tommy whopping the TV set would not have discommoded them much, but it had been a dreary rainy Saturday, the boys inside all day, prelims less than a week off, and Emma fearful that somehow, in defiance of modern chemistry, she had gotten pregnant again. She would not have minded

582

especially, except that if Flap passed everything and got a job they would be moving just as the baby was due, and she had dreary visions of herself having a baby in someplace like Nebraska, where they knew no one, no doctors, no nurses, no one to take care of the boys. Flap had spent the day having dismal visions too, visions of pages full of questions, none of which he had any idea how to answer; visions of disgrace and a job teaching Sanskrit drama at Houston Baptist College, a fate that sometimes befell terminal M.A.s. All in all they were in no mood to hear the sound of a stick horse whopping a TV set repeatedly. When the boys had departed the table and trouped in to watch *Flipper* it had seemed to both their parents that they had been given a small blessing, thirty minutes' respite from questions, grievances, decisions, talk of any kind. Thirty minutes of silence and coffee was something to live for, and at that moment neither of them could think of anything else.

Now, it seemed, even that was being taken away. Emma pushed back her chair and got up. She didn't like the look on Flap's face. It was the look of a man who was about to go wallop a child, and she didn't want Tommy spanked, not just then. She didn't want any spankings, any tears, any scenes. Maybe she could clear the picture, somehow.

But the picture, when she got there, was hopelessly dim and snowy. Tommy stood by the set with his stick horse in his hand, tears of fury on his cheeks. Teddy sat on the floor directly in front of the set, too appalled even to cry. He was very fish-oriented and *Flipper* was the high point of his week.

"Me TV broken," he said pathetically, looking at his mother.

"I'll see," Emma said. "Maybe I can make it come back on." But she had little heart. Apparently a tube was going. When it got snowy it had to be turned off and left to refresh itself in some mysterious way.

"Fiddle with it," Tommy said frantically. "Fiddle with it. We're missing something. I know we are. We're missing a dangerous part."

"I'm fiddling," Emma said, wanting to cry. The best she could get was a blur in which the moving figures were just discernible as moving figures. That was awful. She liked it better completely blank, but the boys didn't. They clung to hope that the blurs would turn back into the people they had been watching.

"I can't get it, honey," she said finally. "We've just got to get it fixed, that's all there is to it."

"But you said you would," Tommy said. "You said you would the morning we missed the cartoons, remember? That was a long time ago. Why haven't you got it fixed yet?"

"I just haven't," she said, feeling criminal. "I'm sorry."

"Oh, we're missing *minutes* of it," Tommy said, jumping up and down. "Maybe if I hit it just once, *real* hard."

"You do and I'll hit your spanker real hard," Flap said from the doorway. His look bespoke severe exasperation.

"But *you* hit it and it came on," Tommy said. "Remember?"

"I guess that was luck," Flap said. "Anyway, I hit it with my hand, not with a stick horse."

Teddy wandered over to his father, thinking that perhaps it was a matter that took masculine attending to. "Me TV broken," he said, looking at Flap.

"Well, I can't help it," Flap said.

"Why don't you try hitting it?" Tommy said. "We're missing minutes."

"You might as well," Emma said. "It did work once."

Flap went over and hit the TV set five or six times with the heel of his hand. Only the Sunday before, during a pro football game, he had made it come on that way. But it didn't work a second time. The snow changed to waves while he was hitting it, then to wrinkles, then back to snow. He hit the turn-off button and the set went dark. "No soap," he said.

"Now we'll miss it all," Tommy said. "It might have come back on."

The boys took it in their different ways. Teddy began to cry loudly, standing where he was. Emma reached over and grabbed him and pulled him into her lap. He fought for a bit and then sat there crying. Tommy flung himself on the couch and began to kick it. His face gathered, as if he would cry, but his angers were deeper and colder than his brother's, and though his mouth trembled he didn't cry.

"I won't watch it next Saturday night," he said. "I'll never watch it again."

"Sure you'll watch it again," Flap said.

"I won't ever watch TV again," Tommy said, cold and sure. "I won't watch cartoons either."

"Tommy," Emma said, "don't be that way. It was my fault for not getting the set fixed. That's like saying you wouldn't ever eat candy again if I didn't give you a piece just when you wanted it."

"Well," Tommy said, "if I really wanted it and you wouldn't give it to me I would never eat candy again."

"Don't argue with him when he's sulking," Flap said.

"Well, he has a right to sulk. Nobody likes to miss their favorite things."

Tommy suddenly jumped up and without a word ran out of the room, his face pinched and furious. Emma looked at Flap helplessly, bereft of all spirit. Sometimes she could take Tommy's angers calmly and sometimes they broke her up. She could feel herself breaking up. He had taken, when hurt, to running into the small pantry and crawling onto the lowest shelf, making a place for himself amid whatever canned goods were there. Once there, he was apt to stay an hour. Emma could never cajole him out; he did not want her to come into the pantry. Flap could drag him out, but he was loath to do it and she was loath to make him. Once Teddy tried to climb up in the same shelf and got a kick in the mouth; so when Tommy went to the pantry everybody left him alone, uneasily. Flap tried to make light of it. It was obviously a normal thing for a sensitive boy to do. But nothing he ever said made Emma feel less worried or less wretched. She did not think she could stand an hour of Tommy in the pantry, not just then.

"Please see if you can make him come out," she said. "And don't beat him or anything."

"It's not like I beat him every day," Flap said morosely and went to see what he could do. After a while Emma heard his voice. She couldn't hear what he was saying, but the tones that came from the kitchen were patient and she felt grateful and wiped her eyes on her apron. Teddy had forgotten about the disaster with the TV and, glad to have his brother out of the room, came over to Emma rather shyly and with a big grin held out a pack of cards. It was his favorite game and he almost never got to play it just as he liked to play it, which was with his mother and no one else. Tommy was an aggressive card player and knew rules that involved Teddy having to give up every card he really wanted. Emma, on the other hand, knew no rules; when she and Teddy played, all was merry. They dealt each other hands with great formality and examined them with great secrecy, and despite Emma's elaborate precautions Teddy invariably managed to get all the kings and queens and jacks, the cards he liked best. With him so happy it was hard to be too downcast, but Emma kept seeing, from time to time, Tommy curled on the pantry shelf, and kept listening for a change in Flap's voice, half expecting it to rise into anger. But it didn't, and after twenty minutes Tommy marched in looking cheerful and took command of the card game. Teddy turned sullen immediately and clutched such cards as he had in a death grip.

"We really do need new cards," Tommy observed. "These are a little sticky. It's Teddy's fault. He drools on them."

Teddy got up and took his hand across the room. When Tommy got up to go after him he flung them down indifferently, as if cards had lost all appeal.

"Pick 'em up, Ted," Flap said. He sat down on the couch, looking a little drained.

"Gosh, you're a genius," Emma said. "Thank you. How'd you do it?"

"I guess we're going to the planetarium tomorrow. Pick those cards up, Ted. We don't throw cards on the floor."

Teddy put his foot on a card and scooted it back and forth, a calm reflective look on his face as he considered his father's command. "Me throw 'em down," he said, looking up cheerfully, as if it should be obvious that he could not pick up what he had thrown down.

"Please pick them up," Emma said.

"Me throw 'em *down*," Teddy insisted, still cheerful. He grinned slyly, picked up one card, came and dropped it in Emma's lap and moved rapidly off in the direction of his fire engine. Emma rolled her eyes in despair and Flap stood up, swooped Teddy up and dangled him horizontally a few inches above the cards until he grew red in the face from laughing. When he was set down he casually picked up the rest of the cards.

"He hasn't learned very many manners," Tommy said. "Not near as many as I know."

"I agree," Emma said. "Could you go run your bath?"

Later, the boys asleep, she emerged from the bathroom in her nightgown and surprised Flap in a strange state. He was watching the late news, the TV set having refreshed itself in the interim. As she came into the room barefooted, he turned and saw her and quickly brushed his hand across his eyes as if to wipe away tears. She pretended not to notice and went to the kitchen and fixed some coffee, but she felt scared. There had been a time just after his father died when Flap had been prone to depressions and occasional tears, but that had been three years before and it had been understandable. He and his father had been very close—they sailed a lot in a sailboat that Flap had had to sell when his father passed away. She went in with the coffee and saw that she had been right. His face looked hollow.

"What's the matter with you?" she said, alarmed. "Are you mad at me?"

"No. Why should I be? You're bringing me coffee, just like you're supposed to."

"Quit joking," she said. "Tell me why you're sad. I don't like you being forlorn. It scares me."

"I'm not very forlorn," he said. "Maybe it's the goddamn TV. I hate scenes like the one with Tommy. I don't like a child of mine getting wrought up over a porpoise."

"It's not just a porpoise," she said. "For god's sake. Come out of your ivory tower. Didn't you get wrought up over Lassie?"

"I guess," he said. "You needn't get mad."

"I always get mad when I'm scared," she said. "Why were you crying? Is it me or is it prelims?"

"Quit acting neurotic," he said, grinning a little. "Fat girls are not supposed to be neurotic."

"It wasn't you," he added. "I was just thinking about Daddy and the boys—never getting to know one another, I mean. They would have liked one another so well." And despite himself his eyes filled at the thought.

"Why didn't you say so?" Emma said. "Poor man. At least he got to see Tommy."

"Tommy was too little to remember him, though."

Emma sat down by the couch and put her head on his knee; Flap rubbed her neck meditatively. "Tommy is a lot more like him than Teddy is," she said.

"Oh, sure. Teddy has no recognizable progenitors."

"He does too. He has us. We progenited him right in this room."

"How do I know that?" Flap asked lightly. "He's not serious or demented enough to be my son. You might have begot him with a passing stranger."

"I'm too fat and unneurotic for passing strangers," she said. "My father wasn't as interesting as yours."

"He was in his way," Flap said, though only to be nice. He and her father had had no rapport. Her father had considered his daughter thrown away on a bum like Flap. He had made a small fortune but had not expected to die when he did; most of his estate went in inheritance taxes. Emma's mother still kept the large family house in River Oaks, a house she could ill afford. She had grown extremely tight with her money and spent most of her time talking about whether she should sell the house and take an apartment. She and Flap got on indifferently but were not actively hostile to each other.

"I wish we had the Carpenters' money," Flap said. "Then we could afford sitters and could go out on Saturday night and have more fun than anybody. Instead we sit home with our broken TV. Do you suppose Teddy will ever learn to say 'my' instead of 'me'?"

"Don't rush him. I have to have a baby."

"Sure, but there's no point in retarding Teddy. You can have a real baby."

"I don't want to yet. Not until we get moved and see if we like it."

Flap sighed and was silent. "Quit that," Emma said. "You can't possibly fail. Besides, I don't like you envying Jim and Patsy. I bet they're sitting home squabbling, just like we are."

"I bet their TV works, at least," he said. "I don't think about *them,* particularly. I just envy them their money. Are they really going to buy the Duffin house?"

"Patsy can't make up her mind. She's so strange these days. Jim's being an invalid is having a bad effect on her. I don't think they're getting on too well."

"They never have," Flap said. "Why should they start now?"

"They have too. They just argue a lot. We argue, don't we?"

"You snipe at me. I bear it with dignity. We don't argue like they argue."

"Jim changes his mind too often," Emma said. "If he'd ever decided what to be, Patsy would be okay."

"Let's go to bed. I hate to sit and look at a blank TV on Saturday night."

He went and brushed his teeth and they lay in bed reading for more than an hour. Flap was poring morosely over a large red history of English literature, written by Baugh, Brooke, Chew, Malone, and Sherburn. He had been poring over it for six months and Emma had come to hate it. Each page contained thirty dates and thirty titles, and there were eleven hundred pages, or so Flap said, making something like sixty-six thousand facts he might be asked. Emma was reading *The Prime of Miss Jean Brodie.* She was very fond of Muriel Spark and fancied that if she ever took up writing she would write like her. From time to time she rubbed Flap's stomach, hoping he would finish with Baugh, Brooke, Chew, Malone, and Sherburn and talk to her. It was not the best Muriel Spark, she didn't think.

"How you coming on facts?" she asked.

"I'm coming. It's theories and interpretations that are beginning to worry me now."

"How many of those are there?"

"Roughly sixty-six thousand," he said. "Approximately one for every fact."

"Are you planning to make a pass at me? I'm sleepy."

"It's an idea," Flap said. "I've got a malaise tonight."

"I know," she said, closing her book. "I wish your dad had met Teddy, even if they aren't alike."

"Me too," Flap said quietly. He put the book on the floor

with a heavy thump, went to the bathroom, and came back and turned out the light.

"Check on Teddy, please, while you're up," Emma said. "Unwad his blanket from around his neck. He has a compulsion to smother himself and it's muggy tonight." Flap turned the light back on and went to the boys' room and Emma remembered that she had let Tommy go to bed with a heavy undershirt on and got up herself to see if he was too hot.

"Look at him," Flap said, indicating Teddy, who was sprawled on his back. "He's soaked."

Emma went over briefly and touched her son, and indeed Teddy's chest and neck were slick with sweat where he had had his blanket wound. But it didn't worry her. "Oh, he gets that way every night," she said. "He'll cool. I think I'll take Tommy's nightshirt off." She began to, tugging it up, but it was very difficult to get one of Tommy's elbows out of the armhole and he half awoke and frowned in protest and then his face softened into sleep again immediately when she got the nightshirt off. She took the nightshirt and put it on the boys' bureau and turned in surprise at a strange sound from Flap. He was standing with his elbows on the rail of Teddy's baby bed, looking at Teddy and sniffing back tears. Emma was not disquieted, as she had been earlier. She folded the nightshirt and went over and stood by him, her arm around his waist. Teddy, luxurious in his sleep, lay on his back, one knee drawn up slightly, one bare foot curled slightly in, his mouth open, sleeping as if all peace and all security were his. So sweet, Emma thought, reaching in to straighten his plastic pants where they had been tucked under his diaper uncomfortably.

"He is sort of like Dad," Flap said, still racked with memory. "It just doesn't show yet."

"It must to you," she said, leaning her head against his shoulder for a minute. Then she left him and went back to bed and in a few minutes Flap came too, much calmed. He gave his wife a kiss when he got in bed. Neither of them felt sexy, but they didn't feel sleepy either, and they lay awake for an hour, talking of Flap's father and of Emma's, and holding hands.

20

By the end of October Patsy knew in full what was meant by
duplicity. In spirit and in flesh, she knew, and it was no
mere romantic schizophrenia, a matter of being two women
in the same skin. She was two women in two different
skins—women of differing minds and differing hearts. Her
days lost all consistency; pleasure and distress, desire and
shame beset her by turns, and she never knew in the
morning which skin she would wear in the afternoon. "Who
said love was fun?" she said one day, tugging on a blue
sweater. She was the old Patsy, shamed, stiff, depressed. Her
hair was tangled. But when Hank kissed her she grew soft
and sullen and felt like biting. "It's something but it's not
fun," she said a few minutes later. And once she had
changed skins again she looked wearily at the rumpled bed
where she had been when she was someone else. "Of course
it's not love, either," she said, putting her comb in her
purse.

Hank yawned; he didn't believe her. For him it was
certainly love. He was as blank in his desire as he had been
at first. Patsy looked at him hostilely, angry that he still
understood her so little. He really noted nothing except her
body—it was her body he knew, not her. He behaved as if,
so far as he knew, they would go on making love every day
forever. He hadn't noticed that something had already
changed, that she no longer came to him every day so
suffused with feeling that she couldn't think. She might
come eagerly, she might come reluctantly, she might be
happy or she might be sad, but she was no longer mindless,

and she was seldom carried out of herself, no matter how well they made love.

She sat on the bed, dressed to leave, and looked at him, aware of an odd disappointment. There were so many men in the world—who was he, from whose bed she had just risen? Why him? He scarcely spoke to her. There must be many for whom she could feel everything she had first felt for him. It made her feel strange. She wanted him to be unique and irreplaceable, the only man she could care about, someone who could hold her. And yet the moment she thought it she knew it wouldn't be so.

"Something's changing," she said.

"You're getting sexier," Hank said.

Patsy shook her head, though it was true enough. Physically things were very satisfactory between them.

"That's not what I meant," she said. "I meant it when I said it wasn't love."

Hank was silent, his usual defenses were caught unprepared by her directness.

"Maybe I was just desperate for someone to want me the way you do," she said, looking him in the eye. Hank was scared by the calmness in her face when she spoke. He would have fallen back on his second defense, which was sex, but Patsy was dressed to go and he knew he couldn't reach her. He didn't say anything.

"Okay," she said. "I warned you. Enjoy your delusions. If you want to be the love of my life you've got to do more than screw me.

"I just thought I'd tell you," she added as she was leaving. He looked pained and puzzled, and she felt sorry for him as she walked home. He didn't really know anything else *to* do. That night at home she became very silent and felt more completely alone than she had ever felt. She had two men, two nice men, even; and no confidence that either of them was going to do.

Before the month was gone she had had to recognize that something was dying. The season was taking with it a version of herself, one Patsy of the two that had come to exist. She knew that the summer had changed her, but she was a long time admitting that the change was permanent.

She wanted to go back to being the Patsy she had been before the summer—the Patsy who lived with and cared for Jim. The other Patsy, the Patsy who slept with Hank, was not acceptable. That Patsy had no right to exist; she deserved no recognition and no consideration. She was the result of some unwanted revolution of the blood—she was illegal and irresponsible. One thing both Patsys agreed upon was that the two of them could not possibly co-exist, not in the same town, in the same garments, moving among the same people.

October came and went, more like summer than fall, and yet like fall also. Patsy felt a terrible solstice approaching; she didn't want it to come but she knew of no way to avert it. For her it was no mellow season, but a time of gorging, of swollen hours that the cool, quiet, fastidious woman that she sometimes was could not recollect pleasantly. Only occasionally, in between times, was she the Patsy she was sure of.

Those times were always when she was home, with Jim and Davey. Then, more than ever, she dreaded the solstice. When she was in quiet moods the thought of change seemed dreadful—why should anything change? It was emotion that blurred everything; if only she could keep calm and look at matters clearly for a few days then she might be able to straighten herself out, align her emotions with her responsibilities and keep anything really bad from happening. Calmness and clarity were what she needed, and a few simple feelings that she could not doubt.

Davey, at least, was still simple, and at times Jim seemed simple too. At night, watching television with him, or reading beside him in bed, he sometimes seemed far nicer than she gave him credit for being. His needs were not desperate or extreme and he was probably less complex than she made him out to be. It occurred to her at times that all he needed was humoring, of a skillful and considerate kind. He needed lightness and chatter and food and for her to be lovely, and Davey well, and a pursuit to be involved in, and a modicum of sex—for so little as that he could be happy, a thought that only made her the more distressed with herself. Even the little that he needed seemed not easily providable. She had the maddening feeling that something was ruining them, and the most maddening thing about the feeling was the sense that if she could ever for one moment put her finger on the exact cause of the decay, she could stop it. Probably the root of the trouble was herself: her selfishness, her feverishness, her foolish destructive desire for things Jim could not give. Half the time she was convinced that their troubles were all her fault; the other half she was convinced they were all *his* fault. She could not rid herself of the conviction that he was playing games he ought to have outgrown. He didn't want enough; she wanted too much. Neither of them could quite determine the nature of what it was that was lacking.

Four times in one week, in the middle of October, she had fits of causeless incoherent weeping because she felt the hopelessness of ever having what she wanted. And yet she was as distrustful of her sorrows as she was of her happiness, on the days when she was happy. Some days, when things went well with Hank, her spirits rose very high, and she felt it was more natural to be happy than to be unhappy. It might only be a matter of sticking to simple tasks. Davey was a good age to be taken about in the world, and taking him about was a delight. Safety, happiness, normalcy, even gaiety seemed to lie in the simplest domestic tasks—in cooking breakfast, in buying new sheets, in giving Davey his bath. Breakfasts and baths and shopping she handled splendidly. If happiness lay in handling such things splendidly then she was enviable. But if happiness lay in large things rather than small, in the fulfillment of major needs and adequacy to major responsibilities, then she felt lost. Honor and honesty, fidelity, responsibility, duty, love, all did less for her spirits than buying baby clothes and cooking waffles. There were days when the ability to cook a good breakfast seemed the only hope for her character.

William Duffin was reading a great deal of psychology, prefatory to attempting a major biography, and he had devoted most of his fall seminar to a discussion of psychoanalytic biography and its possibilities. Jim dutifully brought home the works of the various psychologists Duffin recommended, and Patsy, who still could not resist snooping in whatever he was reading, read sections of books by

Ernest Jones, Erik Erikson, Norman O. Brown, Philip Rieff, and R. D. Laing. At first she felt intensely interested and cheered and rather hopeful. She skipped from book to book, always with the sense that the next chapter or the next page might reveal to her why she was in trouble and tell her what she might do to get out. Everything seemed somehow applicable, and yet, as it turned out, nothing she came to was precisely applicable, or even helpful. She still fought with Jim, yearned to be out of trouble, slept with Hank; she was even beginning to fight with him too. Before long the psychology began to depress her. The terminology that had been briefly fascinating began to seem turgid, and the insights that for a time had seemed dramatic began to seem monotonous and depressing. At the end of two weeks she went back to magazines and fiction. Every time she opened one of the psychologists she ended up feeling more hopeless than she had been feeling. The books were not going to help.

They did increase her vocabulary, though, and made her more formidable in argument.

"I'm getting rid of you any day now," she told Hank one morning. "You're nothing but an ego support. I'll find someone else to support my feeble ego." For no good reason she had gone from one bed directly to another and she was disgusted with herself.

"I love you," he said. "What's wrong with me? You're always criticizing me now." It was true, and it puzzled him.

"In the main you're rather uninteresting," she said, yawning.

"In the main?"

"Sure. Isn't that a good graduate school phrase? In the main you're kind of dull." And she smiled at him cheerfully, in a way that bothered him; he couldn't tell if she really thought he was dull or not.

"Why do you sleep with me then?" he asked, offended.

"Why not?" she said, twisting a lock of hair around her finger. "Ladies are sometimes attracted to dullards, I guess. My wretched body has an affinity for you. So what? I'll conquer it yet."

"You talk too much," Hank said, turning on his stomach.

"So I've been told," she said.

* * *

That night at home she had a fit, and for very little reason. She had only seen Hank for an hour that morning, and short visits left her with an edge. When she took the edge home and it encountered some tension there, such grip as she had on herself was destroyed and anything might happen.

In this case the fit was over books. Rice had secured, for one year, a famous visiting professor, an old crony of Duffin's whose specialty was the nineteenth-century novel. Jim and most of the other graduate students had been herded into his seminar, and Jim soon had another hero to worship. He began buying books again, this time nineteenth-century novels. When Patsy got home from Hank's a large box had arrived from a bookseller in Scotland and the very sight of it made her fume. All their bookshelves were full, there was absolutely no room for more books until they moved, if they moved, and it annoyed her that he had ordered more. She had read more of the books than he had, anyway, and the new box was a very large one.

The contents, it turned out, were forty-four volumes, twenty-six of George Eliot and eighteen of George Meredith. Jim unpacked them after supper, delightedly, while she was putting Davey to bed. Davey liked to lie on his back and contemplate the ceiling when put to bed, and Patsy would often stand by the baby bed awhile, tickling his stomach or letting him clutch her fingers. He had developed a vocabulary of meaningless sounds, which she interpreted and answered as she chose. It was a pleasant time. When Davey got sleepy he generally rolled abruptly on his stomach and was gone as quickly, it seemed to her, as Jim went when he was ready for sleep. Such little resemblances, already noticeable, touched her and disquieted her. It was fine that he should have his father's charm, but not all of his father's habits, and she had the feeling that there might be very little she could do about it.

When she turned from Davey, Jim was sitting on the couch writing his name in pencil in each of the books. She came over and sat down on the couch and picked up a volume of George Meredith, frowning.

"Why do you write your name in every volume?" she asked. "Why not just in the first volume?"

"Oh, habit," he said. "Suppose someone borrowed *Felix Holt the Radical* and didn't get around to reading it for a year. They might forget whose it was."

"Personally I'd be just as glad if someone carried off *Felix Holt the Radical* and kept it forever," she said.

"You're a woman. You have no sense of the comprehensive."

"I don't like remarks prefaced by 'You're a woman.' My sex has nothing to do with it and I don't see where comprehensiveness comes in."

"If you're going to have an author you might as well have him complete," Jim said.

"I think that's dull. It makes more sense just to have the books you like. I'm never going to want to read *Felix Holt the Radical* and neither are you."

"How do you know? Maybe I'll have to do a paper on it someday."

"Great. Where do we put them while we're waiting for you to get assigned one of them?"

"I guess they can go in a closet until we move," he said. "Or else I'll box some of the paperbacks and put them in a closet."

"No fair," Patsy said, picking up another volume of George Meredith. "I read the paperbacks. Who is this man? I never heard of him."

"Sure you have. George Meredith."

But Patsy had never heard of George Meredith, that she could remember, and was irked to be made to feel that she ought to have. "I'm not a graduate student," she said. "I don't know everything. What did he write that's good?"

"You've heard of him," Jim insisted. He was rather pleased that she hadn't—she had few enough glaring gaps. *"The Ordeal of Richard Feverel* and *The Egoist."*

"Oh, yeah," she said. "I think there was something by him in *My Book House*. Did he write children's books?"

"I'm not too big on him but the set was so cheap I couldn't resist."

"I don't understand you," she said. "Why did you have to buy these now? There must be a set of George Eliot closer than Scotland that you could get if you needed to write on her. Or you could even use a library book for a change."

"Why not buy them? They were cheap."

"That's no reason to buy something. It's a terrible reason to buy a book. I'd be willing to bet you won't read ten pages of any one of these books in the next five years."

"Bet me enough and I'll read ten pages right now. If you'd hurry and go look at the Duffin house maybe we could move in January and then we'd have plenty of book space."

"Oh, hell," she said. "That's a fine goddamn reason to buy a house. If you think I'm going to buy that house and sit and watch you turn into William Duffin you're crazy."

"What do you want a house for, then?" he asked. "It was your idea."

"I want a house big enough that I can get away from you without going outdoors," she said hotly. The sight of the stacks of books plus his patient quiet assurance that sooner or later she would decide what they should do angered her uncontrollably. For a moment all she wanted was revenge. She reached out a foot and kicked over a stack of George Meredith. Jim looked up. He was surprised to see how angry she was.

"What are you doing?" he asked.

She got up as if to leave the room, but instead kicked the box the books had come in. "I want a house so maybe I can be happy," she said, ashamed of herself for kicking the books.

"You wouldn't be happy in Buckingham Palace," he said. "Don't be so goddamn childish. You don't know that I won't read these. I may read every one of them."

"You're too spoiled to be happy," he added, as if in afterthought. "If that's why you want a house, let's forget it. You'd just be disappointed once we moved in."

"Go to hell," she said. "You're no one to call me spoiled. I took care of your son all summer while you played games with cameras and older women and went to rodeos and all that. You don't care whether your son has a room of his own or not. It never occurs to you what other people might need."

"Oh, it occurs to me. You've pointed out to me what you think you need every second day since we've been married."

"A lot of goddamn good it's done me," she said. "Nothing's changed yet."

"Yes it has, you're twice as profane," he said. "You didn't use to yell curses, just complaints. If I had a dollar for every time you've complained we could make a down payment on a house."

"I wouldn't live in that house if they gave it to us," she said. "If you don't like my language you can leave. This place is big enough for Davey and me."

She began to cry and Jim tried to apologize, but every time he said anything to her she yelled at him and it woke Davey up and he cried too and was very agitated. She was a long time calming him. As she was standing by the baby bed stroking Davey's back the anger went out of her and she felt terribly in the wrong and ashamed of herself.

"I'm terribly sorry," she said when Davey was asleep again. Jim was on the bed, resting his hip and looking gloomy. "I don't know why I attacked you."

"It's all right. I guess it was unnecessary, buying those books."

"No, buy all the books you want to. Why not? One of us will read them someday. But we have to have a house, see? So Davey can get away from us when I pick a fight with you."

"I agree. The Duffins are certainly eager to sell."

He tried to rub her back, to soothe her, but she didn't want any back rubbing. "Do you think I ought to see a psychiatrist?" she asked.

"Why?" He was surprised.

"Because we keep having fights."

"I'm sure everybody has fights."

"But we don't have anything else any more."

Jim turned off the light and tried to pull her close to him, to comfort her. She didn't resist, but as soon as he was asleep she began to edge away from him. Since his return she had not liked to sleep close to him. Every night she edged away and awoke in the morning to find herself on the very edge of the bed. She always awoke before he did and got up while he was asleep, so he didn't notice. He had not noticed anything; only that her rages were more violent. Otherwise he treated her as if she were the Patsy she had been before the summer. It was partly a relief, partly a disappointment. He didn't know who she was, and while that was good, it was also bad. She didn't like feeling herself a stranger to her own husband.

The next morning Jim reminded her that he had asked Hank to dinner that evening. It was an occasion he insisted on and she dreaded it. For three weeks she had postponed it with one excuse after another, but there seemed no way to postpone it any longer. Yet the thought of it made her sick with tension. That afternoon, while Jim was in his nineteenth-century novel seminar, she went to Hank's and was sick at her stomach from the tension. She lay on his couch fully dressed and white and cold at the contemplation of the evening and the mess her life was in.

Hank was sulky. He had hoped to make love. He was reading *The End of the Road*. The sight of the book made Patsy the more depressed. For some reason she connected the beginning of the end of her romance—her romance, as opposed to her affair—with her own reading of it, which had occurred about a month before. The book had been lying around Hank's apartment for months before she grabbed it one day while hastening to the john. She read it straight through, growing more and more depressed with each turned page. She hated it but it fascinated her. She didn't like anyone in it, neither Jacob Horner nor either of the Morgans, and she decided privately that the reason the book fascinated her was because it was a time in her life when she really didn't like anyone, herself included. Only Davey was exempt from her blanket dislike. Emma was okay, but Emma was a pillar of virtue against which she could not comfortably lean. Jim and Hank and herself were as wretched a threesome as the one in Barth, it seemed to her.

Somehow the book made clear to her something that she didn't want to know: that she was not in love with Hank. For a month or two she had had the strong if sporadic illusion that she was. She had been illusioning herself a grand passion, and at first, when everything was new, the illusion worked. Feeling blurred her vision for a while and life was beautiful; then, despite herself, her vision began to clear and she could not help seeing the man she was involved with. And the man she was involved with was not so remarkable as she had first supposed him to be. What it boiled down to, she had come to fear, was that he just happened to be a good lay, or the kind of lay she just happened to need at that time. Otherwise, he was really no better than Jim—not as smart, actually, and no stronger, if as strong. He had more animal stubbornness, but it was of a very selfish kind. For a while he kept her dazed with sex, and she was glad; she didn't want to be objective about him. But then it ceased to daze her in quite the same way; she began to grow objective even before she left the bed.

At times she was angry with Nature herself for making her so physically vulnerable to someone who was going to turn out to be temporary, after all. She knew that even the best relationships were supposed to have gaps, but except for sex theirs was practically all gap. For one thing, Hank was too soft. The longer she knew him the more convinced she was that the only part of him that was ever hard was his penis. Otherwise he was quite yielding. He really didn't want her to hang around long, once they had made love, because if she did they invariably got in an argument and Patsy invariably won. There was almost no point he wouldn't yield if she pressed him hard enough. He was capable of temper, but not capable of really standing up against her onslaughts. She told him not to let her have her way, but he did, anyway, to her disgust.

When disappointment first began to dawn she tried to hide it from herself. She tried very hard to be in love. Sex was her way of trying, and it seemed, for a time, that it might be a sufficient way. She only realized it wasn't going to be when it occurred to her one day that she wouldn't want to marry him; there were too many things she didn't like about him. She could not really visualize them outside his apartment. The thought that, after all, they were only temporary frightened her, and to escape from it she turned back to sex with a kind of voracity that amazed her. For a time she had only two modes, the carnal and the maternal. At home, in the late afternoon, she would bathe Davey and powder him and then sit with him in her lap, smelling his neck or behind his ears, thinking how very different a baby smelled from a man. She pressed her face against Davey's neck and listened to him gurgle, or let him pull her hair, still calmed and subdued from the things she had done in the afternoon, only an hour or two earlier, when her face had been pressed against Hank's neck, in a room where there were quite different smells.

Only Jim, slowly recovering, was left out of it all. He was nice; she was nice to him, but never came close enough to him to notice that he had a smell. It saddened her. She wept for him and for them sometimes when she noticed him looking lonely, or when it occurred to her how much he must need; but he could do nothing about her and she could do nothing about herself.

And he seemed to suspect nothing at all about Hank, which was the reason she had not been able to get out of the awkward dinner. "Couldn't you pretend to be sick?" she asked, looking over at Hank, who was still reading.

"No," he said. "I did that once. I could bring Kenny. He loves your dinners. Or would you rather I brought a date."

"Shut up," she said. "Would you get me a Coke?"

He did, and she sipped it unhappily. "How did it get this way?" she asked. "It was wonderful for a month or two, and now it's a hopeless mess."

"Maybe I should go away again," he said without looking at her.

Patsy gave him a dark look. "Why?" she said.

"To end the mess."

"Sure," she said. "Go on, desert me. It's exactly what I deserve. When are you thinking of going? Shall I pack you a lunch?"

"I wasn't thinking of going. I just said it."

"Oh, yes," she said. "I remember now. Your remarks originate in the larynx, not the brain." She belched and felt a little better.

He looked hurt, and she began to feel sorry for him. "Don't leave," she said later. The fact that she didn't really love him didn't change much. She was still involved with him, still wanted him to come sit by her. "There's no reason a mess can't go on forever," she said when he came and sat by her.

"It will drive you crazy."

"So what," she said. "Anything for novelty. You've never asked me to leave him and marry you, you know."

"I know you too well," Hank said.

"I don't like being known that well," she said and was silent. She lay blankly for fifteen minutes; she had ceased to believe in anything—love, decency, peace, anything. A fog of depression covered her; somehow Hank sneaked into it and aroused her. The fog dispersed, but there were problems even in the sunlight. She had grown more uninhibited—there was no point in being an inhibited adulteress, that she could see—and wanted to do something new, but Hank wouldn't let her. He was prudish about himself; he liked to do it his own simple way. Several times, trying to explore her new feelings, she had been rebuffed. It hurt her; she couldn't understand it or make him talk about it, but she kept hoping. It hurt again that he rebuffed her, but she was too glad to be out of the fog to want to fight about it.

They did it his way and it went well, so well, unfortunately, that Hank was moved to brag. "Pretty effective, huh?" he said.

She didn't answer; the cold fog had moved back in. She got up and didn't touch him the rest of the day. "I wish you weren't coming to dinner," she said as she was leaving.

"Why?"

"Because you make me feel small," she said. And she cried a few tears of self-pity on the way home. She couldn't believe she would ever have a grand passion or a man who was really right for her; she was not even having as wild an affair as she could have handled. Dreariness was what she deserved, and dreariness was what she was going to get.

The dinner, however, turned out to be pleasant, and the thanks were largely due to Kenny Cambridge. Kenny was going to pieces as spectacularly as it was possible for someone unspectacular to go to pieces. The university had long since come to regret its investment in him, but so much had been invested that there was nothing to do but lead him along the path toward the Ph.D. His hair was as long as it would grow, but it refused to hang down and stuck straight out from his head. He had adopted old fatigues as his uniform, with a yellow scarf for color, and his beard hung down in the way his hair ideally should have. He had decided, improbably and at the last minute, that he wanted to be a medievalist, as a means of escaping the sterility of modern literature, and had decided to make his thesis a verse translation of *Bevis of Hamptoun*. The department had okayed the project, mostly because they were too bored with Kenny to help him think up a viable topic; but as it became apparent that he was giving *Bevis* an extremely free, almost Ginsbergian, rendering, opposition to his project had begun to mass itself.

His chubby mistress had dropped out of school and gone to work for the phone company, to help support them, but she had gotten fired. Her parents, who had moved to Houston, would not have tolerated her living with Kenny, so it was necessary for him to pretend he was living somewhere else. What that meant was that he had to keep his clothes in a suitcase in the garage. They were not many, but it was still inconvenient, and if her mother happened to appear too early in the morning he would have to hide in a closet while she chattered with her daughter. To make the arrangement even more bizarre, they had decided to get a pet; not liking dogs, they got a parakeet. Unfortunately they had not noticed that the parakeet had only one leg. It seemed a small matter, but, as it developed, the bird's one leg got tired from time to time and he would collapse off his perch with much fluttering and racket, usually while Kenny and his girl were making love. Kenny took a huge enjoyment in the idiosyncrasy of his own decline, and also a huge enjoyment in Patsy's veal scallopini, which was quite good. The chubby mistress was there also, bland and silent as a fruit.

Patsy was happy all evening. She did not feel awkward with Hank at all. He was too silent. It was pleasant to see him in a normal context rather than one of unadorned adultery. The talk was all of the staples of graduate school: professors, papers, seminars, books of scholarship, read and unread. When the company all left, Patsy put on her yellow robe and sat in her rocker, a little high from what she had drunk. She felt mellow, very pleased that such a potentially tricky evening had gone so well. She and Hank had behaved like hostess and guest. It was surprising to her that such was possible.

Later, still rather dreamy, she was lying on the bed on her stomach, not really reading a *New Yorker*. Jim came in from his ablutions and stroked her calf. She had shaved her legs that afternoon and her calf was very smooth.

"Nice dinner party," he said. "We ought to have Hank over more often."

"Huum," she said. "He didn't have much to say."

"He never does. But he's still pleasant. Actually I think he's scared of you."

"Scared of me?" she said, irked by the remark.

"Sure. He doesn't really know what to do with women. He was the same way around Clara last year—very quiet. I think she must have been too much for him."

"It might be that he just didn't like her, you know," she said, but her mood was spoiled. Jim's tone, though chatty, sounded insufferably pretentious. She wanted to kick him and shout at him but knew it was an impulse to resist. She did kick his hand off her calf and rolled across to her side of the bed. She kept looking at *The New Yorker,* but she was sulky and swollen with anger and afraid that Jim, hot with a conviction of superiority, was going to make a serious pass. But what upset her most was mention of Clara. It made it all seem smaller and drearier. A year before, Clara had been his mistress; now she was. A knot formed in her stomach, traveled up her back, between her shoulder blades—it lodged behind her eyes and swelled and filled her head. She began to cry.

Jim was startled; he had just switched off the bed light and was under the impression that she was in a good mood.

"Are you sick?" he asked, switching the light on again.

"No," she said with a sob of misery. "Nothing's wrong."

Jim was very confused; he didn't understand it at all. He tried to pull her close to him, but she stiffened. "No," she said. "Go on to sleep. Just go on to sleep."

"Okay," Jim said a little angrily. He was silent for a few minutes. "I'll never understand you," he said.

Patsy didn't answer and didn't care. She didn't want to be understood. She had felt good for an hour, felt in possession of herself, and suddenly, because of a few words from Jim, she felt worthless again and unsure of everything. Jim was silent and patient, sure that she would calm down and be apologetic. While he was waiting, his mind wandered and he went to sleep. The fact registered itself on Patsy and she became calmer at once. When he was in bed with her and awake she could not feel calm. It was like listening to the ticking of a human bomb, and the bomb, she knew, inside her. If he were to jostle her she might explode, and she lay tensely, hoping not to be jostled in the wrong way. As soon as he went to sleep the ticking stopped and she relaxed.

She got up and washed her face, rueful at the thought of how puffy she would look in the morning. Back in bed, she felt wakeful and turned on her reading light and reached across Jim to get her *New Yorker*. The sight of him asleep made her feel guilty for having been upset over so little. He had disposed of his beard, and looking at his quiet familiar face made her wonder what he would feel if he really knew her. How would it change his face, knowing what she had become? What would he do? What sort of man would he become, in the face of her disloyalty? Would he beat her, leave her, weep, blame it on Hank, be quietly hurt, forgive her, be blasé? She couldn't predict; his feeling for her was too indefinite in the forms it took for her to be able to predict. Worse, she couldn't decide which of the various reactions she would like him to have. Her feelings were just as indefinite as his, but when she turned off the light again and heard his quiet breathing she felt calm and safe, not to have been discovered. Better to stay calm and safe, with husband and son. All the other wildness could not really be worth as much as it seemed. There was no permanency in it. So long as she was not jostled the familial darkness was nice.

The next morning she was making French toast when the resolve to have a house awakened in her. Davey was scuttling around at her feet on the cold floor, mumbling and exclaiming and discoursing. He was fascinated with her fuzzy yellow house shoes and she had taken one off and given it to him, to keep him out from under her feet. He rubbed it against his face and sneezed and then beat it against the floor for a while; then he came and got underfoot anyway, convinced the other house shoe was more desirable. She took it off and scooted him back from the stove and finished breakfast barefooted, watching him happily mouth the shoe. It was time for a house. There was no point in more shilly-shallying. What if her midnight fits were penetrating to Davey in some way, worrying him in ways that didn't show?

When Jim staggered into the bathroom a half hour later Patsy was on the phone talking to Lee Duffin, and, two hours after that, while Davey was having a morning nap, she left Jim to baby-sit and went to see the house. The morning was fresh, bright, not nippy exactly but refreshingly cool, and she felt extremely good and extremely businesslike. She felt like doing something smart and positive. As she passed Albans Road it occurred to her that if she had happened to meet Hank just then she could have dispatched him from her life with a smile. She was in a mood to dispatch things.

The Duffins were awed by her mood. Bill was hung over and could not quite get with it. He tried being laconic with Patsy and found that she was even more laconic with him; she was not really seeing him at all, or listening to him. She was inspecting the house with strict concentration. He became grave and formal and then decided to hell with it and left for school, leaving Lee to deal with Patsy. Lee had no trouble. She assimilated herself to Patsy's mood and showed the house from attic to basement. When the tour was done she poured them coffee and brought it into the living room. Patsy was looking at the windows and brooding about drapes. She looked at Lee and smiled; they were both in sweaters and skirts. Lee's face was quiet.

"How much do you want?"

"Thirty. We arrived at that figure the night we agreed to offer it to you."

Patsy sipped some coffee, leaned back on the comfortable sofa and looked at the long windows again, picturing them with drapes. Her drapes. Lee's drapes were beige and not quite bright enough for the room, she thought.

"We can offer twenty-seven five," she said, considering the high bookcases.

Lee smiled as if pleased with something. "Did you arrive at that figure the night we offered to sell?" she asked.

"No, just now. I'm so glad the third floor's carpeted. It's perfect for Davey."

"We'll take twenty-eight," Lee said.

"Okay," Patsy said.

They chatted for a while about various aspects of the

house, which Patsy had come immediately to consider hers. As they were standing up, Patsy about to leave, it seemed to occur to Lee that the house had in some way ceased to be her own, that soon she would be without the beautiful dark floors of her living room and its lovely afternoon light. There was a look of unhappiness in her eyes, as if she already foresaw herself placeless. She kept glancing out her living-room windows, as if remembering the light. Some of the briskness left Patsy too when she thought of moving. Inadequate as the old apartment was, it had been her first home as a woman and she loved it. She didn't feel business-like any more.

"How is Peter?" she asked, a little startled by her own question.

Lee showed no surprise. "He's fine," she said. "He's a perfect darling. No one could help loving him."

"That was my impression," Patsy said.

Lee looked up, brightening by an effort of will. "Well, now that we've done the essential dealing let's leave the details to the men." They walked out on the steps and looked up at the shedding elm. When Patsy left she had the impression that, however glad Lee may have been to have the house selling done, the larger part of her was sad at the thought of losing the house, or Peter, or both. Passing back by Albans Road, she herself felt much less clear and positive, much less in a mood to dispatch anyone from her life. Her mood of decision had passed. Who was she to be making such positive moves, a woman with so little certain in her life? It was almost winter. Someday soon she would have to take Davey to the zoo and see if Peewee Raskin had returned to his favorite job on the zoo train.

At home a sense of briskness returned. She felt she had accomplished something major. Jim and Davey were on the floor, playing with each other somewhat disgruntledly, Davey slapping petulantly at the toys Jim held out to him. Jim was mildly peeved to have been left out of the house dealing, while Davey seemed to be annoyed at the world in general.

"We can move in January," she said. The thought of the house and all the bookcases soon lifted Jim's spirits and he went off to the library. Patsy remembered that she had forgotten to pick up her laundry, and she got Davey's sweater and a neat-looking fall cap she had bought him and carried him underarm downstairs to his stroller, which they kept in the garage.

Wheeling him back toward Bissonnet in the bright fall sunlight, the trees on South Boulevard beautifully green, she felt a great surge of spirits. They would have a whole house, finally. There was a whole floor for Davey, narrow and piney, but just right for a little boy. The stairs were of a nice wood too, and she could not stop thinking about drapes for the living room.

Her launderer was a small jolly man named Mr. Plum. He thought she was gorgeous and was always telling her so; often when she was low his cheeriness and his fondness for her were a help. When she wheeled Davey in, her eyes sparkling, he saw that she was in an exceptional humor and immediately, in his wry way, began to seek the cause. Patsy was not reticent.

"Since you're my only real friend you get to be the first to know," she said, grinning with delight. "We've just bought a house."

"Not far away, I hope," he said. "Look at him, pretty soon he'll reach it."

Davey was standing up in his stroller, straining to reach the penny gum machine, in front of which Patsy invariably parked him. It was one of the mysteries of his life, the round globe full of gum. He could not quite reach it from the stroller and his face grew red with straining.

"You can't chew it yet," Patsy said. "It takes more teeth."

But she stooped to lift him out of the stroller, and her hair fell over his head as she struggled to disengage one of his feet. Unless she gave him a close look at the gum machine he would cry all the way home. Once she had him out, she set him on her hip and watched him happily as he explored the mystery further, rubbing his hands on the glass, still unable to understand why the gum could not be touched. She held him with one hand and straightened her hair with the other, looking to see if Mr. Plum shared her delight in Davey's obsession.

"I wish I could make a piece come out without having to give it to him," she said. Mr. Plum wanted to know all about the house; he chided her for not having a contractor check the foundation. "I know I should have," she said, "but I just couldn't resist it. I had to get a house for this big boy of mine." Her falling hair and his own straining hand had turned Davey's cute cap awry. "I'm so happy about it," she said, and she found a Kleenex and wiped Davey's slobbers off the gum machine. She looked keenly pleased, like a young woman who had never known unhappiness, but a little abstracted by the rush of her own thoughts. She stuffed Davey back in his stroller, got the laundry, and in a moment was poised on the lip of Bissonnet, looking one way and another for a break in the traffic and hoping one would come before Davey grew fretful at being stopped. She didn't want him trying to turn around in the stroller; with one hand full of clothes hangers it was hard enough to manage. She patted her foot a little impatiently while the cars swished by. Her hair was blowing again and she had many things on her mind.

BOOK IV

Summer's Lease

MOVING ON

"Sh," Jim was telling me. "How big's that boy now?"
...someone... "He's sitting on my lap."
..., Roger said... "Did the two of you ever give that little
proposition I made you any thought? About letting this old
worn-out ranch..."
"Goodness," she said... "I completely forgot to tell him
about it. He had an accident and it wiped everything else
right out of my..."
"Whats this?" Jim asked... She took over, explained his
accident as best she could, and listened to Roger's prompt-
ing. Patsy broke in to say goodbye... When Roger... off. She
...Davey... dialed about... and left him... to play with the...

===**1**===

One evening in early November, only two or three days after
they decided to buy the Duffin house, Roger Wagonner
called. Patsy was cooking supper. A real norther had blown
in and the windows were rattling. The trees in the Whitneys'
back yard were scraping the roof. The sound of rattling
windows felt wintry and went well with the smell of the
lamb chops she was cooking. It was almost dark. Davey was
underfoot, where he almost always was, fretting a little
because he was hungry and playing with one of the few
remaining blocks from the block truck Dixie had given him
during the summer. Patsy stood by the stove, in a comfortable mull, thinking about rugs and chairs. Jim answered the
phone, and though she listened with one ear to what he was
saying it took a minute or two to realize who he was talking
to. Since deciding to buy the house she had more or less
forgotten that she was unhappy with Jim and she seldom
really listened to what he was saying. When she realized he
was talking to Roger she turned from the stove at once,
causing Davey to wail with impatience. She picked him up,
turned the lamb chops off, and went to the bedroom to the
other phone.

When she picked up the receiver Roger was in the midst of
a leisurely report on the weather in his part of the country,
but he interrupted it to ask how she was.

"Fine, of course," she said. "So's Davey. Is it snowing up
there?"

"No, it ain't warm enough."

"We just bought a house," she said. "We can't move in for
two months."

"So Jim was telling me. How big's that boy now?"

"Enormous. He's sitting on my hip."

"Say," Roger said. "Did the two of you ever give that little proposition I made you any thought? About taking this old worn-out ranch?"

"Goodness," she said. "I completely forgot to tell him about it. He had an accident and it wiped everything else right out of my mind."

"What's this?" Jim asked. He took over, explained his accident as best he could, and listened to Roger's proposition. Patsy broke in to say goodbye and wish Roger well. She put Davey in his highchair and fed him, listening with one ear to Jim's half of the conversation. Roger's voice had sounded exactly the same. It was rather pleasant to sit and poke baby goop into Davey's mouth; she had grown so expert at it that only relatively small amounts got on his hands or into his hair. Jim sounded very interested in the ranch, and that too was okay. She could contemplate owning a house and rugs and chairs and tables, but a ranch was beyond her scale. Better to leave it to the men. Davey could hear his father's voice and kept twisting his head about to look for him, causing Patsy to hit his cheek with a spoonful of spinach. Finally Jim hung up and came in and sat down. Patsy sighed. "If you like him so much, he can feed you," she said, handing Jim the spoon. She wiped her hands on the dishtowel and went back to the stove.

Jim continued the feeding. He was obviously feeling happy, and he had developed some fatherly skills, enough at least to keep Davey amused when she needed him not to be under her feet. She opened some small peas and watched Davey bang his fist on the white apron of his highchair. They were a nice father and son; she felt well disposed toward them. The routine of meals was one routine she liked, for her kitchen was a pleasant bright place, cozy on winter evenings, and Davey was always doing something she and Jim could chatter about. The small routines of her life were attractive to her. It seemed they were gradually wearing the edge off the sword of her differences with Jim. It had seemed such a terribly sharp sword at one time that she could never have supposed anything could dull it, but breakfasts and suppers and Davey seemed to be doing it. It could still cut, particularly if they were in bed, but they were not always in bed, and in the kitchen, with her dinner taking shape, it could be forgotten.

"What did Roger tell you?" she asked.

"Just that he wants us to have his ranch," he said. "How could you forget to tell me? Think of that. A ranch."

"I take it that means you want it," she said, bringing the chops and peas to the table. She had put a loaf of French bread in the oven and went back to see about it.

"Of course I want it," Jim said. "Don't you? He doesn't have anyone else to leave it to. Do you know what land is worth these days? It must be a couple of hundred dollars an acre, even out there."

"That much?" she said, sniffing at some cottage cheese.

"Besides, Davey and I could ride," he said.

"He ought to have had a son of his own," she said. "I think it's sad. He would have made a fine father."

As soon as the bread was hot they sat down to eat. Davey was given a spoon and banged it against his tray. His hair was longer and getting darker. They were having a mild debate about whether to get his hair cut when the phone rang again.

"I'll get it," Patsy said. "I forgot to bring the butter."

She had a bite of bread in her mouth when she picked up the hall receiver, and her hello was a little muffled.

"Pat," Emma said. Her tone was very strange.

"Yah?" Patsy said. "How you?"

"He's done it," Emma said. "He . . . shot himself." She said no more and Patsy heard her breath catch as she struggled with tears. The sound of Emma's voice, as much as her words, made her feel weak and shaky.

"Okay, I'm coming," she said. "I'm coming right now."

"Please hurry," Emma said in a heavy voice. "I don't want to leave the boys with the neighbors."

"I'm coming right now," Patsy said, but Emma had hung up.

"Oh, oh," she said, going to the kitchen. She leaned against the cabinet, feeling very faint.

"What is it?" Jim asked.

"Flap shot himself," she said, rocking against the sink. It was not believable.

Jim jumped up and started for the phone and then stopped. "Is he dead?"

"I don't know," she said. "I didn't ask."

For a moment the only sound was the sound of Davey banging his spoon on the white plastic tray. Then Patsy remembered what she had promised. She shook her head and untied her apron.

"I've got to go," she said. Jim had come near, but he was a blur.

"I ought to come," he said. "I'll have to."

"Not now, she needs me quick," she said. "You'll have to wait until Juanita can get here. I have to go right now. Put him to bed and try to get Juanita."

She grabbed a purse and a coat. "Look, call me," he said as she was leaving.

"Okay," she said, but she could not think of anyone but Emma, and the fright in her voice. And when she got to the Hortons', Emma was the only person she could see, really see. An ambulance with a whirling red light was pulling away as she drove up; neighbors were on the sidewalk talking quietly. Patsy ran through them, up the steps, and found more neighbors inside, and Emma sitting on the couch, her best coat on, hugging the two boys, who were not crying. Emma was not crying either, but her face was worse than tears could have made it, as if the effort she was making to hold in her fright had pulled her features out of alignment. She plainly did not really see the neighbors who filled the room. Her face changed a little when she saw Patsy.

"Do you need to go on?" Patsy asked. As if released, Emma stood up. A boy had each hand. Teddy seemed merely amazed that so many people were there, but Tommy was scared and seriously inquisitive.

"Mommy, are you going in an ambulance too?" he asked.

"No, I'll go in the car," she said. "You and Ted stay with Patsy. She'll put you to bed and stay till I come back."

"Me choo-choo story," Teddy said. He released his mother's hand and went to find his favorite book, *The Little Engine That Could*. Tommy held on for a moment.

"Did he hurt himself badly or is it just a little hurt?" he asked, trying to get Emma's eyes.

"I don't know, honey," she said. "Not too bad, maybe. I'll call Patsy when the doctor tells me."

Teddy came back with his book and thrust it into Patsy's hand. The neighbors had begun to leave. Patsy knelt and tried to get Tommy to look at her. "What's your favorite book?" she asked. "I'll read it too."

"I don't want any story." He wouldn't look at her.

"Well, you be nice," Emma said and disengaged her hand. "Momma's got to go."

She looked at Patsy and left quickly. Some of the neighbors stayed, asking how they could help. Patsy only wanted them to go. She wanted to keep Tommy talking. She was dreadfully worried; he looked as if he might close up in his fear at any moment. She began to want very much to ask one of the women about Flap, but there was no way she could. Finally the last of the women left and she took Teddy in her lap and sat on the couch. "Goodness, when there's an accident everybody comes," she said.

"Me choo-choo story," Teddy said, and she read it. Tommy sat with his chin down and his heels pressed together.

"He's not in his pajamas," he said. "He'll make you read it again."

"That's not so bad. We'll get your pajamas on and have another story then."

"I would rather my daddy came back," Tommy said quietly. "He reads stories very well."

"Me story *agin,* me p.j.s," Teddy said, trying to get her attention. He wiggled out of her lap and went to find his pajamas. While they were in the bathtub she called Jim and told him what little she knew. He had not been able to get Juanita or a baby-sitter and was very distracted. Davey was crying in the background. "I'll call again when I find out something," she said.

She read Teddy his choo-choo story again and was in the middle of a Babar book when the phone rang. It was Emma, sounding not so terrible.

"I'm at Ben Taub," she said. "God. It isn't very bad, really. It just looked bad because it was in the neck and there was so much blood. He says it was really an accident but I don't know. I called Mother, she'll be over to spend the night with the boys. How are they?"

"Okay. One of them is a little uptight. We're reading stories. Don't worry."

"I think he heard the shot," Emma said. She sighed, and Patsy heard the sound of someone shouting, through the phone.

"Terrible here," Emma said. "Butchered-up people all around."

"Want me to come when your mother gets here?"

"Would you? I really don't quite know what to say to Flap."

"I won't either, but I'll come. Did he really fail his exams, or what?"

"Oh, I don't know. I don't even think he knows. He didn't come home until late. He's been sulking around the library lately. I didn't even know he was in the garage. Apparently he sat down there fiddling with his dad's old pistol and feeling sorry for himself until he got it to go off and shoot him. He probably hasn't failed. I don't know what to think about him. I'm glad it was just a .22."

"Don't think for a while. I'll come as soon as I can."

"Tell Tommy Flap's okay. Flap can explain it all to him sometime. He can explain it to me too."

Both boys were asleep before Emma's mother arrived. She was a fat woman, as fat, Patsy supposed, as Emma would be someday if she wasn't careful. And she was as complacent as she was fat. It had always irked Patsy a little that she cheerfully let her daughter live in squalor while she herself still kept a beautiful house in River Oaks, though it had occurred to her, watching them together, that it had simply not occurred to Mrs. Greenway that *her* daughter might lack for anything. The fact of the Hortons' poverty seemed not quite to have penetrated her consciousness, something hard for Patsy to understand. Her own mother would not have drawn a happy breath if she and Jim were in similarly straitened circumstances. But Mrs. Greenway seemed to assume that both the world and her own were as they should be and it would have taken a very dramatic occurrence to convince her otherwise. Even Flap shooting himself was not dramatic enough. She came in as unhurriedly as if she were merely dropping by to say hello to her grandchildren. Her face wore no expression of alarm, and in chatting with her it seemed clear that Emma had protected her mother from the ambiguities of the facts. She supposed that Flap had had a simple accident with a gun.

It irked Patsy a little, with Emma. Why must she be so overprotective of a woman fifty-five years old? But then she remembered that she had done something of the same in regard to Miri and her own mother.

"I suppose he thought it was unloaded," Mrs. Greenway said, setting her purse on a table. "It's always the unloaded gun that shoots people, isn't it? How have you been, dear? I haven't seen David in months. He must be walking by now."

"Not quite, but he's thinking about it," Patsy said. "I think the boys are okay. Tommy was sort of worried. I told Emma I'd go by the hospital and see how things were."

Mrs. Greenway looked around the Hortons' living room as if surprised to find herself there. It seemed to horrify her slightly to realize that she was expected to spend the night. "That's kind of you, dear," she said. "She said they took him to Ben Taub. I believe that's the one where they take all the Negroes after they cut themselves up. Why do you suppose she picked that one?"

"The emergency treatment there is supposed to be very good," Patsy said. "Really, it was very frightening. I think Flap lost a lot of blood."

"My husband died in Methodist," Mrs. Greenway said vaguely. "Goodness, you know I've never spent the night at Emma's. I wonder if she had time to change the sheets?"

"No, I'm sure she didn't but I'll be glad to if you like," Patsy said, white with anger.

"Oh, no, dear, I can manage," she said, bending over slowly to switch on the TV. "A little housework will be good for me."

When Patsy got outside she discovered that Mrs. Greenway had left her Cadillac parked a good yard and a half from the curb. It was ancient, as Cadillacs go; she had nosed it toward the curb and left the tail fins pointing out into West Main. Patsy stood on the sidewalk indecisively, trying to decide whether to go back in and get the keys and park the car properly, but she was too irritated to trust herself with Mrs. Greenway and went on to the hospital.

Finding Emma and Flap was no simple matter. The registration room was crowded with indigent sufferers and their relatives. Though it was nine at night the line to the information desk was twenty people long and seemed not to move; most of the people sitting on benches were asleep, their heads in their arms. Most were Negro, but there were whites and Mexicans waiting as well. Many of the women held children in their arms, children whose faces, asleep or awake, already held something of the hopelessness of the women who held them. The sight of the children, pigtailed in some cases, chubby-fisted like her own child, all their faces a stupor of weariness, made Patsy wince inside. She wanted to leave the room, so she wouldn't have to see the children. The longer she stood the more depressed she became. She knew that even if there was something that could be done about such things, she would never do it, but would go on day by day for years, leading a clean, extravagant, comfortable liberal life. After a time a feeling of dullness came over her and she stepped out of line and called Jim.

"I haven't found them yet," she said. "You may as well go to bed. He's not badly hurt. Maybe I'll get home in time for breakfast."

They talked for a while about why Flap had done it, but without coming to any conclusions. Patsy went back to the line and by the time she reached the head of it had come to feel more vegetable than animal. For a time she listened to conversations around her, or to the arguments the sufferers were having with the nurse at the registration desk, but that grew old and painful. There were quibbles and belligerence from all parties and it was evident from the tone of the talk that nobody was going to be satisfied with the outcome. After a while Patsy tuned out; her ears ceased to pick up the conversation. She became a person waiting in a hospital. She didn't move, except to shift her purse from one hand to another, shift her weight from one hip to another. The light in the room was as flat as she felt, and the gritty floors unpleasant to stand on, like the floors in a traffic court. After thirty or forty minutes something happened to her time axis: the waiting room seemed like a continuum, something eternal, to which the vegetable approach was the only approach possible. She could not remember a time when she had not been there waiting, and could not envision a time when she might be somewhere else. It was a shock to find herself suddenly at the desk, confronted by the nurse. She had been dreading the nurse. She had a twangy East Texas voice and had been cutting people down with it ever since Patsy had been in earshot. But to Patsy she was politeness itself; she was not tempted to cut down anyone white and middle-class.

"They're on four," she said. "No room, honey, we're full. Just look in the halls."

And it was in a corner of one of the fourth-floor corridors that she found the Hortons finally. Flap was by no means the only patient without a room; the halls were full of wheezing bulks and silent bulks. Emma sat in a straight chair at the head of the bed. Patsy tip-toed up, supposing Flap to be asleep or unconscious, but then she saw his eyes move. The corridor was shadowed, but there was a light coming in the window behind Emma, enough that Patsy could see that she had been crying.

Patsy didn't know which of them to speak to. She couldn't see them well enough to judge what the emotional terrain was like. Flap was looking at her.

"Hi, Pat," he said.

"How are you?" she asked, bending over him. She felt relieved. She had expected him to look crazed or doped, and he didn't. His face was hollow, but the look he gave her was sheepish, not crazed.

Flap sighed, as if he too were relieved. "I'm feeling much better," he said. "Very good of you to come. Will you help me with Emma? I'm having trouble with her."

She looked at her friend, but Emma wouldn't look at her. Emma looked lonely.

"What's the matter?" Patsy asked, not sure who she was addressing the question to.

"See if you can persuade her not to treat me like a leper," Flap said.

"I'm not going to do any such thing. You shouldn't have shot yourself. My god. What did you think you were doing?"

"He doesn't know what he was doing," Emma said in a flat tone.

"Emma, I do too," Flap said. He tried to turn so he could see her but moving hurt his neck and he couldn't make it. He sighed and was silent.

"What did Momma say?" Emma asked.

"Very little," Patsy said, trying to suppress her irritation with Mrs. Greenway.

"What did she do to tick you off?" Emma asked, looking up for the first time.

Patsy sighed. "She wondered if you had time to change the sheets."

Emma smiled and after a moment bent over and began to cry, hiding her face in her arms, almost as Teddy had. Patsy looked at Flap and tried to be angry with him but couldn't. He didn't seem very upset by the crying. For a man who had just done the unpredictable, he looked very dependable. After Emma had cried awhile he reached awkwardly back with one arm, trying to get Emma to take his hand, but she wouldn't and he gave up and raised his eyebrows at Patsy.

"I hope you're not crying because your mother wondered if you'd changed the sheets," he said. "That's just the way she thinks. There's nothing so bad about it."

"I wish I had a chair," Patsy said, and she went and found one several beds away. When she brought it back Emma was drying her tears and Flap was reaching for her hand again and still getting nowhere. For Emma's sake Patsy decided to help him. It was incumbent that the two of them get cheered up.

"I'm afraid I may have spoiled Teddy," she said. "I ended up reading him the same story three times."

"God," Flap said. "He'll be trying to get me to shoot myself every day."

"Oh, hush!" Emma said, so loudly Patsy was afraid it would wake the hall. "He doesn't really know what you did. Tommy doesn't really know either."

Flap sighed and looked at Patsy to be sure she was on his

side. He looked very tired, as if he wanted to go to sleep, but he made an effort for Emma's sake. "I'll tell them," he said.

"I don't want you to tell them. I don't want them to know."

"I'll tell them, anyway," Flap insisted. "I didn't commit any crime against God. I was very depressed and I was sitting there thinking about suicide, I admit, but I didn't intend to kill myself."

"Bullshit!" Emma said. "Patsy knows it's bullshit too. Who do you think you're fooling?"

"I don't know anything," Patsy said. "I wasn't a spectator."

"Well, I know. I don't care what you two decide about it. It's just an accident I'm not a widow right now. You don't sit around thinking about killing yourself and then shoot yourself in the neck without there being some connection."

"I never said there was no connection. I was examining how it felt to face a loaded gun. I knew it was loaded. I thought I was pointing it past my head."

"Why did it shoot, then? You don't usually shoot guns past your head."

"I squeezed too hard," he said. "Quite accidentally. Even if it wasn't accidental, so what? Maybe I wanted to scare myself. It was in the nature of a warning shot. It worked too. I feel a lot more sensible now. I certainly found out I don't like to shoot myself."

"Well, I'm glad you did," Emma said, her voice still breaking.

Flap tried again to get her hand and finally did, and she scooted her chair a little closer to the bed so his arm would not be twisted so awkwardly. He seemed relieved and subdued. They were all silent for several minutes. Patsy could think of absolutely nothing to say.

"It's eerie taking prelims," Flap said. "I had to do something to get it off my mind."

"That's a weak excuse," Emma said instantly.

"I know, but it's the only one I've got."

"How inconsiderate can you be?"

"Pretty inconsiderate," Flap said quietly.

Patsy felt lighter all of a sudden. The Hortons would go on arguing forever. She looked behind Emma, out the window, and could see, beyond the trees, the wall of another, larger hospital, with only a few of its many rooms lit. It had begun to mist; the streets would be wet. When she looked back Flap was asleep and Emma more composed. "Can you stay while I find a john?" she asked.

"Want me to stay all night?" Patsy asked when Emma returned. "We could take shifts."

"Doing what? There's no place to lie down. You might as well go."

Patsy looked doubtful. "No, I'm okay," Emma added. "I just get mad at him every time I think of him doing that. It's so unfair to the boys."

"I think it's probably like he said. He needed some kind of a jar."

"Not that bad, he didn't. If he'd waited a week he might have found out he passed with flying colors. He can't expect me to forgive him for doing that. It's too unfair."

It was true; Patsy looked down. For a moment she felt more kinship with Flap than with Emma. Emma didn't know what it was to do something that was completely unfair. Emma had never done anything that threatened everything. Patsy didn't know what to say, but nothing was necessary. Emma sighed and rubbed her eyes.

"Well, there's no use brooding over it," she said. "I didn't think he would die, you know, even when I was so scared. I just couldn't believe it. I knew the minute I started going with him years ago that I'd never get rid of him and I just couldn't believe he would die."

They were silent. Emma rested her cheek on Flap's arm.

"I wish you had at least a cot," Patsy said.

"Damn it. Now we have to stay in this cruddy hospital for days. It's going to seem like years."

Patsy saw there was no use in staying longer and got up to go. "Let me know what you want done," she said. "We can keep the boys. One of us could stay with Flap while you go home and rest, maybe tomorrow."

"He's not that sick," Emma said. "If we ever get in a ward he can stay by himself. There is one big favor I need you to do. I hate to ask it."

"Well ask it."

"Go over early in the morning and clean up the blood," Emma said, looking up at her. "I don't want the boys discovering it."

"Sure. What time do they get up?"

"I guess you ought to go by seven."

Flap had begun to snore softly, his mouth open. As she had been coming to the hospital it had begun to rain; the wind had died. She took a silk scarf out of her purse and bent over to look at Flap as she was tying it around her head. "So that's what you have to sleep with every night of your life," she said, joshing a bit. "I always wondered how he looked asleep."

Emma looked at him and smiled. "That's it," she said. "Fool that I am. Thanks for coming."

The smell of the soft rain on the sidewalks and the grass, and the patter of it on the tops of cars in the parking lot was so nice, after the hospital, that Patsy almost wished she could go in and get Emma and bring her out in it. It made a mist in the high branches of the trees in Hermann Park, and the street lights were misty golden circles. She drove slowly, her window down, enjoying the swish of her tires on the wet street and the shine of neon through the rain. Though it was November, the night had turned warm. The wind was gone and the rain held nothing of winter. She yawned and pulled the scarf off her head as she drove.

It was a relief knowing that Flap Horton was not going to die. Having to mop his blood off the garage floor at seven in the morning was not going to be convenient, but convenience was nothing compared to what might have happened. As she turned off Sunset she thought of Hank and slowed down. Albans Road was only a block away. She had never been there at night. Jim was doubtless already asleep and anyhow she had a perfect excuse. Good excuses were rare—there might never be another. Lately she had been able to see him only twice a week, at best. She drove around the block, debating as she drove. She wanted to tell him about Flap, but she wanted even more just to go up and see what he was doing. She parked near his house, but slightly past it, so that someone coming out wouldn't notice the

Ford. She sat under the wheel for several minutes, tapping it with her fingernails, trying to decide. What if Kenny were there? What if she met him at the door? What could she invent? It wouldn't do to spread the story of Flap's near suicide.

As she was sitting pondering it all, the light in Hank's front room went off. No one was there. She got out and hurried across the squishy grass and up the stairs. When she tapped on his door he asked who was there.

"Let me in," she said.

He was very surprised, and Patsy, once in, found that she was trembling. It was always an adventure—always scary. He had been taking off his shirt and it was unbuttoned. "Your hair's misty," he said.

"I've been at the hospital." She told him, swearing him to secrecy. Once she calmed down she found that she was hungry and got herself a glass of milk and a peanut butter sandwich.

"I was just going to bed," Hank said.

Patsy took her milk and sandwich to the bedroom and snooped through his bedside books while she ate. There was a fat red anthology of the Romantics open on the bed. There was also a book on Defoe.

"Aren't you reading any books? These all seem to be studies. I could never live with you. Who wants someone who's always reading studies?"

He bent to kiss her but she fended him off with her milk glass.

"Quit," she said.

"Jim reads studies," he pointed out.

"No, he doesn't. He just carries them home and carries them back. That's better than someone who reads them. Flap reads them and look how he turned out."

He had gone to turn off the light in the kitchen.

"Why are you turning off the lights?" she asked. She put her plate on the floor. Hank sat on the bed and began to untie his shoes. She put her hand under his shirttail and rubbed the smooth curve of his back. "A nice back," she said. "Guess I'll be going, since you're sleepy. If you had a book I'd stay and read awhile, but I don't like to read studies."

"Keep doing that," he said, and she did. He scooted back in the bed more comfortably, so that he sat in the curve of her body. It was very relaxing. Patsy's mind had gone back to the hospital, to Flap's hollow face and Emma sitting in the straight chair, and the children in the waiting room, their faces either too thin or bloated-looking. Hank noticed that she was a little depressed and began to rub her neck. The bed light was in his eyes and he turned it off. "Come on," he said, meaning undress. He took off his shirt, but Patsy sat as she was, her lips thoughtfully against the skin of his shoulders.

"I ought to go home," she said, but she didn't feel like moving. The prospect of a night there, enclosed by darkness and the arms that were already around her, was too delicious to allow, even as a thought. Hank pulled her blouse out of her skirt and put his hand under it, low on her back, touching her where she had been touching him. She put her face against his shoulder while he stroked her back, and as he touched her lightly the faces in the hospital faded, the need for thought slipped from her attention, and the time axis swung again, but in a better way. They undressed sitting on the bed, in a timeless darkness. For months time had controlled them; the need for haste had been with them at every meeting; heat could be worked off but often the working off was rushed and not very subtle. It was fighting or sex, sex or fighting. Unknowingly, Flap had given them a fine gift, a time to be together unhastily. Patsy had never been so awake to the light touch, the cool or gentle touch, to breath and skin and the feel of arm against arm and leg against leg. It was so long after they had made love.

Once she felt a flutter of fear, a tug of home, but it was not strong enough to make her get up. She raised up on her elbows, for a time, and saw her driveway, the dark room where Jim and Davey were sleeping, saw Emma in the chair at the hospital, and then she lay back down and put her fingers on Hank's lips. The darkness seemed to add a different quality to it all; it made the nearness of each other's bodies seem so natural that it seemed something that would go on forever, or until it got light. They slept and awoke together, as if by plan, and made love again, almost too greedily, reducing the small subtle tastes to a single taste. Then, a little numb, they recovered and talked companionably, their voices as soft as the gray rainy dawn that eventually lighted the room. Patsy sat up to watch it, idly straightening her hair, and Hank sat behind her, both arms around her shoulders.

"I didn't mean to do this," she said. "Suppose Jim found out somehow. I'd be hung."

"It was worth it," Hank said, yawning.

Patsy closed her eyes for a minute. "Right now it is," she said. "How do I know how I'd feel about it if it really happened?"

The clock said six-thirty. She got up and showered, came back, combed her hair, put her panties on, collected her clothes and brought them to the bed. Hank was dozing. She sat down on the bed to sort out her garments. Hank woke and looked at her strangely, as if he were surprised to see her on his bed at that hour of the morning, untwisting her bra straps. She fastened the bra, making a small grimace at the effort it took, and went to the window. Her hair was loose about her shoulders and her face still softened by the night. "I love this kind of rain," she said. "You can go back to sleep." He held out a hand to her and she sat back down for a minute, tapping her fingers on his chest. "I hope you enjoyed all this," she said.

"Why?"

Patsy looked at him thoughtfully. "Because enjoying it's the only security we'll ever have," she said. "I have to go attend to some gore."

The morning rain was colder than it had looked through the window. For a time Patsy was in two places at once. She was driving to the Hortons', but at the same time she hadn't quite left the bedroom. It made mopping up the dried blood no task at all—it didn't affect her. She mopped carefully but automatically, her mind carrying her backward and forward. Then she took the bucket of water and emptied it behind the garage, wrung out the old mop, and hung it on Emma's clothesline. The back yard was soppy. When she had gone in to get the mop there had been sounds in the boys' room, so she decided to go up and fix them breakfast. She came upon both boys in the kitchen, and both were looking forlorn. Tommy had climbed up on the cabinet and was eating Quisp straight from the box, by the handful. Teddy had been unable to negotiate the cabinet and sat on the floor looking up at Tommy. Occasionally Tommy let two or three pieces of cereal fall to the floor and Teddy picked them up and ate them, looking very small and woebegone. When Patsy turned on the kitchen light they blinked.

"No one was around to feed us," Tommy said.

"So I see."

"We were very hungry."

"Well, don't make a big thing of it. It's only seven and I'm here to feed you. How you, Teddy?"

"Me no have bery much Quisp," Teddy said, sighing. He got up and went like a streak to his highchair, convinced that now that an adult female had appeared breakfast must inevitably follow. Sure enough it did. She managed to get a respectable amount of juice, toast, cereal and egg down them. Both clamored for bacon but she couldn't locate any. "Bacon," Teddy kept saying brightly, as if by tossing the word at her he would eventually force her to produce some.

"Hush," she said. "There's no bacon today. Nibble on your toes, or something."

Both boys regarded the remark as immensely amusing and risqué. Tommy repeated it and Teddy broke into hysterical laughter. Then he peered at his toes to see if the suggestion seemed practical. Patsy obliged Teddy by reading descriptions of what could be had from various cereal companies. The chatter was lively, but in her mind she kept going back to the place where she had been all night. Teddy, the bon vivant, blew her kisses from his sticky palm. While they were chattering, Mrs. Greenway arose and swept in like a Spanish galleon, her enormous purple housecoat billowing about her. Her hair also billowed. "I might have known you boys would be up before me," she said.

"We're always up before everybody," Tommy assured her.

Just as Patsy was about to leave, Emma called. Her voice sounded cracked.

"You okay?" Patsy asked.

Emma said she was and that she would be home in an hour, and Patsy left. Driving home, she began to feel tired. The night had become last night, not something she was still in, though her body still held the memory of it. She parked the Ford and yawned and stretched and got out. Perhaps Davey would let her sleep. She found them in the kitchen— Davey was getting his breakfast. After the din at the Hortons' it was almost abnormally quiet for a scene in a kitchen. Davey grinned when he saw her, but not Jim. She was pulling her wet scarf off her head when she looked at Jim, and saw at once, with a shock like a fist hitting her chest, that everything was changed. Something had happened. His face was terrible. Even before they spoke she knew what had happened, knew that, after all, she was hung.

2

"What's wrong? What happened?" she said, her wet scarf in her hand. She knew, but thought for a second that it might be something else, some catastrophe in his family or hers. It needn't be her that had changed his face so.

"You know what's wrong," Jim said, giving Davey another bite of baby food.

Patsy walked past them to the cabinet, to the place where she had stood when the news of Flap came. She was numbed and frightened past speech. She didn't want to turn around and look at Jim.

"No, I don't," she said with her back to them.

"Emma called just after you left the hospital last night. She forgot to tell you to ask me to bring Flap some books."

Patsy was silent. A lie occurred to her. She could say she fell asleep in the car in the hospital parking lot. Or that she went to the Hortons' to clean up the garage and fell asleep there. But the lie never got to her throat. She didn't have the energy to lie, or the pride. She felt too numb, and anyway, she could not lie to Jim with him looking so hurt. Lying was easy when he was complacent, when he was happily taking her for granted, but it was not possible when he was sitting feeding Davey and looking crushed.

She turned and went over to the table. Davey smiled at her. The smile didn't reach her, but she bent and kissed him on the forehead from habit.

"Want to fix his bottle?" Jim asked. "He won't eat much more of this."

Patsy looked vaguely at Davey and got up to fix the bottle. She forgot for a moment where the bottles were, so numb was her mind. She began to wish Jim would talk. It was a time when speech would have helped, even the bitterest, angriest speech. But he seemed as voiceless as she was.

When she had fixed the bottle she got a rag and wiped Davey's face and hands and took him out of the highchair. He leaned back in her lap and guzzled his milk, but his presence didn't matter, for once. It didn't lighten anything.

"Please go on and accuse me," she said, facing Jim finally. "I'm not worth your getting that hurt about. Did you think I was off getting murdered or something?"

"Oh, for a few minutes I did. Then it occurred to me where you were."

"How?"

"I'm not so dumb," Jim said. "Hank doesn't have a girl this year and you get strange every time I mention him. I was thinking about spying on you but this saved me the trouble."

"You could have asked," she said. "I might have told you the truth."

"Would you have?"

"I don't know," she said tiredly. "Maybe if you'd asked at the right time. Maybe not. I really don't know."

He stood up and got himself another cup of coffee. "Want some?" he asked politely, but she shook her head. "Why him?" he asked when he sat back down. "That's what I've been wondering most of the night."

Patsy shrugged, flat and discouraged and ashamed. "I don't know," she said honestly. The sick feeling that filled her made the question unanswerable. Why Hank? The night that only an hour before had seemed worth much turned its other side to her memory. With Jim's new, older face looking at her from across the table the hours that had seemed beautiful while they were happening seemed in memory only common and sordid. She could not remember them as being worth very much, certainly not what they had cost her.

"I don't guess I understand you very well," Jim said. "I thought you were the most virtuous woman alive."

Patsy winced; feeling tightened her throat, but she didn't cry. "Don't say that," she said. "Don't say things like that."

"Okay," Jim said mildly. "I guess I idealize you too much. I guess in a way it's mostly my fault."

But Patsy liked that even less. She shook her head, bent over and knocked Davey's baby bottle out of his hand accidentally. He was indignant and she picked it up.

"You needn't go assuming the fault," she said. "I was the one who was out all night."

Davey looked at his bottle and popped the nipple back into his mouth. He looked up at his mother as he sucked, and Patsy smiled at him. She loved the way his jaws worked.

"Well, I mean I probably drove you away."

He got up and left the room and Patsy sat where she was while Davey took the bottle. She felt tired and slightly sick; she felt immobile. It was an effort to move her fingers. Then, when Davey was finished, she had a moment of worry about Jim and went to the bedroom. He was dressed to go out.

"I'll take Flap some books," he said.

"Are you okay?" she said, coming closer. "I don't want you imitating him, no matter how bad I've been."

"I wasn't planning on it."

She sighed, very troubled. Jim puzzled her, but she didn't feel she had any right to question him or criticize him. The room seemed unfamiliar. She was not sure she had any right in the room at all, or any right anywhere. There was a very long silence. It seemed to her that much ought to be being said, but she could not start it. She could only wait for whatever was going to be meted out to her. It was disturbing to think that nothing was going to be meted out to her, that nothing would be said and the terrible indefiniteness allowed to continue. Anything would be better than prolonged indefiniteness, it seemed to her.

Jim was staring at the books in the bookcases. "I thought maybe you just went by to tell him about Flap," he said. "I even got a taxi at two A.M. and dashed over to see if that was where you were. Maybe I should have come up and had a fight with him and drug you home. But it would have involved leaving Davey too long. As it was I was only gone about four minutes. Do you think I should have come up?"

She tried to turn her mind to it but found the scene unimaginable. "No," she said, "I would just have been mad at you for leaving Davey."

"Probably," he said.

"So what now?"

"I don't know," he said.

"Do you want a divorce?"

"No."

She felt a quick relief. Davey had crawled over and was pulling himself up by clutching her clothes. The relief lasted only a minute and then was smothered by the stupor she felt.

"Why aren't you beating me?" she said. "You used to say you'd kill me if I ever slept with anyone else."

"That was when I didn't believe it could happen," Jim said. "That's just the kind of thing you say. I don't feel much like beating you. I feel more like holding on to you.

"I guess I don't even feel much like beating him, really," Jim said. "I'd sleep with you if I were him and got the chance.

"Of course you have to quit seeing him," he added, looking at her.

"Of course," Patsy said automatically. But then it struck her how extremely complicated every day was going to be from then on, and she dropped her head dispiritedly.

"Cheer up," Jim said, attempting to look brisk. "We haven't died. We'll work it out. It's not the end of everything." When Patsy looked up he bent to kiss her. She took the kiss on her cheek and caught a glimpse of his eyes as he raised up. There was more hurt in them than in his words. He didn't look like himself.

"Oh, I'm sorry," she said.

But Jim attempted to be light. He juggled Davey a bit and picked up the books to go.

"When will you be back?" she asked. She wanted to have something to expect.

"Oh, after lunch."

She stood up, suddenly distraught at the thought that he might meet Hank.

"Are you going to see him?" she asked.

"I'd just as soon not. I think I'll cut the seminar today."

They were silent again, both of them pondering the new complications of ordinary academic intercourse.

"I guess you'd better tell him to go away," Jim said.

Patsy nodded, again automatically. "Shit," she said. "I've ruined everybody. He went away once on account of me. If you hadn't gone away I don't think he would ever have come back. Now he'll never get a degree and it's all because I couldn't behave."

Suddenly she began to cry; the sense of the mess that she had made overwhelmed her. She sat down on the couch crying. Davey was distressed and Jim became impatient. Her tears seemed to annoy him more than her adultery.

"Now hush, damn it," he said. "He had as much to do with it as you did, probably more. If he has to go, too bad. He's a lousy graduate student, anyway—he'll never get a doctorate. I don't like you crying about him."

"I'm not . . . just crying . . . about him," she said. "I'm crying . . . about everything I've . . . ruined."

She went on crying and Jim got a raincoat and wrapped the books he was taking in a newspaper. "I'm going to take these books to Flap," he said. "It's better than watching you cry."

Patsy felt a moment of hatred for him after he had gone. She hoped he might have forgotten something and would have to come back, so she could tell him, while she felt it, that it was all his fault, that if he only wouldn't run out on her at such times she wouldn't have needed anyone else. But he didn't come back and she couldn't sustain the hatred. Why shouldn't he go? Why should he stay to watch her cry? He was quite right. It was not his fault but hers for being weak, foolish, selfish, disloyal. And what she was going to do about it she had no idea, for she was still as weak, foolish, selfish, and disloyal as she had been before she was discovered.

Davey got used to her crying and she got a pillow off the bed and lay on the floor, so as to be at his level, and cried and sniffed and blew her nose while he played with his blocks, babbling emphatically.

While she was crying Emma called, asking if Jim had left with the books. Flap was better, she said, and she sounded better. She heard the tears in Patsy's voice and asked what was wrong.

"Oh, nothing. We just had a fight. It's nothing."

"I guess the reason I feel so much better is because it's not the sort of thing Flap would ever do twice," Emma said. "What the hell. I can always *live* with him."

"I'm not sure I can always live with Jim," Patsy said. "However, I'm not going to bore you with my troubles after the kind of night you've had."

"Your troubles don't bore me. I don't suppose you want the boys this afternoon. Momma seems to have a date."

"Sure," Patsy said, though she didn't at all want the boys. It turned out, though, that they were a godsend. She spent a bad morning, tired, sick with herself, irresolute. She tried to sleep but Davey wouldn't let her. She couldn't think, couldn't decide anything, didn't feel she had the right to decide anything. All she could do was wait for Jim to tell her what he wanted of her, so she could try to do it. She gave little thought to Hank, who had even fewer rights in the matter than she did.

But when Jim returned, just before lunch, it was clear he had reached no important decisions. He looked tired and unhappy, but not desperate and not at all decisive. He couldn't even decide what kind of sandwich he wanted. The kitchen was dirty and Patsy cleaned it up in silence. They had lunch in silence. Davey napped and Jim read *Time* magazine. The afternoon looked like a completely unbridgeable gap of time. There was nothing to do but sit and feel sick and apprehensive. It was hard to imagine anything good happening, that afternoon or any time.

Thus the Horton boys were a welcome interruption. At Jim's suggestion they all went to the zoo. Mrs. Greenway had bought the boys new red winter jackets and they were in the best of spirits and on their best behavior. The rain had blown away but the foliage and even the air were still wet.

They gave the boys bags of popcorn, to Davey's envy, and walked all over the zoo. For supper they got hamburgers and French fries and when Mrs. Greenway showed up, the boys were greasy and ketchupy and she looked somewhat disapproving.

"I've never known what people see in hamburgers," she said.

But the afternoon had been passed, and during it Patsy and Jim achieved a state of complete politeness. It was so complete that she began to wonder if it might not last forever. They read all evening. Only at bedtime did Jim mention the problem again.

"When are you going to tell him?" he asked.

Patsy had given it no thought. "I don't know," she said. "When do you think I should?"

"Why put it off?" he said.

"Okay," she said, shrugging. "I'll tell him tomorrow." The problem was less immediate than another. Jim was in bed and she was still at her dressing table. "Would you mind if I slept on the couch tonight?" she asked timidly.

Jim looked surprised. "Why should you do that?" he asked.

Patsy was at a loss. It seemed obvious to her, but she had no clear position on anything any more. She wanted to sleep on the couch but that scarcely seemed an important reason why she should; it was probably one more reason why she shouldn't.

She said no more; she got in bed. But asking had been a mistake.

"Is there something wrong with me?" he asked angrily.

"No," Patsy said. "Don't be that way. Just forget I asked."

"I'm not very good at forgetting the things you do," he said. "Some night when we're not so tired I want you to explain it all to me. There are a lot of things I'd really like to know."

"Maybe we should consult an oracle. I doubt I can be very helpful. I don't understand it myself."

She knew from the way he looked at her that he was disgusted with that answer. He thought she knew exactly why she had done it and was merely too selfish to tell him.

But it had been too long a day. She could not afford to take every disgusted look seriously. She turned off her light and went to sleep, and, through the night, kept as far as possible to her side of the bed.

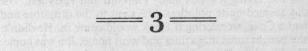

3

She awoke not knowing what was going to happen—went through a day not knowing what was going to happen. Physically she felt worse than she had the day before. She had slept poorly and awoke with a knot in her stomach. It was raining again, and blowy, and she sat at the breakfast table wishing for some easy out, like the flu, that would give her an excuse to go to bed for a few days and hold all problems in abeyance. Jim and Davey were very cheerful at breakfast; she could not respond and was even a little annoyed by Jim's cheerfulness. His resilience seemed to her a little too easy, and his cheerfulness either false or stupid. There was nothing to be cheerful about. He had pursued her across the bed during the night and had his arm across her body when she awoke. She had not liked it. It was that that had given her the knot. She didn't want to be touched, and cheerful was nothing she was ever likely to be again.

Jim went off to the library and she moped through the morning. Juanita came but Patsy did not go out. She felt no desire to see Hank, no eagerness at all to make him go away or not go away, no inclination to do anything about anything. She sat in the rocking chair most of the morning, trying to read a fat novel by Doris Lessing. Jim had lugged it home from the library, but she couldn't read it. Doris Lessing's problems were as dull as her own. When Jim came in at lunch and deduced from the fact that she was still in her bathrobe that she had not gone out to give Hank the gate, he was annoyed with her, though he suppressed it as best he could.

After lunch she dressed and paid Flap a visit. Emma was not there. He was in a large ward mostly filled with Negroes. He was not very talkative and neither was Patsy. "You look hollow-eyed," he said, appraising her. "Been sitting up all night reading Ginsberg?"

"No, but I like his beard," she said, yawning. They both felt like taking a nap. Finally Flap did and Patsy left. The day seemed quite pointless. She went to the drugstore and had a Coke, wondering if Hank would come in. He didn't; she bought some magazines and went home. Jim was home. She kept her silence, washed her hair, and read magazines until it was time to cook dinner. She had not had the energy to go to the grocery store and fell back on soup and rather uninspired bacon and tomato sandwiches. After supper, while she sat on the bed admiring Davey in his brand new winter pajamas, Jim got tired of suppressing his annoyance.

"You didn't do it, did you?" he said.

"No, he wasn't home."

"It's rather cruel of you not to look him up. He might be sick with worry." There was an edge in his voice.

"Okay," she said, sighing. "I promise to look him up tomorrow if you'll drop it right now. I don't like to talk about it while I'm playing with Davey."

"Oh, shit," he said. "You have a lot of refinement for someone who's been sleeping around."

"Shut up," she said. "I haven't been sleeping around."

Jim shrugged. "It's just a phrase," he said. "Anywhere that's not here is around, as far as I'm concerned. But I apologize. I think it's a little silly not to want to mention it in front of Davey. He doesn't understand."

"So I'm silly," she said. "I'm a silly overrefined adulteress. Are you sure you want to keep bothering with me? I may be too frivolous for the scholarly life."

Jim withdrew and let it drop. They spent the evening being strictly polite.

* * *

The next morning Patsy awoke with the same knot in her stomach and decided that, inasmuch as she felt bad already, she would go get it over with with Hank. She found him barely up and when he reached for her she brushed his arm aside with a movement of her shoulders and sat on the couch, her coat on and her purse in her lap.

"You look sick," he said. "Where were you yesterday?"

"I was sick yesterday. I'm sick today and I'll probably be sick tomorrow and for years to come, and it serves me right. We've been discovered."

She watched him closely, hoping for some helpful reaction, but all he did was frown and sit down by her. "I guess that night was a mistake," he said.

He reached for her but she made herself unapproachable. "Don't touch me," she said. "It won't do any good. Off you go again, back to your goddamn plains. Too bad for your career."

Hank shrugged and pushed her back on the couch. She didn't fight but neither would she take off her coat or let go of her purse.

"Jim said you were a lousy graduate student," she said. "Is that right? I assumed you were brilliant. You're so silent I had to assume it."

"I'm so-so," he said. "My mind hasn't been in the groove this year."

"I'm well aware of what groove your mind's been in. I ought to be, since it's ruined my life. If you're not brilliant you ruined me under false pretenses, you bastard." She smiled a little. For a moment it ceased to seem so awful.

He made her let go of her purse, and caught her hands. "Quit," she said. "I never meant to be ruined by a lousy graduate student. Boy, am I dumb. I could have been ruined by William Duffin if I'd wanted to. Why'd I pick you?"

For a moment it all ceased to seem serious. It was just another morning. The change that had taken place had taken place in the other world. Their world was still the same. It might not be enough, but it was the same. He smoothed her hair and she felt comfortable and welcome. She had to tug hard at her mind to remember that there was another, sterner world, in which she had duties. Her hus-

band, at that moment, was waiting for her to come home
and tell him she had put an end to something. She had
forgotten how she meant to do it.

"I wish I felt as bleak here as I do at home," she said.
"Then it would all be easy. You could be shot down without
impunity, you know. Or with impunity, whichever it is.
Now your career is in ruins and you're losing your true love.
Why aren't you bereft?"

But, looking at his face, she knew why. He was thinking
about sex. He didn't really take what she was saying
seriously. She didn't like it. The look on his face, so familiar
and so thoughtless, made it all seem serious again.

"We could run away, I guess," he said. "Ever consider
that?"

"No," she said. "You never gave me any reason to
consider it. You don't want to marry me. You wouldn't
know what to do with me, married, no more than Jim does.
Don't go fantasizing any miraculous elopement. What do
you think I am? We just bought a house. The contract is
signed. We have a child. I'm not going to run away."

"I don't like you living with him," Hank said, as if it were
something that had just occurred to him.

Patsy felt cold. "Thanks," she said. "This is a great time
for you to turn purist. Suddenly you're an absolutist. I leave
my husband for you or you go away. What happens to me
then is no concern of yours, I guess. You'll have your
purity." She had quickly become very agitated.

"We're good for one another," Hank said, as if that too
had just occurred to him.

"Good for one another!" she said. "What have we done
for one another that was so good up to now? All we did was
screw a lot!"

"I love you," he said, trying to kiss her.

"I don't want to talk about love," she said, jerking back.
"I don't know anything about love. I don't love you—I
never said I loved you, not in a sane moment, anyway."

"You have too!" he said, his voice rising. Her agitation
startled him, scared him. "Think of the other night. What
about that?"

"I don't remember the other night," she said bitterly. "I

don't want to, either. Think about what? So we screwed to our hearts' content, so what. It's nothing to bank on. I happen to have real obligations to live up to, thank you. Important ones. Just because you don't, doesn't mean I don't. I don't love you and that won't ever happen again."

She looked at him coldly and contemptuously and Hank, unable to stand it, suddenly hit her in the mouth, knocking her off the couch. He immediately caught the lapels of her coat and helped her back on the couch. They were both surprised and silent, and both were shaking.

"You do love me," he said.

"No I don't," she said, shaking her head. "No I don't." She began to cry. "I don't love anybody." She hadn't felt the blow at all but her lips felt numb.

Hank wiped her tears away with his fingers and then tried to kiss her. He was gentle about it and she let him, sensing that he was trying to make up for having hit her. She saw how agitated he was and raised her face to him. They kissed and were tender for a few minutes, sitting on the edge of the couch, but then the tenderness got lost in their separate confusions. They kept kissing but it changed. Wanting to be close so badly, they missed it, passed it somewhere, and began to move toward sex, hoping it would make them close. Neither felt sure about it but they moved toward it, anyway, hoping it would change something. It was awkward, since neither was sure. In time they got to the bed, in time got their clothes off, but they were sluggish at every stage and beneath it depressed and almost desperate. Patsy was waiting, hoping that the feeling that had always been there would be there again, so strong and clear that it would solve everything, make her know what to do, make her want to hold him. But they were trembling and hot and scared, not in touch with each other. Patsy lost it all, thought of Jim, grew sick with herself in the midst of it. She got up immediately, crying, suddenly sick with fear that Jim would suddenly decide to come looking for her. Hank got up and tried to calm her, but futilely.

"I'm sorry," he said. "Quit crying."

"Oh, don't be sorry," she said, gathering up her clothes. "You did me a favor. You made it as bleak here as it is at home. I'm sure it will all be a lot easier now. You go back to your desert and I'll go back to my family. This is just how we deserve to end."

"I haven't left yet," he said.

"I'll be glad when you do," she said. "Had you rather we went on like this?"

He sat on the bed and twisted a sock around his hand. "Maybe I can get a job in a hillbilly band," he said, trying to be light. "Follow in my father's footsteps."

He was trying to joke, but there was a plaintive tone in his voice that angered Patsy beyond control. Lost in fury, she turned, dropped her clothes, went to the closet, yanked the old guitar out of its case and swung it at the wall. It didn't break. She hit the closet door with it, crying, then brought it down against the bedpost as hard as she could. The bottom cracked; she swung again and it splintered. Hank had been too surprised to act, but he recovered, stepped in and wrestled with her. Her face was twisted. She wouldn't turn loose of the guitar. "No, you won't, you won't get to . . ." she said. He finally got the ruined guitar out of her hands and tried to hold her against him. She strained back and he had to settle for making her sit on the edge of the bed. Her body was shaking and heaving and she was still furious, but she became so weak that he was afraid she would be sick. She let him hold her, and gradually she calmed down.

"You can't leave me and go sit around feeling sorry for yourself," she said coldly, by way of explanation.

"I don't want to leave you."

'I don't wish to argue. We'll see what you do. I'm all right now. Please let me dress."

They both dressed and she left with no more said. She softened just slightly, enough that they could manage a little lightness. He refused to say goodbye and she allowed it to stand that she would see him at least once more. But after she was out, all the spleen and hurt and anger came back and seethed in her for hours. Everything was ugly, she felt. Jim, it turned out, was at the library; he did not get back to see that she had done her duty for almost three hours. It made her the more angry and resentful. When he did come he noticed that her mouth was swollen and made a point of not commenting on it, which made her even more resentful. But in time she calmed a little, of herself.

He avoided the topic until they were at the dinner table and then asked her what Hank had said.

"It doesn't matter," she said. "He'll leave."

"He must have said something."

"He's not a talkative man. *I* said a number of things. I also got socked, as you can see."

"Undeservedly?" he asked.

Patsy felt chilled and looked at him silently for a long minute. "It would be easier if you were on my side," she said.

"I am."

She looked down at the small peas she didn't feel like eating. "You're awfully serene," she said. "You don't know me. You couldn't be on my side."

"Come on. I know you well."

"No," she said. "Why didn't you beat him up and see that he quits socking me and dragging me into his bed?"

"Because I think that's melodramatic," Jim said. "You did it, you ought to be the one to finish it. That's only civilized."

"I *am* melodramatic," she said. "And if you knew me you'd know I'm not civilized."

"I guess you aren't," Jim said and politely finished his meal.

643

The next morning, as soon as Jim was gone, she called Hank to apologize for smashing the guitar. She had awakened thinking about him, and instead of feeling bitter and furious, as she had the day before, she felt softened and lonely for him. The ugliness and anger of the day before seemed unreal.

"I wish I could come over again," she said. "I wish I could come right now."

"Come on."

"I oughtn't to." But she looked at her watch to see how long it was before Juanita was due.

"If he comes back and finds me gone he'll know where I am," she said. "I'd just as soon not have a three-way scene."

"I don't think he'll come here," Hank said.

Patsy reflected, and was inclined to agree. Jim had left the house in high spirits. He seemed to feel that the matter was settled, and was letting bygones be bygones. "I could be telling you goodbye, I guess," she said. "You're going, aren't you?"

"I guess," he said. "Jim and I are having a hard time avoiding one another now, and it's only been two days."

"I'll come over," she said, glancing at Davey. He was trying to wad a sheet of the morning newspaper into his mouth. "All he can do is kill me. Maybe we can work in a few days of goodbyes."

The day before she had taken the world into his room, but she did not repeat the mistake. She simply left the world for two hours—let it wait. What they had might not be a great love—undoubtedly wasn't—but it was something real, and she wanted to enjoy what little there was left of it. She cried when she saw the smashed guitar, but once she had cried she felt much better. They discussed the matter of his leaving very calmly. Once they were agreed to the step, Patsy came to feel that the loss of all future gave them rights to a day or two, a meeting or two. Once it was known that it was only a day or two, she managed, by a twist of her mind, to forget that it was so and to enjoy three morning visits as if they were mornings of normal time in a normal life. They were very quiet visits, only talk and bed. It seemed possible not to make a big thing of parting, and very easy to make a good thing of the mornings. Their sex had not been wrecked, as she had feared; it came back, as strong as ever. On the next to last visit Patsy could not help but be merry. She felt very good in body and sat on the bed later than she should have, clutching her knees and chatting about books. A good feeling lingered all through the day.

But the next morning, which was the last morning, she knew why it had been possible to be gay and peaceful and even merry. It had been because she was good at twisting her mind. On the last morning she couldn't hold the twist. Part of his belongings were in the Oldsmobile, and the sight of the loaded car stunned her, as it had the first time he went away. He was going away and it was real. She couldn't stop it. She would be alone. It seemed once more like a terrible desertion, a betrayal of what had been. Even if it wasn't love, it was important. She didn't want to lose him. He was hers, in some way; and, in some way, she was his. Despite herself she broke into hopeless reproaches.

"You could live on the other side of town," she said miserably. "You could go to the University of Houston. They have an English department. You may not be able to live right here on Albans Road and see me every day, but you don't need to go a thousand miles away, either." Though part of her knew it was terrible to reproach him, or to expect him to stay in hiding just for her sake, another part of her thought it was quite natural and something he should have thought of for himself. She lay on the couch during the whole visit, feeling tight and distant from him, as if through sheer perversity he was inflicting a terrible hurt on her. He should be able to do something besides go away, desert her, leave her alone. Hank kept repeating over and over again, monotonously, she felt, that it was no good for her to divide herself between himself and Jim. It made her sullen, and all the more resentful. Jim seemed irrelevant to her. She had hardly taken notice of him since the discovery. It was hard for her to fix her eyes on him, literally hard. She kept looking past him, away from him.

"Why do you keep bringing him up?" she said coldly. "He's not involved."

"Of course he is. He is as long as you're living with him."

"Not really," she said. "Not him as a person."

"If it's not him as a person then you oughtn't to stay."

"Oh, I know it," she said restlessly. Her unfairness to Jim was so obvious and so terrible that she thought it was merely cruel of Hank to bring it up. Jim wasn't at issue. At issue was his going away.

"If I don't leave you'll go on being divided until you collapse," Hank said.

"Oh, shit!" she said. "I'm not divided! Why have you suddenly come up with this division theory? It's just your excuse. I haven't been divided since the day you kissed me the first time. Please quit talking about it."

"You're fooling yourself," he insisted, and they were silent, stuck, not knowing what to do or how to proceed.

"But you won't stay?" she asked.

"No. I won't settle for two hours a week."

"Because you're selfish. Will no hours be better, do you think?"

"I don't know. We'll find out."

Patsy had not cried for four days. She had determined to give it up. It annoyed Jim so much that she had finally decided his annoyance was justified. It was her way of remaining childish, she decided. She was going to have to grow up, as he kept reminding her, and she might as well begin by learning to control her tears. She had not cried since smashing Hank's guitar. At home she and Jim conversed in polite sarcasms and the tone she maintained through her days was a tone of adult sarcasm. The three nice mornings with Hank had seduced her out of it, into a pleasanter mood and a pleasanter tone, but she closed and became sarcastic again once she left him, and in that mood she had no need for tears.

While she lay on the couch arguing about his going away, she kept tight. The skin around her eyes felt tight, and breathing was hard, but she was not conscious of a need to cry. Only when the argument played out and they were lying side by side on the couch, confronted with a hopeless disagreement which they both knew could not be resolved, did Patsy loosen.

She felt petulant and sullen and for a moment almost glad that he was going. She felt herself closing to him, and it was just as well; once she closed that part of herself that only he entered, life would be simpler. But she found herself looking at his hands. He was propped up on his elbows, and his hands were on the end of the couch, near her face. She had always liked them; his fingers were long and strong. They had touched her in a way that no other hands had, and it hurt her to think they were going to stop touching her. And yet, they were helpless. They could always touch her, never keep her. She put out her own hand and stroked the back of his, up to his wrists. She traced one of her fingers down the back of his hand and touched the little creases where the fingers joined. She stroked the back of his hands lightly and he turned them and opened his fingers to join them with hers. But she wanted to touch hands, not hold hands. She put her palm against one of his, curled her fingers in his palm and let him close his hand over hers, then opened her hand again and touched the insides of his fingers. In touching his hands the worth of what she was losing struck her fully and she could not hold herself tight.

"Oh, damn," she said, "damn, damn," and began weeping. Her body was very still. The tears seemed to empty from her eyes alone. She didn't move at all as she cried. A half-hour later they both felt it might as well be then and they went to the door. Patsy was almost wordless, her face wet and stunned with pain as she looked up at him. "Take care of yourself," she said, and Hank came as far as the car with her. He said he would get off about three.

She stumbled blindly up the alley and home and shut herself in the bathroom to try and cry herself out, out of

sight of Juanita. Time gnawed at her. It was only one
o'clock. He would be in the city for two more hours. It
seemed terrible to waste two whole hours; she remembered
again the night they had spent together, how long the
separate minutes had seemed. Two hours might be like
months. And yet they had parted. She couldn't go back.
They had parted with a good feeling too; if she went back
she would probably spoil it. She didn't know, and she stayed
in the john, crying. She tried to stop crying by reading this
book and that from the john bookcase, but her tears hid the
pages and even when they didn't she scarcely saw the words.

In the end she compromised. At two-thirty she put Davey
in his stroller and tried to dry her eyes as she wheeled him
along to Albans Road. Hank's car was still there. She
wouldn't talk to him again, but she would see him as he left,
perhaps even wave. The car seemed packed full. She turned
the stroller up the street, away from his apartment, and
wheeled Davey up and down the block while she waited.
There was a wind and the fallen leaves were swirling in the
street. Davey was not in sympathy with repetitious trips up
and down the same block of sidewalk. He stood up in the
stroller, tried to reach leaves, tried to twist around, and
managed to pull his cap off. Patsy shushed him and talked to
him automatically, watching for Hank. When he came out
finally she didn't know what to do, whether to let him see
her or not. But the sidewalk where she was was crossed with
sunlight and shadow from the high waving trees, and Hank
did not see her. He got in the car and drove around the
corner to the filling station a block away. Patsy wheeled
Davey to the corner and stood watching him. He was out of
the car, wearing the same suede coat he had been wearing
the first time she saw him. The hood of the car was raised
and he was chatting with the filling station man about oil or
the motor or something, the wind blowing his hair. He never
looked her way. By the corner near the same station was
where she had been sure he would kiss her the first time,
though he hadn't. She would have liked to walk by while the
car was being gassed and say goodbye in a nice voice, or
wave, or have Davey wave, but she knew she couldn't
manage it and squatted down by the stroller on her heels,
waiting while he paid for the gas and got back in the car.

Davey grabbed her hair just then, a habit she had not been able to break him of, and when she looked up again the Oldsmobile was pulling out of the filling station drive. In a second it turned onto Sunset and was gone.

Davey still had hold of her hair. Patsy leaned over and rested her forehead a moment against the cool bar of the stroller. Then she saw someone looking strangely at her from a passing car and she straightened up and went on to the park with Davey, walking deliberately. She swung Davey for ten minutes, then carried him over to the smaller of the slides and came down it with him in her lap. He loved to slide. After that she sat in the grass and Davey crawled. A friendly dog that knew them came over and licked Davey in the face and she called the dog to her. It was a small female border collie who belonged to a rather sloppy young couple from Rice. The collie was evidently not loved and was insecure; her coat, which might have been beautiful, was dull. Her name was Felicity. She was desperate for friends and often bowled Davey over in his crawls. Patsy rubbed her head and scratched her nose. Various mothers were about with their varied offspring. Some boys were playing basketball on a nearby court and Davey sat watching them, a very tiny boy, not even a year old, nothing more harmful in his mouth than a few stray blades of autumn grass.

The wind kept blowing. She managed not to make a spectacle of herself. She didn't cry in front of the mothers. She didn't feel that anything was ended. She would have liked to be riding with him. She never had, except the one night when he had taken her to Yum-Yum's Lounge. The wind blew in her face and she let herself imagine riding with him. Since she had not done it she felt she could indulge in imagining it. She didn't imagine getting there, only the driving. She had scarcely so much as driven into the country since she and Jim had returned from their rodeo trip. How would it be to go back into the same spare country, only with Hank? She didn't know, but she could picture his hands on the wheel and the shaggy hair at the back of his neck, pushing over the collar of his suede coat. Davey got tired of watching and began to crawl on, toward the basketball game, evidently feeling it was something he would like to get in on, and Patsy sighed and got up and inserted him back in his stroller. He kicked indignantly. On the way out of the park a young Rice mother stopped her. Her husband taught anthropology, they had been there less than a year and were lonely, and Patsy accepted an invitation for dinner on Saturday evening. Perhaps it was time she tried to do more with the social round, she reflected, walking home.

Hank drove all night toward the plains. The wind grew stronger as he rose from the coast. Sometimes it rocked the cars on the highway. He went through the little silent towns that spotted the darkness. When he got into rolling country he could often see their lights twenty miles away, then lose them, then see them again, and lights of the towns, at a distance in the darkness, distinct as stars, were always more beautiful than the empty towns themselves. Before dawn he topped the cap rock and had breakfast at a truck stop in the town of Shallowater. He liked to drive and could do it without thinking; he did not feel too bad. The waitress, a talkative old lady, took a fancy to him. "All the way from Houston?" she said. "Good lord a' mercy. You're as crazy as my boy. He'd take off and drive anywhere. Must be a girl out here somewhere, for you to drive all that way at night. Blonde or brunette?" And she smiled at him in a motherly way.

"Brunette," he said, sugaring his coffee.

═════ 5 ═════

For a few days Patsy felt exempt—exempt from hope, exempt from feeling, exempt from duty. She had no feeling of relief or satisfaction, no sense that she deserved any credit for having done a hard but necessary thing. She didn't know whether it had been necessary or not, and anyway she had not done it. It had accomplished itself, or Hank had done it, or Jim, but she was not ready to applaud anyone for it. She felt flattened, generally flattened. She could not call the feeling hoplessness; she could think of things to hope for, she supposed. But she had no definite expectations. Worst of all, she had ceased to expect much of herself. She saw that Jim was patiently waiting for her to recover, that he expected her to straighten up and become the old Patsy, or perhaps a new and better Patsy, and it made her quietly contemptuous of him. It struck her as stupid, expecting things of her. Only Davey could expect good treatment at her hands, it seemed to her.

She didn't mope, particularly. She went about her chores and read and sat and walked Davey and cooked dinners and watched television and chatted with Jim about school, about books, about Davey. Anything that could be chatted about they welcomed, for it relieved the silences that sometimes grew too long, and it meant they did not really have to talk, seriously talk. But nothing was moving inside her, and she made no real moves. Jim kept mentioning the house they had bought, talking about things they might do to it, obviously wishing she would throw herself into a frenzy of buying and planning. Patsy couldn't. She accepted the house as a sort of permanent topic of conversation, second only to Davey for its convenience, but the thought of the house made nothing move inside her. She had no feeling about it, and anyway, the Duffins were still in it and would be for a while.

Emma it was who wrought the first change in her. Flap was home from the hospital and back in school. It turned out that, quite as everyone but himself had expected, he had passed his prelims by an ample margin and, except for a general recommendation that he read more medieval literature, was only a dissertation away from his degree and a good job. If there were suspicions around school that he had done something unstable they were politely muffled, and he spent his short convalescence writing letters of inquiry to two hundred and fifty schools.

But Emma's nerves had been scraped raw by the whole experience. She became for a time irritable and difficult, more direct even than usual and, so Flap and the boys thought, even less tolerant of their human shortcomings. She was no longer inclined to yawn and let things pass, let time take care of them. She came over one afternoon nervous but determined, looked Patsy in the eye, and made known her problem.

"Look, Jim's driving us crazy," she said. "Did you know it?"

Patsy was startled; she hadn't. "No," she said. "Jim? How?"

"He comes to see Flap every afternoon," Emma said. "He usually stays two or three hours, drinking coffee and talking. Flap will let him, you see. Flap can't say no to anybody. I don't know what to do. I don't want to make you mad, and I don't know what I'd do without you, but please do something about him. I don't want him in my kitchen three hours a day. I don't think he realizes he stays so long. He seems to be a writhing mass of insecurities these days."

"Oh, dear," Patsy said, stricken and ashamed. There was a silence.

"Are you mad?" Emma asked.

"Of course not. Thanks for telling me. I'll make him quit bugging you, don't worry. I guess I'm what's the matter with him."

"It's not even me so much," Emma said. "I just don't want anyone aggravating Flap's bad tendencies. I want him to get cheerful and get on that dissertation and get us out of here. If he sits around yakking with Jim he won't get it done and he'll get morbid and scared and it will start all over again. What *is* the matter with Jim?"

Patsy shook her head, wanting badly to cry. She was afraid to bring it out. Emma might quit her and then she would have no friend. She shook her head again.

"Hank went away again," Emma said. "Nobody can figure that out. It was because of you, wasn't it?"

She nodded miserably, unable to lie.

"I thought so," Emma said. "You quiver when I mention his name."

"Do you suppose anyone else has noticed?" Patsy asked fearfully.

"Flap has, but I won't let him discuss you around me. He fancies himself a great analyzer of women and he doesn't know a damn thing about them, basically. You fascinate him. He decided a year ago you were having an affair with Hank."

"He may know more about women than you think," Patsy said. "I wasn't, a year ago, though. I'm not sure what I've had. Affair sounds too technical. I don't like it."

"So how'd Jim find out?"

"Oh, he just did. Now I feel like I ought to be stoned."

Emma was silent. She had not believed it, quite, even after months of listening to Flap marshal the evidence. She could not imagine her friend being in two beds, with two different men. It was a shock, but a mild enough shock because she couldn't imagine it. The distress in Patsy's face was there and it was real.

"Come on," Emma said. "Don't look like that. I would only stone you out of jealousy. I always sort of fancied him myself."

Patsy had begun to cry; Emma chewed a fingernail until she finally stopped.

"But you wouldn't have done it," Patsy said.

"How do you know?" Emma said thoughtfully. "I never was able to say no to anybody who really wanted me. It just turned out that Flap was about the only one who did. Maybe

I'm lucky no one does. I don't know all that much about it. I don't know what I might do."

"You wouldn't," Patsy insisted.

"Oh, shut up," Emma said angrily. "I can't stand being glorified. What it boils down to is that I haven't had any good opportunities to stray, and you have. Frankly, I think you deserved Hank. Jim's too wishy-washy about you. At least Flap isn't wishy-washy."

"Jim's perfectly decent," Patsy said meekly. "I have to straighten up and get him out of your hair."

When they parted, Patsy felt better. Emma was still her friend, after all. She felt in a mood to straighten herself out. There was no excuse for moping or self-pity; her problems were hardly unsolvable. All she had to do was take herself and her husband in hand and behave sensibly about life.

She confronted Jim the minute he stepped in the door and told him in no uncertain terms that he was not to spend any more afternoons at the Hortons'.

"Look, I'm the one that hurt you," she said. "I'm the one you have the problems with. Talk to me about it. Even if Flap understood he couldn't say anything that would really help."

Jim was surprised and annoyed. He was mostly ticked off at Emma for not complaining directly to him, but he was also mad at Patsy.

"You haven't been the easiest person in the world to talk to lately," he said. "I do try to talk to you, you just don't remember it. Some little door clicks shut in your brain every time I look at you, much less try to talk to you."

"Keep knocking until it opens, then," she said. "I'm not that formidable and Flap's certainly no psychiatrist. What could he say that would help?"

"Nothing. He's just easy to talk to."

She dropped it, convinced he would stay clear of the Hortons. That night at the supper table she found herself in the pleasantest mood she had had for days, and while in it she took a close look at Jim. Her eyes had avoided him for weeks, and what she saw when she finally did look closely was enough to worry her very much. If she had come to wear a different skin because of Hank, so had Jim, and it was no improvement on the one he had had. He didn't look aged, he looked younger, and uncertain, a scared and unhappy boy. And there was nothing he could be certain about—not himself, and not her. There was Davey, but he was little help.

It scared her, seeing how scared he was, but she was in a strong mood and she tried to begin changing the look in his eyes. She was as pleasant and cheerful as she could be and was able to believe for a few hours that things might gradually right themselves. She was going to profit by her mistake and start considering Jim and being positive about him.

Jim was delighted that she was cheerful, delighted that she would look at him again. She seemed like the old Patsy, the one he had fallen in love with, the one he could handle. He took her cheerfulness to mean a change of heart. Though it was really only a change of mood, it was a mood he might have built on, had he known how to nurse it and encourage it. But he took it as something more dramatic, something that should be capitalized on, something he ought to match immediately. He took it to mean that she had returned to him and that their marriage was on again.

When bedtime came and she was still cheerful and was quietly reading Frazer he decided such amiability was as near to a sexual invitation as he was likely to get, and he pursued it as such. It destroyed the evening and such small purchase of each other as they had regained. Patsy's mood had changed but her body hadn't. She was relaxed in bed for the first time in almost a month and was hurt that Jim would take advantage of her first little bit of softening. He felt that if he didn't she would feel he was neglecting her, and anyway, he wanted to. Patsy couldn't deny him; for even as she felt betrayed she also felt that he had every right to take advantage of her and that she owed him what he wanted. But despite all debts and duties it left her clenched against him, and him angry at her.

She could yield but she couldn't respond; it was not something she could call forth to anneal a wound or pay a debt. Later she felt that if only he had waited, come closer to her gradually, through several more cheerful moods, he might have succeeded in calling it forth again, little by little. As it was she felt abused; she couldn't help it. And Jim felt cheated. He couldn't help it either. It had been no fun.

They didn't talk that night; they were both, in their separate ways, too bitter, dissatisfied with themselves and with each other. They knew better than to talk—that much at least they had learned.

The next day Jim had a new perspective on it all. He was convinced that sex was their whole problem. He brooded about it all day and that night insisted they discuss it. Patsy had a cold and didn't really feel like discussing anything, much less sex, but Jim was not to be put off. He was convinced the cold was psychosomatic, merely a means of avoiding sex, and he insisted on talking about it. He had convinced himself that not only the otherwise inexplicable affair with Hank but all their previous marital difficulties stemmed from Patsy's irrational attitudes about sex. She saw it coming and grew sullen.

"Look, if you're going to tell me I'm frigid again, don't," she said. "I don't want to be told I'm frigid. It might make it come true."

"I don't think you're frigid," he said judiciously. "You just aren't reasonable about it. You're too emotional. You can't be emotional about it year in and year out. It's like being emotional about what you're going to have for dinner."

"That's an awful analogy. *I'm* emotional about what I have for dinner. Year in and year out I'm emotional. I'm an emotional girl. If you don't like that, I don't see how you can ever like *me.*"

Jim made a face. "I don't mind that you're emotional," he said. "I just don't see why you have to be in a high emotional state to enjoy sex. You know, you do it with your body. You don't have to work yourself up and throw yourself over a precipice emotionally just to enjoy it."

Patsy felt the more sullen. "I don't like the way you talk about it," she said. "I don't throw myself over a precipice—I just need to feel a little warm."

"And you never feel warm toward me?"

She sighed, not knowing what to say. She did and she didn't, but how could that be said nicely? While she was brooding he flew into one of his rare rages and accused her of never liking him in their whole married life. She denied it, but when he tried to pin her down as to when she had liked him she couldn't remember and began to cry. He was doubly annoyed and issued an edict on conjugal rights, to the effect that she owed them to him and he wanted them and she would just have to adjust. Patsy agreed that she owed them to him but when he told her she would have to adjust she said, "I don't know how."

"Well, you'll never adjust if we don't ever do it," Jim said. "If we avoid it, it just gets worse. It's silly. There's nothing wrong with me. There's probably nothing wrong with us that a lot of good sex wouldn't cure."

Patsy could only pass. She neither agreed nor disagreed, but she went to bed from then on in deep apprehension and too often her apprehensions were justified. Jim determinedly put his edict into effect. He wanted her and saw nothing to be gained by postponement. He had waited before, and lost through it. He made love to her considerately and knew she was not liking it, but he thought that once she accepted the fact that he really wanted her she would begin to want him in return. Patsy had ceased to doubt that he wanted her, but it didn't make her want him at all. The nights quickly grew worse; her days were mostly spent in dreading them. They stopped talking about it but it hung in the air all day. Patsy wanted to tell him to please stop—not only was it not making her like him better, it was making her hate him— but she simply couldn't bring it up. Her only tactic was to ignore it, while it was happening and while it wasn't, and hope that Jim could catch on and let her alone for a while. Had she said as much, Jim would have let her alone. He had convinced himself by his own arguments, but he was aware it wasn't working. Patsy could have unconvinced him had she spoken, but her silent reluctance was more difficult for him to interpret. It made him feel defensive about his own feelings and he felt that he had to keep demonstrating that he wanted her if she was ever to accept it.

In ten days his attempts to join them through sex ended by severing them more terribly than her adultery had severed them. One night Patsy had almost succeeded in getting to sleep unscrewed, when Jim decided he wanted her. He was angry with her because she wouldn't speak to him or make any move to be near him at all. Any token of affection would have made him wait, or would have made him tender, but Patsy's affections were frozen. As a result he felt brutal and she felt brutalized. Afterward she couldn't sleep. She began to tremble. Finally she got up, took her pillow to the couch, got sheets and a blanket, and huddled there.

"Why are you doing that?"

"So I won't get sick. I'm going to sleep here from now on, so I won't get sick."

He saw that his plan had come to ruin, and he felt a failure. He felt he had treated her badly and would have apologized if he had not sensed that she was too alienated to be touched by apology.

"How do you feel?" he asked finally.

"Animal," Patsy said. "I don't want to talk."

"Animal?"

She raised up and looked at him. "I feel like a domestic animal. Domestic animals are used without their consent. I was used without my consent. Don't you touch me any more. You don't have that kind of rights over me."

Jim let it go. He knew from the way her voice trembled that arguing would only make things worse. The next day they tried to assess the extent of the disaster and it seemed incalculable.

"Well, at least forgive me," Jim said. "You know I didn't mean to be that awful. I was just trying to get you back."

Patsy could not look at him. "You never wait for anything," she said. "If you had waited and been kind I might have come back by myself."

"No, you wouldn't have," he said. "You would just have thought I was neglectful."

She chuckled bitterly. "You get full points for not being neglectful," she said. "Boy, are you not neglectful!"

They talked around in circles for several days. Sometimes they had the illusion that they were getting somewhere, in talking; other times it just made them feel the more hopeless. Patsy slept on the couch. They gradually worked back to a condition of politeness, but there they stopped. Nothing he said could bring Patsy back to the bed. A week passed and their nerves were in terrible states. Patsy had begun to fly off the handle at Davey. Jim stayed away from home as much as possible. At night she slept poorly, half afraid he would come to the couch and touch her, and he slept fitfully, felt wronged, and didn't know whether she would ever sleep with him again.

One morning at breakfast psychiatry occurred to them. For some reason it had never entered their minds that they should go to psychiatrists, and the idea struck them like a revelation. It was the only hopeful idea they had had in weeks. They spent the day asking around, rather fruitlessly. The Hortons knew no psychiatrists. Flap had meant to go to one after his trouble, but once he got his spirits back he became too busy to bother. Finally Jim asked Bill Duffin, who knew one. Lee had gone to him for two weeks, after they moved to Houston. Patsy called to ask her about him. She and Lee had developed a sort of cynical compatibility. Lee had not asked about Hank, but Patsy took it for granted that she had figured it out.

"The man's absurd," Lee said of the psychiatrist. "He'll do to talk at but don't expect much feedback. I wouldn't let you go to him except that I expect you need some laughs."

It was not an encouraging report, but the two of them were too cheered by the idea of psychiatry to look further. They called the doctor, whose name was Fuller, and intimated that they had a problem.

Dr. Fuller suggested that they come in singly, but both on the same day, for what he termed exploratory conversations. Jim went first and told Dr. Fuller that his wife had had an affair and didn't like to sleep with him, and that he didn't know what to do. Jim talked rapidly for fifty-five minutes. Patsy went in an hour later and found it difficult to talk at all. Dr. Fuller looked more like a pediatrician than a psychiatrist, and, moreover, he had copies of *The Ford Times* in his waiting room, which prejudiced Patsy against him to begin with. He looked robust and healthy and so completely Protestant and trustworthy that it seemed unlikely he had ever committed a sin. Patsy felt guilty just being near him. She managed, rather haltingly, to get out the chronology of her marriage and her affair and he maintained such a determined silence when she spoke of the latter that she felt even guiltier.

"What do you do for fun, Mrs. Carpenter?" he asked, flabbergasting Patsy completely. She hadn't had any in some time, and the last she could remember had involved Hank and a bed.

"I mean, what are your amusements?" he asked by way of clarification.

When she finally said she liked to read he nodded, as if it were very meaningful. When the hour was finally waning, with nothing significant having been said, Dr. Fuller briskly picked up the phone and made them appointments for a battery of psychological tests.

"Then we'll know something," he assured her merrily.

They took the tests the next day, Patsy in the morning, Jim in the afternoon. Patsy enjoyed them; she had always been good at tests. The man who gave them was a grave middle-aged gentleman named Mr. Penny. He took his job seriously and explained the tests in such detail that they would have been comprehensible to a three-year-old. She enjoyed the verbal tests and had a great time with the Rorschach.

Jim was not so lucky. After a year in graduate school, tests in which one arranged circles and triangles and matched words struck him as silly. He didn't see how it was going to help. For him, the Rorschach was an absolute calamity. Virtually every blot looked like a vagina. Mr. Penny became even more grave and finally grew visibly upset.

"Are you sure you're looking hard enough?" he asked after eight straight blots had been vaginas.

"There may be something wrong with my vision," Jim said morosely. "I'm sorry, but that's what it looks like."

So did the next one, but he decided to lie in order to spare Mr. Penny's sensibilities. He saw a pelvis.

"Well, that's less specific," Mr. Penny said hopefully, shifting his blots.

By stretching his imagination to the utmost, Jim managed to see a couple of crabs, a spider, and a butterfly. At his vaguest he saw a cloud. But there were still a scandalous number of blots that looked like nothing more than vaginas. Mr. Penny was deeply offended.

"Surely you can see something else," he said sternly.

"No," Jim said.

Mr. Penny searched among the blots to find one that could not possibly look like a vagina. "Your wife saw a coach-and-four," he said nostalgically, after Jim saw another vagina.

"She would," Jim said bitterly.

Their second interviews with Dr. Fuller were very dampening. "Your Rorschach was frankly appalling," he told Jim immediately. "You saw fifty-two vaginas. Sex is not that important. You've got it out of proportion. It's just one of a number of things we humans do. You shouldn't keep it on your mind so much."

"How can I help it?" Jim said. "My wife doesn't like it with me."

"Your wife is immature," Dr. Fuller said. "Let's forget her for the moment. You have to take yourself in hand. An obsession with sex is not going to help you. Mature people try to balance their activities."

He told Jim that above all he should be firm with Patsy and realize that her feelings of repugnance were not personal but were the result of her own instability. They spent the last ten minutes of the hour discussing the vagaries of the Rice football team.

Patsy's interview was even less satisfactory.

"You realize, don't you, that your husband is very unhappy?" Dr. Fuller said.

"We're both unhappy," she said.

"Don't you agree that it's a wife's duty to make her husband happy?" he asked, beaming at her.

"I guess. I'm sure it is. I just don't know how to do it."

"He doesn't have much confidence right now," Dr. Fuller went on. "Sexually, he's very insecure. He thinks you don't like to sleep with him."

"I don't, very much," Patsy said meekly.

"But, young lady," Dr. Fuller said in his most jovial pediatrician's voice, "you're his wife. You're grown up. Mature people can't afford to be highly emotional about their duties. There are simply things we must do, for the good of our loved ones."

Patsy was at a loss. It was not what she had expected of

psychiatry. Reading the books Jim had brought home had grown depressing, but they all did seem to assume that life was rather complicated. Dr. Fuller clearly didn't think so. No one had ever made her feel more unequivocally guilty.

"You and your husband have to take yourselves in hand," he said. "You have to be adult. You're both being rather childish. I have an idea you don't go out enough. Go to some movies. Make him take you dancing. Enjoy yourselves. The more activities you share the better you'll get along."

"Isn't there something more specific wrong with us?" she asked.

"Well, of course at the moment you're both suffering from the consequences of your affair with the young man. I hope nothing like that will happen again. These things have no moral base, you realize. It's no more than a form of escapism. What you must do is buckle down to reality."

Patsy reported that bit of advice to Lee the next day and Lee laughed long and feelingly. "My own triumph was forcing him to utter the word cunnilingus," she said. "I think he would rather have bitten his tongue off. Go buy some smart clothes. It's really more cheering than psychiatry."

Patsy went, but she had not been in the store more than five minutes when an awful depression came over her. She didn't want to buy clothes. Why? Who for? What good would it do? When she got home Jim saw how depressed she was and asked her what was the matter.

"Everything," she said. "I almost spent a lot of money today. I'm too young for that. You're supposed to save that for when you're forty or so."

"Maybe we should buy things together," Jim said. "Dr. Fuller said we should do things together." The thought depressed them both. They could not even think of a pleasant way to spend money together. That night they went to their separate places of rest feeling very glum. Jim would have liked to ask her to come back to bed but held his peace. Patsy had begun to miss Hank. From time to time she was seized by a strong desire—she wanted to hear his voice, to feel his hands. The desire assailed her very strongly just after the lights were turned out. The room was silent in the way rooms are when they contain two waking people who are not in accord but who have grown wary of putting their discords into words. They might have talked, but neither could think of a way to start a conversation; and a conversation started on a bad note, in the wrong tone, could lead to anger, spleen, tears, and a tense sleepless night which neither of them wanted. What was hard to do was to have an after-dark conversation that might end nicely, with them feeling closer rather than more separated. It had grown almost impossible, and they played safe and stayed silent, each depressed. In only one week psychiatry had failed them, and neither of them knew where they might turn next.

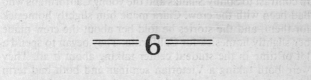

6

Jim began to wonder if he could sleep with Clara Clark. Patsy had forbidden him the Hortons, so he took to spending his days around school looking for someone to talk to. Flap had launched into his dissertation and couldn't be kept at coffee for more than fifteen minutes, so he wouldn't do. Kenny Cambridge was sometimes someone to talk to, but he was lazy and generally lay around his apartment until the middle of the afternoon. He usually showed up just as it was time for Jim to go home. Most of the more intelligent older graduate students were writing dissertations and were as inaccessible as Flap, and none of the younger first-year people had yet emerged as interesting. That left Clara, and, as it happened, Clara was as much at loose ends as Jim.

Both of them were beginning to have serious doubts about their scholarly futures, and their doubts made a convenient conversation topic. The first year of study had been easy. Reading was pleasant and scholarship rather interesting, in an esoteric way. Writing papers was good mental exercise. The university seemed a handleable scene, as Clara put it.

But their summers changed all that. Clara had done nothing particularly unusual with hers; she had spent it in Santa Barbara, screwing and getting high. She had grown too old to surf, but she spent a lot of time on the beaches and had a satisfying summer. The difficulty was that during it she had ceased to feel very intellectual or very competitive or very interested in a degree and a job. Screwing and getting high were more her kind of scene.

Jim had done none of either, but he had not been back in class long before he discovered that it wasn't all as pleasant as it had been the year before. Taking pictures on the movie set had been pleasant. The work, the talk, and the people had all been amusing. In contrast the people in graduate school did not seem very vivid. Even Flap seemed pedantic in contrast to Sonny Shanks and the young Californians who had been with the crew. Clara made him slightly homesick for them, and the stories he told her about the crew made her slightly homesick for California. They began to spend a lot of time in the student center talking about it all. They were both taking a Victorian seminar and both had term papers hanging over their heads, tasks they were eager to avoid. One day Jim confessed his marital problems. It was hard to write about Victorian poetry with something like that on his back, he said. Clara was sympathetic. His marital problems seemed nothing unusual, but she too was unable to think of anything coherent or original to say about Victorian poetry. They had a mutual recognition over coffee: they didn't really like writing about literature and couldn't possibly do it professionally all their lives. Being companions in failure made them feel closer, and they went to the zoo.

It almost turned out badly for Jim. No sooner were they inside than he ran into Peewee Raskin, returned again to his old job on the zoo train. He looked no older, no larger, and no more prosperous than he had the winter before. Peewee didn't see them, but it gave Jim a start and made him realize that nothing was simple. Patsy could be there, for all he knew, or Emma and her boys could be there. He was nervous; Clara didn't mind. She had merely gone along with the zoo suggestion to keep him with her. She would rather have gone to her place and to bed. She had always liked Jim's looks. She felt fine and was very pleasant and vivacious. She knew that bed was where they were heading. If not today, tomorrow.

Jim hesitated only one day, brooding about what would happen, wondering if he could get away with it. But he remembered Eleanor Guthrie and what had happened when he hesitated with her. He didn't mean for that to happen with Clara. He didn't feel as emotional about Clara as he had about Eleanor, but he still had no intention of passing her up. Patsy was so remote—he didn't know if he could ever get her back. He was anxious to have somebody, and Clara seemed willing.

Her willingness, when he finally tested it, was one of the surprises of his life. Patsy had taken a good deal of winning, when he had won her years before. Eleanor had taken more than he could manage. Clara took practically none. She was a girl who liked to screw. They went to her apartment the next day on the feeble pretense of getting a book she needed. There was an awkward moment or two, and then they seduced each other.

"I've been keen on you for a year," Clara said afterward, stretching. "I thought you were never going to get around to me. I was interested in you even before I had that thing with Hank. You're just more my type."

Jim had never been convinced that he was more anybody's type than anyone, but Clara soon showed him she meant it. Not only did she like to screw, she liked very much to screw with him. Her enthusiasm more than counterbalanced his guilt feelings. After all, Patsy had had hers, he had a right to his and even if that had not been so he would have had a hard time relinquishing Clara. She quickly convinced him of what he had always suspected, that his sex life with Patsy had been absurdly inhibited and constrained and that Patsy either didn't like sex or didn't like it with him in the way that she should. Clara liked it and liked it. She seemed to Jim an incredible example of sanity and health—just what a well-adjusted female should be. She was not obsessed about anything but was just a girl who liked what there was to do in bed better than what there was to do in other places.

They grew fond of each other, in a light and unfrantic way, and it seemed to him that was an ideal way to relate to another person.

Somewhat guiltily, he began to discuss Patsy with her, knowing full well that if Patsy ever found out he had she would never forgive him. He sketched out for Clara what seemed to him to be Patsy's problems and Clara listened and said nice things about him. She was discreet and careful where Patsy was concerned. She never asked for more information than Jim was willing to give, and she never criticized Patsy sharply, though she sometimes made general criticisms that Jim thought very perceptive.

Clara had always had a fine touch for what would go with a certain man and what wouldn't. She had known Hank was going to be short-term even before she slept with him, and she made the most of the term. Jim was something else. She wasn't hot to marry, but she had decided he just might be long-term. It didn't bother her that he wasn't very sure of himself; she was sure of him. He wasn't any more ambitious than she was. He just needed someone who liked him and who wouldn't give a damn whether he ever did anything or not. He needed someone who would enjoy drifting with him and not make him feel like a failure for drifting. She could hardly wait to get him in bed. She didn't want him all twisted up with romantic longing; she wanted them to make it while they were friends, and to make it nicely enough that he wouldn't need to worry for a while about whether he loved her or not. And she disarmed his suspicions by telling him as much.

"I like friends who are attracted to me," she said. "If I'm attracted to them, it's great. I don't know about marriage. Everyone who's been married expects hang-ups. Like you. You expect hang-ups with me. But there doesn't need to be any. Why should there be? This is a good way to spend time, isn't it?"

Jim thought it was, but then of course Clara didn't have a wife and son to go home to. When he left her she took a walk or a nap or watched television the rest of the day. She had no tensions to cope with, and the next day when he came in she would be just like he had left her, pleasant, lovely, and very touchable. She liked being naked, and her usual indoor costume was a sweater and an old pair of corduroy pants, both of which she shed readily and put on again when he went to the door to leave.

"I was made to live on a beach and not wear many clothes," she said. "At least till I start having kids."

She fully expected to begin desiring children someday; she would not have dreamed of not having them. She just had not come to that point yet. It worried Jim a little. If she should turn up pregnant, explaining it to Patsy would turn his hair white. But Clara told him to forget it; she didn't look forward to an abortion but would certainly get one rather than make trouble.

Sometimes Jim grew paranoid. He had found out about Patsy through sheer accident. Mightn't she find out about Clara the same way? Fortunately her apartment lay directly on his way to school. If surprised he could always be borrowing a book. He always carried a book for just such an emergency. But it didn't allay his fears. He didn't know what to do. He was not going to give up his afternoons with Clara, though; he knew that. He tried to put the thought of discovery out of his mind and he gave as little thought as possible to where it might all be leading. For a month he lived day by day and night by night.

Clara didn't push. She wanted what was going on to continue. She didn't want him forced into any choice between her and Patsy—not then. She didn't want any crisis at all. She wanted good afternoons, if she could get them. And she was not jealous of Patsy; she was mildly curious about her and mildly contemptuous of her. Such a great-looking girl, and so unnecessarily hung up. So far as she was concerned Patsy was lucky someone hadn't taken Jim away from her years before. It hadn't taken her two weeks to convince him he was a prize, and Patsy had left him in doubt on that score for years. Clara was really dubious about what went on in marriage. It amazed her that someone who liked to screw as much as Jim did could go for months without screwing his wife. It made no sense to her.

It made no sense to Jim either, once he thought about it. Patsy had drawn into herself again—she had closed in some way. She seemed younger, demure, and girlish. Sometimes he sat in bed at night and watched her making a maidenly bed on the couch and felt sorry for her. It seemed a pity. She might not know what fun she was missing. But then it occurred to him that she had slept with Hank Malory and had kept on doing it. He knew her well enough to know she wouldn't have kept on if she hadn't liked it. So what did that mean? He didn't know. Clara liked it with him. It occurred to him that perhaps *he* had changed, that the Jim Patsy was averse to was an earlier Jim. Perhaps with Clara he had learned something that Patsy didn't know he knew. Often he was tempted to approach her, to try once more to make love to her. Perhaps the change would communicate itself; perhaps it was not too late for her to start liking him. But he put it off, not quite convinced that it could be. And the more he screwed Clara, the easier it became to put off.

And the more afternoons the two of them spent in bed, the less they gave a damn about Victorian poetry or the Ph.D. Bill Duffin and one or two of the other professors noted their slackening interest, but Bill Duffin was in the process of packing his books and had ceased to give a damn about Jim. Often in the afternoons, lying around, their hands on each other, Jim and Clara discussed in an idle, indefinite fashion what they might do if they both dropped out of school at the end of the semester.

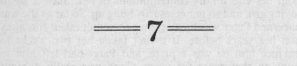

7

One afternoon, a week before Christmas holidays began, Hank called. It was an afternoon when Jim would normally have been in a seminar. So far as Patsy knew, he *was* in a seminar. Had she known he was at Clara's she would have been extremely surprised, much more surprised than she was when she heard Hank's voice. She had been expecting

him to call, more or less, and had figured out that he would
remember which afternoons were safe. Even so, the sound
of his voice was a shock. It took her breath for a moment.

"Well, it's my old pal," she said. "Where are you, old
pal?"

"Portales," he said. "But not for long."

"Why not?"

"No job."

"You mean they got someone else at the filling station?"
Patsy said. "How inconsiderate. If only you wouldn't keep
running off to Houston to try and be an intellectual. Not
only do you get in trouble with people's wives, but you lose
your niche."

"How are you?" he asked.

"As well as I deserve to be."

"Jim?"

"Sort of distant. Okay."

They both fell silent, struck by a feeling of helplessness.
Neither of them wanted to talk about the present, and the
past was unmanageable in the few minutes they felt they
had. Both started at once to try and locate the future. It was
easier for Hank. He had to get a job. He was thinking of
working in Lubbock and enrolling at Texas Tech for the
spring semester.

"Aha," she said. "Still trying to be an intellectual. What
innocent wife will you ruin there?"

"I'll be too depressed to ruin anyone," he said.

"I doubt it," she said. "There must be innocents, even in
Lubbock. One of them will entice you, probably."

"You can't see them for the sand," he said. "I miss you."

"I miss you too," she said, unable to deny it. At the end of
the conversation he told her he loved her. She didn't doubt
it, but both of them had trouble believing that the feeling
would ever again do them any good. The feeling was
genuine, but it was useless, and after Patsy hung up she grew
deeply depressed. What good was it? What good had it
been? Her depression went below tears. She had wanted him
to call but couldn't help wishing he hadn't. The silence had
been easier to handle. His voice was enough to stir her
memory, to make her yearn for what she couldn't have.
Yearning was no fun. It was better simply to be blank.

The call echoed through her mind that evening and all the next day. She was very troubled, could not think, could not assemble herself. Her mind was either entirely vacant or else distant from the rest of her. But that evening the depression lifted. It lifted as she was putting Davey to bed. At bedtime they played a little game of peekaboo, with Davey holding on to the headboard of his bed and bobbing up and down. Patsy began playing rather mechanically—it was simply part of the bedtime ritual—but Davey was full of zest and looked particularly impish, and his merriment reached her. It lifted her out of her gloom and she began to play for real. They played too long, overexciting Davey. He was a long time going to sleep.

Patsy went in and washed her hair. She had been as conscious of her depression as if it had been a headache, and she was just as conscious that it was gone. Things seemed very clear, and much simpler than they had. It had been real, whatever she had had with Hank, absolutely real. As she massaged her scalp she thought of it without regret for the first time. It was something she would not have wanted to miss—it had been too good. But still, it was over. He was far away and would never be more than an occasional voice again. She had somehow made a decision, and it had been to stay with Jim and Davey. So it was time she stopped mooning, stopped feeling sorry for herself, stopped being childish. If she was going to stay she might as well really play, as she had with Davey. It had worked with him and it might work with Jim, if she forced herself to go through the mechanics.

Later, watching Jim, who was reading in bed, she began to feel sympathetic to him and forgave him for the misuse of a few weeks before. How could he have been expected to know better? He had probably been desperate. It had been a long time since she had really been accommodating, and he had known she had accommodated someone else. How could he have been blamed? Since then he had been kind and patient. He hadn't even asked her to come back to bed. She had really been selfish long enough. If she was going to stay married it was time she started thinking of him. They had a new house to move into, and Christmas was coming. They couldn't sleep separately at her parents' house; such a clear hint that something was wrong would spoil her mother's whole Christmas. It was time to start trying again.

She sat in her rocking chair until her hair was dry. Jim had quit reading and was watching the *Tonight* show. She went over and sat on the bed and, when he looked up, asked if he wanted to make love. It sounded strange to her. She had never asked in that way before, but she was afraid that after what she had said the other night he would ignore any other kind of invitation.

Jim was startled. He had been contentedly watching the show, but it didn't occur to him to say no to Patsy's question. He was disconcerted, though. He had made love to Clara that afternoon and for a moment, absurd though he knew it was, he was fearful that the fact would somehow reveal itself. Patsy lifted her gown off over her head and sat on the edge of the bed for a moment, thoughtful. He was struck by how much slimmer she was than Clara; Clara was a strongly built girl. "Seen enough?" she asked, nodding toward the TV, and when he nodded she went over and bent to turn it off. He saw the hang of her breasts before the TV darkened.

"I'm sorry I've been so silly," she said, coming back to the bed.

"Oh, it's okay," Jim said, hugging her rather awkwardly, her cool breasts against his arms.

But it proved far from okay. Patsy had made a decision and acted on it in good faith, but her decision had caught them both cold. It was, in its way, the equivalent of Jim's earlier efforts to make them work through sheer will, and it failed as miserably. They tried to make love on sympathy—neither of them had any hunger. They moved together, but mechanically; they went nowhere. Neither came or even came close to coming. After a while they simply stopped and lay side by side.

"Well, I guess it's back to the couch," she said finally.

"The living-room couch or the psychiatrist's couch?" he asked, very glum.

"Either one," she said. "Both, maybe. Hell. I guess I am frigid. It's finally come true."

Jim didn't say anything. He had no answers, but he was more tired than she was and soon went to sleep. After a while Patsy got up and put on her gown and went back to the couch.

The memory of that attempt stayed in Jim's mind for days and gradually began to swell. It began to seem a worse failure than it had been, more awkward, more awful, more final. He could conceive of no way to come back from it, and for the first time began to entertain the notion that he and Patsy could not go on living together. The idea, like most of his ideas, soon ran away with him, and he quickly came to think of his marriage as something impossible. It was not that he had stopped caring for Patsy. He knew that he cared about her. He still wanted her sexually, for that matter. She still turned him on. But she was simply too difficult and he didn't want the difficulties any longer. He didn't know why she had slept with Hank. Probably in time she would start sleeping with someone else. He could not handle her emotions. They were either so vague as to be undetectable or so violent that they unnerved him. He didn't know what to do about her sexually. There seemed to be no meeting ground. For him she was virtually all difficulty.

And with Clara there were no difficulties. She was easy for him in every way. He was beginning, at moments, to feel that he loved her, and he had come to depend on her, not just for sex but for intimacy. He and Patsy had no intimacy any longer, only a kind of politeness. It dissatisfied them both, but it seemed the best they could do. Clara became both mistress and confidante. He began to talk of leaving Patsy. Clara said she thought it would be best for both of them, but she let him feel his way slowly toward the decision. She didn't push, but she did tell him she wouldn't see any other man until he made up his mind. She hadn't been seeing other men, anyway, but the fact that she stated it made a difference. Jim was pleased; to have gained an exclusive purchase on someone as experienced as Clara made him feel better about himself.

He found at home that his sense of the impossibility of it going on was swelling inside him, just as his memory of their bad experiences had swelled. Every night he wanted to talk about it, have it out in the open; but he hated the thought of the night that would buy them, and so long as Patsy was quiet and nominally content he let it ride.

Once or twice Clara said quietly that she wished he were free. "You could drive me home for Christmas," she said. "I could show you some of California."

"I wish I were too," he said.

That night he wished it more; the calm at home broke down. He had been supposed to see a man about some painting they were going to have done on the new house, and he had put it off. It was the third time he had put it off; having painting done had simply ceased to interest him. But it made Patsy furious: all she wanted him to do was to get an estimate on how much it would cost.

"Look," she said, "if you don't want to do that, I'll do it. I would have done it already if you hadn't told me three times you'd be glad to take care of it. *Why* don't you take care of it? What have you got to do that's so important you can't take thirty minutes to go see a painter?"

"I was working on my term paper," Jim said, but it was a miserable lie, the more miserable because he had done nothing at all about his term paper other than decide vaguely to write on Arthur Hugh Clough. He was well aware that the fact would soon come out and that he would have the task of explaining why he had collapsed academically in the course of one semester. Either that or he was going to have to work terribly hard for a month, and he knew he wasn't going to do that. He had no good defense and sat silent while Patsy poured out her spleen. Finally she exhausted it and stopped, ashamed of herself. Such minor failings had been characteristic of Jim ever since she had known him and she didn't like herself any better for blasting him so.

Jim felt hopeless. He was on the verge of confessing all and telling her they ought to call it quits. The idea of leaving, of driving Clara to California, seemed marvelous to him, a bold but on the whole rational way out. He had to make a break. He and Patsy would only go on until they broke each other down. And if he sent Clara to California alone she might find another man, she might not come back, she might conclude that he would never have the nerve to leave Patsy. He didn't want that. He didn't want to let things cool between them. He had let things cool too long with Patsy and had discovered what a mistake it had been.

Yet he couldn't quite come out of it. He quailed at the thought of what it might do to Patsy. He really didn't know if it would crush her or make her murderous. He put it off a day and the next evening Patsy accidentally opened it all up.

She had been brooding about sex and had convinced herself that she had all but destroyed Jim, in that way. She felt she had to do something to reverse the trend and to make it up. What she had done the last time had been the wrong way to try. She hated talking about it, but he wasn't doing anything about it and she felt it was entirely her fault that he wasn't. That night she went to the bed and tried to tell him what she thought might help.

"Look," she said, "I was wrong the last time. I sort of decided it in my head. I know I've been awful and I'm not mad at you now. You don't have to wait for me to raise a flag or anything. I'm not going to knife you if you touch me."

Jim looked up at her. He saw that she was trying to be nice, but it irritated him that she took the tone that she took. It annoyed him that she should think he needed telling what to do in regard to sex. It seemed to him that she was the one who needed telling.

"I should just let it come naturally, hum?" he asked.

"Sure," she said, not meaning it. There was an edge in his tone that cut her and she knew if he should want to let it come naturally right then it would affect her as badly as it had the last time. But she let the point stand and went to the kitchen to do the dishes. When she returned she felt okay again, but Jim didn't. The more he thought about it the more presumptuous her remarks seemed, and the more he resented them. Not only did she imply that she needed help, but she had also implied that he had been leaving her alone because he was scared of her. He longed to point out that she was not necessarily the most wantable female in the world, that he knew another who was a great deal more fun in bed. But he controlled himself to the extent of being oblique.

"You know, I think you gave up on psychiatry too soon," he said. "There must be more intelligent psychiatrists than Dr. Fuller. It wouldn't hurt you to try one more."

Patsy was at her dresser. She turned and looked at him. She caught the drift of the insinuation. They were both so honed by tension that obliquities were seldom missed. Patsy could have caught his meaning if she had had to lip read.

"What did I say to make you think that?" she asked.

"Nothing. I just don't think you understand yourself."

"You mean sexually?"

"That way and other ways."

"But you're not talking about the other ways," she said, facing him. "Why don't you quit hinting? Do you think I'm Lesbian, or what?"

Jim was silent. He had said all he wanted to say.

"After all," she said, "you're the one who saw fifty-two vaginas. Why don't you go to another psychiatrist? I saw perfectly normal things."

"You didn't see any penises, did you?" he asked.

The hostility between them was so great for a moment that if they had been armed with guns one or both would have fired. But they had only words to fire.

"No, but so what?" she said, shrugging. "I never particularly liked to look at them. If looking at vaginas is what you really like to do you can look at mine any time."

Jim got up without another word and went to the closet and got his suitcase. He opened it across the bed and began to pack. He was too angry to talk.

"Okay, go," Patsy said. She hadn't moved.

"I didn't ask your permission to sleep with you and I don't need your permission to go," he said.

"Where are you planning on going?"

"To a friend's place."

"You're not going to the Hortons'," she said. "I won't have that."

"I wasn't planning on going to the Hortons'," he said. "Just shut up."

"Well, that leaves Kenny. Shall I call and tell him you're coming?"

Even in his anger he had some inclination to spare her, but it vanished. "I'm going to a *girl* friend's," he said. "Someone who knows I like to do more than look."

It was a bolt quite from the blue. She had had no suspicion at all. Her first thought was Lee Duffin. She had the awful certainty that Lee had silently fulfilled her old prophecy, and just as she was getting to like her for a friend. She waited for Jim to say, "I'm sleeping with Lee."

"I'm probably going to go away with Clara," he said instead.

Patsy was stunned. If he had said Lee she might have screamed. As it was she looked at him and sat down in the rocking chair, her mouth trembling. Clara. She had had them both.

"You're right," she said. "I better see some more doctors. I must have a lot to learn."

"If you hadn't been so goddamned sure all along that you didn't, it would never have happened," he said.

"When was I ever sure of anything?" she asked, beginning to cry.

"Look, I'm going," he said. "There's no point in us trying any longer. Don't sit there crying and looking tragic all night. I'll probably come by tomorrow and get some of the books."

She looked at the bookshelves rather than at him. "You better get them tonight," she said. "Take the car full. Anything you leave here may be ashes in the morning."

"Oh, Patsy, stop talking that way," he said. "Don't be so melodramatic."

"You don't want to talk to me," she said. "Go on. If you hear a fire engine in the next few minutes you can chalk it all up to melodrama. Is *she* unmelodramatic?"

"I'll be by tomorrow," he said and left, just ahead of Patsy's rage. When it ended most of his books were in a great pile on the floor and Davey was awake and crying. Patsy was so choked with tears that she couldn't comfort him very well; she rocked him and rocked him and finally he went back to sleep and she sat down on the floor and straightened out the books she had thrown in a pile. There was no point in ruining them. Then she got in bed, knowing she couldn't sleep, that she had no recourse but to lie alone thinking about it. She couldn't call Hank; she would only get his aunt. Emma was the only possible person, and she wasn't ready to call Emma.

Once she calmed down a little she regretted bitterly that she had let Jim leave so abruptly. She *knew* nothing really, and it was a time when knowing particulars might have helped. As it was, she had a statement in a void: "I'm probably going to go away with Clara." Going away where? How long had it been going on? Had he been sleeping with her ever since Hank stopped? Or had she driven him to it recently by her own resistance? Could she blame him or must it be all her fault?

She was not aware that she slept at all, but she was aware, time after time, of jerking awake with it all on her mind, of turning one way and then another, trying to quit thinking about it. But the one fact she knew was that he was with Clara, and that probably they were talking about her, and it was not a fact that would let her sleep. If he had stayed, fought with her, wanted to forgive and be forgiven, that would have been one thing. But he left and let her know where he was going and that was different. It hurt all night.

Next morning, feeding Davey, it occurred to her that the night had paid her back for the one he spent when she had stopped at Hank's. He had been deliberate and she hadn't, but it amounted to the same quality of pain. Her hand was shaky with the spoon. The fact that they were even did not strike her as a cause for optimism. They were even, but they were also quits.

After breakfast she went in and put his books back in the bookcases, leaving no evidence of her blind fit except a few wrinkled pages and a copy of *On the Road* that she had ripped in two. She put on a white blouse and a skirt and sat in the rocking chair for the rest of the morning, watching Davey play. Her stomach was unsettled, but otherwise she was very quiet. No tides of emotion swept through her. A strange, formal feeling came. The only time she felt like weeping was when Davey dragged one of Jim's house shoes out from under the bed. What would he do for a father, their little boy? But Davey soon left the house shoe and Patsy left the question, for a time. Her mind was too blank to deal with it.

Jim came about noon. Patsy had feared she would fly into a rage at the sight of him, but she didn't. The formal feeling prevailed. He seemed to have it too. She gave him coffee and asked him politely about the things that had troubled her during the night. And when he revealed that it had not been going on quite a month she felt a small, cautious relief. Perhaps it was not quite the bitter end. And in their polite conversation they were awkwardly circumlocutory in their efforts to avoid flat statements that would make it the bitter end.

"Would you mind if I leave most of the stuff here?" he asked. "I really don't know yet what I'm going to do." But when he said a little later that he was going to drive Clara to California for Christmas, Patsy frowned. She didn't like it and couldn't hide it. Jim quickly tried to put a good therapeutic face on it.

"Look, we've got to get away from one another for a while and look things over," he said. "We'll kill one another if we go on like this."

"You don't have to get away from me with her," she said. "You could just get away by yourself. You don't have to go all the way to California, either."

Jim looked discouraged. He was very ambivalent about it. He had convinced himself he wanted nothing more than to drive Clara to California, but since he had committed himself to doing it he had not been so sure. Leaving Patsy and Davey at Christmastime did not seem very fair. When he left he had felt savage toward her. But seeing her again, sad and familiar, made him feel different. He did not feel savage toward her at all. He felt troubled. Everything looked dim. But he had told Clara he would take her. She considered it settled and was looking forward to it happily. He could not imagine how he could get out of it, and he was only half sure he wanted to.

"I've promised, I guess," he said. "I don't know. I think it might be better if we were far apart for a while. If I stay here we'll keep on fighting even if we aren't living in the same house."

When he said he had promised, Patsy's spirits dropped a notch, and they had been low enough to begin with. If he had given Clara such a promise, so soon, there was really no hope. She did not even feel angry, just low.

"I guess you two will go to Dallas, won't you?" Jim said.

"Oh, I guess." Christmas was unimaginable.

"So is it okay if I leave my stuff awhile?"

"Sure," she said. "Why not?" Then it occurred to her: they had bought a house. They were to move in mid-January.

"But what about the house?" she said. "We bought it, you know. We have to move next month."

Jim shrugged. It seemed to him the least of their worries. "Well, maybe you and Davey could live there and I should live here," he said half jokingly. "I don't know that we have to decide about it today. Maybe things will be clearer next month."

"They couldn't very well be less clear, " she said, and she meant it. The thought of herself and Davey having to move into the huge house alone was appalling. It was all wrong. It spoiled everything.

But Jim refused to talk about it. He didn't want any more fights. He was relieved that Patsy remained as composed as she did and he wanted to leave her composed. They chatted a little longer, sitting at the kitchen table, with Davey fretting and trying to open one of the lower doors of the cabinet. He could never get it open and it bugged him. Patsy asked Jim when he was thinking of leaving and Jim said he didn't know. Possibly that weekend, he added. There was no point in hanging around. Patsy said she supposed not, though without conviction. Jim stayed long enough to distract Davey from the frustrating cabinet and then left.

After he left she began to hurt. She could not understand it, could not believe it. That he would sleep with Clara, yes; but that in the space of four days he would simply leave her and go somewhere with another woman? It didn't seem real, didn't seem possible. It didn't seem like Jim. They had hurt each other in all sorts of ways and perhaps they didn't love each other in the right ways but still such an action chilled her and hurt her in the breast. It didn't seem possible.

She spent the afternoon as she had spent the morning, except that she took Davey for a short walk in his stroller. She contemplated the Hortons but didn't turn in their direction. She had a feeling she would collapse if she went there. She walked a few blocks and went home again.

The next day Jim came again. Classes were out on Friday and he and Clara had decided to leave that night. He felt in a terrific state of tension and wanted to leave before something exploded. Clara had been ideal during it all, quiet and comforting, not pushing and not pulling. She was a steady girl and she was fond of him. He felt very guilty but made no move to back out. It seemed to him he had done Patsy an irreparable wrong. There was no use in doing something equally bad to Clara.

Patsy was no longer so composed, but she had broken in the direction of tears rather than anger. She couldn't understand it and despite herself kept weeping.

"I don't see what's so hard to understand," he said. "You know how we've been."

"Oh, I know," she said. "But it all seems so minor compared to this. I mean, four years. Haven't they meant anything to you?"

"Of course they've meant something."

"Then I don't understand. Don't I mean anything to you? Are you really all that in love with her?"

"I never said I was in love with her," Jim said.

"Oh, please make more sense. Why are you leaving me to go to California with her if you don't even love her?"

"Because I have to leave you anyway," he said. "We just do one another harm. I have to leave so we'll stop. I'd just as soon go to California as anywhere else. It makes just as much sense."

"It doesn't to me," Patsy said, sobbing. "It doesn't at all. Not right at Christmastime."

Jim saw the argument was getting nowhere, so he got a few more of his things, mostly cameras, and got ready to leave. He decided in the end not to take any books, a bit of whimsey that turned Patsy abruptly from sorrow to fury.

"All right, don't take them!" she yelled. "You better be back and do something about them before I have to move or you'll never see a goddamned one of them again. I'm not going to move your goddamned books for you. If you think you can leave me to cart around the results of your stupid hobbies while you're off screwing that bitch you can think again."

Jim left her raging. He came back once more, on Friday afternoon, and stayed half an hour. They were desperately superficial the whole time; they didn't feel they dared be themselves. Though Jim was going, he felt terribly undecided; once out of the house and in the new Mustang he had bought for the trip he felt that if only Patsy had given him some sign that she wanted him he would have broken with Clara and stayed. Patsy, once he had shut the screen door, sat and cried. She felt she had been beseeching him the whole time he was there, and yet he had ignored her. Two days later, when he called from Phoenix to find out how they were, all they did was disagree about their last meeting. Each felt the other had done the spurning.

The afternoon he left, Patsy put aside her pride and went to the Hortons'. The Hortons were prepared. Flap had had it from Jim, and Emma had been sitting by the telephone for two days waiting for Patsy to break down and call. Flap had tried to get Emma to call her, but Emma stubbornly refused. She knew Patsy would call when she was ready. Flap was irritated at both of them.

"God damn it, what are you?" he said. "Why don't you call her?"

"I just better not," Emma said. She really didn't know whether she was right not to or not, but she kept sitting by the phone waiting. "Then why doesn't *she* call?" Flap said. "You called her when I shot myself. Why can't she call you now?"

"Oh, shut up!" Emma yelled at him. "They aren't the same kind of emergencies. Not at all."

"No, but they're both emergencies. In an emergency you call your best friend."

"I don't want to talk about it," Emma said.

So they were both terribly relieved when Patsy and Davey showed up at the doorstep and Patsy was relieved she had come, once the first moments were over. She cried a little but remained mostly composed and sat and talked with them for almost an hour at what normally would have been the boys' suppertime. The boys sensed the seriousness in the air and were model children for once. They took over Davey and amused him highly by making faces at him. Emma and Flap were very quiet about it all. They didn't say bad things about Jim, or offer any advice, though Flap told her she ought not to do anything hastily.

"Like seeing a lawyer or anything," he said. "Give it some time."

"Oh, I will. I don't feel like divorcing him. I don't feel like doing anything drastic."

"Eat supper with us," Emma suggested, and Patsy went in the kitchen with her and helped her fix it. It was chicken spaghetti and they had some wine with it. Their tensions loosened and the three of them became a little high. The children ceased to be models at once. Teddy was insecure and belligerent because Davey was in his highchair, and Tommy was repeating TV commercials in a very loud voice. After supper Flap took her home. He was very kind and carried Davey's stroller up the stairs for her.

"How's your dissertation coming?" she asked, taking real note of him. She had been lost in the swirl of her own problems and remembered that only a few weeks before he had had problems just as bad.

"I'm grinding at it," he said. They could think of nothing more to say; he said good night awkwardly and left. Just as he did, Emma called.

"Want company?"

"Sure."

She came after a while and they sat and talked until midnight. The wine and the company had lifted Patsy above the really bad feelings; she knew they were there and that she would have to feel them again, in some hour when she could not draw comfort from the Hortons. But she was not melancholy with Emma. They talked about their Christmases, small disasters they could remember, fun Christmases, disappointments, what Emma and Flap were getting the boys, what Patsy might get them, whether it was worth it planning a New Year's party. Finally they got around to Clara.

"I don't know—it was just such a surprise," she said. "But it shouldn't have been. I hurt *him*."

"You didn't go to New Mexico," Emma pointed out mildly.

"Do you know her?"

"No. I picked her out right away as someone who would

682

screw husbands and took pains to keep Flap out of her way."

"Oh, hell," Patsy said. "That guy loves you. He wouldn't cheat on you."

"Yeah, I know he does," Emma said. She was compulsively unraveling the sleeve of her green sweater. Patsy hated the sweater and was thinking she would be glad when Emma got it completely unraveled. "He's just human, though. I doubt he could resist a new body if one were dangled in front of his eyes often enough."

"Maybe not," Patsy said. "I swear I feel like I've been a child up until this week. I don't understand people at all, I guess."

"Well, you're just human too," Emma said.

"What is that supposed to mean?"

"You don't calculate all the time, like I do," Emma said.

"I think I'm ready to start. Only now I don't have anyone to calculate about."

"She doesn't strike me as the permanent type," Emma said. "Jim will come back if you let him."

Patsy sighed. "I probably would," she said. "I would if he approached me nicely, I guess."

They dropped it and talked about places where Flap might get a job. The most likely possibilities were in the Midwest. "Picture me in Des Moines," Emma said, growing glum suddenly. "Or Lincoln, Nebraska. What'll I do? You won't ever come and see us."

"Oh, I will. Sure I will. I'll always come and see you."

"I wouldn't come and see you if you were there," Emma said, yawning. "You'd have to make the best of it." She stood up to go.

"You haven't finished unraveling your sweater," Patsy said. "Why hurry off?"

"It's awful, isn't it?" Emma said, looking at her sleeve. "I should give it to the poor. They're having a toy drive at Tommy's school and he's very puzzled as to who the poor are. Flap and I consider that we're the poor, and it's confused him."

"Well, next year there'll be no confusion. You'll be solid academic middle class."

"Yep, in goddamn Des Moines," Emma said.

8

For almost the whole distance to California Jim had the feeling that he was going the wrong way. He had had the feeling before on drives, when he had missed a turn or something and would realize it or suspect it and yet drive on, half knowing he was driving in the wrong direction but never quite sure. There was always a chance that the place he was looking for would appear somewhere ahead.

But he had never had the feeling of going the wrong way so strongly, or for so long a time. It was a strange feeling and it took his appetite. Everything about the trip was strange, including the car. He could not take the Ford and leave Patsy carless. He could have left her the new car but there was no certainty the Ford was up to a trip to California and he didn't like the prospect of being broken down somewhere in the desert on his first trip with Clara. It seemed more sensible to leave the Ford and get a new car. He talked it over with Clara, who had no strong opinion. A car was a car. He got a red Mustang because he had always liked red, and he felt good about it until Patsy saw it one day when he was carrying down some of his clothes. She didn't say anything but he knew from the look on her face that she didn't like the car or the color. It affected him. Once he and Clara were on the road he realized he didn't really like the color either. He would have been better off with dark green or even black.

They left at dark on Friday, intending to drive all night. But something depressed them both, and right away, almost before they were out of Houston. They didn't admit depression—to themselves or to each other—it was just some late-afternoon malaise. But three hours later, when they got to Austin, it was still with them. They stopped for coffee and decided they didn't want to drive all night.

"Jesus, it's six hundred miles to El Paso," Jim said. "I didn't realize it was that far."

They were at a stoplight on the western edge of Austin. The thought of the six hundred dark and almost empty miles didn't help their malaise. They felt strangers to each other suddenly. What were they doing, setting off across the country together? Clara had never driven between Texas and California before. She looked at the road map glumly. Six hundred more miles of Texas seemed incredible.

Jim suggested they stop and get a motel, and they did. It cut the malaise a little. They got in bed immediately and watched television. It made them feel better. It was little different from being in Clara's apartment watching television. Naked in bed, they were familiar to each other again, and the strangeness went away. Jim decided it had been a temporary thing. Seeing Clara's clothes in the car instead of Patsy's, no car seat for Davey, and the car itself brand-new—it had all disoriented him. In bed he was not so disoriented. The motel was on Town Lake and they had a view of downtown Austin across the water.

He dropped into pockets of moody regret, thinking about Patsy and Davey, but Clara didn't let him stay in them long. She had felt miserable all afternoon. It occurred to her, once they actually left, that she might be getting into something that would be hard to handle. In Houston she and Jim got on fine. There was nothing to keep them from it. They talked and watched TV and ate and balled. But in California there were complications—her family for one. They were a tolerant bunch, but still, Jim would have to be explained. And there was the time after Christmas—what would happen then? She had gotten out of the habit of thinking ahead, and could scarcely remember when she had been a zippy career graduate student. Jim not particularly knowing what to do hadn't mattered in Houston, but it might in California. Clara felt a little nervous. She might have let herself in for a difficult scene.

But in the motel she didn't have to think about it. What to

do was obvious again. They watched TV and then balled. It was Clara's word but Jim had taken it up. It took care of them for the night.

But the next day, crossing the gray wastes of West Texas, the feeling of going the wrong way pulled at Jim hard. It was a long six hundred miles to El Paso, and he and Clara both felt flat the whole way. She leaned against the car door and smoked and they listened to what they could get on the radio and said very little to each other. She saw he was having bad thoughts and left him alone with them. She smoked and listened to the radio and waited to see how he moved. If he had decided to put her on a plane in El Paso and go back she would not have been very surprised, nor blamed him much, nor been very upset. If he really wanted to, that would be okay with her. If he didn't want to, that was okay too. Once they got to California, things might pick up.

It was a gray winter day, the sky above them gray as the land they were driving through. The rock music from the station in Austin contrasted with it sharply. Clara napped her way across most of the Edwards Plateau. Jim drove and felt strange; he had begun to wonder about himself. He had always assumed that he was basically okay, and lucky and perhaps even gifted, and that things would turn out well once he found out what he really liked to do. But he wondered. And he began to drive in memory all the drives he had driven with Patsy. The drives around Dallas, when he was courting her, and the drive to Abilene, to their first rodeo. The long drive west to Phoenix. Soon he would be recrossing ground he had crossed with Patsy and Peewee on that drive. Clara's face was hidden; he could only see her red hair. He didn't want to turn around and go back to Patsy, exactly, but he wanted very much to *be* back. If there had been some way to be back without the complications of going, he would have welcomed it. He didn't merely feel flat; he felt lonely. He forgot how difficult things had been with Patsy—how angry they got with each other, how fouled up their sex life was, how glad he had been that Clara liked him and how much he had wanted at various times to go away from Patsy.

In Fort Stockton he had an impulse to stop and call her

but he knew if he stopped Clara would wake up and he didn't want to try and explain a call. He drove for two more hours, wishing he could hear Patsy's voice and be with her again. It seemed to him he had not meant to leave. Bad luck of various kinds had forced them apart. But then it occurred to him that she probably wouldn't want him back, that his leaving had been something final, and he simply felt lonely and confused. Clara woke up, a little puffy, still silent, and she made him feel no better.

"How much farther to El Paso?"

"Two hours."

It seemed a week, but they finally got there and into a motel. They were too tired to ball. The inclination had left them. Jim thought for long stretches about calling Patsy but he didn't, not until the next day, when they were stopped in Phoenix.

"Is Davey okay?" he asked.

Patsy's voice sounded strained. "That's a fatuous thing to ask, under the circumstances," she said bitterly. "Nothing's wrong. We're both making out fine."

"You don't have to sound so tough," he said, and then they argued about the last visit. They got nowhere. He was in a phone booth and a woman stood outside waiting impatiently. He hoped Patsy would ask him when he intended to come home, but she didn't and they didn't mention Clara.

That night they made Yuma, both of them silent and despondent. They had looked forward to the trip as an adventure, and it had turned out to be merely a hard drive. It had seemed lovely in prospect; in fact it was merely tiring. If they had been deeply involved they might have fought, but as it was they were not at all angry with each other. They were in separate depressions. They knew well enough that they were not deeply involved. They didn't think it likely that they would stay with each other forever, or even for long, but their states were such that they would have been lonelier apart than they were together.

"Well, screw the desert," Clara said. "It's ugly, isn't it?"

"Most of it."

Then Jim recalled that he had a buddy in Los Angeles, a college chum from Dallas who worked for IBM. "Maybe we ought to see him when we go through. He could probably get me a job. Imagine me at IBM."

"Maybe he can get me one too," Clara said. "Imagine *me* at IBM."

The next morning their spirits lifted. Patsy began to slip out of Jim's mind for longer and longer stretches. It was so far back to Texas that it was ludicrous to think of returning until he had actually seen California. They crossed the mountains and drove into San Diego, and Clara's spirits rose higher and higher as they approached the coast. She became more girlish; her sober driving mood gave way to a mood more whimsical. It was a fine sunny day. "Hey, there's a great zoo here," she said. "Let's go see it. You took me to a zoo, now I'll take you to one." So they spent two hours wandering the San Diego zoo and then drove up the coast toward L.A. listening to a wild soul station. The music no longer seemed out of tune with the country.

"God, I'm glad you came with me," Clara said suddenly. "It's so much better to come home with somebody. I can show you some really good places."

"Just show me how to get through L.A.," Jim said. He had meant to stop also and call his friend, and perhaps Sonny Shanks, who had an apartment in L.A., but it began to seem too complicated and they decided to go straight on to Santa Barbara.

As they drew nearer to Los Angeles, the freeway widened; soon they were moving in a wide current of cars. Jim was used to freeways, but he had never seen so many cars. It was growing dark and the cars were beginning to turn their lights on. There were thousands of tailights in front of him, thousands of headlights behind him. Clara was swinging her hands with the music. All the cars were moving fast, seventy, seventy-five. The freeway widened again and was still full. After three days of desert, the great emptiness that had stretched for half a continent, the suddenness and speed of the cars in their thousands was unnerving. It was only as the great current of traffic swept them into L.A. that Jim began to relax a little. He began to feel secure in his spot, in his lane, and the spectacle of the river of cars was astonishing, almost majestic. After years on the tributaries he had finally reached the Father of Waters, where traffic was concerned. From every entrance cars poured into the freeway. Jim was in a strange, tired, trancelike state and for a few miles he enjoyed the flood of cars. It was as if the whole country was emptying itself into the freeways of Los Angeles—cars from all over America, leaving garages, creeping down country roads, moving out of little towns, swarming out of suburbs, millions of them flowing toward the river he was in, leaving the long regions of the country empty again, not even Indians to disturb it, not even buffaloes. Everyone had come to California, or if not, they were on their way.

With Clara's expert help he made it through Los Angeles and followed a thinner flow on north, out of the Los Angeles basin and into Santa Barbara. When they got there Clara decided she didn't feel up to her folks just then. It had been a long day, the third long day in a row. "Let's arrive about noon tomorrow," she said, so once again they got a motel, went to bed, and watched TV.

9

When Jim had been gone three days Patsy finally got around to grappling with the problem of Christmas cards. She had the cards picked out and the envelopes addressed but the problem was how to sign the cards. Jim's one call had been very unsatisfactory, and as the silence lengthened, the colder and bitterer she felt toward him. Yet, alternating with the bitterness, she had periods of worry. She even reproached herself for letting him go. She could have stopped him if she really cared to, and it seemed to her that going to

California with Clara Clark was a folly he ought not to have been permitted. He was probably very unhappy; she kept feeling that she ought to think of some way to get him out of the stupid mess he was in. She ought to make him come back home, and she ought to really try to make the marriage work.

But he didn't call, and it made her cold and sad and ate at what hope she had for them. He could call. If he didn't, there was nothing she could do.

She had planned to sign the cards "Patsy, Jim, and Davey," but his absence made that seem wrong. She could sign them "The Carpenters," but she didn't like that. She could sign them "Patsy and Davey," but she liked that even less. One morning she sat at what had been Jim's desk desultorily signing them "Patsy, Jim and Davey," on the grounds that they might all be together again, when there was a knock at the door and a delivery boy handed her a box with a dozen long-stemmed roses in it. She was amazed. She could not remember when anyone had given her flowers. Since her marriage she had always bought them for herself. There was no card with them and she puzzled about it while she arranged them. Bits of the ferns they were packed with dropped to the floor, and Davey, who was at his usual station at her elbow, picked the bits off the kitchen floor, surveyed them, and tasted them.

They were not likely to be from Hank. He had not called again, either, and would not send flowers, because he didn't know that Jim was gone. That being the case, they were more likely to be from Jim. Either he had sent them out of pure guilt, or in a moment of fondness, or as a means of preparing the way for his homecoming. On the whole Patsy suspected the latter. It had probably blown up with Clara. He was probably driving back and had sent the roses to soften her up.

For a while the possibility perked her up. Whether she wanted him back for good was one question, but it would be nice to have him back at least temporarily in order to settle that question. Nothing could be much sloppier than the situation as it stood.

Her spirits rose, and while they were high the phone rang.

690

She was prepared for Jim—for his nicest apologetic voice. Instead she got the voice of Sonny Shanks.

"Mornin'," he said.

"Oh, mornin' yourself," she said. "You sound like Gary Cooper."

"Wish I did. How's Texas?"

"Fine. Where are you?"

"I'm one block from the famous Sunset Strip, in Los An-geles. Far enough to suit you?"

"Perfect. Why are you calling, if I may ask?"

"To see if you got them flowers I sent you," he said.

"Oh, shit," she said, her spirits taking an immediate downcurve.

"You're welcome," Sonny said blithely.

"Oh, hush. I didn't say thank you. I'm most ungrateful. They're very nice roses, but really."

"Really what?"

Patsy wanted to cry. If he had sent them it meant the situation was as sloppy as ever.

"Oh, I don't know. I'm upset. Why did you send me roses, now of all times?"

"I thought you might be blue. Your wanderin' husband called last night from Santa Barbara. Wants me to get him a job in pictures."

"I see," she said. "So you're pouncing, are you? When will I have to chase you off my doorstep?"

"Uh, not before late February, I guess," Sonny said. "That's when the rodeo comes to Houston. I ain't in pictures no more, so I'll probably be there. I sent you the flowers because I thought you might be blue, like I said."

"Well, you were right, I'm blue," she said, chastened. "Thank you, Sonny."

"No time of year for you to be down in the mouth," he said.

"I am anyway. How did he sound?"

"Just like Jim."

"Did he have any plans, beyond a career in pictures?"

"I think he just mostly wanted to know if I was around. I imagine if he comes to L.A. I'll be gettin' to see a lot of him."

"Well, you deserve to. If you hadn't given him that tacky

job last summer he would never have left and about a hundred bad things might not have happened. You ought to have to take care of him for a while."

"I can barely take care of myself."

"The hell you can't," she said. "You can take care of yourself. You should leave babes in the woods like us alone. Did he mention a girl?"

"Yeah. He sort of drew me a picture."

"I wish the bastard would draw me one. I'm sick of the picture I'm looking at."

"You ought to come out and join the fun. I gotta go to Las Vegas tomorrow. Be glad to have you along."

"Sorry," she said. "I'm afraid I'd just spoil the fun. Thank you again for the roses."

"Sure. Stay beautiful like you are."

"My looks are wrecked," she said. "Probably if you could see me you wouldn't bother sending me flowers. Could I ask you a favor? It doesn't seem like he intends to call and let me know what he's doing. If you learn of any serious plans I wish you'd let me know. Do it collect."

"Sure," he said. "Maybe I'll pay you a visit in February."

"Why not? I'll have a house then. If you'll promise to be very proper you can come and I'll serve you tea."

"I always act proper in Texas. It's crazy places like L.A. that stir me up."

"Thanks for calling," she said. "Have fun in Las Vegas."

She fixed the roses and finished the Christmas cards and went out and got a tiny tree big enough for a small corner table she had. While she was cooking supper Jim called from a phone booth in Santa Barbara.

"I don't believe it," she said. "She let you out of her sight long enough for you to call."

"Don't bitch at me," he said. "I called twice and you were out."

"Does your friend bitch at you?"

"If you just want to fight I'm going to hang up," Jim said.

"You know my evil disposition. Your friend Sonny Shanks called this morning. He also sent me flowers. I understand you've spread the word about us."

"I didn't see any reason not to tell him."

"I suppose there isn't any. I also understand you're hoping to get into the movies."

"I was just inquiring. I might stay out here awhile if I could get some kind of job."

Patsy ceased to feel hard. She felt hurt. "I don't understand you," she said. "Did I not know you all that time? Haven't you missed us at all?"

"Oh, sure," he said. "God, yes. But if I come right back you know we'll just fight and fight and fight over all this."

"Fighting's better than nothingness," she said. "What about our house?"

"It doesn't seem central. It's nice, but what's the good of living together if we just do nothing but fight? A house wouldn't make that much difference."

"Okay," she said. "It seems central to me. How do you know how we'd be in a house?"

"We'd be the same people, wherever we were."

Patsy gave up. The more she said, the more humiliated she felt. He asked about Davey; she told him what little there was to tell. He said he could call again Christmas and she said she would probably be in Dallas. When he hung up she felt desperately low and called Hank. She got his aunt. He was in Lubbock, looking for a job, and was not expected back for two or three days. Patsy left word for him to call her whenever he arrived, and she felt a little better. After she had cried her depression out she felt it was just as well Hank hadn't been there. She would have been unable to resist asking him to come back at once, and it was still too soon for that. Besides, she didn't love him, she only missed him; it would just make things messier. Jim had sounded very uncertain beneath his assurance. He could still make any number of unforeseen moves.

The following evening, just after she had had a long and harrowing telephone conversation with her mother, in which she had agreed to come to Dallas for Christmas, a knock came at the door and Pete Tatum stood on the landing. For a moment she was dumbfounded.

"Good evenin'," he said. "Tried to call but your line was busy."

"You cowboys," she said. "Peewee's at the zoo, Sonny calls—you had to be next. Where's Boots?"

She held the door open and Pete came in. He looked heavier than he had; his face was too fleshy. When she looked at him closely she saw that he didn't look well. He went straight over to Davey, who had stopped in mid-crawl when he saw a strange man enter. Pete squatted down and said hello to him. Davey was as dumbfounded as his mother had been, and he looked to her for reassurance.

"No Boots?" she asked again.

"No," he said. "She's in Fort Worth, pregnant as hell. We may get the stork this year instead of Santy Claus."

"Oh, good," Patsy said, delighted. "Will it really be that soon?"

"It may be sooner. I just hope I get home in time. Where's old Jim?"

"Well, it's a long story," she said. "If I can keep your mind off the stork long enough to feed you, let me go fix some dinner and I'll tell you while we eat."

"Okay," he said. "While you're cooking I'll get acquainted with your son."

As she cooked, she heard the low sounds of Pete's voice talking to Davey. She had not been eating much and her larder was not too well stocked, but she decided against running out to replenish it. She had canned soup, a green salad, and sandwiches of peppered beef and cheese. Fixing the meal brought her spirits up. She didn't like to cook just for herself and it was not yet possible to cook for Davey. Jim and the whole situation slipped out of her mind and she hummed as she set the table.

Once Davey accepted someone, he accepted them without reservations, and he had accepted Pete. It was difficult to talk during supper, he accepted him so well. He kept banging spoons and spluttering and otherwise trying to keep Pete's attention. Patsy didn't try to tell the long story; they chatted. She felt cheerful, but it was not the blind cheerfulness she had once been prone to, and watching Pete across the table troubled her. Though he had kept his presence and his small ironic smile, he was not quite the same man. The heaviness of his face bespoke a sadness, a disappointment, and it was particularly evident when he dropped into silence for a moment. He told her he had quit clowning, or almost quit. Although he was returning to Fort Worth from working a rodeo in Harlingen, it was the only show he had worked in three months. He had finally accepted a job as a car salesman for his father-in-law in Fort Worth.

"It was about my best out," he said. "Traveling wasn't no fun for Boots, once she got big, and she don't like for me to go off and leave her. I wasn't making enough money at it, anyway, not really."

"I'm glad you quit," Patsy said. "It was a ridiculous profession, anyway, and you know it. It's okay for a nut like Sonny who's got no dependents. He sent me those flowers in the living room when he heard Jim left me. It was high time you quit rodeo."

But part of her could not believe her own words, not when she looked at him. He was dressed as she had always seen him dressed, in Levi's and a faded Western shirt. It was hard to imagine him in a white shirt, and tie and a cheap suit, standing on a windy car lot in Fort Worth. It would only be dull for him, and empty, and the dullness and emptiness were already settling in his face.

"Still, I guess you miss it," she said, remembering the night he had taken her so firmly by the arm to lead her in to her unconscious husband. And the day they stopped to eat breakfast together on the drive to Laramie. And the time they had held hands in the park in Cheyenne. And he and Boots leaving Amarillo, with Boots in tears because Joe Percy had given her a box of candy.

"Were you glad about the baby?" she asked, looking at him. It struck her that he could scarcely be expected to be glad about it, since it had taken him from so much that he was part of: the West, all that country, those drives he and Boots loved, and rodeo, horses and bulls, the whole movement of the arena. For all that it was dumb and dull to her, it kindled something vital in Pete. He matched with it in some way. So did Sonny. Even Peewee matched with it, in his way. On the zoo train he was just a sad uneducated kid in a big city, doing a silly job. Pete would look just as sad on a car lot, it seemed to her. It had already taken something away from him. He no longer looked like a man who could move faster than a bull.

"Oh, yeah, I was glad enough," he said. "It was time for Boots to settle down. I didn't want her barrel racing forever. Just as well now as later."

Patsy didn't know. She went in and put Davey to bed and came back and made coffee. She felt a little askew thinking about it. Boots grown up? Settled down? PTA? Dresses like other mothers wore? A husband who sold secondhand cars, like other husbands? She told Pete her story, over three cups of coffee, and wasn't dramatic about it. Her mind wasn't on her problem. It was on Boots and Pete and their problems. They were going to become people she wouldn't even know, or even want to know.

When they went into the other room Pete saw the flowers from Sonny and an unhappy look crossed his face. Patsy saw it. He said nothing, but the look stayed on his face and the tone of the visit changed. What she had very faintly feared the moment she saw him on the doorstep became so: he wanted her. Her husband was far away and she was alone; there was no natural check to his wanting her and the awkwardness showed in his face. His wife was in Fort Worth, almost ready to bear him a child, but it didn't change it. The want was there.

Patsy felt it and tensed against it at once. In Cheyenne his desire had surprised her; she hadn't known what to think about it and could only flutter uncertainly in response. But things were different, and she was different. She knew many things to think about it. At once she began to try and talk him past it, and she failed. They had told their stories, they had little more to talk about, and her small talk only exposed his desire the more clearly. She asked questions about Boots's pregnancy, about her doctor, about whether they were hoping for a boy or a girl, all in hopes of bringing his mind back to his wife. He answered, but underneath it he was wanting her.

They had stopped looking at each other's faces. She looked past his face; he looked past hers. She kept forming a sentence in her mind: "Look, old friend, you have to go—I can't sleep with you." But she couldn't get the sentence from her mind to her lips. Pete stood up and moved indecisively about the room looking at things. Patsy stood up too, hoping he was about to say he had to be going. But as she moved past him to turn on a little lamp he stepped toward her quickly and caught her with one arm. She was surprised and embarrassed. She didn't want to struggle and didn't want to speak, so she put her face against his shoulder and her arms around him lightly, trying to pretend it was a friendly hug. But they had never hugged, in friendship or otherwise, and her pretense was awkward. She was not in front of him but beside him, her hip against his hip. He tried to turn her, to shift her in front of him, but she stiffened hard. "Un-uh," she said. He bent his face toward her but she kept hers hidden. She could not get angry. All she felt was a deep dreadful embarrassment that would not let her look at him. She was cold with embarrassment and didn't want to see his face. He pulled but she only stiffened the more, and then, with a sigh that made her wish he were a thousand miles away, he let her go. "I'm sorry," she said, quickly stepping away. "It's the last thing I need." Davey cried out and she went to the baby bed. He had twisted himself into a corner, very uncomfortably. She straightened him out and he rolled onto his back and grunted, as if complaining in his sleep. She put her hand under his pajamas for a second, on his hot little stomach, and smiled when he made another small grunt.

Pete was sitting on the couch, his head down. He clearly felt wretched. The tension had gone away, and she wanted to see his face. She went over and squatted down in front of him. "Come on," she said. "Forget it. It's not like you had committed a major sin."

Pete raised his head and looked at her. They looked into each other's faces for the longest they had looked since the minute under the waterspout in Cheyenne. Their faces had changed, Patsy's hollowed by the worries of her fall, Pete's fattened by the worries of his. He saw in her the girl he had always seen, the girl who reminded him of his first wife, and tried to smile at her, but the constant smile of his profession was costing him his true smile, the wry smile that had once made him so appealing. Patsy saw in the smile and the look a man who was more depressed than he knew; soon he would have to learn to call his depression happiness in order to endure it. But he was not gone. His face was thickening but it was still a face she liked. There was not just a problem in his face, there was still Pete, only so close to the end of what he had been that she felt she might never see him again. And stupidly she had never touched him. She put her arms around his neck and pulled his head against her shoulder. He had not shaved and she felt the slight rasp of his beard against her throat.

"Snap out of it," she said. "You've got to hit the road and beat the stork home. I'm not going to have you driving along thinking it's the end of the world because you made a small pass at me."

"I feel like I ought to be shot," he said.

"No, just kicked. And me too, for not telling you to get the whole notion out of your head the minute I saw you had it in your head. But not shot."

Pete looked again at the roses Sonny had sent her, and again he frowned. "What is it?" she asked. "He's not that bad, is he? He certainly never got anywhere with me."

"He got somewhere with my first wife," he said. "It was just her bad luck to grow up in his home town. They broke up and she married me and we broke up and she took up with him again, for a while."

"Oh," Patsy said. "That's why you had the famous fight I've heard about."

Pete sighed. "Partly. He bought me a dirty movie, one night in Juárez when we was drunk, and gave it to me and told me the reason I never got along with Marie was because I didn't know anything about screwing. I was supposed to watch the movie and learn. I threw it in the Rio Grande and we had the fight on the bridge."

"For god's sake," Patsy said.

In a few minutes she sent him on. She did her best, in the few minutes, to get his spirits up, but for all her efforts he went away depressed, and once he was gone she too became depressed. She sat on the couch for a long time holding a magazine but not reading it. Somehow, all along the way, they had missed each other, had only really come close to each other for a few ambiguous minutes in Wyoming, and even then timidly, uncertainly. Whatever possibility there had been was finished, Pete was gone for good, and it seemed a shame that they had drawn so near only to miss. She told herself that it was sentimental to think of things that way, but it made her feel no less strange. She couldn't see the pages of the magazine. The story of his old trouble with Sonny stuck in her mind and haunted her. Perhaps Sonny had been right; perhaps Pete's confidence had always turned to awkwardness with Marie, just as it had with her. It was a gloomy thought, and while she was thinking it the phone rang. It was Hank, calling from Lubbock. He had got the message from his aunt. Patsy felt suspended. She was in no mood at all. She told him Jim was gone but didn't ask him to come back. She didn't want anyone. Hank had got a job at a tiny art-film house in Lubbock.

"Why, that's perfect," she said. "Antonioni and sand-storms. We're going to Dallas day after tomorrow and won't be back until after Christmas."

Hank tried to make her promise to see him, but she wouldn't. She didn't get angry, she just wasn't promising anything. She cried a little when she hung up, out of general depression. She found she couldn't remember him very well, and wondered as she was going to bed why it had been him instead of Pete. The next morning she decided proximity had made the difference. Hank had been at the drugstore, where she could find him, just often enough. The conclusion made her feel shallow, but it remained her conclusion.

Dallas was far worse than it had been the year before. Miri was still not home. Patsy tried several times to reach her on the phone and couldn't. Her father had been out to see her and had been so shaken by the circumstances he found her in that he could scarcely describe them. He was sure it would only be a matter of time before she went crazy or ended up in jail. He had never imagined he would have a daughter who would go two years without coming home. The whole problem baffled him. He drank and watched football games. Patsy employed Davey in the manner that would do most to cheer up her mother. She also promised to go out and see about Miri herself, once she got moved, and she called Boots and found out there was no baby yet. Jim called on Christmas day but the connection was terrible and they did little more than shout assurances that they were well. Patsy kept herself cut off. The only times she cut on were late at night, when her mother and father were asleep. Then she lay on the couch in her parents' den and watched the latest possible movie on TV. It didn't matter how bad the movies were. They were all at least as real and as amusing as her life.

10

Eleanor spent her Christmases at the ranch, dispensing the sort of largesse which was traditional. The cowboys all got cash bonuses and sides of beef. There was an ascending scale of presents to be given, scaling up to Lucy, whom she always gave something for her house. Lucy owned a house in town, to which she planned to retire on some mythical and distant day when her mistress no longer needed her. Some of her boys lived there. Eleanor gave her a color TV, knowing they would all enjoy it.

It was a cold winter day; there was a light snow just before Christmas and a keen wind all day. She had a dinner invitation in Dallas and had rather meant to go, but finally decided not to. She spent Christmas evening on her leather sofa in front of a huge fire of mesquite logs. The logs crackled and burned beautifully. She was reading *Valley of the Dolls* without enthusiasm and talking off and on to Sonny on the telephone. He was in Las Vegas, judging a Miss

Rodeo America pageant. He kept calling every few hours and badgering her to go somewhere with him for New Year's. She felt lonesome for him and was quite willing but they could not agree on a place. He wanted to go to Acapulco and she didn't, and the only compromise he had offered was Mexico City, which she didn't favor either.

The sixth or seventh call of the day came at midnight, when she was in bed but not asleep. They picked the argument up where they had left it two hours before.

"Why won't you go anyplace where there's not a Hilton hotel?" she asked.

"It wouldn't have no airport."

"What do you do between these calls? You either gamble or else you've got something brewing with Miss Rodeo America. Which is it?"

"I generally watch TV," he said.

"You could have spent Christmas with me."

"I wish I had, now. If you'd get over not liking Acapulco we'd go and have a happy New Year. I thought that was where you jet-set types hung out this year."

"I'm too old to be jet set," she said. "I'm a sedate middle-aged woman and I don't want to go to any tacky resorts. Why don't we go to the Orient? We could spend New Year's in Tokyo. I'll get the tickets if you're too tight."

"Too much air time," he said. "I hate long plane rides. I don't want to go noplace we can't get to in four hours in the air."

"Well, South America, then. Peru. I've never been there."

"Nope. If you ain't been there it's bound to be too far."

"You're impossible," she said. "I want to go to sleep. It's a mistake to decide anything on Christmas Day, anyway. We'll argue sometime in the morning."

"Not too early, we won't," he said. "I was thinking of heading back to L.A. tonight. I've fucked around here long enough."

"This late?"

"It ain't any special time here. I feel like driving. Anyhow, Coon's here. If I don't feel like driving he can drive. That's what I keep him around for."

"Well, what time will you call?"

"Whenever I wake up. Tomorrow afternoon."

"I miss you," she said. "Holidays always make me lonesome for you. Why don't you come here?"

Sonny considered it. "I ain't got enough pills for that long a drive," he said. "And I don't like to drive that far with Coon. I'd kick him out before we got to Albuquerque. I may kick him out, anyway, but if I do I can get to L.A. with no trouble."

"I wish you'd get off those pills."

"Naw, I was thinking of getting on more of them," Sonny said. "I was just thinking, maybe what I need to do is let my hair grow and take lots of speed and LSD and turn into a cowboy hippie. Maybe it ain't too late for me yet. I could sort of be the Joe Namath of rodeo, you know."

"Who?" she asked, mildly amazed by the picture he was drawing and yet mildly disturbed too, for she knew he was just as apt to do it as not, if the mood to do it persisted.

"He's a quarterback," Sonny said.

"Even you couldn't get away with long hair around a rodeo," she said. "Half the drunks in the West would be wanting to fight."

"That'd be okay. I could whip a few of them and the publicity wouldn't hurt. They might even make me into a television series."

"Well, you just be careful tonight, speedy."

"Be nice if I was where you could rub my back," he said thoughtfully.

"Wouldn't it, though. You wouldn't have to drive here, necessarily. I could send the plane in the morning. Your young friend could take the hearse back to L.A."

"Naw, I'm too pepped up," he said. "I want to drive and, anyway, I don't want to fuck around here all night. I'll see you in a day or two, soon as we make up our minds where to go for New Year's. Want to get married?"

"I don't know that I'm that lonesome," she said. "You want to? You think I'd be better for you than long hair and LSD?"

"Hard to say," he said. "I guess it's watching all this gambling that makes me ask. It wouldn't be no more foolish than anything else."

"You just remember what a good back rubber I am," she

said. "I knew you'd eventually begin to appreciate my domestic skills. You think we should sleep on it? We've only known one another fifteen years."

"You sleep on it," he said, "and I'll run on over to L.A."

"Proposals are usually accompanied by a declaration of love," Eleanor said, smiling.

"I'm in too big a rush to get off to start in on anything like that," he said. "I wouldn't mind being snuggled up with you right now, though. You're good to have around in a norther."

"Okay," she said. "Don't strain yourself trying to think of compliments. I'm very fond of you too, and I'm going to sleep. Call me when you wake up, okay?"

"Yeah, sleep tight," he said.

Coon was disgruntled that they were leaving. He thought Las Vegas was a great place, much better than L.A. In Las Vegas nobody looked down on him for dressing like a cowboy, at least no one did in the places he was allowed in. Being a cowboy in L.A. was increasingly unrewarding. Hippies with hair three feet long were treated better than he was, it seemed to him. Girls didn't put them down, and in L.A. girls put him down constantly. None had put him down in Las Vegas, because he hadn't spoken to any. He just looked. On the whole, from a looker's standpoint, the girls of Las Vegas had it over the girls of L.A. Too many of the girls he ran into in L.A. had something wrong with them—crooked noses or something. Las Vegas girls didn't seem to have discouraging defects. They were out of reach, but nice to look at.

Miss Rodeo America made him ache. Her name was Wanda Lou Rawlins and she hailed from Waxahachie, Texas. She was a petite brunette who never took her Stetson off. Coon ached, and Wanda Lou did her best to make up to Sonny, who was her official escort on a couple of occasions. She was tired of Waxahachie and wanted to live in L.A. and be in Sonny's next movie, if there was one. She would have considered it an honor to sleep with him, and most probably a pleasure too. All Coon could do was watch. He had watched before, so often in fact that he had come to derive a kind of vicarious satisfaction from Sonny's conquests. He dreamed about them while sleeping in the hearse, where he slept when he was driving for Sonny. He had watched Miss Rodeo America go around for three days with her tongue virtually hanging out and he gave her some thought at night while resting in the hearse and watching the lights along the Strip. Thus it was actually a disappointment when Sonny told him to bring the hearse around—they were leaving. He couldn't understand why Sonny would just walk off from a piece like Wanda Lou without so much as a sniff. It made him restless. He felt double deprived. It was wasteful. Sonny could at least have screwed her once, if only for courtesy's sake. Coon felt chivalric toward her. It was no way to treat a queen. After all, there was only one Miss Rodeo America.

Soon they were thirty miles into the desert, gliding toward Barstow at an easy eighty-five. Sonny had elected to drive, but he was not quite ready for the real speed. He was feeling his seat, meditating. He liked the desert, had crossed it at night endless times in his years of rodeoing. He had taken two Dexamyls and was feeling good. Eleanor stayed on his mind. It would be very pleasant to sit on the couch with her and drink bourbon in front of the mesquite fire. It was time he went to Texas; he hadn't been there since the summer, when the movie production moved to L.A. For a few miles he considered possibilities, regretting that he had not taken the road straight south to Needles. Then he could have shot across to Texas on Sixty-six and been there in twenty hours. He could have doubled back, but the prospect didn't please him. It wasn't worth it. In fifty miles he resolved it in his mind and found his seat and moved up to ninety-five. He could fly to Dallas the next day and have Eleanor send the plane for him. She could send it all the way to L.A., for that matter. He was settling down to enjoy the run to Hollywood when Coon voiced his disgruntlement in regard to Wanda Lou.

"I don't see why you wanted to run off," he said. "Wouldn't catch me running off from a woman that good-looking."

"What good-looking?" Sonny said absently. He had completely forgotten Wanda Lou.

"You know," Sonny said irritably. "Wanda." It seemed to

him a token of intimacy that she had allowed him to use her first name.

Sonny was a little amused. "You like her, huh?" he said.

"Well, who wouldn't. You could have screwed her if you'd halfway tried."

"Tried?" Sonny said. "I was afraid to get on an elevator with her unless somebody else was in it."

"Yeah, that's what I mean," Coon said. "And you pass it up."

"I got city ways now," Sonny said. "A girl from Waxahachie is just as apt to have ticks as not. You every had a tick on your balls?"

Coon was sullenly silent. The glamour of being Sonny's driver was wearing off and he was oppressed by the unfairness of life. Not only was he not getting girls, he was not improving as a bronc rider either, and the only reason he had stopped being a bronc rider was to get what girls Sonny didn't want. He was convinced that in another day in Las Vegas Wanda Lou might have come to him for consolation. It seldom happened, but he brooded about it and decided it would have, in her case.

"Fucking desert," he said. "What a big fucking desert. Fucking Sahara desert."

Sonny was mildly amused and mildly irritated. He was in the mood for a quiet drive.

"You should have told me you was in love with her," he said. "I might could have fixed you up. You might as well quit cussing the desert. It ain't the desert's fault you're dumb and ugly."

He meant it jokingly, but Coon's bad mood was getting out of hand. He felt very aggrieved. "Merry Christmas, motherfuckers," he said to two shivering hitchhikers they zoomed past. Both had beards.

"Goddamn hippies," he said. "I guess their last ride got tired of smelling them. I hate those fucking hippies. That's what I liked about Las Vegas. No goddamn hippies around."

"You're just full of peace on earth, ain't you?" Sonny said. "All because you got no pussy for Christmas. You could have bought you some for a Christmas present if you weren't so tight. Half the women in Las Vegas are for sale."

"I don't buy it," Coon said righteously, though he bought it on occasion.

Sonny suddenly lifted his foot and let the hearse coast. When it was down to fifty he braked and pulled to the side of the road. He turned and reached into the back, got Coon's dufflebag, and politely handed it to him.

"And a Merry Christmas to you," he said.

Coon was stunned. He was well aware that Sonny was given to arbitrary decisions, but he had not been expecting an arbitrary decision of such a nature just then.

"What'd I do?" he asked.

But Sonny had torn a check off his checkbook and was scribbling a note on the back of it. He turned on the cab light. "Here," he said, handing the note to Coon, who looked at it blankly.

Dear Wanda Lou:
   Coon can't wait to have a date with you. Be nice to him, honey, he's a real good old boy.

                                                          Sonny

"She won't gimme no date," Coon said. "You crazy?"

"I may be and I may not be. The one thing I'm sure of is that I'm tired of listening to you talk. If you get out here and start back you might get to meet them hippies."

"I don't wanta meet 'em. Can't I ride with you? I'll be quiet."

"No, you need a little desert air and I need a little solitude. Better put that Levi jacket on. It's cold out there."

"Just to Barstow?" Coon said. "Be a lot easier hitching out of there."

"I'm not going to slow down in Barstow. I guess if you want to take a chance on jumping out, you can."

Coon knew there was no point in arguing. Sonny was drumming his fingers impatiently on the wheel.

"Reckon she'd give me a date if I give her the note?" Coon asked.

"Ain't but one way to find out. See you by and by."

Coon got out without another word and Sonny spun the hearse back on the highway and was off. There would be no more interruptions, but the exchange with Coon had broken his mood, the mood he had been in since talking with Eleanor. He had been feeling mellow. The thought of the big ranch and the good food and the fireplace and Eleanor had seemed very desirable, very resting. But his mood had switched. He wanted speed instead of rest.

The hearse sliced through the desert at close to a hundred and ten, and the farther he drove the faster he wanted to drive. Barstow was passed, a few lights in the night, and then Victorville, and he bore down on San Bernardino, made it and swung west into the traffic of the San Bernardino freeway. The traffic annoyed him. He got into boxes of traffic and honked until one or another of the cars gave way for him; then he swept on. He wanted more driving. It seemed like no time since he had left Las Vegas and already L.A. was only fifty miles away. He wanted more driving than that, but for once he had no clear notion of where he wanted to go. He felt too pilled up to stop. There were too many places to go, and anyway he wanted to go faster than he could drive on the San Bernardino freeway.

He thought of turning south and shooting down to Tijuana. It would serve Eleanor right if he made her come to Tijuana for New Year's. Instead of getting married they could watch the donkey show. But he didn't turn toward Tijuana; the urge wasn't strong enough. He could go to Palm Springs, make her come there. They could fuck for a while in Palm Springs and if they wanted to get married they could easily do it there. The traffic swept him on, but he tried to outrun it; he kept the hearse close to a hundred on the open stretches. Or he could go to Texas after all. That feeling felt best. Back to Texas, with Coon got rid of and the whole clear dark desert to drive through. The lights of the cars ahead annoyed him. He didn't feel like seeing taillights. He passed strings of cars, schools of cars, scores of them. He wanted the clear desert, with the headlights whitening the straight road. Then he could open the hearse up and really drive.

But he kept on toward L.A., and there kept on being lights in front of him. His saddle was in L.A. For some reason he had forgotten to put it in the hearse and had not taken it to Las Vegas. He decided then what to do—he would run on to

L.A., get his saddle and some pills, and split down Highway Ten for Texas. He could make Arizona by breakfast, and Arizona was fine to drive through. Hitchhikers could drive when he came down. Or he could drive all the way. It would be a great drive, Las Vegas to L.A. and then back to Texas. No taillights ahead that he couldn't pass. No more California, no more movies. There was a rodeo in Denver just after New Year's. They could spend New Year's in Colorado, in the Broadmoor, or in Denver or in Aspen. Once with another driver he had driven all the way from Calgary to Baton Rouge in three days to make a rodeo. That had done in his first hearse; that had been fifteen years ago. Vegas to L.A. and back to Texas, with no other drivers—it appealed to him. All he needed was his saddle and some pills.

But what was hard, what was annoying, what bugged him, was slowing down for L.A. He was primed for speed, for some straight drive, and the traffic and the lights really bugged him. He should have taken the saddle to Las Vegas, so he could have gone straight to the Guthrie ranch. Cops were out for Christmas. He saw many cars pulled over, but he had always been lucky; no cops threatened him and he swung at eighty-five through the interchanges and past downtown L.A., saw it glow in the midnight smog. Some people thought the hearse was an ambulance and gave way for it reflexively. But some didn't. He was boxed in and couldn't get out and in annoyance swung off the freeway onto Sunset Boulevard. It was a bad move. His apartment was a hundred blocks up the Boulevard, above the Strip. He shot up the dinky, dingy downtown end of the Sunset, but after the open desert and the fast freeway his timing was off. He kept hitting lights. There was no way to make the speed of the hearse match the speed inside him. He would gun it up to seventy-five in a few blocks and then hit another light. For once he couldn't relax, make his own rhythm match the rhythm of the lights. He was too hyped, too impatient. He wanted his saddle and then to be gone to Texas.

Then he remembered the pills and made a screeching right-hand turn. The pills he could get at a place on Hollywood Boulevard. No problem there, it would only take a minute. He could even double-park. Then he could get his saddle and be gone. He cut the few blocks north at sixty, feeling better, hitting lights again. Half an hour and he would be on the desert again. He approached the Boulevard at the point where the Hollywood freeway passed underneath it. The light turned yellow when he was half a block away, but Sonny didn't stop. He had had enough of stopping. Let the traffic wait. He was going fast enough that they could see he wasn't stopping.

But a stoned young driver in an old Buick full of hippies didn't see. They were all listening to a soul station and not thinking much, swaying and talking, and someone's head and swinging hair was between the driver and the approaching hearse, and the driver himself was swinging with the radio. He hit the intersection early, just as Sonny hit it late. He saw the Buick's movement too late, and the driver, listening to his sounds and blinded by lights and hair, never saw the hearse at all. He was accelerating fully when the two vehicles struck each other. Sonny, with a great reflex, sensed the collision a second before it happened and tried to swing out of his turn, to shoot straight across the Boulevard and onto the downgoing entrance ramp. But though he whipped his body right, as he would have whipped it riding a turning bull, he could not whip the heavy hearse that quickly. The Buick hit him, knocked the hearse across the Boulevard, where a Chrysler driven by a swinger from Van Nuys whirled into the entrance ramp from the other direction, also in full acceleration, and hit the hearse again. Sonny, knocked half loose by the Buick, had nonetheless hung on to the steering wheel and hit his own footfeed hard, hoping to outspeed the Chrysler. But he didn't, and when the Chrysler hit him his own speed and the sharp downward drop of the ramp caused the hearse to lift as it rolled, to slide along the railing and drop twenty feet to the Hollywood freeway, the bottles, the clothes and bandages, the ropes and old boots and some woman's forgotten scarf, the mattress, the bridles, and all the gear from the back end falling over Sonny as the white hearse fell.

It was not, as wrecks go on that freeway, a very disastrous wreck. The hearse hit a spot in the traffic and it was late enough that the pile-up was not bad. Only nine cars were involved. Three people were hurt seriously but not as seriously as they might have been, and of the fourteen people injured only one, Sonny Shanks, World's Champion Cowboy, was killed.

=== 11 ===

Patsy was in Houston when she heard of the death. She had flown back the morning after Christmas. Davey was in the process of having his first cold, and she wanted him home before he got any sicker. She did not want to be trapped for three or four days in her parents' house, having to cope both with Davey and with her mother's nursing. Davey was feverish and fretful and took coping enough, and she wanted him where his own doctor could see him in case his cold got worse.

Juanita had been given a key, and was there ahead of her, and the rooms were nice and clean and warm. In the afternoon Patsy walked to the drugstore to get some cough syrup for Davey and some shampoo for herself and saw Lee Duffin and two of her daughters sitting at the counter. The girls were both taller than Lee and had long dark hair, and both were wearing jeans and sweaters and chattering happily while Lee sipped her coffee and looked melancholy. When Patsy came over she brightened a little and introduced her girls.

"Ah, yes, I know your sister," the older girl said. Her face was like her mother's, good sharp features, but she was very merry and her mother was not.

"My goodness," Patsy said. "Do you? I'm very angry with her right now. She seems to think of herself as in exile. We haven't seen her in two years."

"I know," Melissa said. "She hates Dallas. I guess she hates all of Texas. I don't see too much of her but we do live in the same house."

Patsy picked Melissa's brain for a while, but Melissa carefully avoided telling her any of the scary things she knew about Miri and boys and Miri and drugs. The other girl was looking through *Newsweek*. When Patsy ran out of questions they were all silent for a moment, each looking absently at their images in the mirror behind the counter.

"I was sorry to read about your friend Mr. Shanks," Lee said, looking at her. "Of course I only met him that once but I liked him."

"What about him?" Patsy asked.

"He was killed last night. It was in the morning paper, but there wasn't much detail. He was killed in a car wreck in Hollywood."

"Oh, no," Patsy said. A flat feeling struck her. They were silent, except for the young girl, who made a sucking sound with her straw trying to get the last few drops of her Coke.

"He seemed like a charming man, in his way," Lee said.

"In his way," Patsy said. "I'm sorry he's dead."

Though she knew it was true, it was hard to believe. Sonny dead? They walked out of the drugstore together and Lee stopped with her a minute on the blowy corner while the girls walked on. "As soon as they leave I'm going to pack," she said. "You can bring things over in stages, if you want. Bill's at the MLA again. Are you expecting Jim back in time for the move?"

"No," Patsy said. "I'm not really expecting anything." What's to expect? she thought.

"I think I know how you feel," Lee said. "I've got to get on. Cheer up. I hope Davey's better tomorrow."

As she was walking up her steps Patsy saw the browned stems of Sonny's roses sticking out of the garbage can. Juanita had just thrown them away. She went in, unrolled the morning paper, and found the story, one column on page three. The picture with it had been taken during the movie work—Sonny, no hat on, his black hair tousled as always. She felt no great pain about it but she did feel a strange clear sorrow that stayed with her until the evening. After Davey went down, with the thought that perhaps she hadn't read the paper or hadn't heard, she called Dixie. But Dixie had heard, and when Patsy said his name her aunt broke into tears.

"I know, I'm going to the funeral," she said. "It's in Borger, if you want to go. He always drove too fast. He was worse than me, even. If we'd got married I guess it would have happened long ago. Did I tell you he wanted to marry me once? Like a fool I turned him down. Can you imagine anyone turning Sonny down and then marrying Squatty? Well, that's me—"

"Come on, dear," Patsy said. "Don't cry. Sonny wouldn't have liked being married to anybody, I don't think."

"That's true," Dixie said. "That's true. I guess I did him a favor without either of us knowing it.

"But he was gorgeous," she added in a quieter voice.

Patsy cried a little after she hung up, no less for her aunt than for Sonny. She didn't believe that Sonny had ever proposed to Dixie, but she knew Dixie would believe it and tell it to everyone as long as she lived, or could remember. Such would be Sonny's few years of immortality, the stories the women he had briefly wanted would tell about him. How many women would beat their husbands with Sonny's ghost in the next few years?

For weeks after that she wanted to call Dixie again and ask if Eleanor Guthrie had been at the funeral, but she never did. The next day in a moment of sentiment she sent flowers, and she walked out of the flower shop after ordering them feeling somehow lightened and cheerful. It occurred to her that as a tribute to Sonny she ought to have gone to the funeral wearing a sign that said, "I'm the one that got away," and she imagined how all the fattening, fading Dixies that might be there would hate her, and how Sonny, could he know, would applaud the joke. Could he know, it would almost make up for her having got away.

But her light mood was deceptive. That afternoon, at the seedy laundrymat that she and Emma used, she broke into tears. An old woman caused it by giving her a laundry cart. The place was crowded, for once, and carts in short supply, and Patsy was carrying a load of sopping clothes to the dryer by hand when the old lady saw her problem and brought her a cart she was just emptying. "Here, honey," she said. "You're getting your skirt wet." It seemed so kind a thing to do that Patsy was undone. Who else would do something kind for her? The Hortons, maybe, but they were her fast friends. Her eyes dripped as the clothes spun in the dryer.

That night Jim called, wanting to talk about Sonny, but she refused to talk about him. She was calm and wanted to stay calm, and besides it seemed fatuous to talk about him as if they had been close friends when they hadn't. Jim surprised her a great deal by telling her he was thinking of taking a job with IBM.

"You?" she said. "At IBM? Why, for god's sake?"

"Because Ed can get me one. If I'm going to stay out here I ought to get some kind of job. That's the one place I've got a contact."

"And you've decided to stay out there?" she asked calmly.

"I think I better, for a while. If I come back right now we'll just start it all again. You know that."

"Okay. I wasn't arguing. I was asking."

"It's tragic," he said, "but we're just at cross-purposes when we're together."

"Oh, shit," she said. "There's nothing tragic about it. We're both just spoiled. Do what you damn well please but don't go tragicizing it, if that's a word. Tell all that to her, if she's still around.

"*Is* she still around?" she asked.

"More or less," Jim said.

"Oh, for god's sake. Don't be so wishy-washy. A person can't be around more or less. She's around and you might as well say so."

"Okay," he said angrily. "She's around."

He didn't tell her that he and Clara had already taken an apartment in Altadena. They finished the conversation on a polite note.

She had scarcely hung up when Hank called. "What are you doing?" he asked.

"Thinking about the quick and the dead," she said. "How are you? Why aren't you at work, bringing art to the masses? I suppose you heard about Sonny Shanks."

"Sure. There are big write-ups out here."

"I'm tired of talking about it. Are you okay?"

"I'd like to come and see you."

She thought about it. "No," she said. "I have to move next week. I can't tell what Jim might do and I don't want any complications until the dust gets settled. You're dusty enough yourself. In fact you're mostly dust. You're probably even worse now that you live in a desert again."

"They have bumper stickers out here that say, 'Lucky Me! I Live in Lubbock.'"

"Send me one. I'll put it in my kitchen to remind me that you exist."

In a week she moved. The Duffins had decided to take a fancy apartment for the spring, one with a heated swimming pool. Patsy hired two gigantic good-natured movers to move her. It only took half a morning. Her possessions—they had almost crowded her out of the apartment—seemed no more substantial than a couple of suitcases in the expanse of the new house. They did not even make a good litter; some rooms remained totally bare. Emma came over and wandered about for an hour marveling at how much room there was. Patsy had ordered a couch and two tables and some rugs and several chairs, but none of them were due to arrive for a few days. The Horton boys made dozens of trips up and down stairs. Patsy's spirits were dropping very badly. The house was cold and too bare and full of half-unpacked boxes; a new lamp she had bought needed to be screwed into a wall and there was no one to do it. She didn't know what to do first; she started on the kitchen and then decided it would be better to do Davey's room first. His room was the whole narrow third floor. It had lots of windows and was a lovely bright room when the sun was shining, but it was a cloudy January day and the room seemed cheerless. Davey didn't agree. He crawled about with great enthusiasm, mumbling to himself, and every three seconds managed to work his way to the head of the stairs. They fascinated him. Patsy had neglected to get stair gates and had horrible visions of him tumbling down.

"Why did we buy it?" she said to Emma. "I'm too helpless for a house." She felt very much like crying. Three stories was too much to be alone in with a little boy. It had been lovely to plan on fixing up the house, but to be dumped on the floor of it on a cold day was depressing. It was awful of Jim. He had wanted the house too, and should not have gone off and left her to cope with anything so major. She felt bitter at the same time that she felt lonely. He had not done his part. In the end, despite her threat, she had moved the books for him. She felt like a sucker, and an abandoned sucker at that. She had forgotten to tell the movers that the TV had to go on the second floor. With it on downstairs she could not hear Davey crying from the third floor. The TV set was too heavy for her to move upstairs. Juanita had the flu and Davey had never quite got over his cold and was a drippy mess, although a cheerful one. The large empty house made her feel lonely and exposed. In the apartment she had at least felt safe and cozy.

Fortunately Emma noticed her depression. "I think I better loan you my husband for the afternoon," she said. "He's handy for shoving things around."

She was true to her word; Flap came in an hour, and all parties were delighted. Flap moved the TV upstairs, put a bed together, and spent most of the rest of the afternoon drinking beer, peering vaguely into boxes, or reading Jim's books. He was wearing an old green army-surplus coat that made him look like a war refugee, but his presence cut the gloom and Patsy brightened up and unpacked the kitchen stuff. The sun came out just before it went down and shone through the windows, making the living room lovely. Patsy stopped and sat for thirty minutes on the arm of a chair, sipping beer and thinking about where things would go, once they came. By griping at him skillfully she managed to get Flap to screw in the lamp.

"Why'd you buy something that had to be screwed into the wall?" he asked. "Women have no sense. There are perfectly good lamps that stand on the floor. I think I've hit a beam. I'm ruining this screw."

Emma had insisted that Flap bring the two of them home for supper, out of the same motive that had prompted her to the loan of Flap. Patsy insisted that Flap pick out a book as a reward for his labors.

"Is it legal?" he asked.

"Who cares? I moved them, I can give you one if I want to. Pick out a book."

"Well, maybe I will," Flap said. "I did screw the lamp in for you." He picked out a neat two-volume Montaigne, blue, Oxford University Press. "I've always supposed I would read Montaigne eventually," he said. "If the two volumes count as one book, that is."

"Sure," Patsy said. "I'm full of largesse. Let's go see what Emma's cooked." She was tugging Davey with difficulty into a blue sweater. He was dripping and looking at Flap.

"I've always supposed I would read him too," she said as they were driving to the Hortons'.

"If the urge really hits you, you can read him at our house. Am I supposed to ask about Jim once in a while?"

"You might, for form's sake. He's trying to get a job with IBM."

"That's as likely a corporation as any," Flap said. He was reading the translator's introduction to the Montaigne. His interest in Jim was not overwhelming. Patsy looked a little tired, but lovely. She was wearing jeans and a brown sweater. He had wondered as he put the bed together that afternoon if he would ever, by some happy fortune, get to sleep with her a time or two. He couldn't help feeling that he deserved that kind of bonus before he ended his days. But the gift of the book had pleased him. Emma was already budgeting them toward their summer move and would not let him buy books. He had always found the publications of the Oxford University Press extremely satisfying. Having them made him feel scholarly, and frequently he liked to read them too. It occurred to him that if he could remember to be helpful while Patsy was setting up her new house, she might give him more; but by the time he finished Emma's supper, which was meat loaf with green peppers in it, he had forgotten that he meant to be helpful. He lay on the couch most of the evening reading the translator's long introduction and didn't quite get around to reading Montaigne.

Patsy spent the evening shelving the books. It was the most relaxing of the many things she might have done. The living room bookcases were built in, and the books looked nice in them. The Hortons wanted to have a semester's-end party. They would not think of letting a semester end without as much revelry as possible, and she was debating whether she should invite Hank to come back from Lubbock for it. She had no clear feeling about it. It would be nice having him back, but once back he might stay, and she didn't like that thought. It was sloppy, she wasn't sure what she felt about him, and it looked too much like tit for tat—just a reaction to what Jim had done. She did not want to go titting for tatting. Not her. She wavered all evening but ended, after she had bathed in the strangely large tub in the strangely large tiled bathroom, with a firm feeling against it. She would simply quite flirting with the idea of Hank for a while. It was no time for it. If Jim never came back, or if she reached a point where she knew she would not let him, then maybe. Until then she would keep aloof, and she went aloofly to bed in the large bare master bedroom. It felt as out of proportion as the bathroom and there was no denying that aloofness was going to be lonely in such an empty, manless house. It was strange having Davey above her, instead of a few yards away behind a partition. It meant that she had to listen for him, and she spent a wakeful, restless, scared first night in their new home, listening almost all night for sounds of distress from her son.

═══ 12 ═══

All the graduate students were desperate to have a
semester's-end party. Flap had worked hard on his dissertation and had two chapters done and only three to go, and he
had secured a job, a better one than he had expected, at the
University of Iowa, in Iowa City. Emma was gloomy for a
few days at the thought of Iowa, but then someone told her
that there was a big writing center there, with hundreds of
lively writers in it. The news cheered her a bit. She sat
around for several days reading *Letting Go* and imagining
herself slimmed up and having an affair with a young writer
of some kind.

"If worst comes to worst I could even take classes," she
told Patsy. Patsy was making brownies. She had discovered
she liked them.

"Sure," Patsy said, full of encouragement. "Who knows,
you might even be a writer. Maybe you'll be the one to write
the story of all our lives."

To her surprise Emma looked strange for a moment, as if
a memory had caught at her heart. They were sitting in
Patsy's kitchen, which was gradually taking form. Hank *had*
sent her a "Lucky Me! I Live in Lubbock" sticker and she
had pasted it above the cabinet. Emma looked like she
might cry, but she didn't. Patsy decided she was probably
just sad at the prospect of going away. The prospect of
Emma going away made *her* sad, in fact. Who would she
have to sit in the kitchen with?

"Well, are you going to have the party or am I going to
have the party?" Emma asked. That was the ostensible
subject of the conversation.

"I will. It can be a housewarming too. What's Kenny doing? I haven't seen him in weeks."

"Writing a thesis on the novels of Rose Macaulay," Emma said. "He decided he wasn't doctoral material and is taking a terminal M.A. Are you going to divorce Jim?"

"We haven't decided anything," she said with a light sigh. She was more interested in her brownies.

"You don't look crushed," Emma said.

"Why should I spend my life being crushed? Once I got sort of used to him being gone it was such a relief not having those constant arguments that I couldn't keep feeling crushed. I don't like having terrible fights all the time. Now I just feel sort of light. Maybe I'm just shallow. Who will we have to the party?"

They drew up a list, and on her own hook Patsy decided to invite Peewee Raskin. She had seen him two or three times at the zoo and for some reason had avoided asking him to dinner. Harmless as he was, she just didn't want it. He was too worshipful to ask to dinner, but a party was different. She went to the zoo and asked him, and she and Davey rode all around the zoo on the zoo train. Peewee drove erratically, mostly because he kept looking back and trying to tell her things. He agreed somewhat gingerly to come to the party. He literally could not imagine what kind of people might be there.

That night at the Gulf-Air he had a long speculative conversation about intellectuals. Roscoe was as vocal as ever.

"What you oughta do is take us to that party," he said. "We could hold our own. I'm an expert on half a dozen things myself."

"You're an expert on horseshit," Skeets said. "At least you ought to be, as much of it as you put out."

Roscoe was not offended. "You're an expert on losing at dominoes, yourself. Why don't you bring your egghead friends over here sometimes, Squirt? I'd like to talk to them."

Peewee was evasive. He had no intention whatever of exposing Patsy to the vulgarities of Roscoe. The mere thought made him cringe. He agonized over the party for three days, sure that he would seem hideously out of place no matter how well he behaved. He could not decide whether to wear his hat. Patsy had told him it would be a very casual party, but that was no help. When it came time to go he put on his cleanest Levi's and a new Western shirt he had bought especially for the occasion, and after a good deal of fidgeting took down his hat and put it on. He wore it on the bus going over, thinking that if he changed his mind he could stick it under a bush and pick it up when he left the party.

As it happened, though, he had no difficulties at the party at all. At the last minute he forgot to stick his hat under a bush and wore it in and made a great hit, hat and all. For him the party was a wild delight. The Hortons immediately took him to their hearts and plied him with questions about his trade. Various other sloppily dressed graduate students drifted over to listen and Peewee, discovering that he knew more than he thought, at least about rodeo, expanded two inches and spent the whole evening talking, jiggling slightly in time with whatever record was on, drinking an occasional beer at somebody's insistence but mostly eating hundreds of Fritos with cheese dip, to punctuate his remarks. He had never been to a party where there were so many odd things to eat strewn about, and besides Fritos and dip stuffed himself with nuts, pretzels, and rye crackers.

Kenny Cambridge, once he arrived, took an especial liking to Peewee and they spent an hour talking about motor bikes. Finding out that Patsy's people were interested in some of the same things he was interested in was a warming revelation to Peewee, and made him feel good about life. Once in a while he passed a conversation where everyone was talking about books he had never heard of, but he didn't let it spook him. He hurried on to the nearest dip bowl, thinking of the triumphant report he would make at the Gulf-Air the next evening. His only disappointment was that Patsy didn't talk to him much. She was being a hostess and dancing and occasionally running upstairs. She wore a sweater and a short red skirt and looked very lovely.

Peewee didn't suspect it, but Patsy was the one person at the party who wasn't having a good time. As the evening was beginning she fell into a strange depression that she tried every possible way to lift herself out of, with no success.

Something was wrong, not with the evening, not with the people, but with her. It was something irrational, for the house was a great house for a party and everyone was in a party mood. Things were clicking; there was no stiffness, not even initially. A tall graduate student from Chicago insisted on smoking pot and she grew mildly irritated with him for passing it around so freely, but he was not the source of her depression. What sort of hostess would protest against marijuana? She had invited the Duffins, to let them see what she had done with the house. Lee was complimentary, and Patsy danced a lot with Bill. For a while she enjoyed it; it covered the depression. Then she went upstairs to check on Davey. She had asked Juanita to sleep in for the evening, for she knew with the party going on she would never hear him if he cried. Juanita was watching television. Davey was sleeping soundly. Patsy poised restlessly on the second floor, feeling oddly irritable. She wanted the phone to ring. Even more, she wanted Hank to show up at the party. She hadn't asked him, but she had mentioned the party in their last conversation and she thought how nice it would be if he surprised her. She was not in the mood to resent a surprise. What she was beginning to resent was the lack of one.

When she went back down into the noise she took the depression with her. It was no good not having a man—for some reason it struck her then. She was without one. Emma had one, Lee had one, all the girls at the party had one. Most of them were men she herself would not want, but still she felt unattended and strange. She missed Jim, as much or more as she missed Hank. He was good at attending her at parties, and she enjoyed dancing with him. When she came downstairs Kenny Cambridge wanted to dance with her. His beard was longer and reddish brown. His pudgy girl friend had left him and he had not managed to replace her. Patsy turned him on, and he looked merrier when turned on.

"Quit leering," she told him.

"It wasn't a leer. It was a look of frank concupiscence."

"Oh, screw," Patsy said. "I think I'll get a drink."

She got a drink and complimented Bill Duffin on his daughters and got another drink and accidentally got drunk. In thirty minutes she was drunk enough to have a sense that she was reeling in some way, not physically, but some way.

She went through moods rapidly. When she began to get high she rose above the depression and had a half-hour of great well-being. Her party was going fine. Everyone was splendid. She felt bound to everyone there. Parties were the answer to loneliness and mortality. The people were fine, and they were her people.

But that mood dropped away. She found herself sitting halfway up the stairs, at a point where the stairs made a turn, and Bill Duffin was with her. She was complimenting him on his daughters again, and though she had a vague sense that she might be repeating herself she didn't stop. Bill didn't care. He reached up from time to time to pat her shoulder or try to hug her. He had drunk a good bit too and was speculating quietly about the affair they hadn't had. Patsy didn't care; she was even vaguely interested, though she wanted to cry. Hank or Jim should have come. Jim was probably at a party himself, with Clara Clark. Bill kept putting his arm around her; he tried to pull her against him.

"I'm just being fatherly," he claimed. "You look forlorn."

"Screw you," she said. "I'm not forlorn. And you're not fatherly. You're fondling me, and you're still scheming. Forget it, buddy. It's too late. I never liked you anyway. I just had my eye on your house."

She giggled at her own meanness. Bill put his hand on her knee and confessed that he had a stomachache.

"Your ulcer, probably," she said. "The price of fame."

"What's the word from Jim and Clara?" he asked.

"So they're Jim and Clara now," she said angrily, jumping up. "How would I know what the word is? I don't even want to."

Bill was unimpressed with her annoyance. She was standing two stairs above him and he could almost see up her skirt. Her legs were lovely and it angered him that she had never let him near her.

"Well, the man who lives with Clara won't get much time for scholarly pursuits," he said, looking into his glass. "Not as I remember her."

"As *you* remember her? My god, did she screw the whole faculty and student body? That's just great."

"I don't know about the student body, but I'm sure she

only gave her favors to a minute portion of the faculty." He used his gravest, most professorial tone.

"That's great," she said and went to the bathroom to cry. Jim had run off with the easiest girl in school. After her cry she went back to the party. Lee, looking quite happy, was dancing with the pot-smoking graduate student. Peewee and Kenny were in a corner talking motor bikes. Patsy felt very much like leaving. All the people depressed her suddenly, and she knew it would be hours before they could be expected to leave.

"Would you look after my party?" she asked Emma. "I'm going to get someone to take me to a bar."

"Why?" Emma was a little tight, and mildly surprised.

"I feel more like being at a bar than like being here."

"Are you going off the deep end?"

"No, I'm just going to a bar, if I can get someone to take me," she said, getting her coat from the coat closet. "If the narcotics squad comes and arrests you tell them they can find me in a bar. I'm not trying to evade my guilt."

She went over and asked Kenny and Peewee if they would like to take her to a bar and though both were very surprised, both said yes. They could not imagine why she wanted to go to a bar with them. Patsy realized she was not entirely sober and made Kenny drive.

"What kind of bar?" he asked.

"I don't care. Peewee must know some bars. So must you."

Peewee had a bad moment. It seemed to him that by some horrible quirk of fate Kenny would drive straight to the Gulf-Air, where everyone would either make fun of him or insult Kenny because of his beard or, worse, insult Patsy, so that he and Kenny would be forced to fight them. Horrible as the vision was, a tiny part of him secretly hoped Kenny *would* take them to the Gulf-Air, so they could all see he really did have a beautiful friend who went to Rice. But Kenny lacked initiative and was unused to driving cars and simply took them to Yum-Yum's.

"I've been here," Patsy said. "Is this the best bar you know?"

"Best for what? It's safe, at least."

"I feel maudlin," she said. "It'll do."

It proved to be an excellent place for crying. They had hardly sat down when the waitress came over and asked about Hank. She was the same thin blonde who had been there the night Hank brought her. Patsy tried to remember when that had been, precisely when it had been, and couldn't. She could barely be sure of the year. It had been a long time ago, when she was very innocent, she knew that. Kenny and Peewee had a stiff conversation about motor bikes, both of them trying hard to ignore the fact that she was crying. She didn't seem desperately unhappy, she even talked with them from time to time, but tears kept streaming down her face. They all drank beer faster than they would have ordinarily, in hopes that she would stop crying. She herself drank four beers while she talked and cried, not exactly conscious of being sad. It was not just missing Hank that caused her to cry. She missed everybody, even some of the people at the party. Everyone was gone away, far away; they were scattered, lost, dead, all the men she liked. The music made her sadder—it was all hillbilly. There was a song about a man whose wife had just left him. He was at the airport, and it was raining:

> *In the early mornin' rain . . .*
> *Out on runway number nine . . .*

The song played over and over and the barmaid brought them more beer and Kenny and Peewee did their best to ignore her tears. Patsy drew circles on the table top and rested her lip against the cool glass of the beer mug. A couple were shuffling nearby, interrupting their dance from time to time in order to argue.

"I miss everyone," she told Kenny in explanation of her tears. Jim more than ever, Hank almost as much as Jim. And Sonny Shanks too, and Joe Percy—they would be fun to go to a bar with. Every time she tried to speak she ended up hiccuping.

Peewee and Kenny became alarmed, for they saw that Patsy would sit there all night, crying and drinking beer and listening to hillbilly music, if she were allowed to. Kenny kept mentioning the party, hoping that she would remember she was the hostess of it. But Patsy had all but forgotten it. She drank beer without really tasting it and imagined that she was with people who weren't there. She spied enviously on the couples dancing. She had no one to dance with, no one to fight with either.

"Sonny's dead," she said to Peewee. "Had you heard?"

"Aw, yeah," Peewee said. "Heard all about it. That's the way it goes."

"Yep, that's the way it goes," Patsy said.

"Quit talking like Hemingway characters," Kenny said. "This isn't *The Sun Also Rises.*"

"Why'd you break up with your girl friend?" Patsy asked.

"Oh, because she was hung up about fucking," Kenny said.

"Live fast, love hard, die young, and leave beau-ti-ful mem-o-ries . . ." Peewee quavered. Patsy and Kenny were startled. He seemed about to sing. But that was all he sang. Sonny had been his idol, and mention of his death had reminded him of that old song. "Won't be no more like him," he said, feeling for a second like he might cry.

Patsy patted him on the hand in sympathy. "There were no more like him, anyway," she said.

Peewee controlled himself, but his near breakdown alarmed Kenny. He was not drunk and he didn't relish the prospect of two drunks on his hands. He demanded they go back to the party. Peewee was not really drunk, and he was just as glad they were going. But Patsy didn't want to go. She was at a clear stage of drunkenness where all she knew was what she didn't want. She went outside with them but then she became petulant and childish and sat down on a curb. She wouldn't talk to them. She just sat down. Peewee was getting a bad feeling. It was going to be the scene in El Paso all over again, only Jim wouldn't be there to handle her. Fortunately Kenny was a man of small patience and he saw no reason why he should bother to be patient with Patsy.

"We're going," he said. "If you don't come you can walk."

"Okay," Patsy said.

Kenny started the Ford. She was still sitting on the curb. Peewee stood uneasily by the car.

"You're stealing my car," Patsy said. "You're a cruel bastard. I think you're both car thieves. Cruel beasts too."

"Oh, fuck off," Kenny said. "We want to go to the party. Get in, Peewee."

Patsy got up. It surprised her that she could walk.

"Take me to your place," she said. "It's too early to go back to the party. It will look suspicious." She squeezed into the back seat and began to giggle.

"*Why* will it look suspicious to go back now?" Kenny asked. "Let me know if you need to puke."

"*Why* would I need to puke?" she said, mocking him. "Let's go to your place. I like dingy places. We could smoke pot. I'm sure you've got some hidden."

"As drunk as you are you don't need to be high," he said. "Besides, we could do that at your place."

Peewee's apprehension deepened. Marijuana was an ominous possibility. He didn't know much about such matters, but he feared the worst. He saw himself hooked on heroin. He saw himself spending years in the Huntsville prison. He was a little drunk and Patsy and Kenny were scaring him slightly.

Patsy felt very odd. Anything to avoid the party. "You could read us your poems," she said, leaning over the front seat.

"You're putting me on," Kenny said.

"Nooo," she said. "I wouldn't do that. I hate parties. I want to hear poems. Peewee's probably never heard a poem."

Though Kenny got back to within a block of the party, Patsy had her way. She leaned over into the front seat and insisted, and since she had stopped crying and seemed to feel happy they both quickly became enchanted with her again. On the curb she had seemed difficult but in the car she only seemed pleasantly drunk and she smelled good. Kenny thought, Why not, and Peewee forgot his visions of the needle.

They went to Kenny's place, which had grown even dingier since the departure of his girl friend. It was only two houses down from the building where Hank's apartment had been, an unfortunate proximity. Walking in, Patsy stopped on the cold lawn and looked at the other building, two houses away, where she had had so much pleasure. The bottom suddenly fell out of her pleasant mood. There was no more pleasure. There, almost next door, her pleasure had ended. She hadn't been touched in two months.

"Come in, it's cold," Kenny said, and she moved reluctantly. The other apartment was in her mind—the time she had spent there, the night she had spent there that had ruined everything. Kenny's room was a mess. The bed wasn't made. But the bad thing, suddenly, was Kenny and Peewee. They were enchanted with her again. They looked at her when she came in as if she were the angel of beauty. She felt queasy and soured and bad and faithless and pleasureless and sordid, and their worshipful looks infuriated her. She glared at them, but they didn't understand. They kept looking at her as if she were someone she wasn't, someone virtuous, ethereal, kind, and chaste. It was hateful. She was different from what they thought. She was no better than the women in the bar, who were probably at that moment getting screwed by the men who had been dancing with them. It was insulting for two little boys like Kenny and Peewee to look at her as if she were pure. They wanted her themselves and were always giving her the eye, and yet they thought she was chaste and virtuous. It was hateful. She churned with resentment and pain.

"Stop looking at me that way," she said. "I didn't come here to be stared at."

It was an unfortunate command. They saw that, inexplicably, she had become furious at them, and it scared them both. Even Kenny, who usually became sullen and stolid when women were angry with him, was made nervous by Patsy's look. She looked wild, like she might start smashing things, including him. When she told them not to look at her they both stared at her the harder.

"Oh, why do you keep looking at me?" she said, gasping with anger. "Turn and look at the wall if you can't stop looking at me like that."

Kenny shrugged. "Like what?" he said. "We weren't giving you the evil eye or anything."

"The evil eye," she said. "Of course you weren't. I didn't say anything about evil eyes. It's worse, what you're doing. I can't stand either of you."

"Well," Kenny said, trying to assume sullenness as a defense. "How come?"

"Because you don't look at me right," she said, advancing on them a step. Peewee was shaken. He didn't know what was happening or how to look at her. He was for turning to face the wall.

"Well, how come?" Kenny said again in the same sullen tone.

"Oh, shit!" Patsy yelled. "If you say how come to me again I'll hit you! You don't know me and you look at me wrong. You look at me like you want to sleep with me but you think I'm too good or something. You think I'm the sort of woman who doesn't sleep with anybody, I know you do."

"Aw, you've got a child," Kenny said.

"I *know* I've got a child," she said. "Don't mention my child. You think I'm untouchable and that I'm virtuous and that I never do anything bad, that's what you think. I'm not so goddamn virtuous. I do the same things other women do. I slept with someone, and I chased my husband off. What do you know about how virtuous I am? I don't want to be on any goddamn pedestals. If she can screw everybody in the goddamn English department I can screw people too, anybody I want to."

"Okay, okay, you're not so good," Kenny said.

"Don't talk to me," Patsy said. "Just shut up. I could sleep with both of you if I wanted to. I don't know why we don't. She slept with everybody. You always want to, both of you always want to, every time you've looked at me for years. I'm sick of you looking at me like that, I'd rather do it right now than see you looking that way. Then you wouldn't think I was so precious." She stumbled past them, taking her coat off, and to their mutual consternation dropped her coat on the floor and began taking off her sweater.

"Hey, no, you don't know what you're doing," Kenny said, grabbing one of her arms. "You're just drunk." He tried to motion Peewee into the fray, but Peewee hung back; he wanted no part of it. Patsy had her sweater hiked up, showing her slip, but Kenny held on to her wrist so she couldn't get the sweater off.

"Let me go," she said. "I want to take it off . . . I want to take it off . . ." But her breath grew short, the fierce anger went out of her voice and out of her eyes. She twisted and pulled, trying to make Kenny let go her wrist. She began to cry, and suddenly the liquor and the beer came up in a rush. She barely had time to bend over. Kenny didn't even try to guide her to the bathroom; he got her to kneel over a wastebasket. She coughed and heaved. Some got on the floor but he didn't care. She wasn't the first girl to barf on his floor. He knew it was all over and was vastly relieved.

Peewee, once he saw that that was really it, Patsy was sick drunk and not any longer possessed of her terrible frenzy, became able to act. He found the bathroom and got a washrag and helped Kenny clean up the mess while Patsy rested, braced on her hands, her head over the wastebasket and her eyes closed, crying, quietening, occasionally still heaving. When she finished and sat back she started automatically to brush back her hair with her hand, but Kenny caught the hand and wiped it clean so she wouldn't get vomit in her hair. With drunk females he was an old and confident hand. They helped Patsy over to a chair and cleaned off her sweater and skirt as best they could.

Kenny talked to her coaxingly and quietly, telling her it was okay, telling her she would feel better by and by. They were both startled by the change in her. The raging, frightening, all but unhandleable woman of a few minutes before was gone and she looked like a girl again, a girl who was pale and who felt sick. They squatted by the chair watching her. Now that she was quiet and helpless they both felt touched, a little enchanted with her again, and loyal and on her side. They felt rather comradely too; they had seen her through it.

After a while she opened her eyes—she obviously felt ghastly.

"Feel well enough for us to get you home?" Kenny asked.

She shook her head weakly. "I don't feel good," she said.

In the end she stayed the night. Kenny made his bed as neatly as possible and Patsy slept on top of the covers, her coat over her legs. Peewee and Kenny sat on the floor and drank beer, talking quietly of this and that, Patsy and Jim, rodeos, motor bikes, and the adventures of their youth. They talked the rest of the night almost. Peewee fell asleep on the floor at four A.M. and Kenny read J. P. Donleavy the rest of the night.

Patsy began to stir at six. She didn't feel much better than she had, but she realized the necessity of getting home.

Davey would be waking. Peewee was a heap in a corner. Kenny had thrown a blanket over him and set his black hat where he could find it when he awoke. The sight of Peewee sleeping was so funny and pathetic that she managed a pained grin. Kenny was cheerful and took her home. "You'll live, you'll live," he kept telling her on the way. She had her eyes shut.

"I don't want to," she said.

She felt awkward, not asking him in for coffee, since he had been so hospitable, but she didn't want Juanita to think she had spent the night with him, so she didn't. Kenny didn't care. He went off whistling, looking very boyish.

She had thirty minutes in which to gain strength before Juanita brought Davey down. She spent it sitting at the kitchen table yawning and feeling queasy. Davey, once he appeared, was all hunger and sunshine, and Juanita quietly sympathetic. "Parties weel wear you out," she said.

As she was dragging herself up to bathe, Patsy found a little note from Emma on the table by the stairs. "Fine pair you picked to go off the deep end with," it read. "Flap was very hurt. Everybody liked your party, and all got drunker. Emma."

13

For six weeks, through the last half of January and all February, nothing happened. It was the soggy part of the Houston winter—not very cold but with much rain. While she was recovering from the party, Patsy caught a low-grade virus of some kind and didn't manage to shake it for two weeks. It was more boring than painful, the only painful part being the shots she kept having to get in her behind.

The rest of the time she felt slightly feverish and dull. Bill Duffin had left a garage half full of wood; after much smoky experimenting she learned to make fires in the fireplace. It made being slightly ill much more pleasant. Her good couch finally came and she arranged it in front of the fireplace, with a good lamp at each end, and spent most of her time on the couch reading. She had had the foresight to make Jim leave her his library card, and every few days she bundled up and sloshed to the Rice library to get an armful of novels. If she didn't feel like novels she went to the drugstore and read magazines. She grew quite lazy and was reluctant to go out at all. She even took to ordering her groceries by phone.

Indeed, for the period of her illness she began to live on the phone. She couldn't go to the Hortons', for fear of giving her virus to the children, so she talked to Emma on the phone. Emma was all hung up on how life would be in Iowa City. Patsy could not herself imagine living in Iowa City, but as a service to her friend she adopted the philosophy that it matters not where you are but how you are. She knew better, but she was good at defending philosophical positions that she didn't really agree with, and she usually managed to cheer Emma up.

Her mother was a different matter. Jeanette was in a period of crisis. Miri was the ostensible cause, but there were other reasons. She had absolutely nothing to do, even less than Patsy. Garland had decided his fortunes were declining and had started feverishly attending to business. He was gone most of the time, and in any case he felt like a failure in regard to Miri and didn't like for Jeanette to talk about it with him; so she talked about it with Patsy. She called four or five times a week to talk about it. Patsy was tolerant as long as the talk was about Miri or her father; she was not tolerant when Jeanette tried to find out what was happening with her and Jim. That she refused to discuss. But she did promise definitely to go to California in March and try to do something about Miri. It allowed Jeanette to talk for more hours about all that might be done.

Generally she heard from Hank once a week, and once a week from Jim. Neither calls were very satisfactory. With Jim she had to walk a narrow line. She did not want to blow her cool, for if she did she fumed and stewed and felt bad inside for hours afterward. In order not to blow her cool she had to be careful. She asked as few questions as possible. She kept off the future, she kept off the past. She kept off them. She told him about Davey, and he told her about life in California. The result was that their conversations were so polite and superficial that they might as well have not talked at all. After such a conversation Jim seemed very remote to her; she could scarcely visualize him. Often, looking at Davey, it pained and puzzled her that the man who had fathered him could have become so remote, so without tangibility as a person.

And when the politeness did not work, when something was said that caused one or the other of them to blow their cool, it was just as bad. What she felt for him then was worse: resentment and bitterness that he could leave her so easily. She forgot the months of fighting; his departure seemed cheap and whimsical. And it seemed to her that cowardice kept him from coming back. It filled her with disgust. Remoteness was easier on her stomach than spleen, so their conversations became politer and politer and she thought of him less and less often and remembered him less and less well.

With Hank's calls the opposite was true. Again there was a narrow line to be walked, but in his case what she had to try and do was keep from remembering him too well. If his voice struck a certain tone then all that she missed became vivid and she missed it more painfully. Sometimes then longing became irritability, and irritability anger, and she fought with him more bitterly than she fought with Jim. All their conversations were chancy, for the sense of missingness was apt to swell terribly after she hung up, and then there was nothing to do but wait for its slow going-away. Gradually she developed a workable middle tone, a style of banter that kept things more or less level.

What energy she had was spent mostly on Davey and on the house. The house absorbed hours of thought. She had very quickly become discontent with having Davey on the third floor, beautiful as the third floor was. It was a mistake. At night she worried about fires. What if one occurred while he was up there? And even in the purest practical sense it was awkward. He still had to be carried, but he had grown heavy, and it was a long carry from the kitchen to the third floor. After three weeks she moved him down a floor. When he got old enough to walk upstairs he could return to the third. Juanita breathed a sigh of relief; constant trips up two flights of stairs were breaking her health, she felt.

But better than the house was Davey himself. As he approached his first birthday and became—every week it seemed—a little less a baby, a little more a small boy, he entered upon a period of very active happiness. He didn't miss his father, he didn't miss anything. From the time he woke up, wanting his mother, wanting attention, wanting food, until after he and she had completed the various little bed games he liked to play, his days were a crude flow of activity, broken only by an afternoon nap. He was good-natured, laughed and babbled more than he cried, and he did not seem overly demanding. Yet, from early morning until evening it seemed that she or Juanita or both of them at once were in constant motion, getting him, cleaning up after him, keeping him out of things, finding toys for him when he was in bed or getting toys out of bed for him when he happened to be on the floor, feeding him, changing him, doing *something* with him. They could both tell from the tone of his wails whether a particular problem was serious trouble or a mere momentary frustration.

He was, it seemed to Patsy, exceptionally communicative. When he wanted her to know something he sought her out. She would be lying in a doze on the couch, still in her bathrobe, warmed by the fire, and would be awakened by Davey yanking on her hair. It was his method of announcing a message. Sometimes the sound of his crawling awakened her, for he crawled rapidly and it was easy to tell when he left the rug and struck the bare floor. For all that he was less than one, he gave the house a kind of masculine center. Patsy talked to him a lot, chattered at him, sang him songs, sat him on her stomach if she was lying down or on her lap if she was sitting up. She was thinking of getting him a dog, and she constantly read pet ads. He had her dark hair, and it was getting longer.

At times the rapport she had with Davey frightened her a little; she wondered if it was abnormal. She missed Hank whenever he called and reminded her of himself, and sometimes in lonely moods she missed Jim, but there were days when she missed neither of them, when Hank was as vague to her as Jim. Even Hank, who had been so tangible, was becoming intangible little by little. Davey was completely tangible, sitting on her stomach chewing on his rubber kitty or pulling her hair, or poking his fingers in her mouth, cheerfully gobbling food, drenching diapers, and kicking merrily while his behind was being powdered. Every night she brought him in from his bath wrapped in a huge towel and plopped him on her bed to be diapered and pajamaed. He quickly made a game of not liking to be diapered and would wiggle out of the towel and dart to the corners of the bed to elude her, naked and giggly, the ends of his hair still wet. Eventually Patsy would catch him by a foot and drag him to the center of the bed, dry his hair roughly, and roll him on his back. Once he had had his play out he generally assented to being dressed, though he really preferred being naked, and would chew on the rubber sleep-with kitty while she pinned the diapers. His little stomach bulged out of his unbuttoned pajamas and Patsy would rub it affectionately as she was buttoning him, or splutter on it while he grabbed her hair and exploded with giggles. She never rocked him at night, but often she rocked him in the afternoon, if he seemed reluctant to nap, and after a great deal of wiggling and looking up to see if she was still there he would go to sleep on her shoulder and she would put him in bed and stand a moment smoothing the long wavy black hair at his temples.

One night when she was absently rubbing his stomach and he just as absently chewing the rubber kitty, Patsy caught herself with a start; she was stroking her son with the same sort of pure tactile enjoyment that she might get from stroking a man. At least it had reminded her of men. She didn't feel depraved, exactly, just thoughtful, and after a time buttoned Davey's pajamas over his stomach and put him to bed.

In a few weeks, when she got over her flu and felt well again, she noticed that she was not unhappy. Lonely at times, but not unhappy. She was becoming cheerful again, cheerful in a way that she had not been for a year. There was a stretch of fine weather in February and she began to delight in the three big trees in the back yard, to plan the back yard, and to look for yard furniture. Shopping and chatting with store people became fun again, and her laundry man told her she was beautiful. At home, Davey kept her and Juanita giggling half the time. At night, when she was low, or thought about it, she wondered about herself—wondered if she was one of those women who didn't need a mate, only a child. She wondered if she would become some kind of cannibal mother, devouring Davey, absorbing him and being absorbed by him in too intense a way. She didn't want to, she didn't mean to, but as the spring approached she found herself being happier and more self-sufficient every day, with no man around but him.

One day she wandered into the Russian section of the library and decided she ought to read a Russian novel. She practically never had, except *Crime and Punishment*, which she hadn't much liked. She decided she would read a Tolstoy, a Dostoevsky, and a Turgenev, and so brought home *Anna Karenina, The Idiot,* and *Fathers and Sons.*

The only one of the three she read was *Anna.* She remembered having tried it in high school; she had stopped after a hundred pages and had never gone on. This time she went on, hurriedly and a little irritably. Kitty and Levin she skipped whenever she could. Their innocence merely annoyed her; it was stupid and there was nothing absorbing in it. She wanted to read about Anna, though it was painful to do so. Anna was so exposed that reading about her was embarrassing; Patsy read page after page with a pinched frown and yet went on, as if it were a medicine she must take, and at the end, when she closed the book with Anna dead, she felt more depressed than she had at any time since Hank and Jim went away.

The depression lasted two days and then lifted as suddenly as it had come. Some discrepancy between the novel and her own life discouraged her terribly. Her own sins had been so small-time; her marriage, and her affair as well, so weak and short-term. She hadn't sustained anything for years against all sorts of obstacles, as Anna had done. She wasn't dead, nor even ruined, and neither were her husband and her lover. Even the dull psychiatrist hadn't been very interested in a problem as ordinary as hers. She was not even meat for a good case history, much less a novel. It had all been trivial, and probably in the end amounted to nothing more than that she had run into someone she liked sex with better than she liked it with her husband. Society didn't care what she did—not really. She wasn't being persecuted, or insulted at operas; she wouldn't lose her child; she had money and friends and looks and not even any reason to feel overwhelmingly guilty, since so far as she could tell, her husband was going to be happier in his new life than he had ever been with her. It was too near to nothing, all of it, and she didn't know why it had seemed so intense and so crucial and so much the end of everything when it had been all the time such an ordinary episode. She had scorned Jim for calling it tragic, yet there were times when she herself assumed it must be: tragic that they could not make a harmony out of their feelings, tragic that they could not be what they ought to be. But when she finished *Anna* she felt bruised by a sense of the triviality of her marriage, the timidity of her affair. The worst of it was that her memory was so bad. The passion Anna had felt for Vronsky was more easily remembered than anything she had felt for Hank. She could barely remember the good parts of her marriage or her affair. Her thoughts took her in circles, and in small ordinary circles, at that. In her depression she felt drab and worthless, just a shallow young woman who had managed to screw up two men, one of them her husband.

But when finally the depression lifted, it occurred to her that it was silly to go around moping because she wasn't Anna Karenina. It was sillier than any of the other things she had done. She took Davey with her to Mr. Plum's and let him try a piece of chewing gum. A blue piece. He swallowed it, but not before a dribble of blue coloring had run out his mouth, down his chin, and onto his white sweater. "I keep the gum there to make business for myself," Mr. Plum said. She took Davey into the park and sat on the jungle gym while he moved around and around it below, squinting up at her. Emma was driving by on her way home from taking Flap to Rice, and she stopped to yak awhile. She was looking peaked and feeling peaked and their moods clashed a little, for Patsy was just back to delighting in everything after two days of moping because her life lacked scale. She overresponded when Emma told her she had turned up pregnant.

"I'm envious," she said, and she was.

But Emma was in no mood to be envied. "Don't envy me if you want to remain my friend," she said glumly. "I wish I weren't so forgetful. I've got all the kids I need."

"Come on," Patsy said. "You couldn't not like a baby."

Emma sat down on a bench and sighed. "I can't not like a baby but I can damn well not like the idea of one. We'll only have been in Iowa City three months when it comes."

Patsy was tired of the song and dance of cheering Emma up with the possible virtues of Iowa City, so she didn't try. She told her she had been depressed by reading *Anna*. Emma thought she probably would be too, and soon hurried on. Patsy lingered with Davey in the park, thinking of Emma having another baby. The thought led back to herself. When would she have another? When would Davey get brothers and sisters? And who would their father be? It was a shivery thing to think about, and she felt too good to dwell on it, so she put Davey in his carriage and wheeled him briskly home. It was a warm February morning, and she found it difficult not to believe that something good would happen. What, when, with whom, she didn't know, but she could not feel downhearted on such a bright day. She had a fine son and a very pleasant house in which to wait.

===14===

Within a week something did happen, but instead of a new man coming into her life, an old man went out of it. She was feeding Davey spinach and making a mess of it, one day at lunch, when Roger Wagonner's sister called to tell her Roger was dead. His sister was older than he had been and had a dry cracked voice and the accents of West Texas.

"How did you know to call me?" Patsy asked, stunned. She had scarcely taken in the details, which were that Roger had had a stroke and had been dead two days when the mailman found him.

"Well, Roger wrote us about you, honey, when he decided to leave his property to you."

"I'm sorry," Patsy said. "I just can't think. What can I do?"

"Not much more to be done," the old lady said. "You know how thoughtful Roger was. He paid the funeral home two years ago, they told us. All we have to pay is the increase in price."

"Oh, dear. When will the funeral be?"

Tomorrow, she was told, and the old lady rambled on in her twangy small-town schoolteacher's tone about how good Roger had been, how methodical, how he had arranged with a neighbor to take care of his animals in such an event. Patsy numbly agreed, though she had never thought of him as methodical and couldn't, any more than she could immediately think of him as dead. Even in her numbness, though, she felt a certain embarrassment, and a fear that his sister would resent her because of the land. But before she could say anything the old lady relieved her mind.

"Honey, don't you be worried about us wanting that land," she said kindly. "We ain't got long to live ourselves and of course I guess he told you about us losing our boy, so don't you worry about it. If Billy had lived we would have wanted him to have it, but me and my husband can't hardly take care of what we've got in Wilbarger County, much less Roger's old place. We told him ourselves he ought to leave it to somebody young—somebody who could enjoy it."

"Oh, thank you," Patsy said, though she did not believe that she would ever enjoy it. The kindliness of the voice on the wire was so akin in tone to that of the man who was dead that it was causing her to cry. Her inclination was not to go to the funeral, or near the ranch at all for many months until her memories had worn smooth again, but then she recalled that Roger had driven all the way to Houston because she had had a child. The least she could do was go to his funeral, since he had died. She said she would be there and hung up.

She lay down on her couch to weep, but then got up and immediately began packing, still crying. She didn't want to give herself any time to think. In an hour and a half she, Juanita, and Davey were in the Ford and on the way to Dallas. Davey was cheerful and excited, bouncing on his car seat, patting Patsy's shoulder, and occasionally grabbing her hair. Juanita was worried about proprieties. She would be staying in Dallas to help Jeanette with Davey, and she had had to pack in such a hurry that she was sure she had come off without something that might be socially essential. Her weeks in Dallas while Jim had been recuperating had not intimidated her, exactly, but they had informed her. She knew Jeanette expected of her what one should expect of a maid, while Patsy's expectations were lighter and, she could not help feeling, somewhat erratic and eccentric. She loved Patsy dearly but she had always been a little worried about her behavior. Every few miles she bethought herself of something she might have left, and turned and rummaged in her handbag to see if it was there.

It was a bright cold March day, with a few small high clouds and a keen wind that caused the Ford some strain; it had not been on the open road in months and ran peculiarly, Patsy thought. Had she been able to keep her mind on it, she would have worried, but the state of the car she was driving was the last thing on her mind. It was as if Roger's death had caused all the silt and sediments of uncertainty to sift out of her emotions; they were a pure water as she drove. For the long hundred-mile stretch of the freeway that cut through the pine forests from Houston to Madisonville she was happy in the drive, the sun and blue sky and bright green of the trees all pleasing to her. Occasionally she tilted her head to the side and let her hair tickle Davey, who giggled and shoved her away. But mostly she just drove, and she scarcely looked around when he grew fretful with his car seat and Juanita took him out. He wailed deafeningly for ten miles and then went to sleep. She drove, untouched by Davey's wails or Juanita's worries. It was pleasant to drive and her destination and her reason for going were not in her mind, either.

But when she left the freeway and drove through the opening country Roger did come to her mind. That he was dead came to her mind—the country brought the fact in now and then. Some horses standing on a hill, a gray farmhouse standing in isolation far off the road, the pickups parked at a country store at a little crossroads community—such things reminded her. After three hours, when she was beyond the heavy forests, the loosening and spreading of the land itself as it began its long roll westward toward the plains, that too reminded her. She would cross a roll of land and see farther than she had seen in months, see the land spreading away for thirty miles under the gathering afternoon clouds, colder land than the forests and covered still with winter grass. When she thought of Roger her eyes filled—not really from pain, but from a kind of sorrow, sorrow that she had not gone to see him again, sorrow that she would not talk with him again. Of all the people she missed in life there was suddenly one that she must miss forever. No more words would pass between them. It was an awful thought.

"We cry but it does them no good," Juanita said nervously. Crying was for the house, to her mind, not for a crowded highway.

"I'm not crying for him," Patsy said calmly. "He was happy enough. I wished he had lived until Davey was older."

And she glanced back at Davey, asleep on his stomach on

the seat, his face mashed into the crack of the seat and one foot bare. He would not remember the old man who had taken him riding; that would belong to her and not to him.

She decided to spend the night in Dallas and drive on to the funeral in the morning. At dinner, offhandedly, in telling her mother and father what kind of man Roger Wagonner had been, she mentioned that he had left his ranch to Jim and herself. To her surprise, instead of seeing it as a generous but, all circumstances considered, reasonable act, they both became terribly upset, particularly when she told them she would probably spend a day or two there, seeing what shape things were in and what the details of the inheritance really were.

"But he was not really related to you," Jeanette said. "Why would he leave his land to you?"

"He had no one else. Besides, he left it to both of us, not just to me."

"Well, it seems to me Jim is the one who ought to be looking into it," Garland said stiffly. "You don't know anything about things like that and besides it won't look good. If you ask me you ought to call him."

"I mean to, but it's two hours earlier there. He's barely off work. He's not likely to come, though. I can do it. It should be fairly simple. After all, I'll be there."

Jeanette, to Patsy's surprise, was extremely flustered. "But you aren't related to him," she said again. "I'm sure it won't seem the usual thing at all, to the people who knew him. I think your father just means it would be better if you waited until some time when Jim is with you."

"Why?" Patsy asked. "I thought I explained to you that so far as I know, Jim won't be with me any more. I simply have to do things on my own now."

Then it dawned on her what they were upset about—that the townspeople would construe it that she had somehow seduced Roger in order to get the land. Her parents thought that people would see her as a siren who had appeared at the eleventh hour and acquired all an old man had worked for all his life. The recognition of how they assumed people would look at it made her white with anger, and she put down her fork.

"You never fail, do you?" she said. "Why did you have to

think that? Do I look that bad? Why did you have to think that?"

The sight of her anger was enough to switch her parents' mood. They instantly decided their apprehensions had been ridiculous, but the damage had been done, so far as Patsy was concerned.

"His own sister told me she was glad about it," she said. "I don't care what you think people might think about *me*, but what do you think people think about *him*? He lived there all his life. Do you think people saw him as a fool? Or a lecher? He was a fine man."

"Well, we just didn't know him," Garland said, very humble pie. "If we had we wouldn't have said it."

Patsy was so disturbed that she decided not to spend the night. Her anger wore off, but she didn't want to be exposed to her parents' way of thinking through the evening. Before she left, her parents had become so apologetic about it all that she was doubly glad to be leaving.

But once she got out of Dallas into the open country she almost regretted her haste and her moodiness. Driving at night by herself was very different from driving in the daytime with Davey and Juanita. She had never driven any distance alone at night. At Denton she turned off the big well-trafficked highway onto a small state road and for a stretch of thirty miles was almost the only car in sight. After the rush of traffic out of Dallas, the road seemed very silent. The Ford's radio had long since ceased to work, so she hadn't even that company. The Ford itself was still making peculiar sounds, and she couldn't help wondering what she would do if it broke down. She saw now and then the yellow light of a farmhouse window off the road, but couldn't really imagine herself walking across the fields to such a house. There would be giant dogs, probably. On the other hand, she didn't want to stand by the road and present herself to the uncertain mercies of midnight travelers. She felt frightened just driving, and it annoyed her. After weeks alone she should be above such girlishness. But in Houston there were houses, not dark fields and pastures, and street lights at a comfortable height on the corners, not the countless cold stars far above. When she had driven the West with Jim, the vastness and the stars at night had delighted her, but with

Jim she had felt safe within the car, and alone she didn't feel safe at all. What the whole evening had done was persuade her again that she needed a man. She wished Jim had been home for her calls. The inheritance, contrary to what she had said, might have been just the thing to bring him back. At the moment she wanted him back. Perversely, once it was too late, her parents' flusterments seemed quite natural. What *would* people think when she popped in the day of the funeral to inquire about her land?

In a town called Bowie she stopped at a filling station to consult her map. The little town of Thalia, where Roger was to be buried, was so small she wanted to be sure she wouldn't miss it. She got out and asked the attendant, a young man in a Levi jacket, if he would please look under her hood and tell her if anything was drastically wrong. He immediately informed her that she needed a new fan belt and went off to see if he had one that would fit. The wind from the north swept across the bare bright concrete, very cold; after shivering for a minute Patsy decided to wait inside the warm office. It was heated by a gas stove, the flames flickering and blue, and was so warm that the plate-glass windows had fogged over. The lights outside were a strange blur. She decided she wanted a Coke and while the young man changed her fan belt she sat on a small iron bridge chair, all the paint worn off, sipping a Coke and eating a package of cheese crisps. There was a radio on the desk next to the green credit-card machine, and it was playing a hillbilly song. A late-night high-watt station in Fort Worth was trying to sell an album of hillbilly favorites from yesteryear, fifty songs for two ninety-eight. The album was called *The Teardrop Special*. She heard "Take These Chains from My Heart," and then the announcer went into a three- or four-minute spiel about the album. The announcer was everybody's friend and had always been everybody's friend:

"Folks, these are songs you've all heard many times, songs we all love. Some of the singers you'll hear are dead now, but I know most of you haven't forgotten them and I know you'll want this album. Why, it'll bring all these great country singers into your homes again, just like old times, you know, when all you had to do to hear 'em was turn your radio dial. Just as soon as I tell you what you have to do to get this fine album we're going to play another song, this one'll be the old 'Panhandle Rag,' by Monroe Malory, the old Wichita Ranger, but first get out your pencil and paper and take down this address . . ."

It scarcely registered; Patsy crumpled up the cellophane the cheese crisps had come in. When it did register, the announcer was going on about how they could receive the album C.O.D. She waited, not sure she had heard aright, but it turned out she had. Finally, after the announcer had repeated the address four times, she heard the voice of Hank's father:

> *I was ram-bul-lin' throooough*
> *A Texas border tooown . . .*

and on through a little story about a traveling man who met a woman. They fell in love but it didn't work out and the man went on to ramble through other towns. It was not a convincing song; the rhythm was too snappy for the story. There were tones in the voice that were like tones in Hank's, but the person Monroe Malory's voice really reminded her of was her own father. There was whiskey in the voice, and the same falseness of tone; it brought back to her her father's red-faced confusion at the supper table, confusion perpetually trying to wear the mask of good nature. The young attendant came in while the song was playing and Patsy got some change and walked across the street to a phone booth near a street light. It seemed to be the only phone booth in town. Hank was not at his apartment but she got him at the movie theater where he worked. He was just closing up. It was a bad connection, as if the cold north wind were blowing through the phone.

"Hi," she said. "I'm on my way to a funeral and I just heard one of your father's records."

She told him about it and they both laughed a little at the incongruity of their positions in the world, he in an art theater on the cap rock, she in a spidery phone booth in Bowie. "Amazing invention, the phone," she said.

When she told him where she was going he was silent a

minute and she knew why. It was less than two hundred miles from where he was. He wanted to come and see her. She had considered it as she walked across the street, and she didn't feel against it. She felt for it. So when he asked she said okay. He agreed to come the day after the burial.

"I'll be at the ranch house, I guess," she said. "I'm getting all these houses lately. You'll have to ask someone how to get there. I don't really remember."

The connection got dramatically worse and they gave up on the conversation. Patsy got in the Ford and went on. For forty-five miles she drove through a townless stretch of ranch country, rolling, scarcely wooded at all, no lights except those of distant oil rigs or oil flares. The little town, when she finally came to it, was on a hill, or a ridge, so that she saw its lights miles away. Once she did get there she realized how stupid she had been not to wait until morning, for it was obvious that everyone in the tiny hotel was long since asleep. There was a light over the desk and in lieu of a bell there was a horseshoe which could be struck with a piece of iron if the management had to be summoned. Patsy felt very silly. She carried in her suitcase, in order to delay striking the horseshoe. She was tempted to try and sleep in the car, but it was too cold. Finally, reluctantly, she hit it. It made an amazingly loud sound, but the silence of the hotel, and of the town, was as complete as ever once the sound had died. She had to strike it twice more before she heard a thump upstairs. Very shortly an old man came running downstairs and crashed into the desk alarmingly hard. It startled her a great deal. In his grogginess he had accidentally built up speed and had to keep running to keep from falling. He wore a flannel robe of faded maroon and had a mop of tousled gray hair.

"Excuse me," he said, holding his side and grimacing. "I ain't got my wits about me. I started downstairs thinking I was in a dream, and when I woke up I was about to fall on my face. Good thing the desk was between me and the window, I'd a run right through it and cut myself up."

"I'm sorry," Patsy said. "It's my fault for coming in so late." He was obviously in pain from having hit the desk so hard, and she felt herself to be an inordinate lot of trouble, especially since the room she took only cost three dollars.

"That's very cheap," she said, wondering what the room would be like.

"Yeah, about the only people who sleep here are folks who break out of jail," he said. "It's just across the alley. You must have read your map wrong, or you wouldn't be here. This ain't exactly the crossroads of the world."

"No, I came for a funeral. I'll just be here one night."

"Oh, Roger, I guess," he said, still rubbing his ribs. "Knew him all my life. Been funny if I had killed myself coming down to register you, wouldn't it? They could have buried me and Roger together, except they'd have had to bury me on credit."

The morning took some getting up to. The old man, whose name was Holiday, had provided her with ample cover and she slept so well and warmly that when she awoke she was extremely reluctant to exchange the comfort and snugness of the bed for the grimness of everything around it. The night before the room had seemed all right. In the flat morning light it was bare and dusty and ugly, a hotel room out of Dreiser or some Midwestern novelist, chair, scratched yellow pine dresser, white gas stove which she had no way of lighting. The rug was frayed. It was a room for males, and males who didn't intend to use it more than a night or two. The shade was only half drawn and beyond it she could see the housetops of the town, and the country beyond the town. The sky was gray, almost the color of dust, though she didn't know if the dustiness was in the sky or on the unwashed windows. It didn't look like a world worth getting up to, particularly since it was very cold. She solved the heat problem by skipping in and running a hot bath in the narrow tub. Fifteen minutes' soaking left her warm enough to dress in the sober dress she had brought, and when she got downstairs Mr. Holiday, looking as if he still hadn't his wits fully about him, told her not to worry, it was due to warm up in the afternoon.

At the little cafe where she ate breakfast they fried eggs exactly as Roger had fried them. A couple of cowboys were there, and a civil servant or two, having coffee. All looked at her curiously.

The funeral was to be in a small red brick church, with cedar trees flanking the door. Patsy sat in front, in the Ford, with the motor running and the heater on, waiting for the crowd to gather. Roger's sister found her easily. She was as tall and angular as he had been, and looked twenty years older than he had looked, with white hair and furrows of powder on her cheeks. She and her heavy, silent bald husband, along with Patsy, constituted Roger's family, and they sat in the front of the church. Soon the church filled with his friends. The men looked uncomfortable in their suits, and in contrast to them the two heavy young men from the funeral home, in attempting to appear suave, appeared dandified. With their pompadours and heavy self-seriousness they reminded her of the show steers she had seen at the stock show. Roger's sister—Mrs. Daniels, she was—kept whispering details of this and that as the church filled and the organist began to play.

Perhaps because of the ushers, perhaps because of Mrs. Daniels, perhaps because she couldn't really connect it with Roger, the funeral didn't touch her. She was dry-eyed and not sorrowful at all. It was a generally quiet funeral. No one seemed near hysterics. Mrs. Daniels' long narrow face was grave, but scarcely racked by emotion. Two ministers gave modest eulogies; a fat woman sang "The Old Rugged Cross"; and an aged preacher, considerably shakier than Roger had ever been, gave a short sermon on the theme of dust to dust. Patsy's mind was on Hank. She was getting a slight case of cold feet, a slight sense that it had been a mistake to agree to let him come.

Passing out of the church, she glanced at the dead man as briefly as was decent; she didn't want to see him. It was the only time she had ever seen him in a tie; the oddness of that was enough to cause her to turn away. At the graveyard, watching the people who stood around waiting for the casket to be lowered, it occurred to her that probably the only times Roger had worn ties was at funerals, his own or someone else's. The tall rawfaced men stuck out of their department store suits as angularly and awkwardly as the bare mesquites around the graveyard stuck out of the wintry earth. They were all wrists and necks, but afterward, when several of them grouped together to smoke, they made a good windbreak. The sprays of flowers looked odd against the cold clods and gray mesquite grass. They were real flowers, but were so unnatural there that they looked like plastic. Mrs. Daniels introduced her to a number of the old ladies; they were so kindly that they made her feel shy, and their stockings were twisted. The graveyard stood on the northeast edge of the ridge that held the town, and the wind that sang across the rolling gray plains rustled the old ladies' veils. In the northeast the gray clouds were breaking a little, and patches of sky could be seen. It was far from warm and Patsy was glad when they could go. She felt quite calm.

Mrs. Daniels took her to the house of a friend, where they had lunch. It was a small squat house whose living room was almost filled with ugly china dogs. The two old ladies talked about their high school romances, and Roger's, while their husbands and Patsy ate in silence the fried chicken, mashed potatoes, and green beans that were available in quantity.

After lunch she was introduced to Roger's lawyer, a paunchy man who apparently owned the best suit in town. Her duty done, Mrs. Daniels and her husband departed for their home in Wilbarger County, assuring Patsy that there was everything at the ranch house that she would need. The lawyer looked her over circumspectly and came straight to the point, which was oil leases. Various companies had drilled with no success, but various others wanted to drill.

"Be funny if they were to bring in a big well now, after he lived there bone poor all his life," he said. "That's the way it happens half the time."

Patsy told him her father was an oil man; she would ask him about it. She thought of Roger, and of Jim, and became depressed. Roger's gift had shown a faith in them that they had not lived up to. She left the law office feeling slightly cheap but equipped with numerous keys and the name of a neighbor whom she could contact if anything puzzled her. On the way out of town she stopped at a filling station to find out how to get to the ranch. They told her, of course, that the owner of the ranch had just that day been buried and were very surprised when she told him she was his heir.

The warming that Mr. Holiday promised had come, after all. It was three in the afternoon when she left the town; all the morning's clouds had blown away, the western sky was a lovely deep blue, and the sun was just beginning to drop in its short arc. It had grown so much warmer in only a few hours that she shrugged her coat off and turned down the heater in the Ford.

As soon as she got to the brown road turning off into the pastures, she felt secure about the way and began to feel happy, though it was a little strange to be spending a night in the country absolutely alone. Once she slipped off in a rut that had been made by some heavy vehicle after a rain, and the Ford bounced and squirmed the whole length of the rut before climbing out. "Atta boy," she said, patting the dashboard. When deprived of all other companions she often talked to the Ford. In the corner of the back seat was one of Davey's boot socks, kicked off while he was napping and overlooked, giving her a vision of him scrabbling about her mother's house with one foot bare. A covey of bobwhites scurried across the road in front of her and she slowed so as to miss a laggard. After the grim cloudiness of the morning the bright sun was beautiful, touching the grass and the wires of the fences, the coats of the small hurrying birds, and the old fraying bark that still clung to the fence posts. A longing took her for Jim. If she had been able to get him, and he had come home, and could be driving with her, surely it would fix them and they would be all right. She regretted having called Hank at all. She should have kept on until she got Jim. It was Jim Davey needed, or would need.

The ranch house was unusually, almost uncomfortably, clean and spic and was well provisioned, along certain lines. There were three cakes on the kitchen table, an angel food, a chocolate, and a coconut, each minus one slice. There was also a huge neatly covered plate of cold fried chicken and a bowl of cole slaw—all gifts of the funeral party.

Out of habit, Patsy went into the bedroom where she and Jim had stayed, took off her sober funeral dress, put on blue jeans and sneakers and a sweater, and combed her hair. As she was looking out the window a red pickup drove past and stopped at the barn. A tall man in a Levi jacket got out and went quickly into the barn. For a second she was frightened,

749

but then she remembered that someone had described the neighbor she was supposed to rely on as a tall fellow. That was probably the man. She looked up his name in her address book and saw that it was Melvin Huston. She decided to be bold and go and meet him. She got her leather jacket, the most Western thing she owned, and left the house.

When she got to the barn and peeped in, Melvin was standing in the hallway sacking oats, scooping them out of a bin with a big scoop shovel and easing them skillfully into a sack set between his legs. Patsy felt shy about making her presence known. Melvin was as tall as Roger, at least twice as heavy, and was very absorbed in sacking oats.

"Hi," she said. "You must be Mr. Huston."

Melvin deftly sacked the scoopful of oats he had in hand, looked up at her in blank surprise for a second, then gave her the sort of grin that is said to be as big as all outdoors. It certainly seemed to stretch across the hallway of the old barn.

"Why, howdy, howdy," he said, coming over and shaking her hand. "Mrs. Carpenter, I bet."

He said it so vigorously and quickly that Patsy assumed a lively stream of conversation would follow. None did. Just Melvin's grin. Having said her name he seemed mildly bewildered as to what to say to her next, but he kept smiling to assure her of his good will.

"Are those oats?" Patsy asked, more or less rhetorically.

"Uh, yeah, them's oats," Melvin assured her. "Sacking up a few for them old horses. Actually Roger told me a year ago if it ever come to this to pasture the horses and take what horse feed there was. Never figured you'd need it, I guess."

"No, I certainly don't need it," Patsy said, peeping into the various stalls of the barn. "You're welcome to it all." She opened a door latch with a piece of leather and saw a room full of miscellaneous junk. There were numerous buckets, a couple of very old saddles, a motor, a shotgun leaning against the wall, and many smelly gallon bottles that had once held some kind of crude medicine. Melvin surveyed the room with a look of slight embarrassment, as if its disordered condition was somehow his fault.

"Little bit of everything in there," he said in an instructional tone. "That's a shotgun—old single shot."

"I see," Patsy said, deciding not to ask him to explain much to her.

"Say, I'm plumb sick I didn't make the funeral," Melvin said, and a really sorrowful look crossed his face. "Long as me and Mr. Waggoner been neighbors, wouldn't seem like there was no excuse, but I been calving my young heifers this month and I was right in the middle of trying to get a calf out and didn't have no help and didn't hardly see how I could turn it loose. In fact I'd a given what the calf is worth to have had Mr. Waggoner there to help me. He was as good as a vet at that kind of thing."

"Don't feel bad about it," she said, seeing that, despite the calf, he did feel bad about it. "It was a very quick funeral."

"I guess it was," Melvin said. He had resumed his sacking and was working efficiently, glancing at her now and then. "I come on in as soon as I got cleaned up, hoping to catch up with it at the graveyard at least, but everybody had done left and there wasn't much I could do but kick a few clods around. Don't nothing ever happen convenient for me."

There was the sound of the shovel hitting oats and then of oats sifting into the filling sack.

"Course it wasn't convenient for Mr. Waggoner, either," he added, still working. "Me and him was gonna dehorn his yearlings this week."

The way he kept calling Roger Mr. Waggoner stabbed at her suddenly. Though he must have known Roger for years it was clear that he had never called him anything but Mr. Waggoner; and the thought of Melvin, in whatever kind of suit he could own, the blood of birth barely off his hands, alone at the filled-in-grave, hit her hard. It had the sort of poignance the funeral had utterly lacked. She went outside while Melvin finished sacking the oats, and dipped her fingers in the icy water of the watering trough. Her eyes and lashes were wet. The animals were gone. No horses, no milk cow, no chickens. When Melvin came out and with a grunt heaved the heavy sack into his pickup she had recovered and asked him about them.

"Oh, my wife got the chickens yesterday," he said. "I

guess we'll deep freeze 'em. We don't keep no hens. The milk cow's got a fresh calf, so I got her over where I can milk her handier. Bet you think I'm running off with all your livestock. Jump in and I'll show you what you got left."

She got in the red pickup and as the late winter sun fell, Melvin, talking a blue streak at last, gave her a bouncy tour of her new estate. He took her to four pastures, pointing out what he took to be the salient features of each in his hearty tones. Here and there were cattle grazing amid the leafless trees. In each of the pastures, when he came to what seemed to him a strategic spot, Melvin stopped and stood on the running board of the pickup, the door open, calling the cattle. Occasionally he honked the pickup horn, but only as a kind of accompaniment to his own voice. She had never heard cattle called, and though it was a little deafening she liked to listen. In the still, clear late-evening air Melvin's strong voice carried far across the pastures. At times she heard its echo, though what it was echoing off of she couldn't imagine. The cattle heard and responded. She could see cows half a mile away lift their heads, listen a minute, and then immediately move toward the pickup, often bellowing in answer.

Melvin seemed to count the incoming rush of cattle with some amazing computer in his head, for forty or fifty animals would sweep in and mill around the pickup, bumping it with their hips, and in five seconds Melvin would lean in with a slightly worried look on his big face and say, "Forty-six here, that's missing nine, must be a little pocket over in the southwest corner that can't hear me, sure would like to see 'em," and then would step down, alternately whoop and cluck at the cows as if they were giant hens, and would dole them out a little trail of cowfeed from a sack he kept handy in the back. By the time the cows had lined up to eat, shoving at one another, and their calves trying to shove in to be near them, Melvin would be back in the cab and they would be off again to another pasture. "Got to get away quick," he said. "I never gave them but a little dribble. Didn't want 'em to think I'd call 'em in for nothin'." In his walk down the line of cows he would have acquired all manner of intimate information which he conveyed to Patsy as he drove, assuming, apparently, that she would remember the cows he was talking about. One had had a calf she hadn't brought to the feed ground; one was looking like she was due to calve that night or in a day or two; one was getting hoof rot, though he didn't know how, no more rain than there'd been; and a number had disposition or personality problems that displeased and worried him.

"Goodness, you seem to know them as well as Roger did," she said, a little awed. She had assumed that Roger's way with animals was a rare and magical thing, and it was surprising to hear a big pleasant goon like Melvin talking about them in the same tones, and so informedly. It occurred to her that if one could relate to animals, country life might not be so lonely.

"Well, we neighbored a lot," Melvin said. "He knowed mine about as well as I knowed his."

When the tour of the pastures was finished the sun was just down. Melvin let her out at her back gate and got out and stood by the gate a minute while Patsy thanked him for his kindness and rather awkwardly attempted to work out some arrangement where he would be caretaker of the land and do or have done whatever needed to be done. It was obvious to her that Melvin was going to do whatever needed doing anyway, and she wanted him to be fairly paid.

The subject embarrassed him considerably. He pushed his hat back off his windburned forehead, slapped himself on the thigh with his gloves, chewed a grass blade, inspected the ground, inspected the sky, kicked his pickup tire, shook a post in the yard fence to see if it needed replacing, and acknowledged, finally, that although his time wasn't worth a whole lot he guessed he could take a little something for looking after the cows until he could find a good buyer for them. He supposed fifty dollars a month and Patsy, assuming he was underpaying himself by at least half, insisted on a hundred. Melvin, red-faced, finally agreed because he figured it wouldn't take more than a month or two to get the cattle sold.

"Nice little bunch of cows," he said. "Wisht I had the money to buy 'em myself."

Patsy was hoping he would say that and said, "Why don't you? I'm not pressed for money. You could pay me in installments, if you needed to."

"Ma'am, I couldn't raise an installment on one cow, much less two hundred," he said. "Many thanks, anyway."

Patsy let it go, determined to pursue it later, when they were better acquainted. As she went into the yard Melvin looked at her worriedly, as if it had just dawned on him that she intended to spend some time there all by herself. Clearly, at some point during the drive through the pastures, she had revealed herself to him as a city girl.

"Say, Miss Pat," he said, "you run up against anything you can't handle while you're here be sure and give us a call. We don't live but two miles over there, won't take no time for my wife or me to get there. We ain't good for much but we do believe in neighboring."

"Thanks. I will if you'll call me Patsy," she said, touched. "But I'll only be here tomorrow and tomorrow night. A friend's coming by to see me. If I don't see you again this trip I'll see you next time I'm up. Please call me collect when there's anything I should know about."

Melvin promised and touched his hat to her and was soon in the red pickup, bouncing over the cattle guard. A towsack blew out, but he didn't notice. She walked through the yard and picked it up and hung it on the yard fence near the gate, where Melvin could find it next time he came.

Walking through the back yard, she remembered that she had forgotten to ask about Bob, the old dog. He was nowhere to be seen, so she assumed the Hustons had adopted him too. With the failing of the light the yard and the long sloping plain to the west of the house had a colder, grayer look, as did the house, the old smokehouse, everything but the few black angular mesquite trees and the glowing spot on the western horizon where the sun had just disappeared. Bob would have been someone to talk to.

In the darkening house the three gashed cakes, the plate of chicken, and the bowl of coleslaw faced her like so many unwanted bridal gifts for whom thank-you notes had to be written. She looked more closely and saw that Mrs. Daniels had pasted the name of the owner to each plate, so she could return them when she passed through town. Patsy felt a bad, lonely depression building up and only managed to stave it off by building a fire in the living-room fireplace. It took her thirty minutes, but the cheer it produced was more than worth it. She dragged the couch over—Rosemary's couch, and probably not sat on three times since her death—and made herself a sandwich with the last of the peanut butter she had bought so long ago. She ate and drank milk and began a MacKinlay Kantor novel in one of the twenty or so *Reader's Digest* condensed books, which, with a Bible and a Sunday School teachers' handbook, piles of *Reader's Digests* and *The Cattleman,* a half-dozen J. Frank Dobie books, and a small nineteenth-century edition in blue floral binding of Owen Meredith's *Lucile,* filled the little glass-fronted bookcase by the fireplace, constituting the Waggoner library. When she finished the MacKinlay Kantor novel she went back to the kitchen for milk and discovered that the chocolate cake was not at all bad. She reduced its girth considerably. There was lots of dry mesquite wood. She returned and lay late by the fire. After MacKinlay Kantor she read Daphne Du Maurier. She felt untroubled; the fire was nice, the logs popped loudly, making virtually the only noise.

It was the silence of the house and land that made her slightly conscious of how isolated she was, and the sense was heightened when she stepped out on the cold front porch for a minute. It was not terribly cold, but cold enough, and the stillness, the moonlight and the stars over the plains gave the night air a cleanness and clarity that were tangible; everything in sight was very distinct: the cedars, the yard gate, the old swing at the end of the porch. It was the opposite of Houston, whose warm, foggy, mushy nights melted everything together, made neons pastel and figures blur. The night was so beautifully clear that it was disturbing, and too dry even for smells. And while the keen air felt good on Patsy's skin, the goose-bumpy cold prickling her ankles and neck, she could not help missing her own front yard at night, with its misty light and spunky odor and wet leaves.

Upstairs, she poked a little, discovering that the TV set she had assumed the Hustons had liberated with the livestock was still in Roger's bedroom. She turned it on, but the reception was awful and she quickly turned it off again. The deep cedar closet in the hall smelled of mothballs and there were still ladies' dresses hanging in it, dresses of the forties, dresses that ought to be given to museums. There were boxes of bank statements and boxes of snapshots, but she was too tired to snoop seriously. There was also, in the big closet, an old windup phonograph with a few thick seventy-eight records in its record cabinet. She found some needles and by winding with one hand and holding the needle arm with the other managed to play a part of a badly scratched Jimmy Rodgers' record:

> *My mothah was a lady,*
> *And yours I would allow,*
> *And you may have a sis-tah*
> *Who need pro-tecshun now . . .*

Quaint as it was, she soon decided it was not worth the effort it took to wind it. In her room and gowned and in bed she discovered that it was possible to make do with the overhead light as a reading light if she burrowed under the covers and poked her head out where her feet would ordinarily have been, so that the light was directly above her. The quilts that were on the bed must have been resurrected by Mrs. Daniels, for they smelled of mothballs and long years in a cedar shelf, a lovely smell to go sleep with, and when the quilts had made her yawn and Daphne Du Maurier had made her yawn several times, she tiptoed and turned out the light and, leaving the morrow for the morrow, went to sleep.

15

It was when she awoke, alone in his house, that the knowledge that Roger was dead struck her. She woke early, warm under the quilts but aware that she was in a strange place. Outside, the sharp keen starshot darkness had changed to vague gray. Patsy tried to go back to sleep, but she was not sleepy. Every time she looked out the window the light had become a little stronger and she could see a little more of the slope leading to the barn. The ground was white with frost; everything was absolutely silent in the house. There was no creaking of boards as Roger walked down the hall, no sounds of bootheels on the stairs, no water running, no toilet flushing, no muffled sounds from the kitchen as he made breakfast. There was only her own breath and the creak of the bedsprings when she turned on her side. She marked his absence in the absence of the sounds she had been accustomed to him making on her few visits.

A little later, when she got up and sat shivering in her bathrobe, tying her sneakers, she looked out the window and saw the slope, white with frost and sparkling beautifully with sunlight, and saw the empty lots, the barn with no animals near it, the chickenless chicken house, and marked again, quietly enough, the absence of Roger. The land was there still, but not the man, and the morning light that had always called Roger forth would call him forth no more. She cried a little in the bathroom, not through any excess of grief, but because she saw his razor. She was snooping in the bathroom cabinet and it was still there, an old razor, all the silver plating long ago worn off, so that it was like a brass artifact. It still had a blade in it, but she took it out and

757

decided to keep the razor. After a bit she felt all right and went down and made oatmeal in an improvised double boiler and then cleaned out the cabinets thoroughly and washed all the wooden-handled knives and forks.

She was standing by the cabinet drying them with a coarse dishtowel when she heard the cattle guard rattle and in a minute saw Hank drive up to the back gate and park his old Oldsmobile beside the Ford. He got out and peeked in the Ford, as if to reassure himself by the familiar clutter in the back seat that she was somewhere about. His hair was a little longer but otherwise he seemed the same as he had seemed when she watched him leave the filling station. He still wore the brown suede coat.

She went to the screen and met him, attempting to look critical and severe, but it didn't work. She had been lonely and he was very much the same—more greedy than talkative. In less than an hour they were attempting to restore the quilts and sheets of the bed to some sort of order. Patsy went over and raised the window. The day was warming, but the bedroom was still cold enough to raise goose bumps all over her body and she hoped to let some warm air in. She felt somewhat snippy and irritable about the rapidity of the proceedings. Hank looked complacent, and the look annoyed her a little. She got in bed and turned her back on him, so as not to see it. He immediately tried to turn her over, but she clutched the post at the head of the bed. One nice thing about the bed was that it had something she could hang on to.

"Quit," she said. "Go rope a cow or something. Why bother me? Thirty minutes you've been here and you've already got seduction out of the way and can get on with your work, whatever it is. Quit tugging."

He tugged and she clung to the bedpost, gritting her teeth. She felt very determined.

"What's wrong?" he asked. "Aren't you happy?"

"No," she said. "I have a very bad character, or I wouldn't let myself be seduced so quickly."

He decided her mood was best ignored, and got up and went to the kitchen. When he came back he had a plate of cold chicken, a large hunk of cake, and some milk. Patsy was feeling somewhat better. He sat on the bed eating chicken, cake, and milk while Patsy lazed and threw out small criticisms from the depths of the quilts.

"What an eye," she said. "You spotted that chicken in two seconds, while you were chasing me through the kitchen. I have a feeling I'm little better than a chicken to you."

"You're warmer than this one," he said, folding the end of the quilt over his bare feet.

He put the cake plate on the floor and Patsy leaned out of the covers and broke herself off a piece. She had some milk from his glass.

"Don't get crumbs in the bed," he said.

"Why not? There's everything else in here." She reached down and after some searching came out with the *Reader's Digest* condensed book that she had read the night before. It had been kicked aside during the lovemaking.

They spent the morning in bed making up for months of separateness. She got seduced again, more satisfyingly, and when she finally got up insisted that he help her wrestle the old phonograph downstairs. Then they went out. The day had warmed up and was very sunny. They fiddled awhile with a tractor that was behind the barn and finally decided it was inoperative. Then they climbed up into the loft and sat in the open loft door looking across the land. Patsy became pensive and worried. Everything was so uncertain.

"What if Jim wants all this?" she asked. "He might come back and decide to be married to me now that we own a ranch."

Hank had no views on what Jim might do. As they were about to go down she saw him eyeing a pile of hay. "Uh-oh," she said. "I have a feeling I'm about to hear a hackneyed metaphor." But for whimsey's sake they inspected the hay together. It was the leavings of several barnloads of alfalfa and baled oats and was stubbly and scratchy and quite uninviting, even as a place to sit. "It would be like doing it on a bed of nails," she said.

In the afternoon she decided it would be pleasant to retrace in the Ford the tour she had taken with Melvin, so they set out. They couldn't find any real cowfeed, but she insisted that Hank put a few pounds of oats in a sack, in case cows came up and acted ravenous. "It's my obligation to feed them if they approach, I believe," she said, somewhat worried about it. She did not want to disappoint her own cows.

"Who would have thought I'd end up responsible for a bunch of cows?" she said, concentrating intently on her driving. The road was narrow, very bumpy, and full of roots, ruts, and what seemed to be small stumps. In the first two pastures they didn't see a single cow, much to Patsy's chagrin. Worried though she was about what to do if a lot came, she still wanted to show Hank that she had them. He was irreverent and skeptical and it was a relief, in the third pasture, to see twenty or more grazing with their calves among the mesquite, not far from the road. One or two cows raised their heads when they passed, but most paid the car no attention at all.

"We have no rapport yet," she said. "They're going to be sold, so I guess we never will."

They came to the place where Melvin had done the feeding the day before. It was ringed with piles of dung. Patsy drove on adventurously; since the road was getting no worse it would be fun to see where it went. It ended a mile farther on, at a long shallow-looking pool of water with an earthen dam at one end. As they pulled up and stopped a large gray crane rose from the shallows and flew away. His take-off was so heavy and awkward it seemed he might not clear the mesquite, but as he rose higher he flew more swiftly and more gracefully and soon disappeared to the north.

They got out and sat on the dam of the tank for a while, plinking little stones into the water. "I wish Davey were here," Patsy said. "He'd love all this." She wished also that a few cows would come by. It seemed to her that she remembered that cows came to water in the afternoons, and it would be a nice way to meet some. It had grown quite warm.

"Too bad it isn't summer," he said. "We could go swimming."

"You could. For all you know these tanks have alligators. I'm not swimming in unauthorized waters, even if I own them."

When they got tired of sitting on the dam they went back to the Ford. In the course of some light necking Hank developed an urgent desire for her. She fanned it a bit, for amusement, only to discover that he was serious.

"Come on," she said. "What can you be thinking of? This is a family car."

"It's my life's ambition," he said.

"I can believe that—it's your only ambition." She surveyed the Ford hastily, not really opposed, only a little skeptical. But he laid her in the front seat, and they managed, almost comfortably. The front seat was warm from the sun shining through the glass, a little too warm, and the outside air felt cool on her bare legs. She held to the steering wheel with one hand and Hank with the other. Afterward, standing barefoot on the short prickly grass, nude from the waist down and trying to untangle her rolled-together jeans and panties she felt it was all very silly, the whole business—what ridiculous moments it involved.

"I'm glad no cows came by," she said.

It seemed to be a day for doing it. That night they ate the rest of the chicken, all the coleslaw, and most of the angel food cake, then built a fire and lay in front of it on the couch, watching very blurred television. They brought down some quilts and eventually ended up wearing quilts rather than clothes. Television was dull as well as blurry and sex easily drove it out. Aunt Rosemary's couch, though not ideal, was more comfortable than the Ford. Afterward Patsy sat on the hearth, feeding the fire, her front warm and her back cool, basking, feeling wonderfully dreamy and lazy. They went to sleep scrunched on the couch and only hours later, when the fire was out and both were uncomfortable, did they manage to drag themselves and the quilts up to the bedroom. The sheets were icy.

When they awoke the next morning the floors were icy and the sheets warm, and their clothes were downstairs. It was bright and sunshiny outside but very cold in the bedroom, which made conditions ideal for dawdling. They dawdled and argued about the future, all pleasantly. Patsy got up, tiptoed to the john, and came back a mass of goose bumps, to snuggle gratefully back into the warm bed. Hank was for staying a day or two, but she was firm against it. "I have to get back to Dallas," she said. "Anyway, I'd just sap your manhood if we stayed any longer."

Hunger eventually drove them up, but the only thing left to eat was oatmeal. She made some brittle toast from bread that was a week old, and then firmly sent him off. "Maybe I'll meet you every full moon, or something," she said. She felt very good, glad that he had gone without a scene, and went into the house to get a washrag and the broom. The Ford needed cleaning out. She scrubbed the front seat and fished from between the seats a quarter Juanita was always complaining about having lost. She loosened the back seat a little and found another quarter, a nickel, two dusty pennies, a map of Salt Lake City, a blue comb, a ball-point pen, a tie clasp of Jim's that she had not seen in years, toothpicks and chewing gum wrappers in quantity, and a dusty crumpled letter from Emma, written only three months after she and Jim married, when Emma was pregnant with Teddy. She reread the letter, which was full of the miseries of pregnancy, and of Flap's neglect and general intransigence, all cheerfully related in the very literary epistolary style they had used in their letters in those days.

For a minute she was sad. She put the letter and Jim's tie clasp in the glove compartment. He had liked it, she remembered; she could mail it to him. Working for IBM must require one to wear ties. It was sad, but the little gold tie clasp made the Jim she had once known and once married more vivid than anything the present Jim had done in many months. She sniffed at the car seat, to reassure herself, and then got out. It was still early and cold. The sun was turning the frost to water and it shone on the grass of the slope. The white moon was just fading in the sunlight, but it could still be seen, a faint half-moon hanging in the blue west over the road where Hank was driving. Once again, with Hank gone, the land and the buildings looked too empty; they registered the absence of all that Roger had brought to them. Patsy got the broom and washrag and hurried in to wash the pan of oatmeal before the oatmeal stiffened and became hard to remove.

Later, her bag packed and the dishes washed, she tidied

up the house. Best to leave it, for a time, as it had been. She shoved the couch back into its usual place; it was easy to position because of the dust that had been beneath it on the bare floor. In tidying, Mrs. Daniels had not thought to sweep under the couch, little supposing it would be moved. What that lady or the lady whose couch it had been would have thought of the goings on of the night before did not disturb her; she had come, by the act of inheritance, to think of it as her house. She folded the quilts and put them back in the closet, thinking that if there was a ghost in the house it was the ghost of a man who had never spent much time in the living room. She returned the *Reader's Digest* book to the glass-fronted case. Next trip she would bring some books and some food and some reading lamps and probably Davey, if all went well.

She washed the three cake plates, the chicken plate, and the bowl the coleslaw had been in and, on the way through town, dropped them at the minister's house, near the church where the funeral had been held. He was still shaky, but kindly and inquisitive, and promised to get the plates to their respective owners. He said he hoped to see her in church when she was up. "We got a fine little nursery school," he said. Patsy thanked him for everything and left for Dallas, her conscience clear.

16

It was a pleasant drive to Dallas, the pleasanter because there was no Davey squalling and no Juanita fidgeting and sucking in her breath every time they passed a car. In almost every little town along the way there was a roadside antique shop, and Patsy stopped to poke in almost every one of them. All she bought was a few funny turn-of-the-century postcards, but it was fun to stop and poke. She stopped in a town called Decatur and walked around a huge grotesquely ugly old courthouse. She pretended she was in France looking at cathedrals, and the old men spitting and whittling on a bench on the courthouse lawn looked at her as if she were an invader from a century they did not want to live in. Mostly she stopped in order to walk. She felt extraordinarily good, light and loose and fresh, and she kept smiling as she walked. It had been so long since she had had sex that she had forgotten what it could do for her, and she felt several twinges of regret that she had not stayed at the ranch another day. The minute Hank had driven away she had begun to miss him. But as she got closer to Dallas she began to develop a strong desire to be in her own house, and she determined to bundle up Davey and Juanita and drive straight on.

She discovered, however, that in her absence another mission had been prepared for her.

The first person she saw when she walked in was her mother, and the look on Jeanette's face was so awful that it sent a current of shock and weakness through Patsy. Jeanette looked past tears, as if something had happened from which there could be no possible recovery. Patsy immediately assumed it had happened to Davey.

"Where is he?" she said. "What's happened?" Then she heard his voice babbling from another room, and she stepped past her mother and there he was, in blue overalls, as merry and healthy as ever. She grabbed him up and kissed his neck and, holding him, went back to her mother.

"Thank god you've come," Jeanette said. "I wanted to call but Garland didn't want me to. He said you'd be back today."

"What is it, Mother? What is it? Is somebody dead?"

Jeanette sat down on a sofa shaking her head. "It's Miri."

Patsy was impatient. "Well, what? Is she dead or sick or in jail or pregnant or what?" When she said pregnant her mother's blank pained face twisted and began to cry.

"She's pregnant," she sobbed. Davey was twisting, trying to get to the floor, and Patsy squatted down and watched his blue bottom as he rapidly crawled into the other room.

Jeanette was sobbing so wrenchingly that Patsy could do nothing until she quieted. She sat by her on the couch and put her arms around her. Finally Jeanette grew calmer.

"Come on, dear. It's not the end of the world," Patsy said. "Where's Daddy?"

"Oh, it is, it is," Jeanette insisted.

"No. We'll just have to get her back here where we can take care of her. Who's the boy?"

It turned out they didn't know. Indeed, they knew next to nothing. A daughter of an old family friend had seen Miri and reported that she was pregnant—that was all. They could not get her on the phone. Garland had started to go out and find her but had decided to wait for Patsy's return. He came in an hour later, red-faced and not very coherent. He too regarded it as the end of the world and had been drinking heavily. It made Patsy angry. He had a reservation on a six o'clock flight to San Francisco. Once the facts were known to all and they had speculated fruitlessly about the possible father and what ought to be done, a silence fell over the room. Patsy was very angry at her sister for not having called, but then she had not been calling Miri and couldn't really complain. But she was even angrier at her parents, an anger she tried hard to curb, because she felt sorry for them at the same time. It was plain that they were beaten. Their only plan was to find Miri and the boy and force them to marry. It was the only approach to such a problem that they knew. Even in her irritation with them Patsy kept away from stating some of the more awkward possibilities, such as that Miri might not know who the father was, or that he might be a Negro, Arab, Chinese—there was really no telling. She decided that the first order of business was to block any confrontation between her parents and Miri. She had better go herself and find Miri and get the facts.

Once she made up her mind to go, she wasted no time. Garland surrendered his reservation with clear relief. "I guess it would be better if I stayed here to look after Mother," he said, sighing.

"I think you two can use some mutual looking after," Patsy said and left them and went to see Juanita. She got a report on Davey and took him out in her parents' large sunny back yard and played with him for an hour and a half before she had to bathe and leave. While she was bathing she began to have apprehensions. Perhaps she was not up to the job she was taking on. She didn't know California, and what she had read of the hippie scene made it seem rather different from the one camping weekend she had spent in Yosemite years before. But it was not really the thought of a strange city that scared her; it was the thought of a strange sister. They had never been the sort to exchange every confidence, but neither of them had supposed when Miri left for Stanford that such a time would elapse before they saw each other again. Miri had simply not come back, and Patsy couldn't help wondering what sort of girl she would find when she found her.

In any case, as she packed, the desirability of some masculine help began to seem more and more clear. It occurred to her that while she was out there she might as well see Jim. It was absurd to go on allowing him to be a sort of floating man in her life. "You know," she said, "maybe I ought to go see Jim first. If we can work something out he might come help me with Miri. If we can't then I have an old friend in Los Angeles who might help. Let's see if I can switch my flight."

Her parents were cheered. They welcomed any effort toward reconciliation, on any front. The switching was no problem; the two flights left within minutes of each other, and in a very short time Patsy was flying west. It was a beautiful flight, with the sun setting just ahead of them for two and a half hours. Almost at once, it seemed, they were over the desert. Patsy had a seat by a window and looked down at the brown land and brown lakes and tiny towns whose names she didn't know. She had a vague idea they must be flying over Lubbock and thought how strange it would be if Hank were still driving on one of the highways she was flying over. The only town the pilot mentioned by name was Las Vegas, and she was on the wrong side of the plane to see it. She had a gin and tonic for the sake of her

nerves. The fields of clouds were made beautiful by the
setting sun. She dozed for a little and awoke with a sense of
pressure and a sense of disorientation. She felt very unprepared. Only a few hours before she had been in her
bathrobe, being hugged, Hank's arms around her and her
back against his car, with the silent house and the clear
morning and the still pastures around them. The sun that
had risen while the two of them lay snugly in the bed had
beaten her to the coast and dropped into the Pacific clouds.
The land below was no longer bright with evening but was
gray, sprinkled with faint lights, and soon, before she could
clear her head, the plane had banked and was descending
into the white smog of Los Angeles. Just before they landed
she glimpsed a freeway below and rows of cars with their
lights on.

As the plane taxied in among the strange smog-hidden
terminals of the L.A. International and her fellow passengers gathered up purses and briefcases, Patsy became very
oppressed by the hastiness of what she had done. The desire
to keep her father in Dallas had wiped out her judgment, she
felt. She had not called Jim, she had no hotel reservations,
she didn't know where Altadena was, or even where to find
her luggage.

She found the latter with no real difficulty, but when she
had carried her suitcase to a phone she found she could not
call Jim. A course of action that had once been natural had
become impossible. She had already put in her dime, but
she could not imagine what she would say if she got Clara, so
she got her dime back instead and stood for several minutes
in a state of tense dejection. The longer she stood by the
phone the less clear she felt about everything.

Finally she wrestled her suitcase into a locker and in a
kind of torpor wandered into the main terminal and stood
in a travelers' shop looking at overpriced stuffed animals for
Davey. She felt like going back to Texas and had to exert an
effort of will to go check on flights to San Francisco, thinking
she might as well go on there. But everybody wanted to go to
San Francisco, it seemed. The length of the waiting line
dejected her still more and in order to give it time to shrink
she called Joe Percy. The sound of his voice saying hello was

one of the most welcome sounds she had ever heard. It was amazing that one of the two people she knew in the whole city should be at home when she called. It was very cheering.

"Help," she said. "Help, help, help. I've come to be a burden."

"Why, Patsy Carpenter," Joe said, with no surprise. "I knew you'd call if I sat by the phone long enough. I hope you've come to see me and not that fugitive husband of yours."

"What do you know about him?"

"He buzzed me about a job. It was about the time Sonny got killed. I haven't heard from him since, but I assume if you're here he must be too."

"He's in someplace called Altadena. It's a long story. Could you come and get me?"

"Not there," Joe said. "It would take hours. What you should do is take a limo to the Ambassador. I'll meet you there."

"A what?"

"Limousine. And please plan to stay here. I have a nice guest room."

"Okay," she said, relieved. "Gee, I'm in Hollywood."

"No, you're at the airport," he said. "Hollywood is another country."

The fact of having found Joe cheered her up and she found her limo and squeezed in between two stone-silent businessmen. The lights and the speed and the heavy enclosing presences of the businessmen lulled her again; she felt already that she had slipped out of the normal stream of time and event. Anything was apt to happen. She rather expected the limousine to run all night through the freeways, for she had no idea how distant the hotel might be and the traffic around them was so fast and thick it was hard to imagine really getting out of it.

But when she arrived at the Ambassador, Joe Percy was there, having a conversation with one of the doormen. He came over and hugged her, and the businessmen hurrying to register bumped them with their briefcases.

A few hours later they were at his house and Patsy was drunk. Joe was apologetic, because he had helped her get drunk without meaning to. They had eaten at a quiet restaurant and he had had a natural number of drinks. Patsy was telling her story and had seemed to want a few drinks too, and he had let her have them, assuming she knew her capacity. When they finished eating and he saw she couldn't walk straight he realized she had been drinking out of relief, or out of distress, and got her to his house, hoping she wouldn't get sick. She was pale, and had cried a fair amount, and was talking around and around the same questions, which were when and how to give up a person one was married to, and how to know if a person one loved or liked was a good bet to marry. On the latter point Joe had no advice, but he did make it clear that he thought the time had come for her to give up on Jim. Patsy agreed, and soon came back to the same question again, a little paler and a little sicker. Joe gauged it beautifully and got her to the bathroom just when she needed to be there. Then he put her to bed.

She slept, but not well. She didn't want to have got drunk. Irritation with her own stupidity kept her awake. She felt too bad to move. She heard the sound of television from the other room, just loud enough that she could not stop hearing it and go to sleep. When she did finally sleep she had a vague fitful dream involving Hank and Roger's ranch house. She felt weak and wretched when morning came, but was glad, nonetheless, that the night was over.

Joe Percy insisted that she get up and sit with him while he breakfasted. He made himself a good breakfast, but the sight of it did not please her. She sat in a chair across from him and sipped a little orange juice.

"I look awful," she said. "It's nothing to how I feel, though."

"You look like you were drunk last night," he said. "I didn't know you couldn't drink or I would have watched you better."

"I can't do anything like that," she said. "I'm unsuited to all but the most basic wickedness. Even my milkshakes have to be vanilla."

"About noon you'll feel like living again," she said.

"But I was supposed to do things! I was going to be brisk today. I was going to clear that girl out of Jim's life and we were going to San Francisco to rescue my little sister from a bad end. That was the general plan."

"You really want him back? I never thought you two were all that interested in one another."

"We must have been at one time. We got married, didn't we?"

Joe shrugged. He was wearing a light green pullover sweater and looked in top spirits.

"Maybe you stopped being, then."

"I was raised not to accept reasons like that."

Joe shrugged again. "Screw raisings," he said. "You've got fifty-odd years to live."

"I agree," Patsy said. "I agree completely." There were many windows in his house, some looking out on the bare brown shoulders of the Hollywood hills, but most looking out on the houses beyond and below. It seemed to be a sunny day, but the white smog diluted the sunlight and made it paler. The paleness made the outside look too cool and rather uninviting. She felt chilly even in her bathrobe.

"I know just the thing for you," Joe said, "but unfortunately it will have to wait until lunch."

"If it involves much action on my part it had better wait until lunch *tomorrow.*"

"No, today. You stay here and take it easy while I go work awhile."

"What are you creating?"

"A TV script about a hippie who becomes a cop. It's a shitty idea, but who knows?"

He left and she devoted the morning to recovery, most of it spent in the comfortable guest-room bed watching the hills outside her window become browner and more distinct as the sun burned through the smog. She read the L.A. *Times* and an issue of *Variety* and recovered to the point of wanting coffee. She made some and wandered around the living room looking at Joe's books and magazines. Most of the books in his bookcases were upside down for some reason, but a fair number of them were interesting books, once they were turned over.

On impulse she went and dialed Jim's number and let it ring seven times, her heart pounding. Then she decided she was silly and took a hot bath. Since her general plan had been destroyed, she felt at a loss. She had no secondary plan, but her weak feeling went away, at least. She had not really drunk so much. When Joe came back she felt somewhat like seeing the town. They climbed in his Morgan and he took her at once to a mod dress shop on the Sunset Strip and insisted that she buy herself a wild dress. As he had predicted, it was just the thing for her spirits. She bought a short bright yellow dress, with no back at all, wondering all the while what possible occasion she could have to wear it. The shop was full of teenage girls, their hair as long and as beautifully kept as the manes of show ponies, and they glanced at her from time to time with a certain hostility, as if she were far too old to be in their dress shop. Joe Percy they regarded with frank contempt, and he was relieved when Patsy finished and they could leave.

"Those kids looked at me as if I embodied the System," he said. "Imagine it. Me embodying the System."

"You embody more of it than they do," Patsy said. They had lunch in a large dark-paneled restaurant on Hollywood Boulevard, and she had a chance to observe her escort closely. The closer she looked, the more she was inclined to feel that his high spirits were superficial. He looked tired. It made her feel odd, for she had just begun to feel good again. She had the strange feeling that she had somehow passed him her sorrow.

"Will the movie you made with Sonny ever be released?" she asked.

"Nope," Joe said. "If it was ready now, it could be, but they're still screwing around with it. Now that he's dead and forgotten it would bomb. It makes a good tax write-off."

"He's not entirely forgotten," Patsy said. "I remember him."

"Me too," Joe said. "For a nut he was a good poker player."

The Boulevard was warm and sunny when they went outside, and they walked a bit. "I want to go to Altadena," Patsy said.

"Sucker."

"I know."

"IBM is just over on Wilshire. It's a lot closer."

"No, Altadena."

771

He got her a cab and went back to work, and Patsy rode with a silent Latin cabbie down the Hollywood freeway, out the Pasadena freeway, beneath slopes and tall brown palms, and then north up a long street almost to the foot of a mountain. When the mountain was very close the driver turned off and parked beside a vast apartment building. The apartments were terraced and spread over a whole block, sunk into the gentle slope that spread back toward Los Angeles. She didn't want to be stranded in Altadena and asked the driver to wait. There were no cars at all in the empty street, and it was strange that it should be so empty. All the cars were back where she had come from, in L.A. The sidewalks that ran into the maze of apartments were just as deserted as the streets. It was almost frightening. She encountered an old lady in shorts and sneakers walking a poodle. The old lady was taken aback. "We don't live here," she said. "We're just walking through."

"It seems nice," Patsy said, for the old lady was a bit belligerent and seemed to expect a reply.

"It's not fit to live in, if you're lookin'," she said. "They won't take you if you're over fifty, and they won't take no children and they won't take no pets. We live down the street. Homosexuals everywhere too." With that she went on, tugging the poodle away from a faucet he was licking.

Patsy went on too, and almost immediately encountered two well-tanned young men. They were having a lovers' quarrel by one of the swimming pools and they looked up as she passed and for a moment both focused their hostility on her. They didn't speak, but it frightened her. She had seldom run into faces that said so clearly that they disliked her and resented not only her presence near their swimming pool but her very existence as well. She felt they might have grabbed her and drowned her if she had dared to speak.

When she found Jim's apartment all she did was stand in front of it a few minutes feeling silly. It was curtained, and though she peeped as best she could all she could see was the end of a sofa with some newspapers on it. The curtains were off-white and the sofa brown. Very quietly, as if she were a spy, she tried the door, but it was locked. The apartment, like all the others, was done in a rough unpainted shingle,

772

vaguely English. There was really nothing more to do. She could not imagine what kind of lives Jim and Clara led, inside the door, and she found that she had little curiosity and even less possessiveness in regard to Jim. She had just wanted to see the place, and was not sure she would have rung the doorbell even if she had known he was there and alone. She walked back through the winding sidewalks, among the heavy glossy shrubs, not even bothering to avoid the pool. The young men had settled their quarrel and were stretched out side by side, both on their backs, both in heavy sunglasses, taking the sun. Neither moved a muscle when she walked by; the only sound was the sound of her heels. She would not have supposed it could be so silent anywhere in L.A. The cab driver was listening to Mexican music on his radio and seemed displeased that she was back. She told him to take her to the IBM building on Wilshire Boulevard.

The one thing she felt certain about was that she no longer had any inclination for a big scene about Clara Clark. Too much time had passed. The issues had grown vague, and her feelings had grown vague also. All she wanted in that regard was to avoid Clara completely. But Jim was different. Avoiding him completely did not seem right. The best plan that came to mind was to wait outside his office building and surprise him when he got off work. Once she got to Wilshire and scrutinized the building, curiosity began to nibble at her. Perhaps, as Joe suggested, she wasn't very interested in Jim, but she was nonetheless curious to see what he looked like and who he had become. She tried to project the man she had known who had sat around for two years fiddling with cameras and scholarship into the IBM building, and it was hard. She walked down Wilshire for almost a mile and sat for a while in an Orange Julius bar. The men there were talking about the Lakers, all except two hippies. The hippies of L.A. had fantastic hair; it made her realize what an inferior breed of hippie she had been exposed to in Texas.

The elevators were busy when Patsy went in, but soon they became even busier. Every time one reached the ground floor a score of young men and women stepped out and hurried toward the street. The building began to empty itself of its hundreds, of its thousands. At first Patsy watched each elevator load intensely, expecting Jim to be in each one. She was very nervous. But by the time twenty elevator loads of people had poured out before her eyes her nervousness had changed to confusion and then to a kind of light discouragement that was akin to her feeling of silliness as she stood in front of the apartment in Altadena. She felt like she didn't know what she was doing. It was hard to believe that Jim, any Jim she knew, would come out of one of the elevators. All the young men looked rather alike, their suits gray or blue or brown. Almost in unison, when the elevators opened, they began to fish sunglasses from their pockets and put them on. Those who didn't already had them on. And the elevators kept coming, emptying hundreds of nice-looking young men, some with their hair short, some with their hair longish; and girls with their hair longish, in short skirts and colored stockings, all heading for the street. After ten or fifteen minutes Patsy's discouragement deepened. It occurred to her that in such a throng she might not notice Jim, or might not recognize him. His face could be turned the wrong way. Several times she had thought she had seen him, only to find that it was merely someone who resembled him slightly. It occurred to her that she might have missed him already. He might have passed within twenty feet, wearing sunglasses and a suit she wouldn't recognize. Finally she simply let go of it, the whole plan, the whole pursuit, stepped into the departing rush and was back on Wilshire Boulevard, no more enlightened than when she went in. With some difficulty she got a cab and went to Joe Percy's. He was there having a martini. Patsy took some sherry and listened meekly as Joe told her she was going about things in a very silly way.

"This is the age of appointments," he said. "You use the phone. Doctors, lawyers, ex-husbands, it doesn't matter. Wait an hour and a half and call him."

"Okay," she said listlessly.

"Look," he said. "Make up your mind. Are you here to rescue your sister or to get your husband back. If it's your sister, I can help you. I've got the whole weekend, and I know San Francisco. Jim probably doesn't."

She shook her head, genuinely uncertain. "I don't much want him back. It's just so messy, being married in absentia. I guess I think *he* ought to do something about it, if he wants us to be together again."

She dialed Altadena, but no one was there. "Let's do something wild to take my mind off it," she said. "Why don't you take me dancing? We could go to the Whiskey Au Go-Go or someplace extremely wild and I could wear that dress you bought me."

Joe frowned. "Aren't I supposed to wear it?" she asked.

"I was frowning at the thought of Whiskey Au Go-Go," he said. "I think it's sort of had its hour. But we can go see."

The dress was absolutely backless and she had no bra she could wear with it, which made her feel both shy and very daring. She smiled at the thought of what her mother would think if she knew that, instead of rescuing Miri, she was going off to a night club wearing no bra. Joe praised her lavishly and she blushed.

"My goodness, I feel odd," she said. "I'm not sure I could wear it if I were going with anyone but you."

Joe, seeing her blush, was all the more delighted with his purchase. She looked a girl again, looked like she had in Phoenix the night they met—only something had been added.

"Look, it's six hours too early to do anything," he said. "Why don't I show you a little of the town."

He did, and Patsy loved it. They went in the Morgan and her hair blew wildly. They went to Santa Monica and drove along the beach. Then he took her up the Miracle Mile and then to the Beverly Hills shopping center, where they got out and walked awhile. As they were passing a drugstore a dark beautiful woman came out adjusting her sunglasses. She was dressed in white, and she said hello to Joe, who said hello in return. "Who was that?" Patsy asked, feeling she ought to remember.

"Dolores Del Rio," Joe said, taking her arm. She was still shy about her dress, though no one seemed to pay her the slightest mind.

As it grew dark he drove her into the hills and gave her a view of the lights of Los Angeles. Still early, they went to the

Go-Go and danced amid a thin motley crowd of youngsters. Though colorfully dressed, most of them looked stoned, and the looks on their faces didn't fit with the frenetic music. Patsy had never danced without a bra and could not get over being self-conscious about the movement of her breasts. A young man in a red shirt open to the navel, with a black armband on one arm, kept ogling her, though he was with a tall lovely girl who looked part Indian and part Negro. Patsy felt constrained and they soon left.

"That guy was an American Nazi," Joe said. "Thus the armband."

"Goodness. I supposed someone in his family was dead."

They went back to Joe's place and he fixed them a great, exotic omelet, with Patsy helping and advising. Between them they made short work of it and then sat in Joe's living room having coffee. His living-room window did not look out on all L.A., but it did have a nice view of the Hollywood hills, with enough lights to make the night lovelier. It was an intimate vista, very different from the dazzling one he had shown her in Beverly Hills.

Patsy felt quiet and relaxed, as if her head had just cleared after a long stretch of fogginess. She felt as if she had gone through some kind of crisis, of a sort she did not understand; all she knew was that she felt she was through it. In such moods it was possible for her to notice other people in ways that she didn't when her mind was hazed with her own problems. She noticed once again that her host looked melancholy.

"You make a good omelet, Joe," she said. "Why are you depressed?"

"Me?" he said.

"Don't kid me. I've seen you depressed before."

"Oh, yes, the night Dixie raped me. How is she, by the way?"

"Fine. I remember you telling me she would always be fine, and why."

"I was talking through my hat. Dixie could take a tumble any time."

"Don't beat around the bush," she said. "I tell you my troubles constantly. Why are you depressed?"

776

"I'm trying to keep from falling in love inappropriately," he said. "That's the sum of it. It's very hard not to let yourself love when you see someone lovable, you know."

"Who is she?"

"The wife of an English screenwriter. Married about a year. She's something like you, only a little younger. As lovely a woman as I've seen in years."

"Uh-oh," Patsy said. "What about her husband?"

"He's queer and she doesn't realize it. She knows something's wrong but it'll be a long while before she realizes it's that simple. On the surface he's the opposite of queer. I shudder to think how much she'll have to take before she figures out that he really doesn't like her at all.

"I see a lot of them socially, and she likes me," he added. "That makes it tricky. It would shock her out of her mind if she thought I was in love with her, and I almost already am."

"You already am," Patsy said. "No almost about it. What endless messes. I'm going to call Jim while I feel sensible."

She dialed, and Clara Clark answered. "Could I speak to Jim, please," Patsy said.

"Uh, who's calling?"

"Mrs. Carpenter," Patsy said very matter-of-factly.

"Oh."

"Hi," Jim said cautiously, after a moment. "Where are you?"

"In Hollywood."

There was a silence and Patsy could picture the two of them making startled faces at each other and trying to figure out what it meant. Despite her matter-of-factness the sound of Clara's voice had irked her.

"What brings you?" he asked. "Are you going into pictures?"

He sounded defensive—as if her proximity made it necessary for him to maneuver in some way. It irked her more.

"Don't get in a panic," she said. "I'm not here to make trouble for you. I'm here to do something about Miri. She's pregnant."

"In L.A.?"

"In San Francisco. I stopped here thinking we might

ought to see one another and straighten some things out. Since your companion is there I guess it would put you on the spot to ask if you wanted to see me?"

"I guess it would," Jim said, sounding very conscious of the spot he was on. "Where are you?"

"At Joe's."

"Why are you staying with *him?*" he asked, as if it irked him.

"Why not? He's the only friend I've got in this part of the world."

"You pick strange friends."

Patsy sighed. Nothing much had changed. "Okay," she said. "Don't let's go into that. I was thinking you might want to go help me with Miri. I hate to be blunt but what else can I be. Do you want to or not?"

Jim was silent.

"I realize this is probably a bad time to call," she said. "I've called before and missed you. Several times. Roger Wagonner died the other day. I went to the funeral and then came right out here."

"Goodness," Jim said. "I wish you'd got me. What did he die of?"

In telling about Roger they grew a little friendlier and less edgy, but when the subject was exhausted they were left with the same question: Did he want to go, or not?

"I can't manage it right now," Jim said. There was a tone of regret in his voice and Patsy softened a little.

"Could you manage it if I were calling at a better time?"

"I don't think so," he said finally. "Miri never liked me, anyway. I'd probably just make it more complicated."

"That's right," she said, angered. "We don't want to try anything hard or complicated, do we?"

"I will if you insist," he said.

"I don't. I'm very bad at arm twisting."

"No you aren't."

"Well, I don't like to do it, anyway," she said. "If you don't want to, forget it. Don't you think we might as well start thinking about divorce?"

"I've been thinking about it."

"Any conclusions?"

"None that I want to talk about right now. How long will you be in town?"

"Just tonight."

"That's too bad," he said, the tone of regret in his voice again.

"Yes, it's too bad," she said. "I can't help it. I should be in San Francisco now. We have no idea who she's pregnant by, or how far along she is."

"I see," he said.

"Well, look, I'm sorry I bothered you and put you on the spot. It's my fault. I should have planned better. Will you let me know when you come to some conclusions about divorce? I'll probably be back in Houston by Monday or Tuesday."

"I'll let you know," he said. "I'm sorry."

"For what?" she asked crossly.

"Generally, I guess."

"Oh, screw," she said. "I don't like your being sorry. Just forget it. Good night."

He said good night and she hung up. Joe was attempting to look noncommittal. "That's that," she said.

He nodded sagely. Patsy paced about the room, very dissatisfied. "I wish we were back at that place dancing," she said. "Would you have let me dance with that Nazi if he had asked?"

"No," Joe said.

"Why not? I think that's small of you. I'm a free woman and can dance with whom I please. What if I had made a scene?"

"I'd have bawled you out."

"Oh, I'm just mad at myself for being so bitchy with Jim," she said. "I get so harsh when I talk to him. Do you suppose I could still love him?"

"No."

"I don't think so either."

"It's been my observation that resentment lasts longer than love," he said, so pontifically that it amused her. She went in and changed out of the barebacked dress. She put on a gown and robe and came and lay on his couch; in a few minutes she recovered her good humor. Joe drank Scotch and she sipped wine and they watched old movies on TV until very late. First they watched *Algiers,* with Hedy Lamarr and Charles Boyer. "I guess you know them, don't you?" Patsy said.

"I've seen them around."

After *Algiers,* when they were both a little bit tipsy, they watched a strange, hilarious Italian superspy movie, with Terry Thomas and Marissa Mell. It was about a thief so talented that he gradually drove a small European country into bankruptcy. In the end the government was forced to melt all its remaining gold reserves into one giant twenty-ton ingot, something they assumed no thief could steal. But the thief, whose name was Diabolik, managed. As the ingot was being shipped out of the country on a special train, he dynamited a causeway. The train and the ingot fell into the sea. Diabolik then affixed giant balloons to the ingot and towed it to his secret hideaway. Joe and Patsy laughed and laughed. They had both been in a state of suppressed gloom, but under the impress of drink, each other's company, and the ridiculous movie their gloom spent itself in bursts of hilarity.

"It's a relief to know there are people making worse movies than us," Joe said.

Patsy was lying full length on the couch, very relaxed, her head on a green pillow and her ankles crossed and propped on the end of the couch. She was barefooted and kept wiggling her toes. Joe was reminded several times of the girl he had fallen in love with, whose name was Bettina; she had nice legs and ankles too, but instead of being brunette she had ashy blond hair and was taller than Patsy, an awkward long-legged young beauty who had not yet learned to handle her body.

"Are you going to seduce her or aren't you?" Patsy asked, divining the drift of his thoughts.

"I'm twice her age," he said. "I don't think I could really do her any good. Maybe I should hold off and let someone younger find her."

"Don't be so noble," Patsy said. "She'd be lucky to get you."

He got up and switched channels, but they were tired of

movies. He turned the TV off and they sat looking at the lights of the Hollywood hills.

"It's a miserable town for a girl, really," he said. "Two thirds of the men are queer and the others are predatory. They're not looking for anything but pussy."

"I'd become a drunkard if I lived here," Patsy said. "Does TV go on all night?"

"All night. It's a bad town for girls but a great town for insomniacs."

"You really want to go help me with my sister?" she asked, yawning.

"Absolutely."

"Okay. Do we drive or fly?"

They couldn't decide. Both of them were too sleepy. But when Patsy went to bed Joe was still sitting in the chair in his living room, drinking and staring somberly at the lights.

=== **17** ===

Joe woke her early. Sometime during his midnight deliberations he had decided he wanted to drive to San Francisco. "It's a nicer drive than the one from here to the airport," he said. Patsy was in her bathrobe, still half asleep, having coffee. But when she succeeded in showering herself awake she found that she felt rather good. Joe was putting the top up on the Morgan. She protested, but he put it up, anyway. "You'd get windburned," he said.

At times, as they zipped north in the fast morning traffic, Patsy was a little frightened. Joe was a silent, intense driver, and the traffic around them was intense without being silent. Sometimes they shot into valleys between two huge trailer trucks, and Patsy could look out and see huge tires looming higher than her head, only a yard or two away. It seemed to her that a sudden gust of wind could blow the Morgan right under such a truck and she was always relieved when they slipped ahead and were back among ordinary cars.

They stopped and breakfasted in Santa Barbara, debating how much time to give to the drive. Joe wanted to drive the coast highway. Patsy had never been on it and had no objection. At San Luis Obispo Joe got out and took the top down, and they spent the day driving slowly up the beautiful coast. Joe regaled her all day with Hollywood stories while the curves of the coast unfolded themselves before her. At midafternoon they stopped and ate cheese and crackers and wieners, parked on a little point that looked down on the sea. Before they reached Big Sur it was evening. They saw the last of the sun, and the country and the sea turned gray. Before they reached Monterey they were driving in a thick fog. Joe became an intense driver again. By the time they were back on 101, Patsy was asleep. Joe shook her awake almost two hours later as they were passing South San Francisco. "We're nearly there," he said. "Sit up and look."

Patsy got her eyes open but found that sitting up was not easy. Sleeping in a Morgan was not as comfortable as sleeping in the Ford, and as she tried to uncramp herself she was for a moment lonesome and homesick for Texas and her house and her car and her son. She was cold as well. "There's no place quite like it," Joe said sentimentally as the city of San Francisco appeared before them. He obviously loved it. Patsy felt that he had made the drive for that moment, when the lights of the city came into view. For herself, she felt little, though the lights had a certain beauty in the fog, and the way they were grouped together on the cluster of hills was more appealing than the millions of lights in the sprawl of L.A. She was cold and rumpled and in no mood to appreciate the singularity of San Francisco.

A little later, when Joe drove them up to a very formidably posh hotel off a large square, with a cable car running in front of it, it was her rumpledness that worried her the most. She was not comfortable until the door of her room was shut behind her. Joe had offered to show her the town, but she felt far too exhausted.

When she had bathed and was warm again she sat at her window looking down on the thronged streets; she watched the cable cars and called Miri. A message said that the number was no longer in use. It scared her. Where could Miri be? How could she be found? She lay awake a long time worrying about it, hearing the muffled clang of the cable cars.

When she awoke the city was gray and she felt rather gray herself. Miri was going to seem a stranger, she was sure, and it might not even be possible to find her. All she had was the address where the phone had once been. She had a vision of herself having to hire a private detective to find her sister, a grubby detective, of the sort one saw on late TV. She called Joe, and after a time he answered, in a voice indicating that he had been asleep.

"I'm sorry. I guess you were out late."

"Um." His tone reminded her of Teddy Horton.

"Do you mind if I wake you up?"

"No," he said gallantly.

"You sleep awhile," she said. "I just wanted to be sure you got in safely. I'll call you if I really need you."

"Be awake in a minute," he mumbled, but she quietly hung up. She was a little irritated with him for having picked such a splendid hotel. Whatever she wore that would look good enough to get her through the lobby was going to look awfully haut monde wherever she came upon Miri. Fortunately her choice was limited. She wore her dark green suit and had an expensive breakfast, with good marmalade, in the hotel coffee shop.

The house where the phone had been was in the center of a steeply sloping block between Fillmore and Van Ness. It was a gray three-story house, amid a block of gray and light green and white three-story houses. There were six mailboxes outside the door but Miri's name was not on any of them and she felt a growing distress. Miri was indeed gone. She tried the door but it was the sort that had to be opened either by a key or a buzzer, and she turned back, very discouraged. She was about to go down to the street when she noticed that the name on one of the mailboxes was Melissa Duffin. She hesitated again, conscious that it was a little too early to be ringing doorbells in California—

particularly the doorbells of people one hardly knew. But she was there and Melissa was the only person she could think of in the whole city who might know where Miri was. She rang the bell. Almost immediately the buzzer sounded and she pushed open the door, realizing only after it had closed behind her that she had forgotten to check the number of the apartment. Fortunately Melissa came out almost as soon as Patsy was in. She looked down the stairwell from the third floor and Patsy saw her.

"Oh, hi," Melissa said. "You're Patsy. Come on up. I thought you were the postman bringing me a package from Momma. Today's my birthday."

"No, it's only me, empty-handed."

"And I bet I know why you're here," Melissa said. "I was wondering when her folks were going to show up. I'm glad it's you instead."

"Did I get you up?"

"Oh, no." Patsy could believe it. Melissa looked lovely and wide awake and fresh. She wore a long loose black dress. It surprised Patsy for a moment, but once they were inside the apartment the dress seemed ideal. It was a clean, light white-walled apartment, very pleasant, and Melissa's dark hair and the dark dress were perfect for it. The floor was bare and instead of furniture there was a profusion of cushions and a mattress covered with a nice orange spread.

"We love cushions," Melissa said. "Won't you have some oranges? I was having some for breakfast."

Patsy was taking in the room, looking at the three or four drawings on the wall and out the little bay window. There was a chair near the bay window, the only chair in the room, small, done in a smooth unpainted wood, with a rope bottom. "A friend of ours made that for us," Melissa said. "He's a carpenter of sorts."

"A good sort, I'd say. I will have an orange, if I may."

The morning paper was spread out in the middle of the floor. Melissa was reading it while she ate oranges. Patsy got a blue cushion and joined her. "I see you put your seeds on the want ads," she said. "I was always slovenly with mine. Your boy friend must have you well trained."

"He does," Melissa said. "Hey, Barry, get up. There's someone I want you to meet."

Outside, the morning mist had just broken and the sun shone on the houses across the street. The room, which was already light, became even lighter and more pleasant. While Patsy was peeling her orange there was the sound of a male dressing in the room past the little kitchen, and in a minute in walked Barry, an amazingly tall, lanky young man with a nice red beard and a shy grin. He was barefooted, in chinos and a blue tee shirt. He stood scratching his head.

"I was determined to get someone taller than Daddy," Melissa said. "You want oranges or not?"

"Is there any coffee?" Barry asked politely.

"No, because I didn't know I was going to wake you up so soon," Melissa said. "Have an orange and I'll make some."

Barry sat down and peeled his orange, grinning shyly at Patsy now and then. "Gee," he said, "I'm not usually up so early. I'm a nut for all-night movies."

"I'm afraid I'm responsible," Patsy said. "If it's any consolation, I like your beard."

"Thanks," he said, his face lighting up. "Melissa's nuts for it too."

"Now that he's up you can come in and see the bedroom," Melissa said. "That's our real view."

Patsy went in, and agreed, for the bedroom window looked out over the southern part of San Francisco, over thousands of slanting roofs and white buildings, with churches in the distance. She looked down into the tiny yard below and saw a calico cat walking along a fence. The bedroom was like the living room, furnished with a mattress and cushions, a bookcase with a vase of yellow flowers sitting on it, and a small TV on the floor. There was a tiny balcony just off the bedroom. "It's a great place for smoking pot," Melissa said, indicating the balcony. "It's just great on foggy nights."

Melissa's dark hair had been loose, but as they walked back to the living room she gathered it and hastily bound it with a rubber band. Watching her move, it struck Patsy how like Lee she was, although she was tall. She moved like Lee; and the rooms, for all that they were expressive of Barry and Melissa, were like Lee's rooms in their cleanness and colors and receptivity to light. Even Barry brought Lee to mind— as tall as Bill, as gentle and shy as Peter.

She found, as she sipped a cup of Melissa's coffee, that she liked Melissa and Barry very much and enjoyed being at breakfast with them. They were clearly happy, and very sweet to each other, Melissa chattering, Barry mumbling and looking at her mischievously and shyly. Patsy felt odd and old and not quite normal. It had been so long since she had been with people who seemed fully happy with each other that it was hard to get used to. Melissa ate more oranges than anyone she had ever known, and Barry became hungrier as he grew wide awake and soon went to the kitchen to make himself a peanut butter sandwich. "Don't put the peanut butter knife in the honey jar," Melissa said. "It gloms up the honey."

"I never do," Barry said mildly.

"You do every time I don't mention it," Melissa claimed.

Barry came back eating his sandwich and trying to keep the honey from dribbling onto his beard. "Hard to eat," he said. "Only bad thing about beards."

Patsy would have liked just to sit and visit with them and perhaps find out what they did or ate or worked at that made them both look so healthy; but the morning was passing and she was no nearer to her sister. When she finally brought her up, Melissa and Barry looked at each other a little guiltily.

"We don't really know where they are," Melissa said, "but I'm sure I can find some guys who can find them. I guess it was that girl friend of Miri's who told about her being pregnant. Last week she got very paranoid and was sort of expecting her folks to show up any minute and drag her back to Texas. They moved somewhere over near the Hashbury. She really doesn't want to go back to Texas."

"They?"

"That's kind of the bad part," Melissa said. "I don't know if you know it, but Miri doesn't have much sense about guys. The guy she's living with is a very hostile person."

"Negro."

Melissa nodded. "We don't know that he's the father, though. He's been around long enough, but some others were around too."

"He might not be the father," Barry said quietly. "She was fucking lots of guys, for a while."

"How pregnant is she?" Patsy asked, suddenly quite depressed by the prospect before her.

Melissa and Barry looked at each other indecisively. "Four or five months," Melissa said. "It's hard to say."

"Not to put down Miri or anything," Barry said, "but we were sort of glad when they left. Stone was bad to have around."

"Stone?"

"That's his name. He was always hitting us for money. Or trying to. I think your folks must have cut her off, or something, to try and get her to come back—I don't know. They were pretty broke. Then he tried to come on with me one day and Barry was going to beat him up, but Stone was gone and I managed to cool Barry off before he got back. It was just a deteriorating scene."

"I can imagine," Patsy said. "How did Miri get mixed up with him?"

"He found her at a party, probably. I always thought it was more a hate thing than a love thing. Stone needs a white chick to hate and Miri was glad to have someone hate her, for a while. She was very down on herself, and she stayed high a lot."

Patsy's depression deepened. She went into Melissa's kitchen and rinsed the orange juice off her hands.

"I should have come a year ago," she said. "My folks should have come eighteen months ago, it sounds like. I better go find her, if you can tell me where the boys live."

"Sure. The guys are over on Clay Street. They're really nice, and I think a couple of them were pretty hung on Miri, but Stone scared them off."

Barry stood up and scratched his head and looked pained. "Listen, maybe we better go with you," he said. "That guy's rough. He beat the crap out of Miri two or three times that I know of. I think he's got her scared to leave him. You want me to come along?"

"I'll go with her," Melissa said. "You have to go to work."

Barry, it turned out, worked part time in a bookshop on Polk Street. Melissa worked part time in a laundry. "It ticks my folks off, but it's not bad," she said. "Neither of us wants to work all the time." She disappeared into the bedroom and came out shortly, clad in jeans and a heavy sweater. Barry was still looking pained.

"It's not so important to go to work on time," he said. "I can call and tell them I'll be late. I don't want you two getting into it with that guy."

"Look, I can handle Stone," Melissa said. "I did, didn't I?"

"Once," Barry said. "This time he might handle you. Set him off and he's liable to beat the piss out of all three of you."

Though she had never seen him, Patsy was beginning to be distinctly frightened of the man named Stone, and for all Melissa's assurance, she was for having a man along. She remembered the one time she had almost been beaten up, the night Sonny Shanks had abducted her in Phoenix, and she thought how nice it would be if her old menacer could be there to take her into the Hashbury. When it came to violence he was the one person who came to mind who could be put up against anybody. Barry, for all his height, looked too basically gentle, and Joe Percy had sounded in no shape for trouble.

But Melissa carried the day. They left Barry standing in the kitchen looking pained and trying to decide if he wanted another sandwich. "He's overprotective of me," Melissa said as they went down the steps. "He's got to learn sometime." They walked over a street and into a little park that just covered the top of a hill. From it they could see the bay and one end of the Golden Gate. The edges of the fog had not yet receded from the hills to the north of the bridge. The bay was very blue in the sunlight and the houses sloping down all around the park were white and gray.

"I see why people like this city," Patsy said.

"Oh, it's great," Melissa said, as if they were discussing the value of air.

They walked down the hill, along Clay Street and across Fillmore, and up a slope beside another little park, one that seemed to be terraced and flat on top. Melissa rang at a brown house and they went in and woke up an apartmentful of boys. They all had long, long hair and the same friendly slightly sheepish air that Barry had. Some remained in sleeping bags and smiled out at Patsy from beneath their hair, but two dressed and wandered around looking pained at the sudden invasion of girls. One devoted himself at once to getting a record on the phonograph. They approached the question of Miri's whereabouts delicately, as if they had to feel their way to it, and one boy named Martin finally told Melissa that Miri was living somewhere near Clement Street. A good bit of mumbling went on while Patsy stood by feeling awkward. Martin finally located an actual address, and Melissa thanked him.

"What a lot of nice-looking boys," Patsy said, once they were on the street again. "Why do they all act so shy?"

Melissa shrugged. "A lot of guys are like that out here," she said. "They don't quite know what to do about girls. Some of them try to come on but most of them just sort of hang around being brotherly. Barry was even that way with me, for a while. It's great, though, once you get them trained not to be scared of you."

They walked back to Fillmore, Melissa brooding. "He wasn't so much scared of me," she elaborated. "I think he was just scared I'd leave him, for a while. I had been hung up with this anthropology professor at Cal and the guy was a lot older than Barry and more experienced and I guess Barry thought I'd go back to him."

"From what I've seen of Barry, he needn't worry," Patsy said.

"Isn't he great?" Melissa said, coloring. "He's six five."

The address Martin had given them was several blocks off Clement Street, near the neck of Golden Gate Park. The apartment was in a drab two-story house on a very unadorned street of drab two-story houses. "The flat parts of town just aren't as nice," Melissa said. But Patsy had passed beyond aesthetics into a state of shaky apprehension at the thought of suddenly coming face to face with Miri—and possibly her lover as well. She knew she must look like the most WASP of WASPs and almost wished she had borrowed some less middle-class clothes from Melissa. She felt strange in her stomach, and very uncertain as to what she must say or do. Again, Miri's name was not on the mailbox, but the address said apartment five, and they went in.

Melissa too looked a little apprehensive. "Maybe Stone won't be here," she said.

But Stone opened the door of apartment five. Patsy had been expecting a large man, someone heavy. Stone was medium height and thin and rather light. He wore a green fatigue jacket with the collar turned up and dirty Levi's. He had a thin straggle of mustache and a Ho Chi Minh goatee, and he looked no less threatening for being thin. He focused on Melissa, not Patsy, and his look was one of instant resentment. Behind him Patsy could see the edge of a green couch, a pulled-down windowshade, and a cigarette smoking in an ashtray.

"Who you want?" Stone asked.

"I want Miri," Patsy said, and meant it. Few certainties had ever come to her as quickly. Stone turned his resentful eyes toward her, but Miri had heard her and stepped into view behind him. She wore a thin gray sweatshirt that showed the slight bulge of her pregnancy, and her hair had grown very long. Her face, which Patsy remembered as rounded and girlish, was pale and very thin. She was very surprised, and for a moment her face opened and betrayed a quick delight at the sight of her sister, but then Stone turned and looked at her with hard hostility and the look turned Miri's face into a mirror of his, so that even before Stone spoke his hostility was reflected in Miri's gray eyes.

"Just go away," Miri said. "I don't want you and I don't need you."

But Patsy was not to be put off. She stepped past Stone into the room and Melissa followed her.

"You're not invited in here," Stone said, but Patsy didn't look at him. Miri repeated what she had said, her lips trembling. She had drawn very tight.

"Then get some manners and invite me in here," Patsy said, looking at the room. It was rugless and wretchedly furnished, with a sofa and a mattress and a small white portable TV. "I'm your sister and I've come a long way to see you," she went on. "Why shouldn't I be invited in?"

She turned to face Miri, and before anyone could speak or move Miri unwound. She hit Patsy in the face, a wild hard slap that rocked her back two steps and left her momentarily stunned and dizzy. Patsy sank onto the green couch, holding her cheek and looking at her sister in disbelief. The slap had connected squarely, and it took a minute for her head to clear. Miri had drawn tight again. Melissa looked worriedly at Patsy. Stone turned and walked to the other end of the room, quite impassive, as if he had decided to pretend the two women weren't there.

"What did I say to deserve that?" Patsy asked. But the feeling that welled up in her as she looked at the cheap dusty room and at Miri's legs, a bruise on one shin, and at her dingy black skirt, was that the slap should have been for Garland and Jeanette, who had fiddled and worried for two years and been afraid to do anything; and for her too, for forgetting her sister for so long, for pretending that Miri could take care of herself, just because she was nineteen. The slap was for all of them, for not having come sooner.

"Oh, baby, I'm sorry," Patsy said tearfully.

"I won't go back," Miri said, still fierce. "I won't live in Texas. I'm staying with Stone. I won't live with them. They don't want me."

It was true enough. As she stood, Garland and Jeanette would not want her. She was not the daughter they loved, or thought of themselves as loving, whichever it was. She was thin, bedraggled, pregnant, and defiant.

"No, I don't want you to live with them," Patsy said. "I want you to live with me, in Houston. I have a house now. Jim's gone."

"Don't talk about it!" Miri yelled, almost screaming. "I won't talk about it." She drew back her hand as if to slap Patsy again but then stopped and began to bite her lips.

Stone was standing across the room looking sullenly away from them all. Melissa stood behind Miri and was trying to tell Patsy something with her lips, but Patsy couldn't make it out.

Patsy's head had quit swimming and she stood up looking at her sister. "Listen," she said, "if you think I'm going back and leave you in this mess just because you cut loose and walloped me one you better think again. Have you been to a doctor yet?"

"Just to see if I was," Miri said sullenly. She kept glancing at Stone, but he wouldn't look at her.

"You could introduce me to your lover, at least," Patsy

said. "He doesn't have to stand in the corner just because
I'm here. My glance doesn't turn to stone, or anything, no
pun intended."

Stone turned and gave her a look that would have turned
her to ash, could it have been converted into heat.

"His name's Stone," Miri said.

"Which name? Is it the fashion just to have one these
days?"

Stone didn't leave his place near the corner. "Who the
fuck are you to come in here?" he said.

"I'm Patsy Carpenter," she said, deciding to treat it as an
introduction. "I'm Miriam's sister. I'm sorry, but I didn't
get your first name, Mr. Stone." She saw Melissa smile
slightly, but Miri looked embarrassed and scared.

"We never asked you," he said. He had a low voice, with a
touch of college in it. "You're not going to come in here and
bust up our life. You're not taking her back to Texas."

"Why not?" Patsy asked, facing him. "I can't see that you
want her. You don't even look at her."

Stone crossed in front of her with a sullen shrug, as if to
say all conversation between them would be automatically
irrelevant, and raised the windowshade and stared resentfully into the street. Two Italian children were attempting to
learn to skateboard on the sidewalk across the street. Patsy
saw that Miri was crying. Streams of tears wet her thin face.
Melissa put her arm around her and was trying to get her to
sit on the couch. Miri resisted but Melissa kept murmuring
to her and pulling her toward the couch and finally Miri sat
down. Her arms were trembling. Melissa went over and
rummaged near the mattress; she came back with a shawl,
which she gave to Miri.

"You should have kept in touch with us, honey," Melissa
said. "We didn't know where you were living. We had to ask
the guys."

"It's not really ours," Miri said. "We just borrowed it for a
few days from a guy who's out of town. We were gonna move
across the park when we got some bread."

Stone turned when she began to speak and looked at her
with the same look of hostility he had given her at the door.

"Listen, tell these cunts to get out," he said. "They're your people, you tell them to go. We don't need two bad cunts in here criticizing where we at and how we live. They think you're too fuckin' good for me an' that's all they've got to say and we already heard that, didn't we?"

Miri was still crying. "I'm not too good," she said pathetically.

"You sleazy bastard," Melissa said, furious suddenly. She went over to face him. "Anybody human's too good for you the way you act. I wouldn't let you keep my cat. This is her sister—do you know what a sister is?"

"I don't care what a sister is," he said, looking back out the window. "I know what a bad cunt is and that means you. And her in the green too."

Patsy felt at a loss. She knew what she meant to do but not how to accomplish it. Miri simply looked sick. Her eyes were strange, and though she was clearly reacting to a great strain, she seemed barely aware of what was happening. The cigarette had burned itself out and the room smelled of ash. What she wanted most was to get her sister out of the room where Stone was, so she could try and talk to her. But there was no other room, only a small bathroom. There was no kitchen. A carton of soft drinks sat by the mattress.

She decided the best thing to do was to join Melissa in the verbal fray. Perhaps they could drive him out, at least for a while.

"Look, Mr. Stone," she said, "I don't know how good or how bad you are but I have a friend coming in a little while and if you call me names like that when he's here there's apt to be trouble. I just thought I'd warn you."

"There you are, now," Stone said, looking down at Miri. "Didn't I tell you? They got the marines right outside. They going to take you right back to Dallas, and it don't matter what you want and it don't matter what I want. And they didn't have no trouble finding us. You told those mother-fuckers on Clay Street right where we'd be."

"No, listen," Patsy said. "All I have outside is one middle-aged friend, and I'm perfectly willing to listen to what you and Miri want. There are plenty of things I'd like to know about this but I don't see why I can't talk about them without being slapped and called names."

793

"Well, ask your little sister," Stone said oversweetly. "Just ask your little sister." And with a scowling glance at Melissa he turned and went quickly out the door. He didn't look at Miri at all.

"He left," she said vaguely. "Why did you make him go?"

She got up suddenly and began to rummage in the pile of clothes near the mattress. Melissa quickly came to Patsy and began to whisper.

"That bastard left just to panic her," she said. "She's high as the hills. We better just go with her and not try to stop her from looking for him. She might really tear loose if we try to stop her. Maybe we can ease her off a little if we walk."

Miri was muttering to herself as she searched in the clothes. She pulled a thick black sweater on over her sweatshirt and dropped her skirt and struggled into a pair of jeans, but she stopped before she got them buttoned and ran to the window to look out. The terror in her face and the bulge of her abdomen over the cheap cotton panties shook Patsy and she tried to talk to Miri calmly.

"We'll go with you to find him," she said, but Miri had become oblivious to them. She rummaged in the clothes until she found a heavy chain with a medallion on it and she put that on her neck and then hastened to the door, wearing no shoes.

"She's barefoot," Patsy said. Melissa looked around quickly, but she didn't spot any shoes, and shrugged. "Won't hurt," she said.

Miri was two or three doors ahead of them when they got to the street. They could hear her, still muttering.

"I just didn't want us to lose her," Melissa said. "If she got away from us and ran into Stone she'd really be gone. He'd hide her but good. As long as we stay with her we're all right."

"I don't know what I'd do without you," Patsy said.

Miri stopped at the first corner and looked around indecisively. They caught up with her and she seemed quite friendly toward them, but Patsy saw that she was without a sense of who they were. Her sense of who they were had grown dimmer and dimmer since the moment of the slap. She had hit her sister as hard as she could and then ceased to notice that she was her sister. Patsy was aware that she didn't know how to talk to Miri and was content to let Melissa do it.

"You two been eating lately?" Melissa asked. "Maybe Stone went off to eat a meal."

Miri shrugged, as if it were irrelevant. "We had a pizza," she said but didn't say when. Once or twice they met hippies as they approached the park. Miri stopped and asked them if they'd seen Stone. Both looked as if they had either just got up or else were looking for a good place to lie down. Neither had seen Stone.

Soon they angled into the park, Miri walking ahead. Patsy worried about what they would do if they found Stone. She had called earlier to give Joe the address, and was wondering what would happen if he and Stone arrived at the same time. She also wondered what had happened to all the things Miri had taken to college with her, clothes, phonograph, records, and such. There had been practically nothing in the tiny apartment. She had on heels, because of the St. Francis, and once they got in the park was hard put to keep up with Melissa and Miri. The grass was damp and in spots fairly long. Then they bumped into a couple of guys the girls knew. One had a serape and the other a sheepskin jacket and both had shoulder length hair and mustaches. Melissa, by a few snaps of her fingers, enlisted them in the cause, and they reversed their directions and joined the troupe.

One whose name was Frank dropped back and walked with Patsy. "Hi," he said conspiratorially. "I understand we're chasing Stone but why do we want to find him? I'd just as soon lose him."

"I'm with you," Patsy said. "We're just trying to hold Miri together, actually. She was threatening to fly apart."

"Yeah," Frank said sagely, as if he knew all about it.

Then, as they were almost across the park, they passed a scene which for a time took Patsy's mind off her sister. Fifteen or twenty motorcycles were there, and their riders were there too, and their riders' women. Patsy glanced at them without much curiosity, for she had seen motorcycle gangs before. But what she saw hit her almost as hard as the

slap Miri had given her. Most of the cyclists were drinking
beer and talking with what seemed to be the instrument
man of a rock band; at least he was uncoiling wires and
fiddling with a large pile of electronic gear. He seemed
nervous and apprehensive and straightened up occasionally
to whip his hair out of his eyes. But it was three cyclists
somewhat to the side that gave Patsy the start. They were no
hairier or dirtier or more disagreeable-looking than the
others, but they had their pants down and were quite
exposed. One thin one was leaning back against his cycle, a
can of beer in one hand, while his woman, a hefty-looking
creature in a black shirt and jeans leaned across the cycle
and languidly pumped his penis with one hand. Another
woman, whose back was to Patsy, was kneeling on the
grass in front of a large cyclist who had a hairy stomach
and a penis that was half erect. As Patsy looked, the
woman reached up and grasped it, pulling it down. Patsy
stumbled and looked away, dreadfully shocked, so stunned
she felt weak for a moment. Neither Miri nor Melissa
seemed to take more than glancing notice of the scene,
or to think it unusual, but both the boys looked over
cautiously.

"What in the world?" Patsy said, unable to keep from
looking once more to be sure she had seen it. Several more
of the cyclists had wandered over and partially blocked her
view of the kneeling woman, but there was no doubt that she
had seen it. The thin cyclist was still leaning against his cycle
and the hefty girl still held his penis.

Frank noticed her confusion and seemed to have some
sympathy for it. "New scene?" he asked, smiling pleasantly
at her. "It's the Angels. I think, I don't know, they're
warming up for some birthday party or something. They
won't bother us if we go on. Those guys over there are taking
their lives in their hands." He nodded at a straggle of
younger hippies, four boys and a girl, who were standing
near a tree staring at the Angels.

"You don't want to just stand and watch them," Frank
said. "It makes them want to do their thing, which is to beat
the shit out of people."

"But how can they get away with that?" Patsy asked,
confused. "In the middle of the day. In *public?*"

"Well, it's the park," Frank said, shrugging. "Nobody bugs you in the park, much."

Soon they crossed out of the park into a section of old houses and small grocery stores. Most of the houses were iron gray, but on some the paint was peeling. Some had psychedelic posters in the windows and a few of the cars parked along the street were weirdly painted. At the first corner a teenager of fifteen or sixteen asked Frank if he could spare some change. The boy wore a good corduroy coat and black new-looking knee boots. Frank turned him down. "Fifty-dollar boots and he's scrounging change," he said disgustedly.

The day had clouded over again, at least in the part of the city they were in. Once in a while Patsy caught a distant glimpse of white buildings with the sun on them, but the clouds over the Haight-Ashbury were as gray as the houses. Miri had slowed a little. Whenever she passed a cluster of hippies she stopped to ask about Stone, always with negative results. She stopped and went into a little poster shop. Patsy and Frank caught up with Melissa and the other boy, whose name was George. They had a consultation. George wore the serape and had not perceived that the true object of their quest was to avoid Stone, not to find him.

"Why are we looking here?" he said. "He's no head. He's probably down on Fillmore somewhere."

"What do you think?" Patsy asked Melissa.

"She's awfully zingy," Melissa said. "This isn't getting us anywhere. I don't think she even knows where she is. She knows Stone doesn't like this part of town. He hates hippies. You really going to take her to Texas?"

"I sure am."

"Why?" George asked. "Isn't it a bad place? Half the heads I know come from there. They all say it's a bad place."

"It may be a bad place for heads but it's a nice place for expectant mothers," Patsy said. "I'm taking her back. The only question is how to go about it."

"I'm glad I'm not you," Melissa said. "If you're going to do it, I guess you ought to do it quick. Once you get her on a plane there's not much she or Stone can do about it. We can stick with you until you get her to the airport, if you want us to."

"I want you to," Patsy said.

When Miri came out of the store she noticed Patsy again and they walked together back through the park, the other three behind them.

"Did you see Momma and Daddy?" Miri asked. "When are they going to send me some money? We can't even buy grass. We're going to have a party when we get some more money."

"You should have called me. I'd have sent you money."

But Miri seemed not really concerned about that or about anything. She walked along looking restlessly one way and another. The thought that she was going to have to bear a child when she was only a thin bewildered child herself hurt Patsy and made her all the angrier at her parents. When they got back to Miri's street Joe Percy was there, sitting under the wheel of the Morgan. He was wearing a sports jacket and a tweed cap and was looking worried. "Is Stone here?" Miri asked him quickly.

"Well, somebody's in apartment five. All I got was his attitude."

Miri ran in and up the stairs and the five of them stood on the sidewalk looking downcast and indecisive.

"We can't all go up," Melissa said. "I don't know which of us would make him the least mad."

"I'm going up," Patsy said after a moment. "She's my sister and if it makes him mad that's tough. If I need any help I guess I can yell."

Joe and Melissa looked uneasy, but neither of them said anything and Patsy went in and up the stairs. She was very scared, as scared as she had been the night Sonny abducted her in his hearse, but in a different way. She was afraid of Stone on the one hand and afraid too that if she mismanaged things her sister might have a serious breakdown, something far beyond her power to cope with. But going away without Miri had become unthinkable. She went up despite her fear and knocked on the door of apartment five.

"Yeah," Stone said.

"I'm Mrs. Carpenter," she said. "I'd like to come in."

The door didn't open. "What for?" he asked.

"To get my sister and her things," Patsy said.

"You are fucking crazy," he said. "You think I'm gonna let you come in here and walk off with my piece?"

The way he said it angered her uncontrollably and she kicked the door as hard as she could. It was a thin door and rattled loudly. "Open that goddamn door," she said.

He did, immediately, with a little sardonic smile. "Is that the way you kick niggers down in Texas?" he asked. Miri had taken off the black sweater and the jeans and was fumbling in the clothes as if she were trying to put them in some sort of order. She didn't look around when Patsy came in.

Patsy was quivering with tension and anger. She let the remark about niggers pass. "I'm trying not to hate your guts," she said, "but you do make it hard."

"Well, don't try," he said softly. "Just go at it."

"I'm going to take my sister to Texas," she said. "We're leaving as soon as I can get her things together, if she has any things left. If you want to make a fight out of it, okay. I'll get my friends and lawyers and policemen and the marines if I have to, and if that's what you want, okay."

But Stone had turned sullen again. He shrugged and resumed his stance at the window. Miri was pulling on a gray skirt. Stone was silent, closed up. Patsy did not believe she had ever seen a human being as hard to handle. It was incredible to her that Miri, who had always been completely open, should have taken as her lover a man who seemed completely closed.

She went over and knelt by Miri to see what should be salvaged of the garments there. There were mostly sweaters and jeans, with a few skirts and no bras and a pair or two of panties. Miri sat on the couch and looked at Stone. Patsy could find no shoes at all.

"My god," Patsy said. "You must have some shoes. Where are her shoes?"

"She left 'em someplace," Stone said. "We been living light."

To Patsy's great relief he seemed to have turned off his hostility. He suddenly looked totally apathetic. Miri, again reflecting him, seemed apathetic too. But in a way it confused the scene even more. She had come up the stairs prepared for any sort of wildness—blows, screams, curses, and police. She expected to have to drag Miri away inch by inch. But Stone stood at the window and Miri sat on the couch and they both looked as if they had forgotten what was happening and had no interest in it. Patsy was at a loss. There was nothing to gather up, no suitcases to pack, nothing. The few garments by the mattress were simply not worth bothering about. There seemed literally nothing else to do but take Miri by the hand and lead her out. Stone had shrugged it off and Miri, once she was in his company, seemed to be completely passive. Patsy didn't know what to do. She sat down beside her sister.

"Is it your child?" she asked, looking at Stone. The problem just occurred to her.

"Might be."

"Oh, shit," Patsy said. "What an incredible goddamn mess. I have a genius for screwing up and even I couldn't screw up this bad."

"No mess," Stone said. "You just takin' her away. I knew somebody would, sometime. It's always happenin'. You get mixed up with some chick with redneck kinfolks 'n' sooner or later some redneck gonna come and take her away."

Patsy didn't want to argue. She wanted to leave. "You think anything you want of me and I'll think anything I want of you," she said. "Since we don't know one another, that's what we'll have to do. Could you at least tell me what my sister's been taking to make her like this? I might need to tell a doctor."

He looked a Miri wearily, as if he wished they were both gone. "She takes this and that," he said. "Little speed, little acid, smoke some grass, few pills—whatever we run into."

"No wonder she doesn't know where she is," Patsy said. "Look, I'm not trying to banish you from her life forever. I don't know what I think about the future. I just know she's in wretched shape and needs to be healthier. I assume you had your chance to take care of her and now I'm going to have mine. But I'll give you my address and phone number and you might give me an address where I could reach you. I don't know what might come up."

Stone shook his head, as if talk of addresses was completely senseless. "You leavin', Miri?" he asked in the gentlest voice he had used, but the way he said it was ambiguous. Patsy could not tell if it was a question or a statement.

"Isn't there going to be a party somewhere?" Miri asked.

"Come on, honey," Patsy said, taking her arm. Miri stood up and looked at Stone briefly, but whatever impulse had caused him to speak gently had been only momentary and he was looking at both of them with clear hostility again, the same hostility that had been in his face when he first came to the door that morning.

"Goodbye," Patsy said. Stone turned away and said nothing.

When they were in the hall, on the stairs, Miri looked at Patsy hostilely and said, "Why didn't you invite him too?"

"Not now," Patsy said.

Joe and Melissa were relieved to see them. The two young men were looking at the Morgan as if it were a beautiful piece of sculpture. But the Morgan was a problem. There were six of them. Since Stone had been no trouble, Melissa decided the young men were dispensable, but that still left four. Finally Patsy and Miri and Melissa took a taxi and Joe followed in the Morgan as a kind of rear guard. Miri was silent, but quite passive. They decided to go to Melissa's house, where Miri could clean up a bit. Once in the taxi, Patsy relaxed—a little too soon, as it happened. Miri was sitting on the outside, and when the taxi stopped for a light on California Street she simply opened the door and got out. She was out before Patsy could move. It was very awkward, for the light changed just then. Miri got across ahead of it, and it was hard to pursue. Fortunately, though, she was not running, nor even trying to lose them. She wandered into a big grocery store, where they caught her, and once caught she was quite passive and went back with them to the taxi, talking about the grapefruit in the store.

Barry was gone when they got to Melissa's. Miri seemed to recognize the house and did not seem frantic. Melissa showed her the bathtub and she immediately wanted to take a bath. While it was running Melissa offered to run out and buy Miri some shoes and a decent sweater and skirt and Patsy gave her some money. Joe made plane reservations and went back to the hotel to check the two of them out. They were a well-functioning team; only Patsy had nothing to do. There was a plane to Dallas in four hours.

Once Joe and Melissa were gone, Patsy kept hearing the water running in the bathroom and became worried. Perhaps Miri was drowning herself. She peeked, very cautiously. Miri had filled the tub to the very top, and was sitting in it. All her clothes were stuffed in the bathroom wastebasket. Her hair was wet and she was fingering the medallion around her neck and humming softly. It was an old deep 1920s tub; the water covered Miri's breasts.

Patsy was relieved and went and sat in Melissa's quiet, bright room, in the rope chair by the bay window. She could see a corner of the little park where they had walked. She heard the tub draining, in the silence, and then heard it begin to fill again. She was puzzled, and peeked a second time. Miri was standing with her back to the door, her feet on a towel, waiting for the tub to fill again. Her hips seemed very slim.

She was still bathing when Melissa returned with the clothes. In the end she emptied and filled the tub four times. Melissa said let her, it was harmless enough. They put the clothes inside the door. Then they dropped their guard again and Miri almost got away. Patsy wanted to see the view from the bedroom again, and while she looked Melissa sat on the mattress sewing up a hole in one of Barry's sweaters. They were chatting, not worried about Miri at all, when they heard the living room door shut. "Barry?" Melissa asked, surprised. But it was Miri leaving. She had slipped quietly out. They rushed out and caught her before she had gone a block, but it gave Patsy the jitters. She was glad when Joe returned. Miri sat in the living room plunking softly on Barry's guitar, her black hair still damp from the several washings she had given it. Joe Percy sat down by her and began to talk to her as if they were old friends, and Miri warmed to him and began to chatter, still playing the guitar. They talked about Simon and Garfunkel, and about the Jefferson Airplane. Then Miri got up and began to walk restlessly around the room, carrying the guitar.

"Let's go on to the airport," Joe said. "We can walk around until the plane leaves."

Melissa decided to stay with them until the end, and Patsy was just as glad. They called a taxi and just as it arrived Barry arrived too, carrying a sackful of vegetables and a paperback copy of *One Flew Over the Cuckoo's Nest*. He decided to come along and folded himself into the front seat of the cab while the four of them squeezed in the back. Miri was silent. She looked strained again, and a little wild. As the taxi curved onto the Bayshore freeway Patsy glanced back at the hills and white houses and wished for a moment that all was different, that she could walk around with Joe and Barry and Melissa and see the city. As it was, she could scarcely be conscious of anything but the troubled face of her sister. She could hardly believe that Miri seemed to know her so little, so intermittently.

At the airport they thought to pass time by watching the planes come in, but Miri's face was tightening. She looked wild and tense and scared of the crowds, and they were all worried. "Maybe we ought to feed her," Joe suggested. Patsy was dubious, but it proved a good suggestion. The airport restaurant was not too crowded. Melissa ordered Miri some chicken noodle soup, while the rest of them had coffee. The waitress brought a little plate of crackers and Miri ate them all before the soup came. Then she ate all the soup and did not protest when Patsy asked if she would like a grilled cheese sandwich. Patsy ordered it and Miri ate it all.

It dawned on the four of them simultaneously that Miri was starving. They ordered her a salad and some milk and a hot roast beef sandwich. Miri ate the sandwich and asked for another. While it was coming, she asked Patsy what color Davey's eyes were. "I couldn't tell from the pictures you sent," she said, wiping her mouth. Barry regarded her with wonder and a certain amount of envy. He was hungry but Melissa wouldn't let him spend their money in an airport restaurant. "Could I have some ice cream?" Miri asked. She felt her hair to see if it was dry. She had ice cream and pie and coffee and leaned back in the booth, looking like a sane, clean, and somewhat somnolent girl who would like to take a nap. The rest of them, excepting Barry, felt almost slack with relief. Barry had not been tense. Patsy took advantage of the lull to call Jeanette. She told her to have Davey and Juanita ready. They were all going to Houston that night.

Miri was okay but might react badly to Dallas. Jeanette was numb with gratitude and agreed to everything.

On the way to the loading gate Miri walked ahead with Barry, talking rapidly. Joe and Patsy and Melissa all felt bushed, although Melissa made a pretense of it being all in the day's routine. Patsy felt so grateful to all of them that she feared she would start crying if she tried to express it. At the gate she thanked Melissa rather awkwardly and Melissa smilingly passed it over by giving her messages to Lee, messages which it would not matter if she forgot. Barry put his arm around Melissa as they were waiting. They made a great tall couple, Patsy thought. She resolved to sing their praises to Lee and Bill. Patsy had brought nothing to read and Barry pulled the Kesey book out of his jacket and pressed it on her, assuring her he could get another the next day at the bookstore. As Miri was quiet, and waiting awkward, they waved and wandered off to window-shop in the airport stores.

Miri was sitting comfortably in one of the seats in the waiting room yawning and looking out the window, and Patsy and Joe stood at the railing that separated passengers from guests, talking awkwardly about things that didn't interest them. Joe looked a little ragged, and Patsy remembered that he had his love problem. She had wanted to talk to him about it, but she felt too odd and choked to want to do it there in the airport; she felt she had only a few threads of control left. Joe apparently felt somewhat the same way and they chatted without hearing each other and looked out at the blue sky over the brown hills of the peninsula. Tiny cars sped by at the foot of the hills. When the flight was called they were both glad, and they looked at each other finally. Tears started in Patsy's eyes.

"Okay, thanks, buddy," she said. "Please don't get your dumb heart broken."

Joe shrugged and grinned, as if to say such things were not in his power to prevent, and then he reached across the rail and hugged and kissed her. Patsy picked up her purse and got her ticket ready; Miri got in line with her, still yawning. Joe stood at the rail watching. "I'd know you for sisters anywhere," he said. "What a pair of broads." They both looked pleased.

"Hollywood to the end," Patsy said, turning to wave goodbye.

"I accompany you," he said. "Call me if I can help."

"Oh, Joe," she said, and the line pressed her into the plane.

"Want to read?" Patsy asked when they were both settled, but Miri merely nodded. They were both silent as they waited for the plane to fill, and silent as it taxied out the runway. But their silence was pensive, not awkward or hostile. Both looked out the window at the hills with the cars speeding at their feet, or at the planes coming in one after another over the water. It was a pleasant silence, as if both were glad that for a few hours nothing would be expected of either of them except that they sit. They were flying first class and it was very comfortable. As they went up, the white bank of evening fog was just pushing at the line of hills; the sun shone on the fog and made it brilliantly white, white as a cloud. In a few minutes they were over the Sierras, very beautiful and rough and capped with snow. Patsy had never seen mountains so clearly from the air. They shone beneath the plane, and all California stretched beside them, brown and white and blue at the horizons. Joe and Melissa and Barry would scarcely be back in the city. And then Joe would be driving intensely down the freeways, most of the night probably, unless he chose to stay in San Francisco and drink. She hoped Melissa and Barry would ask him to dinner; she didn't like to think of him drinking alone. It had been a hard day. She was tempted to have a gin and tonic but remembered that she had to drive to Houston. She could not afford to get too relaxed.

She was not allowed to relax, anyway, for as they were passing over Nevada, Miri, who had been sitting quietly, leafing through the Kesey book, opened her little purse and before Patsy noticed what she was doing took out a marijuana cigarette and lit it. Patsy caught the faint odor and looked around to discover to her horror that Miri was offering marijuana to the well-dressed middle-aged couple who sat across the aisle. The man looked startled for a second but immediately recovered his aplomb and he and his wife declined and spoke kindly to Miri, who offered the cigarette to Patsy. The stewardess came just at that time to take dinner orders; though she must have observed what Miri was smoking she treated it with the utmost cool and merely let down their trays. "Look, please put it out," Patsy said. "Please. Wait until we get home. I don't want you having your baby in jail."

After one more draw Miri complied. "I guess I better save it," she said, looking into her purse. "I don't know anyone to buy it from in Texas."

She ate her food when it came, but Patsy hardly touched hers. She was tight with apprehension. It occurred to her that the cool stewardess had probably told the pilot, who would probably radio the Dallas police. Narcotics agents would be waiting for them when they got off the plane. She thought of making a personal appeal to the stewardess, or of having Miri flush it, but she knew Miri wouldn't want to and in any case her paranoia was accompanied by a kind of fatalistic lethargy. All she did was sit and worry. The land darkened; lights winked far below. Miri read in the Kesey book. "I met him," she said, and talked in her light voice about a party, but Patsy was too glazed with worry to hear.

As they left the plane in Dallas Patsy tried to think of what to say to the agents, but no agents appeared. They left the airport unmolested, and the relief carried her through an awkward half-hour at her parents'. Miri was extremely uncomfortable there. She moved restlessly from one room to another; Patsy tried to pack the Ford and yet stay in the same room with her, because it was obvious she would leave if a chance arose. Garland and Jeanette had no idea what to do or say, and Miri shut within herself and would not say a word to them. Patsy made all the conversation, to Garland, to Jeanette, to Miri, to Juanita. Davey had been asleep but woke as they were transferring him to the Ford. Patsy put Miri in the back seat with him, Juanita in the front with her, and they drove off, leaving Garland and Jeanette standing in their driveway, puzzled, awkward, and helpless. The best she had been able to do for them was to promise they could come and visit when things quieted down.

Davey had come wide awake and wanted to be in his car seat, and once he was put in it wanted to twist around and look at Miri. She seemed pleased with him and offered him a finger to hold. He held it solemnly. "Can I smoke pot now?" Miri asked.

Patsy was past caring. "I guess," she said, glancing at Juanita to see how she would take it. Juanita was worried about car wrecks, not marijuana. "What if I get stopped for speeding?"

"I could swallow it."

"Okay." Soon Davey got in the back seat and lay on his back; Miri smoked pot and tickled his stomach and played with his feet and he gurgled and babbled and sang.

It made Patsy miss him; she glanced back at him much oftener than Juanita would have liked. "Maybe your sister would like to drive," she said. "You can play with Davey." She was not above needling Patsy.

"Listen," Patsy said. "My sister is flying, can't you tell? She's high above us, in a marijuana airplane. You might as well get used to seeing her up there. She's one of those people who get high."

"I weel be high if I get to heaven," Juanita said, yawning.

"Only my sister Patsy is going to heaven," Miri said with a little giggle. "She's the only one in the world who only does right things."

"Give me peace," Patsy said. "It used to be only Davey and Juanita against me. Now I'll have to buck all three of you."

"That's right," Juanita said, looking shyly at Miri. "We make you toe the line from now on. We run the house an' you pay the bills."

They bantered for a while and Davey babbled, and then they all went to sleep and gave her peace. It was almost too much peace, for she was tired too, and three long hours from Houston. The smell of marijuana lingered in the car. To keep awake Patsy turned on the radio and, as she could get nothing else very clearly, listened to a hillbilly station in Shreveport. It reminded her of Hank. She had not called him since they had seen each other. In only a few rapid days it had become strange again, and unreal. She had no sense, as she drove, that they would ever get together again. Her immediate future was in the back seat. She could not see a future through the windshield. Ahead was the back of a truck with many license plates on it. She could not give her attention to the dark country stretching west. What she wanted was to get home, and once she got back on the long wide stretch of Interstate she pushed the Ford to its top speed, which was seventy-five. There was a mushy fog when she arrived in Houston. The downtown lights were pink and green. Davey didn't wake up as he was transferred into the house, and Juanita scarcely did. Miri woke up and was downstairs playing a record when Patsy had changed into her nightgown. She went down for a minute.

"I'm half dead," she said. "I'm going to sleep. Please don't run off."

"I'm just playing your records," Miri said. "We had to sell my phonograph."

Patsy left it at that. The next morning Juanita found Miri asleep on the couch and covered her. Davey came and stared at her and babbled mightily, but Miri slept until noon.

18

With Miri's return, a different sort of time began, different from any Patsy had known. It could not be called a bad time, and yet it was not good either, not for Patsy. March passed, and half of April and Houston was hot again. Davey had learned to walk and toddled all over the house and the yard and the park and wherever else he was let to be. Patsy mothered him, and sistered Miri, and bossed Juanita. She ruled efficiently, often irritably, always reluctantly, over her small domain. She brooded, but could not decide whether it was a life she had made because it was the life she secretly wanted, or merely a life circumstance had thrust upon her despite herself.

Miri changed, Davey changed, but she herself did not change, and in her worst moments she felt it to be unlikely that she would ever change again. She could not foresee anything happening that would make her much different than she was.

Where Miri was concerned, only the first week was scary. All that week there was a strangeness in her, an intermittent restlessness. She constantly rearranged her room, she wandered restlessly about the house, and she took baths at the rate of four or five a day. Patsy could not be sure at night that she would awake and find her still there. But Miri didn't leave. Toward the end of the week she had an eighteen-hour spell of franticness. She wanted Stone and looked at Patsy hostilely for having taken her away from him. She began to try and call him. She called everyone she knew in San Francisco, trying to find him, leaving word for him to call; but she didn't find him and he didn't call. For two days she was almost catatonic with despair; she sat by the phonograph for hours playing rock songs until Patsy thought the whole household would go crazy.

Then, gradually, Miri began to feel better. She did not become the old Miri—Patsy knew she never would—but she became happier. She became friendly again in a quiet way, and soon she began to get her looks back. For a while she was always hungry and ate enormously. Patsy was afraid she would gain too much weight and made sure she saw her doctor regularly. Her cheeks filled out, she lost her pallor, and in a month her complexion was good again. At times she was quite rosy, and once in a while would burst into a peal of laughter at something Davey did. Her periods of restlessness became less intense, and her periods of withdrawal less impenetrable. With everyone except her parents she became talkative and sociable.

Garland and Jeanette came down twice; their visits were horrors of awkwardness. They all skated constantly on the thinnest ice of convention. The visits left Patsy with terrific headaches, left Miri hostile, left Garland and Jeanette hurt and confused. Parents and children could find no safe ground to stand on. They couldn't talk with pleasure. Jeanette so overflowed with gratitude to Patsy that Patsy felt she would drown in it. By the end of the second visit Garland and Jeanette realized they were at an impasse, and after that they called. It was easier on everyone. Over the phone everyone could believe that everyone else was fine. Garland and Jeanette could hope for a miraculous eleventh-hour proper marriage of some kind, with someone, and Patsy did not get headaches.

Soon Miri was making friends. Emma and Flap liked her but she was a tiny bit suspicious of them, regarding them as Patsy's allies. Her first friend was Juanita, who soon loved Miri and could not do enough for her. Juanita became the only person who really looked forward to Miri's baby. If it was Miri's, it could not but be a precious child, whoever its father was. Juanita talked about babies constantly and could hardly wait.

Miri's second friend was Kenny Cambridge. He stopped one night to chat and he and Miri sat up all night talking and listening to records. He quickly became a suitor, taking her out to movies and on long walks around Rice. He also became her source of pot. Patsy decided she would have to allow it, but she told them both her largesse extended only to pot. "No acid," she said. But Kenny introduced Miri to a good many students and one night in April acid turned up at a party and Miri dropped it. It gave Patsy a serious scare. For two days Miri was again in her most downcast state—remote, sometimes crying, sometimes goofy, silent for long stretches, and defensive about her own exaltation. Patsy was very out of patience with her but she was too worried to explode and it passed off. Miri brightened again and seemed to have lost no ground.

It was after that, during the course of laying down the law, that the question of Stone came up for the first and only time. It was late; she and Miri were in the living room. The TV had been moved back down, so that she and Miri could watch it while she played records. Patsy was giving an anti-LSD lecture and Miri was arguing, but rhetorically, with little spirit. She had been cheerful all day but seemed low and lonely. It occurred to Patsy that perhaps she loved the boy. There might well have been a lovable side to him, one that had had no chance to show itself. She had to admit that she had seen him under the worst of circumstances.

"Do you miss Stone?" she asked.

Miri was surprised. Hearing his name caused her face to change. "Why would you care?" she asked, looking hostile.

"Don't be hostile," Patsy said. "I care about you and what affects you."

Miri looked down at the chair, a deep chair done in brown. Her hair was very long and when she bent forward it lay on the arms of the chair. "How can you not miss someone?" she asked.

"I took you away from there because you looked sick," Patsy said. "You were sick, and you know it. I didn't say you never could see him again, if you love him. I know I didn't see him under good circumstances."

"I don't think you saw him at all," Miri said. Talking about him seemed to weigh on her. She sounded very discouraged.

"I saw a very hostile person," Patsy said. "But I don't claim to have seen the whole of him. Please don't look so blue. Talk to me about him."

"No, I don't want to."

"Would you marry him if you could?"

"I don't want to marry anybody. It's stupid to get married."

"Oh? Why?" Pronouncements about marriage by someone who had never been married had come to amuse her.

"Nobody loves anybody very long."

"Don't be so cynical. I'm sure people do. You're too young to be cynical."

"I'm not so young," Miri snapped. "You didn't love Jim long, did you, and he was nice. You don't love Hank any more, either."

"I'm not sure I ever loved him," she said.

"Well, there's no point in having a lover if he's not around so you can fuck," Miri said dogmatically.

Patsy had no answer to that. Miri picked up one of Davey's socks; he was always losing them. She stretched it and smoothed it across her knee.

"Stone's already forgotten me," she said and then added

in a different, apologetic tone, "He doesn't have a very good memory," as if it were his housekey he was prone to forget.

"Was it that one-sided?"

Miri got up and went upstairs to her room without answering the question, and Patsy never asked about Stone again. When it came time to decide upon a last name for the baby, Stone was not considered. They talked it over among themselves—Miri, Patsy, and Juanita, with Emma an occasional consultant. The phone book stayed on the kitchen table for a month. Often, while Patsy idled over lunch, or drank iced tea or read magazines with her feet propped on the table, Miri, who would be just up and having breakfast pushed at her by Juanita, would read out names and the three of them would discuss their qualities. They also discussed stories for Jeanette and Garland to tell their friends. Miri was resistant on that point; she didn't want to tell any lies at all.

"Look, don't be so selfish," Patsy said. "Think of them a little. It's terrible for them. The point is that any good story we make up about it they'll come to believe, and it will be better for them to believe a sort of decent lie that they can tell their friends. It's awful for people like Momma and Daddy not to have something reasonably acceptable to tell their friends."

"Okay," Miri said finally. "You make it up."

Patsy had been putting them off by telling them that Miri simply wouldn't talk about it. Finally what she told them was that Miri had been engaged and had gotten pregnant just as she and the boy found they weren't right for marriage. She invented a fictional boy named Raymond Hammett, amalgamating the name one night when Kenny Cambridge, a detective-story buff, was haranguing them about the respective merits of Dashiell Hammett and Raymond Chandler. Miri listened almost with awe as Patsy gave their parents, via the telephone, a description of young Mr. Hammett, making him seem a highly desirable, proper, respectable, but confused and impetuous young man. She also made them promise to leave him strictly alone and told them he was paying all the bills and acquitting himself respectably, under the circumstances.

"How was that?" Patsy asked when she finished.

"Great, except I'd never screw anyone like that," Miri said. "Also you forgot to tell them he was a spade."

"Well, according to you, maybe he wasn't," Patsy said. "We'll cross that bridge when and if we come to it."

From then on, when they were in good moods, they sat around and made up stories about Raymond Hammett. Miri confused the issue by referring to him as Dashiell Chandler, or, as she usually put it, "my former lover, Dashiell Chandler." Eventually even Juanita came to believe someone named Raymond was the father. They were particularly prone to talking about Raymond Hammett-Dashiel Chandler when Kenny was around. He took detective writing as seriously as he had once taken Augustine Birrell and felt that the girls were being a little too frivolous. It irked him too that neither of them would read *The Maltese Falcon* or *The Big Sleep* or anything else he wanted them to read. He and Miri did not agree on records, though, and spent hours and hours discussing Bob Dylan, whom they both idolized. They went to see his movie four times.

For a time Patsy had a feeling that Miri and Kenny were going to get thick, and they might have had not Kenny introduced her around so much. One of the people he introduced her to was a boy named Eric Flanigan, and within a week Eric became her accepted boy friend. He was a first-year graduate student from Menlo Park, California, and he and Miri had an immediate meeting point in that they were both nostalgic for the Bay Area generally. Patsy liked Eric almost as much as Miri did and soon he was a regular feature at supper. He was slightly unhappy in graduate school and spent his free afternoons playing tennis, at which he was quite good. Often Miri would go to the court and meet him and walk with him to Dunstan Street. He would come in in his tennis clothes and gratefully consume quantities of Patsy's food while Miri chattered. He was a good-looking boy, blond and loose, with a short beard—one of those young Californians who, it seemed to Patsy, must almost constitute a new breed, they were so healthy and so alike. For Eric was a sort of shorter Barry, shy, immediately friendly, bright, but so quiet it took weeks for his brightness to show itself. He was so relaxed and at home with himself physically that it was a comfort to have him around. He was charming to watch with Miri, because she pecked and chattered and sniped at him and he took it so quietly that it was hard to decide whether he was afraid of her or merely tolerant. Eric liked Patsy's house better than his own apartment, and he spent most of his evenings there. He was having difficulties with his eighteenth-century seminar and would sit on the floor frowning mildly, usually still in his tennis shorts, reading Collins and Gray and the Whartons while Miri tussled with Davey if he was still up, or listened to records or watched TV if he wasn't. Patsy generally lay in splendor on her couch, wearing a long green caftan and watching TV or arguing with Miri or debating with Eric the merits of the various writers he was reading. She had debated most of them with Hank the year before. Eric, like Flap, was in awe of Jim's scholarly library, though it had not grown by one book since Jim had left.

Sometimes the sight of Eric and Miri sitting on the floor together, both of them pleasant and rather placid, made Patsy feel that even the five years that separated them was a long gap in generation. They were so beautiful as they were, in the present, that it bothered her a little when she tried to project them a future. Miri had simply stepped aside, stepped out of the groove of her upbringing, and she was not going to go back.

Once when Jeanette came they tried to buy her clothes, thinking a lot of new clothes might cheer her up. Miri was not resentful, she was just openly bored. She was not interested in clothes, maternity or otherwise. She wore jeans and sweatshirts, or jeans and blouses, or a cheap cotton dress she had bought herself one day. She was not interested in money, either. Patsy was a little embarrassed about it and told Miri to please ask when she needed some, and Miri did. She seldom asked for more than twenty dollars a week, and only that much when she wanted to buy records. Kenny and Eric gave her pot, and Patsy gave her food. Patsy did not see her changing back, going back to a life where one dressed up, went to classes, got married. They talked about her getting into Rice, and she didn't want to, though sociology interested her and she did consider sitting in on an urban problems seminar.

Patsy was glad to see Eric come along, for it was clear that Eric cared about Miri, and whatever her future, she had ceased to be unhappy with her present. And Eric, for all his easygoingness, was not idle or indifferent or lazy. When he got excited he got tremendously excited; he talked, he flushed, he moved. Sometimes Patsy and Miri would carry Davey over to the tennis courts and sit on the grass in the spring sun watching Eric play. He was not overserious about his tennis, but he played hard, with lots of ardor and considerable grace, and it was pleasant to sit on the green spring grass and watch.

Within two weeks Eric and Miri became such solid chums that Patsy rather regretted the invention of Raymond Hammett. Miri's pregnancy seemed no deterrent to Eric, and Miri was very delighted with him. She couldn't keep her hands off him, walked home from the tennis courts with her arm around him, and often used him as a pillow when they were stretched out on the floor. Her affection often embarrassed Eric, but it was a becoming embarrassment. He looked at once excited and shy. It came to be the rule that two or three nights a week they would wander off together to the library and then spend the night at his apartment, wandering back together the next morning when it was time for him to go to school. Patsy was delighted. He seemed to be just what Miri needed. She became stable to the point of laziness and had no more dramatic sinkings of spirit.

Patsy found that she was not without a certain dull envy, and it was particularly prone to make itself felt on nights when Miri was at Eric's. There were hours when life was noticeably empty, when she didn't want to read or watch television or visit anyone there was to visit. She had restless hours, and very few ways to work off the restlessness. Various of the graduate students seemed always on the verge of asking her out, but none did, whether intimidated by the thought of Jim, or Hank, or simply her, she couldn't tell. There were some she would have accepted dates with, but none she cared to pursue, so she never went out unless Eric and Miri were going to a movie and asked her along.

At such times, feeling manless and over the hill and resenting both feelings, she usually called Hank and, often as not, picked a fight with him. Her own ambivalence toward him seemed to provide fertile seed for argument. She wanted him back, and yet she didn't. If he were there he would probably eventually con her into marrying him, and she didn't want to. She had a feeling that as a husband he would be more of a burden than a support, and having just dropped one burden she was not anxious to pick up another. She didn't want him to come—she just wanted him to be there, without coming or being asked. It was an impossible desire. He was broke, and his car was broken down, but the unreasonableness of her desire did not keep it from being strong. It led to fights that neither of them expected and that neither of them could stop. Later, after an hour or two of resentment and self-pity, Patsy would usually break down and call back, and some sort of reconciliation would be effected, better than nothing, but a poor substitute for all that she missed. It was decided that in late April they would meet at the ranch again, and in brooding on it Patsy could not decide whether to leave Davey and go up alone or whether to take them all, Eric included. One day she felt one way, one day another. There were certain things the ranch house needed to make it fully habitable and she was more or less inclined to go up alone and buy them and move them in. But the date was a month away and on dull nights what she needed more than anything was something immediate to look forward to.

It was on such a night that Jim called to present his conclusions on divorce. His calls had become increasingly infrequent and light and impersonal, and Patsy had come to take it for granted that his conclusions, once he got around to presenting them, would be positive for divorce. She even assumed that he would never get around to presenting them unless she or Clara prodded him. Thus it was a considerable surprise when he called and said he wanted to talk about it, and then said he didn't want a divorce, he wanted to get them back together again.

"What did you say?" she asked. "Are you serious?"

"Of course I am. I still love you. If you're fond of me at all

I could make you love me now, I think. I'm smarter than I was."

Patsy was silent, troubled, not sure what to say.

"You can't have lost all your fondness for me," Jim said.

"Maybe I haven't," she said, "but it's certainly not going to increase while you're out there living with her. You are still living with her?"

"Yes, but I can break it off."

"I wish you'd done it before you called."

"I can," he said.

"Okay," she said. "You can, but you're not willing to until you're sure of me, right?"

"Why are you always so skeptical of me?" he asked.

"I don't know."

He went on, but not so confidently as he had begun. It turned out he wanted Patsy to sell the house and bring Davey to L.A.

"For god's sake why?"

"I like my job and I like California."

"You like Los Angeles?" she said.

"Sure. You weren't here long enough to be able to appreciate it."

"It seemed long enough to me," Patsy said. "Anyway, that's impossible. I have Miri now, remember. She's doing fine and she's going to stay right here where Juanita and I can take care of her until she has her baby."

She could tell by his silence that he was annoyed, that he felt she was more concerned with Miri than with saving their marriage. But he held his annoyance in.

"Well, that won't be too long," he said. "I could break off with Clara and once Miri's okay you could come on out."

"Oh, Jim," she said. "That will be months. We'll have half forgotten one another by then. We've half forgotten one another now."

"So you don't really want to stay married?"

"I don't want to move to Los Angeles," Patsy said. "Any time. I like this house very much and I don't want to move out of it."

"I suppose it's convenient," he said. "You can see your boy friend."

817

"I haven't. Not since I went to California. I think we can leave him out of it."

"Why?" he said. "It's tit for tat. You want me to give up Clara."

"It's not tit for tat. I'm not living with him and I never have."

They were both silent, uncertain as to where to go with the conversation. "Why don't you come back here if you want to stay married?" Patsy asked. "If you like your job so much maybe you could get transferred. I'm sure there's an IBM office here. I don't want Davey growing up in Los Angeles. It's too provincial."

"Oh, shit," he said. "Don't be so provincial."

They reached a point where they both wanted to stop talking. Suddenly the idea of reuniting struck them both as absurd. They ceased to be angry and rang off as politely as casual acquaintances.

But Jim was not quite through with it. He called again three days later and said he was looking into the transfer possibility. For a moment Patsy felt receptive. She had been thinking about it for three days, and in the abstract, detached from the actuality of Jim, a reconciliation seemed highly reasonable and highly desirable. It would simplify the future enormously. She would not have to move, not have to get a divorce, not have to make any hard decisions. She would simply have a husband again, and one who was a known quantity. Hank, considered as a husband, was only a question mark. He had never even really proposed.

Thus, she was thinking affirmatively of a reconciliation, but when Jim actually called and spoke of returning she did a quick switch within herself. Something hardened. She didn't like his tone. It was the tone he used when he was thinking of abandoning one line of work and starting another.

"Are you sure it's me you want back?" she asked. "Or are you just tired of what you're doing?"

"I knew you'd ask that," he said bitterly. "Every time I try to approach you, you ask something like that. You don't believe in me at all. You block me at every goddamn turn with some question."

"Well, I'm sorry," Patsy said, and she was, a little. "It's my future too."

"I do want you," he said. "I do. Maybe I'm a little confused right now, but I do. If I can get a transfer I'm sure I can get some kind of job in Houston. I could go back to graduate school, if worst comes to worst. It isn't as if we need money."

The more he talked the more she hardened, and the surer she felt in her resistance. He began to talk about all they could do, the ways they could improve themselves, and in the midst of his projection of the future she cut him off.

"No," she said. "No, no. I'm sorry. I don't want it."

"What?" he said, a little panicky. "Don't want what?"

"Oh, I don't know," she said, weary of talk. "I don't want what you're imagining. I don't want you, either. I just don't want any more of anyone's confusion. I can barely cope with my own. If I marry again I'm going to marry someone who knows what he's doing, even if he's sixty years old."

Jim had trouble believing that she meant it. "But you have to be a little tolerant, my god," he said. "Everyone's a little confused."

"I should be but I don't have to be," Patsy said. "I'm just not tolerant—I'm sorry. I don't want to talk about it any more. I'll do anything you want to about a divorce. I'll go to Juárez if you want me to."

He wouldn't believe it, not that night or the next or the next. He called every night, and they argued. The arguments flared into fights, she wept, her stomach hurt, Jim threatened to come, they rehashed all their old grievances against each other, and always it came out the same. "Quit badgering me," she said finally. "Do something if you want something to change. I don't want to go through this every night."

Jim quit calling, but it did not improve her mood. For a week she felt bad about herself. Through sheer obstinacy she had succeeded in welding him to another woman. It annoyed her that he was never able to break her down, for it left her feeling that she was hard and domineering. But there it was. She got her way whether she really wanted it or not. And probably she would be the same with Hank or anyone—hard, obstinate, and unmovable. She doubted that anyone could really cope with her willfulness, or that anyone would really want to for long.

One afternoon late in April, she found herself in a deep midafternoon depression, sick of everything. She was sick of giving orders to Juanita, sick of walking Davey to the same park every day, sick of cooking meals for Miri and Eric, sick of watching them hold hands, sick of thinking about Jim, and sick of thinking about Hank. She was sick of Emma, whose problems depressed her more than her own, and sick of Houston, with its stagnant, fishy morning smells. She was sick of everything. She moved about the house in a state of near-desperate disgust with everything, herself, her wretched temperament, and the general conditions of life. She was even constipated and was in the bathroom laying unsuccessful siege on her intestines. She looked at herself in the bathroom mirror and decided to cut her hair. She got her scissors and came back and cut it immediately. Davey was just up from his nap and waddled in while she was doing it. He picked up some of the fallen tresses and soon had hair all over his clean corduroy overalls. "Oh, get out of here," Patsy said, very irritated. She dragged him out, gave him a sharp little splat on his behind, shut the door, and continued to cut, not heeding Davey's offended wails. She did a rough job of cutting, but when she finished, her hair was short. Unevenly short, but short. She gathered up the fallen hair and stuffed it in the bathroom wastebasket, then lay on her bed and cried until her face was puffy. Davey came in while she was crying, tugged one of her house shoes off, and took it away. He was still very fond of house shoes.

Juanita, Miri, and Emma in turn tiptoed around the subject of her hair. They were all startled when she appeared roughly shorn, and they all complimented her insincerely on her new hair style. She did not bother to challenge the insincerity; she didn't care. It was three days before anyone asked her why she cut it, and then it was Eric who asked. Patsy had cooked spaghetti and Eric was eating it all. Miri was upstairs changing. They were all going to a movie.

"How come you cut your hair?" he asked mildly. "I liked it better long."

Patsy gave him a black look, but he was draining his glass of milk and the look was lost on him.

"If you knew anything about women you wouldn't ask one why she cut her hair," she said coldly.

Eric looked slightly disconcerted, as if until that moment he had taken it for granted that one could suppose he knew the slightest thing about women. It was only when it dawned on him that Patsy was out of temper that he grew embarrassed about his question. To conceal it he poked Davey in the ribs with one finger and Davey giggled and writhed in his highchair and knocked a ring of plastic spoons to the floor.

"Well, it'll grow back, I guess," Eric said. Eric looked on the bright side, and when he encountered a flame that needed damping, his customary procedure was to smother it with optimistic truisms. Patsy was well aware of the habit; it was one of the few things she didn't like about him. Davey wailed for his spoons, stretching his fingers piteously toward the floor.

"Oh, pick up his goddamn spoons," she said. "Shut up about my hair or I'll throw this spaghetti at you. Don't say anything optimistic, either. For all you know I may go bald."

But it was hard for Eric to choke off his optimism so abruptly. "You could get a nice wig," he said, and then, looking at her, decided he would take Davey into the living room and wait for Miri there.

By the time they got back from the movie Patsy's pet had passed off and she apologized for her rudeness. He shrugged. "I guess it was a symbolic gesture," he said sagely.

"Right," Patsy said. "A symbolic gesture meaning fuck everything."

He and Miri had come in rather timorously, prepared for an attack, and Eric was so relieved that Patsy was in a better mood that he gave vent to more optimism. "Well, you'll probably feel better about something soon," he said.

"No, that's the point. I'm not going to feel better. I'm resigned to a wasted life. I deserve one and I'm going to have one."

"Why?" Miri asked.

"Don't ask me why."

"I agree, you know," Eric said. "I'm resigned to one too. Got any coffee? We have to study."

"We? What's she studying?"

"Babies," Miri said. She had used Eric's library card and checked out all the books on babies that Patsy had read a year and a half before. Raymond Hammett's child was beginning to interest her. Seeing the books gave Patsy a sense of déjà vu, and it got worse, for in a little while Miri stretched out on the floor and had with Eric the conversation about *Tristram Shandy* that she had had with Hank when he was trying to read it. Eric didn't like it either, and Patsy loved it and joined in the argument. In a minute she was arguing with Eric about Norman Mailer. They both got very excited.

Patsy eventually won the argument over Sterne, but Eric wore her down on the subject of Mailer. She got up yawning and left the living room to the lovers. "Even if we started talking about *Beowulf* I bet we'd end up talking about Norman Mailer," she said. "If I had any more hair I'd go cut it off."

"Have a baby," Miri suggested. "It takes your mind off literature."

"Not a bad idea," Patsy said. "If you see Dashiell Chandler have him look me up."

The next day her midafternoon gloom recurred, though not quite so severely, and she went to the drugstore and attempted to cut it with a milkshake and a couple of fashion magazines. Bill Duffin came in while she was reading and once again managed to survey what she was reading before she noticed him.

"You see more bosom in *Vogue* than you see in *Playboy* these days," he said. "Better bosom too."

In an attempt to conceal the damage she had done she wore a blue scarf around her head, but the change was not lost on William Duffin.

"You have a lovely neck," he said. "I always suspected it."

Patsy went on reading.

"I wish I had back all the compliments I've wasted on you," he said, looking at her with exasperation.

"They've been rather common, as I remember," Patsy said. "I shouldn't think their loss would have bankrupted your imagination."

"Your neck is certainly lovelier than your disposition."

"Yes, I'm in touchy temper these days. I'm likely to trample your middle-aged sensibilities if you're not careful."

"I hear you saw my daughter and liked her young man."

"Oh, very much."

"I hear he's taller than me."

"He is. Sweeter too." She smiled. Bill smiled too. "Trampling your sensibilities is like trampling ball bearings," she said.

"I'm really nicer, now that I've quit trying to s-c-r-e-w you."

She was amused. "Whose modesty are you sparing?" she asked. "You never really tried very hard, you know."

"I'm aging. I need easy conquests."

"Every time I see you in this drugstore all we do is talk about sex. Can't we have an ordinary conversation?"

"Good milkshake?" he said, to oblige her.

"Yep, they keep calling me back. Would you and Lee like to come to dinner in your former house next week? I didn't get a chance to make Melissa any sort of return for all the kind things she did for me. The least I can do is feed her parents."

"We'd love to," Bill said.

He prevailed upon her to let him pay for her milkshake for once. The invitation had been quite spur-of-the-moment, but she was glad she had done it. The Duffins would be a pleasant change from Eric and Miri. She walked home feeling better. Perhaps she would invite the Hortons. A strong temptation came over her to call Hank and insist that he come and be her date. It would be a nice occasion on which to have a date. She envisioned it as being very pleasant and gay—her debut as a woman of the world.

But when she talked to Hank next she changed her mind and didn't mention the dinner. In the end she called Kenny Cambridge and asked him to be her date. "You'll wear a tie and you'll pour the wine," she said.

"Am I supposed to be a date or a waiter?" he asked good-humoredly.

"A date with many duties and few privileges," she said. "This is your big chance, you realize."

Kenny actually wore a tie, poured the wine, corrupted himself by talking scholarship politely with Bill and Flap, and grinned at the end of the evening when Patsy gave him a handshake as a reward. Earlier, Bill Duffin had praised her cooking and had bent down majestically and kissed her on the cheek. Lee, clearly in a down phase, had been silent all evening, subdued and a little bitter-looking.

"This isn't what I had in mind," Kenny said. "My services merit a better reward."

"Well, possibly. What did you have in mind?"

"Jim has a copy of Gary Snyder's first book," he said. "He's my favorite poet. Could I have it?"

"Good god," she said. "Help yourself, if you can find it. It's what I get for asking a literary man to be my date. You could have asked for me. Next time I'll get me a cowboy. I wish I could remember the name of the first one who ever tried to seduce me. He pissed on my car. He wouldn't have been thinking of Gary Snyder in such a situation."

"That's the way it goes," Kenny said, and as he went out he too kissed her on the cheek.

19

The week after she had the Duffins in to dinner, Patsy received an invitation which surprised her. It was from a couple called the Caldwells, an older couple who were friends of Jim's parents. She and Jim scarcely knew them, but twice, on grand occasions, they had been asked to dinner at the Caldwells' and had gone and been bored in a quiet but high style.

The Caldwells were of the very wealthy; their fortune was

one of the most respectable and the most respected in the state, but it was respected within a certain circle only, for they were in no sense flamboyant. The Caldwells were not of the Hunts, the Mecoms, or the Murchisons. They built no hotels, bought no football teams, owned no newspapers; they had no links with the White House, raced no horses, bred no fancy cattle. The Caldwells had no image at all or, at least, none comparable to the size of their fortune. They were known nationally only to those who knew finance, and locally as regular, dutiful contributors to charity and to the arts. They lived much as Jim's parents lived, quietly if restlessly, and occupied their time with travel and rather haphazard art collecting. They were not extraordinarily memorable, or extraordinarily likable, but they were pleasant, they were kindly, they seemed like people who had been able to occupy themselves for sixty years without going crazy and hoped, with luck, to keep it up another decade or so. The dinners Jim and Patsy attended had been stiff. The Caldwells knew only the wealthy and enjoyed only a small fraction of the wealthy they knew—mostly rather quiet conservative people like themselves who, despite their fortunes, seemed bent on nothing more ambitious than not going crazy. The talk at the dinners was not unpleasant, just uninspired. A little politics, a little gossip, usually pedestrian and fairly good-natured, a little sport, a little art, and mostly places—places everyone had been, places everyone would go again, in particular Mexico.

Mrs. Caldwell was a thin graying woman who gave an impression of feebleness. She smoked a great deal and the hand she held her cigarette with shook. Hostessing seemed an effort for her, but she worked at it. Individual guests were sometimes taken for long distances into the interior of the huge house to be shown particular works of art. Patsy had once been shown three Rothkos.

The dinner party of the evening was larger than the ones she and Jim had attended. Some twenty people were there, enough to fill the small paneled den where cocktails were being served. The den held no Rothkos, only an English oil portrait. Mr. Caldwell—Ted, he liked to be called—was a small dapper man; he was fond of Patsy, twinkled at her, and shook her hand at length. Mrs. Caldwell kissed her, as she always did, and as always Patsy found it difficult not to notice that at some point Mrs. Caldwell had had a face-lifting operation. While Mr. Caldwell was shaking her hand and telling her an anecdote about Jim's parents, whose path he had crossed in New York, of all places, Patsy looked past him into the room and saw, with a strange shock of surprise, that Eleanor Guthrie was there. It should have been no surprise, for in terms of fortune Eleanor and the Caldwells were peers, and in Texas peers of that class all knew one another. But she was a person Patsy had never expected to see again, and there she was, sitting across the room. The attentions of three men were focused on her, one sitting on each side of her, drink in hand, one standing looking down at her, swirling his drink; but Eleanor's attention seemed not to be focused anywhere. She too held a drink and seemed to be listening only in the most perfunctory way to the remarks the three men made. She was dressed in brown, and very soberly, and her heavy dark blond hair was combed long.

Patsy was taken and introduced to the two youngest couples there. They were standing in a corner, rather apart, talking of Antonioni. *Blow-Up* had been the rage two years before and Patsy was a little surprised to find people still talking about it, but she was ever quick with an opinion and chatted pleasantly until dinnertime. One of the men was a broker, the other in oil. Their wives were Eastern girls, smart and very pretty; they fluttered as gallantly as possible in the stiff social shrubbery of Houston. Patsy liked them and hoped they liked her. She felt in need of new friends. But all the while, as she talked, she was slightly conscious of Eleanor Guthrie behind her. What she really wanted to do was go over, cut through the men, and talk with Eleanor. She wanted to, but she didn't; she didn't even get to speak to her as they were moving in to dinner. She noticed, though, that Eleanor seemed heavier, not only her body but her face. Her legs seemed thin. Her weight, which she had once worked at keeping well distributed, had gone to her middle, to her stomach and hips, and she moved more slackly than she had. She was seated at the side of her host, Ted Caldwell, and Patsy was almost at the opposite end of the table, next to a bald and very shrewd-looking investment counselor who talked to her learnedly of wines. When he saw that his connoiseurship was boring her a little he grew silent, and to encourage him Patsy told him she had a certain amount of money and wondered if she ought to come to him for counseling. He asked her how much, and when she told him he very tactfully explained why he could not handle accounts of that size. She felt a little deflated, for she had always supposed herself to be a girl with money. Jim's having so much more had never mattered to her, and it was a mild shock to find that, in comparison to the other people at the table, she had little more financial weight than a ribbon clerk at Woolworth's.

It was difficult, even after dinner, for her to get near Eleanor, and so far as she could tell, Eleanor had not recognized her, probably because of her short hair. When they left the table the two young Eastern wives caught Patsy again, and the same three men caught Eleanor, and Patsy was afraid she might actually leave without them speaking. Finally she excused herself and went and stood slightly behind the two men and Eleanor looked up from her brandy and saw her. There was a strained expression on her face, the effect of trying to be polite in a situation that simply didn't reach her.

"Why, Mrs. Carpenter," she said and stood up and took Patsy's hand. The men had been like a wall, but when Eleanor stood up they sank back. She managed, merely by the way she spoke to Patsy, to cut them off, to make them understand that a person she wished to talk to had appeared. The men were perfunctorily introduced and moved a little distance away, politely and mutually annoyed, but aware that they were powerless. For a minute or two Patsy was aware of them as slightly antagonistic presences nearby, but then she forgot them, as Eleanor clearly had.

For a second after saying hello they both fell awkwardly silent, Eleanor adjusting to her surprise, Patsy simply not sure what to say. Eleanor recovered first.

"You've cut your hair," she said. "That's why I didn't recognize you. I kept thinking as I was eating that I heard a familiar voice, somewhere around the table. How have you been?"

"Oh, fine," Patsy said. She felt odd and almost regretted having spoken to Eleanor, for where could it lead? They didn't know each other well enough to talk—not to talk personally—and yet, because of the people, the men they had known, they knew each other too well for dinner party chitchat to be absorbing. She might as well have stayed across the room with the young Eastern women, talking of Antonioni. The men from whom she had taken Eleanor were still there, waiting to draw around her again. Fortunately Eleanor sensed the feeling and knew what to do about it.

"I have to go to the powder room for a minute," she said. "Would you like to come along? I've got so I can't think in rooms full of people."

She picked up a small purse from a lamp table and as she turned gave the three men a look of sullen annoyance, as if to warn them away. Patsy followed her to the powder room, which was large, with white walls and a very blue rug.

"God, I don't like this rug," Eleanor said. "Every time I come in this room I wish I were a thousand miles away. The rest of the house is nice." There were two or three chairs and a long mirror and Eleanor sat down in one of the chairs, turning it around first so that her back was to the mirror. She lit a cigarette and for a second her face was concealed by the smoke. She slumped a little in her chair and sighed as if she were very tired.

"Who were those men?" Patsy asked. "They certainly were monopolizing you."

"Oh, a bachelor and two philanderers," Eleanor said. "You'll probably be hearing from one or another of them in a few days."

"Me? They weren't paying any attention to me. I think they were mad at me for butting in."

"That will pass," Eleanor said.

Patsy looked in the very bright mirror and touched her hair. In the white room, with a good mirror, the shortness of it looked all the more odd. She frowned and took out her comb, but all she could do was rough it out a bit. There was no way it could be made to look like it had. Eleanor turned and glanced at her.

"They were just after me tonight," she said. "Next week one of them will have a dinner party and ask you. You're a fresh face. I bet one of the philanderers is pumping Ted Caldwell about you now. You must have noticed that we seem to attract the same men."

"Ugh," Patsy said. "Not those, surely."

Eleanor was looking at Patsy's hair. She reached up with a frown to straighten her own. "Mine needs thinning," she said. "I never seem to get around to anything these days. Did Jim's breaks heal well?"

"Finally," Patsy said, a little nervously.

"I hear from Joe Percy that the two of you are separated. I hope you don't mind my mentioning it."

"I don't." She bent over and opened a lipstick but then closed it again without using it and sat down. The room had affected her as it affected Eleanor. It was too bright—not a room to stay in more than five minutes. And yet she didn't feel like going back amid the guests.

"I wish I'd brought my brandy," Eleanor said. "If we unscrewed a few light bulbs it wouldn't be so bad in here."

"I saw Joe a month or so ago," Patsy said.

"Yes, he mentioned that when he mentioned Jim. I suppose I may have played a minor part in your troubles, and if so I apologize."

"Forget it," Patsy said. "Everybody played a minor part in our troubles. I'm sure we insisted on everyone participating."

"The sad thing is that Jim is very nice," Eleanor said. "He doesn't really dislike anyone. What am I doing? Of all things to say. I'm really not very alert this time of night."

"No, it's true," Patsy said. "Did Joe tell you about his love problem?"

"Yes. He told me. I wouldn't worry too much about Joe. His real love is dead; it's why he's such an invaluable sympathizer. I made him come and hold my hand for a week, when Sonny was killed. Sooner or later I imagine he'll help the young lady rescue a sister or get over the death of a lover or not feel so bad because her husband's the way he is.

He likes women so much he can cheer anyone up, if he's given a chance."

Just then Mrs. Caldwell looked in, obviously a little worried by their disappearance. "Anything the matter?" she asked, concern in her face.

"Oh, no, Beth," Eleanor said, smiling. "We were just sitting here talking about our friends."

"You're welcome to our upstairs den," Mrs. Caldwell whispered, but Eleanor shook her head.

"No, I'm worn out. I'd like to get back to the hotel." She stood up and straightened her dress.

"I wish I could go with you," Mrs. Caldwell said. "Grady's drunk and letting the niggers have it. We had a scene with him five years ago and I think we're going to have another one tonight."

She went out and Eleanor turned to the mirror and looked at her hair but did nothing with it. In the bright light Patsy saw how much her face had changed. It was not heavier—if anything she had lost flesh in the face. It was as if she no longer cared to carry her beauty and was letting it leave her as it would. Some remained, some had fallen away. Eleanor seemed almost indifferent. Unhappiness showed in her eyes and in the set of her mouth; there was no longer any pride in her expression. Boredom, sorrow, disappointment, were things she was no longer attempting to conceal. She took her purse and they left the powder room and said but little more. "I wish you could come and see my son," Patsy said, but Eleanor did not look interested. She was leaving in the morning, she said.

Several of the party were saying their goodbyes when they came out, and when Patsy said she must leave too, Beth Caldwell arranged for one of the young couples to drive her home. It turned out that Eleanor had an escort, not one of the three pursuers but a short gentle-looking lawyer with a large curved nose. His name was Taylor, and Patsy learned later that he was a widower. They all stepped out into the broad driveway together and Eleanor and Patsy said goodbye as Mr. Taylor was helping Eleanor on with her light spring coat. Though he seemed very nice, Eleanor appeared to be slightly intolerant of him, and when he was slipping her coat on she stepped away and shrugged it on herself; she straightened her collar and swung her head so that her hair hung free. She gave Patsy an odd quick smile as she turned to go, a smile half friendly and half bitter. Then she turned and put her hands in her coat pocket with an authority of movement that, for a moment, brought all her presence back.

An ambulance was screaming up Fannin Street toward the hospital, the *wheeaaaw, wheeaaaw* of its siren becoming louder and louder as it drew near. While still remote, it was almost a pleasant sound, but it soon became louder and rawer and, for a few brief seconds, was much too loud. Nothing cut the sound: not the wall around Shadyside, not the great trees, not the massive houses. For a moment the sound overwhelmed the pleasantries of farewell, and, despite themselves, the people standing in front of the huge ivied house all looked toward it. Two chauffeurs who had got out of two limousines looked toward it too. None of them could see the spinning red light on top of the ambulance but they all knew when it came opposite them. Then the full reverberation of the sound struck them all and quickly began to diminish.

Eleanor turned and said a final word to her hosts and then turned again and began to walk away, Mr. Taylor with her. The hotel where she was staying was just outside the wall, scarcely two blocks away. Patsy got in with one of the nice young couples. They only had a station wagon, and they steered carefully past the two long black cars parked at the head of the driveway. As they turned into the street they passed Eleanor and Mr. Taylor. He was talking, she was walking silently. Patsy was by the window and the window was down, but she didn't wave. Eleanor was looking across the long lawn, and the polite tones of Mr. Taylor's voice, which Patsy heard for a second, seemed more remote from her than they were from Patsy, more remote from her even than they were from the two silent chauffeurs beside the two limousines. Eleanor was inscrutable; she was not to be reached. There loomed beyond the small polite man at her side that other figure, that man who had known her far away from the trees of Houston, in the rougher, rawer country where the two of them had had their life and been, in their strange way, a royal couple.

Her final glimpse of Eleanor made Patsy pensive. To see Eleanor was to remember Sonny. She wondered if she would ever have a man so distinctly hers that she would remind people of him. She doubted it, and it made her sad.

She was not very responsive to the dozens of questions that Miri and Eric asked her about the fancy party she had been to. Later, in bed, she was wide awake. It occurred to her that Jim had been a fool to back away from Eleanor and run away with Clara. But, as Eleanor had said, he was always nice, and he didn't dislike anyone. She thought about him for a moment, but he wouldn't stay on her mind. It was just a quick judgment she passed on him and then forgot. The future and the past were on her mind and she would have been glad of a sleeping pill.

Downstairs, Eric and Miri were talking about her—about what was wrong with her, about what she would do, about Hank, whom Miri had not seen and whom Eric had not known. They went on to talk about marriage, how stupidly most people went into it, how foolish they were about it, how simple it would be to have a good marriage if one were only sensible. They speculated about it far into the night, now passionately, now soberly, stopping from time to time to neck. Patsy, could she have heard, would have gone to sleep amused.

20

It had been decided that Davey should have a dog. They were all at the park on a fine sunny afternoon in late April discussing it—Patsy and Davey, Miri and Eric, and Emma and Tom and Teddy. Tommy no longer liked being called Tommy; he felt that Tom was more adult. Everyone complied with his wish in the matter except Teddy, whose modus vivendi was to comply with as little as possible, at least where his brother was concerned. But, for the moment, names were not at issue. Ostensibly they were all waiting for Flap, who was in a seminar; but none of them were in any hurry for Flap to appear. It was a fine spring day, clear and breezy and unsmogged—a perfect day to sit in the park and talk about dogs.

Patsy was wearing an old sweatshirt that had once been Jim's and blue jeans and sneakers and was perched atop the jungle gym looking down at Davey, who was holding the bottom rail of the jungle gym and looking up at her occasionally. He was used to her being up there when they were at the park and was not disgruntled. A small brown and black mongrel was sniffing Davey's pants leg, and enough other dogs were around to lend point to the discussion. A large Doberman ran by from time to time, and Felicity, the unloved border collie, was sitting nearby, her leash tied to a swing pole, wishing someone would come and pet her. The boys were playing in the sandpile and Emma and Eric and Miri sat at one of the concrete tables being dogmatic about dogs.

Everyone had very firm opinions on the matter except Patsy, who would have to foot the bill, and Davey, whose dog it would actually be. Davey would have liked any reasonable dog, and Patsy was afraid she would too. The longer she contemplated dogs and their infinite variety the less specific she felt. In regard to dogs she was handicapped by an almost total open-mindedness.

Her friends had no such problem. Each of them knew exactly what kind of dog would be best. Even Tom had an opinion. He favored bulldogs, as being effective against burglars.

Emma, the sentimentalist, favored cockers, because she had had one as a child and had loved it and remembered it vividly. "You can't go wrong with cockers," she remarked several times. She wore a new green maternity dress and was showing her pregnancy. She sat filing her nails.

"Oh, hush about cockers," Patsy said, remembering that they were the one kind of dog she didn't much like. "They fawn," she said. "Every one I ever knew fawned."

Emma shrugged and tried to tidy her untidy blond hair. "So?" she said. "Don't be harsh and intolerant. They're very friendly and they need a lot of love. I fawn too. It's the only way I can get any attention in this world."

"Boo hoo," Patsy said. "You and your self-pity."

Actually she and Emma were on great terms, though they carped at each other constantly about self-pity. The only thing they really pitied themselves about was that they would soon lose each other as companions. In three months the Hortons would be gone to Iowa.

"I still think you should get him an Afghan," Eric said. "I've always wanted one."

"But you're hardly Davey," Patsy said. She remembered the beautiful Afghan that had been at the motel in Phoenix. It made her see Eric's point. She too would like an Afghan. It would be the perfect dog for her. She saw herself a woman of mystery, going walking at night in the mist with her beautiful dog. She would walk around on foggy nights and become a legend. Undergraduates would whisper when they caught a glimpse of her, and her Afghan would go everywhere she went.

But she was hardly Davey, either. The dog was for him, and he didn't give her time to be a woman of mystery, anyway. "Davey's too young for an Afghan," she said.

"They're supposed to be very sensitive. A kid would drive one crazy."

Eric did not seem to doubt it. "Scotties?" he said.

"Too much hair," Miri said. "It's too hot for hairy dogs in this town. It wouldn't be able to go outside all summer. Just get him a plain sensible terrier. Any kind of terrier."

Miri had come to feel that she was much more sensible than any of them. Sensible had become her favorite word. Pregnancy and Eric and general good health had made her a little smug. Patsy, remembering the shape Miri had been in only six weeks before, was sometimes amused at her pretensions to sense, and sometimes a little annoyed by her quiet smugness. But in regard to dogs she was forced to admit that Miri was probably right. In view of the climate of Houston, a short-haired dog was indicated.

Eric stood up and stretched. "Let's all go get a milkshake," he said. "Flap won't be out for thirty minutes yet."

Patsy and Emma were silent, not interested. The park was too nice. It was almost four o'clock and soon the park would be full of mothers and young children. Emma was pregnant, Patsy not hungry. They shook their heads. Miri looked up at Eric. She was feeling lazy, but he clearly wanted to go, so she stood up, obedient for the moment. "Want us to take the boys?" she asked Emma.

"Sure, if they want to go."

The boys did. But Teddy's sneakers were untied, and so full of sand they could barely be tied. He had not mastered his knots, and he sat on a bench while Emma tied them. Miri and Eric were holding hands, waiting. Emma brushed some of the sand out of Teddy's brown hair and entrusted Tommy with thirty-one cents. "That's for two two-dip cones," she said.

They departed, Eric and Miri walking slowly, the boys running ahead across the green park. Patsy from her perch and Emma from her table watched them run. They were never quite sure the boys would stop when they got to the street. They did though. It was always a relief. Patsy was tired of sitting on the cross bar of the jungle gym and climbed down. It was necessary, anyway. Davey had not been asked to go to the drugstore but had decided to go on his own and was proceeding past the sandpile, far in the rear of Eric and Miri. Patsy was about to run after him when he tripped and fell. He didn't rise, apparently because he realized the hopelessness of overtaking the party. Emma had opened a book of Updike stories. Being pregnant always made her feel like reading short stories.

"Ever try eating pickles?" Patsy asked as she walked by.

Emma was engrossed and didn't answer. She only had to read two sentences of any story to become engrossed. Patsy skirted the sand pile and went on to where Davey was. He was still lying on his stomach but had raised his head. He had grass on his lip. Patsy sat down by him and he put a hand on her knee. She dragged him into her lap and rocked him back and forth in her arms for a bit. Then she brushed the grass off his lip. "Well, they just abandoned you, old chum," she said. "How could anybody abandon a big boy like you?"

Davey was not interested in her motherly mouthings. He wiggled out of her lap and got up, using her shoulder for support. Behind them, on a court, some boys were playing basketball. Davey was watching them and Patsy turned so she could watch them too. They were in their early teens, very energetic but not very good. They played with much yelling, and were quick to reproach one another for any error or inexpertness. Davey was fascinated. From time to time the boys stopped to catch their breath and get their hair out of their eyes. All but one or two had long hair that swung wildly as they played.

Davey turned loose of Patsy's shoulder and walked toward the court to get a closer look. "Not too close," she said, but he was as engrossed in the basketball as Emma was in the short stories and paid her no mind. Patsy had become used to being ignored at will, even by her own son, and she got off the grass and followed in case she had to rush in and keep him from being trampled.

As it happened, there was no danger. He got to the court just as the boys were taking a breather. They were talking about cars. The basketball had been temporarily abandoned and Davey walked over and took possession of it. The boys glanced at him but didn't seem to mind. He couldn't lift it, but it seemed to give him just as much satisfaction just to bend over and encircle it with his arms. He pushed it, followed it, and bent over it again, grunting a little, full of self-confidence and self-importance and delighted to be playing ball. From time to time he looked at Patsy to make sure she was noticing.

Then the boys all stood up. Davey looked at them cheerfully, equal to equals, as if he expected some new phase of the game to begin. But the boys took the ball as if he didn't exist and began to dribble it and throw it to one another.

Patsy walked onto the court to lead Davey out of the way. "Come on, before you get brained," she said. She reached down and got his hand; but Davey was in a state of shock. He had realized that the boys didn't mean for him to play with them. For a few minutes while he was playing with the ball he had had the illusion that he and they were the same. He had felt himself a big boy. Then they took the ball and he realized it was not so—realized it in a way that he never had before. His mother and his aunt and his maid treated him like a big boy and it was a terrible disappointment to find out that real boys didn't. He tried to pull away from Patsy. She didn't have a good grip on his hand and had to ease him down to the concrete for a minute, for fear he would slip free and really fall. He was crushed; his face took on a look of complete disappointment. His lower lip came out and he began to cry. Patsy was embarrassed, for at the first wail the boys all looked at them with slight disgust. She stooped to pick him up, but when she did, his first dawning disappointment turned to indignation and then wild rage at the unfair state of things. He was a little boy, but he was a little boy in all his fury, and she picked up a wiggling, kicking, screaming bundle.

Emma, halfway across the park, looked up from Updike at the sound of Davey's wails. Patsy had picked him up by the arms but in doing so had not calculated on his being quite so mad. He was kicking her thighs and hips with all his might and she had to set him down again briefly; he was by then incoherent and utterly unsoothable. She tucked him under one arm, held on grimly, and carried him shrieking and kicking across the park. A few of the mothers looked around, but it was not an uncommon sight. Patsy was half amused and half sad about it all—sad because Davey had had such an awful disappointed look on his face when he realized he did not yet have a place in the world of big people.

She sat down at the concrete table across from Emma and tried to soothe him. But he was having a fit, and his fit took a while to wear off. "What's the matter with him?" Emma asked. Patsy shook her head. She was trying to hang on to him and he was growing red in the face from trying to squirm out of her lap. Finally she let him up. He sat down in the dirt and the deafening wails diminished and became the intermittent jerky sobs of a small boy whose fit had almost run its course.

"He's crying because he's not big enough to play basket-ball," she said. "They let him hold the ball a minute and it gave him delusions of grandeur. Poor thing. It's no fun finding out you're little and helpless. Do you suppose I've spoiled him by treating him like he was older than he is?"

She looked to see what Emma thought, for when it came to matters pertaining to the well-being of children Emma was the person she put the most trust in. But Emma wasn't listening. She hadn't heard the question. Her own question had been a purely rhetorical response to Davey's wails. Emma had looked up from her book and was staring across the park, but it was not the park that she was seeing. Her eyes were vacant. They did not take in the mothers and the children, the slides and playground horses, the streets and the green spring grass. Her eyes were fixed on some country of her own, and her mouth was set in a strange way. Patsy, who knew her friend's looks, knew that Emma was about to cry. Unlike herself, Emma did not cry easily. She fought herself, and her face became swollen with pain before she cried. At one time the sight of Emma about to cry had panicked Patsy. She would always try desperately to keep her from actually crying. "What's the matter? What's the matter? Tell me," she would say, and Emma would say, "Nothing, nothing, I'm all right," and then cry, anyway. But Patsy had learned. She looked discreetly away and waited, straightening Davey's hair with her fingertips. In a minute or two she heard the strange sniffing sounds that Emma made when she was crying. Emma was oddly ashamed of tears. They seemed to her immoral, and if she failed to gulp them back she wiped each one away the minute it touched her cheek. When Patsy looked up she was wiping them away, but for once she was weeping faster than she could wipe. Patsy reached in her baby bag and handed her friend a Kleenex.

"My god," she said gently. "A beautiful spring day and everyone's bawling. You're big enough to play basketball. What's the matter with you?"

"Oooh," Emma said, not looking at her. She sniffed some more. Then her face cleared a little and she sighed and shut the book of short stories.

"A story I read reminded me of someone," she said. The remote and inward look was still in her eyes; the tears had not really brought her back to the table. But she sniffed again and looked at her friend.

"My goodness," Patsy said. "I shouldn't have teased you. He's not the sort of writer who usually brings on tears, though."

"No," Emma said. She looked wistful. "Something in a story made me think of Danny Deck," she said.

"Oh. I wish I'd got to know that guy better."

"He didn't write much like Updike," she added.

"Oh, no, not at all," Emma said. She looked sad and turned her eyes on Patsy solemnly, as if she knew a secret and was trying to decide whether to tell it. Patsy was surprised. She did not think of Emma as having secrets.

"What is it?" she asked, but Emma turned away for a moment.

"It's just not fair that he's dead," she said. "It makes me sad, that's all. Everybody else our age is still alive and Danny's dead. I know he is. Sometimes I just miss him. I wish he were alive."

Danny Deck had written one book, had one child, broken up with his wife, and disappeared. His car had been found in Del Rio, Texas, near a bridge that crossed the Rio Grande. Patsy didn't know what to say. She had known before that Emma had had a soft spot for him, but from the look on her face she began to suspect that perhaps the soft spot was of a different nature from what she had supposed. Emma had told her that Flap had deflowered her, and Patsy had always supposed that he had been her one and only. But the look on Emma's face made her think differently.

"It was his wife's fault," Emma said. "I never liked her—she was never any good for him. If it hadn't been for her he never would have run away. He loved her."

"Maybe she was just a bitch like me," Patsy said. "I guess poor Jim loved me. Maybe he still does. Was Danny sweet on you?" She asked it lightly, for Emma's face had loosened and she was talking more easily.

Emma looked shy and a little guilty. "We always liked one another," she said jerkily. "Of course I loved Flap and he loved his wife but it always made Danny feel good to come around and drink with us when things were rough. It made me feel good too—we just liked one another a lot. Like you must have liked that clown you used to talk about."

Patsy felt strange, for she had forgotten that there had been a time when she had talked to Emma about Pete Tatum. The thought of his last visit made her sad. Clearly Emma had no such bad feeling in regard to Danny Deck.

"You were a little in love, huh?" she asked.

"Oh," Emma said, and was never more specific.

She sighed. "He spent the night with me once," she said softly. "Flap was off fishing with his father and I was pregnant with Tommy. I guess I was jealous of Flap's father in those days. Everything Flap did seemed to hurt me, some way. Danny's wife was giving him an awful time too. I guess we were both so unhappy we thought it couldn't hurt."

"Well, it didn't, did it?"

"No," Emma said, a little surprised, forgetting even to wipe a sliding tear. "It didn't, you know. I felt guilty for a long time but I really did like Danny and we were both just unhappy kids when it happened. I think what I felt the guiltiest about was never telling Flap. I just couldn't. He was so hipped on being everything to me in those days. I think he was always a little suspicious of Danny, though they did like one another. I guess he just knew I sort of turned Danny on. I don't know. I just couldn't tell him. I knew it would never happen again—even if Danny had lived, it wouldn't have. I wanted to keep Flap from ever knowing."

"Quit worrying about it," Patsy said. "Flap is unscathed. I don't believe in all this automatic honesty. I think you have to be frank but maybe you don't always have to be full. I'm glad you told me, though. It makes me feel you're not too much better than I am."

"It could never have been anything long, like you and Hank had," Emma said thoughtfully.

They were silent for a bit, thinking of their men. Patsy bristled a little at mention of Hank. Lately she had felt hostile whenever she thought of him. He himself was nice enough but she didn't like to be reminded of all that he reminded her of. He was part of a past she didn't like. More and more she wanted to be totally free of that past, of Hank, of Jim, and of all the distressing memories that they called to mind. At her feet, Davey picked himself up. He decided that, grim though it was, life must go on. He went over and climbed gingerly into the sandbox. He was oddly cautious about the sandbox and put his feet into it slowly, as if he were getting into a wading pool.

"Actually, Danny spent most of the night telling me about his second book," Emma said, smiling at her memories. "It was going to be called *The Man Who Never Learned.* It was about a guy who had terrible troubles with women—I think he had himself in mind. It was structured around a baby bed—his little girl's baby bed—and the point of it was that everybody's apt to sleep with everybody they know, sooner or later."

"In a baby bed? Come on."

"Oh, no," Emma said, trying again to straighten her hair. "It was just that the baby bed got handed from couple to couple and while it was being handed along the couples all got involved with one another in complicated ways. An amazing number of couples were involved."

"I wish he'd written it," Patsy said. "Here comes Flap."

She got up and went to take a small stick away from Davey. Some kids were playing freeze tag near the sandpile and a little boy named James, whose parents Patsy knew slightly, had just been tagged. He froze with one foot off ground. "Hi, James," Patsy said. He had brown hair and large brown eyes. James was straining to keep his balance, and he only grinned. Patsy decided Davey had had enough sand and carried him back and plopped him on the top of the concrete table. Flap walked up, his coat over his shoulder, and smooched Emma behind the ear. He spread his arms to Patsy, inviting her to be hugged, but Patsy made a face at him. It was not a very unpleasant face. Flap seemed to be entering his prime, and it was hard not to be a little delighted by his general high spirits. He had his dissertation all but finished and even had a small article finished. It was on insect lore in Shelley and everyone but Emma kidded him about it. Emma held her peace. Flap was overjoyed with everything. He was glad his wife was pregnant, glad graduate school was over, glad to be leaving Houston. The world was his oyster, at least temporarily. He was wearing old corduroy pants and a green tie that Emma had been wanting to throw away for years. Also he had grown a bushy brown mustache and it suited him. He had washed his hair that morning and it was very unruly.

"You didn't bring me any books," Emma said.

"I was too lazy to check them out. It's too pretty a day to be lugging books around. God, it's a nice afternoon. You've got a book, anyway."

"I'm nearly finished with it," Emma said. "I won't have anything to read tonight."

"Come by and I'll loan you something," Patsy said. "Here comes the gang."

Sure enough, the drugstore crowd was returning. Tom and Teddy were far in the lead; Miri and Eric were strolling very slowly, holding hands. From a distance her pregnancy was more noticeable. It showed in her manner of walking.

"Ever decide what you're going to name it?" Flap asked.

"Not really," Patsy said. "It's not my problem. I named mine, let her name hers."

Tommy dashed up, full of news of a mini-dragon set he had seen in the toy section of the drugstore. His eyes were wide and he talked rapidly of the many wonderful mini-dragons that could be made with it. Emma listened with half an ear but smiled at him.

"Ask your pop," she said. "He's the one who seems to think we're rich these days."

Flap was sitting on one end of the table poking Davey in the stomach with a finger. Davey enjoyed Flap and tried to grab the finger as it came near and poked him and withdrew.

"Hey, guess what," Flap said. "They've abolished all censorship in Denmark."

"So?" Emma said.

"So anything goes in Denmark," Flap said. "I was just passing on a tiny bit of cultural news."

"I wonder what the kids will be doing?" Patsy said.

"Oh, fucking," Flap said. "What else?" He grinned merrily, partly at the idea of the youngsters of Denmark going at it, partly at the sight of Patsy, always one of his favorite sights.

"Watch that," Patsy said. "That's my son you're talking to. I'm sure he'll get around to it but I'd just as soon it didn't turn out to be his first word. His grandmother wouldn't approve."

But words had no effect on Flap when he was in a good humor. Teddy straggled slowly up wearing a mustache of chocolate ice cream. "Oh, wipe his mouth," Emma said, but instead Flap swooped Teddy up and dangled him briefly over one shoulder. In a minute Eric and Miri walked up looking very satisfied with each other. They said hello to Flap and walked on, homeward bound. The Hortons' car was at Patsy's house and they all got up and left the park together, following Eric and Miri.

Patsy carried Davey as far as the sidewalk and then set him down and offered him a finger, thinking they might walk along together. But Davey had not forgotten the humiliation of the basketball court. He was not pleased with his mother and didn't want to talk with her. He slapped at her finger and looked petulant. Then he sat down. He did not intend to walk at all, and especially not with Patsy. He seemed to feel that what had happened on the basketball court was entirely her fault. He was not about to forgive her for the fact that he was small. His look showed clearly enough that he considered her responsible for the whole business.

Patsy squatted down and looked him in the eye, grinning, but Davey looked her back in the eye most unfondly. "I think he's sick of women," Flap said. "Carry my coat and I'll carry him."

Patsy took the coat and Flap, with great fatherly authority, swooped Davey up and sat him on his shoulder. Teddy had been dragging along looking tired, but the sight of a little boy on his father's shoulder stirred his competitive spirit. He livened up and strolled along in the space between Flap and Patsy, weaving from one side of the sidewalk to the other and singing loudly. Singing was his latest accomplishment. He had a varied repertoire of songs and among his favorites was "The Rock Island Line," which he had learned from a Johnny Cash record. His favorite part was near the end, when the train was safely across the bridge, picking up speed, and the engineer says:

> I fooled you, I fooled you,
> I got pig iron, I got pig iron, I got
> Allllll pig iron . . .

What Teddy especially liked was the "Allllll," which he liked to hold as long as possible. So he walked along, sometimes stepping on Patsy's heels, singing, "Pig iron, pig iron, I got allllll . . ." and he sucked in his breath and held the word as long as possible and then sucked in his breath again and on the next go-round held it even longer. He held it so long he had to stop, red in the face, still holding his word. Everyone looked at him and watched him grow red.

"Oh, quit," Emma said. "You'll pop."

"Pound him on the back, someone," Flap said, and Patsy turned around and gave Teddy a playful shaking, so that he finally stopped holding his word and collapsed on the grass, giggling at himself.

"Come on," Patsy said. "Walk with me. Your daddy's got my boy, I get to walk with you."

Teddy got up and contentedly gave her his hand, and they walked along. Tommy, full of energy, was far in front of Eric and Miri, who had slowed and were having a conversation. Emma, still engrossed in a story, was reading as she walked. Teddy was also fond of "The Yellow Submarine." Patsy hummed it as they walked along and Teddy sang a little and giggled and swung backward and forward from her hand, leaning as far as he could toward the grass and occasionally almost pulling Patsy off balance. Davey, from his perch on Flap's shoulder, watched Teddy's performance with interest, his good mood finally restored. Patsy turned once and made as if to grab him away, but Flap quickly stepped back and Davey giggled, one hand clutching Flap's hair.

Flap himself could not have been happier, walking as he was behind his two favorite women. The soft spring sun that fell on Dunstan Street shone through Emma's wispy blond hair like light through a cloud. But it was Patsy whom Flap was mostly thinking about; Emma he could admire at home when in an admiring mood. Patsy he never got enough of. He liked the looseness of her walk, the way her hips moved, the way her body bent to the left when Teddy pulled on her hand. Her black hair had begun to grow out again and was rough in the back and beautifully uneven; the sun touched it with lights when she turned to look down at Teddy. Flap imagined the movement of her waist beneath the old sweatshirt, saw in his greedy mind's eye the nice juncture of her legs and body and the sway of the light breasts that he had never seen but had often imagined. The sight of Patsy almost always made him feel hopeful—as it almost always made him feel horny. Hopeful and horny, he followed her down the sidewalk. Who could say? Someday she might. He could not quite imagine why, could not envision very particularly the circumstances or the occasion that would make it possible; but still there was no telling, someday she might. She was a lovely woman, and there was almost nothing nicer to think about. So he thought about it, strolling along with her son on his shoulder, two steps behind his own beloved slow-walking wife, and was almost as happy as a man could be. For a few moments his pleasure was so keen that he felt himself wonderfully and exclusively privileged, as if it were given only to him to see the real beauty of things which were alive.

Patsy, for once, was unaware of the sexual onceover Flap was giving her. She was dragging Teddy and idly trying to decide whether to take her whole brood—the Dunstan Street Mafia, as they had taken to calling themselves—to the ranch when she went in two weeks. She could take them, or she could go alone and let Hank come. The trip would be such fun for Davey. He could ride in the pickup with Melvin and see the cows, and Eric and Miri could climb up in the loft and dangle their feet. Spring had come; it would have changed the land. It would be lovely, as it had been when she had first seen it that one early morning when she had watched Roger Wagonner walk through the mist to tend his animals. And if she went alone and let Hank come, the visit would undoubtedly go just as the last one had gone. Considered coldly and in the abstract, the prospect of a sexual spree was not quite so pleasing as the thought of Davey riding in a pickup and staring with amazement at the cows. But that was considering it coldly. There were pros and cons. Six of one, but how many of the other? She could not decide—purely could not decide.

"You better call your eldest," she said to Emma. "He's almost out of sight."

"It's all right," Emma said, closing the Updike book and glancing ahead at Tommy. "He's been almost out of sight since three days after he was born."

Eric and Miri slowed down. They stopped a minute, then started again. Eric had turned to face Miri and was walking backward just in front of her. He put up his hands and she put her palms against his and pushed him backward lightly, moving from side to side a little as if they were doing a slow dance. Miri said something neither Patsy nor Emma could hear, but whatever it was gave Eric an enormous charge. His face lit up and he reddened with excitement and pleasure. "No kidding?" he said. "Really? No kidding?"

Patsy and Emma saw how it was; both smiled at the sight of him. Emma glanced back at her husband to see where his wandering eye was wandering—as if she hadn't known. Teddy turned loose of Patsy's hand and dashed ahead, both shoelaces flopping, his hair flopping too, suddenly intent upon catching up with his brother. Eric, still in his moment of excitement, was redder in the face than ever and was doing a little stiff-legged backward dance, and the look of delight he gave Miri was as clear and soft as the evening air, as fresh as the spring which touched the land. Miri turned for a second and looked around to see if anyone was watching them, but she didn't really care, didn't really notice anyone herself. Her far-off look never reached them, and her lightly rounded face was smug.

Well you might be, Patsy thought, noting the smugness. Eric, for a brief moment, made it all real again—all that was not real unless it was there, in the flesh. It would be nice—nice, indeed—to be there when such a beaut of a young man got around to bringing that blood back home, back to the place it nourished, the country that it fed.

"Look at him," Patsy said to her friend. Emma looked. She smiled and nodded and glanced beyond Eric to see if her two sons were going to bother to stop before they crossed the street.